THE COURAGE CONSORT

The Courage Consort

Michel Faber

CANONGATE BOOKS

To all those who sing lustily and with good courage,
and to all who only wish they could.

My thanks, as ever, to Eva, especially for her help
in creating the characters of Ben and Dagmar

First published in Great Britain in 2002 by
Canongate Books Ltd, 14 High Street, Edinburgh EH1 1TE

1 3 5 7 9 10 8 6 4 2

British Library Cataloguing-in-Publication Data
A catalogue record for this book is available on
request from the British Library

ISBN 1 84195 226 5

Typeset by Patty Rennie Production, Portsoy
Printed and bound by WS Bookwell, Finland

www.canongate.net

ON THE DAY THE GOOD NEWS arrived, Catherine spent her first few waking hours toying with the idea of jumping out the window of her apartment. Toying was perhaps too mild a word; she actually opened the window and sat on the sill, wondering if four storeys was enough to make death certain. She didn't fancy the prospect of quadriplegia, as she hated hospitals, with their peculiar synthesis of fuss and boredom. Straight to the grave was best. If she could only drop from a height of a thousand storeys into soft, spongy ground, maybe her body would even bury itself on impact.

'Good news, Kate,' said her husband, not raising his voice though he was hidden away in the study, reading the day's mail.

'Oh yes?' she said, pressing one hand against the folds of her dressing-gown to stop the chill wind blowing into the space between her breasts.

'The fortnight's rehearsal in Martinekerke's come through.'

Catherine was looking down at the ground far below. Half a dozen brightly-dressed children were loitering around in the car-park, and she wondered why they weren't at school. Then she wondered what effect it would have on them to see a woman falling, apparently from the sky, and bursting like a big fruit right before their eyes.

At the thought of that, she felt a trickle of mysterious natural chemical entering her system, an injection of something more effective than her anti-depressants.

'Is . . . is it a school holiday, darling?' she called to Roger, slipping off the sill back onto the carpet. The Berber plush felt hot against her frigid bare feet, as if it had just come out of a tumble-dryer. Taking a couple of steps, she found she was numb from waist to knee.

'School holiday? *I* don't know,' her husband replied, with an edge of exasperation that did not lose its sharpness as it passed through the walls. 'July the sixth through to the twentieth.'

Catherine hobbled to the study, running her fingers through her tangled hair.

'No, no,' she said, poking her head round the door. 'Today. Is today a school holiday?'

Roger, seated at his desk as usual, looked up from the letter he was holding in his hands. His reading glasses sat on the end of his nose, and he peered for-bearingly over them. His PC's digital stomach emitted a discreet *nirp*.

'I wouldn't have the foggiest,' he said. At fifty-two

years old, a silver-haired veteran of a marriage that had remained carefully childless for three decades, he obviously felt he'd earned the right to be hazy on such details. 'Why?'

Already forgetting, she shrugged. Her dressing-gown slipped off her naked shoulder, prompting one of his eyebrows to rise. At the same moment, she noticed *he* wasn't in pyjamas any longer, but fully dressed and handsomely groomed. Hitching her gown back up, she strained to recall how she and Roger had managed to start the day on such unequal footing. Had they got up together this morning? Had they even slept together, or was it one of those nights when she curled up in the guest bedroom, listening to the muted plainsong of his CDs through the wall, waiting for silence? She couldn't remember; the days were a chaos in her brain. Last night was already long ago.

Smiling gamely, she scanned his desk for his favourite mug and couldn't spot it.

'I'll put the kettle on, shall I?' she offered.

He produced his mug of hot coffee out of nowhere.

'Some lunch, perhaps,' he said.

Determined to carry on as normal, Roger picked up the telephone and dialled the number of Julian Hind.

Julian's answering machine came on, and his penetrating tenor sang: *'Be-elzebub has a devil put aside for me-e-e . . . for me-e-e . . . for meeeeeeee!'* – the pitch rising

3

show-offishly to soprano without any loss of volume. Roger had learned by now to hold the telephone receiver away from his ear until the singing stopped.

'Hello,' said the voice then, 'Julian Hind here. If *you* have a devil put aside for me, or anything else for that matter, do leave a message after the tone.'

Roger left the message, knowing that Julian was probably hovering near the phone, his floppy-fringed head cocked to one side, listening.

Next, Roger dialled Dagmar's number. It rang for a long time before she responded, making Roger wonder whether she'd gone AWOL again, mountain-climbing. Surely she'd have given that a rest, though, in the circumstances!

'Yes?' she replied at last, her German accent saturating even this small word. She didn't sound in the mood for chat.

'Hello, it's Roger,' he said.

'Roger who?' There was a horn-like sonority to the vowels, even on the telephone.

'Roger Courage.'

'Oh, hallo,' she said. The words were indistinct amid sudden whuffling noises; evidently she'd just clamped the receiver between jaw and shoulder. 'I was just talking to a Roger. He was trying to sell me some thermal climbing gear for about a million pounds. You didn't sound like him.'

4

'Indeed I hope not,' said Roger, as the nonsense prattle of Dagmar's baby began to google in his ear. 'This is to do with the fortnight in Martinekerke.'

'Let me guess,' said Dagmar, with the breezily scornful mistrust of the State – any State – that came to her so readily. 'They are telling us blah-blah, funding cuts, current climate, regrets . . .'

'Well, no, actually: it's going ahead.'

'Oh.' She sounded almost disappointed. 'Excellent.' Then, before she hung up: 'We don't have to travel together, do we?'

After a sip of coffee, Roger rang Benjamin Lamb.

'Ben Lamb,' boomed the big man himself.

'Hello, Ben. It's Roger here. The fortnight in Martinekerke is going ahead.'

'Good. Sixth of July to twentieth, yes?'

'Yes.'

'Good.'

'Good . . . Well, see you at the terminal, then.'

'Good. 'Bye.'

Roger replaced the receiver and leaned back in his swivel chair. The score of Pino Fugazza's *Partitum Mutante*, which, before the calls, had been glowing on his PC monitor in all its devilish complexity, had now been replaced by a screen-saver. A coloured sphere was ricocheting through the darkness of space, exploding into brilliant fragments, then reassembling in a different hue, over and over again.

Roger nudged the mouse with one of his long, strong fingers. Pino Fugazza's intricate grid of notes jumped out of the blackness, illuminating the screen. The cursor was where Roger had left it, hesitating under something he wasn't convinced was humanly possible to sing.

'Soup is served,' said Catherine, entering the room with an earthenware bowl steaming between her hands. She placed it on his desk, well away from the keyboard as she'd been taught. He watched her as she was bending over; she'd put a T-shirt on underneath her dressing-gown.

'Thanks,' he said. 'Any French rolls left?'

She grinned awkwardly, tucking a lock of her greying hair behind one ear.

'I just tried to freshen them up a bit in the microwave. I don't know what went wrong. Their molecular structure seems to have changed completely.'

He sighed, stirring the soup with the spoon.

'Five to ten seconds is all they ever need,' he reminded her.

'Mm,' she said, her attention already wandering outside the window over his shoulder. Meticulous though she could be with musical tempos, she was having a lot of trouble lately, in so-called ordinary life, telling the difference between ten seconds and ten years.

'I do hope this chateau is a *cheerful* place,' she murmured as he began to eat. 'It would have to be, wouldn't it? For people in our position to bother going there?'

Roger grunted encouragingly, his face slightly eerie in the glow of the monitor through the haze of soup-steam.

Roger Courage's Courage Consort were, arguably, the seventh most-renowned serious vocal ensemble in the world. Certainly they were more uncompromising than some of the more famous groups: they'd never sunk so low as to chant Renaissance accompaniment to New Age saxophone players, or to warble Lennon/McCartney chestnuts at the Proms.

A little-known fact was that, of all the purely vocal ensembles in the world, the Courage Consort had the highest proportion of contemporary pieces in their repertoire. Whereas others might cruise along on a diet of antique favourites and the occasional foray into the twentieth century, the Courage Consort were always open to a challenge from the avant-garde. No one had performed Stockhausen's *Stimmung* as often as they (four times in Munich, twice in Birmingham and once, memorably, in Reykjavik) and they always welcomed invitations to tackle new works by up-and-coming composers. They could confidently claim to be friends of the younger generation — indeed, two of their members were under forty, Dagmar Belotte being only twenty-seven. Fearlessly forward-looking, they were already signed up for the Barcelona Festival in 2005, to sing a pugnaciously post-millennial work called *2K+5* by the *enfant terrible* of Spanish vocal music, Paco Barrios.

And now, they had been granted two weeks' rehearsal time in an eighteenth-century chateau in rural Belgium, to prepare the unleashing of Pino Fugazza's fearsome *Partitum Mutante* onto an unsuspecting world.

Come the sixth of July, the early-morning English air was still nippy but the Belgium midday was absolutely sweltering. The message from God seemed to be that the Courage Consort shouldn't be deceived by the brevity of the plane and train journeys or the trifling difference in geographical latitude: they had crossed a boundary from one world into another.

In the cobbled car-park outside Duidermonde railway station, an eleven-seater minibus was waiting, its banana-yellow body dazzling in the sun. Behind the wheel, a smart young man was keeping an eye out for British singers through a pair of very cool granny specs. He was Jan van Hoeidonck, the director of the Benelux Contemporary Music Festival. Spotting his overdressed guests disembarking from the train, he flashed the headlights of the minibus in welcome.

'The Courage Consort, yes?' he called through the vehicle's side window, as if to make perfectly sure it wasn't some other band of foreign-looking travellers lugging their suitcases through the railway barriers.

Benjamin Lamb, towering over the others, waved in salute. He was grinning, relieved there had been no turnstiles to squeeze through — the bane of his travelling life. The mighty scale of his obesity was easily the most identifiable feature of the Courage Consort, though if anyone who'd never met them before asked for a pointer, Roger would always tactfully advise: 'Look out for a man with silver-grey hair and glasses' — himself, of course.

'But aren't there supposed to be five of you?' asked the director as Roger, Catherine, Julian and Ben approached the side of the minibus.

'Indeed there are,' said Roger, rolling open the sliding door and heaving his wife's huge suitcase inside. 'Our contralto is coming under her own steam.'

Jan van Hoeidonck translated this idiom into Dutch instantaneously, and relaxed behind the wheel while the Consort lugged their belongings. Catherine thought he seemed a friendly and intelligent young man, but was struck by his apparent lack of motivation to come out and help. *I'm in a foreign country*, she told herself. It hadn't been real to her until now. She always slept like a corpse on planes and trains, from the moment of departure to the instant of arrival.

Having loaded his luggage next to hers, Roger walked jauntily round the front of the vehicle and got in next to the director. He consulted no one about this. That was his way.

Catherine climbed into the banana-yellow bus with her fellow Courage Consort members. In true British fashion, each of them sat as far away from the others as possible, spreading themselves across the nine available seats with mathematical precision. Ben Lamb needed two seats to himself, right enough, for his twenty stone of flesh.

Catherine looked aside at Julian. It had been three months since she'd seen him, or so Roger said. It seemed more like three years. In profile, his heavy-lidded, supercilious face, superbly styled black hair and classic cheekbones were like a movie star's, with the same suggestion of jaded, juvenile naughtiness. He might have been the older brother she never had, contemptuously running ahead of her to the haunts of grown-up vice but never quite escaping her memories of him in short trousers and shopping-centre haircut. Yet he was only thirty-seven, and she was ten years older than that.

As the bus pulled away from the station, Catherine reflected that she almost always felt much younger than other people, unless they were clearly minors. This wasn't vanity on her part; it was inferiority. Everyone had negotiated their passage into adulthood except her. She was still waiting to be called.

Jan van Hoeidonck was talking to her husband in the front. The director spoke as if he'd been facilitating cultural events since World War II. But then they all spoke like that, Catherine thought, all these cocky young administrators. The chap at the Barbican was the same — born too late to remember the Beatles, he talked as if Peter Pears might have cried on his shoulder when Benjamin Britten died.

Self-confidence was a funny thing, when you thought about it. Catherine squinted out the window, stroking her own shoulder, as the bus ferried them into a surreally pretty forest. Chauffeured like this, towards a nest prepared for her by admirers, she still managed to feel like a fraud; even under a shimmering sun, travelling smoothly through placid woodland, she felt a vapour of fear breaking through. How was that possible? Here she was, an artist of international standing, secretly wondering whether she looked dowdy and feeble-minded to Jan van Whatsaname, while he, a fledgling bureaucrat with the pimples barely faded from his pink neck, took his own worth for granted. Even Roger listened respectfully as Jan explained his plans to steer the ship of Benelux art into new and uncharted waters.

'Of course,' Jan was saying, as the minibus delved deeper into the forest, 'multi-media events are not so unusual with rock music. Have you seen Towering Inferno?'

'Ah . . . the movie about the burning skyscraper?' Roger was more of a Bergman and Truffaut man himself.

'No,' Jan informed him, 'they are a multi-media music group from England. They have performed a piece about the Holocaust, called *Kaddish*, all over Europe — and in your own country also. The piece used many video projections, an orchestra, the Hungarian singer Marta Sebestyén, many things like this. I hope this piece *Partitum Mutante* will do something similar, in a more classical way.' The director slowed the vehicle and tooted its horn, to scare a pheasant off the road. They had encountered no other traffic so far. 'Wim Waafels,' he went on, 'is one of the best young video artists in the Netherlands. He will visit you here after a week or so, and you will see the projections that you will be singing under.'

Julian Hind, listening in, remarked:

'So, we'll be the Velvet Underground, and this video chap will be Andy Warhol's *Exploding Plastic Inevitable*, eh?'

Roger glanced over his shoulder at Julian in mute incomprehension, but the director nodded and said 'Yes.' Catherine had no idea what any of this was all about, except that Roger didn't like being shown up on matters musical.

Catherine's chest tightened with disappointment as, true to form, her husband took his paltry revenge. She tried to concentrate on the lovely scenery outside, but she couldn't shut her ears to what he was doing: moving the conversation deftly into the area of European arts bureaucracy, a subject Julian knew next to nothing about. He reminisced fondly about the French socialist administration that had made the 1985 Paris Biennale such a pleasure to be involved with, and expressed concern about where the management of the Amsterdam Concertgebouw was heading just now. Catherine's irritation softened into boredom; her eyelids drooped in the flickering sunshine.

'So,' interrupted the director, evidently more concerned about where the conversation was heading than the fate of the Concertgebouw. 'This Consort of yours is a family affair, yes?'

Catherine's ears pricked up again; how would her husband handle this? Nobody in the ensemble was actually a Courage except her and Roger, and she tended to cling to her maiden name as often as she could get away with it, for sheer dread of being known as 'Kate Courage'. She couldn't go through the rest of her life with a name like a comic-book super-heroine.

Suavely, Roger more or less evaded the issue.

'Well, believe it or not,' he said, 'the Consort is not specifically named after me. I regard myself as just one member of the ensemble, and when we were trying to think of a name for ourselves, we considered a number of things, but the concept of courage seemed to keep coming up.'

Catherine became aware of Julian's head tilting exaggeratedly. She watched an incredulous smirk forming on his face as Roger and the director carried on:

'Did you feel maybe that performing this sort of music needs courage?'

'Well . . . I'll leave that to our audiences to decide,' said Roger. 'Really, what we had in mind was more the old Wesleyan adage about hymn-singing, you know: "Sing lustily and with good courage".'

Julian turned to Catherine and winked. '*Did* we have that in mind?' he murmured across the seats to her. 'I find myself strangely unable to recall this momentous conversation.'

Catherine smiled back, mildly confused. While meaning no disloyalty to her husband, she couldn't recall the conversation either. Turning to look out the window of the minibus, she half-heartedly tried to cast her mind back, back, back to a time before she'd been the soprano in the Courage Consort. Hundreds of neat, slender trees flashed past her eyes, blurring into greeny-brown pulsations. This and the gentle thrumming of the engine lulled her, for the third time today, to the brink of sleep.

Behind her, Benjamin Lamb began to snore.

For the last couple of miles of their journey, the chateau was in plain, if distant, view.

'Is that where we're going?' asked Catherine.

'Yes,' replied Jan.

'The wicked witch's gingerbread house,' murmured Julian for Catherine to hear.

'Pardon?' said the director.

'I was wondering what the chateau was actually called,' said Julian.

'Its real name is 't Luitspelershuisje, but Flemings and visitors call it Chateau de Luth.'

'Ah . . . Chateau de Luth, how nice,' repeated Catherine, as the minibus sped through the last mile — or 1.609 kilometres. When the director parked the car in front of the Consort's new home-away-from-home, he smiled benignly but, again, left them to deal with their own baggage.

The Chateau de Luth was more beautiful, though rather smaller, than Catherine had expected. A two-storey cottage built right next to the long straight road between Duidermonde and Martinekerke, with no other houses anywhere about, it might almost have been an antique railway station whose railway line had been spirited away and replaced with a neat ribbon of macadamised tar.

'Luciano Berio and Cathy Berberian stayed here, in the last year they were together,' said the director, encouraging them all to approach and go inside. 'Bussotti and Pousseur too.'

The house was in perfect condition for its age, except for the artful tangle of stag horns crowning the front door, which had been eaten away somewhat by acid rain in the late Eighties. The red brick walls and dark grey roof tiles were immaculate, the carved window-frames freshly painted in brilliant white.

All around the cottage, lushly tasteful woodland glowed like a high-quality postcard, each tree apparently planted with discretion and attention to detail. Glimpsed among the straight and slender boughs, an elegant brown doe froze to attention, like an expensive scale model of a deer added as a *pièce de résistance*.

Catherine stood gazing while Roger took care of her suitcase somewhere behind her.

'It all looks as if Robin Hood and his Merry Men could trot out of the greenery any minute,' she said, as the director ambled up.

'It's funny you say this,' he commented. 'In the Sixties there was a television series filmed here, a sort of French Robin Hood adventure called *Thierry la Fronde*. This smooth road through the forest was perfect for tracking shots.'

The director left her deer-spotting and hurried off to unlock the front door, where the others stood waiting. They were arranged in a tight trio around their bags and cases, Ben at the back and the shorter men in front, like a rock group posing for a publicity shot.

Jan worked on the locks, first with a massive, antique-looking brass key and then with a couple of little stainless-steel numbers.

'Presto!' he exclaimed. Never having seen a conjurer at work, Catherine took the expression as a musical directive. What could he want them to do *presto*? She was in a somewhat *adagio* state of mind.

The chateau's magnificent front room, all sunlight and antiques, was obviously the one where rehearsals would take place. Julian, as he was wont to do, immediately tested the acoustic with a few *sotto voce* Es. He'd done this in cellars and cathedrals from Aachen to Zyrardów; he couldn't help it, or so he claimed.

'Mi-mi-mi-mi-mi,' he sang, then smiled. This was a definite improvement on Ben Lamb's rather muffled sitting room.

'Yes, it's good,' smiled the director, and began to show them round.

Catherine had only been inside a couple of minutes when she began to feel a polite unease finding a purchase on her shoulders. It wasn't anything to do with the atmosphere of the place: that was quite charming, even enchanting. All the furniture and most of the fixtures were dark-stained wood, a little sombre perhaps, but there was plenty of sunlight beaming in through the many windows and a superb smell, or maybe it was an *absence* of smell: oxygen-rich air untainted by industry or human congestion.

All cons, both mod and antique, were on offer: Giraffe upright piano, electric shower, embroidered quilts, microwave oven, fridge, a concert-sized xylophone, an eighteenth-century spinning-wheel, two computers, a complete pre-war set of Grove's *Dictionary of Music and Musicians* (in Dutch), an ornate rack of wooden recorders (sopranino, descant, alto, tenor, plus a flageolet), several cordless telephones, even an assortment of slippers to wear around the house.

No, it wasn't any of these things that troubled Catherine as she accompanied her fellow Consort members on their guided tour of the chateau. It was entirely to do with the number of bedrooms. As the director escorted them from one room to the next, she was keeping count and, by the time he was showing them the galley kitchen, a burnished-wood showpiece worthy of Vermeer, she appreciated there wasn't going to be any advance on four. One for Ben, one for Julian, one for Dagmar, and . . . one for herself and Roger.

'The shops are not so accessible,' the director was saying, 'so we've put some food in the cupboards for you. It is not English food, but it should keep you alive in an emergency.'

Catherine made the effort to look into the

cupboard he was holding open for their appraisal, so as not to be rude. Foremost was a cardboard box of what looked, from the illustration, exactly like the vegetation surrounding the house. 'BOERENKOOL', it said.

'This really is awfully sweet,' she said, turning the almost weightless box over in her hands.

'No,' said Jan, 'it has an earthy, slightly bitter taste.'

So there were limits to his ability to understand his visitors from across the channel, after all.

It was around nine o'clock in the evening, almost nightfall, when Dagmar finally showed up. The director had long gone; the Courage Consort were busy with unpacking, nosing around, eating Corn Flakes ('Nieuw Super Knapperig!'), and other settling-in activities. It was Ben who noticed, through an upstairs window, the tiny cycling figure approaching far in the distance. They all went to stand outside, a welcoming committee for their prodigal contralto.

Dagmar had cycled from Duidermonde railway station with a heavy rucksack on her back and fully laden baskets on both the front and rear of her bicycle. Sweat shone on her throat and plastered her loose white T-shirt semi-transparently against her black bra and tanned ribcage; it darkened the knees of her electric-blue sports tights and twinkled in the unruly fringe of her jet-black hair. Still she seemed to have plenty of energy left as she dismounted the bike and wheeled it towards her fellow Consort members.

'Sorry I took so long; the ferry people gave me a lot of hassles,' she said, her huge brown eyes narrowing slightly in embarrassment. Like all colourful non-conformists, she preferred to zoom past awed onlookers, leaving them gaping in her wake, rather than be examined at leisure as she cycled towards them over miles of dead flat road.

'Not to worry, not to worry, we've not started yet,' said Roger, stepping forward to relieve her of the bicycle, but it was Ben she allowed to take it from her. Despite his massive size, unfeasible for cycling, she trusted him to know what to do with it.

Swaying a little on her Reebok feet, Dagmar wiped her face with a handful of her T-shirt. Her midriff, like all the rest of her skin, was the colour of toffee.

'Well, childbirth hasn't made you any less of an athlete, I see,' commented Julian.

Dagmar shrugged off the compliment as ignorant and empty.

'I've lost a hell of a lot of muscle tone, actually,' she said. 'I will try to get it back while I'm here.'

'Toning up!' chirped Julian, straining, as he always did within minutes of a reunion with Dagmar, to remain friendly. 'That's what we're all here for, isn't it?'

The thought of Dagmar's eight-week-old baby

roused Catherine from her daze. 'Who's taking care of little Axel?' she asked.

'It's not a problem,' Dagmar replied. 'He's going to be staying here with us.'

This revelation made Julian's chin jut forward dramatically. Accepting delivery of Dagmar had already sorely taxed him; the prospect of her baby coming to join her was just too much to take.

'I . . . don't . . . know if that would be such a good idea,' he said, his tone pensive and musical, as if she'd asked him his opinion and he had deliberated long and hard before responding.

'Is that so?' she said coldly. 'Why not?'

'Well, I just thought, if we're being given this space — this literal and metaphysical space — to rehearse in, far away from noise and distractions, it . . . well, it seems odd to introduce a crying baby into it, that's all.'

'My baby isn't a very crying baby, actually,' said Dagmar, flapping the hem of her T-shirt with her fists to let the cooling air in. 'For a male, he makes less noise than many others.' And she walked past Julian, to stake her own claim to the Chateau de Luth.

'Well, we'll find out, I suppose,' Julian remarked unhappily.

'Yes, I guess we will,' Dagmar called over her shoulder. On her back, nestled inside her bulging rucksack, a spiky-haired infant was sleeping the sleep of the just.

*

21

By the time the Courage Consort settled down to their first serious run-through of *Partitum Mutante*, dark had come. The burnished lights cast a coppery glow over the room, and the windows reflected five unlikely individuals with luminous clarity. To Catherine, these mirrored people looked as if they belonged together: five Musketeers ready to do battle.

If she could just concentrate on that unreal image, shining on a pane of glass with a forest behind it, she could imagine herself clinging onto her place in this little fraternity. The rehearsals were always the hardest ordeal; the eventual performance was a doddle by comparison. The audience, who saw them presented on stage as if they were a projection from far away, knew no better than that they were a closely-knit clan, and this allowed them to behave like one. The artificiality of the concert platform was insulated against disturbing events: no one argued, or sulked, or asked her questions she couldn't answer, or expected her to say yes to sex. All they did was sing, in perfect harmony. Or, in the case of Pino Fugazza's *Partitum Mutante*, perfect disharmony.

'F sharp there, Kate, not F natural.'

'Honestly?'

'That's what's written. On *my* print-out, at least.'

'Sorry.'

The trick was lasting the distance from now till the première.

♪♪♪♪♪

Late on the first night in the Chateau de Luth, tucked up in a strange, soft bed next to Roger, Catherine turned the pages of *Extended Vocal Techniques* by the Extended Vocal Techniques Ensemble of California. It was a book she resorted to sometimes to put her to sleep, but tonight it had the additional purpose of keeping physical contact off the agenda.

Roger was reading a coffee-table book on Karel Appel, a Dutch artist, that he had found in a bookshelf downstairs — or rather he was looking at the pictures, she supposed; she didn't think her husband had managed to learn Dutch for this adventure. He *might* have done, but she imagined she'd have noticed something if he had.

Slyly she glanced at him from time to time, without moving her head. He was sinking further down in the bed, inch by inch. Her almost invincible insomnia would give her the edge soon enough, she hoped. She read on.

'Vowels can be defined linguistically by the characteristic band of overtones each contains. These bands are narrowed to specific pitches, so that the singer's voice resonates in a way that reinforces a single harmonic partial of the fundamental being sung. Such reinforced harmonics make it possible to write in eight parts for four singers.'

Catherine wondered if, rather than losing her sanity, she was perhaps merely getting old.

'Crazy character, this Karel Appel,' remarked Roger.

'Mm,' she said, drawing her knees up a little under the quilted eiderdown to better support her book. She wished this new piece by Pino Fugazza didn't require her and Dagmar to do so many things that distorted normal perception. Other people might think it was terribly exciting when two females singing in thirds made the airwaves buzz weirdly, but Catherine was finding that her nerves were no longer up to it. Even the way a sustained A flat tended to make an auditorium's air-conditioning hum gave her the creeps lately. It was as if her face was being rubbed in the fact that music was all soundwaves and atoms when you stripped the Baroque wrapping-paper off it. But too much sonic nakedness wasn't good for the spirit. At least that's what she was finding lately, since she'd started coming . . . adrift. A bit of Bach or Monteverdi might be more healing than what this Pino Fugazza expected of her.

Cowardly sentiments, she knew, from a member of the Courage Consort.

When Roger finally fell asleep, it was long past midnight. She didn't know exactly what time, because the only clock in the room was Roger's watch, hidden underneath his pillow as he breathed gently off the edge of the bed. It was strange the things you forgot to bring with you to a foreign place.

Catherine laid *Extended Vocal Techniques* gingerly on the floor, drew the eiderdown up to her chin, and switched off the bedside light. The silence that descended on her then was so uncompromising that she was unnerved by it. It was as if the whole universe had been switched off.

On the threshold of sleep, she found herself wondering how a person might go about killing herself in an environment like this.

At dawn, there were birds. Nothing on too grand a scale, just a few piccolo chirps and twitterings from species unknown. How strange that in London, in her flat near the half-dozen trees planted by the council, there should always be such a racket in the mornings from throngs of birds making the best of things, while here, in the middle of a forest, so few voices should be raised. Either there were only a handful of birds out there, chirping at the tops of their lungs in a hopeless attempt to fill the vacuum, or else there were millions and millions of them, all keeping silent. Sitting in the branches, waiting for the right moment.

Catherine was aghast to find herself becoming afraid: afraid of all the millions of silent birds, infesting the trees, waiting. And, knowing how irrational this fear was, she despised herself. Surely she was too crazy to live, surely it was high time she cleaned herself off the face of the planet, if she'd sunk to feeling anxiety even at the thought of birds sitting contentedly in a forest. It was as if the frayed and tangled wiring of her soul, submitted to God for repairs, had been entrusted to incompetent juniors instead, and now she was programmed to see danger in every little sparrow, dire warning in music, deadly threat from the love of her own husband.

Roger was sleeping like a stone beside her. He might wake any second, though; he never snuffled or fidgeted before waking, he just opened his eyes and there he was, fully conscious, fully functioning. Catherine looked at his head on the pillow, the head she'd once been barely able to resist stroking and kissing in adoration. She'd been so grateful he wanted her, so in awe of his conviction that he could shape her into something more than just another lost and self-destructive girl with a pretty soprano voice.

'You've got it inside you,' he'd promised her.

Yearning, terrified, she'd left her father's house at long last, and given herself over to Roger Courage instead.

Now she lay next to him in this strange soft bed in Belgium, and she wished she could breathe some magic odourless chloroform into his open mouth, to keep him safely asleep while she worked up the courage to face the day.

She mentioned the unearthly silence of the night to the others, over breakfast. She was light-headed with relief by then: she'd leapt out of bed and got herself ready before Roger was able to rouse himself from an unusually deep sleep. She was already in the kitchen, fully dressed, before he made his way downstairs to join his fellow Consort members. She was cooking *havermout* — porridge by any other name — for a ravenous unshaven Ben, and generally behaving like a sound-minded person.

'Good morning, darling,' she said, as her husband appeared. He looked a bit nonplussed, padding down the stairs in his herringbone-patterned socks. (All the men were in socks, actually, caught between the chateau's house rule against wearing shoes and their own reluctance to wear the leather clogs provided for them.)

Julian, bleary-eyed and elegantly dishevelled, was nursing a coffee without drinking it. As soon as Catherine mentioned the silence, he said he'd noticed it too, and that it wasn't natural. He'd lain awake all night because of it.

Catherine shuddered; the thought of her and Julian lying awake at exactly the same time in the same house, with only a wall between them, was disturbing somehow. It wasn't that she disliked him really, but she was so thin-skinned nowadays, so hypersensitive, that this simultaneous insomnia in a shared darkness was like unwelcome intimacy.

'And the way there's hardly any birdsong, in this big forest: that's a bit unsettling, don't you think?' she suggested hesitantly, wary of stepping into the spotlight of mental frailty but enjoying the idea of communication with her friends.

Dagmar was cutting fresh bread on the kitchen worktop, her snoozing baby lying swaddled in a blanket on the same surface, right near the breadboard, as if she meant to slice him next.

'That silence is what you get if you climb a mountain,' she said, referring to her favourite pastime. 'I like it.'

Having failed to get any joy from womankind, Catherine looked back to the men. Ben was now busy with the *havermout*, however, spooning it through his big soft lips, and Julian had turned his attention to his coffee, so that left only Roger.

Her husband searched his soul briefly for some appropriate observation.

'A vocal acoustic as silent as this must be very rare, when you think about it,' he said. 'I mean, just think of that recording of Hildegard songs by Gothic Voices... There you have Emma Kirkby singing like a lark, and in the background you can hear cars accelerating along the road!'

Julian had to disagree.

'That's because the sound engineers placed the microphones such a long way back from the singers,' he said, 'to try and get that monastery acoustic. They should have miked the singers close up, and put some reverb on later.'

'You can't mean that,' protested Roger. Catherine had ceased to exist, forgotten as she tried to make toast for him under the oven grill. 'The acoustics of a place are unique and precious.'

'For a live performance, yes,' agreed Julian. 'I've never sounded better than in that cellar in Reykjavik, with the stone walls and everything. But Gothic Voices weren't performing, they were making a record. Who needs the Church of St Jude-on-the-Wall in Hampstead if at the flick of a switch or the push of a fader you can have a churchy acoustic, without the bloody Volvo vrooming up the road?'

A smell of burnt toast started to pervade the kitchen. Little Axel coughed uneasily and started flapping his arms gently on the kitchen worktop, as if trying to fly away to a fresher square of air.

'Sorry,' said Catherine.

Partitum Mutante was sheer pleasure for at least one of its performers: Benjamin Lamb. Pino Fugazza was obviously very taken with the sonorous chanting of Tibetan monks, and had written oodles of something very similar for the bass parts of his own piece.

While the other members of the Courage Consort had to learn complicated and athletic melodies in perverse keys, Benjamin was required to hum like an organ for bar after bar after bar. At the very beginning

of the piece, his vocalisations were intended to convey
the birth of the universe, no less, and he tackled this
with an eerie resonance worthy of a holy Himalayan —
indeed, of several.

'Mwoooooooiiiinnng, mwoooooooiiiiinnng, mwoo-
ooooiiiinnng,' he sang, from deep within his huge
belly.

Pino Fugazza was cunning, though: he'd timed low
baritone swoops for Roger to cover Ben's pauses for
breath, creating the illusion of a ceaseless foghorn of
bass. And, just when it seemed that the music was going
to remain abyssally dark forever, Julian came in with a
high, pure voicing of the first articulate word: 'God' —
pitched in G major, of course.

The real trouble came with the entry of the females,
a reflection no doubt on the Italian's philosophy of
human relations as filtered through Judeo-Christian
tradition. The manuscript became alarmingly complex
at this point, the notes crowding the bar lines like
dense troops of ants squashed wholesale on the way to
something irresistible.

Dagmar and Catherine sang till the sweat was falling off their brows onto the pages. They sang until
their throats ached. They sang until they both felt
moved to stare at each other imploringly, like two
plantation slaves willing each other not to collapse, for
that would be to invite a far worse fate. The hours were
passing, not in linear flow, but in endless repetitions

of two minutes here, five minutes there, and then the same two minutes from before, over and over and over.

Finally, as night was again falling, the Consort reached the end of the piece, and, one by one, each of the singers faded away, leaving Catherine to bring *Partitum Mutante* to its close. The very last note was a very high C, to be reached over several bars from two octaves below, then sustained for fifteen seconds, increasing in volume, then diminishing to nothing. Ecstatic that the end was in sight, Catherine sang it with the purity and sureness of a fife.

For several seconds after she had ushered the last traces of the note into oblivion, the rest of the Courage Consort sat mute. In the extraordinary quiet of Martinekerke forest, they breathed like babies, no one wanting to be the first to speak.

'I was worried about that one, I must confess,' said Roger, finally. 'Well done.'

Catherine blushed and concealed her throat behind one hand.

'I just seem to be able to hit higher and higher notes all the time,' she said.

The silence moved in again, as soon as she'd finished speaking, so she pressed on, making conversation to fill the void.

'Maybe if I'd had one of those fearsome Svengali mothers pushing me when I was young I could have been a coloratura by now.'

Dagmar was uncrossing her lotused legs with a wince of discomfort, wiggling her naked feet — her own solution to the house slipper dilemma.

'So what sort of mother did you have?' she asked.

Catherine looked up at the ceiling, to see what might be written there about what sort of mother she'd had.

'She was a cellist, actually,' she replied meditatively, 'in the BBC Symphony Orchestra.'

'But I meant what sort of person was she?'

'Umm . . . I'm not really sure,' murmured Catherine, her vision growing vague as she stared at the delicate mosaic of cracks in the paint overhead. 'She was away a lot, and then she committed suicide when I was twelve.'

'Oh, I'm sorry,' said Dagmar.

It sounded odd, this effete Britishism, coming at robust volume from the German girl. The sharpness of her accent made the condolence sound like something else altogether, and yet there was nothing insincere in her tone: in fact, it was Dagmar's sincerity that really struck the discord. The phrase 'Oh, I'm sorry' must have been composed by the English to be softly sung in a feminine cadence.

'Not your fault,' said Catherine, lowering her gaze to smile at Dagmar. A ghostly blue after-image of the ceiling lamp floated like an aura around the German girl's face. 'It was me who found her, actually. Me or I?

— which is it, Roger?' She glanced at him, but not long enough to notice his frowning, eyebrow-twitching signal for her to stop talking. 'She did it in her bed, with sleeping pills and a polythene bag over her head.'

Dagmar narrowed her eyes and said nothing, imagining the scene and how a child might have taken it in. Julian couldn't contain himself, however.

'Did she leave a note?' he enquired.

'No,' said Catherine. Roger was getting up, rustling papers at the periphery of her attention. 'Though the polythene bag wasn't a plain one. It was a UNICEF one, with pictures of smiling children all over it. I always wondered about that.'

Even Julian couldn't think where to take the conversation from there.

'Tragic business,' he said, getting to his feet to follow Roger into the kitchen.

Dagmar wiped her forehead with one arm. As she did so, the fabric of her top was pulled taut against her breasts, alerting her to the fact that she had leaked milk from her nipples.

'Excuse me,' she said.

'How long has it been, do you think,' enquired Roger in bed that night, 'since we last made love?' Leading a singing group, he'd learned to hide his fault-finding under a consultative guise.

'I don't know,' she said truthfully. 'Quite a long

33

time, I suppose.' It would have been . . . undiplomatic to suggest otherwise, obviously.

The spooky silence of Martinekerke forest was back with them in the inky-black bedroom. Catherine wondered what had become of the moon, which she could have sworn was almost full last night. There must be clouds hiding it just now.

'So, do you think we might have a problem?' said Roger after a while.

'I'm sure it's nothing that won't come good,' said Catherine. 'The doctor did say that the anti-depressants might suppress . . . you know . . . desire.' The word sounded cringe-makingly romantic, a Barbara Cartland sort of word, or else a throwback to William Blake.

> *What is it that women do require?*
> *The lineaments of gratified desire.*

It was partly to save her from having to figure out what such terms as 'lineaments' could possibly mean that Catherine had originally allowed Roger to pluck her out of St Magdalen's College.

'Are you still listening to me?' he prompted now, in the vacuum of the noiseless night.

'Yes,' she assured him. 'I was just thinking.'

'Thinking what?'

'I can't remember now.' She giggled in embarrassment.

Roger lay still for another few seconds or minutes, then rolled onto his side — facing her. Not that she could see his face, but she could feel his elbow digging into the edge of her pillow and could sense, in the centre of the bed near her own thighs, the warmth of his . . . well, his desire.

'You're still a good-looking woman, you know,' he said in a quiet, deep voice.

Catherine laughed out loud, unable to control herself. The faint praise, offered so solemnly, so seductively, at a time when neither of them could see a bloody thing, struck her as unbearably funny somehow.

'I'm sorry, I'm sorry,' she whispered, mortified lest Julian hear them through the wall. 'It must be the anti-depressants.'

Roger slumped onto his back with an emphasis that rocked the bed-springs.

'Maybe you should stop taking them now,' he suggested wearily. 'I mean, have you felt suicidal lately?'

Catherine stared out of the window, relieved to see a pale glow of moonlight seeping into the sky.

'It comes and goes,' she said.

Hours later, when he was asleep, Catherine began to weep in the silence. She wished she could sing to herself, something sweet and tuneful, a little Schubert *lied* or even a nursery rhyme. 'Twinkle, Twinkle, Little Star' would do fine. But of course it wasn't possible. Her throat was sore from singing *Partitum Mutante*, and

35

she lay in dread of waking her husband, in a strange bedroom in a forest in Belgium, with that wicked Julian Hind listening through the wall for her every snuffle. Oh my God, how had things come to this?

Suddenly, she heard a short, high-pitched cry from somewhere quite far away. It wasn't Axel, she didn't think; that boy slept like an angel all night through and, during the day, hardly uttered a sound unless you set fire to a slab of Belgian bread right near his nose.

Catherine's skin prickled electrically as the cry came again. It didn't sound human, or if it was, it was halfway towards something else. She wished she could slide across the bed, into the big protecting arms of someone who could be trusted to do nothing to her except keep her warm and safe. Such people were hard to find, in her experience.

Instead, she drew the bedclothes up to her mouth and lay very still, counting the cries until she fell asleep.

In the morning, she didn't manage to make an appearance at breakfast. She'd hoped to be there, bright-eyed and bushy-tailed, each morning before Roger, but the previous night's insomnia caught up with her and she slept till midday. Roger was long gone by the time she awoke. Score: Roger: one, Catherine: zero, then.

The sun was pouring in through the window, its heat boosting her body's metabolism to an itchy simmer. Just before waking, she'd been having a nightmare of suffocation inside a humid transparent sac; anxiously conscious at last, she fought her way out of the clammy bedclothes and sat up, drenched with sweat.

She showered and dressed, hearing nothing except the sounds she herself was making. Perhaps the others were sitting around downstairs, waiting to sing, but lacking their soprano. Perhaps they'd gone exploring together, leaving her alone in the Chateau de Luth with its spinning-wheels and antique recorders and a bed she didn't know if she could bear to lie in again.

She needn't have worried. Arriving in the kitchen, she found Ben still in his XXL pyjamas, looking slightly sheepish as he sat alone at the sunlit bench, browsing through a four-year-old *Times Literary Supplement*.

He was such a strange man, Catherine thought. The oldest of them all, he was as baby-faced at fifty-five as he'd been when the Courage Consort first formed. He'd always been immense, too, though perhaps marginally bigger now than a couple of decades ago. Quietly competent and poised in every sphere of life, he had just this one area of weakness, his Achilles' stomach. Each concert tour brought more surprises from his store of hitherto unsuspected talents — last year he'd dismantled the engine of a broken-down tour bus and got it going with a necktie and two wedding rings — but he just wasn't terribly good at feeding himself.

'Hello,' he said, and a rumbling noise not a million miles removed from the moans he contributed to *Partitum Mutante* issued from somewhere inside him.

Catherine had no doubt he could have solved whatever physical and intellectual challenges a cooking pot and a box of oats might pose, but, plainly, there was some reason why he couldn't bring himself to tackle them. He looked at Catherine, his eyes sincere in their supplication. He was telling her, with that look, that he loved his own wife dearly, but that his wife was in London and Catherine was here with him, and what were they going to do about it?

'Would you like some porridge, Ben?' she asked him.

'Yes,' he immediately replied, colour rising to his great cheeks.

'Then I'll make us both some,' she said.

It turned out that the Courage Consort had already been lacking its contralto even while its soprano slept the morning away. At first light, Dagmar had cycled off into the forest with Axel, and had not yet returned. Perhaps she'd gone to Martinekerke or Duidermonde to fetch more supplies; perhaps she was merely exercising. She was gone, anyway, so Roger was typing correspondence on one of the computers, Julian was reading a paperback in the sitting room, and Ben had been waiting around for someone to offer him breakfast.

'Say "whoa",' said Catherine as she began to pour the milk.

'Whoa,' he murmured regretfully, when the bowl threatened to overflow.

Overhearing the sounds of nurture, Julian found his way back to the kitchen, where he'd fed himself on tinned rice pudding and coffee a few hours earlier. He was dressed in black jeans, a black T-shirt, black socks. From the top of his blow-dried head to where his ankles began, he looked like a French film star.

'Morning,' he grinned, still holding his book aloft, as if he'd just glanced up from his reading and noticed the kitchen had sidled up to him.

'Hello Julian,' said Catherine, trying not to be sour-faced as the moment of benign simplicity — the bowl of hot oatmeal, herself as provider, Ben Lamb as mute recipient — was ruined. As Julian stepped casually between herself and Ben, she noted that the book spreadeagled in his elegant hands was some sort of thriller with a frightened female face on the cover, and she suddenly thought, *I really, really dislike this man*.

'Julian, would you like some porridge?'

During the first five words of her question his eyes lit up, but they dulled in disappointment when she reached the end.

'No thanks,' he said. 'There's nothing . . . ah . . . more substantial is there?'

'I don't know,' said Catherine, gazing wistfully at Ben spooning the steaming *havermout* into his mouth. 'Porridge is quite filling, isn't it?'

'I was thinking of eggs, actually,' confessed Julian.

'Perhaps Dagmar will bring some back with her.'

'Mm.' Plainly, for Julian, the prospect of asking Dagmar to share food with him was not a realistic one.

Scraping the remnants of the *havermout* into a bowl for herself, Catherine asked Julian how he'd slept.

'Lay awake half the night again,' he grumbled, settling himself on a stool. His paperback nestled on his lap, its glossy image of a wide-eyed beauty staring up from between his slim black thighs.

'You heard the cries, then?' said Catherine.

'Cries?'

'Cries, out there in the forest somewhere.'

'Probably Dagmar's baby,' he suggested. 'Or bats.'

She could tell he hadn't heard anything really.

'I definitely heard them,' said Catherine. 'Human. But terribly forlorn and strange. Just cries, no words.'

Julian smiled indulgently.

'An infant crying in the night, / an infant crying for the light, / and with no language but a cry, eh?' he said, deadpan.

Catherine stared at him in uneasy puzzlement. Julian often came out with this sort of thing: a tanta-

40

lising quote from one of her favourite Victorian or
Romantic poets, delivered with a shrug as if it were an
arch soundbite from a TV commercial or an election
slogan of yesteryear made tacky, or poignant, or
poignantly tacky, by hindsight.

Elsewhere in the house, a telephone rang.

'Ghostbusters,' quipped Julian.

The call was from a young woman called Gina. She
wanted to know if it was convenient for her to drive
over this afternoon and clean 't Luitspelershuisje,
change the bed linen, that sort of thing.

Catherine was relieved when Roger told her this.
She hadn't expected domestic help somehow; after the
director's indifference to their baggage, she'd assumed
it wouldn't be Dutch. But if someone could come and
do something about the sweat-soaked sheets on the bed
she'd have to share with Roger tonight, that would
make a big difference.

Minutes after Roger passed on the message about
the maid, Dagmar returned from her adventures, hot
and bothered. She barged into the kitchen, plastic bags
in each fist, Axel still on her back. He was whimpering
and grizzling.

'*Moment mal, moment mal*,' she chided him, dumping
groceries on the kitchen bench. The *Times Literary
Supplement* was obscured by yoghurts, fresh apricots,
crispbreads, cheeses, avocados, cold meats, coffee,

cartons of 'Vla met echt fruit!', plastic flip-top con-
tainers of baby-wipes — and eggs.

Roger was already gone; Ben Lamb followed him
gracefully, recognising that there wasn't room in the
kitchen for all this bounty, Catherine, Dagmar, Julian,
and himself as well. Julian hesitated, his eyes on the
eggs. He was thinking he might be able to put up with
the irritating noise of the baby if there were omelettes
on the horizon.

But Dagmar sat heavily on a stool right opposite
him and hoisted Axel over her shoulder, depositing
him on her lap. Then, hitching her T-shirt up, she
uncupped one breast and guided her baby's mouth to
the nipple.

'Excuse me,' said Julian, leaving the women to it.

Catherine sat at the kitchen bench, staring abstractedly
into Ben's porridge bowl. It was so clean and shiny it
might have been licked, though she imagined she would
have noticed if that were the case. She herself tended to
half-eat food and then forget about it. Roger didn't
like that for some reason, so, back home in London,
she'd taken to hiding her food as soon as she lost her
appetite for it, in whatever nook or receptacle was
closest to hand. *I'll finish this later*, she'd tell herself, but
then the world would turn, turn, turn. Days, weeks
later, ossified bagels would fall out of coat pockets,
furry yoghurts would peep out of the jewellery drawer,

liquefying black bananas would lie like corpses inside the coffins of her shoes.

She hoped she wasn't doing it here in the Chateau de Luth, though chances were that she was. Roger was probably cleaning up after her, refraining from saying anything because of the other people. Could she perhaps be getting Alzheimer's instead of going crazy? At forty-seven she doubted it was very likely . . . Still: there was something so very blameless and . . . non-negotiable about Alzheimer's. Nobody would think of telling you to pull yourself together, or get impatient for you to return to your sex life. You wouldn't have to take Prozac anymore, and if somebody found a hoard of half-eaten apples behind the television, well, they'd understand.

And when you died, you wouldn't even know what was happening. You'd just dither absentmindedly into the next world, blinking mildly in the light of the Almighty.

Catherine's eyes came into focus on the *Times Literary Supplement*, from which she had removed the food and neatly put it away in refrigerator and cupboards minutes ago. The *TLS* was open at the letters pages, and nine distinguished academics from all over Britain and the USA were arguing about the dedicatee of Shakespeare's sonnets, taking it all very personally. *Correspondence on this matter is now closed*, warned the editor, but after nigh-on four hundred years it was pretty

43

obvious that the sonnets argument, like all arguments, would run forever without resolving anything. As for Catherine, she had no opinion, except that it would be nine different kinds of Hell to be married to these men.

'You can eat any of the food that you want,' Dagmar said.

Catherine had forgotten the German girl was there, and looked up with a start.

'Oh . . . thank you,' she said.

'Except if I'm the only one of us who's going to be shopping, I'll need to have some extra money soon,' added Dagmar. Her baby was still sucking at the breast, placid as a sleeping kitten.

'Just mention it to Roger, he'll take care of it,' said Catherine. She hadn't signed a cheque or set foot in a bank in years. Latterly she had a little plastic card which gave her money out of a slot in the wall, providing she could remember a four-digit number – and the card, of course. There was nowhere in Martinekerke forest where that little plastic card could be inserted.

'How did you sleep last night, Dagmar?' asked Catherine, carrying Ben's bowl to the sink.

'Perfect,' said Dagmar.

'You didn't hear anything unusual, in the small hours of the morning? Like a cry from the forest?'

'Nothing wakes me,' said Dagmar, looking down at Axel, 'except him, of course.'

This seemed unlikely, given the child's almost noiseless functioning, but Dagmar must know what she was talking about. Catherine was struck by how, when the German girl was looking down at the baby at her breast, her slim, taut-skinned face acquired a double chin, adding five years to her age. There was a pale scar on Dagmar's forehead, too, which Catherine had never noticed before. Wrinkles of the future, cicatrices of the past, all the million marks recording a private life that no outsider could ever understand.

'Are you enjoying yourself here?' asked Catherine.

'Sure,' Dagmar replied. 'It's good they provide us with this space. I've been a professional musician now for ten years, and I have a kid; it's about time somebody pays for us to rehearse, yeah?'

'But the place itself, and the piece itself – are you enjoying those?'

'I don't care at all about Pino Fugazza's music,' shrugged Dagmar, removing Axel from her breast. Saliva gleamed on her nipple and areola, prompting immediate loss of eye contact from Catherine. 'I want to sing it well. If I get too bored with the music put in front of me, I should get off my ass and compose some of my own, yeah?'

Catherine, still embarrassed at her own queasiness about the spittly nipple, was even more thrown by this turn the conversation was taking. The American-accented 'ass' instead of 'arse' emphasised Dagmar's foreignness even more than her German accent usually did, and her frank indifference to the commission that had brought them all here was startling. Strangest of all was this notion that you could compose yourself, if you were dissatisfied with the music you were given.

'You write music?' At the bottom edges of her vision, Catherine registered that the T-shirt was coming down, covering the perturbing swell of flesh.

'Sure,' said Dagmar, finding a more convenient spot to lay her boy's wispy head. 'Don't you?'

Catherine had never once dreamt of composing a note. She played the piano competently, could get by on the flute, could hear a piece of music playing in her head just by reading the score — though not as accurately as Roger could hear it, of course. When it came to score-reading, she imagined her brain as an old radio, fading out now and then, and Roger's brain as a CD player, extracting every nuance with digital efficiency. As for the prospect of making her *own* marks on the staves: no, that was inconceivable. The only times she ever sang a note that was different from what had been written for her, Roger was always there to say, "F sharp, Kate, not F natural," or whatever.

'I'm sure I don't have what it takes,' she told Dagmar.

The German girl wasn't passionately motivated to disagree, her brown eyes as dark and opaque as Belgian mocha chocolate.

'If you think so,' she shrugged.

Catherine flinched inwardly: she'd been hoping for reassurance. How strange these Germans were, not understanding that a declaration of unfitness was really a plea for encouragement. Perhaps it was a good thing they hadn't won the Battle of Britain.

'I haven't had the right training, for a start,' Catherine said. 'People like Pino Whatsisname have studied composition for years and years.'

Dagmar was plainly unawed by this reminder of Pino's credentials.

'Humming to yourself in the bath is composing, don't you think?' she said, hugging Axel up onto her shoulder. 'I sing to myself when I'm out cycling, and to my kid. It's not *Partitum Mutante* I'm singing, that's for sure.'

She grinned, and Catherine grinned too. It was a nice, safe place to leave the conversation.

'I'm going to put Axel to bed now,' said Dagmar. 'You should go out for a walk, don't you think? Everything is perfect out there — the weather, the forest, everything.'

'I'd like that,' promised Catherine. 'I really would. But maybe Roger wants us to start now.'

The look she got from Dagmar then was enough to shame her into finding her shoes.

Gina the maid arrived in a little white Peugeot just as Catherine was stepping out the door — excellent

47

timing, since it meant that Roger couldn't be angry about the delay in the rehearsals, could he?

Slightly awed at her own daring waywardness, Catherine cast off from the house without even explaining herself to anyone, hurried into the fringe of the forest, then peered through the sparse trees back at the chateau. Roger and Julian were competing to welcome Gina, who, contrary to expectations, was a blonde twentysomething with a figure like a dancer and work apparel to match. Everything in the Netherlands was of better quality than you thought it would be. Even the vacuum cleaner that Gina was struggling to remove from her vehicle's back seat without the assistance of foreigners looked like a design award-winner that could suck anything into its sleek little perspex body.

To the best of Catherine's knowledge, Roger had never been unfaithful to her. It wasn't his style. Once he made a commitment to something, he stuck with it and never let go, no matter what. No matter what. Nor was a sudden heart attack or stroke likely to take him from her. He was four years older than her, but very fit. They would be together always, unless she died first.

Catherine turned her back on the chateau and wandered deeper into the trees. As she walked she kicked gently at the soft, rustling carpet of fallen leaves and peaty earth, to leave some sort of trail she could follow later if she got lost. The sky was clear, the breeze gentle. Her footsteps would remain, she was sure.

During the war, the Nazis had probably killed people in these woods. The war had come to Belgium, hadn't it? She was vaguely ashamed to concede that she wasn't sure. She didn't really know much about anything except singing. Roger had rescued her from post-adolescent misery at St Magdalen's College and, forever after, had taken responsibility for the world at large. He told her what he thought might interest her, vetted out what in his opinion she'd rather not know. Then again, she was terribly forgetful, especially lately. Roger possibly *had* told her about Belgium and World War II once, but she would have forgotten it by now.

Anyway, assuming there *had* been Nazis in this forest, this would have been a perfect spot to execute people. Catherine wondered what it would be like to be rounded up, herded to the edge of a communal grave, and shot. She tried to feel pity for those who didn't wish to die: women with children, perhaps. All she could think of was what a mercy it would be to have the burden of decision shouldered by someone else: a Nazi to lead you from prevarication to the grave, where he would shoot you in the back of the head, a place you couldn't reach yourself.

Then, a few years later, a French Robin Hood and his Merry Men would ride their horses over your bones, twirling their colourful pennants, delighting children all over Europe.

After fifteen minutes or so, Catherine stopped

walking and squatted against the mossy bough of a cedar, making herself comfortable on the forest bed. The ground was quite safe to rest her bottom — her ass? — on; it seemed to have been designed by Netherlandish scientists to nourish vegetation without staining trousers. The warmth of the sun, diffused by the treetops, beamed vitamin D onto her skin. All around her, pale golden light flickered subtly on the greens and browns, the leaves breathing out their clean, fragrant oxygen.

Composers are often inspired by nature, she thought. Beethoven's *'Pastoral' Symphony*, Vaughan Williams, Delius, that sort of thing. What did nature mean to her? She tried to decide, as if God had just asked her the question.

Nature meant the absence of people. It was a system set up to run without human beings, concentrating instead on the insensate and the eternal. Which was very relaxing now and then. But dangerous in the long run: darkness would fall, and there would be no door to close, no roof over one's head, no blankets to pull up. One wasn't an animal, after all.

Catherine stood up and slapped the leaves and fragments of bark off the seat of her jeans. She'd had enough nature for one day. It was time she was getting back to the house.

Walking back along the path she'd made, she became aware of all the birds that must be sitting in the trees all around and above her. A few were twittering musically, but the vast majority were silent. Looking down at her. It didn't bear thinking about; she concentrated on the sound of her own feet rustling through the undergrowth.

Her quickening breathing sounded amazingly loud in the stillness, and as she walked faster the breaths became more like voiced utterances, with an actual pitch and timbre to them. Exactly like avant-garde singing, really: the vocalisations of a terrorised soul.

She was almost running now, stumbling on loose branches and clods of earth she had kicked up earlier. The sunlight was flickering much too fast through the trees, like malfunctioning fluorescence, lurid and cold. Had she lost track of time again? Was she hours away from home?

What would she do if she heard the cry?

The thought came suddenly, like an arrow shot into her brain. She was alone in the forest of Martinekerke with whatever had wailed out to her during the night. Its eyes were probably on her right now, glowing through the trees. It was waiting for the right moment to utter that cry again, waiting until she had blundered so close that it could scream right in her ear, into the nape of her neck, sending her crashing to her knees in panic. Catherine ran, whimpering anxiously. She would be a good girl from now on, if only Roger would come and rescue her.

Breathless, half-blind, she broke into the clearing. For all the intensity of her dread, she'd taken only a couple of minutes to put the forest behind her; she hadn't strayed very far from home at all. The chateau was right there across the road, and the little white Peugeot parked outside spoke of the impossibility of supernatural cries.

'OK, time for *Partitum Mutante*,' said Roger to her, as soon as she stepped across the threshold.

Rehearsals went badly that day. Ben, Dagmar and Catherine were game enough, but Roger was irritable, strangely unsettled. Julian had his mind on something else and lost his place in the score at every small distraction — like Gina leaving the house, for example. He watched her through the sparkly clean windows as she loaded her equipment into her car, and his cue to sing the words of the Creator God went by unnoticed.

Politely hostile words between Julian and Roger were mercifully interrupted by another phone-call. It was a journalist from a Luxembourg newspaper, trying to find a story in the Benelux Contemporary Music Festival.

Those members of the Consort who were not Roger Courage sat idle while Roger handled the enquiries, the first of which was evidently why Pino Fugazza's piece was called *Partitum Mutante*. This was one of many questions that Catherine had never thought to ask Roger, so she made the effort to listen to his reply.

'Well, my Italian is pretty rudimentary,' he purred into the mouthpiece, implying quite the opposite, 'but I gather the title isn't Italian as such, or even Latin. It's more a sort of multi-layered pun on lots of things. There's a play on *partita*, of course, in the sense of a musical suite, as well as some reference to *partum*, in the sense of birth. *Mutante* then suggests mutant birth, or a mutant musical form . . .'

Catherine's attention wandered to the forest outside. A deer was grazing right near the window. It was really awfully nice out there, seen from indoors. She must go walking in the woods more often, face her fears, not be such a baby.

'I do think it's awfully important to give performers of newly commissioned music adequate rehearsal time,' Roger was saying to the journalist from Luxembourg. 'Too often when you go to a première of a contemporary vocal work, you're hearing singers flying by the seat of their pants, so to speak, on a piece they've only just learnt. There hasn't been time to master it fully, to capture the nuances and inflections. You have to remember that when a traditional vocal group sing Handel's *Messiah* or some such chestnut, they can virtually sing it in their sleep. What we, in the Courage Consort, are trying to do with *Partitum Mutante* here in this splendid chateau is learn it to the point when we can sing it in our sleep. That's when the real work can begin.'

Moments later, when Roger was off the phone and sitting down with his fellow Consort members, Catherine said:

'I thought it meant underpants.'

Dagmar chuckled throatily, a release of tension. Roger looked at his wife as if he had every expectation that she would resume making sense very soon, if he only stared hard enough into her eyes.

'*Mutante*,' Catherine explained. 'I could've sworn it meant underpants.'

'I'm sure it's to do with mutation, dear,' Roger warned her mildly, rolling his eyes from side to side to remind her they were not alone in their apartment now. But she was not to be brushed off like that. She had been to Italy only last year, singing Dowland and Byrd. En route, she'd done a bit of shopping in Rome, thrilled and terrified to be off Roger's leash for an hour.

'I remember when I was in Rome,' she said, 'I needed some briefs. I was in a big department store and I didn't know how to ask. Obviously I couldn't show them my knickers, could I? So I looked up underpants in a guide book. I'm sure it said *mutante*.' She laughed, a little embarrassed. 'That's the sort of thing I do remember.'

Roger smirked wearily.

'On that note,' he said, 'coffee, anyone?'

When they were all sitting together again, Roger informed them that Pino Fugazza himself would be paying a visit to them tomorrow, to see — or rather hear — how they were progressing with his masterpiece. What needed to be discussed before then, obviously, was which parts of *Partitum Mutante* they needed to rehearse most intensively, in order to make the best possible impression on the composer.

It was a tense discussion, at least among those of the Consort who had an opinion on the matter. Julian felt the tenor-rich passages were most underdeveloped, while Dagmar was sure that the contralto and soprano harmonics were far short of ideal; Roger tended towards the view that these weaknesses could be improved at leisure within a binding framework woven by a clean and confident baritone line. An impasse was reached with no singing done. Julian went to the toilet, Roger went for a breath of fresh air, and Dagmar went to look in on Axel.

Left alone with Ben, Catherine said:

'I've still got the briefs, actually. They lasted superbly. I might even have them on right now.'

Ben rested his massive head on his hands and half-closed his eyes, smiling.

In bed that night, Roger finally allowed himself to be badly behaved.

'You don't love me anymore,' he said, as Catherine cringed beside him, rolling herself up into a ball.

'I don't know, I don't know,' pleaded Catherine, her voice strangled to a squeak by tears and too much singing.

'Have you given any more thought to stopping the anti-depressants,' he enquired tonelessly, tugging at the blankets to cover the parts she had exposed.

'I've already stopped,' she said. It was true. It had been true for days. In fact, despite Roger's frequent gentle reminders, back in London, about all the items she should make sure she took with her to Belgium, she had somehow managed to leave those little pills behind. The cardboard box they lived in had got beetroot and mayonnaise soaked into it somehow, and she hadn't been up to fixing the problem. The box of pills, the spilled food, the handbag in which all this had happened: she'd left the whole caboodle under her bed at home. The bed she slept in alone, in the spare room.

'Really?' said Roger, lying right next to her in Belgium. 'So how are you feeling?'

She burst out laughing. She tried desperately to stop, mindful of Julian in the next room, but she couldn't; she just laughed louder, sobbing until her sides were aching.

Later, when the fit had subsided, Roger lay with his head and one hand against her back.

'We have a big day tomorrow,' he sighed, heavy with loneliness on the brink of sleep.

'I won't let you down,' Catherine assured him.

No sooner had his breathing become deep and regular than the first cry echoed eerily in the forest outside.

'Come for a cycle with me,' Dagmar invited her next morning after breakfast.

Catherine blushed, her hands trembling up to her throat. She could not have been more nonplussed if she'd just been asked to go skinny-dipping in Arctic waters with a bunch of fervent Inuits.

'Ah . . . it sounds lovely, Dagmar, really, but . . .'

She looked to Ben for help, but he was busy spooning up the *havermout*, content as a . . . well, a lamb.

'I haven't got a bicycle, for one thing,' she pointed out gratefully.

'I found one at the back of the chateau,' said Dagmar. 'It's an old one, but sound construction. A good Dutch bike. But if you think you can't ride an old one, you can use mine.'

Defeated, Catherine allowed herself to be led out of the house. The German girl's thighs and buttocks flexed like an Olympian's as she walked, the shiny aquamarine of her tights contrasting sharply with the pastel blue of Catherine's evenly faded jeans. There were the two bicycles already parked, side by side at the edge of the road, gleaming in the sun. There was no escape except to say *No, I don't want to*, which had always been impossible for Catherine.

'They say you never forget how to ride a bicycle,' she said, approaching the machines warily, 'but I've forgotten the most amazing things, you know.'

'It's all right, we'll take it easy,' said Dagmar, preoccupied with strapping on the Axel rucksack.

Catherine examined the seats of the two bikes, feeling the leather curves, trying to imagine how hard or soft each might be between her legs.

'Erm . . . which of these is better for someone who hasn't . . . you know . . .'

Dagmar shrugged, quite an achievement for a woman with a six-kilo human being on her back.

'One bike has about a hundred gears, the other has none,' she said. 'But travelling slow on a totally flat road, it makes very little difference.'

And so it began. Catherine's anxiety turned to relief as she discovered she could still ride perfectly well. Her other fear, that Dagmar would speed ahead of her, was equally unfounded. The German girl cycled at a slow and even pace — not because she was making any special effort to be considerate, but because she had simply sent an instruction down to her legs to rotate at a certain number of revolutions per minute. Whatever the reason, Catherine was able to keep up, and, to her growing delight, found herself cycling along the dark smooth road, forest blurring by on either side, a breeze of her own creation blowing through her hair.

After a mile or two, she was even confident enough to speak.

'You know, I really am enjoying this terribly much,' she called across to Dagmar.

Axel, nestled against his mother's back, his face barely distinguishable under a woollen cap, opened his eyes wide. He wasn't used to fellow travellers.

'You will sing better tonight,' Dagmar asserted confidently. 'It's good for the lungs, good for the diaphragm, good for everything.'

'You'll have me going mountain climbing with you next!' It was the sort of comment you could make in the Low Countries, without fear.

'Great idea,' called Dagmar. 'There are some OK mountains just over the German border, in Eifel. Three hundred kilometres' journey, maximum.'

Catherine laughed politely, possibly not loud enough for Dagmar to hear over the whirring of the wheels. In the distance, a church spire gave advance warning of Martinekerke.

It was a proud and glowing Catherine who cycled up to the front door of the Chateau de Luth an hour later. She had been exploring the big wide world, making a bit of a reconnaissance of the local facilities. Now she and Dagmar were bringing back the goodies.

The three men watched them mutely as they, two flushed and sweaty women, carried groceries into the kitchen.

Mind you, Catherine hadn't actually been able to carry much on the bicycle with her, having neglected to bring along any sort of bag. But she'd taken responsibility for the eggs, wrapping them up in a sweater she was too hot to wear, and nestling them safely in the basket of her strange Dutch bike.

'You may need another shower, dear,' Roger suggested *sotto voce* as she was pouring a big glass of milk down her glistening throat. 'Pino Fugazza will be here soon.'

Abruptly, for no apparent reason, little Axel started bawling.

Of all the composers that the Courage Consort had ever met, Pino Fugazza proved to be the least charming. Perhaps they ought to have been forewarned slightly when they'd found out that his sizeable fortune derived not from the honest popularity of avant-garde music but was inherited from the family business of automatic weapons. However, in a spirit of not blaming the child for the sins of his parents, they reserved judgement. In any case, as Ben pointed out, Tobias Hume, a favourite composer of the Courage Consort's seventeenth-century repertoire, had actually been a professional killer in his time, and that didn't detract from the merit of the songs he'd written for the viol.

The image of a dashing Tobias Hume laying sword aside to pen the immortal 'Fain would I change that note' was rudely extinguished by the very real arrival, in a black Porsche, of Pino Fugazza. He swanned into the chateau wearing a red Galliano shirt with dozens of little black ears printed on it, black Armani slacks jingling with loose change, and shoes with tassels on them. His smile was startlingly unappealing.

'How do you do,' said Catherine, playing hostess, though she could tell at a glance that she had no desire to know the answer.

'*Prima, prima*,' exclaimed the composer, bounding into the house with a lightness of step possibly achieved by the feeble claims of gravity on his four-foot-eleven frame. Already bald at twenty-nine, he had a face like a macaque. Even Ben Lamb, who was usually most careful not to gape at people with physical peculiarities, couldn't quite believe what Fate had delivered.

Pino had parked his Porsche as close to the front door as possible without driving it into the house, and, as Signor and Signora Courage strove to make him welcome, he kept glancing through the window, as if worried that some delinquent forest animal was liable to drive off with his splendid vehicle.

Calmed at last, he spread his arms beneficently and invited the music to begin.

The Courage Consort sang *Partitum Mutante* — all thirty-one and a half minutes of it, without a break — and they sang it rather well, all things considered. As always, when it came to the challenge of a real performance to an audience — even an audience of one — they moved Heaven and Hell to overcome their differences. Julian managed nuances of some humility, Dagmar conformed for the greater good, Roger slowed his tempo when his wife faltered at one point, gathering her back into the fold. And, at the finish, Catherine sang the last notes with even greater virtuosity than she had before.

Arboreal silence settled on the house as the Courage Consort slumped, exhausted, on the farther shores beyond conventional harmony. They had swum a long way in turbulent sonic waters with barely a pause for breath. Rather disconcertingly, as they struggled up from the sea, they felt themselves being looked down on by a macaque in an infant's pyjama jacket.

'Bravo,' the macaque leered.

Pino Fugazza was, briefly, lavish in his praise, then, at length, lavish in his criticism. As he spoke, he left the score unconsulted at his side; matters of mere pedantic detail did not seem to trouble him. Instead, it was larger issues that he felt the Consort were failing to grasp. Issues like the very essence and spirit of the piece.

Gesticulating balletically, Fugazza swayed before

them, his slacks jingling as he strove to make himself understood in his own avant-garde version of English.

'It shoot be more extrème, but more soft also,' he exclaimed after many abortive attempts. To illustrate some sort of sublime paradox, he threw his stubby claws violently up into the air, then let them float languorously down like dying squidlets. 'Like somesing very lo-o-o-ost, from ze bottom of a well.'

There was a pause.

'Quieter?' Roger attempted to translate.

Fugazza nodded, pleased that progress was being made at last.

'Yes, very much quieter,' he said, 'but wiz no losing of . . . of psychic loudity, you understand? Quiet, but loud inside ze ears . . . Like ze sound of water dripping from a . . . a . . .'

'Tap?'

'Faucet. Dripping in ze night, when everysing is quiet. So it's loud, yes? Silence, amplificated.'

They all pondered this a moment, then Roger said:

'You think we should sing extremely quietly, but have microphones amplifying us?'

'No! No! No microphones!' cried Pino, plucking invisible offending objects from the air in front of him and casting them straight into a lake of fire. 'Ze loudness comes from ze . . . ze intensity, yes?'

'Intensity of emotion?'

'Intensity of . . . of concentration. Concentrated like . . . like . . .'

'Chicken stock cubes?' suggested Dagmar in a poisonous murmur as she played with a strand of her hair.

'Like a bullet,' affirmed the composer in triumph. 'A bullet is very small, yes? But ze effect is . . . is . . .' He grimaced, betrayed yet again by a language so inferior to Italian.

Catherine, resisting the urge to leave her body and float up to the ceiling after her big exertion, tried hard to help him find the right word. She imagined the effect of a bullet entering someone's flesh – someone who didn't want to die.

'Dreadful,' she said.

'I hate him,' hissed Dagmar when he had driven away.

'It's probably a communication problem,' said Roger spiritlessly.

'I hate him,' repeated Dagmar, intently flicking her damp hair with her thumb and index finger. 'That's what I'm communicating to you.'

'Well,' sighed Roger, 'he has *his* idea of the piece, we have ours . . .'

Ben was padding around the house like a bear, going from window to window, opening them all wide. It wasn't until he was opening the biggest, nearest window that his fellow Consort members noticed the whole chateau stank of the sort of perfume probably derived from scraping the scrotums of extremely rare vermin.

United in their dislike of the composer, the Courage Consort devoted the next week to getting on top of *Partitum Mutante*. By day, they did little other than sing. By night, they slept deeply. Even Catherine was less troubled by insomnia than ever before. No sooner had the piercing, plaintive cry of the creature in the forest woken her up than she was drifting off again.

In the Chateau de Luth, she was developing a kind of routine, to which, amazingly for her, she was able to adhere religiously. She who had always seemed programmed to disappoint, abandoning the best-laid late-night plans in the suicidal torpor of dawn, was now getting up early every morning, cooking porridge for Ben, going off for a bike ride with Dagmar, then freshening herself up for a long afternoon's singing. Looking down at herself in the shower as the misty water cascaded over her naked flesh, she wondered if she was merely imagining a more youthful appearance, or if it was real.

Roger was retreating into a hard shell of professionalism, a state he tended to go into whenever a deadline was growing too near. It was by no means unattractive: Catherine liked him best this way. He focused utterly on the task at hand — in this case, the fiendish *Partitum Mutante* — and strove to understand the nature of his fellow singers' difficulties, keen not to dissipate their precious energy or fray their raw nerves. Rather than demanding endless repetition, he was tolerant when things went wrong. 'Let's not waste our breath,' he'd quip gravely, whenever an argument loomed. Afterwards, he'd lie flat on his back in bed at night thinking up ways to make the next performance run more smoothly. Catherine almost felt like embracing him when he was like this. If she could have been sure he'd stay flat on his back, she would have rested her head on his shoulder and stroked his frowning brow.

She wondered if Ben was happy. He was such a mountain of poise, but was he happy? Every night at 11 p.m. sharp, he would retire to his little room, to a bed that could not possibly be big enough for him. What did he do to make himself comfortable? Did he miss his wife? Was his own body, when he was horizontal, intolerably heavy, like an unwanted other person bearing down on him?

Before this fortnight in Martinekerke, it would never have occurred to Catherine to wonder about such things. Each Consort member had his or her separate life, mysterious to the others. Their personal happiness or unhappiness was irrelevant to the purpose that brought them together — at least, that was the way it had always been in the past. They would *rendezvous* at the Lambs' place in Tufnell Park, like five football fans who were going to sit down and watch a televised match together, and with barely a word spoken they would start singing a Josquin *Miserere* or whatever was on the agenda. Ben's wife would make herself scarce, cooking what smelled like very large quantities of Asian food in the kitchen. In all the years the Consort had been doing this, Catherine had never even got around to asking what nationality Mrs Lamb was. She looked Vietnamese or something, and dressed like an American hair-care consultant. At intervals, she would serve her guests coffee and cake: apple and cinnamon slices subtly impregnated with stray aromas of prawns, turmeric, garlic, soy sauce. Now and then Catherine got a hankering to ask Ben a few questions about his wife, but as the years passed she tended to feel she might have missed the right moment to raise the subject.

Julian was an unknown quantity too, although there were signs that he might inspire complex emotions in more people than just his fellow singers. Once, while the Consort were rehearsing at the Lambs' house, a drunken man, shouting unintelligible abuse, had kicked dents into Julian's car parked just outside. Julian went white and sat waiting stoically as the characteristic *bimff* of breaking windscreen resounded in the night air. Again, no one in the Courage Consort asked any questions. Julian's extra-musical activities were his own affair. He could sing the pants off any tenor in England, that was the important thing.

Even Catherine's mental frailties were tolerated, as long as they didn't interfere with the music. Last year, she'd even been able to show up for rehearsals with both her wrists wrapped in snowy white bandage, and nobody had mentioned it. By contrast, if she dared to spend a few minutes too long in Heathrow's toilets when the Consort had a plane to catch, she was liable to hear an admonitory summons over the airport PA.

As for Dagmar, the most recent addition to the group, she'd stuck with the Courage Consort because they gave her fewer hassles than any of her many previous liaisons. After walking out on the Dresden Staatsoper because the directors seemed to think she was too sexually immoral to sing opera (her last rôle for them was Berg's prostitute Lulu, for God's sake!) she'd been a bit wary of these smiling English people, but it had turned out OK. They allowed her to get away with tempestuous love affairs, even illegitimate pregnancy, as long as she showed up on time, and this she had no trouble with. For nine months of ballooning belly she'd never missed a rehearsal; she'd given birth, prudently, during the lull between Ligeti's *Aventures* in Basle and the 'Carols Sacred and Profane' Christmas concert in Huddersfield. That was good enough for Roger Courage, who had sent her a tasteful congratulations card without enquiring after the baby's name or sex.

This strange fortnight in Martinekerke, though,

was making them so much more real to each other as human beings, at least from Catherine's point of view. Living together as a family, cooking for each other, seeing the stubble on each other's faces — well, not on hers, of course — watching each other's hair grow, even ... Catherine was finding it all really quite exciting. She could definitely see herself, before the fortnight was over, asking Ben about his wife, or cycling all the way to Duidermonde.

It was her impression, though, that Julian was not a happy man. As the days in the Chateau de Luth wore on, he was growing increasingly restless. Not restless in the sense of lacking ability to concentrate on the task at hand; he worked as hard on *Partitum Mutante* as any of the Consort. Nor restless in the sense of itching for physical exercise; he was quite content to let Dagmar and Catherine cycle daily to Martinekerke to fetch their supplies. No, it appeared he was restless sexually.

In London, Julian was a lone wolf, never actually seen with a partner. Roger and Catherine had always assumed he must be gay, what with the Freddie Mercury ansaphone message and the waspish comments he was wont to make, but in Martinekerke it became clear that, at the very least, he was prepared to stoop to females if nothing better was available.

Females were in limited supply in the forest, but Julian made the most of what strayed his way. The first time Gina had come to clean the chateau, Julian behaved (Roger told Catherine later) like a gallant lord of the manor receiving an impressionable guest. The girl's flat refusal to let him carry her equipment frustrated this line of approach and so he hurried back indoors to launch Plan B, leaving the formal introductions to Roger. When, less than two minutes later, the time came for Gina to be introduced to Julian Hind, 'our tenor', he was already seated at the piano, playing a piece of Bartók's *Mikrokosmos* with serene intensity. He turned his cheekbones towards her and raised his eyebrows, as if he'd never glimpsed her before this moment, as if she'd just blundered, childlike, into a *sanctum* whose holiness she couldn't be expected to understand. He inclined his head in benign welcome but did not speak. Disappointingly, Gina did not speak either, preferring to get down to business. With the plug of the vacuum cleaner nestled in her hand, she nosed around the room, murmuring to herself: 'Stopcontact, stopcontact' — the Dutch word for power-point, apparently. Once the vacuum cleaner started its noisy sucking, Julian stopped playing the piano and settled for a more passive role. Then, all too soon, Catherine had returned from her walk in the woods, and it was time for *Partitum Mutante*.

The second time Gina came to the chateau, five days later, Catherine was actually there, privileged to witness the changes that Julian's growing discontentment had wrought on him. It was an extraordinary sight, an unforgettable testament to the power of accumulated sexual craving.

To begin with, he welcomed her at the door as if she were royalty – the English rather than the Dutch kind – and immediately tried to get her to sit down with him on the sofa. When she insisted that she had work to do, he followed her from room to room, raising the volume of his velvety tenor to compete with the noise of motorised suction and clanking, sloshing buckets. He guessed, correctly, that she was involved in the expressive arts and only doing this cleaning work as a way of supplementing a government grant. He guessed, correctly, her birth sign, her taste in music, her favourite drink, her preferred animal. Dashing into the bathroom to fetch her some Elastoplast when she'd cut her finger, he returned naked from the waist up and with water combed through his hair, complaining of the heat.

Catherine didn't dare follow them upstairs, so she made herself a cup of tea, wondering despite herself whether there was going to be some sexual activity in the chateau after all. By the time she saw Julian again, ten minutes later, he was installed on the sofa, fully dressed, glowering into a book. A strange sound – bed-springy, rhythmic – from upstairs was eventually decoded as Gina slamming an iron onto a padded ironing board.

Four days before the end of the fortnight, Jan van Hoeidonck dropped in to see how they were getting on. Re-acquainting himself with Catherine Courage, he at first thought she must be the sporty German contralto he'd been told about, she was so tanned and healthy-looking. He'd fixed Catherine in his memory as a slightly stooped middle-aged lady dressed in taupe slacks and a waterproof, with a freshly-washed halo of mousy hair; here she was in green leggings and a berry-stained T-shirt, standing tall, her hair shiny, plastered with sweat. She'd just been for a long cycle, she said.

The real German woman appeared moments later, cradling a sleeping baby in her arms. She shook Jan by the hand, supporting her infant easily in one arm as she did so.

'This is Dagmar Belotte,' said Roger, 'and . . . erm . . . Axel.'

As a way of breaking the ice, Jan made the mistake of asking Dagmar, rather than Roger Courage, what the Consort's impression of Pino Fugazza had been.

'I hate him,' she volunteered. 'He is a nut case and he smells bad.'

'Extraordinary composer, though, of course,' interjected Roger.

'Don't you check them out before you give them money?' said Dagmar.

The director smiled, unfazed. The German girl's

72

frankness made much more sense to him than the strange, twitching discomfiture of the pale Englishman.

'Pino is very crazy, yes,' he conceded. 'Sometimes crazy people make very good music. Sometimes not. We will find out.'

'And if it's bad?' enquired Dagmar.

Jan van Hoeidonck pouted philosophically.

'Bad music is not a problem in our circles,' he said. 'Ten years later, it's completely disappeared. Bio-degradable. It's not like pop music. Bad pop music lasts forever. Johann Strauss. Herman's Hermits. Father Abraham and the Smurfs. These things will never die, even if we put a lot of effort into killing them. But for bad serious music, we don't need to do anything. It just sinks into the ground and it's gone.'

'But Jan, what do *you* think of *Partitum Mutante*?' asked Roger.

'I haven't heard it yet.'

'You've seen the score, surely.'

The director gratefully accepted the steaming cup of coffee being handed to him by Mrs Courage.

'I am a facilitator of musical events,' he explained carefully. 'I read budget sheets. There are enough *crescendos* there, I promise you.' His face was solemn as he said this, though there was a twinkle in his eyes.

Dagmar excused herself and the conversation moved on to more general matters, like the chateau and its facilities. Were the Consort enjoying their stay?

How was the environment suiting them?

The big fat man called Ben Lamb, sitting in the far corner of the room, made a small gesture indicating no complaints. Roger Courage said something to the effect that concentration on a musical project made the outside world cease to exist, but that during the brief moments when his Consort was not beavering away at *Partitum Mutante*, the Chateau de Luth and its setting were very attractive indeed. Julian Hind deflected the question, preferring to discuss with the director the feasibility of a hire-car from Antwerp or Brussels.

'I was wondering,' Catherine said, when Julian, appalled at the high cost of Netherlandish living, had retreated to his room. 'You've had many artists staying in this chateau over the years, haven't you?'

'Very many,' affirmed the director.

'Have any of them ever mentioned strange noises in the night?'

'What kind of noises?'

'Oh . . . cries from the forest, perhaps.'

'Human cries?'

'Mmm, yes, possibly.'

She and Roger were sitting together on the sofa. On the pretence of bending down to fetch his plate of cake off the floor, Roger knocked his knee sharply against hers.

'Excuse me, dear,' he warned, trying to pull her back from whatever brink she was dawdling towards.

Unexpectedly, however, the director had no difficulty with her claims of mysterious cries in the night; in fact, he went pensive, as if faced with something that genuinely might lie outside the scope of art and arithmetic.

'This is a story I have heard before, yes,' he said. 'In fact, it is a kind of legend about the forest here.'

'Really,' breathed Catherine, gazing at him over the top of her steaming coffee mug. Roger was already fading away next to her.

'It began, I think, at the end of the war. A . . .' Jan van Hoeidonck paused, checking the Dutch–English dictionary in his head. 'A mental defective mother . . . can you say this in English?'

'It's all right,' said Catherine, loath to explain political correctness to a foreigner. 'Go on.'

'A mental defective mother ran away from Martinekerke with her baby, when the army, the liberating army, was coming. She didn't understand these soldiers were not going to kill her. So she ran away, and nobody could find her. For all the years since that time, there are reports that a baby is crying in the forest, or a . . . a spirit, yes?'

'Fascinating,' said Catherine, bending forward to put her cup down on the floor without taking her eyes off Jan van Hoeidonck. His own gaze dropped slightly, and she realised, with some surprise, that he was looking at her breasts.

I'm a woman, she thought.

Roger spoke up, pulling the conversation back towards Pino Fugazza and his place in contemporary European music. Had the director, in fact, heard *anything* by the composer?

'I heard his first major piece,' Jan replied, unenthusiastically. '*Precipice*, for voices and percussion – the one that won the Prix d'Italia. I don't remember it so well, because all the other Prix d'Italia entries were played on the same night, and they also were for voices and percussion. Except one from the former Soviet Union, for flügelhorn and ring modulator . . .'

'Yes, but can you remember *anything* about Fugazza's piece?' pursued Roger.

The director frowned: for him, dwelling on musical events that were in the past rather than the future was obviously quite unnatural.

'I only remember the audience,' he admitted, 'sitting there after four hours of singing and whispering and noises going bang without warning, and finally it's over, and they don't know if it's time to clap, and soon they will go home.'

Roger was getting politely exasperated.

'Well . . . if you haven't heard *Partitum Mutante*, what makes you think it'll be any better?'

Jan waved a handful of fingers loosely around his right temple.

'He has since that time had a big mental breakdown,' he said. 'This could be a very good thing for his music. Also, public interest in Fugazza is very high, which is good for ticket sales. He is very famous in the Italian press for attacking his wife with a stiletto shoe at the baggage reclaim of Milan Airport.'

'No!' said Catherine incredulously. 'Is she all right?'

'She is very fine. Soon I think she will be divorced and very wealthy. But of course, the music must stand or fall on its own qualities.'

'Of course,' sighed Roger.

Later, when the director had left, Roger stood at the window, watching the yellow minibus dwindling into the distance, on the long black ribbon towards Brussels. As he watched, the sun was beaming through the window-panes like a trillion-watt spotlight, turning his silver hair white and his flesh the colour of peeled apple. Every age line and wrinkle, every tiny scar and pockmark from as far back as adolescence, was lit up in harsh definition. Eventually the intensity of the light grew too much for him; he turned away, fatigued, blinking and wiping his eyes.

Noticing that Ben Lamb was still sitting in the shady corner of the room, and Catherine lying sweating and sleepy on the couch, he allowed himself to express his first pang of doubt about the value of the project they were all engaged on.

'You know, I'm really rather tired of this glamour that madness is supposed to have, aren't you?' he said, addressing Ben. 'It's the little marks on the score that ought to be sensational, not the behaviour of Italian lunatics at airports.'

Catherine, not happy at the disrespect with which madness was being tossed about here, said:

'Couldn't this Pino fellow just be young and excitable? I wouldn't presume to judge if anyone was definitely mad. Especially an Italian I've only met once. He surely can't be *too* barmy if he drives a Porsche and wears Armani.'

'Poetically put, dear — if somewhat mysterious in reasoning,' remarked Roger.

'No, I meant, he's obviously not . . . um . . . other-wordly, is he?'

There was a pause as the men pondered the significance of this word.

'What do *you* think, Ben?' said Roger.

'I think we should sing as much as we possibly can in the next four days,' said Ben, 'so that, by the time of the première, we can at least be sure of being less confused than Mr Fugazza.'

And so they sang, as the sun blazed in the sky and the temperature inside the chateau climbed towards 30° Celsius. It was worse than being under a full rig of stage lights; all five of them were simmering in their clothes.

'We'll end up performing this in the nude,' suggested Julian. 'That'll put some sensuality into it!'

The others let it pass, appreciating that he was a man on heat.

When, at last, they were all too tired to go on, Roger and Julian went to bed — not with each other, of course, though lately Julian looked as if he might soon consider anything, even his fellow Consort members, as a sexual possibility. His initial disgust at seeing Dagmar breast-feed had, with the passing days, softened to tolerance, and then hardened to a curiosity whose keenness embarrassed everyone except himself. Dagmar, usually indifferent to the petty libidos of unwanted men, grew self-conscious, and the feeding of her baby became an increasingly secret act, perpetrated behind closed doors. In Julian's presence, she tended to fold her arms across her breasts, protectively, aggressively. After half an hour staring Julian down, she would leap up and start pacing back and forth, a dark band across her bosom where her sweaty forearms had soaked the fabric of whatever she was wearing.

On the night of the director's visit, with *Partitum Mutante* finished off and Julian safely gone to bed, Dagmar sat slumped on the couch, Axel at her breast. Ben sat by the open window, staring out at a sky which, even at a quarter to eleven, still had some daylight left in it. The unearthly quiet was descending again, so that even the drip of a tap in the kitchen could be heard from the front room.

Oddly revived by having had her milk sucked from

her, Dagmar decided to take Axel out for a walk in the forest. She did not invite Catherine; the older woman guessed this must be one of those times when Dagmar wanted to have the run of the world alone with her baby, explaining things to him in German.

'Be careful,' said Catherine as they were leaving. 'Remember the legend.'

'What legend?'

'A mother and her child disappeared in that forest once, at the end of the war. Some people say the baby is still out there.'

Dagmar paused momentarily as she made a mental calculation.

'Well, if we meet a fifty-seven-year-old baby on our walk, maybe Axel will like to play with him,' she said, and sauntered into the dark.

Left alone with Ben, Catherine weighed up the pros and cons of going to bed. On the pro side, she was exhausted. But the house had absorbed so much heat that she doubted she would sleep.

'Do you want anything, Ben?' she offered.

'Mm? No, thanks,' he replied. He was still sitting by the window, his white shirt almost transparent with sweat. For all his bear-like bulk, he had no body hair, as far as Catherine could see.

'How are you, anyway?' she asked. It seemed a faintly absurd question, this late in the night.

'Tired,' he said.

'Me too. Isn't it funny how we've lived here together, day after day, and sung together endlessly, and yet we hardly say two words to one another?'

'I'm not much of a conversationalist.'

He closed his eyes and leaned his head back, as if about to release his soul into the ether, leaving his body behind.

'You know,' said Catherine, 'after all these years, I know hardly anything about you.'

'Very little to tell.'

'I don't even know for sure what nationality your wife is.'

'Vietnamese.'

'I thought so.'

Their communication eddied apart then, but not disturbingly. The room's emotional acoustic was not full of shame and failure, like the silences between her and Roger. Silence was Ben's natural state, and to fall into it with him was like joining him in his own world, where he was intimately acquainted with each sleeping soundwave, and knew no fear.

After a while, sitting in the golden-brown front room with Ben in the stillness, Catherine glanced at her watch. It was almost midnight. Ben had never stayed up so late before.

'Did you always want to be a singer?' she asked.

'No,' he said. 'I wanted to carry on coxing.'

She laughed despite herself. 'Carry on *what*?' She was reminded of those dreadful comedy films her father had never allowed her to see, even when she was old enough to be going out with Roger Courage.

'At university,' Ben explained, 'I was a coxswain in a rowing team. I called instructions through a loud-hailer. I enjoyed that very much.'

'What happened?'

'I became involved in the anti-Vietnam war movement. Cambridge wasn't the most left-wing place in those days. I lost most of my friends. Then I got fat.'

You're not fat, Catherine wanted to reassure him, as a reflex kindness, then had to struggle to keep a straight face in the moon face of absurdity. Reassurance is such a sad, mad thing, she thought. Deep inside, everyone knows the truth.

'What do you really think of *Partitum Mutante*, Ben?'

'We-e-ell . . . it's a plum part for a bass, I have to admit. But I don't see us singing it far into the twenty-first century somehow.'

Again the silence descended. Minutes passed. Catherine noticed for the first time that there were no clocks in the Chateau de Luth, except for those inside the computers and the oven, and the wrist-watches worn by the human visitors. Perhaps there had once been splendid old timepieces which some previous guest had stolen — she imagined Cathy Berberian stealthily wrapping an antique clock up in her underwear as she was packing her suitcase to go home. Perhaps there had never been clocks on these walls at all, because the chateau's furnishers had understood that the sound of seconds ticking would have been maddening, intolerable, in the forest's silence.

Suddenly, there was a plaintive, inarticulate wail from outside, a cry that was more high-pitched and eerie than anything Axel was capable of. Catherine's flesh was thrilled with fear.

'There!' she said to Ben. 'Did you hear that?'

But, looking across at him, she saw that his eyes were shut, his great chest rising and falling rhythmically.

Catherine jumped up from the couch, hurried to the front door. She opened it — very quietly so as not to wake Ben — and peered out into the night, which was impenetrably dark to her unadjusted eyes. The forest was indistinguishable from the sky, except that there were stars in one and not the other. Catherine was half-convinced that Dagmar and Axel had been consumed by some lonely demon, swallowed up into the earth, never to be seen again. It was almost disappointing when, minutes later, both mother and baby materialised out of the gloom and strolled up to the chateau, Dagmar's white trainers luminescing.

'Did you hear the cry?' said Catherine as Dagmar reached the threshold.

'What cry?' said Dagmar. Axel was wide-eyed and

full of energy, but his mother was exhausted, overdue for bed. She swayed in the doorway, looking as if she might consider handing her baby over to Catherine for a while.

Next day, Roger telephoned Pino Fugazza, to tell him that there was a problem with *Partitum Mutante*. A technical problem, he said. They'd rehearsed it so thoroughly now, he said, that they were in a position to tell the difference between awkwardnesses that arose from unfamiliarity with the score, and awkwardnesses that might be . . . well, in the score itself.

While Roger spoke, the other members of the Courage Consort sat nearby, wondering how Pino was going to react, especially as Roger was pushed, *poco a poco*, to be more specific about the nature of the problem — which was that, in a certain spot, Pino's time signatures just didn't add up. The Italian's daring musical arithmetic, a tangled thicket of independent polyrhythms, was supposed to resolve itself by the 404th bar (symbolising the 4004 years from Creation to Christ's birth), so that Roger and Catherine were suddenly singing in perfect unison, joined in the next bar by Julian and Dagmar while Ben kept lowing underneath.

'The thing is,' said Roger into the phone, 'by the 404th bar, the baritone is a beat behind the soprano.'

A harsh chattering sound came through the receiver, indecipherable to the overhearers.

'Well . . .' grimaced Roger, adjusting his glasses to look at the computer screen. 'It's possible I've misunderstood something, but three lots of 9/8 and one lot of 15/16 repeated with a two-beat rest . . . are you with me?'

More chatter.

'Yes. Then, from the A flat, it goes . . . Pardon? Uh . . . Yes, I see it right here in front of me, Mr Fugazza . . . But surely thirteen plus eight is twenty-one?'

The conversation was wound up very quickly after that. Roger replaced the telephone receiver on the handset and turned to his expectant fellow members of the Consort.

'He gives us his blessing,' said Roger, frowning in bemusement, 'to do whatever we want.'

It was a freedom none of them would have predicted.

Later that afternoon, while the Courage Consort were taking a break to soothe their throats with fruit juice, a car pulled up to the house. Roger opened the door, and let in a grizzled photographer who looked like a disgraced priest.

'Hello! Courage Consort? Carlo Pignatelli.'

He was Italian, but worked for a Luxembourg newspaper, and he'd been sent to cover the Benelux

Contemporary Music Festival. He had already seen publicity material on the Consort, and knew exactly what he wanted.

Dagmar was nursing a glass of apricot juice alone in the front room while the English members of the group hung around the oven trying to make toast. Pignatelli made a bee-line for the German girl, who was wearing black tights and a white cotton blouse.

'You're Dagmar Belotte, right?' He sounded alarmingly as if he'd learned English from watching subtitled cockney soap operas; in truth, he'd just returned to the bosom of the European press after ten alcoholic years in London.

'That's right,' said Dagmar, putting her drink down on the floor. She was going to need both hands for this one, she could tell.

'You're into mountaineering, right?' said Pignatelli, as if getting a few final facts straight after a gruellingly thorough interview.

'That's right,' said Dagmar.

'You wouldn't have any of your gear with you, would you?'

'What for?'

'A picture.'

'A picture of what?'

'A picture of you in mountaineering gear. Ropes.' He indicated with his hairy hands where the ropes would hang on her, fortunately using his own chest rather than hers to demonstrate. 'Axe.' He mimed a small act of violence against an invisible cliff face.

'There are no mountains here,' said Dagmar evenly.

The photographer was willing to compromise. Quickly sizing up the feel of the chateau's interior, his eyes lingering for micro-seconds on the rack of antique recorders, he said:

'Play the flute?'

'No.'

'Mind holding one?'

Dagmar was speechless for a moment, which he took as assent. Surprisingly fleet on his feet, he bounded over to the recorders and selected the biggest. Handing it over to her, he leered encouragingly, then drew his camera from its holster with a practised one-handed motion. Dagmar folded her arms across her breasts, clasping the recorder in one fist like a police baton.

'Could you put it in your mouth maybe?' suggested the photographer.

'Forget it,' said Dagmar, tossing the instrument onto a nearby cushion.

'Is there a grand piano?' rejoined the photographer, quick as a flash. She surely wouldn't object to leaning in and fingering a few strings, canopied by the lid.

'No, it's a . . .' The word Dagmar was looking for refused to translate itself from German. She considered saying 'erect' but decided against it. 'Not grand,' she said, her big eyes narrowing to slits.

Undaunted, the photographer peered outside to gauge the weather. Mercifully, a loud noise started up from somewhere inside the house, a disconsolate human cry that could not be ignored.

'Excuse me,' muttered Dagmar as she strode off to find her baby.

The photographer turned his attention immediately to Catherine.

'Is it true,' he said, picking up Dagmar's half-finished tumbler of juice, 'a soprano can shatter glass?'

That night, when the singing was over, the chateau was even hotter than the night before. Catherine found herself alone in the front room with Julian, everyone else having gone to bed.

Julian was on his hands and knees in front of a bookcase, peering at the spines. He had finished everything he'd brought with him to Belgium, all the thrillers and exposés, and was now in the market for something else. He read no Dutch, so such tomes as *Het Leven en Werk van Cipriano de Rore (1516–1565)* didn't quite hit the spot, but he was fluent in French and – surprisingly, to Catherine – Latin.

'Really? Latin?' she said, as if he'd just revealed a facility for Urdu or Sinhalese.

'I don't know why you're so surprised,' said Julian, his bottom — ass? — arse? — in the air as he studied the titles. 'We sing Latin texts all the time.'

'Yes, but . . .' Catherine cast her mind back to the last time she'd sung in Latin, and was surprised at the ease with which she recalled the words of Gabrieli's 'O Magnum Mysterium'. Something was happening to her brain lately, an unblocking of the channels, a cleaning of the contours. 'We use translations. Or I do, anyway. Roger prints out parallel English and Latin texts for me, and that's how I learn what it all means.'

'I don't need Roger to tell me what it all means,' muttered Julian as he pulled an ancient-looking volume out of the bookcase. It slid smoothly into his hands, without the billow of dust Catherine might have expected — but then, Gina had dusted there only a few days ago.

'I think I'll go for a walk,' said Catherine.

'You do that,' said Julian. He was in a peculiar, intense state, as if he'd passed right through frustration into whatever lay beyond. Sitting cross-legged on the carpet, he was opening the fragile old book in his lap and bending his head towards its creamy pages, his damp black hair swinging down over his forehead. For Catherine, it was all indefinably unnerving, and her instinct was to get away.

Roger would still be awake, though, in the bed upstairs. Roger, Julian, and the dark forest of Martinekerke:

she was stuck between the devil, and the devil, and the deep blue sea.

Catherine set off into the night, with a windcheater loosely draped over her T-shirt, and only a pencil torch to guide her through the dark. She didn't even switch it on, but kept it in the back pocket of her jeans, hoping that her sight would adjust to the starlight, the way the eyes of people like Dagmar evidently did.

Walking across the road, Catherine felt and heard, but could not see, her feet stepping off the smooth tarmac into the leafy perimeter of the forest. She rustled cautiously forward, trusting her body aura to warn her of approaching trees. Overhead, the sky remained black; perhaps the awful humidity meant that it was cloudy.

She removed the torch from her pocket and shone its thin beam onto the ground before her. A small circle of leaves and earth stood out from the darkness like an image on a television screen. It moved as she tilted her wrist, scooting backwards and forwards through the trees, growing paler. After only thirty seconds of use, the batteries of the torch were getting tired already; the feeble power supply just wasn't up to the challenge of a whole forest full of night. She switched it off, and hoped for the best.

You know what you've come here for, don't you? challenged a voice from inside her. She wasn't alarmed: it was her own voice, intimate and patient, not the terrifying stranger who had once commanded her to swallow poison or slice through the flesh of her wrists. It was just a little harmless internal conversation, between Catherine and herself.

No, tell me: what am I here for? she asked in return.

You're waiting for the cry, came the answer.

She walked deeper into the forest, afraid and unrepentant. A breeze whispered through the trees, merciful after the trapped and stagnant heat inside the house. She was just getting a breath of fresh air, that was all. There was no such thing as ghosts: a ghost would always be revealed, in the clear light of day, to have been an owl, or a wolf, or one's own father standing in the door of one's bedroom, or a plastic bag caught on a branch, waving in the wind. The dead stayed dead. The living had to push on, without help or hindrance from the spirit world.

Catherine's eyes had adjusted to the dark by now, and she could see the boughs of the trees around her, and an impression of the ground beneath her feet. Wary of getting herself lost but wanting to stay in the forest longer, she wandered in circles, keeping the distant golden lights of the house in sight. She clapped her palms against trees as she passed them, swinging around like a child on a pole. The roughness of the bark was heavenly on her hands.

After perhaps half an hour she grew conscious of a

full bladder — all those glasses of fruit juice! — and squatted in a clearing to pee. Her urine rustled into the leaves, and something unidentifiable scratched softly against her naked bottom.

I hope nothing jumps into me while I'm exposed like this, she thought, as, in the chateau, the lights went out.

Next morning, Ben Lamb, waiting for his *havermout*, looked up expectantly as someone entered the kitchen. But it was only Julian, come for his coffee.

'I made a real find last night,' Julian said, as the kettle hissed sluggishly.

'Mm?' said Ben.

'An original edition of Massenet's songs, printed in 1897, including some I'm sure have never seen the light of day, just sitting there on the shelf. Never been looked at!'

'How do you know it's never been looked at?'

'The pages were still uncut. Just think! Totally . . . virgin.'

'And did you cut them, Julian?'

'You bet I did,' grinned Julian. 'And it was a delicious sensation, I can assure you.' He was peering into the refrigerator as Dagmar, fully dressed and with Axel already in her rucksack, passed by the kitchen.

'Save a few eggs for other people, please,' she called over her shoulder.

Julian contorted his face into a gargoyle sneer,

beaming malice in her direction as the front door slammed shut.

'*Jawohl, mein Kommandant!*'

Ben sighed. The Courage Consort were reaching the limit of their ability to coexist harmoniously, at least in such hothouse conditions. It was only 10.30 am now, and the temperature was already stifling; not the best conditions for negotiating the treacherous vocal labyrinths laid out for them by Mr Fugazza. According to an imported *Times* Dagmar had brought back from Martinekerke yesterday, rain was pelting down all over London and the Home Counties: when would the clouds break here?

Roger walked into the kitchen, a veteran of yet another telephone call.

'Wim Waafels, the video artist, is coming here this afternoon,' he said, looking glum.

'Some problem?' enquired Ben.

Roger ran his fingers through his hair, large patches of sweat already darkening the underarms of his shirt, as he searched for a way to summarise his misgivings.

'Let's just say I don't imagine Dagmar is going to like him very much,' he said at last.

'Oooh,' camped Julian, 'fancy that! A soul-mate for me. You never know your luck in a big forest.'

Roger shambled over to the stove, tired of holding his little family together, day after day. He poured himself a cup of tea from the kettle that had boiled, unnoticed.

'Has anyone seen our soprano?' he said, trying to keep his voice light.

Ben shook his head. Julian stared directly into Roger's face, and saw there a look he had a special facility for recognising: the look of a man who is wondering where his wife slept last night.

'She went walkabout,' said Julian. 'After the witching hour.'

Roger sipped at his tea, not a happy man.

Then, a few minutes later, the front door clattered open and footsteps sounded in the hallway. Julian's jaw hardened in anticipation of another German invasion.

Instead, Catherine walked into the kitchen. She walked slowly, dreamily, in no hurry to focus on the men. Her hair was a bird's nest of tangles, her skin was flushed, her eyes half closed. Tiny leaves and fragments of twig clung to the calves of her leggings.

'Are you all right, Kate?' said Roger.

Catherine blinked, acknowledging his existence by degrees.

'Yes, yes, of course,' she responded airily. 'I've been out walking, that's all.'

She padded over to the stove, patting her husband's shoulder as she passed because the poor thing looked so miserable.

'Would anyone like some porridge?' she said, finding Ben's face exactly where she expected it to be and contemplating it with a smile.

Though there were two hours to kill before Wim Waafels was due to arrive, the Consort did not sing. By unspoken mutual agreement, they were giving *Partitum Mutante* a rest while the weather did its worst. Ben sat by the window, nursing a headache and indigestion; the others mooched around the house, fiddling with the musical instruments, books and ornaments. Julian played Beethoven's 'Für Elise' on the piano, over and over, always getting stuck in the same spot; Catherine squatted at the spinning wheel, touching its various parts tentatively, trying to decide if it was meant to be functional or was just for show. Roger sat at the computer, browsing through the score of Paco Barrios's *2K+5*, reminding himself that there would be life after *Partitum Mutante*.

By the time Mr Waafels ought to be arriving, the British members of the Courage Consort had — again by unspoken mutual consent — pulled together, resolved to be philosophical in the face of whatever the visit might bring. Only Dagmar was exempt from the prevailing mood. She sensed something in Roger's manner which made her suspect that the over-extended strings of her tolerance were about to be twanged.

'You've talked to this man, have you?' she queried warily.

'On the phone, yes,' said Roger.

'Is he a nut case?'

'No, no . . .' Roger reassured her breezily. 'He sounds quite . . . focused, really.'

'So he is OK?'

'He . . . he has a very thick Dutch accent. Much thicker than Jan van Hoeidonck's, for example. He's very young, I gather. *Your* age, perhaps. Not an old fuddy-duddy like us, heh heh heh.'

Dagmar's eyes narrowed in contempt. She'd always had a lot of respect for Roger Courage, but right now he was reminding her of the directors at the Dresden Staatsoper.

A vehicle could be heard approaching the Chateau de Luth, though it was half a mile away yet, invisible.

'That'll be him now,' said Roger, smoothly making his escape from Dagmar to take up a position at the window. But when the vehicle came into view, it proved to be not a van or a car, but a motorcycle, roaring through the stillness of Martinekerke forest in a haze of benzine, its rider in grey leather, studded gloves and a silver helmet, like a medieval soldier come looking for Thierry la Fronde and his band of merry men.

Once they invited him in, Wim Waafels proved to be, physically at least, a slightly more impressive specimen

than Pino Fugazza; he could hardly fail to be. Then
again, as he was taking off his helmet and leather jacket
in the chateau's front room, he did cause several
members of the Courage Consort to meditate privately
on the infinite scope of human unattractiveness.

He was a young man — twenty-five, reportedly,
though he looked seventeen, with an overweight
teenager's awkward posture. He wore ochre-coloured
cords, military boots and a large threadbare T-shirt on
which was printed a much-enlarged still from Buñuel's
Un Chien Andalou — the razor blade hovering above the
woman's eye. Waafels's own eyes were bloodshot and
deep-set, full of sincere but rather specialised intelligence. Perspiration and the odd pimple glittered on
his pumpkin face; his head was topped with a bush of
bleached white hair corrugated with gel.

'Erm . . . is it hotter or cooler, driving here on a
motorcycle?' asked Catherine, struggling to make
conversation as she handed him a tall drink of orange
juice.

'Bose,' he replied.

Though Wim's English vocabulary was good, his
accent was so thick that he seemed to have been
schooled by a different process from that used by all the
other Dutch people they'd met — interactive CD roms,
maybe, or those little translator gadgets you saw in
brochures that fell out of the *Radio Times*.

More worrying than his accent was the way he

blushed and stammered when introduced to Dagmar: evidently he had a weakness for big-breasted young German women with muscular limbs, even if they did not look overly friendly. Perhaps he mistook Dagmar's glower for the mock-dangerous pout of an MTV babe.

'Hi. I'm Wim,' he told her.

'Great. Let's see the video,' said Dagmar.

Small talk having reached its apex, they all got promptly down to business. Wim had brought with him a video of his images for *Partitum Mutante*. On the spine of the cassette, in silver felt-tip, he had scrawled '*PArTiTEm M!*' This, more even than Mr Waafels's appearance, caused alarm bells to toll inside the over-heated skulls of the Courage Consort.

There was a slight delay as the television proved not to be connected to the video player. To Wim, this was an eyebrow-raising oddity, something that could only be explained in terms of the Courage Consort having fiddled with the leads and plugs while using digital samplers, MIDI keyboards or other sophisticated technologies. He could not have guessed that the Courage Consort simply did not watch television.

Wim Waafels connected the machines with a practised, casual motion, the closest he came to physical grace. He then asked for the curtains to be drawn so the daylight wouldn't interfere with the clarity of his images. Roger obliged, or attempted to.

'Ken it not be moor dark den dis?' Waafels

enquired uneasily, as the room glowed amber in the muffled sunlight.

Roger fiddled with the curtains, trying out one thing and another.

'That's as dark as we're going to get it,' he said.

They all kneeled around the television, except for Ben, whose massive body did not permit him to kneel; he sat on the divan, insisting he could see perfectly well from a little farther back.

'OK,' announced Wim. 'De oddience is here, you are on de staitch, de lights go out – blekness!'

The tape started to whirr through the machine, and the screen, at first snowy, went perfectly black. It remained perfectly black for what felt like a very long time, though it was probably only thirty seconds – a minute, at most.

'You heff to imegine you are singing, of coorse,' Wim Waafels counselled them.

'Of course,' said Julian, moving a little closer to the television so that he couldn't see Dagmar's face.

The blackness of the screen was finally softening at its core, to a reddish-purple – or maybe it was an optical illusion brought on by eye-strain. But no: there was definitely something taking shape there.

'In de beginning, de ooniverse woss widout form, yes?' explained Waafels. 'Darkness moofs on de face of de deep.' The videotape as it passed along the machine's play heads made a faint squeaking noise which set Catherine's teeth on edge; she wished Ben could be making his sonorous Tibetan moans to give this gloomy void a human soundtrack.

After an eternity, the inky amorphous swirls finally coalesced into . . . into what? Some sort of glistening mauve orifice.

'Now, do you know what iss it?' challenged Waafels.

There was an awkward pause, then Ben spoke up.

'I believe I do,' he said, his voice calm and gently resonant. 'It's a close-up of a larynx, as seen by a laryngoscope.'

'Ferry goot, ferry goot!' said Waafels, happy to have found a soul on his wavelength. 'In de beginning woss de word, yes? De word dat coms from widdin de focal cords of Got.'

Another eternity passed as the larynx trembled open and shut, open and shut, twinkling in its own juices. Catherine felt queasiness accumulate in her stomach as the picture became lighter and pinker, and she glanced sideways at her companions, to see if they were feeling it too. Roger's face was rigid with concentration, loath to miss any crucial details if and when they should come. Julian and Dagmar, though they would probably have hated to be told so, looked strikingly similar: incredulous, open-mouthed, beautiful in their disdain. Catherine longed to turn and look at Ben, but she didn't want to embarrass him, so she reapplied her attention to the yawning aperture of flesh on the screen. Some sort of digital magic was being employed now to morph the larynx; the labia-like *plica vocalis* and *vallecula* were evolving, cell by cell, into the vulva of a heavily pregnant woman. Then, with agonising slowness, silent minute upon silent minute, the vagina dilated to reveal the slick grey head of a baby.

The Courage Consort spoke not a word as the *largo*-speed birth took its vivid and glistening course on the screen before them. They were all intimately aware, though, that the duration of *Partitum Mutante* was a shade over half an hour, and the timer on the video player kept track of every second.

When, at long last, the newborn Adam or Planet Earth or whatever he was supposed to be was squirming out into existence, his slow-motion slither almost unbearably eventful after what had gone before, the Courage Consort began to breathe again. Soon, they knew, the lights would go on.

'Of coorse,' said Wim Waafels by way of qualification, 'it's a total different effect like dis, on only a smol screen.'

'I'm sure it is,' said Roger.

'In de life performance, de immitch will be ferry ferry bik, and you will be ferry smol. It will . . . enfelope you.'

'Mmm,' said Roger, as he might have done if a Bedouin chieftain was watching him eat sheep's eyes at a politically delicate banquet.

'Mmm,' agreed Catherine, suddenly glad to have her husband around to suggest *le mot juste*.

Then, with heavenly timing, little Axel started crying upstairs, and Dagmar's ascension from the room was a *fait accompli* before Wim Waafels had a chance to ask her what she thought. He looked a little crestfallen to have lost the only member of his generation so abruptly, but he turned to the older, less gorgeous members of the Consort without ill feeling.

'Dis giffs you an idea, I hope?' he said to Julian, plainly the next-closest to him in age.

'It does, it does,' said Julian archly. 'I'm sure no one who sees this extraordinary work of yours will ever be able to forget it. My only regret is that I shall be on stage rather than in the audience.'

Waafels hastened to reassure him that this base was covered.

'I will make a video,' he said, 'off de performance.'

'Splendid! Splendid!' crowed Julian, turning away from Roger Courage so as not to be inhibited by the older man's warning stare. 'A video within a video. How very postmodern!'

Waafels smiled shyly as the grinning Julian slapped him on the back.

Later, when Wim Waafels had gone home and Julian had excused himself, the Courages turned to Ben, who was pensively examining the first couple of printed pages of *Partitum Mutante*'s score.

'Well, what do you think, Ben?' sighed Roger.

'I'm too old to claim to know anything about video art,' Ben conceded graciously. 'There is one little thing that worries me, though.'

Still a bit pale and peakish from the slow-motion gush of afterbirth, Catherine waited in silence for him to give voice to his concern.

'While it's utterly dark, in the blackness before the world is born,' mused Ben, 'how are we to see the music?'

The following day was the Consort's second-last in the Chateau de Luth, and they spent most of it arguing.

Things started off civilly enough, in the short-lived morning hours of freshness before the heat set in. Catherine made Ben his *havermout* breakfast as usual, serene with pleasure at this wordless routine of nurture. He ate, she watched, as the sun flowed in on both of them, making them glow like lightbulbs. When it got too bright for comfort, Catherine squinted but did not stop looking, and Ben kept his eyes lowered, smiling into the steam of his porridge.

Julian was holed up in his room, no doubt to avoid a reprise of last night's unpleasantness with Roger over the Waafels affair. Roger had disapproved of Julian's sarcasm on the grounds that Waafels, if he'd taken it to heart, would have regarded Julian as speaking for the Courage Consort as a whole; Julian retorted that he damn well hoped he *was* speaking for the Courage Consort as a whole and that if Roger had any deep-seated enthusiasm for singing inside a pair of labia the size of a barn door he'd better come clean with it immediately.

In the wake of this altercation, there'd been a curious change to the chateau's atmosphere, sonically speaking. Julian had removed the television from the public domain and carried it upstairs in his arms, claiming that if he was going to endure another sleepless night he needed something to keep him from going ga-ga. And, indeed, by midnight Catherine was hearing, from her own bed, the muted sounds of argument and tender Dutch reconciliation coming through the wall. It was a change from the uncanny silence, but not necessarily a welcome one.

This morning, although she couldn't hear any identifiable television sounds filtering down into the kitchen, Catherine had a feeling it was probably still chattering away to Julian in his room, because the purity seemed to have been taken out of the silence somehow. There was an inaudible fuzz, like the sonic equivalent of haze from burning toast, obscuring Catherine's access to the acoustic immensity of the forest. She would have to go out there soon, and leave that haze behind.

Inconveniently, Dagmar didn't want to go for a cycle. Looking fed up and underslept, she came into the kitchen with no discernible purpose except to check that Julian hadn't touched the eggs in the fridge.

'My nipples are cracking up,' she grouched, causing Ben to blush crimson over his *havermout* behind her. 'First, one was still OK, now it's both of them. Today, it must rain — must, must, must. And I don't understand why you people let that asshole Wim Waafels go without hurting him.'

Having run out of non sequiturs, she slammed the door of the refrigerator and tramped out of the kitchen.

Catherine and Ben sat in silence as they heard Dagmar ambush Roger in the next room and start an argument with him. The German girl's voice came through loud and clear, an angry contralto of penetrating musicality. Roger's baritone was more muted, his words of pained defence losing some of their clarity as they passed through the walls.

'There was never any suggestion,' he was saying, 'that we had any choice . . .'

'I'm a singer,' Dagmar reminded him. 'Not a doll for nut cases to play with.'

Roger's voice droned reasonably: '. . . multi-media event . . . we are only one of those media . . . problem with all collaborations . . . compromise . . . I'm not a Catholic, but I sing settings of the Latin Mass . . .'

'This is the Dresden Staatsoper all over again!'

On and on they went, until the listeners ceased to take in the words. Instead, Catherine and Ben let the sound of the arguers' voices wallow in the background, an avant-garde farrago of *Sprechstimme*.

By and by, Julian came downstairs and, smelling blood, gave mere coffee and toast a miss and joined the fray instead.

This was too much for Roger: fearing unfair odds, he called a meeting of the Consort as a whole, and the five of them sat in the front room where they had sung *Partitum Mutante* so endlessly, and bickered.

'The way to stop this sort of fiasco ever happening again,' declared Julian, 'is to price ourselves right out of the loony market.'

'What on earth do you mean by that, Julian?' sighed Roger.

'Sing much more popular repertoire and command higher ticket prices. Do more recordings, get our pretty faces known far and wide. Then, whenever we're offered a commission, we pick and choose. And keep some sort of right of veto. No Italian arms dealers, no gynaecology buffs.'

'But,' Roger winced, 'hasn't our strength always lain in our courage? — that is, our . . . um . . . willingness to be open to new things?'

Catherine started giggling, thinking of the yawning vulva that was waiting to 'enfelope' them all.

'Perhaps Kate is, in her own way, reminding us of

the need for a sense of humour,' Roger suggested rather desperately.

'No, no, I was just . . . never mind,' said Catherine, still chortling into the back of her hand. Roger was staring at her mistrustfully, imploringly: she knew very well he was trying to decide how crazy she was at this moment, how badly she might let him down. He needed her to be on his side, mentally frail or not; he needed her to see things his way, however impishly her inner demons might prevent her articulating it sensibly. She didn't have the heart to tell him that there weren't any inner demons making her laugh anymore; she just had more important things on her mind right now than the Courage Consort.

'The King's Singers went across a bomb at the Proms,' persisted Julian.

Roger bridled at this; it was a sore point with him. 'Look, I didn't cast my boat out on the dangerous sea of *a cappella* music,' he remarked testily, 'to sing "Obla-di, Obla-da" to a crowd of philistines in funny hats.'

'A very *large* crowd,' Julian reminded him. 'How many people are going to be hearing us at the Benelux Contemporary Music Festival?'

'For God's sake, Julian, are you suggesting we sing Andrew Lloyd Webber and "Raindrops Keep Falling on My Head" in motet style?'

'Oh bravo, Mr Courage: *reductio ad absurdum*!' Julian was rearing up alarmingly, balletic with pique. 'I'm merely hummmmmbly suggesting you give a *thought* to what might put some reasonably intelligent *bums* on seats. The Beatles, it may *astound* you to know, inspire greater love than Pino Fugazza and Mr Waffle put together — if such a pairing can be imagined without an ejaculation' — he gasped for breath — 'of vomit.'

'Yes, but . . .'

'You know what would make a great encore for us?' raged Julian, quite crazed by now. 'Queen's "Bohemian Rhapsody", arranged for five voices.'

Dagmar snorted loudly.

'You think I'm joking?' exclaimed Julian, fizzing with mischief. 'Listen!' And he burst into song, a snatch of "Bohemian Rhapsody" showing off his own range from horrible *faux*-bass to fiercely accurate falsetto: 'Bis-mil-lah! No-o-o-o! We will not let you go — Let him go-o-o-o! Will not let you go — Let him go-o-o-o! No, no, no, no, no, no, no — Mama mia, mama mia, mama mia let me go . . .'

Mercifully, Julian's fury dissipated before he reached the 'Beelzebub has a devil put aside' section so familiar from his answering machine, and he slumped back onto his knees.

'You are insane,' pronounced Dagmar, awed, as silence settled again on the sweltering room.

'What do *you* think, Ben?' pleaded Roger.

Ben breathed deeply, blinking as bad vibes continued to float through the thick air.

'I think one thing is not in question,' he said. 'We've been contracted to sing *Partitum Mutante* at the Benelux Contemporary Music Festival. If we do it, some people may question our judgement. If we refuse to do it, many more people will question our professionalism.'

Dagmar shook a heavy lock of hair off her face in a paroxysm of annoyance.

'You are all so British,' she complained. 'You would kill yourself so the funeral company wouldn't be disappointed. Why can't we tell the Benelux Music Festival to shove their Fugazzas and Waafels up their ass?'

'Aahh . . . Perhaps we should approach this from the other end, so to speak,' said Roger, with grim optimism. 'We all seem to be assuming that the fall-out from this event is going to be bad for our reputation — but who's to say it won't be the best thing that ever happened to us? If *Partitum Mutante* outrages everybody and gets the press steamed up, that'll generate a lot of word of mouth about the Consort. In that sense, whatever we may feel in our heart of hearts, the whole affair may push us up to another level of recognition.'

'Oh, you slut, Roger,' said Julian with a sarky pout.

'I *beg* your pardon?'

'I meant it good-naturedly.'

Plainly, the discussion was doomed to be all down-hill from here, but unfortunately there were still many hours of the day to get through. On and on, inexorable as a body function, the argument spasmed blindly along. Catherine, though she was kneeling in the midst of the battle, watched it as if from a distance. She knew Roger wouldn't ask her opinion, not after she'd giggled; he'd be too afraid she'd disgrace him by chattering about underpants. Or he might be worried she'd just stare back at him in a soulless daze, as though he'd tried to summon her from the bottom of a deep, deep well. He didn't realise she was elsewhere now.

It didn't impress her, actually, all this bluster about *Partitum Mutante* and the Consort's future, and she took pleasure in the fact that it didn't impress Ben either. As often as she could get away with it, short of embarrassing them both, she turned to look at him and smiled. He smiled back, pale with tiredness, while between him and Catherine the stinging voices ricocheted.

She thought: *Dare I do something that might lead to the end of two marriages?*

In the end, it was Axel who came to the rescue again. Strange how this unmusical little creature, this uninvited marsupial whom they'd all imagined would meddle constantly with the serious business of singing, had left them to commune with *Partitum Mutante* uninterrupted for two solid weeks, only making himself heard when he could exercise his preferred role as peace broker.

Today, he'd allowed the Consort to argue the

morning and afternoon away, content at first to impose no more ambitious restrictions than to remind them, every few hours, to take a short break for food and drink. However, when night-time came and they were still hard at it, Axel decided that drastic intervention was needed. Screaming at the top of his lungs, his mission was to lure his mother to his feverish little body, which he'd marinated in sufficient puke and ordure to earn himself a bath. Dagmar, interrupted just as she was about to announce her defection from the Anglo-German alliance, swallowed her words, stomped upstairs – and did not return.

With her departure, some séance-like bond of hostility was broken, and the Courage Consort dispersed, exhausted. They had resolved nothing, and the rain still hadn't come. Julian slunk off to be comforted by the murmurings of Dutch television; Roger said he was going to bed, though the expression of wounded stoicism on his face suggested he might be going to the Mount of Olives to pray.

Catherine and Ben sat in the rehearsal room, alone. Through the windows, the trees of the forest were furry black against the indigo of the night sky.

After a time, Catherine said:

'What are you thinking, Ben?'

And he replied:

'Time is short. It would have been better if we'd done some singing.'

Catherine nestled her cheek inside her folded arms, her arms on the back of the couch. From this angle, only one of her eyes could see Ben; it was enough.

'Sing me a song, Ben,' she murmured.

With some effort he raised himself from his chair, and walked over to a glass cabinet. He swung open its doors and fetched out an ancient musical instrument — a theorbo, perhaps. Some sort of lute, anyway, creaking with its own oldness, dark as molasses.

Ben returned to his chair, sat down, and found the least absurd place to rest the bulbous instrument on his bulbous body. Then, gently, he began to strum the strings. From deep inside his chest, sonorous as a saxhorn, came the melancholy lyrics of Tobias Hume, *circa* 1645.

> *Alas, poore men*
> *Why strive you to live long?*
> *To have more time and space*
> *To suffer wrong?*

Looking back at a lifetime devoted to warfare and music, dear old Tobias might well have left it at that, but there were many more verses; the music demanded to go on even if there was little to add to the sentiments. Ben Lamb sang the whole song, about nine minutes altogether, strumming its sombre minimalist accompaniment all the while. Then, when he had finished, he got up and carefully replaced the lute in its display case. Catherine knew he was going to bed now.

'Thank you, Ben,' she said, her lips breathing against her forearm. 'Goodnight.'

'Good night,' he said, carrying his body away with him.

An hour later, Roger and Catherine made love. It seemed the only way to break the tension. He reached out for her, his strange and unreachable wife, and she allowed herself to be taken.

'I don't know anymore, I don't know anymore,' he moaned, lonely as she stroked his damp back.

'Nobody knows, darling,' she murmured abstractedly, smoothing his hair with her hands. 'Go to sleep.'

As soon as he had drifted off, she uncovered herself, imagining she was glowing like an ember in the heat. The house was perfectly quiet; Julian's relationship with the television must have run its course. Outside in the forest, the smell of impending rain dawdled over the tree-tops, teasing.

At the threshold of sleep, she thought she was already dreaming; there were disturbing sounds which seemed to be inside her body, the sounds of a creature in distress, struggling to breathe, vibrating her tissues. Then suddenly she was roused by a very real cry from outside herself. A child's cry, frightened and inarticulate. She was pretty sure it was Axel's, but some instinct told her that it was being provoked by something Dagmar couldn't handle alone.

Roger was dead to the world; she left him sleeping as she threw on her dressing-gown and hurried out of the room.

'*Hilfe!*' called Dagmar breathlessly.

Catherine ran into the German girl's room, but Axel was in there alone, squirming and bawling on a bed whose covers had been flung aside.

'Help!'

Catherine rushed into the room next door, Ben's room. Ben was sprawled on the floor next to his narrow bed, his pyjamas torn open to expose his huge pale torso. Dagmar was hunched over him, apparently kissing him on the mouth. Then, drawing back, she laid her hands on his blubberous chest, clasping one brown palm over the other; with savage force she slammed the weight of her shoulders down through her sinewy arms, squashing a hollow into Ben's flesh.

'Airway. Take over,' she panted urgently, as she heaved herself repeatedly onto where she trusted the well-hidden sternum to be. Ben's mountainous chest was so high off the floor that with every heave her knees were lifting into the air.

Catherine leapt across the room and knelt at Ben's head.

'Roger! Julian!' she screamed, then pressed her lips directly over Ben's. In the pauses between Dagmar's rhythmic shoves, she blew for all she was worth. Filling her lungs so deep that they stabbed her, she blew and blew and blew again.

Please, please breathe, she thought, but Ben did not breathe.

Julian burst into the room, and was momentarily overwhelmed by the sight of the two women, Dagmar stark naked and Catherine in a loose gown, kneeling on the floor with Ben.

'Eh . . .' he choked, eyes popping, before the reality dawned on him. He flew out of the room, bellowing, in pursuit of a telephone in the dark.

The light in the Chateau de Luth was dim and pearly on the day that the Courage Consort were due to go home. The weather had broken at last. Baggage cluttered the front room like ugly modern sculpture forcibly integrated with the archaic spinning-wheels, recorders, leather-bound books, lutes.

Jan van Hoeidonck would be arriving any minute now, in his banana-yellow minibus, and then, no doubt, after the house was safely vacated, Gina would come to clean it. A couple of items in the hallway had been badly damaged by the ambulance people as they'd pulled Ben's body out of the narrow aperture, but the owners of the chateau would just have to be understanding, that was all. Antiques couldn't be expected to last forever; sooner or later, the wear and tear of passing centuries would get to them.

Standing at the window, blindly watching the millions of tiny hail-stones swirling and clattering against the panes, Roger at last raised the subject that must be addressed.

'We have to decide what we're going to do,' he said quietly.

Dagmar turned her face away from him, looking down instead at her baby, cradled tight in her arms. She had a pretty good idea what she was going to do, but now was not the time to tell Roger Courage about it.

'The festival isn't yet,' she said, rocking on Catherine's absurdly big plastic suitcase.

'I know, but it's not going to go away either,' said Roger.

'Give it a rest, Roger,' advised Julian softly, hunched over the piano, stroking his long fingers over all the keys without striking any.

Roger grimaced in shame at what he was about to say, what he could not help saying, what he was obliged by his own personal God to say.

'We could manage it, you know,' he told them. 'The bass part of *Partitum Mutante* is the most straightforward, by a long shot. I know a man called Arthur Falkirk, an old friend of Ben's. They sang together at Cambridge . . .'

'No, Roger.'

It was Catherine speaking. Her face was red and puffy, unrecognisable from crying. Before she'd finally calmed down this morning, she had wept more passionately, more uninhibitedly, than she'd done since she was seven. And, as she'd howled, the torrent of rain had dampened the acoustic of the Chateau de Luth, allowing her lament to take its place alongside the creaking of ancient foundations, the clatter of water from drainpipes and guttering, the burring of telephones. Her voice was hoarse now, so low that no one would ever have guessed she sang soprano.

Roger coughed uneasily.

'Ben was very conscientious,' he said. 'He would've wanted . . .'

'No, Roger,' repeated Catherine.

The telephone rang, and she picked up the receiver before her husband could move a muscle.

'Yes,' she croaked into the mouthpiece. 'Yes, the Courage Consort. This is Catherine Courage speaking. Yes, I understand, don't be sorry. No, of course we won't be performing *Partitum Mutante*. Perhaps Mr Fugazza can find another ensemble. A recording might be a more practical option at this late stage, but I'm sure Mr Fugazza can make up his own mind . . . A dedication? That's very kind of you, but I'm not sure if Ben would have wanted that. Leave it with me, let me think about it. Call me on the London number. But not for a few days, if you would. Yes. Not at all. 'Bye.'

Roger stood at the window, his back turned. His hands were clasped behind his back, one limp inside the other. Against the shimmering shower of hail he was almost a silhouette. Outside, a car door slammed; the others hadn't even heard Jan van Hoeidonck's minibus arrive, but it was here now.

Catherine sat next to Dagmar on the suitcase; it was so uselessly big that there was ample space on its rim for both of them.

'Thanks for travelling with us this time,' she whispered in the German girl's ear.

'It's OK,' stated Dagmar flatly. Tears fell from her

cheeks onto her baby's chest as she allowed Catherine to clasp one of her hands, those steely young hands that had proved unequal to the challenge of punching the life back into Ben Lamb's flesh.

The sound of a rain-swollen front door being shouldered open intruded on the moment. A great gust of wet, fragrant, earthy air swept into the house, as Jan van Hoeidonck let himself in. Without speaking, he walked into the front room, seized hold of two suitcases − Roger's and Ben's − and began to lug them out the door. Dagmar and Catherine slipped off Catherine's suitcase and allowed Roger to trundle it away, though it might just as well have been left behind. It was full of clothes she hadn't worn, and food she hadn't eaten. She would travel lighter in future, if there was a future.

Oh Christ, don't start that again, she thought. *Just get on with it*. And she hurried out into the pelting rain.

The yellow minibus was roomier than she remembered, even though, with the addition of Dagmar and Axel, there were more passengers than there'd been last time − in number, if not in mass. Roger sat next to Jan van Hoeidonck as before. The director pulled away from the Chateau de Luth, tight-lipped, concentrating on the view through the labouring windscreen wipers; the chances that he and Roger would take up the threads of their discussion on the future of the Amsterdam Concertgebouw seemed slim. Julian sat at the back of the bus, gazing at the cottage as it dwindled into perspective, a picture postcard again, misty behind the deluge.

They had not been driving five minutes when the sky abruptly ran out of rain, and the forest materialised into view as if out of a haze of static. Then, dazzlingly, the sun came out.

Radiating through the tinted glass of the minibus window, the warmth bathed Catherine's face, soothing her cheeks, stinging the raw rims of her eyelids. With the rain gone, the world's acoustic was changing again: the gentle thrum of the engine surfaced from below, and birds began to twitter all around, while inside the bus, the silence of Ben's absence accumulated like stale breath. It was awful, deadly.

Instinctively, to fill the void, Catherine began to sing: the simplest, most comforting little song she knew, an ancient round she had sung before she'd even been old enough to learn its meaning.

Sumer is icumen in
Loude sing cuckoo,
Groweth seed and bloweth mead,
And spring'th the woode now.
Sing cuckoo . . .

Catherine's soprano came out of her hoarse throat shaky and soft, barely in tune. She stared out of the window, not caring what the others thought of her; they could brand her as a nut case if they needed to. The terrible silence was receding, that was the main thing.

Beginning the second verse, she was bewildered to find herself being joined by Julian, a delicate tenor counterpoint offering its assistance to her faltering lead.

> *Ewe bleateth after lamb,*
> *Low'th after calfe cow,*
> *Bullock sterteth,*
> *Bucke verteth,*
> *Merry sing cuckoo.*

Roger had joined in by now, and Dagmar, though she didn't know the words, improvised a strange but fitting descant *sans paroles*.

> *Cuckoo cuckoo*
> *Well singst thou cuckoo,*
> *Ne swicke thou never now.*

> *Sing cuckoo now,*
> *Sing cuckoo,*
> *Sing cuckoo,*
> *Sing cuckoo now . . .*

On and on they sang, not looking at each other, heading home.

Wilt

Tom Sharpe was born in 1928 and _____ _____ Lancing College
and at Pembroke College, Cam_____ _____. his National
Service in the Marines befo__ _____ ___th Africa in 1951,
where he did social work _____ ___ European Affairs
Department before tea_____ _____. He had a photographic
studio in Pietermaritzbu___ ___ 1957 until 1961, when he was
deported. From 1963 to 19__ he was a lecturer in History at the
Cambridge College of Arts and Technology. He is married and
lives in Dorset.

Also by Tom Sharpe
in Pan Books

Riotous Assembly
Indecent Exposure
Porterhouse Blue
Blott on the Landscape
The Great Pursuit
The Throwback
The Wilt Alternative
Ancestral Vices
Vintage Stuff

Wilt
Tom Sharpe

Pan Books in association with
Secker & Warburg

First published in Great Britain 1976 by Martin Secker and Warburg Ltd
This edition published 1978 by Pan Books Ltd,
Cavaye Place, London SW10 9PG
in association with Martin Secker and Warburg Ltd
39
© Tom Sharpe 1976
ISBN 0 330 25360 3
Printed and bound in Great Britain by
Richard Clay Ltd, Bungay, Suffolk

for
Meat One

1

Whenever Henry Wilt took the dog for a walk, or, to be more accurate, when the dog took him, or, to be exact, when Mrs Wilt told them both to go and take themselves out of the house so that she could do her yoga exercises, he always took the same route. In fact the dog followed the route and Wilt followed the dog. They went down past the Post Office, across the playground, under the railway bridge and out on to the footpath by the river. A mile along the river and then under the railway line again and back through streets where the houses were bigger than Wilt's semi and where there were large trees and gardens and the cars were all Rovers and Mercedes. It was here that Clem, a pedigree Labrador, evidently feeling more at home, did his business while Wilt stood looking around rather uneasily, conscious that this was not his sort of neighbourhood and wishing it was. It was about the only time during their walk that he was at all aware of his surroundings. For the rest of the way Wilt's walk was an interior one and followed an itinerary completely at variance with his own appearance and that of his route. It was in fact a journey of wishful thinking, a pilgrimage along trails of remote possibility involving the irrevocable disappearance of Mrs Wilt, the sudden acquisition of wealth, power, what he would do if he was appointed Minister of Education or, better still, Prime Minister. It was partly concocted of a series of desperate expedients and partly in an unspoken dialogue so that anyone noticing Wilt (and most people didn't) might have seen his lips move occasionally and his mouth curl into what he fondly imagined was a sardonic smile as he dealt with questions or parried arguments with devastating repartee. It was on one of these walks taken in the rain after a particularly trying day at the Tech that Wilt first conceived the notion that he would only be able to fulfil his latent promise and call his life his own if some not entirely fortuitous disaster overtook his wife.

Like everything else in Henry Wilt's life it was not a sudden decision. He was not a decisive man. Ten years as an Assistant

Lecturer (Grade Two) at the Fenland College of Arts and Technology was proof of that. For ten years he had remained in the Liberal Studies Department teaching classes of Gasfitters, Plasterers, Bricklayers and Plumbers. Or keeping them quiet. And for ten long years he had spent his days going from classroom to classroom with two dozen copies of *Sons and Lovers* or Orwell's *Essays* or *Candide* or *The Lord of the Flies* and had done his damnedest to extend the sensibilities of Day-Release Apprentices with notable lack of success.

'Exposure to Culture', Mr Morris, the Head of Liberal Studies, called it but from Wilt's point of view it looked more like his own exposure to barbarism, and certainly the experience had undermined the ideals and illusions which had sustained him in his younger days. So had twelve years of marriage to Eva.

If Gasfitters could go through life wholly impervious to the emotional significance of the interpersonal relationships portrayed in *Sons and Lovers*, and coarsely amused by D. H. Lawrence's profound insight into the sexual nature of existence, Eva Wilt was incapable of such detachment. She hurled herself into cultural activities and self-improvement with an enthusiasm that tormented Wilt. Worse still, her notion of culture varied from week to week, sometimes embracing Barbara Cartland and Anya Seton, sometimes Ouspensky, sometimes Kenneth Clark, but more often the instructor at the Pottery Class on Tuesdays or the lecturer on Transcendental Meditation on Thursdays, so that Wilt never knew what he was coming home to except a hastily cooked supper, some forcibly expressed opinions about his lack of ambition, and a half-baked intellectual eclecticism that left him disoriented.

To escape from the memory of Gasfitters as putative human beings and of Eva in the lotus position, Wilt walked by the river thinking dark thoughts, made darker still by the knowledge that for the fifth year running his application to be promoted to Senior Lecturer was almost certain to be turned down and that unless he did something soon he would be doomed to Gasfitters Three and Plasterers Two – and to Eva – for the rest of his life. It was not a prospect to be borne. He would act decisively. Above his head a train thundered by. Wilt stood watching its dwindling lights and thought about accidents involving level crossings.

'He's in such a funny state these days,' said Eva Wilt, 'I don't know what to make of him.'

'I've given up trying with Patrick,' said Mavis Mottram studying Eva's vase critically. 'I think I'll put the lupin just a fraction of an inch to the left. Then it will help to emphasize the oratorical qualities of the rose. Now the iris over here. One must try to achieve an almost *audible* effect of contrasting colours. Contrapuntal, one might say.'

Eva nodded and sighed. 'He used to be so energetic,' she said, 'but now he just sits about the house watching telly. It's as much as I can do to get him to take the dog for a walk.'

'He probably misses the children,' said Mavis. 'I know Patrick does.'

'That's because he has some to miss,' said Eva Wilt bitterly. 'Henry can't even whip up the energy to have any.'

'I'm so sorry, Eva. I forgot,' said Mavis, adjusting the lupin so that it clashed more significantly with a geranium.

'There's no need to be sorry,' said Eva, who didn't number self-pity among her failings, 'I suppose I should be grateful. I mean, imagine having children like Henry. He's so uncreative, and besides children are so tiresome. They take up all one's creative energy.'

Mavis Mottram moved away to help someone else to achieve a contrapuntal effect, this time with nasturtiums and hollyhocks in a cerise bowl. Eva fiddled with her rose. Mavis was so lucky. She had Patrick, and Patrick Mottram was such an energetic man. Eva, in spite of her size, placed great emphasis on energy, energy and creativity, so that even quite sensible people who were not unduly impressionable found themselves exhausted after ten minutes in her company. In the lotus position at her yoga class she managed to exude energy, and her attempts at Transcendental Meditation had been likened to a pressure-cooker on simmer. And with creative energy there came enthusiasm, the febrile enthusiasms of the evidently unfulfilled woman for whom each new idea heralds the dawn of a new day and vice versa. Since the ideas she espoused were either trite or incomprehensible to her, her attachment to them was correspondingly brief and did nothing to fill the gap left in her life by Henry Wilt's lack of attainment. While he lived a violent life in his imagination, Eva, lacking any imagination at all, lived violently in fact. She threw herself into things, situations, new friends, groups and happenings with a reckless abandon that concealed the fact that she lacked the emotional stamina to stay for more than a moment. Now, as she backed away from her vase, she bumped into someone behind her.

'I beg your pardon,' she said and turned to find herself looking into a pair of dark eyes.

'No need to apologize,' said the woman in an American accent. She was slight and dressed with a simple scruffiness that was beyond Eva Wilt's moderate income.

'I'm Eva Wilt,' said Eva, who had once attended a class on Getting to Know People at the Oakrington Village College. 'My husband lectures at the Tech and we live at 34 Parkview Avenue.'

'Sally Pringsheim,' said the woman with a smile. 'We're in Rossiter Grove. We're over on a sabbatical. Gaskell's a biochemist.'

Eva Wilt accepted the distinctions and congratulated herself on her perspicacity about the blue jeans and the sweater. People who lived in Rossiter Grove were a cut above Parkview Avenue and husbands who were biochemists on sabbatical were also in the University. Eva Wilt's world was made up of such nuances.

'You know, I'm not at all that sure I could live with an oratorical rose,' said Sally Pringsheim. 'Symphonies are OK in auditoriums but I can do without them in vases.'

Eva stared at her with a mixture of astonishment and admiration. To be openly critical of Mavis Mottram's flower arrangements was to utter blasphemy in Parkview Avenue. 'You know, I've always wanted to say that,' she said with a sudden surge of warmth, 'but I've never had the courage.'

Sally Pringsheim smiled. 'I think one should always say what one thinks. Truth is so essential in any really meaningful relationship. I always tell G baby exactly what I'm thinking.'

'Gee baby?' said Eva Wilt.

'Gaskell's my husband,' said Sally. 'Not that he's really a husband. It's just that we've got this open-ended arrangement for living together. Sure, we're legal and all that, but I think it's important sexually to keep one's options open, don't you?'

By the time Eva got home her vocabulary had come to include several new words. She found Wilt in bed pretending to be asleep and woke him up and told him about Sally Pringsheim. Wilt turned over and tried to go back to sleep wishing to God she had stuck to her contrapuntal flower arrangements. Sexually open-ended freewheeling options were the last thing he wanted just now, and, coming from the wife of a biochemist who could afford to live in Rossiter Grove, didn't augur well for the future. Eva Wilt was too easily influenced by wealth, intellectual status and new acquaintances to be allowed out with a woman who believed that clitoral stimulation oralwise was a concomitant part of a fully emancipated relationship and that unisex was here to stay. Wilt had enough troubles with his own virility without having Eva demand that her conjugal rights be supplemented oralwise. He spent a restless night thinking dark thoughts about accidental deaths involving fast trains, level crossings, their Ford Escort and Eva's seat belt, and got up early and made himself breakfast. He was just going off to a nine o'clock lecture to Motor Mechanics Three when Eva came downstairs with a dreamy look on her face.

'I've just remembered something I wanted to ask you last night,' she said. 'What does "transexual diversification" mean?'

'Writing poems about queers,' said Wilt hastily and went out to the car. He drove down Parkview Avenue and got stuck in a traffic jam at the roundabout. He sat and cursed silently. He was thirty-four and his talents were being dissipated on MM 3 and a woman who was clearly educationally subnormal. Worst

of all, he had to recognize the truth of Eva's constant criticism that he wasn't a man. 'If you were a proper man,' she
was always saying, 'you would show more initiative. You've
got to assert yourself.'

Wilt asserted himself at the roundabout and got into an
altercation with a man in a mini-bus. As usual, he came off
second best.

'The problem with Wilt as I see it is that he lacks drive,' said
the Head of English, himself a nerveless man with a tendency
to see and solve problems with a degree of equivocation that
made good his natural lack of authority.

The Promotions Committee nodded its joint head for the
fifth year running.

'He may lack drive but he *is* committed,' said Mr Morris,
fighting his annual rearguard on Wilt's behalf.

'Committed?' said the Head of Catering with a snort. 'Committed to what? Abortion, Marxism or promiscuity? It's bound
to be one of the three. I've yet to come across a Liberal
Studies lecturer who wasn't a crank, a pervert or a red-hot
revolutionary and a good many have been all three.'

'Hear, hear,' said the Head of Mechanical Engineering, on
whose lathes a demented student had once turned out several
pipe bombs.

Mr Morris bristled. 'I grant you that one or two lecturers
have been ... er ... a little overzealous politically but I resent
the imputation that ...'

'Let's leave generalities aside and get back to Wilt,' said
the Vice-Principal. 'You were saying that he is committed.'

'He needs encouragement,' said Mr Morris. 'Damn it, the
man has been with us ten years and he's still only Grade Two.'

'That's precisely what I mean about his lacking drive,' said
the Head of English. 'If he had been worth promoting he'd
have been a Senior Lecturer by now.'

'I must say I agree,' said the Head of Geography. 'Any man
who is content to spend ten years taking Gasfitters and Plumbers is clearly unfit to hold an administrative post.'

'Do we always have to promote solely for administrative

reasons?' Mr Morris asked wearily. 'Wilt happens to be a good teacher.'

'If I may just make a point,' said Dr Mayfield, the Head of Sociology, 'at this moment in time it is vital we bear in mind that, in the light of the forthcoming introduction of the Joint Honours degree in Urban Studies and Medieval Poetry, provisional approval for which degree by the Council of National Academic Awards I am happy to announce at least in principle, that we maintain a viable staff position in regard to Senior Lectureships by allocating places for candidates with specialist knowledge in particular spheres of academic achievement rather than—'

'If I may just interrupt for a moment, in or out of time,' said Dr Board, Head of Modern Languages, 'are you saying we should have Senior Lectureships for highly qualified specialists who can't teach rather than promote Assistant Lecturers without doctorates who can?'

'If Dr Board had allowed me to continue,' said Dr Mayfield, 'he would have understood that I was saying . . .'

'I doubt it,' said Dr Board, 'quite apart from your syntax . . .'

And so for the fifth year running Wilt's promotion was forgotten. The Fenland College of Arts and Technology was expanding. New degree courses proliferated and more students with fewer qualifications poured in to be taught by more staff with higher qualifications until one day the Tech would cease to be a mere Tech and rise in status to become a Poly. It was the dream of every Head of Department and in the process Wilt's self-esteem and the hopes of Eva Wilt were ignored.

Wilt heard the news before lunch in the canteen.

'I'm sorry, Henry,' said Mr Morris as they lined up with their trays, 'it's this wretched economic squeeze. Even Modern Languages had to take a cut. They only got two promotions through.'

Wilt nodded. It was what he had come to expect. He was in the wrong department, in the wrong marriage and in the wrong life. He took his fish fingers across to a table in the corner and ate by himself. Around him other members of staff sat discussing A-level prospects and who was going to sit on the course board next term. They taught Maths or Economics or English, subjects that counted and where promotion was easy. Liberal Studies didn't count and promotion was out of the question. It was as simple as that. Wilt finished his lunch and went up to the reference library to look up Insulin in the Pharmacopoeia. He had an idea it was the one untraceable poison.

At five to two, none the wiser, he went down to Room 752 to extend the sensibilities of fifteen apprentice butchers, designated on the timetable as Meat One. As usual they were late and drunk.

'We've been drinking Bill's health,' they told him when they drifted in at ten past two.

'Really?' said Wilt, handing out copies of *The Lord of the Flies*. 'And how is he?'

'Bloody awful,' said a large youth with 'Stuff Off' painted across the back of his leather jacket. 'He's puking his guts out. It's his birthday and he had four Vodkas and a Babycham . . .'

'We'd got to the part where Piggy is in the forest,' said Wilt, heading them off a discussion of what Bill had drunk for his birthday. He reached for a board duster and rubbed a drawing of a Dutch Cap off the blackboard.

'That's Mr Sedgwick's trademark,' said one of the butchers, 'he's always going on about contraceptives and things. He's got a thing about them.'

'A thing about them?' said Wilt loyally.

'You know, birth control. Well, he used to be a Catholic, didn't he? And now he's not, he's making up for lost time,' said a small pale-faced youth unwrapping a Mars Bar.

'Someone should tell him about the pill,' said another youth lifting his head somnolently from the desk. 'You can't feel a thing with a Frenchie. You get more thrill with the pill.'

'I suppose you do,' said Wilt, 'but I understood there were side-effects.'

'Depends which side you want it,' said a lad with sideburns.

Wilt turned back to *The Lord of the Flies* reluctantly. He had read the thing two hundred times already.

'Now Piggy goes into the forest . . .' he began, only to be stopped by another butcher, who evidently shared his distaste for the misfortunes of Piggy.

'You only get bad effects with the pill if you use ones that are high in oestrogen.'

'That's very interesting,' said Wilt. 'Oestrogen? You seem to know a lot about it.'

'Old girl down our street got a bloodclot in her leg . . .'

'Silly old clot,' said the Mars Bar.

'Listen,' said Wilt. 'Either we hear what Peter has to tell us about the effects of the pill or we get on and read about Piggy.'

'Fuck Piggy,' said the sideburns.

'Right,' said Wilt heartily, 'then keep quiet.'

'Well,' said Peter, 'this old girl, well she wasn't all that old, maybe thirty, she was on the pill and she got this bloodclot and the doctor told my auntie it was the oestrogen and she'd better take a different sort of pill just in case and the old girl down the street, her old man had to go and have a vasectomy so's she wouldn't have another bloodclot.'

'Buggered if anyone's going to get me to have a vasectomy,' said the Mars Bar, 'I want to know I'm all there.'

'We all have ambitions,' said Wilt.

'Nobody's going to hack away at my knackers with a bloody great knife,' said the sideburns.

'Nobody'd want to,' said someone else.

'What about the bloke whose missus you banged,' said the Mars Bar. 'I bet he wouldn't mind having a go.'

Wilt applied the sanction of Piggy again and got them back on to vasectomy.

'Anyway, it's not irreversible any more,' said Peter. 'They can put a tiny little gold tap in and you can turn it on when you want a nipper.'

'Go on! That's not true.'

'Well, not on the National Health you can't, but if you pay they can. I read about it in a magazine. They've been doing experiments in America.'

15

'What happens if the washer goes wrong?' asked the Mars Bar.

'I suppose they call a plumber in.'

Wilt sat and listened while Meat One ranged far and wide about vasectomy and the coil and Indians getting free transistors and the plane that landed at Audley End with a lot of illegal immigrants and what somebody's brother who was a policeman in Brixton said about blacks and how the Irish were just as bad and bombs and back to Catholics and birth control and who'd want to live in Ireland where you couldn't even buy French letters and so back to the Pill. And all the time his mind filled itself obsessively with ways and means of getting rid of Eva. A diet of birth-control pills high on oestrogen? If he ground them up and mixed them with the Ovaltine she took at bedtime there was a chance she'd develop bloodclots all over the place in no time at all. Wilt put the notion out of his head. Eva with bloodclots was too awful to stomach, and anyway it might not work. No, it would have to be something quick, certain and painless. Preferably an accident.

At the end of the hour Wilt collected the books and made his way back to the Staff Room. He had a free period. On the way he passed the site of the new Administration block. The ground had been cleared and the builders had moved in and were boring pile holes for the foundations. Wilt stopped and watched as the drilling machine wound slowly down into the ground. They were making wide holes. Very wide. Big enough for a body.

'How deep are you going?' he asked one of the workmen.

'Thirty feet.'

'Thirty feet?' said Wilt. 'When's the concrete going in?'

'Monday, with any luck,' said the man.

Wilt passed on. A new and quite horrible idea had just occurred to him.

2

It was one of Eva Wilt's better days. She had days, better days, and one of those days. Days were just days when nothing went wrong and she got the washing-up done and the front room vacuumed and the windows washed and the beds made and the bath Vimmed and the lavatory pan Harpicked and went round to the Harmony Community Centre and helped with Xeroxing or sorted old clothes for the Jumble Sale and generally made herself useful and came home for lunch and went to the library and had tea with Mavis or Susan or Jean and talked about life and how seldom Henry made love to her even perfunctorily nowadays and how she had missed her opportunity by refusing a bank clerk who was a manager now and came home and made Henry's supper and went out to Yoga or Flower Arrangement or Meditation or Pottery and finally climbed into bed with the feeling that she had got something done.

On one of those days nothing went right. The activities were exactly the same but each episode was tainted with some minor disaster like the fuse blowing on the vacuum-cleaner or the drain in the sink getting blocked with a piece of carrot so that by the time Henry came home he was either greeted by silence or subjected to a quite unwarranted exposé of all his faults and shortcomings. On one of those days Wilt usually took the dog for an extended walk via the Ferry Path Inn and spent a restless night getting up and going to the bathroom, thus nullifying the cleansing qualities of the Harpic Eva had puffed round the pan and providing her with a good excuse to point out his faults once again in the morning.

'What the hell am I supposed to do?' he had asked after one of those nights. 'If I pull the chain you grumble because I've woken you up and if I don't you say it looks nasty in the morning.'

'Well, it does, and in any case you don't have to wash all the Harpic off the sides. And don't say you don't. I've seen you. You aim it all the way round so that it all gets taken off. You do it quite deliberately.'

'If I pulled the chain it would all get flushed off anyway and you'd get woken up into the bargain,' Wilt told her, conscious that he did make a habit of aiming at the Harpic. He had a grudge against the stuff.

'Why can't you just wait until the morning? And anyway it serves you right,' she continued, forestalling his obvious answer, 'for drinking all that beer. You're supposed to be taking Clem for a walk, not swilling ale in that horrid pub.'

'To pee or not to pee, that is the question,' said Wilt helping himself to All-Bran. 'What do you expect me to do? Tie a knot in the damned thing?'

'It wouldn't make any difference to me if you did,' said Eva bitterly.

'It would make a hell of a lot of difference to me, thank you very much.'

'I was talking about our sex life and you know it.'

'Oh, that,' said Wilt.

But that was on one of those days.

On one of her better days something unexpected happened to inject the daily round with a new meaning and to awake in her those dormant expectations that somehow everything would suddenly change for the better and stay that way. It was on such expectations that her faith in life was based. They were the spiritual equivalent of the trivial activities that kept her busy and Henry subdued. On one of her better days the sun shone brighter, the floor in the hall gleamed brighter and Eva Wilt was brighter herself and hummed 'Some day my prince will come' while Hoovering the stairs. On one of her better days Eva went forth to meet the world with a disarming goodheartedness and awoke in others the very same expectations that so thrilled her in herself. And on one of her better days Henry had to get his own supper and if he was wise kept out of the house as long as possible. Eva Wilt's expectations demanded something a sight more invigorating than Henry Wilt after a day at the Tech. It was on the evenings of such days that he came nearest to genuinely deciding to murder her and to hell with the consequences.

*

On this particular day she was on her way to the Community Centre when she ran into Sally Pringsheim. It was one of those entirely fortuitous meetings that resulted from Eva making her way on foot instead of by bicycle and going through Rossiter Grove instead of straight down Parkview Avenue which was half a mile shorter. Sally was just driving out of the gate in a Mercedes with a P registration which meant it was brand new. Eva noted the fact and smiled accordingly.

'How funny me running into you like this,' she said brightly as Sally stopped the car and unlocked the door.

'Can I give you a lift? I'm going into town to look for something casual to wear tonight. Gaskell's got some Swedish professor coming over from Heidelberg and we're taking him to Ma Tante's.'

Eva Wilt climbed in happily, her mind computing the cost of the car and the house and the significance of wearing something casual at Ma Tante's (where she had heard that starters like Prawn Cocktails cost 95p) and the fact that Dr Pringsheim entertained Swedish professors when they came to Ipford.

'I was going to walk to town,' she lied. 'Henry's taken the car and it's such a lovely day.'

'Gaskell's bought a bicycle. He says it's quicker and it keeps him fit,' said Sally, thus condemning Henry Wilt to yet another misfortune. Eva made a note to see that he bought a bike at the police auction and cycled to work in rain or snow. 'I was thinking of trying Felicity Fashions for a shantung poncho. I don't know what they're like but I've been told they're good. Professor Grant's wife goes there and she says they have the best selection.'

'I'm sure they must have,' said Eva Wilt, whose patronage of Felicity Fashions had consisted of looking in the window and wondering who on earth could afford dresses at forty pounds. Now she knew. They drove into town and parked in the multi-storey car park. By that time Eva had stored a lot more information about the Pringsheims in her memory. They came from California. Sally had met Gaskell while hitch-hiking through Arizona. She had been to Kansas State but had dropped out to live on a commune. There had been other men in her life. Gaskell loathed cats. They gave him hay fever. Women's Lib meant more than burning your bra. It meant total commitment to the programme of women's superiority over men. Lóve was great if you didn't let it get to you. Compost was in and colour TV out. Gaskell's father had owned a chain of stores which was sordid. Money was handy and Rossiter Grove was a bore. Above all, fucking had to be, just *had* to be fun whichever way you looked at it.

Eva Wilt received this information with a jolt. In her circle 'fuck' was a word husbands used when they hit their thumbs with hammers. When Eva used it she did so in the isolation of the bathroom and with a wistfulness that robbed it of its crudity and imbued it with a splendid virility so that a good fuck became the most distant and abstract of all her expectations and quite removed from Henry's occasional early morning fumblings. And if 'fuck' was reserved for the bathroom, fucking was even more remote. It suggested an almost continuous activity, a familiar occurrence that was both casual and satisfying and added a new dimension to life. Eva Wilt stumbled out of the car and followed Sally to Felicity Fashions in a state of shock.

If fucking was fun, shopping with Sally Pringsheim was a revelation. It was marked by a decisiveness that was truly breathtaking. Where Eva would have hummed and haaed, Sally selected and having selected moved on down the racks, discarded things she didn't like leaving them hanging over chairs, seized others, glanced at them and said she supposed they would do with a bored acceptance that was infectious, and left the shop with a pile of boxes containing two hundred pounds' worth of shantung ponchos, silk summer coats, scarves and blouses. Eva Wilt had spent seventy on a pair of yellow lounging pyjamas and a raincoat with lapels and a belt that Sally said was pure Gatsby.

'Now all you need is the hat and you'll be it,' she said as they loaded the boxes into the car. They bought the hat, a trilby, and then had coffee at the Mombasa Coffee House where Sally leant across the table intensely, smoking a long thin cigar, and talking about body contact in a loud voice so that Eva was conscious that the women at several nearby tables had stopped talking and were listening rather disapprovingly.

'Gaskell's nipples drive me wild,' Sally said. 'They drive him wild too when I suck them.'

Eva drank her coffee and wondered what Henry would do if she took it into her head to suck his nipples. Drive him wild was hardly the word and besides she was beginning to regret having spent seventy pounds. That would drive him wild too. Henry didn't approve of credit cards. But she was enjoying herself too much to let the thought of his reaction spoil her day.

'I think teats are so important,' Sally went on. Two women at the next table paid their bill and walked out.

'I suppose they must be,' said Eva Wilt uneasily. 'I've never had much use for mine.'

'Haven't you?' said Sally. 'We'll have to do something about that.'

'I don't see that there is much anyone can do about it,' said Eva. 'Henry never takes his pyjamas off and my nightie gets in the way.'

'Don't tell me you wear things in bed. Oh you poor thing. And nighties, God, how humiliating for you! I mean it's typical of a male-dominated society, all this costume differentiation. You must be suffering from touch deprivation. Gaskell says it's as bad as vitamin deficiency.'

'Well, Henry is always tired when he gets home,' Eva told her. 'And I go out a lot.'

'I'm not surprised,' said Sally, 'Gaskell says male fatigue is a symptom of penile insecurity. Is Henry's big or small?'

'Well it depends,' said Eva hoarsely. 'Sometimes it's big and sometimes it isn't.'

'I much prefer men with small ones,' said Sally, 'they try so much harder.'

They finished their coffee and went back to the car discussing Gaskell's penis and his theory that in a sexually undifferentiated society nipple stimulation would play an increasingly important role in developing the husband's sense of his hermaphroditic nature.

'He's written an article on it,' Sally said as they drove home. 'It's called "The Man As Mother". It was published in *Suck* last year.'

'Suck?' said Eva.

'Yes, it's a journal published by the Society for Undifferentiated Sexual Studies in Kansas. G's done a lot of work for them on animal behaviour. He did his thesis on Role Play in Rats there.'

'That sounds very interesting,' said Eva uncertainly. Roll or role? Whichever it was it was impressive and certainly Henry's occasional pieces on Day Release Apprentices and Literature in the *Liberal Studies Quarterly* hardly measured up to Dr Pringsheim's monographs.

'Oh I don't know. It's all so obvious really. If you put two male rats together in a cage long enough one of them is simply bound to develop active tendencies and the other passive ones,' said Sally wearily. 'But Gaskell was absolutely furious. He thought they ought to alternate. That's G all over. I told him how silly he was being. I said, "G honey, rats are practically undifferentiated anyway. I mean how can you expect them to be able to make an existential choice?" and you know what he said? He said, "Pubic baby, rats are the paradigm. Just remember that and you won't go far wrong. Rats are the paradigm." What do you think of that?'

'I think rats are rather horrid,' said Eva without thinking. Sally laughed and put her hand on her knee.

'Oh Eva, darling,' she murmured, 'you're so adorably down to earth. No, I'm not taking you back to Parkview Avenue. You're coming home with me for a drink and lunch. I'm simply dying to see you in those lemon loungers.'

They turned into Rossiter Grove.

If rats were a paradigm for Dr Pringsheim, Printers Three were a paradigm for Henry Wilt, though of a rather different sort. They represented all that was most difficult, insensitive and downright bloodyminded about Day Release Classes and to make matters worse the sods thought they were literate because they could actually read and Voltaire was an idiot because he made everything go wrong for Candide. Coming after Nursery Nurses and during his Stand-In period, Printers Three brought out the worst in him. They had obviously brought out the worst in Cecil Williams who should have been taking them.

'It's the second week he's been off sick,' they told Wilt.

'I'm not at all surprised,' said Wilt. 'You lot are enough to make anyone sick.'

'We had one bloke went and gassed himself. Pinkerton his name was. He took us for a term and made us read this book *Jude the Obscure*. That wasn't half a depressing book. All about this twit Jude.'

'I had an idea it was,' said Wilt.

'Next term old Pinky didn't come back. He went down by the river and stuck a pipe up the exhaust and gassed himself.'

'I can't say I blame him,' said Wilt.

'Well I like that. He was supposed to set us an example.'

Wilt looked at the class grimly.

'I'm sure he had that in mind when he gassed himself,' he said. 'And now if you'll just get on and read quietly, eat quietly and smoke so that no one can see you from the Admin block, I've got work to do.'

'Work? You lot don't know what work is. All you do is sit at a desk all day and read. Call that work? Buggered if I do and they pay you to do it . . .'

'Shut up,' said Wilt with startling violence. 'Shut your stupid trap.'

'Who's going to make me?' said the Printer.

Wilt tried to control his temper and for once found it impossible. There was something incredibly arrogant about Printers Three.

'I am,' he shouted.

'You and who else? You couldn't make a mouse shut its trap, not if you tried all day.'

Wilt stood up. 'You fucking little shit,' he shouted. 'You dirty snivelling . . .'

'I must say, Henry, I'd have expected you to show more restraint,' said the Head of Liberal Studies an hour later when Wilt's nose had stopped bleeding and the Tech Sister had put a Band-Aid on his eyebrow.

'Well it wasn't my class and they got my goat by gloating about Pinkerton's suicide. If Williams hadn't been off sick it wouldn't have happened,' Wilt explained. 'He's always sick when he has to take Printers Three.'

Mr Morris shook his head dispiritedly. 'I don't care who they were. You simply can't go around assaulting students . . .'

'Assaulting students? I never touched . . .'

'All right, but you did use offensive language. Bob Fenwick was in the next classroom and he heard you call this Allison fellow a fucking little shit and an evil-minded moron. Now, is it any wonder he took a poke at you?'

'I suppose not,' said Wilt. 'I shouldn't have lost my temper. I'm sorry.'

'In that case we'll just forget it happened,' said Mr Morris. 'But just remember if I'm to get you a Senior Lectureship I can't have you blotting your copybook having punch-ups with students.'

'I didn't have a punch-up,' said Wilt, 'he punched me.'

'Well, let's just hope he doesn't go to the police and charge you with assault. That's the last sort of publicity we want.'

'Just take me off Printers Three,' said Wilt, 'I've had my fill of the brutes.'

He went down the corridor and collected his coat and brief-case from the Staff Room. His nose felt twice its normal size and his eyebrow hurt abominably. On his way out to the car park he passed several other members of staff but no one stopped to ask him what had happened. Henry Wilt passed unnoticed out of the Tech and got into his car. He shut the door and sat for several minutes watching the piledrivers at work on the new block. Up, down, up, down. Nails in a coffin. And one day, one inevitable day he would be in his coffin, still unnoticed, still an Assistant Lecturer (Grade Two) and quite forgotten by everyone except some lout in Printers Three who would always remember the day he had punched a

Liberal Studies lecturer on the nose and got away with it. He'd probably boast about it to his grandchildren.

Wilt started the car and drove out on to the main road filled with loathing for Printers Three, the Tech, life in general and himself in particular. He understood now why terrorists were prepared to sacrifice themselves for the good of some cause. Given a bomb and a cause he would cheerfully have blown himself and any innocent bystanders to Kingdom Come just to prove for one glorious if brief moment that he was an effective force. But he had neither bomb nor cause. Instead he drove home recklessly and parked outside 34 Parkview Avenue. Then he unlocked the front door and went inside.

There was a strange smell in the hall. Some sort of perfume. Musky and sweet. He put his brief-case down and looked into the living-room. Eva was evidently out. He went into the kitchen and put the kettle on and felt his nose. He would have a good look at it in the bathroom mirror. He was halfway upstairs and conscious that there was a positively miasmic quality about the perfume when he was brought to a halt. Eva Wilt stood in the bedroom doorway in a pair of astonishingly yellow pyjamas with enormously flared trousers. She looked quite hideous, and to make matters worse she was smoking a long thin cigarette in a long thin holder and her mouth was a brilliant red.

'Penis baby,' she murmured hoarsely and swayed. 'Come in here. I'm going to suck your nipples till you come me oral-wise.'

Wilt turned and fled downstairs. The bitch was drunk. It was one of her better days. Without waiting to turn the kettle off, Henry Wilt went out of the front door and got back into the car. He wasn't staying around to have her suck his nipples. He'd had all he could take for one day.

3

Eva Wilt went downstairs and looked for penis baby half-heartedly. For one thing she didn't want to find him and for another she didn't feel like sucking his nipples and for a third she knew she shouldn't have spent seventy pounds on a raincoat and a pair of beach pyjamas she could have got for thirty at Blowdens. She didn't need them and she couldn't see herself walking down Parkview Avenue looking like The Great Gatsby. Besides, she felt a bit sick.

Still, he had left the kettle on so he must be somewhere. It wasn't like Henry to go out and leave the kettle on. She looked in the lounge. It had been the sitting-room until lunchtime when Sally called her sitting-room a lounge. She looked in the dining-room, now the diner, and even in the garden but Henry had vanished, taking with him the car, and her hopes that nipple-sucking would bring new meaning to their marriage and put an end to her body contact deprivation. Finally she gave up the search and made herself a nice pot of tea and sat in the kitchen wondering what on earth had induced her to marry a male chauvinist pig like Henry Wilt who wouldn't have known a good fuck if he had been handed one on a plate and whose idea of a sophisticated evening was a boneless chicken curry at the New Delhi and a performance of *King Lear* at the Guild-hall. Why couldn't she have married someone like Gaskell Pringsheim who entertained Swedish professors at Ma Tante and who understood the importance of clitoral stimulation as a necessary con-something-or-other of a truly satisfying interpersonal penetration? Other people still found her attractive. Patrick Mottram did and so did John Frost who taught her pottery, and Sally had said she was lovely. Eva sat staring into space, the space between the washing-up rack and the Kenwood mixer Henry had given her for Christmas, and thought about Sally and how she had looked at her so strangely when she was changing into her lemon loungers. Sally had stood in the doorway of the Pringsheims' bedroom, smoking a cigar and watching her movements with a sensual calculation that had made Eva blush.

'Darling, you have such a lovely body,' she had said as Eva turned hurriedly and scrambled into the trousers to avoid revealing the hole in her panties. 'You mustn't let it go to waste.'

'Do you really think they suit me?'

But Sally had been staring at her breasts intently. 'Booby baby,' she murmured. Eva Wilt's breasts were prominent and Henry, in one of his many off moments, had once said something about the dugs of hell going dingalingaling for you but not for me. Sally was more appreciative, and had insisted that Eva remove her bra and burn it. They had gone down to the kitchen and had drunk Tequila and had put the bra on a dish with a sprig of holly on it and Sally had poured brandy over it and had set it alight. They had to carry the dish out into the garden because it smelt so horrible and smoked so much and they had lain on the grass laughing as it smouldered. Looking back on the episode Eva regretted her action. It had been a good bra with double-stretch panels designed to give confidence where a woman needs it, as the TV adverts put it. Still, Sally had said she owed it to herself as a free woman and with two drinks inside her Eva was in no mood to argue.

'You've got to feel free,' Sally had said. 'Free to be. Free to be.'

'Free to be what?' said Eva.

'Yourself, darling,' Sally whispered, 'your secret self,' and had touched her tenderly where Eva Wilt, had she been sober and less elated, would staunchly have denied having a self. They had gone back into the house and had lunch, a mixture of more Tequila, salad and Ryvita and cottage cheese which Eva, whose appetite for food was almost as omnivorous as her enthusiasm for new experiences, found unsatisfying. She had hinted as much but Sally had poohpoohed the idea of three good meals a day.

'It's not good caloriewise to have a high starch intake,' she said, 'and besides it's not how much you put into yourself but what. Sex and food, honey, are much the same. A little a lot is better than a lot a little.' She had poured Eva another Tequila, insisted she take a bite of lemon before knocking it back and had helped her upstairs to the big bedroom with the big bed and the big mirror in the ceiling.

'It's time for TT,' she said adjusting the slats of the Venetian blinds.

'Tea tea,' Eva mumbled, 'but we've just had din din.'

'Touch Therapy, darling,' said Sally and pushed her gently back on to the bed. Eva Wilt stared up at her reflection in the mirror; a large woman, two large women in yellow pyjamas lying on a large bed, a large crimson bed; two large women without yellow pyjamas on a large crimson bed; four women naked on a large crimson bed.

'Oh Sally, no Sally.'

'Darling,' said Sally and silenced her protest oralwise. It had been a startlingly new experience though only partly remembered. Eva had fallen asleep before the Touch Therapy had got well under way and had woken an hour later to find Sally fully dressed standing by the bed with a cup of black coffee.

'Oh I do feel bad,' Eva said, referring as much to her moral condition as to her physical.

'Drink this and you'll feel better.'

Eva had drunk the coffee and got dressed while Sally explained that post-contact inhibitory depression was a perfectly natural reaction to Touch Therapy at first.

'You'll find it comes naturally after the first few sessions. You'll probably break down and cry and scream and then feel tremendously liberated and relieved.'

'Do you think so? I'm sure I don't know.'

Sally had driven her home. 'You and Henry must come to our barbecue Thursday night,' she said. 'I know G baby will want to meet you. You'll like him. He's a breast baby. He'll go crazy about you.'

'I tell you she was pissed,' said Wilt as he sat in the Braintrees' kitchen while Peter Braintree opened a bottle of beer for him. 'Pissed and wearing some godawful yellow pyjamas and smoking a cigarette in a long bloody holder.'

'What did she say?'

'Well if you must know, she said, "Come here ..." No, it's too much. I have a perfectly foul day at the Tech. Morris tells me I haven't got my senior lectureship. Williams is off sick again so I lose a free period. I get punched in the face by a great lout in Printers Three and I come home to a drunk wife who calls me penis baby.'

'She called you what?' said Peter Braintree, staring at him.

'You heard me.'

'Eva called you penis baby? I don't believe it.'

'Well you go round there and see what she calls you,' said Wilt bitterly, 'and don't blame me if she sucks your nipples off oralwise while she's about it.'

'Good Lord. Is that what she threatened to do?'

'That and more,' said Wilt.

'It doesn't sound like Eva. It really doesn't.'

'It didn't fucking look like her either, come to that. She was all dolled up in yellow beach pyjamas. You should have seen the colour. It would have made a buttercup look drab. And she'd got some ghastly scarlet lipstick smeared round her mouth and she was smoking ... She hasn't smoked for six years and then all this penis baby nipple-sucking stuff. And oralwise.'

Peter Braintree shook his head. 'That's a filthy word,' he said.

'It's a perfectly filthy act too, if you ask me,' said Wilt.

'Well, I must say it all sounds pretty peculiar,' said Braintree, 'God knows what I'd do if Susan came home and started insisting on sucking my teats.'

'Do what I did. Get out of the house,' said Wilt. 'And anyway it isn't just nipples either. Damn it, we've been married twelve long years. It's a bit late in the day to start arsing about oralwise. The thing is she's on this sexual liberation kick. She came home last night from Mavis Mottram's flower arrangement do jabbering about clitoral stimulation and open-ended freewheeling sexual options.'

'Freewheeling what?'

'Sexual options. Perhaps I've got it wrong. I know sexual options came into it somewhere. I was half asleep at the time.'

'Where the hell did she get all this from?' asked Braintree.

'Some bloody Yank called Sally Pringsheim,' said Wilt. 'You know what Eva's like. I mean she can smell intellectual clap-trap a mile off and homes in on it like a bloody dung-beetle heading for an open sewer. You've no idea how many phoney "latest ideas" I've had to put up with. Well, most of them I can manage to live with. I just let her get on with it and go my own quiet way, but when it comes to participating oralwise while she blathers on about Women's Lib, well you can count me out.'

'What I don't understand about Sexual Freedom and Women's Lib is why you have to go back to the nursery to be liberated,' said Braintree. 'There seems to be this loony idea that you have to be passionately in love all the time.'

'Apes,' said Wilt morosely.

'Apes? What about apes?'

'It's all this business about the animal model. If animals do it then humans must. Territorial Imperative and the Naked Ape. You stand everything on its head and instead of aspiring you retrogress a million years. Hitch your wagon to an orang-outang. The egalitarianism of the lowest common denominator.'

'I don't quite see what that has to do with sex,' said Braintree.

'Nor do I,' said Wilt. They went down to the Pig In A Poke and got drunk.

It was midnight before Wilt got home and Eva was asleep. Wilt climbed surreptitiously into bed and lay in the darkness thinking about high levels of oestrogen.

In Rossiter Grove the Pringsheims came back from Ma Tante's tired and bored.

'Swedes are the bottom,' said Sally as she undressed.

Gaskell sat down and took off his shoes. 'Ungstrom's all right. His wife has just left him for a low-temperature physicist at Cambridge. He's not usually so depressed.'

'You could have fooled me. And talking about wives, I've met the most unliberated woman you've ever set eyes on. Name of Eva Wilt. She's got boobs like cantaloupes.'

'Don't,' said Dr Pringsheim, 'if there's one thing I don't need right now it's unliberated wives with breasts.' He climbed into bed and took his glasses off.

'I had her round here today.'

'Had her?'

Sally smiled, 'Gaskell, honey, you've got a toadsome mind.'

Gaskell Pringsheim smiled myopically at himself in the mirror above. He was proud of his mind. 'I just know you, lover,' he said, 'I know your funny little habits. And while we're on the subject of habits what are all those boxes in the guest room? You haven't been spending money again? You know our budget this month ...'

Sally flounced into bed. 'Budget fudget,' she said, 'I'm sending them all back tomorrow.'

'All?'

'Well, not all, but most. I had to impress booby baby somehow.'

'You didn't have to buy half a shop just to ...'

'Gaskell, honey, if you would just let me finish,' said Sally, 'she's a manic, a lovely, beautiful, obsessive compulsive manic. She can't sit still for half a minute without tidying and cleaning and polishing and washing up.'

'That's all we need, a manic compulsive woman around the house all the time. Who needs two?'

'Two? I'm not manic.'

'You're manic enough for me,' said Gaskell.

'But this one's got boobs, baby, boobs. Anyway I've invited them over on Thursday for the barbecue.'

'What the hell for?'

'Well, if you won't buy me a dishwasher like I've asked you a hundred times, I'm going out to get me one. A nice manic compulsive dishwasher with boobs on.'

'Jesus,' sighed Gaskell, 'are you a bitch.'

'Henry Wilt, you are a sod,' Eva said next morning. Wilt sat up in bed. He felt terrible. His nose was even more painful than the day before, his head ached and he had spent much of the night expunging the Harpic from the bowl in the bathroom.

He was in no mood to be woken and told he was a sod. He looked at the clock. It was eight o'clock and he had Bricklayers Two at nine. He got out of bed and made for the bathroom.

'Did you hear what I said?' Eva demanded, getting out of bed herself.

'I heard,' said Wilt, and saw that she was naked. Eva Wilt naked at eight o'clock in the morning was almost as startling a sight as Eva Wilt drunk, smoking and dressed in lemon yellow pyjamas at six o'clock at night. And even less enticing. 'What the hell are you going about like that for?'

'If it comes to that, what's wrong with your nose? I suppose you got drunk and fell down. It looks all red and swollen.'

'It *is* all red and swollen. And if you must know I didn't fall down. Now for goodness sake get out of the way. I've got a lecture at nine.'

He pushed past her and went into the bathroom and looked at his nose. It looked awful. Eva followed him in. 'If you didn't fall on it what did happen?' she demanded.

Wilt squeezed foam from an aerosol and patted it gingerly on his chin.

'Well?' said Eva.

Wilt picked up his razor and put it under the hot tap. 'I had an accident,' he muttered.

'With a lamp-post, I suppose. I knew you'd been drinking.'

'With a Printer,' said Wilt indistinctly and started to shave.

'With a Printer?'

'To be precise, I got punched in the face by a particularly pugnacious apprentice printer.'

Eva stared at him in the mirror. 'You mean to say a student hit you in the classroom?'

Wilt nodded.

'I hope you hit him back.'

Wilt cut himself.

'No I bloody didn't,' he said, dabbing his chin with a finger. 'Now look what you've made me do.'

Eva ignored his complaint. 'Well you should have. You're not a man. You should have hit him back.'

32

Wilt put down the razor. 'And got the sack. Got hauled up in court for assaulting a student. Now that's what I call a brilliant idea.' He reached for the sponge and washed his face.

Eva retreated to the bedroom satisfied. There would be no mention of her lemon loungers now. She had taken his mind off her own little extravagance and given him a sense of grievance that would keep him occupied for the time being. By the time she had finished dressing, Wilt had eaten a bowl of All-Bran, drunk half a cup of coffee and was snarled up in a traffic jam at the roundabout. Eva went downstairs and had her own breakfast and began the daily round of washing up and Hoovering and cleaning the bath and ...

'Commitment,' said Dr Mayfield, 'to an integrated approach is an essential element in ...'

The Joint Committee for the Further Development of Liberal Studies was in session. Wilt squirmed in his chair and wished to hell it wasn't. Dr Mayfield's paper 'Cerebral Content and the Non-Academic Syllabus' held no interest for him, and besides, it was delivered in such convoluted sentences and with so much monotonous fervour that Wilt found it difficult to stay awake. He stared out of the window at the machines boring away on the site of the new Admin block. There was a reality about the work going on down there that was in marked contrast to the impractical theories Dr Mayfield was expounding. If the man really thought he could instil Cerebral Content, whatever that was, into Gasfitters Three he was out of his mind. Worse still, his blasted paper was bound to provoke an argument at question time. Wilt looked round the room. The various factions were all there, the New Left, the Left, the Old Left, the Indifferent Centre, the Cultural Right and the Reactionary Right.

Wilt classed himself with the Indifferents. In earlier years he had belonged to the Left politically and to the Right culturally. In other words he had banned the bomb, supported abortion and the abolition of private education and had been against capital punishment, thus earning himself something of a reputation as a radical while at the same time advocating a return to the craft of the wheelwright, the blacksmith and the handloom weaver which had done much to undermine the efforts of the Technical staff to instil in their students an appreciation of the opportunities provided by modern technology. Time and the intransigent coarseness of Plasterers had changed all that. Wilt's ideals had vanished, to be replaced by the conviction that the man who said the pen was mightier than the sword ought to have tried reading *The Mill on the Floss* to Motor Mechanics Three before he opened his big mouth. In Wilt's view, the sword had much to recommend it.

As Dr Mayfield droned on, as question time with its ideological arguments followed, Wilt studied the pile hole on the building site. It would make an ideal depository for a body and there would be something immensely satisfying in knowing that Eva, who in her lifetime had been so unbearable, was in death supporting the weight of a multi-storey concrete building. Besides it would make her discovery an extremely remote possibility and her identification out of the question. Not even Eva, who boasted a strong constitution and a stronger will, could maintain an identity at the bottom of a pile shaft. The difficulty would be in getting her to go down the hole in the first place. Sleeping pills seemed a sensible preliminary but Eva was a sound sleeper and didn't believe in pills of any sort. 'I can't imagine why not,' Wilt thought grimly, 'she's prepared to believe in just about everything else.'

His reverie was interrupted by Mr Morris who was bringing the meeting to a close. 'Before you all go,' he said, 'there is one more subject I want to mention. We have been asked by the Head of Engineering to conduct a series of one-hour lectures to Sandwich-Course Trainee Firemen. The theme this year will be Problems of Contemporary Society. I have drawn up a list of topics and the lecturers who will give them.'

Mr Morris handed out subjects at random. Major Millfield got Media, Communications and Participatory Democracy about which he knew nothing and cared less. Peter Braintree was given The New Brutalism in Architecture, Its Origins and Social Attributes, and Wilt ended up with Violence and the Break-Up of Family Life. On the whole he thought he had done rather well. The subject fitted in with his present preoccupations. Mr Morris evidently agreed.

'I thought you might like to have a go at it after yesterday's little episode with Printers Three,' he said, as they went out. Wilt smiled wanly and went off to take Fitters and Turners Two. He gave them *Shane* to read and spent the hour jotting down notes for his lecture. In the distance he could hear the pile-boring machines grinding away. Wilt could imagine Eva lying at the bottom as they poured the concrete in. In her lemon pyjamas. It was a nice thought, and helped him with his notes. He wrote down a heading, Crime in the family, sub-heading (A) Murder of Spouse, decline in since divorce laws.

Yes, he should be able to talk about that to Trainee Firemen.

4

'I loathe parties,' said Wilt on Thursday night, 'and if there's one thing worse than parties it's university parties and bottle parties are worst of all. You take along a bottle of decent burgundy and end up drinking someone else's rotgut.'

'It isn't a party,' said Eva, 'it's a barbecue.'

'It says here "Come and Touch and Come with Sally and Gaskell 9PM Thursday. Bring your own ambrosia or take pot luck with the Pringsheim punch." If ambrosia doesn't mean Algerian bilgewater I'd like to know what it does mean.'

'I thought it was that stuff people take to get a hard-on,' said Eva.

Wilt looked at her with disgust. 'You've picked up some choice phrases since you've met these bloody people. A hard-on. I don't know what's got into you.'

'You haven't. That's for sure,' said Eva, and went through to the bathroom. Wilt sat on the bed and looked at the card. The beastly thing was shaped like a ... What the hell was it shaped like? Anyway it was pink and opened out and inside were all these ambiguous words. Come and Touch and Come.

Anyone touched him and they'd get an earful. And what about pot luck? A lot of trendy dons smoking joints and talking about set-theoretic data-manipulation systems or the significance of pre-Popper Hegelianism in the contemporary dialectical scene, or something equally unintelligible, and using fuck and cunt every now and then to show that they were still human.

'And what do you do?' they would ask him.

'Well, actually I teach at the Tech.'

'At the Tech? How frightfully interesting,' looking over his shoulder towards more stimulating horizons, and he would end the evening with some ghastly woman who felt strongly that Techs fulfilled a real function and that intellectual achievement was vastly overrated and that people should be oriented in a way that would make them community coordinated and that's what Techs were doing, weren't they? Wilt knew what Techs were doing. Paying people like him £3500 a year to keep Gasfitters quiet for an hour.

And Pringsheim Punch. Planters Punch. Printers Punch. He'd had enough punches recently.

'What the hell am I to wear?' he asked.

'There's that Mexican shirt you bought on the Costa del Sol last year,' Eva called from the bathroom. 'You haven't had a chance to wear it since.'

'And I don't intend to now,' muttered Wilt, rummaging through a drawer in search of something nondescript that would demonstrate his independence. In the end he put on a striped shirt with blue jeans.

'You're surely not going like that?' Eva told him emerging from the bathroom largely naked. Her face was plastered with white powder and her lips were carmine.

'Jesus wept,' said Wilt, 'Mardi Gras with pernicious anaemia.'

Eva pushed passed him. 'I'm going as The Great Gatsby,' she announced, 'and if you had any imagination you'd think of something better than a business shirt with blue jeans.'

'The Great Gatsby happened to be a man,' said Wilt.

'Bully for him,' said Eva, and put on her lemon loungers.

Wilt shut his eyes and took off his shirt. By the time they left the house he was wearing a red shirt with jeans while Eva, in spite of the hot night, insisted on putting on her new raincoat and trilby.

'We might as well walk,' said Wilt.

They took the car. Eva wasn't yet prepared to walk down Parkview Avenue in a trilby, a belted raincoat and lemon loungers. On the way they stopped at an off-licence where Wilt bought a bottle of Cyprus red.

'Don't think I'm going to touch the muck,' he said, 'and you had better take the car keys now. If it's as bad as I think it will be, I'm walking home early.'

It was. Worse. In his red shirt and blue jeans Wilt looked out of place.

'Darling Eva,' said Sally, when they finally found her talking to a man in a loincloth made out of a kitchen towel advertising Irish cheeses, 'you look great. The twenties suit you. And so this is Henry.' Henry didn't feel Henry at all. 'In period costume too. Henry meet Raphael.'

The man in the loincloth studied Wilt's jeans. 'The fifties are back,' he said languidly, 'I suppose it was bound to happen.'

Wilt looked pointedly at a Connemara Cheddar and tried to smile.

'Help yourself, Henry,' said Sally, and took Eva off to meet the freest but the most liberated woman who was simply dying to meet booby baby. Wilt went into the garden and put his bottle on the table and looked for a corkscrew. There wasn't one. In the end he looked into a large bucket with a ladle in it. Half an orange and segments of bruised peach floated in a purple liquid. He poured himself a paper cup and tried it. As he had anticipated, it tasted like cider with wood alcohol and orange squash. Wilt looked round the garden. In one corner a man in a chef's hat and a jockstrap was cooking, was *burning* sausages over a charcoal grill. In another corner a dozen people were lying in a circle listening to the Watergate tapes. There was a sprinkling of couples talking earnestly and a number of individuals standing by themselves looking supercilious and remote. Wilt recognized himself among them and selected the least attractive girl on the theory that he might just as well jump in the deep end and get it over with. He'd end up with her anyway.

'Hi,' he said, conscious that already he was slipping into the Americanese that Eva had succumbed to. The girl looked at him blankly and moved away.

'Charming,' said Wilt, and finished his drink. Ten minutes and two drinks later he was discussing Rapid Reading with a small round man who seemed deeply interested in the subject.

In the kitchen Eva was cutting up French bread while Sally stood with a drink and talked about Lévi-Strauss with an Ethiopian who had just got back from New Guinea.

'I've always felt that L-S was all wrong on the woman's front,' she said, languidly studying Eva's rear, 'I mean he disregards the essential similarity ...' She stopped and stared out of the window. 'Excuse me a moment,' she said, and went out to rescue Dr Scheimacher from the clutches of Henry Wilt. 'Ernst is such a sweetie,' she said, when she came back, 'you'd never guess he got the Nobel prize for spermatology.'

Wilt stood in the middle of the garden and finished his third drink. He poured himself a fourth and went to listen to the Watergate tapes. He got there in time to hear the end.

'You get a much clearer insight into Tricky Dick's character quadraphonically,' someone said as the group broke up.

'With the highly gifted child one has to develop a special relationship. Roger and I find that Tonio responds best to a constructional approach.'

'It's a load of bull. Take what he says about quasars for example ...'

'I can't honestly see what's wrong with buggery ...'

'I don't care what Marcuse thinks about tolerance. What I'm saying is ...'

'At minus two-fifty nitrogen ...'

'Bach does have his moments I suppose but he has his limitations ...'

'We've got this place at St Trop ...'

'I still think Kaldor had the answer ...'

Wilt finished his fourth drink and went to look for Eva. He'd had enough. He was halted by a yell from the man in the chef's hat.

'Burgers up. Come and get it.'

Wilt staggered off and got it. Two sausages, a burnt beef-burger and a slosh of coleslaw on a paper plate. There didn't seem to be any knives or forks.

'Poor Henry's looking so forlorn,' said Sally, 'I'll go and transfuse him.'

She went out and took Wilt's arm.

'You're so lucky to have Eva. She's the babiest baby.'

'She's thirty-five,' said Wilt drunkenly, 'thirty-five if she's a day.'

'It's marvellous to meet a man who says what he means,' said Sally, and took a piece of beefburger from his plate. 'Gaskell just never says anything straightforwardly. I love down-to-earth people.' She sat down on the grass and pulled Wilt down with her. 'I think it's terribly important for two people to tell one another the truth,' she went on, breaking off another piece of beefburger and popping it into Wilt's mouth. She licked her fingers slowly and looked at him with wide eyes. Wilt chewed the bit uneasily and finally swallowed it. It tasted like burnt mincemeat with a soupçon of Lancôme. Or a bouquet.

'Why two?' he asked, rinsing his mouth out with coleslaw.

'Why two what?'

'Why two people,' said Wilt. 'Why is it so important for two people to tell the truth?'

'Well, I mean ...'

'Why not three? Or four? Or a hundred?'

'A hundred people can't have a relationship. Not an inti-mate one,' said Sally, 'not a meaningful one.'

'I don't know many twos who can either,' said Wilt. Sally dabbed her finger in his coleslaw.

'Oh but you do. You and Eva have this real thing going between you.'

'Not very often,' said Wilt. Sally laughed.

'Oh baby, you're a truth baby,' she said, and got up and fetched two more drinks. Wilt looked down into his paper cup doubtfully. He was getting very drunk.

'If I'm a truth baby, what sort of baby are you, baby?' he asked, endeavouring to instil the last baby with more than a soupçon of contempt. Sally snuggled up to him and whispered in his ear.

'I'm a body baby,' she said.

'I can see that,' said Wilt. 'You've got a very nice body.'

'That's the nicest thing anybody has ever said to me,' said Sally.

'In that case,' said Wilt, picking up a blackened sausage, 'you must have had a deprived childhood.'

'As a matter of fact I did,' Sally said and plucked the sausage from his fingers. 'That's why I need so much loving now.' She put most of the sausage in her mouth, drew it slowly out and nibbled the end. Wilt finished off the coleslaw and washed it down with Pringsheim Punch.

'Aren't they all awful?' said Sally, as shouts and laughter came from the corner of the garden by the grill.

Wilt looked up.

'As a matter of fact they are,' he said. 'Who's the clown in the jockstrap?'

'That's Gaskell. He's so arrested. He loves playing at things. In the States he just loves to ride footplate on a locomotive and he goes to rodeos and last Christmas he insisted on dressing up as Santa Claus and going down to Watts and giving out presents to the black kids at an orphanage. Of course they wouldn't let him.'

'If he went in a jockstrap I'm not in the least surprised,' said Wilt. Sally laughed.

'You must be an Aries,' she said, 'you don't mind what you say.' She got to her feet and pulled Wilt up. 'I'm going to show you his toy room. It's ever so droll.'

Wilt put his plate down and they went into the house. In the kitchen Eva was peeling oranges for a fruit salad and talking about circumcision rites with the Ethiopian, who was slicing bananas for her. In the lounge several couples were dancing back to back very vigorously to an LP of Beethoven's Fifth played at 78.

'Christ,' said Wilt, as Sally collected a bottle of Vodka from a cupboard. They went upstairs and down a passage to a small bedroom filled with toys. There was a model train set on the floor, a punchbag, an enormous Teddy Bear, a rocking horse, a fireman's helmet and a lifesize inflated doll that looked like a real woman.

'That's Judy,' said Sally, 'she's got a real cunt. Gaskell is a plastic freak.' Wilt winced. 'And here are Gaskell's toys. Puberty baby.'

Wilt looked round the room at the mess and shook his head. 'Looks as though he's making up for a lost childhood,' he said.

'Oh, Henry, you're so perceptive,' said Sally, and unscrewed the top of the Vodka bottle.

'I'm not. It's just bloody obvious.'

'Oh you are. You're just terribly modest, is all. Modest and shy and manly.' She swigged from the bottle and gave it to Wilt. He took a mouthful inadvisedly and had trouble swallowing it. Sally locked the door and sat down on the bed. She reached up a hand and pulled Wilt towards her.

'Screw me, Henry baby,' she said and lifted her skirt, 'fuck me, honey. Screw the pants off me.'

'That,' said Wilt, 'would be a bit difficult.'

'Oh. Why?'

'Well for one thing you don't appear to be wearing any and anyway why should I?'

'You want a reason? A reason for screwing?'

'Yes,' said Wilt. 'Yes I do.'

'Reason's treason. Feel free.' She pulled him down and kissed him. Wilt didn't feel at all free. 'Don't be shy, baby.'

'Shy?' said Wilt lurching to one side. 'Me shy?'

'Sure you're shy. OK, you're small. Eva told me ...'

'Small? What do you mean I'm small?' shouted Wilt furiously.

Sally smiled up at him. 'It doesn't matter. It doesn't matter. Nothing matters. Just you and me and ...'

'It bloody well does matter,' snarled Wilt. 'My wife said I was small. I'll soon show the silly bitch who's small. I'll show . . .'

'Show me, Henry baby, show me. I like them small. Prick me to the quick.'

'It's not true,' Wilt mumbled.

'Prove it, lover,' said Sally squirming against him.

'I won't,' said Wilt, and stood up.

Sally stopped squirming and looked at him. 'You're just afraid,' she said. 'You're afraid to be free.'

'Free? Free?' shouted Wilt, trying to open the door. 'Locked in a room with another man's wife is freedom? You've got to be joking.'

Sally pulled down her skirt and sat up.

'You won't?'

'No,' said Wilt.

'Are you a bondage baby? You can tell me. I'm used to bondage babies. Gaskell is real . . .'

'Certainly not,' said Wilt. 'I don't care what Gaskell is.'

'You want a blow job, is that it? You want for me to give you a blow job?' She got off the bed and came towards him. Wilt looked at her wildly.

'Don't you touch me,' he shouted, his mind alive with images of burning paint. 'I don't want anything from you.'

Sally stopped and stared at him. She wasn't smiling any more.

'Why not? Because you're small? Is that why?'

Wilt backed against the door.

'No, it isn't.'

'Because you haven't the courage of your instincts? Because you're a psychic virgin? Because you're not a man? Because you can't take a woman who thinks?'

'Thinks?' yelled Wilt, stung into action by the accusation that he wasn't a man. 'Thinks? You think? You know something? I'd rather have it off with that plastic mechanical doll than you. It's got more sex appeal in its little finger than you have in your whole rotten body. When I want a whore I'll buy one.'

'Why you little shit,' said Sally, and lunged at him. Wilt scuttled sideways and collided with the punchbag. The next moment he had stepped on a model engine and was hurtling across the room. As he slumped down the wall on to the floor Sally picked up the doll and leant over him.

In the kitchen Eva had finished the fruit salad and had made coffee. It was a lovely party. Mr Osewa had told her all about his job as underdevelopment officer in Cultural Affairs to UNESCO and how rewarding he found it. She had been kissed twice on the back of the neck by Dr Scheimacher in passing and the man in the Irish Cheese loincloth had pressed himself against her rather more firmly than was absolutely necessary to reach the tomato ketchup. And all around her terribly clever people were being so outspoken. It was all so sophisticated. She helped herself to another drink and looked around for Henry. He was nowhere to be seen.

'Have you seen Henry?' she asked when Sally came into the kitchen holding a bottle of Vodka and looking rather flushed.

'The last I saw of him he was sitting with some dolly bird,' said Sally, helping herself to a spoonful of fruit salad. 'Oh, Eva darling, you're absolutely Cordon Bleu baby.' Eva blushed.

'I do hope he's enjoying himself. Henry's not awfully good at parties.'

'Eva baby, be honest. Henry's not awfully good period.'

'It's just that he . . .' Eva began but Sally kissed her.

'You're far too good for him,' she said, 'we've got to find you someone really beautiful.' While Eva sipped her drink, Sally found a young man with a frond of hair falling across his forehead who was lying on a couch with a girl, smoking and staring at the ceiling.

'Christopher precious,' she said, 'I'm going to steal you for a moment. I want you to do someone for me. Go into the kitchen and sweeten the woman with the boobies and the awful yellow pyjamas.'

'Oh God. Why me?'

'My sweet, you know you're utterly irresistible. But the sexiest. For me, baby, for me.'

Christopher got off the couch and went into the kitchen and Sally stretched out beside the girl.

'Christopher is a dreamboy,' she said.

'He's a gigolo,' said the girl. 'A male prostitute.'

'Darling,' said Sally, 'it's about time we women had them.'

In the kitchen Eva stopped pouring coffee. She was feeling delightfully tipsy.

'You mustn't,' she said hastily.

'Why not?'

'I'm married.'

'I like it. I like it.'

'Yes but . . .'

'No buts, lover.'

'Oh.'

Upstairs in the toy room Wilt, recovering slowly from the combined assaults on his system of Pringsheim Punch, Vodka, his nymphomaniac hostess and the corner of the cupboard against which he had fallen, had the feeling that something was terribly wrong. It wasn't simply that the room was oscillating, that he had a lump on the back of his head or that he was naked. It was rather the sensation that something with all the less attractive qualities of a mousetrap, or a vice, or a starving clam, had attached itself implacably to what he had up till now always considered to be the most private of his parts. Wilt opened his eyes and found himself staring into a smiling if slightly swollen face. He shut his eyes again, hoped against hope, opened them again, found the face still there and made an effort to sit up.

It was an unwise move. Judy, the plastic doll, inflated beyond her normal pressure, resisted. With a squawk Wilt fell back on to the floor. Judy followed. Her nose bounced on his face and her breasts on his chest. With a curse Wilt rolled on to his side and considered the problem. Sitting up was out of the question. That way led to castration. He would have to try something else. He rolled the doll over further and climbed on top only to decide that his weight on it was increasing the pressure on what remained of his penis and that if he wanted to get gangrene that was the way to go about getting it. Wilt rolled off precipitately and groped for a valve. There must be one somewhere if he could only find it. But if there was a valve it was well hidden and by the feel of things he hadn't got time to waste finding it. He felt round on the floor for something to use as a dagger, something sharp, and finally broke off a piece of railway track and plunged it into his assailant's back. There was a squeak of plastic but Judy's swollen smile remained unchanged and her unwanted attentions as implacable as ever. Again and again he stabbed her but to no avail. Wilt dropped his makeshift dagger and considered other means. He was getting frantic, conscious of a new threat. It was no longer that he was the subject of her high air pressure. His own internal pressures were mounting. The Pringsheim Punch and the Vodka were making their presence felt. With a desperate thought that if he didn't get out of her soon he would burst, Wilt seized Judy's head, bent it sideways and sank his teeth into her neck. Or would have had her pounds per square inch permitted. Instead he bounced off and spent the next two minutes trying to find his false tooth which had been dislodged in the exchange.

By the time he had got it back in place, panic had set in. He had to get out of the doll. He just had to. There would be a razor in the bathroom or a pair of scissors. But where on earth was the bathroom? Never mind about that. He'd find the damned thing. Carefully, very carefully he rolled the doll on to her back and followed her over. Then he inched his knees up until he was straddling the thing. All he needed now was something to hold on to while he got to his feet. Wilt leant over and grasped the edge of a chair with one hand while lifting Judy's head off the floor with the other. A moment later he was on his feet. Holding the doll to him he shuffled towards the door and opened it. He peered out into the passage. What if someone saw him? To hell with that. Wilt no longer cared what people thought about him. But which way was the bathroom? Wilt turned right, and peering frantically over Judy's shoulder, shuffled off down the passage.

•

Downstairs, Eva was having a wonderful time. First Christopher, then the man in the Irish Cheese loincloth and finally Dr Scheimacher, had all made advances to her and been rebuffed. It was such a change from Henry's lack of interest. It showed she was still attractive. Dr Scheimacher had said that she was an interesting example of latent steatopygia, Christopher tried to kiss her breasts and the man in the loincloth had made the most extraordinary suggestion to her. And through it all, Eva had remained entirely virtuous. Her massive skittishness, her insistence on dancing and, most effective of all, her habit of saying in a loud and not wholly cultivated voice, 'Oh, you are awful' at moments of their greatest ardour, had had a markedly deterrent effect. Now she sat on the floor in the living-room, while Sally and Gaskell and the bearded man from the Institute of Ecological Research argued about sexually interchangeable role-playing in a population-restrictive society. She felt strangely elated. Parkview Avenue and Mavis Mottram and her work at the Harmony Community Centre seemed to belong to another world. She had been accepted by people who flew to California or Tokyo to conferences and Think Tanks as casually as she took the bus to town. Dr Scheimacher had mentioned that he was flying to New Delhi in the morning, and Christopher had just come back from a photographic assignment in Trinidad. Above all, there was an aura of importance about what they were doing, a glamour that was wholly lacking in Henry's job at the Tech. If only she could get him to do something interesting and adventurous. But Henry was such a stick-in-the-mud. She had made a mistake in marrying him. She really had. All he was interested in was books, but life wasn't to be found in books. Like Sally said, life was for living. Life was people and experiences and fun. Henry would never see that.

In the bathroom Wilt could see very little. He certainly couldn't see any way of getting out of the doll. His attempt to slit the beastly thing's throat with a razor had failed, thanks largely to the fact that the razor in question was a Wilkinson bonded blade. Having failed with the razor he had tried shampoo as a lubricant but apart from working up a lather which even to his jaundiced eye looked as though he had aroused the doll to positively frenzied heights of sexual expectation the shampoo had achieved nothing. Finally he had reverted to a quest for the valve. The damned thing had one somewhere if only he could find it. In this endeavour he peered into the mirror on the door of the medicine cabinet but the mirror was too small. There was a large one over the washbasin. Wilt pulled down the lid of the toilet and climbed on to it. This way he would be able to get a clear view of the doll's back. He was just inching his way round when there were footsteps in the passage. Wilt stopped inching and stood rigid on the toilet lid. Someone tried the door and found it locked. The footsteps retreated and Wilt breathed a sigh of relief. Now then, just let him find that valve.

And at that moment disaster struck. Wilt's left foot stepped in the shampoo that had dripped on to the toilet seat, slid sideways off the edge and Wilt, the doll and the door of the medicine cabinet with which he had attempted to save himself were momentarily airborne. As they hurtled into the bath, as the shower curtain and fitting followed, as the contents of the medicine cabinet cascaded on' to the washbasin, Wilt gave a last despairing scream. There was a pop reminiscent of champagne corks and Judy, finally responding to the pressure of Wilt's eleven stone dropping from several feet into the bath, ejected him. But Wilt no longer cared. He had in every sense passed out. He was only dimly aware of shouts in the corridor, of someone breaking the door down, of faces peering at him and of hysterical laughter. When he came to he was lying on the bed in the toy room. He got up and put on his clothes and crept downstairs and out of the front door. It was 3AM.

5

Eva sat on the edge of the bed crying.

'How could he? How could he do a thing like that?' she said, 'in front of all these people.'

'Eva baby, men are like that. Believe me,' said Sally.

'But with a doll . . . .'

'That's symbolic of the male chauvinist pig attitude to women. We're just fuck artefacts to them. Objectification. So now you know how Henry feels about you.'

'It's horrible,' said Eva.

'Sure it's horrible. Male domination debases us to the level of objects.'

'But Henry's never done anything like that before,' Eva wailed.

'Well, he's done it now.'

'I'm not going back to him. I couldn't face it. I feel so ashamed.'

'Honey, you just forget about it. You don't have to go anywhere. Sally will look after you. You just lie down and get some sleep.'

Eva lay back, but sleep was impossible. The image of Henry lying naked in the bath on top of that horrible doll was fixed in her mind. They had to break the door down and Dr Scheimacher had cut his hand on a broken bottle trying to get Henry out of the bath . . . Oh, it was all too awful. She would never be able to look people in the face again. The story was bound to get about and she would be known as the woman whose husband went around . . . With a fresh paroxysm of embarrassment Eva buried her head in the pillow and wept.

'Well that sure made the party go with a bang,' said Gaskell. 'Guy screws a doll in the bathroom and everyone goes berserk.' He looked round the living-room at the mess. 'If anyone thinks I'm going to start clearing this lot up now they'd better think again. I'm going to bed.'

'Just don't wake Eva up. She's hysterical,' said Sally.

'Oh great. Now we've got a manic obsessive compulsive woman with hysteria in the house.'

'And tomorrow she's coming with us on the boat.'

'She's what?'

'You heard me. She's coming with us on the boat.'

'Now wait a bit . . .'

'I'm not arguing with you, G. I'm telling you. She's coming with us.'

'Why, for Chrissake?'

'Because I'm not having her go back to that creep of a husband of hers. Because you won't get me a cleaning-woman and because I like her.'

'Because I won't get you a cleaning-woman. Now I've heard it all.'

'Oh no you haven't,' said Sally, 'you haven't heard the half of it. You may not know it but you married a liberated woman. No male pig is going to put one over on me . . .'

'I'm not trying to put one over on you,' said Gaskell. 'All I'm saying is that I don't want to have to . . .'

'I'm not talking about you. I'm talking about that creep Wilt. You think he got into that doll by himself? Think again, G baby, think again.'

Gaskell sat down on the sofa and stared at her.

'You must be out of your mind. What the hell did you want to do a thing like that for?'

'Because when I liberate someone I liberate them. No mistake.'

'Liberate someone by . . .' he shook his head. 'It doesn't make sense.'

Sally poured herself a drink. 'The trouble with you, G, is that you talk big but you don't do. It's yakkity yak with you. "My wife is a liberated woman. My wife's free." Nice-sounding talk but come the time your liberated wife takes it into her head to do something, you don't want to know.'

'Yeah, and when you take it into your goddam head to do something who takes the can back? I do. Where's petticoats then? Who got you out of that mess in Omaha? Who paid the fuzz in Houston that time . . .'

'So you did. So why did you marry me? Just why?'

Gaskell polished his glasses with the edge of the chef's hat. 'I don't know,' he said, 'so help me I don't know.'

'For kicks, baby, for kicks. Without me you'd have died of boredom. With me you get excitement. With me you get kicks.'

'In the teeth.'

Gaskell got up wearily and headed for the stairs. It was at times like these that he wondered why he had married.

Wilt walked home in agony. His pain was no longer physical. It was the agony of humiliation, hatred and self-contempt. He had been made to look a fool, a pervert and an idiot in front of people he despised. The Pringsheims and their set were everything he loathed, false, phoney, pretentious, a circus of intellectual clowns whose antics had not even the merit of his own, which had at least been real. Theirs were merely a parody of enjoyment. They laughed to hear themselves laughing and paraded a sensuality that had nothing to do with feelings or even instincts but was dredged up from shallow imaginations to mimic lust. *Copulo ergo sum*. And that bitch, Sally, had taunted him with not having the courage of his instincts as if instinct consisted of ejaculating into the chemically sterilized body of a woman he had first met twenty minutes before. And Wilt had reacted instinctively, shying away from a concupiscence that had to do with power and arrogance and an intolerable contempt for him which presupposed that what he was, what little he was, was a mere extension of his penis and that the ultimate expression of his thoughts, feelings, hopes and ambitions was to be attained between the legs of a trendy slut. And *that* was being liberated.

'Feel free,' she had said and had knotted him into that fucking doll. Wilt ground his teeth underneath a streetlamp.

And what about Eva? What sort of hell was she going to make for him now? If life had been intolerable with her before this, it was going to be unadulterated misery now. She wouldn't believe that he hadn't been screwing that doll, that he hadn't got into it of his own accord, that he had been put into it by Sally. Not in a month of Sundays. And even if by some miracle she accepted his story, a fat lot of difference that would make.

'What sort of man do you think you are, letting a woman do a thing like that to you?' she would ask. There was absolutely no reply to the question. What sort of man was he? Wilt had no idea. An insignificant little man to whom things happened and for whom life was a chapter of indignities. Printers punched him in the face and he was blamed for it. His wife bullied him and other people's wives made a laughing-stock out of him. Wilt wandered on along suburban streets past semi-detached houses and little gardens with a mounting sense of determination. He had had enough of being the butt of circumstance. From now on things would happen because he wanted them to. He would change from being the recipient of misfortune. He would be the instigator. Just let Eva try anything now. He would knock the bitch down.

Wilt stopped. It was all very well to talk. The bloody woman had a weapon she wouldn't hesitate to use. Knock her down, my eye. If anyone went down it would be Wilt, and in addition she would parade his affair with the doll to everyone they knew. It wouldn't be long before the story reached the Tech. In the darkness of Parkview Avenue Wilt shuddered at the thought. It would be the end of his career. He went through the gate of Number 34 and unlocked the front door with the feeling that unless he took some drastic action in the immediate future he was doomed.

In bed an hour later he was still awake, wide awake and wrestling with the problem of Eva, his own character and how to change it into something he could respect. And what did he respect? Under the blankets Wilt clenched his fist.

'Decisiveness,' he murmured. 'The ability to act without hesitation. Courage.' A strange litany of ancient virtues. But how to acquire them now? How had they turned men like him into Commandos and professional killers during the war? By training them. Wilt lay in the darkness and considered ways in which he could train himself to become what he was clearly not. By the time he fell asleep he had determined to attempt the impossible.

At seven the alarm went. Wilt got up and went into the bathroom and stared at himself in the mirror. He was a hard man, a man without feelings. Hard, methodical, cold-blooded and logical. A man who made no mistakes. He went downstairs and ate his All-Bran and drank his cup of coffee. So Eva wasn't home. She had stayed the night at the Pringsheims. Well that was something. It made things easier for him. Except that she still had the car and the keys. He certainly wasn't going to go round and get the car. He walked down to the roundabout and caught the bus to the Tech. He had Bricklayers One in Room 456. When he arrived they were talking about gradbashing.

'There was this student all dressed up like a waiter see. "Do you mind?" he says, "Do you mind getting out of my way." Just like that and all I was doing was looking in the window at the books . . .'

'At the books?' said Wilt sceptically. 'At eleven o'clock at night you were looking at books? I don't believe it.'

'Magazines and cowboy books,' said the bricklayer. 'They're in a junk shop in Finch Street.'

'They've got girlie mags,' someone else explained. Wilt nodded. That sounded more like it.

'So I says "Mind what?"' continued the bricklayer, 'and he says, "Mind out of my way." His way. Like he owned the bloody street.'

'So what did you say?' asked Wilt.

'Say? I didn't say anything. I wasn't wasting words on him.'

'What did you do then?'

'Well, I put the boot in and duffed him up. Gave him a good going-over and no mistake. Then I pushed off. There's one bloody grad who won't be telling people to get out of his way for a bit.'

The class nodded approvingly.

'They're all the bloody same, students,' said another bricklayer. 'Think because they've got money and go to college they can order you about. They could all do with a going-over. Do them a power of good.'

Wilt considered the implications of mugging as part of an intellectual's education. After his experience the previous night he was inclined to think there was something to be said for it. He would have liked to have duffed up half the people at the Pringsheims' party.

'So none of you feel there's anything wrong with beating a student up if he gets in your way?' he asked.

'Wrong?' said the bricklayers in unison. 'What's wrong with a good punch-up? It's not as if a grad is an old woman or something. He can always hit back, can't he?'

They spent the rest of the hour discussing violence in the modern world. On the whole, the bricklayers seemed to think it was a good thing.

'I mean what's the point of going out on a Saturday night and getting pissed if you can't have a bit of a barney at the same time? Got to get rid of your aggression somehow,' said an unusually articulate bricklayer, 'I mean it's natural isn't it?'

'So you think man is a naturally aggressive animal,' said Wilt.

'Course he is. That's history for you, all them wars and things. It's only bloody poofters don't like violence.'

Wilt took this view of things along to the Staff Room for his free period and collected a cup of coffee from the vending machine. He was joined by Peter Braintree.

'How did the party go?' Braintree asked.

'It didn't,' said Wilt morosely.

'Eva enjoy it?'

'I wouldn't know. She hadn't come home by the time I got up this morning.'

'Hadn't come home?'

'That's what I said,' said Wilt.

'Well did you ring up and find out what had happened to her?'

'No,' said Wilt.

'Why not?'

'Because I'd look a bit of a twit ringing up and being told

53

she was shacked up with the Abyssinian ambassador, wouldn't I?'

'The Abyssinian ambassador? Was he there?'

'I don't know and I don't want to know. The last I saw of her she was being chatted up by this big black bloke from Ethiopia. Something to do with the United Nations. She was making fruit salad and he was chopping bananas for her.'

'Doesn't sound a very compromising sort of activity to me,' said Braintree.

'No, I daresay it doesn't. Only you weren't there and don't know what sort of party it was,' said Wilt rapidly coming to the conclusion that an edited version of the night's events was called for. 'A whole lot of middle-aged with-it kids doing their withered thing.'

'It sounds bloody awful. And you think Eva ...'

'I think Eva got pissed and somebody gave her a joint and she passed out,' said Wilt, 'that's what I think. She's probably sleeping it off in the downstairs loo.'

'Doesn't sound like Eva to me,' said Braintree. Wilt drank his coffee and considered his strategy. If the story of his involvement with that fucking doll was going to come out, perhaps it would be better if he told it his way first. On the other hand ...

'What were you doing while all this was going on?' Braintree asked.

'Well,' said Wilt, 'as a matter of fact ...' He hesitated. On second thoughts it might be better not to mention the doll at all. If Eva kept her trap shut ... 'I got a bit slewed myself.'

'That sounds more like it,' said Braintree, 'I suppose you made a pass at another woman too.'

'If you must know,' said Wilt, 'another woman made a pass at me. Mrs Pringsheim.'

'Mrs Pringsheim made a pass at you?'

'Well, we went upstairs to look at her husband's toys....'

'His toys? I thought you told me he was a biochemist.'

'He is a biochemist. He just happens to like playing with toys. Model trains and Teddy Bears and things. She says he's a case of arrested development. She would, though. She's that sort of loyal wife.'

'What happened then?'

'Apart from her locking the door and lying on the bed with her legs wide open and asking me to screw her and threatening me with a blow job, nothing happened,' said Wilt.

Peter Braintree looked at him sceptically. 'Nothing?' he said finally. 'Nothing? I mean what did you do?'

'Equivocated,' said Wilt.

'That's a new word for it,' said Braintree. 'You go upstairs with Mrs Pringsheim and equivocate while she lies on a bed with her legs open and you want to know why Eva hasn't come home? She's probably round at some lawyer's office filing a petition for divorce right now.'

'But I tell you I didn't screw the bitch,' said Wilt, 'I told her to hawk her pearly somewhere else.'

'And you call that equivocating? Hawk her pearly? Where the hell did you get that expression from?'

'Meat One,' said Wilt and got up and fetched himself another cup of coffee.

By the time he came back to his seat he had decided on his version.

'I don't know what happened after that,' he said when Braintree insisted on hearing the next episode. 'I passed out. It must have been the vodka.'

'You just passed out in a locked room with a naked woman? Is that what happened?' said Braintree. He didn't sound as if he believed a word of the story.

'Precisely,' said Wilt.

'And when you came to?'

'I was walking home,' said Wilt. 'I've no idea what happened in between.'

'Oh well, I daresay we'll hear about that from Eva,' said Braintree. 'She's bound to know.'

He got up and went off and Wilt was left alone to consider his next move. The first thing to do was to make sure that Eva didn't say anything. He went through to the telephone in the corridor and dialled his home number. There was no reply. Wilt went along to Room 187 and spent an hour with Turners and Fitters. Several times during the day he tried to telephone Eva but there was no answer.

'She's probably spent the day round at Mavis Mottram's weeping on her shoulder and telling all and sundry what a pig I am,' he thought. 'She's bound to be waiting for me when I get home tonight.'

But she wasn't. Instead there was a note on the kitchen table and a package. Wilt opened the note.

'I'm going away with Sally and Gaskell to think things over. What you did last night was horrible. I won't ever forgive you. Don't forget to buy some dog food. Eva. P.S. Sally says next time you want a blow job get Judy to give you one.'

Wilt looked at the package. He knew without opening it what it contained. That infernal doll. In a sudden paroxysm of rage Wilt picked it up and hurled it across the kitchen at the sink. Two plates and a saucer bounced off the washing-up rack and broke on the floor.

'Bugger the bitch,' said Wilt inclusively, Eva, Judy, and Sally Pringsheim all coming within the ambit of his fury. Then he sat down at the table and looked at the note again. 'Going away to think things over.' Like hell she was. Think? The stupid cow wasn't capable of thought. She'd emote, drool over his deficiencies and work herself into an ecstasy of self-pity. Wilt could hear her now blathering on about that blasted bank manager and how she should have married him instead of saddling herself with a man who couldn't even get promotion at the Tech and who went around fucking inflatable dolls in other people's bathrooms. And there was that filthy slut, Sally Pringsheim, egging her on. Wilt looked at the post-script: 'Sally says next time you want a blow job ...' Christ. As if he'd wanted a blow job the last time. But there it was, a new myth in the making, like the business of his being in love with Betty Crabtree when all he had done was give her a lift home one night after an Evening Class. Wilt's home life was punctuated by such myths, weapons in Eva's armoury to be brought out when the occasion demanded and brandished above his head. And now Eva had the ultimate deterrent at her disposal, the doll and Sally Pringsheim and a blow job. The balance of recrimination which had been the sustaining factor in their relationship had shifted dramatically. It would take an act of desperate invention on Wilt's part to restore it.

'Don't forget to buy some dog food.' Well at least she had left him the car. It was standing in the carport. Wilt went out and drove round to the supermarket and bought three tins of dog food, a boil-in-the-bag curry and a bottle of gin. He was going to get pissed. Then he went home and sat in the kitchen watching Clem gulp his Bonzo while the bag boiled. He poured himself a stiff gin, topped it up with lime and wandered about. And all the time he was conscious of the package lying there on the draining board waiting for him to open it. And inevitably he would open it. Out of sheer curiosity. He knew it and they knew it wherever they were, and on Sunday night Eva would come home and the first thing she would do would be to ask about the doll and if he had had a nice time with it. Wilt helped himself to some more gin and considered the doll's utility. There must be some way of using the thing to turn the tables on Eva.

By the time he had finished his second gin he had begun to formulate a plan. It involved the doll, a pile hole and a nice test of his own strength of character. It was one thing to have fantasies about murdering your wife. It was quite another to put them into effect and between the two there lay an area of uncertainty. By the end of his third gin Wilt was determined to put the plan into effect. If it did nothing else it would prove he was capable of executing a murder.

Wilt got up and unwrapped the doll. In his interior dialogue Eva was telling him what would happen if Mavis Mottram got to hear about his disgusting behaviour at the Pringsheim's. 'You'd be the laughing stock of the neighbourhood,' she said, 'you'd never live it down.'

Wouldn't he though? Wilt smiled drunkenly to himself and went upstairs. For once Eva was mistaken. He might not live it down but Mrs Eva Wilt wouldn't be around to gloat. She wouldn't live at all.

Upstairs in the bedroom he closed the curtains and laid the doll on the bed and looked for the valve which had eluded him the previous night. He found it and fetched a footpump from the garage. Five minutes later Judy was in good shape. She lay on the bed and smiled up at him. Wilt half closed his eyes and squinted at her. In the half darkness he had to admit that she was hideously lifelike. Plastic Eva with the mastic boobs. All that remained was to dress it up. He rummaged around in several drawers in search of a bra and blouse, decided she didn't need a bra, and picked out an old skirt and a pair of tights. In a cardboard box in the wardrobe he found one of Eva's wigs. She had had a phase of wigs. Finally a pair of shoes. By the time he had finished, Eva Wilt's replica lay on the bed smiling fixedly at the ceiling.

'That's my girl,' said Wilt and went down to the kitchen to see how the boil-in-the-bag was coming along. It was burnt-in-the-bag. Wilt turned the stove off and went into the lavatory under the stairs and sat thinking about his next move. He would use the doll for dummy runs so that if and when it came to the day he would be accustomed to the whole process of murder and would act without feeling like an automaton. Killing by conditioned reflex. Murder by habit. Then again he would know how to time the whole affair. And Eva's going off with the Pringsheims for the weekend would help too. It would establish a pattern of sudden disappearances. He would provoke her somehow to do it again and again and again. And then the visit to the doctor.

'It's just that I can't sleep, doctor. My wife keeps on going off and leaving me and I just can't get used to sleeping on my own.' A prescription for sleeping tablets. Then on the night. 'I'll make the Ovaltine tonight, dear. You're looking tired. I'll bring it up to you in bed.' Gratitude followed by snores. Down to the car ... fairly early would be best ... around ten thirty ... over to the Tech and down the hole. Perhaps inside a plastic bag ... no, not a plastic bag. 'I understand you bought a large plastic bag recently, sir. I wonder if you would mind showing it to us.' No, better just to leave her down the hole they were going to fill with concrete next morning. And finally a bewildered Wilt. He would go round to the Pringsheims'. 'Where's Eva? Yes, you do.' 'No, we don't.' 'Don't lie to me. She's always coming round here.' 'We're not lying.

We haven't seen her.' After that he would go to the police.

Motiveless, clueless and indiscoverable. And proof that he was a man who could act. Or wasn't. What if he broke down under the strain and confessed? That would be some sort of vindication too. He would know what sort of man he was one way or another and at least he would have acted for once in his life. And fifteen years in prison would be almost identical to fifteen, more, twenty years at the Tech confronting louts who despised him and talking about Piggy and the Lord of the Flies. Besides he could always plead the book as a mitigating circumstance at his trial.

'Me lud, members of the Jury, I ask you to put yourself in the defendant's place. For twelve years he has been confronted by the appalling prospect of reading this dreadful book to classes of bored and hostile youths. He has had to endure agonies of repetition, of nausea and disgust at Mr Golding's revoltingly romantic view of human nature. Ah, but I hear you say that Mr Golding is not a romantic, that his view of human nature as expressed in his portrait of a group of young boys marooned on a desert island is the very opposite of romanticism and that the sentimentality of which I accuse him and to which my client's appearance in this court attests is to be found not in *The Lord of the Flies* but in its predecessor, *Coral Island*. But, me lud, gentlemen of the Jury, there is such a thing as inverted romanticism, the romanticism of disillusionment, of pessimism and of nihilism. Let us suppose for one moment that my client had spent twelve years reading not Mr Golding's work but *Coral Island* to groups of apprentices; is it reasonable to imagine that he would have been driven to the desperate remedy of murdering his wife? No. A hundred times no. Mr Ballantyne's book would have given him the inspiration, the self-discipline, the optimism and the belief in man's ability to rescue himself from the most desperate situation by his own ingenuity ...'

It might not be such a good idea to pursue that line of argument too far. The defendant Wilt had after all exercised a good deal of ingenuity in rescuing himself from a desperate situation. Still, it was a nice thought. Wilt finished his business in the lavatory and looked around for the toilet paper. There wasn't any. The bloody roll had run out. He reached in his pocket and found Eva's note and put it to good use. Then he flushed it down the U-bend, puffed some Harpic after it to express his opinion of it and her and went out to the kitchen and helped himself to another gin.

He spent the rest of the evening sitting in front of the TV with a piece of bread and cheese and a tin of peaches until it was time to try his first dummy run. He went out to the front door and looked up and down the street. It was almost dark now and there was no one in sight. Leaving the front door open he went upstairs and fetched the doll and put it in the back seat of the car. He had to push and squeeze a bit to get it in but finally the door shut. Wilt climbed in and backed the car out into Parkview Avenue and drove down to the round-about. By the time he reached the car park at the back of the Tech it was half past ten exactly. He stopped and sat in the car looking around. Not a soul in sight and no lights on. There wouldn't be. The Tech closed at nine.

6

Sally lay naked on the deck of the cabin cruiser, her tight breasts pointing to the sky and her legs apart. Beside her Eva lay on her stomach and looked downriver.

'Oh God, this is divine,' Sally murmured. 'I have this deep thing about the countryside.'

'You've got this deep thing period,' said Gaskell steering the cruiser erratically towards a lock. He was wearing a Captain's cap and sunglasses.

'Cliché baby,' said Sally.

'We're coming to a lock,' said Eva anxiously. 'There are some men there.'

'Men? Forget men, darling. There's just you and me and G and G's not a man, are you G baby?'

'I have my moments,' said Gaskell.

'But so seldom, so awfully seldom,' Sally said. 'Anyway what does it matter? We're here idyllicstyle, cruising down the river in the good old summertime.'

'Shouldn't we have cleared the house up before we left?' Eva asked.

'The secret of parties is not to clear up afterward but to clear off. We can do all that when we get back.'

Eva got up and went below. They were quite near the lock and she wasn't going to be stared at in the nude by the two old men sitting on the bench beside it.

'Jesus, Sally, can't you do something about soulmate? She's getting on my teats,' said Gaskell.

'Oh G baby, she's never. If she did you'd Cheshire cat.'

'Cheshire cat?'

'Disappear with a smile, honey chil', foetus first. She's but positively gargantuanly uterine.'

'She's but positively gargantuanly boring.'

'Time, lover, time. You've got to accentuate the liberated, eliminate the negative and not mess with Mister-in-between.'

'Not mess with Missus-in-between. Operative word missus,' said Gaskell bumping the boat into the lock.

'But that's the whole point.'

'What is?' said Gaskell.

'Messing with Missus-in-between. I mean it's all ways with Eva and us. She does the housework. Gaskell baby can play ship's captain and teatfeast on boobs and Sally sweetie can minotaur her labyrinthine mind.'

'Mind?' said Gaskell. 'Polyunsaturated hasn't got a mind. And talking of cretins, what about Mister-in-between?'

'He's got Judy to mess with. He's probably screwing her now and tomorrow night he'll sit up and watch *Kojak* with her. Who knows, he may even send her off to Mavis Contracuntal Mottram's Flower Arrangement evening. I mean they're suited. You can't say he wasn't hooked on her last night.'

'You can say that again,' said Gaskell and closed the lock gates.

As the cruiser floated downwards the two old men sitting on

the bench stared at Sally. She took off her sunglasses and glared at them.

'Don't blow your prostates, senior citizens,' she said rudely. 'Haven't you seen a fanny before?'

'You talking to me?' said one of the men.

'I wouldn't be talking to myself.'

'Then I'll tell you,' said the man, 'I've seen one like yours before. Once.'

'Once is about right,' said Sally. 'Where?'

'On an old cow as had just dropped her calf,' said the man and spat into a neat bed of geraniums.

In the cabin Eva sat and wondered what they were talking about. She listened to the lapping of the water and the throb of the engine and thought about Henry. It wasn't like him to do a thing like that. It really wasn't. And in front of all those people. He must have been drunk. It was so humiliating. Well, he could suffer. Sally said men ought to be made to suffer. It was part of the process of liberating yourself from them. You had to show them that you didn't need them and violence was the only thing the male psyche understood. That was why she was so harsh with Gaskell. Men were like animals. You had to show them who was master.

Eva went through to the galley and polished the stainless-steel sink. Henry would have to learn how important she was by missing her and doing the housework and cooking for himself and when she got back she would give him such a telling-off about that doll. I mean, it wasn't natural. Perhaps Henry ought to go and see a psychiatrist. Sally said that he had made the most horrible suggestion to her too. It only went to show that you couldn't trust anyone. And Henry of all people. She would never have imagined Henry would think of doing anything like that. But Sally had been so sweet and understanding. She knew how women felt and she hadn't even been angry with Henry.

'It's just that he's a sphincter baby,' she had said. 'It's symptomatic of a male-dominated chauvinist pig society. I've never known an MCP who didn't say "Bugger you" and mean it.'

'Henry's always saying "Bugger",' Eva had admitted. 'It's bugger this, and bugger that.'

'There you are, Eva baby. What did I tell you? It's semantic degradation analwise.'

'It's bloody disgusting,' said Eva, and so it was.

She went on polishing and cleaning until they were clear of the lock and steering downriver towards the open water of the Broads. Then she went up on deck and sat looking out over the flat empty landscape at the sunset. It was all so romantic and exciting, so different from everything she had known before. This was life as she had always dreamt it might be, rich and gay and fulfilling. Eva Wilt sighed. In spite of everything she was at peace with the world.

In the car park at the back of the Tech Henry Wilt wasn't at peace with anything. On the contrary, he was at war with Eva's replica. As he stumbled drunkenly round the car and struggled with Judy he was conscious that even an inflatable doll had a will of its own when it came to being dragged out of small cars. Judy's arms and legs got caught in things. If Eva behaved in the same way on the night of her disposal he would have the devil's own job getting her out of the car. He would have to tie her up in a neat bundle. That would be the best thing to do. Finally, by tugging at the doll's legs, he hauled her out and laid her on the ground. Then he got back into the car to look for her wig. He found it under the seat and after rearranging Judy's skirt so that it wasn't quite so revealing, he put the wig on her head. He looked round the car park at the terrapin huts and the main building but there was no one to be seen. All clear. He picked the doll up and carrying it under his arm set off towards the building site. Halfway there he realized that he wasn't doing it properly. Eva drugged and sleeping would be far too heavy to carry under his arm. He would have to use a fireman's lift. Wilt stopped and hoisted the doll on to his back, and set off again weaving erratically, partly because, thanks to the gin, he couldn't help it, and partly because it added verisimilitude to the undertaking. With Eva over his shoulder he would be bound to weave a bit. He reached the fence and dropped the doll over. In the process the wig fell off again. Wilt groped around in the mud and found it. Then he went round to the gate. It was locked. It would be. He would have to remember that. Details like that were important. He tried to climb over but couldn't. He needed something to give him a leg up. A bicycle. There were usually some in the racks by the main gate. Stuffing the wig into his pocket Wilt made his way round the terrapin huts and past the canteen and was just crossing the grass by the Language Lab when a figure appeared out of the darkness and a torch shone in his face. It was the caretaker.

'Here, where do you think you're going?' the caretaker asked. Wilt halted.

'I've ... I've just come back to get some notes from the Staff Room.'

'Oh it's you, Mr Wilt,' said the caretaker. 'You should know by now that you can't get in at this time of night. We lock up at nine thirty.'

'I'm sorry. I forgot,' said Wilt.

The caretaker sighed. 'Well, since it's you and it's just this once ...' he said, and unlocked the door to the General Studies building. 'You'll have to walk up. The lifts don't work at this time of night. I'll wait for you down here.'

Wilt staggered slowly up five flights of stairs to the Staff Room and went to his locker. He took out a handful of papers and a copy of *Bleak House* he'd been meaning to take home for some months and hadn't. He stuffed the notes into his pocket and found the wig. While he was about it he might as well pick up an elastic band. That would keep the wig on Judy's head. He found some in a box in the stationery cupboard, stuffed the notes into his other pocket and went downstairs.

'Thanks very much,' he told the caretaker. 'Sorry to have bothered you.' He wove off round the corner to the bike sheds.

'Pissed as a newt,' said the caretaker, and went back into his office.

Wilt watched him light his pipe and then turned his attention to the bicycles. The bloody things were all locked. He would just have to carry one round. He put *Bleak House* in the basket, picked the bike up and carried it all the way round to the fence. Then he climbed up and over and groped around in the darkness for the doll. In the end he found it and spent five minutes trying to keep the wig on while he fastened the elastic band under her chin. It kept on jumping off. 'Well, at least that's one problem I won't have with Eva,' he muttered to himself when the wig was secured. Having satisfied himself that it wouldn't come off he moved cautiously forward skirting mounds of gravel, machines, sacks and reinforcing rods when it suddenly occurred to him that he was running a considerable risk of disappearing down one of the pile holes himself. He put the doll down and fumbled in his pocket for the torch and shone it on the ground. Some yards ahead there was a large square of thick plywood. Wilt moved forward and lifted it. Underneath was the hole, a nice big hole. Just the right size. She would fit in there perfectly. He shone the torch down. Must be thirty feet deep. He pushed the plywood to one side and went back for the doll. The wig had fallen off again.

'Fuck,' said Wilt, and reached in his pocket for another elastic band. Five minutes later Judy's wig was firmly in place with four elastic bands fastened under her chin. That should do it. Now all he had to do was to drag the replica to the hole and make sure it fitted. At this point Wilt hesitated. He was beginning to have doubts about the soundness of the scheme. Too many unexpected contingencies had arisen for his liking. On the other hand there was a sense of exhilaration about being alone on the building site in the middle of the night. Perhaps it would be better if he went home now. No, he had to see the thing through. He would put the doll into the hole to make quite sure that it fitted. Then he would deflate it and go home and repeat the process until he had trained himself to kill by proxy. He would keep the doll in the boot of the car. Eva never looked there. And in future he would only blow her up when he reached the car park. That way Eva would have no idea what was going on. Definitely not. Wilt smiled to himself at the simplicity of the scheme. Then he picked Judy up and pushed her towards the hole feet first. She slid in easily while Wilt leant forward. Perfect. And at that moment he slipped on the muddy ground. With a desperate effort which necessitated letting go of the doll he hurled himself to one side and grabbed at the plywood. He got to his feet cautiously and cursed. His trousers were covered with mud and his hands were shaking.

'Damned near went down myself,' he muttered, and looked around for Judy. But Judy had disappeared. Wilt reached for his torch and shone it down the hole. Halfway down the doll was wedged lightly against the sides and for once the wig was still on. Wilt stared desperately down at the thing and wondered what the hell to do. It – or she – must be at least twenty feet down. Fifteen. Anyway a long way down and certainly too far for him to reach. But still too near the top not to be clearly visible to the workmen in the morning. Wilt switched off the torch and pulled the plywood square so that it covered the hole. That way he wouldn't be in danger of joining the doll. Then he stood up and tried to think of ways of getting it out.

Rope with a hook on the end of it? He hadn't a rope or a hook. He might be able to find a rope but hooks were another matter. Get a rope and tie it to something and climb down it and bring the doll up? Certainly not. It would be bad enough climbing down the rope with two hands but to think of climbing back up with one hand holding the doll in the other was sheer lunacy. That way he would end up at the bottom of the hole himself and if one thing was clear in his mind it was that he didn't intend to be discovered at the bottom of a thirty-foot pile hole on Monday morning clutching a plastic fucking doll with a cunt dressed in his wife's clothes. That way lay disaster. Wilt visualized the scene in the Principal's office as he tried to explain how he came to be ... And anyway they might not find him or hear his yells. Those damned cement lorries made a hell of a din and he bloody well wasn't going to risk being buried under ... Shit. Talk about poetic justice. No, the only thing to do was to get that fucking doll down to the bottom of the hole and hope to hell that no one spotted it before they poured the concrete in. Well, at least that way he would learn if it was a sensible method of getting rid of Eva. There was that to be said for it. Every cloud had . . .

Wilt left the hole and looked around for something to move Judy down to the bottom. He tried a handful of gravel but she merely wobbled a bit and stayed put. Something weightier was needed. He went across to a pile of sand and scooped some into a plastic sack and poured it down the hole, but apart from adding an extra dimension of macabre realism to Mrs Wilt's wig the sand did nothing. Perhaps if he dropped a brick on the doll it would burst. Wilt looked around for a brick and ended up with a large lump of clay. That would have to do. He dropped it down the hole. There was a thump, a rattle of gravel and another thump. Wilt shone his torch down. Judy had reached the bottom of the hole and had settled into a grotesque position with her legs crumpled up in front of her and one arm outstretched towards him as if in supplication. Wilt fetched another lump of clay and hurled it down. This time the wig slid sideways and her head lolled. Wilt gave up. There was nothing more he could do. He pulled the plywood back over the hole and went back to the fence.

Here he ran into more trouble. The bicycle was on the other side. He fetched a plank, leant it against the fence and climbed over. Now to carry the bike back to the shed. Oh bugger the bicycle. It could stay where it was. He was fed up with the whole business. He couldn't even dispose of a plastic doll properly. It was ludicrous to think that he could plan, commit and carry through a real murder with any hope of success. He must have been mad to think of it. It was all that blasted gin.

'That's right, blame the gin,' Wilt muttered to himself, as he trudged back to his car. 'You had this idea months ago.' He climbed into the car and sat there in the darkness wondering what on earth had ever possessed him to have fantasies of murdering Eva. It was insane, utterly insane, and just as mad as to imagine that he could train himself to become a cold-blooded killer. Where had the idea originated from? What was it all about? All right, Eva was a stupid cow who made his life a misery by nagging at him and by indulging a taste for Eastern mysticism with a frenetic enthusiasm calculated to derange the soberest of husbands, but why his obsession with murder? Why the need to prove his manliness by violence? Where had he got that from? In the middle of the car park, Henry Wilt, suddenly sober and clear-headed, realized the extraordinary effect that ten years of Liberal Studies had had upon him. For ten long years Plasterers Two and Meat One had been exposed to culture in the shape of Wilt and *The Lord of the Flies*, and for as many years Wilt himself had been exposed to the barbarity, the unhesitating readiness to commit violence of Plasterers Two and Meat One. That was the genesis of it all. That and the unreality of the literature he had been forced to absorb. For ten years Wilt had been the duct along which travelled creatures of imagination, Nostromo, Jack and Piggy, Shane, creatures who acted and whose actions effected something. And all the time he saw himself, mirrored in their eyes, an ineffectual passive person responding solely to the dictates of circumstance. Wilt shook his head. And out of all that and the traumas of the past two days had been born this *acte gratuit*, this semi-crime, the symbolic murder of Eva Wilt.

He started the car and drove out of the car park. He would go and see the Braintrees. They would still be up and glad to see him and besides he needed to talk to someone. Behind him on the building site his notes on Violence and the Break-Up of Family Life drifted about in the night wind and stuck in the mud.

7

'Nature is so libidinous,' said Sally, shining a torch through the porthole at the reeds. 'I mean take bullrushes. I mean they're positively archetypally phallus. Don't you think so, G?'

'Bullrushes?' said Gaskell, gazing helplessly at a chart. 'Bullrushes do nothing for me.'

'Maps neither, by the look of it.'

'Charts, baby, charts.'

'What's in a name?'

'Right now, a hell of a lot. We're either in Frogwater Reach or Fen Broad. No telling which.'

'Give me Fen Broad every time. I just adore broads. Eva sweetheart, how's about another pot of coffee? I want to stay awake all night and watch the dawn come up over the bull-rushes.'

'Yes, well I don't,' said Gaskell. 'Last night was enough for me. That crazy guy with the doll in the bath and Schei cutting himself. That's enough for one day. I'm going to hit the sack.'

'The deck,' said Sally, 'hit the deck, G. Eva and I are sleeping down here. Three's a crowd.'

'Three? With boobs around it's five at the least. OK, so I sleep on deck. We've got to be up early if we're to get off this damned sandbank.'

'Has Captain Pringsheim stranded us, baby?'

'It's these charts. If only they would give an exact indication of depth.'

'If you knew where we were, you'd probably find they do. It's no use knowing it's three feet—'

'Fathoms, honey, fathoms.'

'Three fathoms in Frogwater Reach if we're really in Fen Broad.'

'Well, wherever we are, you'd better start hoping there's a tide that will rise and float us off,' said Gaskell.

'And if there isn't?'

'Then we'll have to think of something else. Maybe someone will come along and tow us off.'

'Oh God, G, you're the skilfullest,' said Sally. 'I mean why couldn't we have just stayed out in the middle? But no, you had to come steaming up this creek wham into a mudbank and all because of what? Ducks, goddamned ducks.'

'Waders, baby, waders. Not just ducks.'

'OK, so they're waders. You want to photograph them so now we're stuck where no one in their right minds would come in a boat. Who do you think is going to come up here? Jonathan Seagull?'

In the galley Eva made coffee. She was wearing the bright red plastic bikini Sally had lent her. It was rather too small for her so that she bulged round it uncomfortably and it was revealingly tight but at least it was better than going around naked even though Sally said nudity was being liberated and look at the Amazonian Indians. She should have brought her own things but Sally had insisted on hurrying and now all she had were the lemon loungers and the bikini. Honestly Sally was so authora . . . authorasomething . . . well, bossy then.

'Dual-purpose plastic, baby, apronwise,' she had said, 'and G has this thing about plastic, haven't you, G?'

'Bio-degradably yes.'

'Bio-degradably?' asked Eva, hoping to be initiated into some new aspect of women's liberation.

'Plastic bottles that disintegrate instead of lying around making an ecological swamp,' said Sally, opening a porthole and dropping an empty cigar packet over the side, 'that's G's lifework. That and recyclability. Infinite recyclability.'

'Right,' said Gaskell. 'We've got in-built obsolescence in the automotive field where it's outmoded. So what we need now is in-built bio-degradable deliquescence in ephemera.'

Eva listened uncomprehendingly but with the feeling that she was somehow at the centre of an intellectual world far surpassing that of Henry and his friends who talked about new degree courses and their students so boringly.

'We've got a compost heap at the bottom of the garden,' she said when she finally understood what they were talking about. 'I put the potato peelings and odds and ends on it.'

Gaskell raised his eyes to the cabin roof. Correction. Deckhead.

'Talking of odds and ends,' said Sally, running a fond hand over Eva's bottom, 'I wonder how Henry is getting along with Judy.'

Eva shuddered. The thought of Henry and the doll lying in the bath still haunted her.

'I can't think what had got into him,' she said, and looked disapprovingly at Gaskell when he sniggered. 'I mean it's not as if he has ever been unfaithful or anything like that. And lots of husbands are. Patrick Mottram is always going off and having affairs with other women but Henry's been very good in that respect. He may be quiet and not very pushing but no one could call him a gadabout.'

'Oh sure,' said Gaskell, 'so he's got a hang-up about sex. My heart bleeds for him.'

'I don't see why you should say he's got something wrong with him because he's faithful,' said Eva.

'G didn't mean that, did you, G?' said Sally. 'He meant that there has to be true freedom in a marriage. No dominance, no jealousy, no possession. Right, G?'

'Right,' said Gaskell.

'The test of true love is when you can watch your wife having it off with someone else and still love her,' Sally went on.

'I could never watch Henry . . .' said Eva. 'Never.'

'So you don't love him. You're insecure. You don't trust him.'

'Trust him?' said Eva. 'If Henry went to bed with another woman I don't see how I could trust him. I mean if that's what he wants to do why did he marry me?'

'That,' said Gaskell, 'is the sixty-four-thousand dollar question.' He picked up his sleeping bag and went out on deck. Behind him Eva had begun to cry.

'There, there,' said Sally, putting her arm round her. 'G was just kidding. He didn't mean ánything.'

'It's not that,' said Eva, 'it's just that I don't understand anything any more. It's all so complicated.'

'Christ, you look bloody awful,' said Peter Braintree as Wilt stood on the doorstep.

'I feel bloody awful,' said Wilt. 'It's all this gin.'

'You mean Eva's not back?' said Braintree, leading the way down the passage to the kitchen.

'She wasn't there when I got home. Just a note saying she was going away with the Pringsheims to think things over.'

'To think things over? Eva? What things?'

'Well . . .' Wilt began and thought better of it, 'that business with Sally I suppose. She says she won't ever forgive me.'

'But you didn't do anything with Sally. That's what you told me.'

'I know I didn't. That's the whole point. If I had done what that nymphomaniac bitch wanted there wouldn't have been all this bloody trouble.'

'I don't see that, Henry. I mean if you had done what she wanted Eva would have had something to grumble about. I don't see why she should be up in the air because you didn't.'

'Sally must have told her that I did do something,' said Wilt, determined not to mention the incident in the bathroom with the doll.

'You mean the blow job?'

'I don't know what I mean. What is a blow job anyway?'

Peter Braintree looked puzzled.

'I'm not too sure,' he said, 'but it's obviously something you don't want your husband to do. If I came home and told Betty I'd done a blow job she'd think I'd been robbing a bank.'

'I wasn't going to do it anyway,' said Wilt. 'She was going to do it to me.'

'Perhaps it's a suck off,' said Braintree, putting a kettle on the stove. 'That's what it sounds like to me.'

'Well it didn't sound like that to me,' said Wilt with a shudder. 'She made it sound like a paint-peeling exercise with a blow lamp. You should have seen the look on her face.'

He sat down at the kitchen table despondently.

Braintree eyed him curiously. 'You certainly seem to have been in the wars,' he said.

Wilt looked down at his trousers. They were covered with mud and there were round patches caked to his knees. 'Yes . . . well . . . well I had a puncture on the way here,' he explained with lack of conviction. 'I had to change a tyre and I knelt down. I was a bit pissed.'

Peter Braintree grunted doubtfully. It didn't sound very convincing to him. Poor old Henry was obviously a bit under the weather. 'You can wash up in the sink,' he said.

Presently Betty Braintree came downstairs. 'I couldn't help hearing what you said about Eva,' she said. 'I'm so sorry, Henry. I wouldn't worry. She's bound to come back.'

'I wouldn't be too sure,' said Wilt, gloomily, 'and anyway I'm not so sure I want her back.'

'Oh, Eva's all right,' Betty said. 'She gets these sudden urges and enthusiasms but they don't last long. It's just the way she's made. It's easy come and easy go with Eva.'

'I think that's what's worrying Henry,' said Braintree, 'the easy come bit.'

'Oh surely not. Eva isn't that sort at all.'

Wilt sat at the kitchen table and sipped his coffee. 'I wouldn't put anything past her in the company she's keeping now,' he muttered lugubriously. 'Remember what happened when she went through that macrobiotic diet phase? Dr Mannix told me I was the nearest thing to a case of scurvy he'd seen since the Burma railway. And then there was that episode with the trampoline. She went to a Keep Fit Class at Bulham Village College and bought herself a fucking trampoline. You know she put old Mrs Portway in hospital with that contraption.'

'I knew there was some sort of accident but Eva never told me what actually happened,' said Betty.

'She wouldn't. It was a ruddy miracle we didn't get sued,' said Wilt. 'It threw Mrs Portway clean through the greenhouse roof. There was glass all over the lawn and it wasn't even as though Mrs Portway was a healthy woman at the best of times.'

'Wasn't she the woman with the rheumatoid arthritis?'

Wilt nodded dismally. 'And the duelling scars on her face,' he said. 'That was our greenhouse, that was.'

'I must say I can think of better places for trampolines than greenhouses,' said Braintree. 'It wasn't a very big greenhouse was it?'

'It wasn't a very big trampoline either, thank God,' said Wilt, 'she'd have been in orbit otherwise.'

'Well it all goes to prove one thing,' said Betty, looking on the bright side, 'Eva may do crazy things but she soon gets over them.'

'Mrs Portway didn't,' said Wilt, not to be comforted. 'She was in hospital for six weeks and the skin grafts didn't take. She hasn't been near our house since.'

'You'll see. Eva will get fed up with these Pringsheim people in a week or two. They're just another fad.'

'A fad with a lot of advantages if you ask me,' said Wilt. 'Money, status and sexual promiscuity. All the things I couldn't give her and all dressed up in a lot of intellectual claptrap about Women's Lib and violence and the intolerance of tolerance and the revolution of the sexes and you're not fully mature unless you're ambisextrous. It's enough to make you vomit and it's just the sort of crap Eva would fall for. I mean she'd buy rotten herrings if some clown up the social scale told her they were the sophisticated things to eat. Talk about being gullible!'

'The thing is that Eva's got too much energy,' said Betty. 'You should try and persuade her to get a full-time job.'

'Full-time job?' said Wilt. 'She's had more full-time jobs than I've had hot dinners. Mind you, that's not saying much these days. All I ever get is a cold supper and a note saying she's gone to Pottery or Transcendental Meditation or something equally half-baked. And anyway Eva's idea of a job is to take over the factory. Remember Potters, that engineering firm that went broke after a strike a couple of years ago? Well, if you ask me that was Eva's fault. She got this job with a consultancy firm doing time and motion study and they sent her out to the factory and the next thing anyone knew they had a strike on their hands . . .'

They went on talking for another hour until the Braintrees asked him to stay the night. But Wilt wouldn't. 'I've got things to do tomorrow.'

'Such as?'

'Feed the dog for one thing.'

'You can always drive over and do that. Clem won't starve overnight.'

But Wilt was too immersed in self-pity to be persuaded and besides he was still worried about that doll. He might have another go at getting the thing out of that hole. He drove home and went to bed in a tangle of sheets and blankets. He hadn't made it in the morning.

'Poor old Henry,' said Betty as she and Peter went upstairs. 'He did look pretty awful.'

'He said he'd had a puncture and had to change the wheel.'

'I wasn't thinking of his clothes. It was the look on his face that worried me. You don't think he's on the verge of a breakdown?'

Peter Braintree shook his head. 'You'd look like that if you had Gasfitters Three and Plasterers Two every day of your life for ten years and then your wife ran away,' he told her.

'Why don't they give him something better to teach?'

'Why? Because the Tech wants to become a Poly and they keep starting new degree courses and hiring people with PhDs to teach them and then the students don't enrol and they're lumbered with specialists like Dr Fitzpatrick who knows all there is to know about child labour in four cotton mills in Manchester in 1837 and damn all about anything else. Put him in front of a class of Day Release Apprentices and all hell would break loose. As it is I have to go into his A-level classes once a week and tell them to shut up. On the other hand Henry looks meek but he can cope with rowdies. He's too good at his job. That's his trouble and besides he's not a bumsucker and that's the kiss of death at the Tech. If you don't lick arses you get nowhere.'

'You know,' said Betty, 'teaching at that place has done horrible things to your language.'

'It's done horrible things to my outlook on life, never mind my language,' said Braintree. 'It's enough to drive a man to drink.'

'It certainly seems to have done that to Henry. His breath reeked of gin.'

'He'll get over it.'

But Wilt didn't. He woke in the morning with the feeling that something was missing quite apart from Eva. That bloody doll. He lay in bed trying to think of some way of retrieving the thing before the workmen arrived on the site on Monday morning but apart from pouring a can of petrol down the hole and lighting it, which seemed on reflection the best way of drawing attention to the fact that he had stuffed a plastic doll dressed in his wife's clothes down there, he could think of nothing practical. He would just have to trust to luck.

When the Sunday papers came he got out of bed and went down to read them over his All-Bran. Then he fed the dog and mooched about the house in his pyjamas, walked down to the Ferry Path Inn for lunch, slept in the afternoon and watched the box all evening. Then he made the bed and got into it and spent a restless night wondering where Eva was, what she was doing, and why, since he had occupied so many fruitless hours speculating on ways of getting rid of her homicidally, he should be in the least concerned now that she had gone of her own accord.

'I mean if I didn't want this to happen why did I keep thinking up ways of killing her,' he thought at two o'clock. 'Sane people don't go for walks with a Labrador and devise schemes for murdering their wives when they can just as easily divorce them.' There was probably some foul psychological reason for it. Wilt could think of several himself, rather too many in fact to be able to decide which was the most likely one. In any case a psychological explanation demanded a degree of self-knowledge which Wilt, who wasn't at all sure he had a self to know, felt was denied him. Ten years of Plasterers Two and Exposure to Barbarism had at least given him the insight to know that there was an answer for every question and it didn't much matter what answer you gave so long as you gave it convincingly. In the fourteenth century they would have said the devil put such thoughts into his head, now in a post-Freudian world it had to be a complex or, to be really up-to-date, a chemical imbalance. In a hundred years they would have come up with some completely different explanation. With the comforting thought that the truths of one age were the absurdities of another and that it didn't much matter what you thought so long as you did the right thing, and in his view he did, Wilt finally fell asleep.

At seven he was woken by the alarm clock and by half past eight had parked his car in the parking lot behind the Tech.

He walked past the building site where the workmen were already at work. Then he went up to the Staff Room and looked out of the window. The square of plywood was still in place covering the hole but the pile-boring machine had been backed away. They had evidently finished with it.

At five to nine he collected twenty-five copies of *Shane* from the cupboard and took them across to Motor Mechanics Three. *Shane* was the ideal soporific. It would keep the brutes quiet while he sat and watched what happened down below. Room 593 in the Engineering block gave him a grandstand view. Wilt filled in the register and handed out copies of *Shane* and told the class to get on with it. He said it with a good deal more vigour than was usual even for a Monday morning and the class settled down to consider the plight of the home-steaders while Wilt stared out of the window, absorbed in a more immediate drama.

A lorry with a revolving drum filled with liquid concrete had arrived on the site and was backing slowly towards the plywood square. It stopped and there was an agonizing wait while the driver climbed down from the cab and lit a cigarette. Another man, evidently the foreman, came out of a wooden hut and wandered across to the lorry and presently a little group was gathered round the hole. Wilt got up from his desk and went over to the window. Why the hell didn't they get a move on? Finally the driver got back into his cab and two men re-moved the plywood. The foreman signalled to the driver. The chute for the concrete was swung into position. Another sig-nal. The drum began to tilt. The concrete was coming. Wilt watched as it began to pour down the chute and just at that moment the foreman looked down the hole. So did one of the workmen. The next instant all hell had broken loose. There were frantic signals and shouts from the foreman. Through the window Wilt watched the open mouths and the gesticula-tions but still the concrete came. Wilt shut his eyes and shuddered. They had found that fucking doll.

Outside on the building site the air was thick with misunder-standing.

'What's that? I'm pouring as fast as I can,' shouted the

driver, misconstruing the frenzied signals of the foreman. He pulled the lever still further and the concrete flood increased. The next moment he was aware that he had made some sort of mistake. The foreman was wrenching at the door of the cab and screaming blue murder.

'Stop, for God's sake stop,' he shouted. 'There's a woman down that hole!'

'A what?' said the driver, and switched off the engine.

'A fucking woman and look what you've been and fucking done. I told you to stop. I told you to stop pouring and you went on. You've been and poured twenty tons of liquid concrete on her.'

The driver climbed down from his cab and went round to the chute where the last trickles of cement were still sliding hesitantly into the hole.

'A woman?' he said. 'What? Down that hole? What's she doing down there?'

The foreman stared at him demonically. 'Doing?' he bellowed, 'what do you think she's doing? What would you be doing if you'd just had twenty tons of liquid concrete dumped on top of you? Fucking drowning, that's what.'

The driver scratched his head. 'Well I didn't know she was down there. How was I to know? You should have told me.'

'Told you?' shrieked the foreman. 'I told you. I told you to stop. You weren't listening.'

'I thought you wanted me to pour faster. I couldn't hear what you were saying.'

'Well, every other bugger could,' yelled the foreman. Certainly Wilt in Room 593 could. He stared wild-eyed out of the window as the panic spread. Beside him Motor Mechanics Three had lost all interest in *Shane*. They clustered at the window and watched.

'Are you quite sure?' asked the driver.

'Sure? Course I'm sure,' yelled the foreman. 'Ask Barney.'

The other workman, evidently Barney, nodded. 'She was down there all right. I'll vouch for that. All crumpled up she was. She had one hand up in the air and her legs was ...'

'Jesus,' said the driver, visibly shaken. 'What the hell are we going to do now?'

It was a question that had been bothering Wilt. Call the Police, presumably. The foreman confirmed his opinion. 'Get the cops. Get an ambulance. Get the Fire Brigade and get a pump. For God's sake get a pump.'

'Pump's no good,' said the driver, 'you'll never pump that concrete out of there, not in a month of Sundays. Anyway it wouldn't do any good. She'll be dead by now. Crushed to death. Wouldn't drown with twenty tons on her. Why didn't she say something?'

'Would it have made any difference if she had?' asked the foreman hoarsely. 'You'd have still gone on pouring.'

'Well, how did she get down there in the first place?' said the driver, to change the subject.

'How the fuck would I know. She must have fallen ...'

'And pulled that plywood sheet over her, I suppose,' said Barney, who clearly had a practical turn of mind. 'She was bloody murdered.'

'We all know that,' squawked the foreman. 'By Chris here. I told him to stop pouring. You heard me. Everyone for half a mile must have heard me but not Chris. Oh, no, he has to go on—'

'She was murdered before she was put down the hole,' said Barney. 'That wooden cover wouldn't have been there if she had fallen down herself.'

The foreman wiped his face with a handkerchief and looked at the square of plywood. 'There is that to it,' he muttered. 'No one can say we didn't take proper safety precautions. You're right. She must have been murdered. Oh, my God!'

'Sex crime, like as not,' said Barney. 'Raped and strangled her. That or someone's missus. You mark my words. She was all crumpled up and that hand ... I'll never forget that hand, not if I live to be a hundred.'

The foreman stared at him lividly. He seemed incapable of expressing his feelings. So was Wilt. He went back to his desk and sat with his head in his hands while the class gaped out of the window and tried to catch what was being said. Presently sirens sounded in the distance and grew louder. A police car arrived, four fire engines hurtled into the car park and an ambulance followed. As more and more uniformed men gathered around what had once been a hole in the ground it became apparent that getting the doll down there had been a damned sight easier than getting it out.

'That concrete starts setting in twenty minutes,' the driver explained when a pump was suggested for the umpteenth time. An Inspector of Police and the Fire Chief stared down at the hole.

'Are you sure you saw a woman's body down there?' the Inspector asked. 'You're positive about it?'

'Positive?' squeaked the foreman. 'Course I'm positive. You don't think ... Tell them, Barney. He saw her too.'

Barney told the Inspector even more graphically than before. 'She had this hair see and her hand was reaching up like it was asking for help and there were these fingers ... I tell you it was horrible. It didn't look natural.'

'No, well, it wouldn't,' said the Inspector sympathetically. 'And you say there was a board on top of the hole when you arrived this morning.'

The foreman gesticulated silently and Barney showed them the board. 'I was standing on it at one time,' he said. 'It was here all right so help me God.'

'The thing is, how are we to get her out?' said the Fire Chief. It was a point that was put to the manager of the construction company when he finally arrived on the scene. 'God alone knows,' he said. 'There's no easy way of getting that concrete out now. We'd have to use drills to get down thirty feet.'

At the end of the hour they were no nearer a solution to the problem. As the Motor Mechanics dragged themselves away from this fascinating situation to go to Technical Drawing, Wilt collected the unread copies of *Shane* and walked across to the Staff Room in a state of shock. The only consolation he could think of was that it would take them at least two or three days to dig down and discover that what had all the appearances of being the body of a murdered woman was in fact an inflatable doll. Or had been once. Wilt rather doubted if it would be inflated now. There had been something horribly intractable about that liquid concrete.

8

There was something horribly intractable about the mudbank on which the cabin cruiser had grounded. To add to their
troubles the engine had gone wrong. Gaskell said it was a
broken con rod.

'Is that serious?' asked Sally.

'It just means we'll have to be towed to a boatyard.'

'By what?'

'By a passing cruiser I guess,' said Gaskell.

Sally looked over the side at the bullrushes.

'Passing?' she said. 'We've been here all night and half the
morning and nothing has passed so far and if it did we wouldn't
be able to see it for all these fucking bullrushes.'

'I thought bullrushes did something for you.'

'That was yesterday,' snapped Sally. 'Today they just mean
we're invisible to anyone more than fifty feet away. And
now you've screwed the motor. I told you not to rev it like
that.'

'So how was I to know it would bust a con rod,' said
Gaskell. 'I was just trying to get us off this mudbank. You
just tell me how I'm supposed to do it without revving the
goddam motor.'

'You could get out and push.'

Gaskell peered over the side. 'I could get out and drown,' he
said.

'So the boat would be lighter,' said Sally. 'We've all got to
make sacrifices and you said the tide would float us off.'

'Well I was mistaken. That's fresh water down there and
means the tide doesn't reach this far.'

'Now he tells me. First we're in Frogwater Beach . . .'

'Reach,' said Gaskell.

'Frogwater wherever. Then we're in Fen Broad. Now where
are we for God's sake?'

'On a mudbank,' said Gaskell.

In the cabin Eva bustled about. There wasn't much space for

bustling but what there was she put to good use. She made the bunks and put the bedding away in the lockers underneath and she plumped the cushions and emptied the ashtrays. She swept the floor and polished the table and wiped the windows and dusted the shelves and generally made everything as neat and tidy as it was possible to make it. And all the time her thoughts got untidier and more muddled so that by the time she was finished and every object in sight was in its right place and the whole cabin properly arranged she was quite confused and in two minds about nearly everything.

The Pringsheims were ever so sophisticated and rich and intellectual and said clever things all the time but they were always quarrelling and getting at one another about something and to be honest they were quite impractical and didn't know the first thing about hygiene. Gaskell went to the lavatory and didn't wash his hands afterwards and goodness only knew when he had last had a shave. And look at the way they had walked out of the house in Rossiter Grove without clearing up after the party and the living-room all over cups and things. Eva had been quite shocked. She would never have left her house in that sort of mess. She had said as much to Sally but Sally had said how nonspontaneous could you get and anyway they were only renting the house for the summer and that it was typical of a male-oriented social system to expect a woman to enter a contractual relationship based upon female domestic servitude. Eva tried to follow her and was left feeling guilty because she couldn't and because it was evidently infra dig to be houseproud and she was.

And then there was what Henry had been doing with that doll. It was so unlike Henry to do anything like that and the more she thought about it the more unlike Henry it became. He must have been drunk but even so . . . without his clothes on? And where had he found the doll? She had asked Sally and had been horrified to learn that Gaskell was mad about plastic and just adored playing games with Judy and men were like that and so to the only meaningful relationships being between women because women didn't need to prove their virility by any overt act of extrasexual violence did they? By which time Eva was lost in a maze of words she didn't understand but which sounded important and they had had another session of Touch Therapy.

And that was another thing she was in two minds about. Touch Therapy. Sally had said she was still inhibited and being inhibited was a sign of emotional and sensational immaturity. Eva battled with her mixed feelings about the matter. On the one hand she didn't want to be emotionally and sensationally immature and if the revulsion she felt lying naked in the arms of another woman was anything to go by and in Eva's view the nastier a medicine tasted the more likely it was to do you good, then she was certainly improving her psycho-sexual behaviour pattern by leaps and bounds. On the other hand she wasn't altogether convinced that Touch Therapy was quite nice. It was only by the application of considerable will-power that she overcame her objections to it and even so there was an undertow of doubt about the propriety of being touched quite so sensationally. It was all very puzzling and to cap it all she was on the Pill. Eva had objected very strongly and had pointed out that Henry and she had always wanted babies and she'd never had any but Sally had insisted.

'Eva baby,' she had said, 'with Gaskell one just never knows. Sometimes he goes for months without so much as a twitch and then, bam, he comes all over the place. He's totally undiscriminating.'

'But I thought you said you had this big thing between you,' Eva said.

'Oh, sure. In a blue moon. Scientists sublimate and G just lives for plastic. And we wouldn't want you to go back to Henry with G's genes in your ovum, now would we?'

'Certainly not,' said Eva horrified at the thought and had taken the pill after breakfast before going through to the tiny galley to wash up. It was all so different from Trascendental Meditation and Pottery.

On deck Sally and Gaskell were still wrangling.

'What the hell are you giving brainless boobs?' Gaskell asked.

'TT, Body Contact, Tactile Liberation,' said Sally. 'She's sensually deprived.'

'She's mentally deprived too. I've met some dummies in my time but this one is the dimwittiest. Anyway, I meant those pills she takes at breakfast.'

Sally smiled. 'Oh those,' she said.

'Yes those. You blowing what little mind she's got or something?' said Gaskell. 'We've got enough troubles without Moby Dick taking a trip.'

'Oral contraceptives, baby, just the plain old Pill.'

'Oral contraceptives? What the hell for? I wouldn't touch her with a sterilized stirring rod.'

'Gaskell, honey, you're so naïve. For authenticity, pure authenticity. It makes my relationship with her so much more real, don't you think. Like wearing a rubber on a dildo.'

Gaskell gaped at her. 'Jesus, you don't mean you've . . .'

'Not yet. Long John Silver is still in his bag but one of these days when she's a little more emancipated. . . .' She smiled wistfully over the bullrushes. 'Perhaps it doesn't matter all that much us being stuck here. It gives us time, so much lovely time and you can look at your ducks . . .'

'Waders,' said Gaskell, 'and we're going to run up one hell of a bill at the Marina if we don't get this boat back in time.'

'Bill?' said Sally. 'You're crazy. You don't think we're paying for this hulk?'

'But you hired her from the boatyard. I mean you're not going to tell me you just took the boat,' said Gaskell. 'For Chrissake, that's theft!'

Sally laughed. 'Honestly, G, you're so moral. I mean you're inconsistent. You steal books from the library and chemicals from the lab but when it comes to boats you're all up in the air.'

'Books are different,' said Gaskell hotly.

'Yes,' said Sally, 'books you don't go to jail for. That's what's different. So you want to think I stole the boat, you go on thinking that.'

Gaskell took out a handkerchief and wiped his glasses. 'Are you telling me you didn't?' he asked finally.

'I borrowed it.'

'Borrowed it? Who from?'

'Schei.'

'Scheimacher?'

'That's right. He said we could have it whenever we wanted it so we've got it.'

'Does he know we've got it?'

Sally sighed. 'Look, he's in India isn't he, currying sperm? So what does it matter what he knows? By the time he gets back we'll be in the Land of the Free.'

'Shit,' said Gaskell wearily, 'one of these days you're going to land us in it up to the eyeballs.'

'Gaskell honey, sometimes you bore me with your worrying so.'

'Let me tell you something. You worry me with your goddam attitude to other people's property.'

'Property is theft.'

'Oh sure. You just get the cops to see it that way when they catch up with you. The fuzz don't go a ball on stealing in this country.'

The fuzz weren't going much of a ball on the well-nourished body of a woman apparently murdered and buried under thirty feet and twenty tons of rapidly setting concrete. Barney had supplied the well-nourished bit. 'She had big breasts too,' he explained, in the seventh version of what he had seen. 'And this hand reaching up——'

'Yes, well we know all about the hand,' said Inspector Flint. 'We've been into all that before but this is the first time you've mentioned breasts.'

'It was the hand that got me,' said Barney. 'I mean you don't think of breasts in a situation like that.'

The Inspector turned to the foreman. 'Did you notice the deceased's breasts?' he enquired. But the foreman just shook his head. He was past speech.

'So we've got a well-nourished woman ... What age would you say?'

Barney scratched his chin reflectively. 'Not old,' he said finally. 'Definitely not old.'

'In her twenties?'

'Could have been.'

'In her thirties?'

Barney shrugged. There was something he was trying to recall. Something that had seemed odd at the time.

'But definitely not in her forties?'

'No,' said Barney. 'Younger than that.' He said it rather hesitantly.

'You're not being very specific,' said Inspector Flint.

'I can't help it,' said Barney plaintively. 'You see a woman down a dirty great hole with concrete sloshing down on top of her you don't ask her her age.'

'Quite. I realize that but if you could just think. Was there anything peculiar about her ...'

'Peculiar? Well, there was this hand see ...'

Inspector Flint sighed. 'I mean anything out of the ordinary about her appearance. Her hair for instance. What colour was it?'

Barney got it. 'I knew there was something,' he said, triumphantly. 'Her hair. It was crooked.'

'Well, it would be, wouldn't it. You don't dump a woman down a thirty-foot pile shaft without mussing up her hair in the process.'

'No, it wasn't like that. It was on sideways and flattened. Like she'd been hit.'

'She probably had been hit. If what you say about the wooden cover being in place is true, she didn't go down there of her own volition. But you still can't give any precise indication of her age?'

'Well,' said Barney, 'bits of her looked young and bits didn't. That's all I know.'

'Which bits?' asked the Inspector, hoping to hell Barney wasn't going to start on that hand again.

'Well, her legs didn't look right for her teats if you see what I mean.' Inspector Flint didn't. 'They were all thin and crumpled-up like.'

'Which were? Her legs or her teats?'

'Her legs, of course,' said Barney. 'I've told you she had these lovely great ...'

'We're treating this as a case of murder,' Inspector Flint told the Principal ten minutes later. The Principal sat behind his desk and thought despairingly about adverse publicity.

'You're quite convinced it couldn't have been an accident?'

'The evidence to date certainly doesn't suggest accidental death,' said the Inspector. 'However, we'll only be absolutely certain on that point when we manage to reach the body and I'm afraid that is going to take some time.'

'Time?' said the Principal. 'Do you mean to say you can't get her out this morning?'

Inspector Flint shook his head. 'Out of the question, sir,' he said. 'We are considering two methods of reaching the body and they'll both take several days. One is to drill down through the concrete and the other is to sink another shaft next to the original hole and try and get at her from the side.'

'Good Lord,' said the Principal, looking at his calendar, 'but that means you're going to be digging away out there for several days.'

'I'm afraid it can't be helped. Whoever put her down there make a good job of it. Still, we'll try to be as unobtrusive as possible.'

Out of the window the Principal could see four police cars, a fire engine and a big blue van. 'This is really most unfortunate,' he murmured.

'Murder always is,' said the Inspector, and got to his feet. 'It's in the nature of the thing. In the meantime we are sealing off the site and we'd be grateful for your cooperation.'

'Anything you require,' said the Principal, with a sigh.

In the Staff Room the presence of so many uniformed men peering down a pile hole provoked mixed reactions. So did the dozen policemen scouring the building site, stopping now and then to put things carefully into envelopes, but it was the arrival of the dark blue caravan that finally clinched matters.

'That's a Mobile Murder Headquarters,' Peter Fenwick explained. 'Apparently some maniac has buried a woman at the bottom of one of the piles.'

The New Left, who had been clustered in a corner discussing the likely implications of so many paramilitary Fascist pigs, heaved a sigh of unmartyred regret but continued to express doubts.

'No, seriously,' said Fenwick, 'I asked one of them what they were doing. I thought it was some sort of bomb scare.'

Dr Cox, Head of Science, confirmed it. His office looked directly on to the hole. 'It's too dreadful to contemplate,' he murmured. 'Every time I look up I think what she must have suffered.'

'What do you suppose they are putting into those envelopes?' asked Dr Mayfield.

'Clues,' said Dr Board, with evident satisfaction. 'Hairs. Bits of skin and bloodstains. The usual trivial detritus of violent crime.'

Dr Cox hurried from the room and Dr Mayfield looked disgusted. 'How revolting,' he said. 'Isn't it possible that there has been some mistake? I mean why should anyone want to murder a woman here?'

Dr Board sipped his coffee and looked wistfully at him. 'I can think of any number of reasons,' he said happily. 'There are at least a dozen women in my Evening Class whom I would cheerfully beat to death and drop down holes. Sylvia Swansbeck for one.'

'Whoever did it must have known they were going to pour concrete down today,' said Fenwick. 'It looks like an inside job to me.'

'One of our less community-conscious students perhaps,' suggested Dr Board, 'I don't suppose they've had time to check if any of the staff are missing.'

'You'll probably find it had nothing to do with the Tech,' said Dr Mayfield. 'Some maniac . . .'

'Come now, give credit where credit is due,' interrupted Dr Board. 'There was obviously an element of premeditation involved. Whoever the murderer was . . . is, he planned it pretty carefully. What puzzles me is why he didn't shovel earth down on top of the wretched woman so that she couldn't be seen. Probably intended to but was disturbed before he could get around to it. One of those little accidents of fate.'

In the corner of the Staff Room Wilt sat and drank his

coffee, conscious that he was the only person not staring out of the window. What the hell was he to do? The sensible thing would be to go to the police and explain that he had been trying to get rid of an inflatable doll that someone had given him. But would they believe him? If that was all that had happened why had he dressed it up in a wig and clothes? And why had he left it inflated? Why hadn't he just thrown the thing away? He was just rehearsing the pros and cons of the argument when the Head of Engineering came in and announced that the police intended boring another hole next to the first one instead of digging down through the concrete.

'They'll probably be able to see bits of her sticking out the side,' he explained. 'Apparently she had one arm up in the air and with all that concrete coming down on top of her there's a chance that arm will have been pressed against the side of the hole. Much quicker that way.'

'I must say I can't see the need for haste,' said Dr Board. 'I should have thought she'd be pretty well preserved in all that concrete. Mummified I daresay.'

In his corner Wilt rather doubted it. With twenty tons of concrete on top of her even Judy who had been an extremely resilient doll was hardly likely to have withstood the pressure. She would have burst as sure as eggs were eggs in which case all the police would find was the empty plastic arm of a doll. They would hardly bother to dig a burst plastic doll out.

'And another thing,' continued the Head of Engineering, 'if the arm is sticking out they'll be able to take fingerprints straight away.'

Wilt smiled to himself. That was one thing they weren't going to find on Judy, fingerprints. He finished his coffee more cheerfully and went off to a class of Senior Secretaries. He found them agog with news of the murder.

'Do you think it was a sex killing?' a small blonde girl in the front row asked as Wilt handed out copies of *This Island Now*. He had always found the chapter on the Vicissitudes of Adolescence appealed to Senior Secs. It dealt with sex and violence and was twelve years out of date but then so were the Senior Secretaries. Today there was no need for the book.

'I don't think it was any sort of killing,' said Wilt taking his place behind the desk.

'Oh but it was. They saw a woman's body down there,' the small blonde insisted.

'They thought they saw something down there that looked like a body,' said Wilt. 'That doesn't mean it was one. People's imaginations play tricks with them.'

'The police don't think so,' said a large girl whose father was something in the City. 'They must be certain to go to all that trouble. We had a murder on our golf course and all they found were bits of body cut up and put in the water hazard on the fifteenth. They'd been there six months. Someone sliced a ball on the dogleg twelfth and it went into the pond. They fished out a foot first. It was all puffy and green ...' A pale girl from Wilstanton fainted in the third row. By the time Wilt had revived her and taken her to the Sick Room, the class had got on to Crippen, Haigh and Christie. Wilt returned to find them discussing acid baths.

'... and all they found were her false teeth and gallstones.'

'You seem to know a lot about murder,' Wilt said to the large girl.

'Daddy plays bridge with the Chief Constable,' she explained. 'He comes to dinner and tells super stories. He says they ought to bring back hanging.'

'I'm sure he does,' said Wilt grimly. It was typical of Senior Secs that they knew Chief Constables who wanted to bring back hanging. It was all mummy and daddy and horses with Senior Secretaries.

'Anyway, hanging doesn't hurt,' said the large girl. 'Sir Frank says a good hangman can have a man out of the condemned cell and on to the trap with a noose around his neck and pull the lever in twenty seconds.'

'Why confine the privilege to men?' asked Wilt bitterly. The class looked at him wth reproachful eyes.

'The last woman they hanged was Ruth Ellis,' said the blonde in the front row.

'Anyway with women it's different,' said the large girl.

'Why?' said Wilt inadvisedly.

'Well it's slower.'

'Slower?'

'They had to tie Mrs Thomson to a chair,' volunteered the blonde. 'She behaved disgracefully.'

'I must say I find your judgements peculiar,' said Wilt. 'A woman murdering her husband is doubtless disgraceful. The fact that she puts up a fight when they come to execute her doesn't strike me as disgraceful at all. I find that ...'

'It's not just that,' interrupted the large girl, who wasn't to be diverted.

'What isn't?' said Wilt.

'It's being slower with women. They have to make them wear waterproof pants.'

Wilt gaped at her in disgust. 'Waterproof what?' he asked without thinking.

'Waterproof pants,' said the large girl.

'Dear God,' said Wilt.

'You see, when they get to the bottom of the rope their insides drop out,' continued the large girl, administering the *coup de grâce*. Wilt stared at her wildly and stumbled from the room.

'What's the matter with him?' said the girl. 'Anyone would think I had said something beastly.'

In the corridor Wilt leant against the wall and felt sick. Those fucking girls were worse than Gasfitters. At least Gasfitters didn't go in for such disgusting anatomical details and besides Senior Secs all came from so-called respectable families. By the time he felt strong enough to face them again the hour had ended. Wilt went back into the classroom sheepishly and collected the books.

'Name of Wilt mean anything to you? Henry Wilt?' asked the Inspector.

'Wilt?' said the Vice-Principal, who had been left to cope with the police while the Principal spent his time more profitably trying to offset the adverse publicity caused by the whole appalling business. 'Well, yes it does. He's one of our Liberal Studies lecturers. Why? Is there ...'

'If you don't mind, sir, I'd just like a word with him. In private.'

'But Wilt's a most inoffensive man,' said the Vice-Principal. 'I'm sure he couldn't help you at all.'

'Possibly not but all the same ...'

'You're not suggesting for one moment that Henry Wilt had anything to do with ...' the Vice-Principal stopped and studied the expression on the Inspector's face. It was ominously neutral.

'I'd rather not go into details,' said Inspector Flint, 'and it's best if we don't jump to conclusions.'

The Vice-Principal picked up the phone. 'Do you want him to come across to that ... er ... caravan?' he asked.

Inspector Flint shook his head. 'We like to be as inconspicuous as possible. If I could just have the use of an empty office.'

'There's an office next door. You can use that.'

Wilt was in the canteen having lunch with Peter Braintree when the Vice-Principal's secretary came down with a message.

'Can't it wait?' asked Wilt.

'He said it was most urgent.'

'It's probably your Senior Lectureship come through at last,' said Braintree brightly. Wilt swallowed the rest of his Scotch egg and got up.

'I doubt that,' he said and went wanly out of the canteen and up the stairs. He had a horrid suspicion that promotion was the last thing the Vice-Principal wanted to see him about.

'Now, sir,' said the Inspector when they were seated in the office, 'my name is Flint, Inspector Flint, CID, and you're Mr Wilt? Mr Henry Wilt?'

'Yes,' said Wilt.

'Now, Mr Wilt, as you may have gathered we are investigating the suspected murder of a woman whose body is believed to have been deposited at the bottom of one of the foundation holes for the new building. I daresay you know about it.' Wilt nodded. 'And naturally we are interested in anything that might be of assistance. I wonder if you would mind having a look at these notes.'

He handed Wilt a piece of paper. It was headed 'Notes on Violence and the Break-Up of Family Life', and underneath were a number of sub-headings.

1 Increasing use of violence in public life to attain political ends.
a Bombing b Hijacking c Kidnapping d Assassination
2 Ineffectuality of Police Methods in combating Violence.
a Negative approach. Police able only to react to crime after it has taken place.
b Use of violence by police themselves.
c Low level of intelligence of average policeman.
d Increasing use of sophisticated methods such as diversionary tactics by criminals.
3 Influence of media. TV brings crime techniques into the home.

There was more. Much more. Wilt looked down the list with a sense of doom.

'You recognize the handwriting?' asked the Inspector.

'I do,' said Wilt, adopting rather prematurely the elliptical language of the witness box.

'You admit that you wrote those notes?' The Inspector reached out a hand and took the notes back.

'Yes.'

'They express your opinion of police methods?'

Wilt pulled himself together. 'They were jottings I was making for a lecture to Sandwich-Course Trainee Firemen,' he explained. 'They were simply rough ideas. They need amplifying of course . . .'

'But you don't deny you wrote them?'

'Of course I don't. I've just said I did, haven't I?'

The Inspector nodded and picked up a book. 'And this is yours too?'

Wilt looked at *Bleak House*. 'It says so, doesn't it?'

Inspector Flint opened the cover. 'So it does,' he said with a show of astonishment, 'so it does.'

Wilt stared at him. There was no point in maintaining the pretence any longer. The best thing to do was to get it over quickly. They had found that bloody book in the basket of the bicycle and the notes must have fallen out of his pocket on the building site.

'Look, Inspector,' he said, 'I can explain everything. It's really quite simple. I did go into that building site ...'

The Inspector stood up. 'Mr Wilt, if you're prepared to make a statement I think I should warn you ...'

Wilt went down to the Murder Headquarters and made a statement in the presence of a police stenographer. His progress to the blue caravan and his failure to come out again were noted with interest by members of the staff teaching in the Science block, by students in the canteen and by twenty-five fellow lecturers gaping through the windows of the Staff Room.

9

'Goddam the thing,' said Gaskell as he knelt greasily beside the engine of the cruiser, 'you'd think that even in this pre-technological monarchy they'd fit a decent motor. This contraption must have been made for the Ark.'

'Ark Ark the Lark,' said Sally, 'and cut the crowned heads foolery. Eva's a reginaphile.'

'A what?'

'Reginaphile. Monarchist. Get it. She's the Queen's Bee so don't be anti-British. We don't want her to stop working as well as the motor. Maybe it isn't the con rod.'

'If I could only get the head off I could tell,' said Gaskell.

'And what good would that do? Buy you another?' said Sally and went into the cabin where Eva was wondering what they were going to have for supper. 'Tarbaby is still tinkering with the motor. He says it's the con rod.'

'Con rod?' said Eva.

'Only connect, baby, only connect.'

'With what?'

'The thigh bone's connected to the knee bone. The con rod's connected to the piston and as everyone knows pistons are penis symbols. The mechanized male's substitute for sex. The Outboard Motor Syndrome. Only this happens to be inboard like his balls never dropped. Honestly, Gaskell is so regressive.'

'I'm sure I don't know,' said Eva.

Sally lay back on the bunk and lit a cigar. 'That's what I love about you, Eva. You don't know. Ignorance is blissful, baby. I lost mine when I was fourteen.'

Eva shook her head. 'Men,' she said disapprovingly.

'He was old enough to be my grandfather,' said Sally. 'He *was* my grandfather.'

'Oh no. How awful.'

'Not really,' said Sally laughing, 'he was an artist. With a beard. And the smell of paint on his smock and there was this studio and he wanted to paint me in the nude. I was so pure in those days. He made me lie on this couch and he arranged my legs. He was always arranging my legs and then standing back to look at me and painting. And then one day when I was lying there he came over and bent my legs back and kissed me and then he was on top of me and his smock was up and . . .'

Eva sat and listened, fascinated. She could visualize it all so clearly, even the smell of paint in the studio and the brushes. Sally had had such an exciting life, so full of incident and so romantic in a dreadful sort of way. Eva tried to remember what she had been like at fourteen and not even going out with boys and there was Sally lying on a couch with a famous artist in his studio.

'But he raped you,' she said finally. 'Why didn't you tell the police?'

'The police? You don't understand. I was at this terribly exclusive school. They would have sent me home. It was progressive and all that but I shouldn't have been out being painted by this artist and my parents would never have forgiven me. They were so strict.' Sally sighed, overcome by the rigours of her wholly fictitious childhood. 'And now you can see why I'm so afraid of being hurt by men. When you've been raped you know what penile aggression means.'

'I suppose you do,' said Eva, in some doubt as to what penile aggression was.

'You see the world differently too. Like G says, nothing's good and nothing's bad. It just is.'

'I went to a lecture on Buddhism once,' said Eva, 'and that's what Mr Podgett said. He said—'

'Zen's all wrong. Like you just sit around waiting. That's passive. You've got to make things happen. You sit around waiting long enough, you're dead. Someone's trampled all over you. You've got to see things happen your way and no one else's.'

'That doesn't sound very sociable,' said Eva. 'I mean if we all did just what we wanted all the time it wouldn't be very nice for other people.'

'Other people are hell,' said Sally. 'That's Sartre and he should know. You do what you want is good and no moral kickback. Like G says, rats are the paradigm. You think rats go around thinking what's good for other people?'

'Well no, I don't suppose they do,' said Eva.

'Right. Rats aren't ethical. No way. They just do. They don't get screwed up thinking.'

'Do you think rats can think?' asked Eva, now thoroughly engaged in the problems of rodent psychology.

'Of course they can't. Rats just are. No *Schadenfreude* with rats.'

'What's *Schadenfreude*?'

'Second cousin to *Weltschmerz*,' said Sally, stubbing her cigar out in the ashtray. 'So we can all do what we want whenever we want to. That's the message. It's only people like G who've got the know bug who get balled up.'

'No bug?' said Eva.

'They've got to know how everything works. Scientists. Lawrence was right. It's all head and no body with G.'

'Henry's a bit like that,' said Eva. 'He's always reading or talking about books. I've told him he doesn't know what the real world is like.'

In the Mobile Murder Headquarters Wilt was learning. He

sat opposite Inspector Flint whose face was registering increasing incredulity.

'Now, we'll just go over that again,' said the Inspector. 'You say that what those men saw down that hole was in actual fact an inflatable plastic doll with a vagina.'

'The vagina is incidental,' said Wilt, calling forth reserves of inconsequence.

'That's as maybe,' said the Inspector. 'Most dolls don't have them but ... all right, we'll let that pass. The point I'm trying to get at is that you're quite positive there isn't a real live human being down there.'

'Positive,' said Wilt, 'and if there were it is doubtful if it would still be alive now.'

The Inspector studied him unpleasantly. 'I don't need you to point that out to me,' he said. 'If there was the faintest possibility of whatever it is down there being alive I wouldn't be sitting here, would I?'

'No,' said Wilt.

'Right. So now we come to the next point. How is it that what those men saw, they say a woman and you say a doll ... that this thing was wearing clothes, had hair and even more remarkably had its head bashed in and one hand stretched up in the air?'

'That was the way it fell,' said Wilt. 'I suppose the arm got caught up on the side and lifted up.'

'And its head was bashed in?'

'Well, I did drop a lump of mud on it,' Wilt admitted, 'that would account for that.'

'You dropped a lump of mud on its head?'

'That's what I said,' Wilt agreed.

'I know that's what you said. What I want to know is why you felt obliged to drop a lump of mud on the head of an inflatable doll that had, as far as I can gather, never done you any harm.'

Wilt hesitated. That damned doll had done him a great deal of harm one way and another but this didn't seem an opportune moment to go into that. 'I don't know really,' he said finally, 'I just thought it might help.'

'Help what?'

'Help ... I don't know. I just did it, that's all. I was drunk at the time.'

'All right, we'll come back to that in a minute. There's still one question you haven't answered. If it was a doll, why was it wearing clothes?'

Wilt looked desperately round the caravan and met the eyes of the police stenographer. There was a look in them that didn't inspire confidence. Talk about lack of suspension of disbelief.

'You're not going to believe this,' Wilt said. The Inspector looked at him and lit a cigarette.

'Well?'

'As a matter of fact I had dressed it up,' Wilt said, squirming with embarrassment.

'You had dressed it up?'

'Yes,' said Wilt.

'And may one enquire what purpose you had in mind when you dressed it up?'

'I don't know exactly.'

The Inspector sighed significantly. 'Right. We go back to the beginning. We have a doll with a vagina which you dress up and bring down here in the dead of night and deposit at the bottom of a thirty-foot hole and drop lumps of mud on its head. Is that what you're saying?'

'Yes,' said Wilt.

'You wouldn't prefer to save everyone concerned a lot of time and bother by admitting here and now that what is at present resting, hopefully at peace, under twenty tons of concrete at the bottom of that pile is the body of a murdered woman?'

'No,' said Wilt, 'I most definitely wouldn't.'

Inspector Flint sighed again. 'You know, we're going to get to the bottom of this thing,' he said. 'It may take time and it may take expense and God knows it's taking patience but when we do get down there—'

'You're going to find an inflatable doll,' said Wilt.

'With a vagina?'

'With a vagina.'

•

In the Staff Room Peter Braintree staunchly defended Wilt's innocence. 'I tell you I've known Henry well for the past seven years and whatever has happened he had nothing to do with it.'

Mr Morris, the Head of Liberal Studies, looked out of the window sceptically. 'They've had him in there since ten past two. That's four hours,' he said. 'They wouldn't do that unless they thought he had some connection with the dead woman.'

'They can think what they like. I know Henry and even if the poor sod wanted to he's incapable of murdering anyone.'

'He did punch that Printer on Tuesday. That shows he's capable of irrational violence.'

'Wrong again. The Printer punched him,' said Braintree.

'Only after Wilt had called him a snivelling fucking moron,' Mr Morris pointed out. 'Anyone who goes into Printers Three and calls one of them that needs his head examined. They killed poor old Pinkerton, you know. He gassed himself in his car.'

'They had a damned good try at killing old Henry come to that.'

'Of course, that blow might have affected his brain,' said Mr Morris, with morose satisfaction. 'Concussion can do funny things to a man's character. Change him overnight from a nice quiet inoffensive little fellow like Wilt into a homicidal maniac who suddenly goes berserk. Stranger things have happened.'

'I daresay Henry would be the first to agree with you,' said Braintree. 'It can't be very pleasant sitting in that caravan being questioned by detectives. I wonder what they're doing to him.'

'Just asking questions. Things like "How have you been getting on with your wife?" and "Can you account for your movements on Saturday night?" They start off gently and then work up to the heavy stuff later on.'

Peter Braintree sat in silent horror. Eva. He'd forgotten all about her and as for Saturday night he knew exactly what Henry had said he had been doing before he turned up on the doorstep covered with mud and looking like death ...

'All I'm saying,' said Mr Morris, 'is that it seems very strange to me that they find a dead body at the bottom of a shaft filled with concrete and the next thing you know they've got Wilt in that Murder HQ for questioning. Very strange indeed. I wouldn't like to be in his shoes.' He got up and left the room and Peter Braintree sat on wondering if there was anything he should do like phone a lawyer and ask him to come round and speak to Henry. It seemed a bit premature and presumably Henry could ask to see a lawyer himself if he wanted one.

Inspector Flint lit another cigarette with an air of insouciant menace. 'How well do you get on with your wife?' he asked.

Wilt hesitated. 'Well enough,' he said.

'Just well enough? No more than that?'

'We get along just fine,' said Wilt, conscious that he had made an error.

'I see. And I suppose she can substantiate your story about this inflatable doll.'

'Substantiate it?'

'The fact that you made a habit of dressing it up and carrying on with it.'

'I didn't make a habit of anything of the sort,' said Wilt indignantly.

'I'm only asking. You were the one who first raised the fact that it had a vagina. I didn't. You volunteered the information and naturally I assumed ...'

'What did you assume?' said Wilt. 'You've got no right ...'

'Mr Wilt,' said the Inspector, 'put yourself in my position. I am investigating a case of suspected murder and a man comes along and tells me that what two eye-witnesses describe as the body of a well-nourished woman in her early thirties ...'

'In her early thirties? Dolls don't have ages. If that bloody doll was more than six months old ...'

'Please, Mr Wilt, if you'll just let me continue. As I was saying we have a prima facie case of murder and you admit yourself to having put a doll with a vagina down that hole. Now if you were in my shoes what sort of inference would you draw from that?'

100

Wilt tried to think of some totally innocent interpretation and couldn't.

'Wouldn't you be the first to agree that it does look a bit peculiar?'

Wilt nodded. It looked horribly peculiar.

'Right,' continued the Inspector. 'Now if we put the nicest possible interpretation on your actions and particularly on your emphasis that this doll had a vagina—'

'I didn't emphasize it. I only mentioned the damned thing to indicate that it was extremely lifelike. I wasn't suggesting I made a habit of ...' He stopped and looked miserably at the floor.

'Go on, Mr Wilt, don't stop now. It often helps to talk.'

Wilt stared at him frantically. Talking to Inspector Flint wasn't helping him one iota. 'If you're implying that my sex life was confined to copulating with an inflatable fucking doll dressed in my wife's clothes ...'

'Hold it there,' said the Inspector, stubbing out his cigarette significantly. 'Ah, so we've taken another step forward. You admit then that whatever is down that hole is dressed in your wife's clothes? Yes or no.'

'Yes,' said Wilt miserably.

Inspector Flint stood up. 'I think it's about time we all went and had a little chat with Mrs Wilt,' he said. 'I want to hear what she has to say about your funny little habits.'

'I'm afraid that's going to be a little difficult,' said Wilt.

'Difficult?'

'Well you see the thing is she's gone away.'

'Gone away?' said the Inspector. 'Did I hear you say that Mrs Wilt has gone away?'

'Yes.'

'And where has Mrs Wilt gone to?'

'That's the trouble. I don't know.'

'You don't know?'

'No, I honestly don't know,' said Wilt.

'She didn't tell you where she was going?'

'No. She just wasn't there when I got home.'

'She didn't leave a note or anything like that?'

'Yes,' said Wilt, 'as a matter of fact she did.'

'Right, well let's just go up to your house and have a look at that note.'

'I'm afraid that's not possible,' said Wilt. 'I got rid of it.'

'You got rid of it?' said the Inspector. 'You got rid of it? How?'

Wilt looked pathetically across at the police stenographer. 'To tell the truth I wiped my bottom with it,' he said.

Inspector Flint gazed at him demonically. 'You did what?'

'Well, there was no toilet paper in the lavatory so I . . .' he stopped. The Inspector was lighting yet another cigarette. His hands were shaking and he had a distant look in his eyes that suggested he had just peered over some appalling abyss. 'Mr Wilt,' he said when he had managed to compose himself, 'I trust I am a reasonably tolerant man, a patient man and a humane man, but if you seriously expect me to believe one word of your utterly preposterous story you must be insane. First you tell me you put a doll down that hole. Then you admit that it was dressed in your wife's clothes. Now you say that she went away without telling you where she was going and finally to cap it all you have the temerity to sit there and tell me that you wiped your arse with the one piece of solid evidence that could substantiate your statement.'

'But I did,' said Wilt.

'Balls,' shouted the Inspector. 'You and I both know where Mrs Wilt has gone and there's no use pretending we don't. She's down at the bottom of that fucking hole and you put her there.'

'Are you arresting me?' Wilt asked as they walked in a tight group across the road to the police car.

'No,' said Inspector Flint, 'you're just helping the police with their enquiries. It will be on the news tonight.'

'My dear Braintree, of course we'll do all we can,' said the Vice-Principal. 'Wilt has always been a loyal member of staff and there has obviously been some dreadful mistake. I'm sure you needn't worry. The whole thing will right itself before long.'

'I hope you're right,' said Braintree, 'but there are complicating factors. For one thing there's Eva ...'

'Eva? Mrs Wilt? You're not suggesting ...'

'I'm not suggesting anything. All I'm saying is ... well, she's missing from home. She walked out on Henry last Friday.'

'Mrs Wilt walked ... well I hardly knew her, except by reputation of course. Wasn't she the woman who broke Mr Lockyer's collar-bone during a part-time Evening Class in Judo some years back?'

'That was Eva,' said Braintree.

'She hardly sounds the sort of woman who would allow Wilt to put her down ...'

'She isn't,' said Braintree hastily. 'If anyone was liable to be murdered in the Wilt household it was Henry. I think the police should be informed of that.'

They were interrupted by the Principal who came in with a copy of the evening paper. 'You've seen this I suppose,' he said, waving it distraughtly. 'It's absolutely appalling.' He put the paper down on the desk and indicated the headlines. MURDERED WOMAN BURIED IN CONCRETE AT TECH. LECTURER HELPING POLICE.

'Oh dear,' said the Vice-Principal. 'Oh dear. How very unfortunate. It couldn't have come at a worse moment.'

'It shouldn't have come at all,' snapped the Principal. 'And that's not all. I've already had half a dozen phone calls from parents wanting to know if we make a habit of employing murderers on the full-time staff. Who is this fellow Wilt anyway?'

'He's in Liberal Studies,' said the Vice-Principal. 'He's been with us ten years.'

'Liberal Studies. I might have guessed it. If they're not poets manqués they're Maoists or ... I don't know where the hell Morris gets them from. And now we've got a blasted murderer. God knows what I'm going to tell the Education Committee tonight. They've called an emergency meeting for eight.'

'I must say I resent Wilt being called a murderer,' said Braintree loyally. 'There is nothing to suggest that he has murdered anyone.'

103

The Principal studied him for a moment and then looked back at the headlines. 'Mr Braintree, when someone is helping the police with their enquiries into a murder it may not be proven that he is a murderer but the suggestion is there.'

'This certainly isn't going to help us get the new CNAA degree off the ground,' intervened the Vice-Principal tactfully. 'We've got a visit from the Inspection Committee scheduled for Friday.'

'From what the police tell me it isn't going to help get the new Administration block off the ground either,' said the Principal. 'They say it's going to take at least three days to bore down to the bottom of that pile and then they'll have to drill through the concrete to get the body out. That means they'll have to put a new pile down and we're already well behind schedule and our building budget has been halved. Why on earth couldn't he have chosen somewhere else to dispose of his damned wife?'

'I don't think . . .' Braintree began.

'I don't care what you think,' said the Principal, 'I'm merely telling you what the police think.'

Braintree left them still wrangling and trying to figure out ways and means of counteracting the adverse publicity the case had already brought the Tech. He went down to the Liberal Studies office and found Mr Morris in a state of despair. He was trying to arrange stand-in lecturers for all Wilt's classes.

'But he'll probably be back in the morning,' Braintree said.

'Like hell he will,' said Mr Morris. 'When they take them in like that they keep them. Mark my words. The police may make mistakes, I'm not saying they don't, but when they act this swiftly they're on to a sure thing. Mind you, I always thought Wilt was a bit odd.'

'Odd? I've just come from the VP's office. You want to hear what the Principal's got to say about Liberal Studies staff.'

'Christ,' said Mr Morris, 'don't tell me.'

'Anyway what's so odd about Henry?'

'Too meek and mild for my liking. Look at the way he accepted remaining a Lecturer Grade Two all these years.'

'That was hardly his fault.'

'Of course it was his fault. All he had to do was threaten to resign and go somewhere else and he'd have got promotion like a shot. That's the only way to get on in this place. Make your presence felt.'

'He seems to have done that now,' said Braintree. 'The Principal is already blaming him for throwing the building programme off schedule and if we don't get the Joint Honours degree past the CNAA, Henry's going to be made the scapegoat. It's too bad. Eva should have had more sense than to walk out on him like that.'

Mr Morris took a more sombre view. 'She'd have shown a damned sight more sense if she'd walked out on him before the sod took it into his head to beat her to death and dump her down that bloody shaft. Now who the hell can I get to take Gasfitters One tomorrow?'

10

At 34 Parkview Avenue Wilt sat in the kitchen with Clem while the detectives ransacked the house. 'You're not going to find anything incriminating here,' he told Inspector Flint.

'Never you mind what we're going to find. We're just having a look.'

He sent one detective upstairs to examine Mrs Wilt's clothes or what remained of them.

'If she went away she'd have taken half her wardrobe,' he said. 'I know women. On the other hand if she's pushing up twenty tons of premix she wouldn't need more than what she's got on.'

Eva's wardrobe was found to be well stocked. Even Wilt had to admit that she hadn't taken much with her.

'What was she wearing when you last saw her?' the Inspector asked.

'Lemon loungers,' said Wilt.

'Lemon what?'

'Pyjamas,' said Wilt, adding to the list of incriminating evidence against him. The Inspector made a note of the fact in his pocketbook.

'In bed, was she?'

'No,' said Wilt. 'Round at the Pringsheims.'

'The Pringsheims? And who might they be?'

'The Americans I told you about who live in Rossiter Grove.'

'You haven't mentioned any Americans to me,' said the Inspector.

'I'm sorry. I thought I had. I'm getting muddled. She went away with them.'

'Oh did she? And I suppose we'll find they're missing too?'

'Almost certainly,' said Wilt. 'I mean if she was going away with them they must have gone too and if she isn't with them I can't imagine where she has got to.'

'I can,' said the Inspector looking with distasteful interest at a stain on a sheet one of the detectives had found in the dirty linen basket. By the time they left the house the incriminating evidence consisted of the sheet, an old dressing-gown cord that had found its way mysteriously into the attic, a chopper that Wilt had once used to open a tin of red lead, and a hypodermic syringe which Eva had got from the vet for watering cacti very precisely during her Indoor Plant phase. There was also a bottle of tablets with no label on it.

'How the hell would I know what they are?' Wilt asked when confronted with the bottle. 'Probably aspirins. And anyway it's full.'

'Put it with the other exhibits,' said the Inspector. Wilt looked at the box.

'For God's sake, what do you think I did with her? Poisoned her, strangled her, hacked her to bits with a chopper and injected her with Biofood?'

'What's Biofood?' asked Inspector Flint with sudden interest.

'It's stuff you feed plants with,' said Wilt. 'The bottle's on the windowsill.'

The Inspector added the bottle of Biofood to the box. 'We

know what you did with her, Mr Wilt,' he said. 'It's how that interests us now.'

They went out to the police car and drove round to the Pringsheims' house in Rossiter Grove. 'You just sit in the car with the constable here while I go and see if they're in,' said Inspector Flint and went to the front door. Wilt sat and watched while he rang the bell. He rang again. He hammered on the doorknocker and finally he walked round through the gate marked Tradesman's Entrance to the kitchen door. A minute later he was back and fumbling with the car radio.

'You've hit the nail on the head all right, Wilt,' he snapped. 'They've gone away. The place is a bloody shambles. Looks like they've had an orgy. Take him out.'

The two detectives bundled Wilt, no longer Mr Wilt but plain Wilt and conscious of the fact, out of the car while the Inspector called Fenland Constabulary and spoke with sinister urgency about warrants and sending something that sounded like the D brigade up. Wilt stood in the driveway of 12 Rossiter Grove and wondered what the hell was happening to him. The order of things on which he had come to depend was disintegrating around him.

'We're going in the back way,' said the Inspector. 'This doesn't look good.'

They went down the path to the kitchen door and round to the back garden. Wilt could see what the Inspector had meant by a shambles. The garden didn't look at all good. Paper plates lay about the lawn or, blown by the wind, had wheeled across the garden into honeysuckle or climbing rose while paper cups, some squashed and some still filled with Pringsheim punch and rainwater, littered the ground. But it was the beefburgers that gave the place its air of macabre filth. They were all over the lawn, stained with coleslaw so that Wilt was put in mind of Clem.

'The dog returns to his vomit,' said Inspector Flint evidently reading his mind. They crossed the terrace to the lounge windows and peered through. If the garden was bad the interior was awful.

'Smash a pane in the kitchen window and let us in,' said the

107

Inspector to the taller of the two detectives. A moment later the lounge window slid back and they went inside.

'No need for forcible entry,' said the detective. 'The back door was unlocked and so was this window. They must have cleared out in a hell of a hurry.'

The Inspector looked round the room and wrinkled his nose. The smell of stale pot, sour punch and candle smoke still hung heavily in the house.

'If they went away,' he said ominously and glanced at Wilt.

'They must have gone away,' said Wilt who felt called upon to make some comment on the scene, 'no one would live in all this mess for a whole weekend without ...'

'Live? You did say "live" didn't you?' said Flint stepping on a piece of burnt beefburger.

'What I meant ...'

'Never mind what you meant, Wilt. Let's see what's happened here.'

They went into the kitchen where the same chaos reigned and then into another room. Everywhere it was the same. Dead cigarette ends doused in cups of coffee or ground out on the carpet. Pieces of broken record behind the sofa marked the end of Beethoven's Fifth. Cushions lay crumpled against the wall. Burnt-out candles hung limply post-coital from bottles. To add a final touch to the squalor someone had drawn a portrait of Princess Anne on the wall with a red felt pen. She was surrounded by helmeted policemen and underneath was written. THE FUZZ AROUND OUR ANNY THE ROYAL FAMLYS FANNY THE PRICK IS DEAD LONG LIVE THE CUNT. Sentiments that were doubtless perfectly acceptable in Women's Lib circles but were hardly calculated to establish the Pringsheims very highly in Inspector Flint's regard.

'You've got some nice friends, Wilt,' he said.

'No friends of mine,' said Wilt, with feeling. 'The sods can't even spell.'

They went upstairs and looked in the big bedroom. The bed was unmade, clothes, mostly underclothes, were all over the floor or hung out of drawers and an unstoppered bottle of Joy lay on its side on the dressing-table. The room stank of perfume.

'Jesus wept,' said the Inspector, eyeing a pair of jockstraps belligerently. 'All that's missing is some blood.'

They found it in the bathroom. Dr Scheimacher's cut hand had rained bloodstains in the bath and splattered the tiles with dark blotches. The bathroom door with its broken frame was hanging from the bottom hinge and there were spots of blood on the paintwork.

'I knew it,' said the Inspector, studying their message and that written in lipstick on the mirror above the washbasin. Wilt looked at it too. It seemed unduly personal.

WHERE WILT FAGGED AND EVA RAN WHO WAS THEN THE MALE CHAUVINIST PIG?

'Charming,' said Inspector Flint. He turned to look at Wilt whose face was now the colour of the tiles. 'I don't suppose you'd know anything about that. Not your handiwork?'

'Certainly not,' said Wilt.

'Nor this?' said the Inspector, pointing to the bloodstains in the bath. Wilt shook his head. 'And I suppose this has nothing to do with you either?' He indicated a diaphragm that had been nailed to the wall above the lavatory seat. WHERE THE B SUCKS THERE SUCK I UNDERNEATH A DUTCH CAP NICE AND DRY. Wilt stared at the thing in utter disgust.

'I don't know what to say,' he muttered. 'It's all so awful.'

'You can say that again,' the Inspector agreed, and turned to more practical matters. 'Well, she didn't die in here.'

'How can you tell?' asked the younger of the two detectives.

'Not enough blood.' The Inspector looked round uncertainly. 'On the other hand one hard bash ...' They followed the bloodstains down the passage to the room where Wilt had been dollknotted.

'For God's sake don't touch anything,' said the Inspector, easing the door open with his sleeve, 'the fingerprint boys are going to have a field day here.' He looked inside at the toys.

'I suppose you butchered the children too,' he said grimly.

'Children?' said Wilt, 'I didn't know they had any.'

'Well if you didn't,' said the Inspector, who was a family man, 'the poor little buggers have got something to be thankful for. Not much by the look of things but something.'

Wilt poked his head round the door and looked at the

Teddy Bear and the rocking horse. 'Those are Gaskell's,' he said, 'he likes to play with them.'

'I thought you said you didn't know they had any children?'

'They haven't. Gaskell is Dr Pringsheim. He's a biochemist and a case of arrested development according to his wife.' The Inspector studied him thoughtfully. The question of arrest had become one that needed careful consideration.

'I don't suppose you're prepared to make a full confession now?' he asked without much hope.

'No I am not,' said Wilt.

'I didn't think you would be, Wilt,' said the Inspector. 'All right, take him down to the Station. I'll be along later.'

The detectives took Wilt by the arms. It was the last straw.

'Leave me alone,' he yelled. 'You've got no right to do this. You've got—'

'Wilt,' shouted Inspector Flint, 'I'm going to give you one last chance. If you don't go quietly I'm going to charge you here and now with the murder of your wife.'

Wilt went quietly. There was nothing else to do.

'The screw?' said Sally. 'But you said it was the con rod.'

'So I was wrong,' said Gaskell. 'She cranks over.'

'It, G, it. It cranks over.'

'OK. It cranks over so it can't be a con rod. It could be something that got tangled with the propshaft.'

'Like what?'

'Like weeds.'

'Why don't you go down and have a look yourself?'

'With these glasses?' said Gaskell. 'I wouldn't be able to see anything.'

'You know I can't swim,' said Sally. 'I have this leg.'

'I can swim,' said Eva.

'We'll tie a rope round you. That way you won't drown,' said Gaskell, 'all you've got to do is go under and feel if there's anything down there.'

'We know what's down there,' said Sally. 'Mud is.'

'Round the propshaft,' said Gaskell. 'Then if there is you can take it off.'

110

Eva went into the cabin and put on the bikini.

'Honestly, Gaskell, sometimes I think you're doing this on purpose. First it's the con rod and now it's the screw.'

'Well, we've got to try everything. We can't just sit here,' said Gaskell, 'I'm supposed to be back in the lab tomorrow.'

'You should have thought of that before,' said Sally. 'Now all we need is a goddam Albatross.'

'If you ask me we've got one,' said Gaskell, as Eva came out of the cabin and put on a bathing cap.

'Now where's the rope?' she asked. Gaskell looked in a locker and found some. He tied it round her waist and Eva clambered over the side into the water.

'It's ever so cold,' she giggled.

'That's because of the Gulf Stream,' said Gaskell, 'it doesn't come this far round.'

Eva swam out and put her feet down.

'It's terribly shallow and full of mud.'

She waded round hanging on to the rope and groped under the stern of the cruiser.

'I can't feel anything,' she called.

'It will be further under,' said Gaskell, peering down at her. Eva put her head under the water and felt the rudder.

'That's the rudder,' said Gaskell.

'Of course it is,' said Eva, 'I know that, silly. I'm not stupid.'

She disappeared under the boat. This time she found the propeller but there was nothing wrapped round it.

'It's just muddy, that's all,' she said, when she resurfaced. 'There's mud all along the bottom.'

'Well there would be wouldn't there,' said Gaskell. Eva waded round to the side. 'We just happen to be stuck on a mudbank.'

Eva went down again but the propshaft was clear too. 'I told you so,' said Sally, as they hauled Eva back on board. 'You just made her do it so you could see her in her plastic kini all covered with mud. Come, Botticelli baby, let Sally wash you off.'

'Oh Jesus,' said Gaskell. 'Penis arising from the waves.' He went back to the engine and looked at it uncertainly. Perhaps there was a blockage in the fuel line. It didn't seem very likely but he had to try something. They couldn't stay stuck on the mudbank forever.

On the foredeck Sally was sponging Eva down.

'Now the bottom half, darling,' she said untying the string.

'Oh, Sally. No, Sally.'

'Labia babia.'

'Oh, Sally, you are awful.'

Gaskell struggled with the adjustable wrench. All this Touch Therapy was getting to him. And the plastic.

At the County Hall the Principal was doing his best to pacify the members of the Education Committee who were demanding a full enquiry into the recruitment policy of the Liberal Studies Department.

'Let me explain,' he said patiently, looking round at the Committee, which was a nice balance of business interests and social commitment. 'The 1944 Education Act laid down that all apprentices should be released from their places of employment to attend Day Release Classes at Technical Colleges ...'

'We know all that,' said a building contractor, 'and we all know it's a bloody waste of time and public money. This country would be a sight better off if they were left to get on with their jobs.'

'The courses they attend,' continued the Principal before anyone with a social conscience could intervene, 'are craft-oriented with the exception of one hour, one obligatory hour of Liberal Studies. Now the difficulty with Liberal Studies is that no one knows what it means.'

'Liberal Studies means,' said Mrs Chatterway, who prided herself on being an advocate of progressive education, in which role she had made a substantial contribution to the illiteracy rate in several previously good primary schools, 'providing socially deprived adolescents with a firm grounding in liberal attitudes and culturally extending topics ...'

'It means teaching them to read and write,' said a company director. 'It's no good having workers who can't read instructions.'

112

'It means whatever anyone chooses it to mean,' said the Principal hastily. 'Now if you are faced with the problem of having to find lecturers who are prepared to spend their lives going into classrooms filled with Gasfitters or Plasterers or Printers who see no good reason for being there, and keeping them occupied with a subject that does not, strictly speaking, exist, you cannot afford to pick and choose the sort of staff you employ. That is the crux of the problem.'

The Committee looked at him doubtfully.

'Am I to understand that you are suggesting that Liberal Studies teachers are not devoted and truly creative individuals imbued with a strong sense of vocation?' asked Mrs Chatterway belligerently.

'No,' said the Principal, 'I am not saying that at all. I am merely trying to make the point that Liberal Studies lecturers are not as other men are. They either start out odd or they end up odd. It's in the nature of their occupation.'

'But they are all highly qualified,' said Mrs Chatterway, 'they all have degrees.'

'Quite. As you say they all hold degrees. They are all qualified teachers but the stresses to which they are subject leave their mark. Let me put it this way. If you were to take a heart transplant surgeon and ask him to spend his working life docking dogs' tails you would hardly expect him to emerge unscathed after ten years' work. The analogy is exact, believe me, exact.'

'Well, all I can say,' protested the building contractor, 'is that not all Liberal Studies lecturers end up burying their murdered wives at the bottom of pile shafts.'

'And all I can say,' said the Principal, 'is that I am extremely surprised more don't.'

The meeting broke up undecided.

11

As dawn broke glaucously over East Anglia Wilt sat in the Interview Room at the central Police Station isolated from the natural world and in a wholly artificial environment that included a table, four chairs, a detective sergeant and a fluorescent light on the ceiling that buzzed slightly. There were no windows, just pale green walls and a door through which people came and went occasionally and Wilt went twice to relieve himself in the company of a constable. Inspector Flint had gone to bed at midnight and his place had been taken by Detective Sergeant Yates who had started again at the beginning.

'What beginning?' said Wilt.

'At the very beginning.'

'God made heaven and earth and all . . .'

'Forget the wisecracks,' said Sergeant Yates.

'Now that,' said Wilt, appreciatively, 'is a more orthodox use of wise.'

'What is?'

'Wisecrack. It's slang but it's good slang wisewise if you get my meaning.'

Detective Sergeant Yates studied him closely. 'This is a soundproof room,' he said finally.

'So I've noticed,' said Wilt.

'A man could scream his guts out in here and no one outside would be any the wiser.'

'Wiser?' said Wilt doubtfully. 'Wisdom and knowledge are not the same thing. Someone outside might not be aware that . . .'

'Shut up,' said Sergeant Yates.

Wilt sighed. 'If you would just let me get some sleep . . .'

'You'll get some sleep when you tell us why you murdered your wife, where you murdered her and how you murdered her.'

'I don't suppose it will do any good if I tell you I didn't murder her.'

114

Sergeant Yates shook his head.

'No,' he said. 'We know you did. You know you did. We know where she is. We're going to get her out. We know you put her there. You've at least admitted that much.'

'I keep telling you I put an inflatable ...'

'Was Mrs Wilt inflatable?'

'Was she fuck,' said Wilt.

'Right, so we'll forget the inflatable doll crap ...'

'I wish to God I could,' said Wilt. 'I'll be only too glad when you get down there and dig it out. It will have burst of course with all that concrete on it but it will still be recognizably an inflatable plastic doll.'

Sergeant Yates leant across the table. 'Let me tell you something. When we do get Mrs Wilt out of there, don't imagine she'll be unrecognizable.' He stopped and stared intently at Wilt. 'Not unless you've disfigured her.'

'Disfigured her?' said Wilt with a hollow laugh. 'She didn't need disfiguring the last time I saw her. She was looking bloody awful. She had on these lemon pyjamas and her face was all covered with ...' He hesitated. There was a curious expression on the Sergeant's face.

'Blood?' he suggested. 'Were you going to say "blood"?'

'No,' said Wilt, 'I most certainly wasn't. I was going to say powder. White powder and scarlet lipstick. I told her she looked fucking awful.'

'You must have had a very happy relationship with her,' said the Sergeant. 'I don't make a habit of telling my wife she looks fucking awful.'

'You probably don't have a fucking awful-looking wife,' said Wilt making an attempt to conciliate the man.

'What I have or don't have by way of a wife is my business. She lies outside the domain of this discussion.'

'Lucky old her,' said Wilt, 'I wish to God mine did.' By two o'clock they had left Mrs Wilt's appearance and got on to teeth and the question of identifying dead bodies by dental chart.

'Look,' said Wilt wearily, 'I daresay teeth fascinate you but at this time of night I can do without them.'

'You wear dentures or something?'

'No. No, I don't,' said Wilt, rejecting the plural.

'Did Mrs Wilt?'

'No,' said Wilt, 'she was always very . . .'

'I thank you,' said Sergeant Yates, 'I knew it would come out in the end.'

'What would?' said Wilt, his mind still on teeth.

'That "was". The past tense. That's the giveaway. Right, so you admit she's dead. Let's go on from there.'

'I didn't say anything of the sort. You said "Did she wear dentures?" and I said she didn't . . .'

'You said "she was". It's that "was" that interests me. If you had said "is" it would have been different.'

'It might have sounded different,' said Wilt, rallying his defences, 'but it wouldn't have made the slightest difference to the facts.'

'Which are?'

'That my wife is probably still around somewhere alive and kicking . . .'

'You don't half give yourself away, Wilt,' said the Sergeant. 'Now it's "probably" and as for "kicking" I just hope for your sake we don't find she was still alive when they poured that concrete down on top of her. The Court wouldn't take kindly to that.'

'I doubt if anyone would,' said Wilt. 'Now when I said "probably" what I meant was that if you had been held in custody for a day and half the night being questioned on the trot by detectives you'd begin to wonder what had happened to your wife. It might even cross your mind that, all evidence to the contrary, she might not be alive. You want to try sitting on this side of the table before you start criticizing me for using terms like "probable". Anything more improbable than being accused of murdering your wife when you know for a fact that you haven't you can't imagine.'

'Listen, Wilt,' said the Sergeant, 'I'm not criticizing you for your language. Believe me I'm not. I'm merely trying as patiently as I can to establish the facts.'

'The facts are these,' said Wilt. 'Like a complete idiot I

made the mistake of dumping an inflatable doll down the bottom of a pile shaft and someone poured concrete in and my wife is away from home and ...'

'I'll tell you one thing,' Sergeant Yates told Inspector Flint when he came on duty at seven in the morning. 'This one is a hard nut to crack. If you hadn't told me he hadn't a record I'd have sworn he was an old hand and a good one at that. Are you sure Central Records have got nothing on him?' Inspector Flint shook his head.

'He hasn't started squealing for a lawyer yet?'

'Not a whimper. I tell you he's either as nutty as a fruit cake or he's been through this lot before.'

And Wilt had. Day after day, year in year out. With Gasfitters One and Printers Three, with Day Release Motor Mechanics and Meat Two. For ten years he had sat in front of classes answering irrelevant questions, discussing why Piggy's rational approach to life was preferable to Jack's brutishness, why Pangloss' optimism was so unsatisfactory, why Orwell hadn't wanted to shoot that blasted elephant or hang that man, and all the time fending off verbal attempts to rattle him and reduce him to the state poor old Pinkerton was in when he gassed himself. By comparison with Bricklayers Four, Sergeant Yates and Inspector Flint were child's play. If only they would let him get some sleep he would go on running inconsequential rings round them.

'I thought I had him once,' the Sergeant told Flint as they conferred in the corridor. 'I had got him on to teeth.'

'Teeth?' said the Inspector.

'I was just explaining we can always identify bodies from their dental charts and he almost admitted she was dead. Then he got away again.'

'Teeth, eh? That's interesting. I'll have to pursue that line of questioning. It may be his weak link.'

'Good luck on you,' said the Sergeant. 'I'm off to bed.'

'Teeth?' said Wilt. 'We're not going through that again are we? I thought we'd exhausted that topic. The last bloke wanted to know if Eva had them in the past tense. I told him she did and ...'

'Wilt,' said Inspector Flint, 'I am not interested in whether or not Mrs Wilt had teeth. I presume she must have done. What I want to know is if she still has them. Present tense.'

'I imagine she must have,' said Wilt patiently. 'You'd better ask her when you find her.'

'And when we find her will she be in a position to tell us?'

'How the hell should I know? All I can say is that if for some quite inexplicable reason she's lost all her teeth there'll be the devil to pay. I'll never hear the end of it. She's got a mania for cleaning the things and sticking bits of dental floss down the loo. You've got no idea the number of times I've thought I'd got worms.'

Inspector Flint sighed. Whatever success Sergeant Yates had had with teeth, it was certainly eluding him. He switched to other matters.

'Let's go over what happened at the Pringsheims' party again,' he said.

'Let's not,' said Wilt who had so far managed to avoid mentioning his contretemps with the doll in the bathroom. 'I've told you five times already and it's wearing a bit thin. Besides it was a filthy party. A lot of trendy intellectuals boosting their paltry egos.'

'Would you say you were an introverted sort of man, Wilt? A solitary type of person?'

Wilt considered the question seriously. It was certainly more to the point than teeth.

'I wouldn't go that far,' he said finally. 'I'm fairly quiet but I'm gregarious too. You have to be to cope with the classes I teach.'

'But you don't like parties?'

'I don't like parties like the Pringsheims', no.'

'Their sexual behaviour outrages you? Fills you with disgust?'

'Their sexual behaviour? I don't know why you pick on that. Everything about them disgusts me. All that crap about Women's Lib for one thing when all it means to someone like

Mrs Pringsheim is that she can go around behaving like a bitch on heat while her husband spends the day slaving over a hot test tube and comes home to cook supper, wash up and is lucky if he's got enough energy to wank himself off before going to sleep. Now if we're talking about real Women's Lib that's another matter. I've got nothing against ...'

'Let's just hold it there,' said the Inspector. 'Now two things you said interest me. One, wives behaving like bitches on heat. Two, this business of you wanking yourself off.'

'Me?' said Wilt indignantly. 'I wasn't talking about myself.'

'Weren't you?'

'No, I wasn't.'

'So you don't masturbate?'

'Now look here, Inspector. You're prying into areas of my private life which don't concern you. If you want to know about masturbation read the Kinsey Report. Don't ask me.'

Inspector Flint restrained himself with difficulty. He tried another tack. 'So when Mrs Pringsheim lay on the bed and asked you to have intercourse with her ...'

'Fuck is what she said,' Wilt corrected him.

'You said no?'

'Precisely,' said Wilt.

'Isn't that a bit odd?'

'What, her lying there or me saying no?'

'You saying no.'

Wilt looked at him incredulously.

'Odd?' he said. 'Odd? A woman comes in here and throws herself flat on her back on this table, pulls up her skirt and says "Fuck me, honey, prick me to the quick." Are you going to leap on to her with a "Whoopee, let's roll baby"? Is that what you mean by not odd?'

'Jesus wept, Wilt,' snarled the Inspector, 'you're walking a fucking tightrope with my patience.'

'You could have fooled me,' said Wilt. 'All I do know is that your notion of what is odd behaviour and what isn't doesn't begin to make sense with me.'

Inspector Flint got up and left the room. 'I'll murder the bastard, so help me God I'll murder him,' he shouted at the

Duty Sergeant. Behind him in the Interview Room Wilt put his head on the table and fell asleep.

At the Tech Wilt's absence was making itself felt in more ways than one. Mr Morris had had to take Gasfitters One at nine o'clock and had come out an hour later feeling that he had gained fresh insight into Wilt's sudden excursion into homicide. The Vice-Principal was fighting off waves of crime reporters anxious to find out more about the man who was helping the police with their enquiries into a particularly macabre and newsworthy crime. And the Principal had begun to regret his criticisms of Liberal Studies to the Education Committee. Mrs Chatterway had phoned to say that she had found his remarks in the worst of taste and had hinted that she might well ask for an enquiry into the running of the Liberal Studies Department. But it was at the meeting of the Course Board that there was most alarm.

'The visitation of the Council for National Academic Awards takes place on Friday,' Dr Mayfield, Head of Sociology, told the committee. 'They are hardly likely to approve the Joint Honours degree in the present circumstances.'

'If they had any sense they wouldn't approve it in any circumstances,' said Dr Board. 'Urban Studies and Medieval Poetry indeed. I know academic eclecticism is the vogue these days but Helen Waddell and Lewis Mumford aren't even remotely natural bedfellows. Besides the degree lacks academic content.'

Dr Mayfield bristled. Academic content was his strong point. 'I don't see how you can say that,' he said. 'The course has been structured to meet the needs of students looking for a thematic approach.'

'The poor benighted creatures we manage to lure away from universities to take this course wouldn't know a thematic approach if they saw one,' said Dr Board. 'Come to think of it I wouldn't either.'

'We all have our limitations,' said Dr Mayfield suavely.

'Precisely,' said Dr Board, 'and in the circumstances we should recognize them instead of concocting Joint Honours degrees which don't make sense for students who, if their

A-level results are anything to go by, haven't any in the first place. Heaven knows I'm all for educational opportunity but—'

'The point is,' interjected Dr Cox, Head of Science, 'that it is not the degree course as such that is the purpose of the visitation. As I understand it they have given their approval to the degree in principle. They are coming to look at the facilities the College provides and they are hardly likely to be impressed by the presence of so many murder squad detectives. That blue caravan is most off-putting.'

'In any case with the late Mrs Wilt structured into the foundations ...' began Dr Board.

'I am doing my best to get the police to remove her from ...'

'The syllabus?' asked Dr Board.

'The premises,' said Dr Mayfield. 'Unfortunately they seem to have hit a snag.'

'A snag?'

'They have hit bedrock at eleven feet.'

Dr Board smiled. 'One wonders why there was any need for thirty-foot piles in the first instance if there is bedrock at eleven,' he murmured.

'I can only tell you what the police have told me,' said Dr Mayfield. 'However they have promised to do all they can to be off the site by Friday. Now I would just like to run over the arrangements again with you. The Visitation will start at eleven with an inspection of the library. We will then break up into groups to discuss Faculty libraries and teaching facilities with particular reference to our ability to provide individual tuition ...'

'I shouldn't have thought that was a point that needed emphasizing,' said Dr Board. 'With the few students we're likely to get we're almost certain to have the highest teacher to student radio in the country.'

'If we adopt that approach the Committee will gain the impression that we are not committed to the degree. We must provide a united front,' said Dr Mayfield, 'we can't afford at this stage to have divisions among ourselves. This degree could mean our getting Polytechnic status.'

There were divisions too among the men boring down on the building site. The foreman was still at home under sedation suffering nervous exhaustion brought on by his part in the cementation of a murdered woman and it was left to Barney to superintend operations. 'There was this hand, see . . .' he told the Sergeant in charge.

'On which side?'

'On the right,' said Barney.

'Then we'll go down on the left. That way if the hand is sticking out we won't cut it off.'

They went down on the left and cut off the main electricity cable to the canteen.

'Forget that bleeding hand,' said the Sergeant, 'we go down on the right and trust to luck. Just so long as we don't cut the bitch in half.'

They went down on the right and hit bedrock at eleven feet.

'This is going to slow us up no end,' said Barney. 'Who would have thought there'd be rock down there.'

'Who would have thought some nut would incorporate his missus in the foundation of a college of further education where he worked,' said the Sergeant.

'Gruesome,' said Barney.

In the meantime the staff had as usual divided into factions. Peter Braintree led those who thought Wilt was innocent and was joined by the New Left on the grounds that anyone in conflict with the fuzz must be in the right. Major Millfield reacted accordingly and led the Right against Wilt on the automatic assumption that anyone who incurred the support of the Left must be in the wrong and that anyway the police knew what they were doing. The issue was raised at the meeting of the Union called to discuss the annual pay demand. Major Millfield proposed a motion calling on the union to support the campaign for the reintroduction of capital punishment. Bill Trent countered with a motion expressing solidarity with Brother Wilt. Peter Braintree proposed that a fund be set up to help Wilt with his legal fees. Dr Lomax, Head of Commerce, argued against this and pointed out that Wilt had, by dismembering his wife, brought the profession into disrepute. Braintree said Wilt hadn't dismembered anyone and that even the police hadn't suggested he had, and there was such a thing as a law against slander. Dr Lomax withdrew his remark. Major Millfield insisted that there were good grounds for thinking Wilt had murdered his wife and that anyway Habeas Corpus didn't exist in Russia. Bill Trent said that capital punishment didn't either. Major Millfield said, 'Bosh.' In the end, after prolonged argument, Major Millfield's motion on hanging was passed by a block vote of the Catering Department while Braintree's proposal and the motion of the New Left were defeated, and the meeting went on to discuss a pay increase of forty-five per cent to keep Teachers in Technical Institutes in line with comparably qualified professions. Afterwards Peter Braintree went down to the Police Station to see if there was anything Henry wanted.

'I wonder if I might see him,' he asked the Sergeant at the desk.

'I'm afraid not, sir,' said the Sergeant, 'Mr Wilt is still helping us with our enquiries.'

'But isn't there anything I can get him? Doesn't he need anything?'

'Mr Wilt is well provided for,' said the Sergeant, with the private reservation that what Wilt needed was his head read.

'But shouldn't he have a solicitor?'

'When Mr Wilt asks for a solicitor he will be allowed to see one,' said the Sergeant. 'I can assure you that so far he hasn't asked.'

And Wilt hadn't. Having finally been allowed three hours sleep he had emerged from his cell at twelve o'clock and had eaten a hearty breakfast in the police canteen. He returned to the Interview Room, haggard and unshaven, and with his sense of the improbable markedly increased.

'Now then, Henry,' said Inspector Flint, dropping an official octave nomenclaturewise in the hope that Wilt would respond, 'about this blood.'

'What blood?' said Wilt, looking round the aseptic room.

'The blood on the walls of the bathroom at the Pringsheims' house. The blood on the landing. Have you any idea how it got there? Any idea at all?'

'None,' said Wilt, 'I can only assume that someone was bleeding.'

'Right,' said the Inspector, 'who?'

'Search me,' said Wilt.

'Quite, and you know what we've found?'

Wilt shook his head.

'No idea?'

'None,' said Wilt.

'Bloodspots on a pair of grey trousers in your wardrobe,' said the Inspector. 'Bloodspots, Henry, bloodspots.'

'Hardly surprising,' said Wilt. 'I mean if you looked hard enough you'd be bound to find some bloodspots in anyone's wardrobe. The thing is I wasn't wearing grey trousers at that party. I was wearing blue jeans.'

'You were wearing blue jeans? You're quite sure about that?'

'Yes.'

'So the bloodspots on the bathroom wall and the bloodspots on your grey trousers have nothing to do with one another?'

'Inspector,' said Wilt, 'far be it from me to teach you your own business but you have a technical branch that specializes in matching bloodstains. Now may I suggest that you make use of their skills to establish . . .'

'Wilt,' said the Inspector, 'Wilt, when I need your advice on how to conduct a murder investigation I'll not only ask for it but I'll resign from the force.'

'Well?' said Wilt.

'Well what?'

'Do they match? Do the bloodstains match?'

The Inspector studied him grimly. 'If I told you they did?' he asked.

Wilt shrugged. 'I'm not in any position to argue,' he said. 'If you say they do, I take it they do.'

'They don't,' said Inspector Flint, 'but that proves nothing,' he continued before Wilt could savour his satisfaction. 'Nothing at all. We've got three people missing. There's Mrs Wilt at the bottom of that shaft ... No, don't say it, Wilt, don't say it. There's Dr Pringsheim and there's Mrs Fucking Pringsheim.'

'I like it,' said Wilt appreciatively, 'I definitely like it.'

'Like what?'

'Mrs Fucking Pringsheim. It's apposite.'

'One of these days, Wilt,' said the Inspector softly, 'you'll go too far.'

'Patiencewise? To use a filthy expression,' asked Wilt.

The Inspector nodded and lit a cigarette.

'You know something, Inspector,' said Wilt, beginning to feel on top of the situation, 'you smoke too much. Those things are bad for you. You should try ...'

'Wilt,' said the Inspector, 'in twenty-five years in the service I have never once resorted to physical violence while interrogating a suspect but there comes a time, a time and a place and a suspect when with the best will in the world ...' He got up and went out. Wilt sat back in his chair and looked up at the fluorescent light. He wished it would stop buzzing. It was getting on his nerves.

12

On Eel Stretch — Gaskell's map-reading had misled him and they were nowhere near Frogwater Reach or Fen Broad — the situation was getting on everyone's nerves. Gaskell's attempts to mend the engine had had the opposite effect. The cockpit was flooded with fuel oil and it was difficult to walk on deck without slipping.

'Jesus, G, anyone would think to look at you that this was a goddam oil rig,' said Sally.

'It was that fucking fuel line,' said Gaskell, 'I couldn't get it back on.'

'So why try starting the motor with it off?'

'To see if it was blocked.'

'So now you know. What you going to do about it? Sit here

till the food runs out? You've gotta think of something.'

'Why me? Why don't you come up with something?'

'If you were any sort of a man ...'

'Shit,' said Gaskell. 'The voice of the liberated woman. Comes the crunch and all of a sudden I've got to be a man. What's up with you, man-woman? You want us off here, you do it. Don't ask me to be a man, uppercase M, in an emergency. I've forgotten how.'

'There must be some way of getting help,' said Sally.

'Oh sure. You just go up top and take a crowsnest at the scenery. All you'll get is a beanfeast of bullrushes.' Sally climbed on top of the cabin and scanned the horizon. It was thirty feet away and consisted of an expanse of reeds.

'There's something over there looks like a church tower,' she said. Gaskell climbed up beside her.

'It is a church tower. So what?'

'So if we flashed a light or something someone might see it.'

'Brilliant. A highly populated place like the top of a church tower there's bound to be people just waiting for us to flash a light.'

'Couldn't we burn something?' said Sally. 'Somebody would see the smoke and ...'

'You crazy? You start burning anything with all that fuel oil floating around they'll see something all right. Like an exploding cruiser with bodies.'

'We could fill a can with oil and put it over the side and float it away before lighting it.'

'And set the reedbeds on fire? What the hell do you want? A fucking holocaust?'

'G baby, you're just being unhelpful.'

'I'm using my brains is all,' said Gaskell. 'You keep coming up with bright ideas like that you're going to land us in a worse mess than we're in already.'

'I don't see why,' said Sally.

'I'll tell you why,' said Gaskell, 'because you went and stole this fucking *Hesperus*. That's why.'

'I didn't steal it. I ...'

126

'You tell the fuzz that. Just tell them. You start setting fire to reedbeds and they'll be all over us asking questions. Like whose boat this is and how come you're sailing someone else's cruiser . . . So we got to get out of here without publicity.'

It started to rain.

'That's all we need. Rain,' said Gaskell. Sally went down into the cabin where Eva was tidying up after lunch. 'God, G's hopeless. First he lands us on a mudbank in the middle of nowhere, then he gefucks the motor but good and now he says he doesn't know what to do.'

'Why doesn't he go and get help?' asked Eva.

'How? Swimming? G couldn't swim that far to save his life.'

'He could take the airbed and paddle down to the open water,' said Eva. 'He wouldn't have to swim.'

'Airbed? Did I hear you say airbed? What airbed?'

'The one in the locker with the lifejackets. All you've got to do is blow it up and . . .'

'Honey you're the practicallest,' said Sally, and rushed outside. 'G, Eva's found a way for you to go and get help. There's an airbed in the locker with the lifejackets.' She rummaged in the locker and took out the airbed.

'You think I'm going anywhere on that damned thing you've got another think coming,' said Gaskell.

'What's wrong with it?'

'In this weather? You ever tried to steer one of those things? It's bad enough on a sunny day with no wind. Right now I'd end up in the reeds and anyhow the rain's getting on my glasses.'

'All right, so we wait till the storm blows over. At least we know how to get off here.'

She went back into the cabin and shut the door. Outside Gaskell squatted by the engine and toyed with the wrench. If only he could get the thing to go again.

'Men,' said Sally contemptuously, 'claim to be the stronger sex but when the chips are down it's us women who have to bail them out.'

'Henry's impractical too,' said Eva. 'It's all he can do to mend a fuse. I do hope he isn't worried about me.'

'He's having himself a ball,' said Sally.

'Not Henry. He wouldn't know how.'

'He's probably having it off with Judy.'

Eva shook her head. 'He was just drunk, that's all. He's never done anything like that before.'

'How would you know?'

'Well he is my husband.'

'Husband hell. He just uses you to wash the dishes and cook and clean up for him. What does he give you? Just tell me that.'

Eva struggled with her thoughts inarticulately. Henry didn't give her anything very much. Not anything she could put into words. 'He needs me,' she said finally.

'So he needs you. Who needs needing? That's the rhetoric of female feudalism. So you save someone's life, you've got to be grateful to them for letting you? Forget Henry. He's a jerk.'

Eva bristled. Henry might not be very much but she didn't like him insulted.

'Gaskell's nothing much to write home about,' she said and went into the kitchen. Behind her Sally lay back on the bunk and opened the centre spread of *Playboy*. 'Gaskell's got bread,' she said.

'Bread?'

'Money, honey. Greenstuff. The stuff that makes the world go round Cabaretwise. You think I married him for his looks? Oh no. I can smell a cool million when it comes by me and I do mean buy me.'

'I could never marry a man for his money,' said Eva primly. 'I'd have to be in love with him. I really would.'

'So you've seen too many movies. Do you really think Gaskell was in love with me?'

'I don't know. I suppose he must have been.'

Sally laughed. 'Eva baby you are naïve. Let me tell you about G. G's a plastic freak. He'd fuck a goddam chimpanzee if you dressed it up in plastic.'

'Oh honestly. He wouldn't,' said Eva. 'I don't believe it.'

'You think I put you on the Pill for nothing? You go around

128

in that bikini and Gaskell's drooling over you all the time –
if I wasn't here he'd have raped you.'

'He'd have a hard time,' said Eva, 'I took Judo classes.'

'Well he'd try. Anything in plastic drives him crazy. Why do
you think he had that doll?'

'I wondered about that.'

'Right. You can stop wondering,' said Sally.

'I still don't see what that has to do with you marrying him,'
said Eva.

'Then let me tell you a little secret. Gaskell was referred to
me ...'

'Referred?'

'By Dr Freeborn. Gaskell had this little problem and he
consulted Dr Freeborn and Dr Freeborn sent him to me.'

Eva looked puzzled. 'But what were you supposed to do?'

'I was a surrogate,' said Sally.

'A surrogate?'

'Like a sex counsellor,' said Sally. 'Dr Freeborn used to
send me clients and I would help them.'

'I wouldn't like that sort of job,' said Eva, 'I couldn't bear
to talk to men about sex. Weren't you embarrassed?'

'You get used to it and there are worse ways of earning a
living. So G comes along with his little problem and I
straightened him out but literally and we got married. A
business arrangement. Cash on the tail.'

'You mean you ...'

'I mean I have Gaskell and Gaskell has plastic. It's an elastic
relationship. The marriage with the two-way stretch.'

Eva digested this information with difficulty. It didn't seem
right somehow. 'Didn't his parents have anything to say about
it?' she asked. 'I mean did he tell them about you helping him
and all that?'

'Say? What could they say? G told them he'd met me at
summer school and Pringsy's greedy little eyes popped out of
his greasy little head. Baby, did that fat little man have penis
projection. Sell? He could sell anything. The Rockefeller
Centre to Rockefeller. So he accepted me. Old Ma Pringsheim
didn't. She huffed and she puffed and she blew but this little

piggy stayed right where the bank was. G and me went back to California and G graduated in plastic and we've been bio-degradable ever since.'

'I'm glad Henry isn't like that,' said Eva. 'I couldn't live with a man who was queer.'

'G's not queer, honey. Like I said he's a plastic freak.'

'If that's not queer I don't know what is,' said Eva.

Sally lit a cigarillo.

'All men get turned on by something,' she said. 'They're manipulable. All you've got to do is find the kink. I should know.'

'Henry's not like that. I'd know if he was.'

'So he makes with the doll. That's how much you know about Henry. You telling me he's the great lover?'

'We've been married twelve years. It's only natural we don't do it as often as we used to. We're so busy.'

'Busy lizzie. And while you're housebound what's Henry doing?'

'He's taking classes at the Tech. He's there all day and he comes home tired.'

'Takes classes takes asses. You'll be telling me next he's not a sidewinder.'

'I don't know what you mean,' said Eva.

'He has his piece on the side. His secretary knees up on the desk.'

'He doesn't have a secretary.'

'Then students prudence. Screws their grades up. I know. I've seen it. I've been around colleges too long to be fooled.'

'I'm sure Henry would never ...'

'That's what they all say and then bingo, it's divorce and bobbysex and all you're left to look forward to is menopause and peeking through the blinds at the man next door and waiting for the Fuller Brush man.'

'You make it all sound so awful,' said Eva. 'You really do.'

'It is, Eva teats. It is. You've got to do something about it before it's too late. You've got to liberate yourself from Henry. Make the break and share the cake. Otherwise it's male domination doomside.'

Eve sat on the bunk and thought about the future. It didn't seem to hold much for her. They would never have any children now and they wouldn't ever have much money. They would go on living in Parkview Avenue and paying off the mortgage and maybe Henry would find someone else and then what would she do? And even if he didn't, life was passing her by.

'I wish I knew what to do,' she said presently. Sally sat up and put her arm round her.

'Why don't you come to the States with us in November?' she said. 'We could have such fun.'

'Oh I couldn't do that,' said Eva. 'It wouldn't be fair to Henry.'

No such qualms bothered Inspector Flint. Wilt's intransigence under intense questioning merely indicated that he was harder than he looked.

'We've had him under interrogation for thirty-six hours now,' he told the conference of the Murder Squad in the briefing room at the Police Station, 'and we've got nothing out of him. So this is going to be a long hard job and quite frankly I have my doubts about breaking him.'

'I told you he was going to be a hard nut to crack,' said Sergeant Yates.

'Nut being the operative word,' said Flint. 'So it's got to be concrete evidence.'

There was a snigger which died away quickly. Inspector Flint was not in a humorous mood.

'Evidence, hard evidence is the only thing that is going to break him. Evidence is the only thing that is going to bring him to trial.'

'But we've got that,' said Yates. 'It's at the bott ...'

'I know exactly where it is, thank you Sergeant. What I am talking about is evidence of multiple murder. Mrs Wilt is accounted for. Dr and Mrs Pringsheim aren't. Now my guess is that he murdered all three and that the other two bodies are ...' He stopped and opened the file in front of him and hunted through it for Notes on Violence and the Break-Up of

Family Life. He studied them for a moment and shook his head. 'No,' he muttered, 'it's not possible.'

'What isn't, sir?' asked Sergeant Yates. 'Anything is possible with this bastard.'

But Inspector Flint was not to be drawn. The notion was too awful.

'As I was saying,' he continued, 'what we need now is hard evidence. What we have got is purely circumstantial. I want more evidence on the Pringsheims. I want to know what happened at that party, who was there and why it happened and at the rate we're going with Wilt we aren't going to get anything out of him. Snell, you go down to the Department of Biochemistry at the University and get what you can on Dr Pringsheim. Find out if any of his colleagues were at that party. Interview them. Get a list of his friends, his hobbies, his girl friends if he had any. Find out if there is any link between him and Mrs Wilt that would suggest a motive. Jackson, you go up to Rossiter Grove and see what you can get on Mrs Pringsheim ...'

By the time the conference broke up detectives had been despatched all over town to build up a dossier on the Pringsheims. Even the American Embassy had been contacted to find out what was known about the couple in the States. The murder investigation had begun in earnest.

Inspector Flint walked back to his office with Sergeant Yates and shut the door. 'Yates,' he said, 'this is confidential. I wasn't going to mention it in there but I've a nasty feeling I know why that sod is so bloody cocky. Have you ever known a murderer sit through thirty-six hours of questioning as cool as a cucumber when he knows we've got the body of his victim pinpointed to the nearest inch?'

Sergeant Yates shook his head. 'I've known some pretty cool customers in my time and particularly since they stopped hanging but this one takes the biscuit. If you ask me he's a raving psychopath.'

Flint dismissed the idea. 'Psychopaths crack easy,' he said. 'They confess to murders they haven't committed or they confess to murders they have committed, but they confess.

This Wilt doesn't. He sits there and tells me how to run the investigation. Now take a look at this.' He opened the file and took out Wilt's notes. 'Notice anything peculiar?'

Sergeant Yates read the notes through twice.

'Well, he doesn't seem to think much of our methods,' he said finally. 'And I don't much like this bit about low level of intelligence of average policeman.'

'What about Point Two D?' said the Inspector. 'Increasing use of sophisticated methods such as diversionary tactics by criminals. Diversionary tactics. Doesn't that suggest anything to you?'

'You mean he's trying to divert our attention away from the real crime to something else?'

Inspector Flint nodded. 'What I mean is this. I wouldn't mind betting that when we do get down to the bottom of that fucking pile we're going to find an inflatable doll dressed up in Mrs Wilt's clothes and with a vagina. That's what I think.'

'But that's insane.'

'Insane? It's fucking diabolical,' said the Inspector. 'He's sitting in there like a goddam dummy giving as good as he gets because he knows he's got us chasing a red herring.'

Sergeant Yates sat down mystified. 'But why? Why draw attention to the murder in the first place? Why didn't he just lie low and act normally?'

'What, and report Mrs Wilt missing? You're forgetting the Pringsheims. A wife goes missing, so what? Two of her friends go missing and leave their house in a hell of a mess and covered with bloodstains. That needs explaining, that does. So he puts out a false trail . . .'

'But that still doesn't help him,' objected the Sergeant. 'We dig up a plastic doll. Doesn't mean we're going to halt the investigation.'

'Maybe not but it gives him a week while the other bodies disintegrate.'

'You think he used an acid bath like Haigh?' asked the Sergeant. 'That's horrible.'

'Of course it's horrible. You think murder's nice or something? Anyway the only reason they got Haigh was that stupid bugger told them where to look for the sludge. If he'd kept his trap shut for another week they wouldn't have found anything. The whole lot would have been washed away. Besides I don't know what Wilt's used. All I do know is he's an intellectual, a clever sod and he thinks he's got it wrapped up. First we take him in for questioning, maybe even get him remanded and when we've done that, we go and dig up a plastic inflatable doll. We're going to look right Charlies going into court with a plastic doll as evidence of murder. We'll be the laughing stock of the world. So the case gets thrown out of court and what happens when we pick him up a second time for questioning on the real murders? We'd have the Civil Liberties brigade sinking their teeth into our throats like bleeding vampire bats.'

'I suppose that explains why he doesn't start shouting for a lawyer,' said Yates.

'Of course it does. What does he want with a lawyer now? But pull him in a second time and he'll have lawyers falling over themselves to help him. They'll be squawking about police brutality and victimization. You won't be able to hear yourself speak. His bloody lawyers will have a field day. First plastic dolls and then no bodies at all. He'll get clean away.'

'Anyone who can think that little lot up must be a madman,' said the Sergeant.

'Or a fucking genius,' said Flint bitterly. 'Christ what a case.' He stubbed out a cigarette resentfully.

'What do you want me to do? Have another go at him?'

'No, I'll do that. You go up to the Tech and chivvy his boss there into saying what he really thinks of Wilt. Get any little bit of dirt on the blighter you can. There's got to be something in his past we can use.'

He went down the corridor and into the Interview Room. Wilt was sitting at the table making notes on the back of a statement form. Now that he was beginning to feel, if not at home in the Police Station, at least more at ease with his surroundings, his mind had turned to the problem of Eva's disappearance. He had to admit that he had been worried by the bloodstains in the Pringsheims' bathroom. To while away the time he had tried to formulate his thoughts on paper and he was still at it when Inspector Flint came into the room and banged the door.

'Right, so you're a clever fellow, Wilt,' he said, sitting down and pulling the paper towards him. 'You can read and write and you've got a nice logical and inventive mind so let's just see what you've written here. Who's Ethel?'

'Eva's sister,' said Wilt. 'She's married to a market gardener in Luton. Eva sometimes goes over there for a week.'

'And "Blood in the bath"?'

'Just wondering how it got there.'

'And "Evidence of hurried departure"?'

'I was simply putting down my thoughts about the state of the Pringsheims' house,' said Wilt.

'You're trying to be helpful?'

'I'm here helping you with your enquiries. That's the official term isn't it?'

'It may be the official term, Wilt, but in this case it doesn't correspond with the facts.'

'I don't suppose it does very often,' said Wilt. 'It's one of those expressions that covers a multitude of sins.'

'And crimes.'

'It also happens to ruin a man's reputation,' said Wilt. 'I hope you realize what you're doing to mine by holding me here like this. It's bad enough knowing I'm going to spend the rest of my life being pointed out as the man who dressed a plastic doll with a cunt up in his wife's clothes and dropped it down a pile hole without everyone thinking I'm a bloody murderer as well.'

'Where you're going to spend the rest of your life nobody is going to care what you did with that plastic doll,' said the Inspector.

Wilt seized on the admission.

'Ah, so you've found it at last,' he said eagerly. 'That's fine. So now I'm free to go.'

'Sit down and shut up,' snarled the Inspector. 'You're not going anywhere and when you do it will be in a large black van. I haven't finished with you yet. In fact I'm only just beginning.'

'Here we go again,' said Wilt. 'I just knew you'd want to

start at the beginning again. You fellows have primary causes on the brain. Cause and effect, cause and effect. Which came first, the chicken or the egg, protoplasm or demiurge? I suppose this time it's going to be what Eva said when we were dressing to go to the party.'

'This time,' said the Inspector, 'I want you to tell me precisely why you stuck that damned doll down that hole.'

'Now that is an interesting question,' said Wilt, and stopped. It didn't seem a good idea to try to explain to Inspector Flint in the present circumstances just what he had had in mind when he dropped the doll down the shaft. The Inspector didn't look the sort of person who would understand at all readily that a husband could have fantasies of murdering his wife without actually putting them into effect. It would be better to wait for Eva to put in an appearance in the flesh before venturing into that uncharted territory of the wholly irrational. With Eva present Flint might sympathize with him. Without her he most certainly wouldn't.

'Let's just say I wanted to get rid of the beastly thing,' he said.

'Let's not say anything of the sort,' said Flint. 'Let's just say you had an ulterior motive for putting it there.'

Wilt nodded. 'I'll go along with that,' he said.

Inspector Flint nodded encouragingly. 'I thought you might. Well, what was it?'

Wilt considered his words carefully. He was getting into deep waters.

'Let's just say it was by way of being a rehearsal.'

'A rehearsal? What sort of rehearsal?'

Wilt thought for a moment.

'Interesting word "rehearsal",' he said. 'It comes from the old French, *rehercer*, meaning . . .'

'To hell with where it comes from,' said the Inspector, 'I want to know where it ends up.'

'Sounds a bit like a funeral too when you come to think of it,' said Wilt, continuing his campaign of semantic attrition.

Inspector Flint hurled himself into the trap. 'Funeral? Whose funeral?'

'Anyone's,' said Wilt blithely. 'Hearse, rehearse. You could say that's what happens when you exhume a body. You rehearse it though I don't suppose you fellows use hearses.'

'For God's sake,' shouted the Inspector. 'Can't you ever stick to the point? You said you were rehearsing something and I want to know what that something was.'

'An idea, a mere idea,' said Wilt, 'one of those ephemera of mental fancy that flit like butterflies across the summer landscape of the mind blown by the breezes of association that come like sudden showers ... I rather like that.'

'I don't,' said the Inspector, looking at him bitterly. 'What I want to know is what you were rehearsing. That's what I'd like to know.'

'I've told you. An idea.'

'What sort of idea?'

'Just an idea,' said Wilt. 'A mere ...'

'So help me God, Wilt,' shouted the Inspector, 'if you start on these fucking butterflies again I'll break the unbroken habit of a lifetime and wring your bloody neck.'

'I wasn't going to mention butterflies this time,' said Wilt reproachfully, 'I was going to say that I had this idea for a book ...'

'A book?' snarled Inspector Flint. 'What sort of book? A book of poetry or a crime story?'

'A crime story,' said Wilt, grateful for the suggestion.

'I see,' said the Inspector. 'So you were going to write a thriller. Well now, just let me guess the outline of the plot. There's this lecturer at the Tech and he has this wife he hates and he decides to murder her ...'

'Go on,' said Wilt, 'you're doing very well so far.'

'I thought I might be,' said Flint delightedly. 'Well, this lecturerer thinks he's a clever fellow who can hoodwink the police. He doesn't think much of the police. So he dumps a plastic doll down a hole that's going to be filled with concrete in the hope that the police will waste their time digging it out and in the meantime he's buried his wife somewhere else. By the way, where did you bury Mrs Wilt, Henry? Let's get this over once and for all. Where did you put her? Just tell me that. You'll feel better when it's out.'

'I didn't put her anywhere. If I've told you that once I've

137

told you a thousand times. How many more times have I got to tell you I don't know where she is.'

'I'll say this for you, Wilt,' said the Inspector, when he could bring himself to speak. 'I've known some cool customers in my time but I have to take my hat off to you. You're the coolest bastard it's ever been my unfortunate experience to come across.'

Wilt shook his head. 'You know,' he said, 'I feel sorry for you, Inspector, I really do. You can't recognize the truth when it's staring you in the face.'

Inspector Flint got up and left the room. 'You there,' he said to the first detective he could find. 'Go into that Interview Room and ask that bastard questions and don't stop till I tell you.'

'What sort of questions?'

'Any sort. Just any. Keep asking him why he stuffed an inflatable plastic doll down a pile hole. That's all. Just ask it over and over again. I'm going to break that sod.'

He went down to his office and slumped into his chair and tried to think.

13

At the Tech Sergeant Yates sat in Mr Morris's office. 'I'm sorry to disturb you again,' he said, 'but we need some more details on this fellow Wilt.'

The Head of Liberal Studies looked up with a haggard expression from the timetable. He had been having a desperate struggle trying to find someone to take Bricklayers Four. Price wouldn't do because he had Mechanics Two and Williams wouldn't anyway. He had already gone home the day before with a nervous stomach and was threatening to repeat the performance if anyone so much as mentioned Bricklayers Four to him again. That left Mr Morris himself and he was prepared to be disturbed by Sergeant Yates for as long as he liked if it meant he didn't have to take those bloody brick-layers.

'Anything to help,' he said, with an affability that was in curious contrast to the haunted look in his eyes. 'What details would you like to know?'

'Just a general impression of the man, sir,' said the Sergeant. 'Was there anything unusual about him?'

'Unusual?' Mr Morris thought for a moment. Apart from a preparedness to teach the most awful Day Release Classes year in and year out without complaint he could think of nothing unusual about Wilt. 'I suppose you could call what amounted to a phobic reaction to *The Lord of the Flies* a bit unusual but then I've never much cared for . . .'

'If you'd just wait a moment, sir,' said the Sergeant busying himself with his notebook. 'You did say "phobic reaction" didn't you?'

'Well what I meant was . . .'

'To flies, sir?'

'To *The Lord of the Flies*. It's a book,' said Mr Morris, now uncertain that he had been wise to mention the fact. Police-men were not noticeably sensitive to those niceties of literary taste that constituted his own definition of intelligence. 'I do hope I haven't said the wrong thing.'

'Not at all, sir. It's these little details that help us to build up a picture of the criminal's mind.'

Mr Morris sighed. 'I'm sure I never thought when Mr Wilt came to us from the University that he would turn out like this.'

'Quite so, sir. Now did Mr Wilt ever say anything disparaging about his wife?'

'Disparaging? Dear me no. Mind you he didn't have to. Eva spoke for herself.' He looked miserably out of the window at the pile-boring machine.

'Then in your opinion Mrs Wilt was not a very likeable woman?'

Mr Morris shook his head. 'She was a ghastly woman,' he said.

Sergeant Yates licked the end of his ballpen.

'You did say "ghastly" sir?'

'I'm afraid so. I once had her in an Evening Class for Elementary Drama.'

'Elementary?' said the Sergeant, and wrote it down.

'Yes, though elemental would have been more appropriate in Mrs Wilt's case. She threw herself into the parts rather too vigorously to be wholly convincing. Her Desdemona to my Othello is something I am never likely to forget.'

'An impetuous woman, would you say?'

'Let me put it this way,' said Mr Morris, 'had Shakespeare written the play as Mrs Wilt interpreted it, Othello would have been the one to be strangled.'

'I see, sir,' said the Sergeant. 'Then I take it she didn't like black men.'

'I have no idea what she thought about the racial issue,' said Mr Morris, 'I am talking of her physical strength.'

'A powerful woman, sir?'

'Very,' said Mr Morris with feelings.

Sergeant Yates looked puzzled. 'It seems strange a woman like that allowing herself to be murdered by Mr Wilt without putting up more of a struggle,' he said thoughtfully.

'It seems incredible to me,' Mr Morris agreed, 'and what is more it indicates a degree of fanatical courage in Henry that his behaviour in this department never led me to suspect. I can only suppose he was insane at the time.'

Sergeant Yates seized on the point. 'Then it is your considered opinion that he was not in his right mind when he killed his wife?'

'Right mind? I can think of nothing rightminded about killing your wife and dumping her body . . .'

'I meant sir,' said the Sergeant, 'that you think Mr Wilt is a lunatic.'

Mr Morris hesitated. There were a good many members of his department whom he would have classified as mentally unbalanced but he hardly liked to advertise the fact. On the other hand it might help poor Wilt.

'Yes, I suppose so,' he said finally for at heart he was a kindly man. 'Quite mad. Between ourselves, Sergeant, anyone who is prepared to teach the sort of bloodyminded young thugs

140

we get can't be entirely sane. And only last week Wilt got into an altercation with one of the Printers and was punched in the face. I think that may have had something to do with his subsequent behaviour. I trust you will treat what I say in the strictest confidence. I wouldn't want ...'

'Quite so, sir,' said Sergeant Yates. 'Well, I needn't detain you any longer.'

He returned to the Police Station and reported his findings to Inspector Flint.

'Nutty as a fruitcake,' he announced. 'That's his opinion. He's quite positive about it.'

'In that case he had no right to employ the sod,' said Flint. 'He should have sacked the brute.'

'Sacked him? From the Tech? You know they can't sack teachers. You've got to do something really drastic before they give you the boot.'

'Like murdering three people, I suppose. Well as far as I'm concerned they can have the little bastard back.'

'You mean he's still holding out?'

'Holding out? He's counterattacking. He's reduced me to a nervous wreck and now Bolton says he wants to be relieved. Can't stand the strain any longer.'

Sergeant Yates scratched his head. 'Beats me how he does it,' he said. 'Anyone would think he was innocent. I wonder when he'll start asking for a lawyer.'

'Never,' said Flint. 'What does he need a lawyer for? If I had a lawyer in there handing out advice I'd have got the truth out of Wilt hours ago.'

As night fell over Eel Creek the wind increased to Gale Force Eight. Rain hammered on the cabin roof, waves slapped against the hull and the cabin cruiser, listing to starboard, settled more firmly into the mud. Inside the cabin the air was thick with smoke and bad feelings. Gaskell had opened a bottle of vodka and was getting drunk. To pass the time they played Scrabble.

'My idea of hell,' said Gaskell, 'is to be huis closed with a couple of dykes.'

'What's a dyke?' said Eva.

Gaskell stared at her. 'You don't know?'

'I know the sort they have in Holland . . .'

'Yoga bear,' said Gaskell, 'you are the naïvest. A dyke is—'

'Forget it, G,' said Sally. 'Whose turn to play?'

'It's mine,' said Eva. 'I . . . M . . . P spells Imp.'

'O . . . T . . . E . . . N . . . T spells Gaskell,' said Sally.

Gaskell drank some more vodka. 'What the hell sort of game we supposed to be playing? Scrabble or some sort of Truth group?'

'Your turn,' said Sally.

Gaskell put D . . . I . . . L . . . D on the O. 'Try that for size.'

Eva looked at it critically.

'You can't use proper names,' she said. 'You wouldn't let me use Squezy.'

'Eva teats, dildo is not a proper name. It's an improper thing. A surrogate penis.'

'A what?'

'Never mind what it is,' said Sally. 'Your turn to play.' Eva studied her letters. She didn't like being told what to do so often and besides she still wanted to know what a dyke was. And a surrogate penis. In the end she put L . . . O . . . V on the E.

'Is a many-splendoured thing,' said Gaskell and put D . . . I . . . D on the L and O.

'You can't have two of them,' said Eva. 'You've got one Dildo already.'

'This one's different,' said Gaskell, 'it's got whiskers.'

'What difference does that make?'

'Ask Sally. She's the one with penis envy.'

'You asshole,' said Sally and put F . . . A . . . G . . . G . . . O on the T. 'Meaning you.'

'Like I said. Truth Scrabble,' said Gaskell. 'Trubble for short. So why don't we have an encounter group instead. Let the truth hang out like it is.'

Eva used the F to make Faithful. Gaskell followed with Hooker and Sally went Insane.

'Great,' said Gaskell, 'Alphabetical I Ching.'

'Wunderkind, you slay me,' said Sally.

'Go Zelda yourself,' said Gaskell and slid his hand up Eva's thigh.

'Keep your hands to yourself,' said Eva and pushed him away. She put S and N on the I. Gaskell made Butch with the B.

'And don't tell me it's a proper name.'

'Well it's certainly not a word I've heard,' said Eva.

Gaskell stared at her and then roared with laughter.

'Now I've heard it all,' he said. 'Like cunnilingus is a cough medicine. How dumb can you get?'

'Go look in the mirror,' said Sally.

'Oh sure. So I married a goddam lesbian whore who goes round stealing other people's wives and boats and things. I'm dumb. But boobs here beats me. She's so fucking hypocritical she pretends she's not a dyke ...'

'I don't know what a dyke is,' said Eva.

'Well let me inform you, fatso. A dyke is a lesbian.'

'Are you calling me a lesbian?' said Eva.

'Yes,' said Gaskell.

Eva slapped him across the face hard. Gaskell's glasses came off and he sat down on the floor.

'Now G ...' Sally began but Gaskell had scrambled to his feet.

'Right you fat bitch,' he said. 'You want the truth you're going to get it. First off, you think husband Henry got into that doll off his own bat, well let me tell you ...'

'Gaskell, you just shut up,' shouted Sally.

'Like hell I will. I've had about enough of you and your rotten little ways. I picked you out of a cathouse ...'

'That's not true. It was a clinic,' screamed Sally, 'a clinic for sick perverts like you.'

Eva wasn't listening. She was staring at Gaskell. He had called her a lesbian and had said Henry hadn't got into that doll of his own accord.

'Tell me about Henry,' she shouted. 'How did he get into that doll?'

Gaskell pointed at Sally. 'She put him there. That poor goof wouldn't know ...'

'You put him there?' Eva said to Sally. 'You did?'

'He tried to make me, Eva. He tried to—'

'I don't believe it,' Eva shouted. 'Henry isn't like that.'

'I tell you he did. He . . .'

'And you put him in that doll?' Eva screamed and launched herself across the table at Sally. There was a splintering sound and the table collapsed. Gaskell scudded sideways on to the bunk and Sally shot out of the cabin. Eva got to her feet and moved forward towards the door. She had been tricked, cheated and lied to. And Henry had been humiliated. She was going to kill that bitch Sally. She stepped out into the cockpit. On the far side Sally was a dark shadow. Eva went round the engine and lunged at her. The next moment she had slipped on the oily deck and Sally had darted across the cockpit and through the door into the cabin. She slammed the door behind her and locked it. Eva Wilt got to her feet and stood with the rain running down her face and as she stood there the illusions that had sustained her through the week disappeared. She saw herself as a fat, silly woman who had left her husband in pursuit of a glamour that was false and shoddy and founded on brittle talk and money. And Gaskell had said she was a lesbian. The full nausea of knowing what Touch Therapy had meant dawned on Eva. She staggered to the side of the boat and sat down on a locker.

And slowly her self-disgust turned back to anger, and a cold hatred of the Pringsheims. She would get her own back on them. They would be sorry they had ever met her. She got up and opened the locker and took out the lifejackets and threw them over the side. Then she blew up the airbed, dropped it into the water and climbed over herself. She let herself down into the water and lay on the airbed. It rocked alarmingly but Eva was not afraid. She was getting her revenge on the Pringsheims and she no longer cared what happened to her. She paddled off through the little waves pushing the lifejackets in front of her. The wind was behind her and the airbed moved easily. In five minutes she had turned the corner of the reeds and was out of sight of the cruiser. Somewhere in the darkness ahead there was the open water where they had seen the dinghies and beyond it land.

Presently she found herself being blown sideways into the reeds. The rain stopped and Eva lay panting on the airbed. It would be easier if she got rid of the lifejackets. She was far enough from the boat for them to be well hidden. She pushed them into the reeds and then hesitated. Perhaps she should keep one for herself. She disentangled a jacket from the bunch and managed to put it on. Then she lay face down on the airbed again and paddled forward down the widening channel.

Sally leant against the cabin door and looked at Gaskell with loathing.

'You stupid jerk,' she said. 'You had to open your big mouth. So what the hell are you going to do now?'

'Divorce you for a start,' said Gaskell.

'I'll alimony you for all the money you've got.'

'Fat chance. You won't get a red cent,' Gaskell said and drank some more vodka.

'I'll see you dead first,' said Sally.

Gaskell grinned. 'Me dead? Anyone's going to die round here, it's you. Booby baby is out for blood.'

'She'll cool off.'

'You think so? Try opening that door if you're so sure. Go on, unlock it.'

Sally moved away from the door and sat down.

'This time you've really bought yourself some trouble,' said Gaskell. 'You had to pick a goddam prizefighter.'

'You go out and pacify her,' said Sally.

'No way. I'd as soon play blind man's buff with a fucking rhinoceros.' He lay on the bunk and smiled happily. 'You know there's something really ironical about all this. You had to go and liberate a Neanderthal. Women's Lib for paleolithics. She Tarzan, you Jane. You've bought yourself a piece of zoo.'

'Very funny,' said Sally. 'And what's your role?'

'Me Noah. Just be thankful she hasn't got a gun.' He pulled a pillow up under his head and went to sleep.

Sally sat on staring at his back venomously. She was frightened. Eva's reaction had been so violent that it had destroyed her confidence in herself. Gaskell was right. There had been something primeval in Eva Wilt's behaviour. She shuddered at

145

the thought of that dark shape moving towards her in the cockpit. Sally got up and went into the galley and found a long sharp knife. Then she went back into the cabin and checked the lock on the door and lay down on her bunk and tried to sleep. But sleep wouldn't come. There were noises outside. Waves lapped against the side of the boat. The wind blew. God, what a mess it all was! Sally clutched her knife and thought about Gaskell and what he had said about divorce.

Peter Braintree sat in the office of Mr Gosdyke, Solicitor, and discussed the problem. 'He's been in there since Monday and it's Thursday now. Surely they've no right to keep him there so long without his seeing a solicitor.'

'If he doesn't ask for one and if the police want to question him and he is prepared to answer their questions and refuses to demand his legal rights I don't really see that there is anything I can do about it,' said Mr Gosdyke.

'But are you sure that that is the situation?' asked Braintree.

'As far as I can ascertain that is indeed the situation. Mr Wilt has not asked to see me. I spoke to the Inspector in charge, you heard me, and it seems quite clear that Mr Wilt appears, for some extraordinary reason, to be prepared to help the police with their enquiries just as long as they feel his presence at the Police Station is necessary. Now if a man refuses to assert his own legal rights then he has only himself to blame for his predicament.'

'But are you absolutely certain that Henry has refused to see you? I mean the police could be lying to you.'

Mr Gosdyke shook his head. 'I have known Inspector Flint for many years,' he said, 'and he is not the sort of man to deny a suspect his rights. No, I'm sorry, Mr Braintree. I would like to be of more assistance but frankly, in the circumstances, I can do nothing. Mr Wilt's predilection for the company of police officers is quite incomprehensible to me, but it disqualifies me from interfering.'

'You don't think they're giving him third degree or anything of that sort?'

'My dear fellow, third degree? You've been watching too

many old movies on the TV. The police don't use strong-arm methods in this country.'

'They've been pretty brutal with some of our students who have been on demos,' Braintree pointed out.

'Ah, but students are quite another matter and demonstrating students get what they deserve. Political provocation is one thing but domestic murders of the sort your friend Mr Wilt seems to have indulged in come into a different category altogether. I can honestly say that in all my years in the legal profession I have yet to come across a case in which the police did not treat a domestic murderer with great care and not a little sympathy. After all, they are nearly all married men themselves, and in any case Mr Wilt has a degree and that always helps. If you are a professional man, and in spite of what some people may say lecturers in Technical Colleges are members of a profession if only marginally, then you can rest assured that the police will do nothing in the least untoward. Mr Wilt is perfectly safe.'

And Wilt felt safe. He sat in the Interview Room and contemplated Inspector Flint with interest.

'Motivation? Now there's an interesting question,' he said. 'If you had asked me why I married Eva in the first place I'd have some trouble trying to explain myself. I was young at the time and ...'

'Wilt,' said the Inspector, 'I didn't ask you why you married your wife. I asked you why you decided to murder her.'

'I didn't decide to murder her,' said Wilt.

'It was a spontaneous action? A momentary impulse you couldn't resist? An act of madness you now regret?'

'It was none of those things. In the first place it was not an act. It was mere fantasy.'

'But you do admit that the thought crossed your mind?'

'Inspector,' said Wilt, 'if I acted upon every impulse that crossed my mind I would have been convicted of child rape, buggery, burglary, assault with intent to commit grievous bodily harm and mass murder long ago.'

'All those impulses crossed your mind?'

'At some time or other, yes,' said Wilt.

'You've got a bloody odd mind.'

'Which is something I share with the vast majority of mankind. I daresay that even you in your odd contemplative moments have ...'

'Wilt,' said the Inspector, 'I don't have odd contemplative moments. Not until I met you anyhow. Now then, you admit you thought of killing your wife ...'

'I said the notion had crossed my mind, particularly when I have to take the dog for a walk. It is a game I play with myself. No more than that.'

'A game? You take the dog for a walk and think of ways and means of killing Mrs Wilt? I don't call that a game. I call it premeditation.'

'Not badly put,' said Wilt with a smile, 'the meditation bit. Eva curls up in the lotus position on the living-room rug and thinks beautiful thoughts. I take the bloody dog for a walk and think dreadful ones while Clem defecates on the grass verge in Grenville Gardens. And in each case the end result is just the same. Eva gets up and cooks supper and washes up and I come home and watch the box or read and go to bed. Nothing has altered one way or another.'

'It has now,' said the Inspector. 'Your wife has disappeared off the face of the earth together with a brilliant young scientist and his wife, and you are sitting here waiting to be charged with their murder.'

'Which I don't happen to have committed,' said Wilt. 'Ah well, these things happen. The moving finger writes and having writ ...'

'Fuck the moving finger. Where are they? Where did you put them? You're going to tell me.'

Wilt sighed. 'I wish I could,' he said, 'I really do. Now you've got that plastic doll ...'

'No we haven't. Not by a long chalk. We're still going down through solid rock. We won't get whatever is down there until tomorrow at the earliest.'

'Something to look forward to,' said Wilt. 'Then I suppose you'll let me go.'

'Like hell I will. I'll have you up for remand on Monday.'

'Without any evidence of murder? Without a body? You can't do that.'

Inspector Flint smiled. 'Wilt,' he said, 'I've got news for you. We don't need a body. We can hold you on suspicion, we can bring you up for trial and we can find you guilty without a body. You may be clever but you don't know your law.'

'Well I must say you fellows have an easy job of it. You mean you can go out in the street and pick up some perfectly innocent passer-by and lug him in here and charge him with murder without any evidence at all?'

'Evidence? We've got evidence all right. We've got a blood-spattered bathroom with a busted-down door. We've got an empty house in a filthy mess and we've got some bloody thing or other down that pile hole and you think we haven't got evidence. You've got it wrong.'

'Makes two of us,' said Wilt.

'And I'll tell you another thing, Wilt. The trouble with bastards like you is that you're too clever by half. You overdo things and you give yourselves away. Now if I'd been in your shoes, I'd have done two things. Know what they are?'

'No,' said Wilt. 'I don't.'

'I'd have washed that bathroom down, number one, and number two I'd have stayed away from that hole. I wouldn't have tried to lay a false trail with notes and making sure the caretaker saw you and turning up at Mr Braintree's house at midnight covered in mud. I'd have sat tight and said nothing.'

'But I didn't know about those bloodstains in the bathroom and if it hadn't been for that filthy doll I wouldn't have dumped the thing down the hole. I'd have gone to bed. Instead of which I got pissed and acted like an idiot.'

'Let me tell you something else, Wilt,' said the Inspector. 'You *are* an idiot, a fucking cunning idiot but an idiot all the same. You need your head read.'

'It would make a change from this lot,' said Wilt.

'What would?'

'Having my head read instead of sitting here and being insulted.'

Inspector Flint studied him thoughtfully. 'You mean that?' he asked.

'Mean what?'

'About having your head read? Would you be prepared to undergo an examination by a qualified psychiatrist?'

'Why not?' said Wilt. 'Anything to help pass the time.'

'Quite voluntarily, you understand. Nobody is forcing you to, but if you want . . .'

'Listen, Inspector, if seeing a psychiatrist will help to convince you that I have not murdered my wife I'll be only too happy to. You can put me on a lie detector. You can pump me full of truth drugs. You can . . .'

'There's no need for any of that other stuff,' said Flint, and stood up. 'A good shrink will do very nicely. And if you think you can get away with guilty but insane, forget it. These blokes know when you're malingering madness.' He went to the door and paused. Then he came back and leant across the table.

'Tell me, Wilt,' he said. 'Tell me just one thing. How come you sit there so coolly? Your wife is missing, we have evidence of murder, we have a replica of her, if you are to be believed, under thirty feet of concrete and you don't turn a hair. How do you do it?'

'Inspector,' said Wilt. 'If you had taught Gasfitters for ten years and been asked as many damnfool questions in that time as I have, you'd know. Besides you haven't met Eva. When you do you'll see why I'm not worried. Eva is perfectly capable of taking care of herself. She may not be bright but she's got a built-in survival kit.'

'Jesus, Wilt, with you around for twelve years she must have had something.'

'Oh she has. You'll like Eva when you meet her. You'll get along like a house on fire. You've both got literal minds and an obsession with trivia. You can take a wormcast and turn it into Mount Everest.'

'Wormcast? Wilt, you sicken me,' said the Inspector, and left the room.

Wilt got up and walked up and down. He was tired of sitting down. On the other hand he was well satisfied with his performance. He had surpassed himself and he took pride in the fact that he was reacting so well to what most people would consider an appalling predicament. But to Wilt it was something else, a challenge, the first real challenge he had had to meet for a long time. Gasfitters and Plasterers had challenged him once but he had learnt to cope with them. You jollied them along. Let them talk, ask questions, divert them, get them going, accept their red herrings and hand out a few of your own, but above all you had to refuse to accept their preconceptions. Whenever they asserted something with absolute conviction as a self-evident truth like all wogs began at Calais, all you had to do was agree and then point out that half the great men in English history had been foreigners like Marconi or Lord Beaverbrook and that even Churchill's mother had been a Yank or talk about the Welsh being the original Englishmen and the Vikings and the Danes and from that lead them off through Indian doctors to the National Health Service and birth control and any other topic under the sun that would keep them quiet and puzzled and desperately trying to think of some ultimate argument that would prove you wrong.

Inspector Flint was no different. He was more obsessive but his tactics were just the same. And besides he had got hold of the wrong end of the stick with a vengeance and it amused Wilt to watch him trying to pin a crime on him he hadn't committed. It made him feel almost important and certainly more of a man than he had done for a long, long time. He was innocent and there was no question about it. In a world where everything else was doubtful and uncertain and open to scepticism the fact of his innocence was sure. For the first time in his adult life Wilt knew himself to be absolutely right, and the knowledge gave him a strength he had never supposed he possessed. And besides there was no question in his mind that Eva would turn up eventually, safe and sound, and more than a little subdued when she realized what her impulsiveness had led to. Serve her right for giving him that disgusting doll. She'd regret that to the end of her days. Yes, if anybody was going to come off badly in this affair it was dear old Eva with her bossiness and her busyness. She'd have a job explaining it to Mavis Mottram and the neighbours. Wilt smiled to himself at the thought. And even the Tech would have to treat him differently in future and with a new respect. Wilt knew the liberal conscience too well not to suppose that he would appear anything less than a martyr when he went back. And a hero. They would bend over backwards to convince themselves that they hadn't thought him as guilty as hell. He'd get promotion too, not for being a good teacher but because they would need to salve their fragile consciences. Talk about killing the fatted calf.

14

At the Tech there was no question of killing the fatted calf, at least not for Henry Wilt. The imminence of the CNAA visitation on Friday, coinciding as it apparently would with the resurrection of the late Mrs Wilt, was causing something approaching panic. The Course Board met in almost continuous session and memoranda circulated so furiously that it was impossible to read one before the next arrived.

'Can't we postpone the visit?' Dr Cox asked. 'I can't have them in my office discussing bibliographies with bits of Mrs Wilt being dug out of the ground outside the window.'

'I have asked the police to make themselves as inconspicuous as possible,' said Dr Mayfield.

'With conspicuous lack of success so far,' said Dr Board. 'They couldn't be more in evidence. There are ten of them peering down that hole at this very moment.'

The Vice-Principal struck a brighter note. 'You'll be glad to hear that we've managed to restore power to the canteen,' he told the meeting, 'so we should be able to lay on a good lunch.'

'I just hope I feel up to eating,' said Dr Cox. 'The shocks of the last few days have done nothing to improve my appetite and when I think of poor Mrs Wilt . . .'

'Try not to think of her,' said the Vice-Principal, but Dr Cox shook his head.

'You try not to think of her with a damned great boring machine grinding away outside your office window all day.'

'Talking about shocks,' said Dr Board, 'I still can't understand how the driver of that mechanical corkscrew managed to escape electrocution when they cut through the power cable.'

'Considering the problems we are faced with, I hardly think that's a relevant point just at present,' said Dr Mayfield. 'What we have got to stress to the members of the CNAA committee is that this degree is an integrated course with a fundamental substructure grounded thematically on a concomitance of cultural and sociological factors in no way unsuperficially disparate and with a solid quota of academic content to give students an intellectual and cerebral . . .'

'Haemorrhage?' suggested Dr Board.

Dr Mayfield regarded him balefully. 'I really do think this is no time for flippancy,' he said angrily. 'Either we are committed to the Joint Honours degree or we are not. Furthermore we have only until tomorrow to structure our tactical approach to the visitation committee. Now, which is it to be?'

'Which is what to be?' asked Dr Board. 'What has our commitment or lack of it to do with structuring, for want of several far better words, our so-called tactical approach to a committee which, since it is coming all the way from London to us and not vice versa, is presumably approaching us?'

'Vice-Principal,' said Dr Mayfield, 'I really must protest. Dr Board's attitude at this late stage in the game is quite incomprehensible. If Dr Board . . .'

'Could even begin to understand one tenth of the jargon Dr Mayfield seems to suppose is English he might be in a better position to express his opinion,' interrupted Dr Board. 'As it is, "incomprehensible" applies to Dr Mayfield's syntax, not to my attitude. I have always maintained . . .'

'Gentlemen,' said the Vice-Principal, 'I think it would be best if we avoided inter-departmental wrangles at this point in time and got down to business.'

There was a silence broken finally by Dr Cox. 'Do you think the police could be persuaded to erect a screen round that hole?' he asked.

'I shall certainly suggest that to them,' said Dr Mayfield. They passed on to the matter of entertainment.

'I have arranged for there to be plenty of drinks before lunch,' said the Vice-Principal, 'and in any case lunch will be judiciously delayed to allow them to get into the right mood so the afternoon sessions should be cut short and proceed, hopefully, more smoothly.'

'Just so long as the Catering Department doesn't serve Toad in the Hole,' said Dr Board.

The meeting broke up acrimoniously.

So did Mr Morris's encounter with the Crime Reporter of the *Sunday Post*.

'Of course I didn't tell the police that I employed homicidal maniacs as a matter of policy,' he shouted at the reporter. 'And in any case what I said was, as I understood it, to be treated in the strictest confidence.'

'But you did say you thought Wilt was insane and that quite a number of Liberal Studies lecturers were off their heads?'

Mr Morris looked at the man with loathing. 'To put the record straight, what I said was that some of them were ...'

'Off their rockers?' suggested the reporter.

'No, not off their rockers,' shouted Mr Morris. 'Merely, well, shall we say, slightly unbalanced.'

'That's not what the police say you said. They say quote ...'

'I don't care what the police say I said. I know what I said and what I didn't and if you're implying ...'

'I'm not implying anything. You made a statement that half your staff are nuts and I'm trying to verify it.'

'Verify it?' snarled Mr Morris. 'You put words into my mouth I never said and you call that verifying it?'

'Did you say it or not? That's all I'm asking. I mean if you express an opinion about your staff ...'

'Mr MacArthur, what I think about my staff is my own affair. It has absolutely nothing to do with you or the rag you represent.'

'Three million people will be interested to read your opinion on Sunday morning,' said Mr MacArthur, 'and I wouldn't be at all surprised if this Wilt character didn't sue you if he ever gets out of the copshop.'

'Sue me? What the hell could he sue me for?'

'Calling him a homicidal maniac for a start. Banner headlines HEAD OF LIBERAL STUDIES CALLS LECTURER HOMICIDAL MANIAC should be good for fifty thousand. I'd be surprised if he got less.'

Mr Morris contemplated destitution. 'Even your paper would never print that,' he muttered. 'I mean Wilt would sue you too.'

'Oh we're used to libel actions. They're run-of-the-mill for us. We pay for them out of petty cash. Now if you'd be a bit more cooperative . . .' He left the suggestion in mid-air for Mr Morris to digest.

'What do you want to know?' he asked miserably.

'Got any juicy drug scene stories for us?' asked Mr MacArthur. 'You know the sort of thing. LOVE ORGIES IN LECTURES. That always gets the public. Teenyboppers having it off and all that. Give us a good one and we'll let you off the hook about Wilt.'

'Get out of my office!' yelled Mr Morris.

Mr MacArthur got up. 'You're going to regret this,' he said and went downstairs to the students' canteen to dig up some dirt on Mr Morris.

'Not tests,' said Wilt adamantly. 'They're deceptive.'

'You think so?' said Dr Pittman, consultant psychiatrist at the Fenland Hospital and professor of Criminal Psychology at the University. Being plagiocephalic didn't help either.

'I should have thought it was obvious,' said Wilt. 'You show me an ink-blot and I think it looks like my grandmother lying in a pool of blood, do you honestly think I'm going to be fool enough to say so? I'd be daft to do that. So I say a butterfly sitting on a geranium. And every time it's the same. I think what it does look like and then say something completely different. Where does that get you?'

'It is still possible to infer something from that,' said Dr Pittman.

'Well, you don't need a bloody ink-blot to infer, do you?'

said Wilt. Dr Pittman made a note of Wilt's interest in blood. 'You can infer things from just looking at the shape of people's heads.'

Dr Pittman polished his glasses grimly. Heads were not things he liked inferences to be drawn from. 'Mr Wilt,' he said, 'I am here at your request to ascertain your sanity and in particular to give an opinion as to whether or not I consider you capable of murdering your wife and disposing of her body in a singularly revolting and callous fashion. I shall not allow anything you may say to influence my ultimate and objective findings.'

Wilt looked perplexed. 'I must say you're not giving yourself much room for manoeuvre. Since we've dispensed with mechanical aids like tests I should have thought what I had to say would be the only thing you could go on. Unless of course you're going to read the bumps on my head. Isn't that a bit old-fashioned?'

'Mr Wilt,' said Dr Pittman, 'the fact that you clearly have a sadistic streak and take pleasure in drawing attention to other people's physical infirmities in no way disposes me to conclude you are capable of murder ...'

'Very decent of you,' said Wilt, 'though frankly I'd have thought anyone was capable of murder given the right, or to be precise the wrong, circumstances.'

Dr Pittman stifled the impulse to say how right he was. Instead he smiled prognathously. 'Would you say you were a rational man, Henry?' he asked.

Wilt frowned. 'Just stick to Mr Wilt if you don't mind. This may not be a paid consultation but I prefer a little formality.'

Dr Pittman's smile vanished. 'You haven't answered my question.'

'No, I wouldn't say I was a rational man,' said Wilt.

'An irrational one perhaps?'

'Neither the one wholly nor the other wholly. Just a man.'

'And a man is neither one thing nor the other?'

'Dr Pittman, this is your province not mine but in my opinion man is capable of reasoning but not of acting within wholly rational limits. Man is an animal, a developed animal, though come to think of it all animals are developed if we are to believe Darwin. Let's just say man is a domesticated animal with elements of wildness about him ...'

'And what sort of animal are you, Mr Wilt?' said Dr Pittman. 'A domesticated animal or a wild one?'

'Here we go again. These splendidly simple dual categories that seem to obsess the modern mind. Either/Or Kierkegaard as that bitch Sally Pringsheim would say. No, I am not wholly domesticated. Ask my wife. She'll express an opinion on the matter.'

'In what respect are you undomesticated?'

'I fart in bed, Dr Pittman. I like to fart in bed. It is the trumpet call of the anthropoid ape in me asserting its territorial imperative in the only way possible.'

'In the only way possible?'

'You haven't met Eva,' said Wilt. 'When you do you'll see that assertion is her forte not mine.'

'You feel dominated by Mrs Wilt?'

'I *am* dominated by Mrs Wilt.'

'She bullies you? She assumes the dominant role?'

'Eva is, Dr Pittman. She doesn't have to assume anything. She just is.'

'Is what?'

'Now there's the rub,' said Wilt. 'What's today? You lose track of time in this place.'

'Thursday.'

'Well, today being Thursday, Eva is Bernard Leach.'

'Bernard Leach?'

'The potter, Dr Pittman, the famous potter,' said Wilt. 'Now tomorrow she'll be Margot Fonteyn and on Saturday we play bridge with the Mottrams so she'll be Omar Sharif. On Sunday she's Elizabeth Taylor or Edna O'Brien depending on what the Colour Supplements have in store for me and in the afternoon we go for a drive and she's Eva Wilt. It's about the only time in the week I meet her and that's because I'm driving and she's got nothing to do but sit still and nag the pants off me.'

'I begin to see the pattern,' said Dr Pittman. 'Mrs Wilt was ... is given to role-playing. This made for an unstable relationship in which you couldn't establish a distinctive and assertive role as a husband ...'

'Dr Pittman,' said Wilt, 'a gyroscope may, indeed must, spin but in doing so it achieves a stability that is virtually unequalled. Now if you understand the principle of the gyroscope you may begin to understand that our marriage does not lack stability. It may be damned uncomfortable coming home to a centrifugal force but it bloody well isn't unstable.'

'But just now you told me that Mrs Wilt did not assume a dominant role. Now you tell me she is a forceful character.'

'Eva is not forceful. She is a force. There's a difference. And as for character, she has so many and they're so varied it's difficult to keep up with them all. Let's just say she throws herself into whoever she is with an urgency and compulsiveness that is not always appropriate. You remember that series of Garbo pictures they showed on TV some years back? Well, Eva was La Dame Aux Camélias for three days after that and she made dying of TB look like St Vitus' dance. Talk about galloping consumption.'

'I begin to get the picture,' said Dr Pittman making a note that Wilt was a pathological liar with sado-masochistic tendencies.

'I'm glad somebody does,' said Wilt. 'Inspector Flint thinks I murdered her and the Pringsheims in some sort of bloodlust and disposed of their bodies in some extraordinary fashion. He mentioned acid. I mean it's crazy. Where on earth does one get nitric acid in the quantities necessary to dissolve three dead bodies, and one of them overweight at that? I mean it doesn't bear thinking about.'

'It certainly doesn't,' said Dr Pittman.

'In any case do I look like a murderer?' continued Wilt cheerfully. 'Of course I don't. Now if he'd said Eva had slaughtered the brutes, and in my opinion someone should have done years ago, I'd have taken him seriously. God help the poor sods who happen to be around when Eva takes it into her head she's Lizzie Borden.'

Dr Pittman studied him predaciously.

'Are you suggesting that Dr and Mrs Pringsheim were murdered by your wife?' he asked. 'Is that what you're saying?'

'No,' said Wilt, 'I am not. All I'm saying is that when Eva does things she does them wholeheartedly. When she cleans the house she cleans it. Let me tell you about the Harpic. She's got this thing about germs ...'

'Mr Wilt,' said Dr Pittman hastily, 'I am not interested in what Mrs Wilt does with the Harpic. I have come here to understand you. Now then, do you make a habit of copulating with a plastic doll? Is this a regular occurrence?'

'Regular?' said Wilt. 'Do you mean a normal occurrence or a recurring one? Now your notion of what constitutes a normal occurrence may differ from mine ...'

'I mean, do you do it often?' interrupted Dr Pittman.

'Do it?' said Wilt. 'I don't do it at all.'

'But I understood you to have placed particular emphasis on the fact that this doll had a vagina?'

'Emphasis? I didn't have to emphasize the fact. The beastly thing was plainly visible.'

'You find vaginas beastly?' said Dr Pittman stalking his prey into the more familiar territory of sexual aberration.

'Taken out of context, yes,' said Wilt sidestepping, 'and with plastic ones you can leave them in context and I still find them nauseating.'

By the time Dr Pittman had finished the interview he was uncertain what to think. He got up wearily and made for the door.

'You've forgotten your hat, doctor,' said Wilt holding it out to him. 'Pardon my asking but do you have them specially made for you?'

'Well?' said Inspector Flint when Dr Pittman came into his office. 'What's the verdict?'

'Verdict? That man should be put away for life.'

'You mean he's a homicidal maniac?'

'I mean that no matter how he killed her Mrs Wilt must have been thankful to go. Twelve years married to that man ... Good God, it doesn't bear thinking about.'

'Well, that doesn't get us much forrader,' said the Inspector, when the psychiatrist had left having expressed the opinion that while Wilt had the mind of an intellectual jackrabbit he couldn't in all honesty say that he was criminally insane. 'We'll just have to see what turns up tomorrow.'

15

What turned up on Friday was seen not only by Inspector Flint, Sergeant Yates, twelve other policemen, Barney and half a dozen construction workers, but several hundred Tech students standing on the steps of the Science block, most of the staff and by all eight members of the CNAA visitation committee who had a particularly good view from the windows of the mock hotel lounge used by the Catering Department to train waiters and to entertain distinguished guests. Dr Mayfield did his best to distract their attention.

'We have structured the foundation course to maximize student interest,' he told Professor Baxendale, who headed the committee, but the professor was not to be diverted. His interest was maximized by what was being unstructured from the foundations of the new Admin block.

'How absolutely appalling,' he muttered as Judy protruded from the hole. Contrary to Wilt's hopes and expectations she had not burst. The liquid concrete had sealed her in too well for that and if in life she had resembled in many particulars a real live woman, in death she had all the attributes of a real dead one. As the corpse of a murdered woman she was entirely convincing. Her wig was matted and secured to her head at an awful angle by the concrete. Her clothes clung to her and cement to them while her legs had evidently been contorted to the point of mutilation and her outstretched arm had, as Barney had foretold, a desperate appeal about it that was most affecting. It also made it exceedingly difficult to extricate her from the hole. The legs didn't help, added to which the concrete had given her a substance and stature approximate to that of Eva Wilt.

160

'I suppose that's what they mean by rigor mortice,' said Dr Board, as Dr Mayfield desperately tried to steer the conversation back to the Joint Honours degree.

'Dear Lord,' muttered Professor Baxendale. Judy had eluded the efforts of Barney and his men and had slumped back down the hole. 'To think what she must have suffered. Did you see that damned hand?'

Dr Mayfield had. He shuddered. Behind him Dr Board sniggered. 'There's a divinity that shapes our ends, rough-hew them how we will,' he said gaily. 'At least Wilt has saved himself the cost of a gravestone. All they'll have to do is prop her up with Here Stands Eva Wilt, Born So and So, Murdered last Saturday carved across her chest. In life monumental, in death a monument.'

'I must say, Board,' said Dr Mayfield, 'I find your sense of humour singularly ill-timed.'

'Well they'll never be able to cremate her, that's for certain,' continued Dr Board. 'And the undertaker who can fit that little lot into a coffin will be nothing short of a genius. I suppose they could always take a sledgehammer to her.'

In the corner Dr Cox fainted.

'I think I'll have another whisky if you don't mind,' said Professor Baxendale weakly. Dr Mayfield poured him a double. When he turned back to the window Judy was protruding once more from the hole.

'The thing about embalming,' said Dr Board, 'is that it costs so much. Now I'm not saying that thing out there is a perfect likeness of Eva Wilt as I remember her ...'

'For heaven's sake, do you have to go on about it?' snarled Dr Mayfield, but Dr Board was not to be stopped. 'Quite apart from the legs there seems to be something odd about the breasts. I know Mrs Wilt's were large but they do seem to have inflated. Probably due to the gases. They putrefy, you know, which would account for it.'

By the time the committee went into lunch they had lost all appetite for food and most of them were drunk.

Inspector Flint was less fortunate. He didn't like being present at exhumations at the best of times and particularly when the corpse on whose behalf he was acting showed such a marked inclination to go back where she came from. Besides he was in two minds whether it was a corpse or not. It looked like a corpse and it certainly behaved like a corpse, albeit a very heavy one, but there was something about the knees that suggested that all was not anatomically as it should have been with whatever it was they had dug up. There was a double jointedness and a certain lack of substance where the legs stuck forwards at right angles that seemed to indicate that Mrs Wilt had lost not only her life but both kneecaps as well. It was this mangled quality that made Barney's job so difficult and exceedingly distasteful. After the body had dropped down the hole for the fourth time Barney went down himself to assist from below.

'If you sods drop her,' he shouted from the depths, 'you'll have two dead bodies down here so hang on to that rope whatever happens. I'm going to tie it round her neck.'

Inspector Flint peered down the shaft. 'You'll do no such thing,' he shouted, 'we don't want her decapitated. We need her all in one piece.'

'She is all in one bloody piece,' came Barney's muffled reply, 'that's one thing you don't have to worry about.'

'Can't you tie the rope around something else?'

'Well I could,' Barney conceded, 'but I'm not going to. A leg is more likely to come off than her head and I'm not going to be underneath her when it goes.'

'All right,' said the Inspector, 'I just hope you know what you're doing, that's all.'

'I'll tell you one thing. The sod who put her down here knew what he was doing and no mistake.'

But this fifth attempt failed, like the previous four, and Judy was lowered into the depths where she rested heavily on Barney's foot.

'Go and get that bloody crane,' he shouted. 'I can't stand much more of this.'

'Nor can I,' muttered the Inspector, who still couldn't make up his mind what it was he was supposed to be disinterring; a doll dressed up to look like Mrs Wilt or Mrs Wilt dressed up to look like something some demented sculptor forgot to finish. What few doubts he had had about Wilt's sanity had been entirely dispelled by what he was presently witnessing. Any man who could go to the awful lengths Wilt had gone to render, and the word was entirely apposite whichever way you took it, either his wife or a plastic doll with a vagina, both inaccessible and horribly mutilated, must be insane.

Sergeant Yates put his thoughts into words. 'You're not going to tell me now that the bastard isn't off his rocker,' he said, as the crane was moved into position and the rope lowered and attached to Judy's neck.

'All right, now take her away,' shouted Barney.

In the dining-room only Dr Board was enjoying his lunch. The eight members of the CNAA committee weren't. Their eyes were glued to the scene below.

'I suppose it could be said she was *in statue pupillari*,' said Dr Board, helping himself to some more Lemon Meringue, 'in which case we stand *in loco parentis*. Not a pleasant thought, gentlemen. Not that she was ever a very bright student. I once had her for an Evening Class in French literature. I don't know what she got out of *Fleurs du Mal* but I do remember thinking that Baudelaire ...'

'Dr Board,' said Dr Mayfield drunkenly, 'for a so-called cultured man you are entirely without feeling.'

'Something I share with the late Mrs Wilt, by the look of things,' said Dr Board, glancing out of the window, 'and while we are still on the subject, things seem to be coming to a head. They do indeed.'

Even Dr Cox, recently revived and coaxed into having some mutton, looked out of the window. As the crane slowly winched Judy into view the Course Board and the Committee rose and went to watch. It was an unedifying sight. Near the top of the shaft Judy's left leg caught in a crevice while her outstretched arm embedded itself in the clay.

'Hold it,' shouted Barney indistinctly, but it was too late.

Unnerved by the nature of his load or in the mistaken belief that he had been told to lift harder, the crane driver hoisted away. There was a ghastly cracking sound as the noose tightened and the next moment Judy's concrete head, capped by Eva Wilt's wig, looked as if it was about to fulfil Inspector Flint's prediction that she would be decapitated. In the event he need not have worried. Judy was made of sterner stuff than might have been expected. As the head continued to rise and the body to remain firmly embedded in the shaft Judy's neck rose to the occasion. It stretched.

'Dear God,' said Professor Baxendale frantically, 'will it never end?'

Dr Board studied the phenomenon with increasing interest. 'It doesn't look like it,' he said. 'Mind you we do make a point of stretching our students, eh Mayfield?'

But Dr Mayfield made no response. As Judy took on the configuration of an ostrich that had absentmindedly buried its head in a pail of cement he knew that the Joint Honours degree was doomed.

'I'll say this for Mrs Wilt,' said Dr Board, 'she do hold on. No one could call her stiff-necked. Attenuated possibly. One begins to see what Modigliani was getting at.'

'For God's sake stop,' yelled Dr Cox hysterically, 'I think I'm going off my head.'

'Which is more than can be said for Mrs Wilt,' said Dr Board callously.

He was interrupted by another awful crack as Judy's body finally gave up the struggle with the shaft. With a shower of clay it careered upwards to resume a closer relationship with the head and hung naked, pink and, now that the clothes and the concrete had been removed, remarkably lifelike at the end of the rope some twenty feet above the ground.

'I must say,' said Dr Board, studying the vulva with relish, 'I've never had much sympathy with necrophilia before but I do begin to see its attractions now. Of course it's only of historical interest but in Elizabethan times it was one of the perks of an executioner ...'

'Board,' screamed Dr Mayfield, 'I've known some fucking swine in my time ...'

Dr Board helped himself to some more coffee. 'I believe the slang term for it is liking your meat cold.'

Underneath the crane Inspector Flint wiped the mud from his face and peered up at the awful object swinging above him. He could see now that it was only a doll. He could also see why Wilt had wanted to bury the beastly thing.

'Get it down. For God's sake get it down,' he bawled, as the press photographers circled round him. But the crane driver had lost his nerve. He shut his eyes, pulled the wrong lever and Judy began a further ascent.

'Stop it, stop it, that's fucking evidence,' screamed the Inspector, but it was already too late. As the rope wound through the final pulley Judy followed. The concrete cap disintegrated, her head slid between the rollers and her body began to swell. Her legs were the first to be affected.

'I've often wondered what elephantiasis looked like,' said Dr Board. 'Shelley had a phobia about it, I believe.'

Dr Cox certainly had. He was gibbering in a corner and the Vice-Principal was urging him to pull himself together.

'An apt expression,' observed Dr Board, above the gasps of horror as Judy, now clearly twelve months pregnant, continued her transformation. 'Early Minoan, wouldn't you say, Mayfield?'

But Dr Mayfield was past speech. He was staring dementedly at a rapidly expanding vagina some fourteen inches long and eight wide. There was a pop and the thing became a penis, an enormous penis that swelled and swelled. He was going mad. He knew he was.

'Now that,' said Dr Board, 'takes some beating. I've heard about sex-change operations for men but ...'

'Beating?' screamed Dr Mayfield, 'Beating? You can stand there cold-bloodedly and talk about ...'

There was a loud bang. Judy had come to the end of her tether. So had Dr Mayfield. The penis was the first thing to go. Dr Mayfield the second. As Judy deflated he hurled himself at Dr Board only to sink to the ground gibbering.

Dr Board ignored his colleague. 'Who would have thought the old bag had so much wind in her?' he murmured, and finished his coffee. As Dr Mayfield was led out by the Vice-Principal, Dr Board turned to Professor Baxendale.

'I must apologize for Mayfield,' he said, 'I'm afraid this Joint Honours degree has been too much for him and to tell the truth I have always found him to be fundamentally unsound. A case of dementia post Cox I daresay.'

Inspector Flint drove back to the Police Station in a state bordering on lunacy.

'We've been made to look idiots,' he snarled at Sergeant Yates. 'You saw them laughing. You heard the bastards.' He was particularly incensed by the press photographers who had asked him to pose with the limp remnants of the plastic doll. 'We've been held up to public ridicule. Well, my God, somebody's going to pay.'

He hurled himself out of the car and lunged down the passage to the Interview Room. 'Right, Wilt,' he shouted, 'you've had your little joke and a bloody nasty one it was too. So now we're going to forget the niceties and get to the bottom of this business.'

Wilt studied the torn piece of plastic. 'Looks better like that if you ask me,' he said. 'More natural if you know what I mean.'

'You'll look bloody natural if you don't answer my questions,' yelled the Inspector. 'Where is she?'

'Where is who?' said Wilt.

'Mrs Fucking Wilt. Where did you put her?'

'I've told you. I didn't put her anywhere.'

'And I'm telling you you did. Now either you're going to tell me where she is or I'm going to beat it out of you.'

'You can beat me up if you like,' said Wilt, 'but it won't do you any good.'

'Oh yes it will,' said the Inspector and took off his coat.

'I demand to see a solicitor,' said Wilt hastily.

Inspector Flint put his jacket on again. 'I've been waiting to hear you say that. Henry Wilt, I hereby charge you with . . .'

16

In the reeds Eva greeted the dawn of another day by blowing up the airbed for the tenth time. It had either sprung a leak or developed a fault in the valve. Whichever it was it had made her progress exceedingly slow and had finally forced her to take refuge in the reeds away from the channel. Here, wedged between the stems, she had spent a muddy night getting off the airbed to blow it up and getting back on to try and wash off the sludge and weeds that had adhered to her when she got off. In the process she had lost the bottom half of her lemon loungers and had torn the top half so that by dawn she resembled less the obsessive housewife of 34 Parkview Avenue than a finalist in the heavyweight division of the Ladies Mud-wrestling Championship. In addition she was exceedingly cold and was glad when the sun came up bringing with it the promise of a hot summer day. All she had to do now was to find her way to land or open water and get someone to ... At this point Eva became aware that her appearance was likely to cause some embarrassment. The lemon loungers had been sufficiently outré to make her avoid walking down the street when she had had them on; with them largely off she certainly didn't want to be seen in public. On the other hand she couldn't stay in the reeds all day. She plunged on, dragging the airbed behind her, half swimming but for the most part trudging through mud and water. At last she came out of the reeds into open water and found herself looking across a stretch to a house, a garden that sloped down to the water's edge, and a church. It seemed a long way across but there was no boat in sight. She would have to swim across and just hope that the woman who lived there was sympathetic and better still large enough to lend her some clothes until she got home. It was at this point that Eva discovered that she had left her handbag somewhere in the reeds. She remembered having it during the night but it must have fallen off the airbed when she was blowing it up. Well she couldn't go back and look for it now. She would just have to go on without it and ring Henry up and tell him to come out in the car and get her. He could bring some clothes too. Yes, that was it. Eva Wilt climbed on to the airbed and began to paddle across. Halfway over the airbed went down for the eleventh time. Eva abandoned it and struggled on in the lifejacket. But that too impeded her progress and she finally decided to take it off. She trod water and tried to undo it and after a struggle managed to get it off. In the process the rest of the lemon loungers disintegrated so that by the time she reached the bank Eva Wilt was exhausted and quite naked. She crawled into the cover of a willow tree and lay panting on the ground. When she had recovered she stood up and looked around. She was at the bottom of the garden and the house was a hundred yards away up the hill. It was a very large house by Eva's standards, and not the sort she would feel at home in at the best of times. For one thing it appeared to have a courtyard with stables at the back and to Eva, whose knowledge of large country houses was confined to what she had seen on TV, there was the suggestion of servants, gentility and a social formality that would make her arrival in the nude rather heavy going. On the other hand the whole place looked decidedly run down. The garden was overgrown and unkempt; ornamental bushes which might once have been trimmed to look like birds and animals had reverted to strange and vaguely monstrous shapes; rusted hoops leant half-hidden in the grass of an untended croquet lawn; a tennis net sagged between posts and an abandoned greenhouse boasted a few panes of lichened glass. Finally there was a dilapidated boathouse and a rowing boat. All in all the domain had a sinister and imposing air to it which wasn't helped by the presence of a small church hidden among trees to the left and a neglected graveyard beyond an old iron fence. Eva peered out from the weeping willow and was about to leave its cover when the French windows opened and a man came out on to the terrace with a pair of binoculars and peered through them in the direction of Eel Stretch. He was wearing a black cassock and a dog collar. Eva went back behind the tree and considered the awkwardness of her situation and lack of attire. It was all extremely embarrassing. Nothing on earth would make her go up to the house,

the Vicarage, with nothing on. Parkview Avenue hadn't prepared her for situations of this sort.

Rossiter Grove hadn't prepared Gaskell for the situation he
found when Sally woke him with 'Noah baby, it's drywise top-
side. Time to fly the coop.'

He opened the cabin door and stepped outside to discover
that Eva had already flown and had taken the airbed and the
lifejackets with her.

'You mean you left her outside all night?' he said. 'Now
we're really up Shit Creek. No paddle, no airbed, no goddam
lifejackets, no nothing.'

'I didn't know she'd do something crazy like take off with
everything,' said Sally.

'You leave her outside in the pouring rain all night she's got
to do something. She's probably frozen to death by now. Or
drowned.'

'She tried to kill me. You think I was going to let her in
when she's tried to do that. Anyhow it's all your fault for
shooting your mouth off about that doll.'

'You tell that to the law when they find her body floating
downstream. You just explain how come she goes off in the
middle of a storm.'

'You're just trying to scare me,' said Sally. 'I didn't make her
go or anything.'

'It's going to look peculiar if something has happened to her
is all I'm saying. And you tell me how we're going to get off
here now. You think I'm going swimming without a lifejacket
you're mistaken. I'm no Spitz.'

'My hero,' said Sally.

Gaskell went into the cabin and looked in the cupboard by
the stove. 'And another thing. We've got a food problem.
And water. There's not much left.'

'You got us into this mess. You think of a way out,' said
Sally.

Gaskell sat down on the bunk and tried to think. There had
to be some way of letting people know they were there and in
trouble. They couldn't be far from land. For all he knew dry
land was just the other side of the reeds. He went out and

climbed on top of the cabin but apart from the church spire in the distance he could see nothing beyond the reeds. Perhaps if they got a piece of cloth and waved it someone would spot it. He went down and fetched a pillow case and spent twenty minutes waving it above his head and shouting. Then he returned to the cabin and got out the chart and pored over it in a vain attempt to discover where they were. He was just folding the map up when he spotted the pieces of Scrabble still lying on the table. Letters. Individual letters. Now if they had something that would float up in the air with letters on it. Like a kite. Gaskell considered ways of making a kite and gave it up. Perhaps the best thing after all was to make smoke signals. He fetched an empty can from the kitchen and filled it with fuel oil from beside the engine and soaked a handkerchief in it and clambered up on the cabin roof. He lit the handkerchief and tried to get the oil to burn but when it did there was very little smoke and the tin got too hot to hold. Gaskell kicked it into the water where it fizzled out.

'Genius baby,' said Sally, 'you're the greatest.'

'Yea, well if you can think of something practical let me know.'

'Try swimming.'

'Try drowning,' said Gaskell.

'You could make a raft or something.'

'I could hack this boat of Scheimacher's up. That's all we need.'

'I saw a movie once where there were these gauchos or Romans or something and they came to a river and wanted to cross and they used pigs' bladders,' said Sally.

'Right now all we don't have is a pig,' said Gaskell.

'You could use the garbage bags in the kitchen,' said Sally. Gaskell fetched a plastic bag and blew it up and tied the end with string. Then he squeezed it. The bag went down.

Gaskell sat down despondently. There had to be some simple way of attracting attention and he certainly didn't want to swim out across that dark water clutching an inflated garbage bag. He fiddled with the pieces of Scrabble and thought once again about kites. Or balloons. Balloons.

'You got those rubbers you use?' he asked suddenly.

'Jesus, at a time like this you get a hard on,' said Sally. 'Forget sex. Think of some way of getting us off here.'

'I have,' said Gaskell, 'I want those skins.'

'You going to float downriver on a pontoon of condoms?'

'Balloons,' said Gaskell. 'We blow them up and paint letters on them and float them in the wind.'

'Genius baby,' said Sally and went into the toilet. She came out with a sponge bag. 'Here they are. For a moment there I thought you wanted me.'

'Days of wine and roses,' said Gaskell, 'are over. Remind me to divorce you.' He tore a packet open and blew a contraceptive up and tied a knot in its end.

'On what grounds?'

'Like you're a lesbian,' said Gaskell and held up the dildo. 'This and kleptomania and the habit you have of putting other men in dolls and knotting them. You name it, I'll use it. Like you're a nymphomaniac.'

'You wouldn't dare. Your family would love it, the scandal.'

'Try me,' said Gaskell and blew up another condom.

'Plastic freak.'

'Bull dyke.'

Sally's eyes narrowed. She was beginning to think he meant what he said about divorce and if Gaskell divorced her in England what sort of alimony would she get? Very little. There were no children and she had the idea that British courts were mean in matters of money. So was Gaskell and there was his family too. Rich and mean. She sat and eyed him.

'Where's your nail varnish?' Gaskell asked when he had finished and twelve contraceptives cluttered the cabin.

'Drop dead,' said Sally and went out on deck to think. She stared down at the dark water and thought about rats and death and being poor again and liberated. The rat paradigm. The world was a rotten place. People were objects to be used and discarded. It was Gaskell's own philosophy and now he was discarding her. And one slip on this oily deck could solve her problems. All that had to happen was for Gaskell to slip and drown and she would be free and rich and no one would ever know. An accident. Natural death. But Gaskell could swim and there had to be no mistakes. Try it once and fail and she wouldn't be able to try again. He would be on his guard. It had to be certain and it had to be natural.

Gaskell came out on deck with the contraceptives. He had tied them together and painted on each one a single letter with nail varnish so that the whole read HELP SOS HELP. He climbed up on the cabin roof and launched them into the air. They floated up for a moment, were caught in the light breeze and sagged sideways down on to the water. Gaskell pulled them in on the string and tried again. Once again they floated down on to the water.

'I'll wait until there's some more wind,' he said, and tied the string to the rail where they bobbed gently. Then he went into the cabin and lay on the bunk.

'What are you going to do now?' Sally asked.

'Sleep. Wake me when there's a wind.'

He took off his glasses and pulled a blanket over him.

Outside Sally sat on a locker and thought about drowning. In bed.

'Mr Gosdyke,' said Inspector Flint, 'you and I have had dealings for a good many years now and I'm prepared to be frank with you. I don't know.'

'But you've charged him with murder,' said Mr Gosdyke.

'He'll come up for remand on Monday. In the meantime I am going on questioning him.'

'But surely the fact that he admits burying a lifesize doll ...'

'Dressed in his wife's clothes, Gosdyke. In his wife's clothes. Don't forget that.'

'It still seems insufficient to me. Can you be absolutely sure that a murder has been committed?'

'Three people disappear off the face of the earth without a trace. They leave behind them two cars, a house littered with unwashed glasses and the leftovers of a party ... you should see that house ... a bathroom and landing covered with blood ...'

'They could have gone in someone else's car.'

'They could have but they didn't. Dr Pringsheim didn't like

being driven by anyone else. We know that from his colleagues at the Department of Biochemistry. He had a rooted objection to British drivers. Don't ask me why but he had.'

'Trains? Buses? Planes?'

'Checked, rechecked and checked again. No one answering to their description used any form of public or private transport out of town. And if you think they went on a bicycle ride, you're wrong again. Dr Pringsheim's bicycle is in the garage. No, you can forget their going anywhere. They died and Mr Smart Alec Wilt knows it.'

'I still don't see how you can be so sure,' said Mr Gosdyke.

Inspector Flint lit a cigarette. 'Let's just look at his actions, his admitted actions and see what they add up to,' he said. 'He gets a lifesize doll . . .'

'Where from?'

'He says he was given it by his wife. Where he got it from doesn't matter.'

'He says he first saw the thing at the Pringsheims' house.'

'Perhaps he did. I'm prepared to believe that. Wherever he got it, the fact remains that he dressed it up to look like Mrs Wilt. He puts it down that hole at the Tech, a hole he knows is going to be filled with concrete. He makes certain he is seen by the caretaker when he knows that the Tech is closed. He leaves a bicycle covered with his fingerprints and with a book of his in the basket. He leaves a trail of notes to the hole. He turns up at Mrs Braintree's house at midnight covered with mud and says he's had a puncture when he hasn't. Now you're not going to tell me that he hadn't got something in mind.'

'He says he was merely trying to dispose of that doll.'

'And he tells me he was rehearsing his wife's murder. He's admitted that.'

'Yes, but only in fantasy. His story to me is that he wanted to get rid of that doll,' Mr Gosdyke persisted.

'Then why the clothes, why blow the thing up and why leave it in such a position it was bound to be spotted when the concrete was poured down? Why didn't he cover it with earth if he didn't want it to be found? Why didn't he just burn the bloody thing or leave it by the roadside? It just doesn't make sense unless you see it as a deliberate plan to draw our attention away from the real crime.' The Inspector paused. 'Well now, the way I see it is that something happened at that party we don't know anything about. Perhaps Wilt found his wife in bed with Dr Pringsheim. He killed them both. Mrs Pringsheim puts in an appearance and he kills her too.'

'How?' said Mr Gosdyke. 'You didn't find that much blood.'

'He strangled her. He strangled his own wife. He battered Pringsheim to death. Then he hides the bodies somewhere, goes home and lays the doll trail. On Sunday he disposes of the real bodies ...'

'Where?'

'God alone knows, but I'm going to find out. All I know is that a man who can think up a scheme like this one is bound to have thought of somewhere diabolical to put the real victims. It wouldn't surprise me to learn that he spent Sunday making illegal use of the crematorium. Whatever he did you can be sure he did it thoroughly.'

But Mr Gosdyke remained unconvinced. 'I wish I knew how you could be so certain,' he said.

'Mr Gosdyke,' said the Inspector wearily, 'you have spent two hours with your client. I have spent the best part of the week and if I've learnt one thing from the experience it is this, that sod in there knows what he is doing. Any normal man in his position would have been worried and alarmed and downright frightened. Any innocent man faced with a missing wife and the evidence we've got of murder would have had a nervous breakdown. Not Wilt. Oh no, he sits in there as bold as you please and tells me how to conduct the investigation. Now if anything convinces me that that bastard is as guilty as hell that does. He did it and I know it. And what is more, I'm going to prove it.'

'He seems a bit worried now,' said Mr Gosdyke.

'He's got reason to be,' said the Inspector, 'because by Monday morning I'm going to get the truth out of him even if it kills him and me both.'

'Inspector,' said Mr Gosdyke getting to his feet, 'I must warn you that I have advised my client not to say another word and if he appears in Court with a mark on him ...'

174

'Mr Gosdyke, you should know me better than that. I'm not a complete fool and if your client has any marks on him on Monday morning they will not have been made by me or any of my men. You have my assurance on that.'

Mr Gosdyke left the Police Station a puzzled man. He had to admit that Wilt's story hadn't been a very convincing one. Mr Gosdyke's experience of murderers was not extensive but he had a shrewd suspicion that men who confessed openly that they had entertained fantasies of murdering their wives ended by admitting that they had done so in fact. Besides his attempt to get Wilt to agree that he'd put the doll down the hole as a practical joke on his colleagues at the Tech had failed hopelessly. Wilt had refused to lie and Mr Gosdyke was not used to clients who insisted on telling the truth.

Inspector Flint went back into the Interview Room and looked at Wilt. Then he pulled up a chair and sat down.

'Henry,' he said with an affability he didn't feel, 'you and I are going to have a little chat.'

'What, another one?' said Wilt. 'Mr Gosdyke has advised me to say nothing.'

'He always does,' said the Inspector sweetly, 'to clients he knows are guilty. Now are you going to talk?'

'I can't see why not. I'm not guilty and it helps to pass the time.'

17

It was Friday and as on every other day in the week the little church at Waterswick was empty. And as on every other day of the week the Vicar, the Reverend St John Froude, was drunk. The two things went together, the lack of a congregation and the Vicar's insobriety. It was an old tradition dating back to the days of smuggling when Brandy for the Parson had been about the only reason the isolated hamlet had a vicar at all. And like so many English traditions it died hard. The Church authorities saw to it that Waterswick got idiosyncratic parsons whose awkward enthusiasms tended to make them unsuitable for more respectable parishes and they, to console themselves for its remoteness and lack of interest in things spiritual, got alcoholic. The Rev St John Froude maintained the tradition. He attended to his duties with the same Anglo-Catholic Fundamentalist fervour that had made him so unpopular in Esher and turned an alcoholic eye on the activities of his few parishioners who, now that brandy was not so much in demand, contented themselves with the occasional boatload of illegal Indian immigrants.

Now as he finished a breakfast of eggnog and Irish coffee and considered the iniquities of his more egregious colleagues as related in the previous Sunday's paper he was startled to see something wobbling above the reeds on Eel Stretch. It looked like balloons, white sausage-shaped balloons that rose briefly and then disappeared. The Rev St John Froude shuddered, shut his eyes, opened them again and thought about the virtues of abstinence. If he was right and he didn't know whether he wanted to be or not, the morning was being profaned by a cluster of contraceptives, inflated contraceptives, wobbling erratically where by the nature of things no contraceptive had ever wobbled before. At least he hoped it was a cluster. He was so used to seeing things in twos when they were in fact ones that he couldn't be sure if what looked like a cluster of inflated contraceptives wasn't just one or better still none at all.

He reeled off to his study to get his binoculars and stepped out on to the terrace to focus them. By that time the manifestation had disappeared. The Rev St John Froude shook his head mournfully. Things and in particular his liver had reached a pretty pickle for him to have hallucinations so early in the morning. He went back into the house and tried to concentrate his attention on a case involving an Archdeacon in Ongar who had undergone a sex-change operation before eloping with his verger. There was matter there for a sermon if only he could think of a suitable text.

*

At the bottom of the garden Eva Wilt watched his retreat and wondered what to do. She had no intention of going up to the house and introducing herself in her present condition. She needed clothes, or at least some sort of covering. She looked around for something temporary and finally decided on some ivy climbing up the graveyard fence. With one eye on the Vicarage she emerged from the willow tree and scampered across to the fence and through the gate into the churchyard. There she ripped some ivy off the trunk of a tree and, carrying it in front of her rather awkwardly, made her way surreptitiously up the overgrown path towards the church. For the most part her progress was masked from the house by the trees but once or twice she had to crouch low and scamper from tombstone to tombstone in full view of the Vicarage. By the time she reached the church porch she was panting and her sense of impropriety had been increased tenfold. If the prospect of presenting herself at the house in the nude offended her on grounds of social decorum, going into a church in the raw was positively sacrilegious. She stood in the porch and tried frantically to steel herself to go in. There were bound to be surplices for the choir in the vestry and dressed in a surplice she could go up to the house. Or could she? Eva wasn't sure about the significance of surplices and the Vicar might be angry. Oh dear it was all so awkward. In the end she opened the church door and went inside. It was cold and damp and empty. Clutching the ivy to her she crossed to the vestry door and tried it. It was locked. Eva stood shivering and tried to think. Finally she went outside and stood in the sunshine trying to get warm.

In the Staff Room at the Tech, Dr Board was holding court. 'All things considered I think we came out of the whole business rather creditably,' he said. 'The Principal has always said he wanted to put the college on the map and with the help of friend Wilt it must be said he has succeeded. The newspaper coverage has been positively prodigious. I shouldn't be surprised if our student intake jumped astonishingly.'

'The committee didn't approve our facilities,' said Mr Morris, 'so you can hardly claim their visit was an unqualified success.'

'Personally I think they got their money's worth,' said Dr Board. 'It's not every day you get the chance to see an exhumation and an execution at the same time. The one usually precedes the other and certainly the experience of seeing what to all intents and purposes was a woman turn in a matter of seconds into a man, an instantaneous sex change, was, to use a modern idiom, a mind-blowing one.'

'Talking of poor Mayfield,' said the Head of Geography, 'I understand he's still at the Mental Hospital.'

'Committed?' asked Dr Board hopefully.

'Depressed. And suffering from exhaustion.'

'Hardly surprising. Anyone who can use language ... abuse language like that is asking for trouble. Structure as a verb, for example.'

'He had set great store by the Joint Honours degree and the fact that it has been turned down ...'

'Quite right too,' said Dr Board. 'The educative value of stuffing second-rate students with fifth-rate ideas on subjects as diverse as Medieval Poetry and Urban Studies escapes me. Far better that they should spend their time watching the police dig up the supposed body of a woman coated in concrete, stretch her neck, rip all her clothes off her, hang her and finally blow her up until she explodes. Now that is what I call a truly educational experience. It combines archaeology with criminology, zoology with physics, anatomy with economic theory, while maintaining the students' undivided attention all the time. If we must have Joint Honours degrees let them be of that vitality. Practical too. I'm thinking of sending away for one of those dolls.'

'It still leaves unresolved the question of Mrs Wilt's disappearance,' said Mr Morris.

'Ah, dear Eva,' said Dr Board wistfully. 'Having seen so much of what I imagined to be her I shall, if I ever have the pleasure of meeting her again, treat her with the utmost courtesy. An amazingly versatile woman and interestingly proportioned. I think I shall christen my doll Eva.'

'But the police still seem to think she is dead.'

'A woman like that can never die,' said Dr Board. 'She may explode but her memory lingers on indelibly.'

In his study the Rev St John Froude shared Dr Board's opinion. The memory of the large and apparently naked lady he had glimpsed emerging from the willow tree at the bottom of his garden like some disgustingly oversized nymph and scuttling through the churchyard was not something he was ever likely to forget. Coming so shortly after the apparition of the inflated contraceptives it lent weight to the suspicion that he had been overdoing things on the alcohol side. Abandoning the sermon he had been preparing on the apostate Archdeacon of Ongar — he had had 'By their fruits ye shall know them' in mind as a text — he got up and peered out of the window in the direction of the church and was wondering if he shouldn't go down and see if there wasn't a large fat naked lady there when his attention was drawn to the reeds across the water. They were there again, those infernal things. This time there could be no doubt about it. He grabbed his binoculars and stared furiously through them. He could see them much more clearly than the first time and much more ominously. The sun was high in the sky and a mist rose over Eel Stretch so that the contraceptives had a luminescent sheen about them, an insubstantiality that was almost spiritual in its implications. Worse still, there appeared to be something written on them. The message was clear if incomprehensible. It read PEESOP. The Rev St John Froude lowered his binoculars and reached for the whisky bottle and considered the significance of PEESOP etched ectoplasmically against the sky. By the time he had finished his third hurried glass and had decided that spiritualism might after all have something to be said for it though why you almost always found yourself in touch with a Red Indian who was acting by proxy for an aunt which might account for the misspelling of Peasoup while removing some of the less attractive ingredients from the stuff, the wind had changed the letters round. This time when he looked the message read EELPOPS. The Vicar shuddered. What eel was popping and how?

'The sins of the spirit,' he said reproachfully to his fourth

179

glass of whisky before consulting the oracle once more. POSH-
ELLS was followed by HEPOLP to be succeeded by SHHLPSPO
which was even worse. The Rev St John Froude thrust his
binoculars and the bottle of whisky aside and went down on
his knees to pray for deliverance, or at least for some guidance
in interpreting the message. But every time he got up to see if
his wish had been granted the combination of letters was as
meaningless as ever or downright threatening. What, for
instance, did HELLSPO signify? Or SLOSHHEEL? Finally, determined to discover for himself the true nature of the occurrence, he put on his cassock and wove off down the garden
path to the boathouse.

'They shall rue the day,' he muttered as he climbed into
the rowing boat and took the oars. The Rev St John Froude
held firm views on contraception. It was one of the tenets of
his Anglo-Catholicism.

In the cabin cruiser Gaskell slept soundly. Around him Sally
made her preparations. She undressed and changed into the
plastic bikini. She took a silk square from her bag and put it
on the table and she fetched a jug from the kitchen and leaning over the side filled it with water. Finally she went into
the toilet and made her face up in the mirror. When she
emerged she was wearing false eyelashes, her lips were heavily
red and pancake make-up obscured her pale complexion.
She was carrying a bathing-cap. She crossed the door of the
galley and put an arm up and stuck her hip out.

'Gaskell baby,' she called.

Gaskell opened his eyes and looked at her. 'What the hell
gives?'

'Like it, baby?'

Gaskell put on his glasses. In spite of himself he did like
it. 'You think you're going to wheedle round me, you're
wrong ...'

Sally smiled. 'Conserve the verbiage. You turn me on,
bio-degradable baby.' She moved forward and sat on the bunk
beside him.

'What are you trying to do?'

'Make it up, babykink. You deserve a curve.' She fondled him gently. 'Like the old days. Remember?'

Gaskell remembered and felt weak. Sally leant forward and pressed him down on to the bunk.

'Surrogate Sally,' she said and unbuttoned his shirt.

Gaskell squirmed. 'If you think . . .'

'Don't think, kink,' said Sally and undid his jeans. 'Only erect.'

'Oh God,' said Gaskell. The perfume, the plastic, the mask of a face and her hands were awakening ancient fantasies. He lay supine on the bunk staring at her while Sally undressed him. Even when she rolled him over on his face and pulled his hands behind his back he made no resistance.

'Bondage baby,' she said softly and reached for the silk square.

'No, Sally, no,' he said weakly. Sally smiled grimly and tied his hands together, winding the silk between his wrists carefully before tightening it. When she had finished Gaskell whimpered. 'You're hurting me.'

Sally rolled him over. 'You love it,' she said and kissed him. She sat back and stroked him gently. 'Harder, baby, real hard. Lift me lover sky high.'

'Oh Sally.'

'That's my baby and now the waterproof.'

'There's no need. I like it better without.'

'But I do, G. I need it to prove you loved me till death did us part.' She bent over and rolled it down.

Gaskell stared up at her. Something was wrong.

'And now the cap.' She reached over and picked up the bathing-cap.

'The cap?' said Gaskell. 'Why the cap? I don't want that thing on.'

'Oh but you do, sweetheart. It makes you look girlwise.' She fitted the cap over his head. 'Now into Sallia inter alia.' She undid the bikini and lowered herself on to him. Gaskell moaned and stared up at her. She was lovely. It was a long time since she had been so good. But he was still frightened. There was a look in her eyes he hadn't seen before. 'Untie me,' he pleaded, 'you're hurting my arm.'

But Sally merely smiled and gyrated. 'When you've come and gone, G baby. When you've been.' She moved her hips. 'Come, bum, come quick.'

Gaskell shuddered.

'Finished?'

He nodded. 'Finished,' he sighed.

'For good, baby, for good,' said Sally. 'That was it. You're past the last.'

'Past the last?'

'You've come and gone, come and gone. It's Styxside for you now.'

'Stickside?'

'S for Sally, T for Terminal, Y for You and X for Exit. All that's left is this.' She reached over and picked up the jug of muddy water. Gaskell turned his head and looked at it.

'What's that for?'

'For you, baby. Mudders milk.' She moved up his body and sat on his chest. 'Open your mouth.'

Gaskell Pringsheim stared up at her frantically. He began to writhe. 'You're mad. You're crazy.'

'Now just lie quietly and it won't hurt. It will soon be over, lover. Natural death by drowning. In bed. You're making history.'

'You bitch, you murderous bitch . . .'

'Cerberuswise,' said Sally, and poured the water into his mouth. She put the jug down and pulled the cap down over his face.

The Rev St John Froude rowed surprisingly steadily for a man with half a bottle of whisky inside him and a wrath in his heart, and the nearer he got to the contraceptives the greater his wrath became. It wasn't simply that he had been given a quite unnecessary fright about the state of his liver by the sight of the things (he could see now that he was close to them that they were real), it was rather that he adhered to the doctrine of sexual non-intervention. God, in his view, had created a perfect world if the book of Genesis was to be believed and it had been going downhill ever since. And the book of Genesis *was* to be believed or the rest of the Bible made no sense at all. Starting from this fundamentalist premise the Rev St John Froude had progressed erratically by way of Blake, Hawker, Leavis and a number of obscurantist theologians to the conviction that the miracles of modern science were the works of the devil, that salvation lay in eschewing every material advance since the Renaissance, and one or two before, and that nature was infinitely less red in tooth and claw than modern mechanized man. In short he was convinced that the end of the world was at hand in the shape of a nuclear holocaust and that it was his duty as a Christian to announce the fact. His sermons on the subject had been of such a vividly horrendous fervour as to lead to his exile in Waterswick. Now as he rowed up the channel into Eel Stretch he fulminated silently against contraception, abortion and the evils of sexual promiscuity. They were all symptoms and causes and causative symptoms of the moral chaos which life on earth had become. And finally there were trippers. The Rev St John Froude loathed trippers. They fouled the little Eden of his parish with their boats, their transistors, and their unabashed enjoyment of the present. And trippers who desecrated the prospect from his study window with inflated contraceptives and meaningless messages were an abomination. By the time he came in sight of the cabin cruiser he was in no mood to be trifled with. He rowed furiously across to the boat, tied up to the rail and, lifting his cassock over his knees, stepped aboard.

In the cabin Sally stared down at the bathing-cap. It deflated and inflated, expanded and was sucked in against Gaskell's face and Sally squirmed with pleasure. She was the liberatedest woman in the world, but the liberatedest. Gaskell was dying and she would be free to be with a million dollars in the kitty. And no one would ever know. When he was dead she would take the cap off and untie him and push his body over the side into the water. Gaskell Pringsheim would have died a natural death by drowning. And at that moment the

183

cabin door opened and she looked up at the silhouette of the Rev St John Froude in the cabin doorway.

'What the hell . . .' she muttered and leapt off Gaskell.

The Rev St John Froude hesitated. He had come to say his piece and say it he would but he had clearly intruded on a very naked woman with a horribly made-up face in the act of making love to a man who as far as a quick glance enabled him to tell had no face at all.

'I . . .' he began and stopped. The man on the bunk had rolled on to the floor and was writhing there in the most extraordinary fashion. The Rev St John Froude stared down at him aghast. The man was not only faceless but his hands were tied behind his back.

'My dear fellow,' said the Vicar, appalled at the scene and looked up at the naked woman for some sort of explanation. She was staring at him demonically and holding a large kitchen knife. The Rev St John Froude stumbled back into the cockpit as the woman advanced towards him holding the knife in front of her with both hands. She was clearly quite demented. So was the man on the floor. He rolled about and dragged his head from side to side. The bathing-cap came off but the Rev St John Froude was too busy scrambling over the side into his rowing boat to notice. He cast off as the ghastly woman lunged towards him and began to row away, his original mission entirely forgotten. In the cockpit Sally stood screaming abuse at him and behind her a shape had appeared in the cabin door. The Vicar was grateful to see that the man had a face now, not a nice face, a positively horrible face but a face for all that, and he was coming up behind the woman with some hideous intention. The next moment the intention was carried out. The man hurled himself at her, the knife dropped on to the deck, the woman scrabbled at the side of the boat and then slid forward into the water. The Rev St John Froude waited no longer. He rowed vigorously away. Whatever appalling orgy of sexual perversion he had interrupted he wanted none of it and painted women with knives who called him a motherfucking son of a cuntsucker among other things didn't elicit his

184

sympathy when the object of their obscene passions pushed them into the water. And in any case they were Americans. The Rev St John Froude had no time for Americans. They epitomized everything he found offensive about the modern world. Imbued with a new disgust for the present and an urge to hit the whisky he rowed home and tied up at the bottom of the garden.

Behind him in the cabin cruiser Gaskell ceased shouting. The priest who had saved his life had ignored his hoarse pleas for further help and Sally was standing waist-deep in water beside the boat. Well she could stay there. He went back into the cabin, turned so that he could lock the door with his tied hands and then looked around for something to cut the silk scarf with. He was still very frightened.

'Right,' said Inspector Flint, 'so what did you do then?'
'Got up and read the Sunday papers.'
'After that?'
'I ate a plate of All-Bran and drank some tea.'
'Tea? You sure it was tea? Last time you said coffee.'
'Which time?'
'The last time you told it.'
'I drank tea.'
'What then?'
'I gave Clem his breakfast.'
'What sort?'
'Chappie.'
'Last time you said Bonzo.'
'This time I say Chappie.'
'Make up your mind. Which sort was it?'
'What the fuck does it matter which sort it was?'
'It matters to me.'
'Chappie.'
'And when you had fed the dog.'
'I shaved.'
'Last time you said you had a bath.'
'I had a bath and then I shaved. I was trying to save time.'

'Forget the time, Wilt, we've got all the time in the world.'

'What time is it?'

'Shut up. What did you do then?'

'Oh for God's sake, what does it matter. What's the point of going over and over the same things?'

'Shut up.'

'Right,' said Wilt, 'I will.'

'When you had shaved what did you do?'

Wilt stared at him and said nothing.

'When you had shaved?'

But Wilt remained silent. Finally Inspector Flint left the room and sent for Sergeant Yates.

'He's clammed up,' he said wearily. 'So what do we do now?'

'Try a little physical persuasion?'

Flint shook his head. 'Gosdyke's seen him. If he turns up in Court on Monday with so much as a hair out of place, he'll be all over us for brutality. There's got to be some other way. He must have a weak spot somewhere but I'm damned if I can find it. How does he do it?'

'Do what?'

'Keep talking and saying nothing. Not one bloody useful thing. That sod's got more opinions on every topic under the flaming sun than I've got hair on my head.'

'If we keep him awake for another forty-eight hours he's bound to crack up.'

'He'll take me with him,' said Flint.' We'll both go into court in straitjackets.'

In the Interview Room Wilt put his head on the table. They would be back in a minute with more questions but a moment's sleep was better than none. Sleep. If only they would let him sleep. What had Flint said? 'The moment you sign a confession, you can have all the sleep you want.' Wilt considered the remark and its possibilities. A confession. But it would have to be plausible enough to keep them occupied while he got some rest and at the same time so impossible that it would be rejected by the court. A delaying tactic to give Eva time to come back and prove his innocence. It would be like giving

Gasfitters Two *Shane* to read while he sat and thought about putting Eva down the pile shaft. He should be able to think up something complicated that would keep them frantically active. How he had killed them? Beat them to death in the bathroom? Not enough blood. Even Flint had admitted that much. So how? What was a nice gentle way to go? Poor old Pinkerton had chosen a peaceful death when he stuck a tube up the exhaust pipe of his car ... That was it. But why? There had to be a motive. Eva was having it off with Dr Pringsheim? With that twit? Not in a month of Sundays. Eva wouldn't have looked twice at Gaskell. But Flint wasn't to know that. And what about that bitch Sally? All three having it off together? Well at least it would explain why he killed them all and it would provide the sort of motive Flint would understand. And besides it was right for that kind of party. So he got this pipe ... What pipe? There was no need for a pipe. They were in the garage to get away from everyone else. No, that wouldn't do. It had to be the bathroom. How about Eva and Gaskell doing it in the bath? That was better. He had bust the door down in a fit of jealousy. Much better. Then he had drowned them. And then Sally had come upstairs and he had had to kill her too. That explained the blood. There had been a struggle. He hadn't meant to kill her but she had fallen in the bath. So far so good. But where had he put them? It had to be something good. Flint wasn't going to believe anything like the river. Somewhere that made sense of the doll down the hole. Flint had it firmly fixed in his head that the doll had been a diversionary tactic. That meant that time entered into their disposal.

Wilt got up and asked to go to the toilet. As usual the constable came with him and stood outside the door.

'Do you have to?' said Wilt. 'I'm not going to hang myself with the chain.'

'To see you don't beat your meat,' said the constable coarsely.

Wilt sat down. Beat your meat. What a hell of an expression. It called to mind Meat One. Meat One? It was a moment of inspiration. Wilt got up and flushed the toilet. Meat One would keep them busy for a long time. He went back to the pale green

187

room where the light buzzed. Flint was waiting for him.

'You going to talk now?' he asked.

Wilt shook his head. They would have to drag it out of him if his confession was to be at all convincing. He would have to hesitate, start to say something, stop, start again, appeal to Flint to stop torturing him, plead and start again. This trout needed tickling. Oh well, it would help to keep him awake.

'Are you going to start again at the beginning?' he asked.

Inspector Flint smiled horribly. 'Right at the beginning.'

'All right,' said Wilt, 'have it your own way. Just don't keep asking me if I gave the dog Chappie or Bonzo. I can't stand all that talk about dog food.'

Inspector Flint rose to the bait. 'Why not?'

'It gets on my nerves,' said Wilt, with a shudder.

The Inspector leant forward. 'Dog food gets on your nerves?' he said.

Wilt hesitated pathetically. 'Don't go on about it,' he said. 'Please don't go on.'

'Now then which was it, Bonzo or Chappie?' said the Inspector, scenting blood.

Wilt put his head in his hands. 'I won't say anything. I won't. Why must you keep asking me about food? Leave me alone.' His voice rose hysterically and with it Inspector Flint's hopes. He knew when he had touched the nerve. He was on to a good thing.

18

'Dear God,' said Sergeant Yates, 'but we had pork pies for lunch yesterday. It's too awful.'

Inspector Flint rinsed his mouth out with black coffee and spat into the washbasin. He had vomited twice and felt like vomiting again.

'I knew it would be something like that,' he said with a shudder, 'I just knew it. A man who could pull that doll trick had to have something really filthy up his sleeve.'

'But they may all have been eaten by now,' said the Sergeant. Flint looked at him balefully.

'Why the hell do you think he laid that phoney trail?' he asked. 'To give them plenty of time to be consumed. His expression "consumed", not mine. You know what the shelf life of a pork pie is?'

Yates shook his head.

'Five days. Five days. So they went out on Tuesday which leaves us one day to find them or what remains of them. I want every pork pie in East Anglia picked up. I want every fucking sausage and steak and kidney pie that went out of Sweetbreads Meat Factory this week found and brought in. And every tin of dog food.'

'Dog food?'

'You heard me,' said Inspector Flint staggering out of the washroom. 'And while you're about it you'd better make it cat food too. You never know with Wilt. He's capable of leading us up the garden path in one important detail.'

'But if they went into pork pies what's all this about dog food?'

'Where the hell do you think he put the odds and ends and I do mean ends?' Inspector Flint asked savagely. 'You don't imagine he was going to have people coming in and complaining they'd found a tooth or a toenail in the Sweetbreads pie they had bought that morning. Not Wilt. That swine thinks of everything. He drowns them in their own bath. He puts them in plastic garbage bags and locks the bags in the garage while he goes home and sticks the doll down that fucking hole. Then on Sunday he goes back and picks them up and spends the day at the meat factory all by himself ... Well if you want to know what he did on Sunday you can read all about it in his statement. It's more than my stomach can stand.'

The Inspector went back hurriedly into the washroom. He'd been living off pork pies since Monday. The statistical chances of his having partaken of Mrs Wilt were extremely high.

When Sweetbreads Meat and Canning Factory opened at eight,

Inspector Flint was waiting at the gate. He stormed into the manager's office and demanded to speak to him.

'He's not here yet,' said the secretary. 'Is there anything I can do for you?'

'I want a list of every establishment you supply with pork pies, steak and kidney pies, sausages and dog food,' said the Inspector.

'I couldn't possibly give you that information,' said the secretary. 'It's extremely confidential.'

'Confidential? What the hell do you mean confidential?'

'Well I don't know really. It's just that I couldn't take it on myself to provide you with inside information ...' She stopped. Inspector Flint was staring at her with a quite horrible expression on his face.

'Well, miss,' he said finally, 'while we're on the topic of inside information, it may interest you to know that what has been inside your pork pies is by way of being inside information. Vital information.'

'Vital information? I don't know what you mean. Our pies contain perfectly wholesome ingredients.'

'Wholesome?' shouted the Inspector. 'You call three human bodies wholesome? You call the boiled, bleached, minced and cooked remains of three murdered bodies wholesome?'

'But we only use ...' the secretary began and fell sideways off her chair in a dead faint.

'Oh for God's sake,' shouted the Inspector, 'you'd think a silly bitch who can work in an abattoir wouldn't be squeamish. Find out who the manager is and where he lives and tell him to come down here at the double.'

He sat down in a chair while Sergeant Yates rummaged in the desk. 'Wakey, wakey,' he said, prodding the secretary with his foot. 'If anyone has got a right to lie down on the job, it's me. I've been on my feet for three days and nights and I've been an accessory after the fact of murder.'

'An accessory?' said Yates. 'I don't see how you can say that.'

'Can't you? Well what would you call helping to dispose of parts of a murder victim? Concealing evidence of a crime?'

'I never thought of it that way,' said Yates.

'I did,' said the Inspector, 'I can't think of anything else.'

In his cell Wilt stared up at the ceiling peacefully. He was astonished that it had been so easy. All you had to do was tell people what they wanted to hear and they would believe you no matter how implausible your story might be. And three days and nights without sleep had suspended Inspector Flint's disbelief with a vengeance. Then again Wilt's hesitations had been timed perfectly and his final confession a nice mixture of conceit and matter-of-factness. On the details of the murder he had been coldly precise and in describing their disposal he had been a craftsman taking pride in his work. Every now and then when he got to a difficult spot he would veer away into a manic arrogance at once boastful and cowardly with 'You'll never be able to prove it. They'll have disappeared without trace now.' And the Harpic had come in useful once again, adding a macabre touch of realism about evidence being flushed down thousands of U-bends with Harpic being poured after it like salt from a salt cellar. Eva would enjoy that when he told her about it, which was more than could be said for Inspector Flint. He hadn't even seen the irony of Wilt's remark that while he had been looking for the Pringsheims they had been under his nose all the time. He had been particularly upset by the crack about gut reactions and the advice to stick to health foods in future. Yes, in spite of his tiredness Wilt had enjoyed himself watching the Inspector's bloodshot eyes turn from glee and gloating self-satisfaction to open amazement and finally undisguised nausea. And when finally Wilt had boasted that they would never be able to bring him to trial without the evidence, Flint had responded magnificently.

'Oh yes, we will,' he had shouted hoarsely. 'If there is one single pie left from that batch we'll get it and when we do the Lab boys will ...'

'Find nothing but pork in it,' said Wilt before being dragged off to his cell. At least that was the truth and if Flint didn't believe it that was his own fault. He had asked for a confession and he had got one by courtesy of Meat One, the apprentice butchers who had spent so many hours of Liberal Studies explaining the workings of Sweetbreads Meat Factory to him and had actually taken him down there one afternoon to show him how it all worked. Dear lads. And how he had loathed them at the time. Which only went to show how wrong you could be about people. Wilt was just wondering if he had been wrong about Eva and perhaps she was dead when he fell asleep.

In the churchyard Eva watched the Rev St John Froude walk down to the boathouse and start rowing towards the reeds. As soon as he had disappeared she made her way up the path towards the house. With the Vicar out of the way she was prepared to take the risk of meeting his wife. She stole through the doorway into the courtyard and looked about her. The place had a dilapidated air about it and a pile of empty bottles in one corner, whisky and gin bottles, seemed to indicate that he might well be unmarried. Still clutching her ivy, she went across to the door, evidently the kitchen door, and knocked. There was no answer. She crossed to the window and looked inside. The kitchen was large, distinctly untidy and had all the hallmarks of a bachelor existence about it. She went back to the door and knocked again and she was just wondering what to do now when there was the sound of a vehicle coming down the drive.

Eva hesitated for a second and then tried the door. It was unlocked. She stepped inside and shut the door as a milk van drove into the courtyard. Eva listened while the milkman put down several bottles and then drove away. Then she turned and went down the passage to the front hall. If she could find the phone she could ring Henry and he could come out in the car and fetch her. She would go back to the church and wait for him there. But the hall was empty. She poked her head into several rooms with a good deal of care and found them largely bare of furniture or with dustcovers over chairs and sofas. The place was incredibly untidy too. Definitely the Vicar was a bachelor. Finally she found his study. There was a phone on the desk. Eva went over and lifted the receiver and dialled Ipford 66066. There was no reply. Henry would be at the Tech. She dialled the Tech number and asked for Mr Wilt.

'Wilt?' said the girl on the switchboard. 'Mr Wilt?'

'Yes,' said Eva in a low voice.

'I'm afraid he's not here,' said the girl.

'Not there? But he's got to be there.'

'Well he isn't.'

'But he's got to be. It's desperately important I get in touch with him.'

'I'm sorry, but I can't help you,' said the girl.

'But ...' Eva began and glanced out of the window. The Vicar had returned and was walking up the garden path towards her. 'Oh God,' she muttered and put the phone down hurriedly. She turned and rushed out of the room in a state of panic. Only when she had made her way back along the passage to the kitchen did it occur to her that she had left her ivy behind in the study. There were footsteps in the passage. Eva looked frantically around, decided against the courtyard and went up a flight of stone steps to the first floor. There she stood and listened. Her heart was palpitating. She was naked and alone in a strange house with a clergyman and Henry wasn't at the Tech when he should have been and the girl on the switchboard had sounded most peculiar, almost as though there was something wrong with wanting to speak to Henry. She had no idea what to do.

In the kitchen the Rev St John Froude had a very good idea what he wanted to do: expunge for ever the vision of the inferno to which he had been lured by those vile things with their meaningless messages floating across the water. He dug a fresh bottle of Teachers out of the cupboard and took it back to his study. What he had witnessed had been so grotesque, so evidently evil, so awful, so prescient of hell itself that he was in two minds whether it had been real or simply a waking nightmare. A man without a face, whose hands were tied behind his back, a woman with a painted face and a knife, the language ... The Rev St John Froude opened the bottle and was about to pour a glass when his eye fell on the ivy Eva had left on the chair. He put the bottle down hastily and stared at the leaves.

Here was another mystery to perplex him. How had a clump of ivy got on to the chair in his study? It certainly hadn't been there when he had left the house. He picked it up gingerly and put it on his desk. Then he sat down and contemplated it with a growing sense of unease. Something was happening in his world that he could not understand. And what about the strange figure he had seen flitting about between the tombstones? He had quite forgotten her. The Rev St John Froude got up and went out on to the terrace and down the path to the church.

'On a Sunday?' shouted the manager of Sweetbreads. 'On a Sunday? But we don't work on a Sunday. There's nobody here. The place is shut.'

'It wasn't last Sunday and there was someone here, Mr Kidney,' said the Inspector.

'Kidley, please,' said the manager, 'Kidley with an L.'

The Inspector nodded. 'OK Mr Kidley, now what I'm telling you is that this man Wilt was here last Sunday and he ...'

'How did he get in?'

'He used a ladder against the back wall from the car park.'

'In broad daylight? He'd have been seen.'

'At two o'clock in the morning, Mr Kidney.'

'Kidley, Inspector, Kidley.'

'Look Mr Kidley, if you work in a place like this with a name like that you're asking for it.'

Mr Kidley looked at him belligerently. 'And if you're telling me that some bloody maniac came in here with three dead bodies last Sunday and spent the day using our equipment to convert them into cooked meat edible for human consumption under the Food Regulations Act I'm telling you that that comes under the head of ... Head? What did he do with the heads? Tell me that?'

'What do you do with heads, Mr Kidley?' asked the Inspector.

'That rather depends. Some of them go with the offal into the animal food bins ...'

'Right. So that's what Wilt said he did with them. And you keep those in the No. 2 cold storage room. Am I right?'

Mr Kidley nodded miserably, 'Yes,' he said, 'we do.' He paused and gaped at the Inspector. 'But there's a world of difference between a pig's head and a ...'

'Quite,' said the Inspector hastily, 'and I daresay you think someone was bound to spot the difference.'

'Of course they would.'

'Now I understand from Mr Wilt that you have an extremely efficient mincing machine ...'

'No,' shouted Mr Kidley desperately. 'No, I don't believe it. It's not possible. It's ...'

'Are you saying he couldn't possibly have ...'

'I'm not saying that. I'm saying he shouldn't have. It's monstrous. It's horrible.'

'Of course it's horrible,' said the Inspector. 'The fact remains that he used that machine.'

'But we keep our equipment meticulously clean.'

'So Wilt says. He was definite on that point. He says he cleaned up carefully afterwards.'

'He must have done,' said Mr Kidley. 'There wasn't a thing out of place on Monday morning. You heard the foreman say so.'

'And I also heard this swine Wilt say that he made a list of where everything came from before he used it so that he could put it back exactly where he'd found it. He thought of everything.'

'And what about our reputation for hygiene? He didn't think of that, did he? For twenty-five years we've been known for the excellence of our products and now this has to happen. We've been at the head of ...' Mr Kidley stopped suddenly and sat down.

'Now then,' said the Inspector, 'what I have to know is who you supply to. We're going to call in every pork pie and sausage ...'

'Call them in? You can't call them in,' screamed Mr Kidley, 'they've all gone.'

'Gone? What do you mean they've gone?'

'What I say. They've gone. They've either been eaten or destroyed by now.'

'Destroyed? You're not going to tell me that there aren't

195

any left. It's only five days since they went out.'

Mr Kidley drew himself up. 'Inspector, this is an old-fashioned firm and we use traditional methods and a Sweetbreads pork pie is a genuine pork pie. It's not one of your ersatz pies with preservatives that ...'

It was Inspector Flint's turn to slump into a chair. 'Am I to understand that your fucking pies don't keep?' he asked.

Mr Kidley nodded. 'They are for immediate consumption,' he said proudly. 'Here today, gone tomorrow. That's our motto. You've seen our advertisements of course.'

Inspector Flint hadn't.

'Today's pie with yesterday's flavour, the traditional pie with the family filling.'

'You can say that again,' said Inspector Flint.

Mr Gosdyke regarded Wilt sceptically and shook his head. 'You should have listened to me,' he said, 'I told you not to talk.'

'I had to say something,' said Wilt. 'They wouldn't let me sleep and they kept asking me the same stupid questions over and over again. You've no idea what that does to you. It drives you potty.'

'Frankly, Mr Wilt, in the light of the confession you have made I find it hard to believe there was any need to. A man who can, of his own free will make a statement like this to the police is clearly insane.'

'But it's not true,' said Wilt, 'it's all pure invention.'

'With a wealth of such revolting detail? I must say I find that hard to believe. I do indeed. The bit about hip and thighs ... It makes my stomach turn over.'

'But that's from the Bible,' said Wilt, 'and besides I had to put in the gory bits or they wouldn't have believed me. Take the part where I say I sawed their ...'

'Mr Wilt, for God's sake ...'

'Well, all I can say is you've never taught Meat One. I got it all from them and once you've taught them life can hold few surprises.'

Mr Gosdyke raised an eyebrow. 'Can't it? Well I think I can

196

disabuse you of that notion,' he said solemnly. 'In the light of this confession you have made against my most earnest advice, and as a result of my firm belief that every word in it is true, I am no longer prepared to act on your behalf.' He collected his papers and stood up. 'You will have to get someone else.'

'But, Mr Gosdyke, you don't really believe all that nonsense about putting Eva in a pork pie, do you?' Wilt asked.

'Believe it? A man who can conceive of such a disgusting thing is capable of anything. Yes I do and what is more so do the police. They are this moment scouring the shops, the pubs and the supermarkets and dustbins of the entire county in search of pork pies.'

'But if they find any it won't do any good.'

'It may also interest you to know that they have impounded five thousand cans of Dogfill, an equal number of Catkin and have begun to dissect a quarter of a ton of Sweetbreads Best Bangers. Somewhere in that little lot they are bound to find some trace of Mrs Wilt, not to mention Dr and Mrs Pringsheim.'

'Well, all I can say is that I wish them luck,' said Wilt.

'And so do I,' said Mr Gosdyke disgustedly and left the room. Behind him Wilt sighed. If only Eva would turn up. Where the hell could she have got to?

At the Police Laboratories Inspector Flint was getting restive. 'Can't you speed things up a bit?' he asked.

The Head of the Forensic Department shook his head. 'It's like looking for a needle in a haystack,' he said, glancing significantly at another batch of sausages that had just been brought in. 'So far not a trace. This could take weeks.'

'I haven't got weeks,' said the Inspector, 'he's due in Court on Monday.'

'Only for remand and in any case you've got his statement.'

But Inspector Flint had his doubts about that. He had been looking at that statement and had noticed a number of discrepancies about it which fatigue, disgust and an overwhelming desire to get the filthy account over and done with before he was sick had tended to obscure at the time. For one thing

197

Wilt's scrawled signature looked suspiciously like Little Tommy Tucker when examined closely and there was a QNED beside it, which Flint had a shrewd idea meant Quod Non Erat Demonstrandum, and in any case there were rather too many references to pigs for his policeman's fancy and fuzzy pigs at that. Finally the information that Wilt had made a special request for two pork pies for lunch and had specified Sweetbreads in particular suggested an insane cannibalism that might fit in with what he had said he had done but seemed to be carrying things too far. The word 'provocation' sprang to mind and since the episode of the doll Flint had been rather conscious of bad publicity. He read through the statement again and couldn't make up his mind about it. One thing was quite certain. Wilt knew exactly how Sweetbreads factory worked. The wealth of detail he had supplied proved that. On the other hand Mr Kidley's incredulity about the heads and the mincing machine had seemed, on inspection, to be justified. Flint had looked gingerly at the beastly contraption and had found it difficult to believe that even Wilt in a fit of homicidal mania could have ... Flint put the thought out of his mind. He decided to have another little chat with Henry Wilt. Feeling like death warmed up he went back to the Interview Room and sent for Wilt.

'How's it going?' said Wilt when he arrived. 'Had any luck with the frankfurters yet? Of course you could always try your hand at black puddings ...'

'Wilt,' interrupted the Inspector, 'why did you sign that statement Little Tommy Tucker?'

Wilt sat down. 'So you've noticed that at last, have you? Very observant of you I must say.'

'I asked you a question.'

'So you did,' said Wilt. 'Let's just say I thought it was appropriate.'

'Appropriate?'

'I was singing, I think that's the slang term for it isn't it, for my sleep, so naturally ...'

'Are you telling me you made all that up?'

'What the hell do you think I did? You don't seriously think

I would inflict the Pringsheims and Eva on an unsuspecting public in the form of pork pies, do you? I mean there must be some limits to your credulity.'

Inspector Flint glared at him. 'My God, Wilt,' he said, 'if I find you've deliberately fabricated a story ...'

'You can't do very much more,' said Wilt. 'You've already charged me with murder. What more do you want? You drag me in here, you humiliate me, you shout at me, you keep me awake for days and nights bombarding me with questions about dog food, you announce to the world that I am helping you in your enquiries into a multiple murder thus leading every citizen in the country to suppose that I have slaughtered my wife and a beastly biochemist and ...'

'Shut up,' shouted Flint, 'I don't care what you think. It's what you've done and what you've said you've done that worries me. You've gone out of your way to mislead me ...'

'I've done nothing of the sort,' said Wilt. 'Until last night I had told you nothing but the truth and you wouldn't accept it. Last night I handed you, in the absurd shape of a pork pie, a lie you wanted to believe. If you crave crap and use illegal methods like sleep deprivation to get it you can't blame me for serving it up. Don't come in here and bluster. If you're stupid that's your problem. Go and find my wife.'

'Someone stop me from killing the bastard,' yelled Flint, as he hurled himself from the room. He went to his office and sent for Sergeant Yates. 'Cancel the pie hunt. It's a load of bull,' he told him.

'Bull?' said the Sergeant uncertainly.

'Shit,' said Flint. 'He's done it again.'

'You mean ...'

'I mean that that little turd in there has led us up the garden path again.'

'But how did he know about the factory and all that?'

Flint looked up at him pathetically. 'If you want to know why he's a walking encyclopedia, you go and ask him yourself.'

Sergeant Yates went out and returned five minutes later. 'Meat One,' he announced enigmatically.

'Meet won?'

'A class of butchers he used to teach. They took him round the factory.'

'Jesus,' said Flint, 'is there anybody that little swine hasn't taught?'

'He says they were most instructive.'

'Yates, do me a favour. Just go back and find out all the names of the classes he's taught. That way we'll know what to expect next.'

'Well I have heard him mention Plasterers Two and Gas-fitters One . . .'

'All of them, Yates, all of them. I don't want to be caught out with some tale about Mrs Wilt being got rid of in the Sewage Works because he once taught Shit Two.' He picked up the evening paper and glanced at the headlines. POLICE PROBE PIES FOR MISSING WIFE.

'Oh my God,' he groaned. 'This is going to do our public image no end of good.'

At the Tech the Principal was expressing the same opinion at a meeting of the Heads of Departments.

'We've been held up to public ridicule,' he said. 'First it is popularly supposed that we make a habit of employing lecturers who bury their unwanted wives in the foundations of the new block. Secondly we have lost all chance of attaining Polytechnic status by having the Joint Honours degree turned down by the CNAA on the grounds that those facilities we do provide are not such as befit an institution of higher learning. Professor Baxendale expressed himself very forcibly on that point and particularly on a remark he heard from one of the senior staff about necrophilia . . .'

'I merely said . . .' Dr Board began.

'We all know what you said, Dr Board. And it may interest you to know that Dr Cox in his lucid moments is still refusing cold meat. Dr Mayfield has already tendered his resignation. And now to cap it all we have this.'

He held up a newspaper, across the top of whose second page there read SEX LECTURES STUN STUDENTS.

'I hope you have all taken good note of the photograph,' said the Principal bitterly, indicating a large and unfortunately angled picture of Judy hanging from the crane. 'The article goes on ... well never mind. You can read it for yourselves. I would merely like answers to the following questions. Who authorized the purchase of thirty copies of *Last Exit From Brooklyn* for use with Fitters and Turners?'

Mr Morris tried to think who had taken FTs. 'I think that must have been Watkins,' he said. 'He left us last term. He was only a part-time lecturer.'

'Thank God we were spared him full-time,' said the Principal. 'Secondly which lecturer makes a habit of advocating to Nursery Nurses that they wear ... er ... Dutch Caps all the time?'

'Well Mr Sedgwick is very keen on them,' said Mr Morris.

'Nursery Nurses or Dutch Caps?' enquired the Principal.

'Possibly both together?' suggested Dr Board sotto voce.

'He's got this thing against the Pill,' said Mr Morris.

'Well please ask Mr Sedgwick to see me in my office on Monday at ten. I want to explain the terms under which he is employed here. And finally, how many lecturers do you know of who make use of Audio Visual Aid equipment to show blue movies to the Senior Secs?'

Mr Morris shook his head emphatically. 'No one in my department,' he said.

'It says here that blue movies have been shown,' said the Principal, 'in periods properly allocated to Current Affairs.'

'Wentworth did show them *Women in Love*,' said the Head of English.

'Well never mind. There's just one more point I want to mention. We are not going to conduct an Evening Class in First Aid with particular reference to the Treatment of Abdominal Hernia for which it was proposed to purchase an inflatable doll. From now on we are going to have to cut our coats to suit our cloth.'

'On the grounds of inflation?' asked Dr Board.

'On the grounds that the Education Committee has been waiting for years for an opportunity to cut back our budget,' said the Principal. 'That opportunity has now been given them. The fact that we have been providing a public service by keeping, to quote Mr Morris, "a large number of mentally unbalanced and potentially dangerous psychopaths off the streets" unquote seems to have escaped their notice.'

'I presume he was referring to the Day Release Apprentices,' said Dr Board charitably.

'He was not,' said the Principal. 'Correct me if I am wrong, Morris, but hadn't you in mind the members of the Liberal Studies Department?'

The meeting broke up. Later that day Mr Morris sat down to compose his letter of resignation.

19

From the window of an empty bedroom on the first floor of the Vicarage, Eva Wilt watched the Rev St John Froude walk pensively down the path to the church. As soon as he had passed out of sight she went downstairs and into the study. She would phone Henry again. If he wasn't at the Tech he must be at home. She crossed to the desk and was about to pick up the phone when she saw the ivy. Oh dear, she had forgotten all about the ivy and she had left it where he was bound to have seen it. It was all so terribly embarrassing. She dialled 34 Parkview Avenue and waited. There was no reply. She put the phone down and dialled the Tech. And all the time she watched the gate into the churchyard in case the Vicar should return.

'Fenland College of Arts and Technology,' said the girl on the switchboard.

'It's me again,' said Eva, 'I want to speak to Mr Wilt.'

'I'm very sorry but Mr Wilt isn't here.'

'But where is he? I've dialled home and ...'

'He's at the Police Station.'

'He's what?' Eva said.

'He's at the Police Station helping the police with their enquiries ...'

'Enquiries? What enquiries?' Eva shrieked.

'Didn't you know?' said the girl. 'It's been in all the papers. He's been and murdered his wife . . .'

Eva took the phone from her ear and stared at it in horror. The girl was still speaking but she was no longer listening. Henry had murdered his wife. But she was his wife. It wasn't possible. She couldn't have been murdered. For one horrible moment Eva Wilt felt sanity slipping from her. Then she put the receiver to her ear again.

'Are you there?' said the girl.

'But I am his wife,' Eva shouted. There was a long silence at the other end and she heard the girl telling someone that there was a crazy woman on the line who said she was Mrs Wilt and what ought she to do.

'I tell you I am Mrs Wilt. Mrs Eva Wilt,' she shouted but the line had gone dead. Eva put the phone down weakly. Henry at the Police Station . . . Henry had murdered her . . . Oh God. The whole world had gone mad. And here she was naked in a vicarage at . . . Eva had no idea where she was. She dialled 999.

'Emergency Services. Which department do you require?' said the operator.

'Police,' said Eva. There was a click and a man's voice came on.

'Police here.'

'This is Mrs Wilt,' said Eva.

'Mrs Wilt?'

'Mrs Eva Wilt. Is it true that my husband has murdered . . . I mean has my husband . . . oh dear I don't know what to say.'

'You say you're Mrs Wilt, Mrs Eva Wilt?' said the man.

Eva nodded and then said, 'Yes.'

'I see,' said the man dubiously. 'You're quite sure you're Mrs Wilt?'

'Of course I'm sure. That's what I'm ringing about.'

'Might I enquire where you're calling from?'

'I don't know,' said Eva. 'You see I'm in this house and I've got no clothes and . . . oh dear.' The Vicar was coming up the path on to the terrace.

'If you could just give us the address.'

'I can't stop now,' said Eva and put the phone down. For a moment she hesitated and then grabbing the ivy from the desk she rushed out of the room.

'I tell you I don't know where she is,' said Wilt. 'I expect you'll find her under missing persons. She has passed from the realm of substantiality into that of abstraction.'

'What the hell do you mean by that?' asked the Inspector, reaching for his cup of coffee. It was eleven o'clock on Saturday morning but he persisted. He had twenty-eight hours to get to the truth.

'I always warned her that Transcendental Meditation carried potential dangers,' said Wilt, himself in a no-man's-land between sleeping and walking. 'But she would do it.'

'Do what?'

'Meditate transcendentally. In the lotus position. Perhaps she has gone too far this time. Possibly she has transmogrified herself.'

'Trans what?' said Inspector Flint suspiciously.

'Changed herself in some magical fashion into something else.'

'Jesus, Wilt, if you start on those pork pies again ...'

'I was thinking of something more spiritual, Inspector, something beautiful.'

'I doubt it.'

'Ah, but think. Here am I sitting in this room with you as a direct result of going for walks with the dog and thinking dark thoughts about murdering my wife. From those hours of idle fancy I have gained the reputation of being a murderer without committing a murder. Who is to say but that Eva whose thoughts were monotonously beautiful has not earned herself a commensurately beautiful reward? To put it in your terms, Inspector, we get what we ask for.'

'I fervently hope so, Wilt,' said the Inspector.

'Ah,' said Wilt, 'but then where is she? Tell me that. Mere speculation will not do ...'

'Me tell you?' shouted the Inspector upsetting his cup of

coffee. 'You know which hole in the ground you put her in or which cement mixer or incinerator you used.'

'I was speaking metaphorically ... I mean rhetorically,' said Wilt. 'I was trying to imagine what Eva would be if her thoughts such as they are took on the substance of reality. My secret dream was to become a ruthless man of action, decisive, unhindered by moral doubts or considerations of conscience, a Hamlet transformed into Henry the Fifth without the patriotic fervour that inclines one to think that he would not have approved of the Common Market, a Caesar ...'

Inspector Flint had heard enough. 'Wilt,' he snarled, 'I don't give a damn what you wanted to become. What I want to know is what has become of your wife.'

'I was just coming to that,' said Wilt. 'What we've got to establish first is what I am.'

'I know what you are, Wilt. A bloody word merchant, a verbal contortionist, a fucking logic-chopper, a linguistic Houdini, an encyclopedia of unwanted information ...' Inspector Flint ran out of metaphors.

'Brilliant, Inspector, brilliant. I couldn't have put it better myself. A logic-chopper, but alas not a wife one. If we follow the same line of reasoning Eva in spite of all her beautiful thoughts and meditations has remained as unchanged as I. The ethereal eludes her. Nirvana slips ever from her grasp. Beauty and truth evade her. She pursues the absolute with a fly-swatter and pours Harpic down the drains of Hell itself ...'

'That's the tenth time you have mentioned Harpic,' said the Inspector, suddenly alive to a new dreadful possibility. 'You didn't ...'

Wilt shook his head. 'There you go again. So like poor Eva. The literal mind that seeks to seize the evanescent and clutches fancy by its non-existent throat. That's Eva for you. She will never dance Swan Lake. No management would allow her to fill the stage with water or install a double bed and Eva would insist.'

Inspector Flint got up. 'This is getting us nowhere fast.'

'Precisely,' said Wilt, 'nowhere at all. We are what we are and nothing we can do will alter the fact. The mould that forms our natures remains unbroken. Call it heredity, call it chance ...'

'Call it a load of codswallop,' said Flint and left the room. He needed his sleep and he intended to get it.

In the passage he met Sergeant Yates.

'There's been an emergency call from a woman claiming to be Mrs Wilt,' the Sergeant said.

'Where from?'

'She wouldn't say where she was,' said Yates. 'She just said she didn't know and that she had no clothes on ...'

'Oh one of those,' said the Inspector. 'A bloody nutter. What the hell are you wasting my time for? As if we didn't have enough on our hands without that.'

'I just thought you'd want to know. If she calls again we'll try and get a fix on the number.'

'As if I cared,' said Flint and hurried off in search of his lost sleep.

The Rev St John Froude spent an uneasy day. His investigation of the church had revealed nothing untoward and there was no sign that an obscene ritual (a Black Mass had crossed his mind) had been performed there. As he walked back to the Vicarage he was glad to note that the sky over Eel Stretch was empty and that the contraceptives had disappeared. So had the ivy on his desk. He regarded the space where it had been with apprehension and helped himself to whisky. He could have sworn there had been a sprig of ivy there when he had left. By the time he had finished what remained in the bottle his mind was filled with weird fancies. The Vicarage was strangely noisy. There were odd creaks from the staircase and inexplicable sounds from the upper floor as if someone or something was moving stealthily about but when the Vicar went to investigate the noises ceased abruptly. He went upstairs and poked his head into several empty bedrooms. He came down again and stood in the hall listening. Then he returned to his study and tried to concentrate on his sermon, but the feeling that he was not alone persisted. The Rev St John Froude sat at his desk and considered the possibility of ghosts. Something very odd was going on. At one o'clock he went down the hall to the kitchen for lunch and discovered that a pint of milk had disappeared from the pantry and that the remains of an apple pie that Mrs Snape who did his cleaning twice weekly had brought him had also vanished. He made do with baked beans on toast and tottered upstairs for his afternoon nap. It was while he was there that he first heard the voices. Or rather one voice. It seemed to come from his study. The Rev St John Froude sat up in bed. If his ears weren't betraying him and in view of the morning's weird events he was inclined to believe that they were he could have sworn someone had been using his telephone. He got up and put on his shoes. Someone was crying. He went out on to the landing and listened. The sobbing had stopped. He went downstairs and looked in all the rooms on the ground floor but, apart from the fact that a dust cover had been removed from one of the armchairs in the unused sitting-room, there was no sign of anyone. He was just about to go upstairs again when the telephone rang. He went into the study and answered it.

'Waterswick Vicarage,' he mumbled.

'This is Fenland Constabulary,' said a man. 'We've just had a call from your number purporting to come from a Mrs Wilt.'

'Mrs Wilt?' said the Rev St John Froude. 'Mrs Wilt? I'm afraid there must be some mistake. I don't know any Mrs Wilt.'

'The call definitely came from your phone, sir.'

The Rev St John Froude considered the matter. 'This is all very peculiar,' he said, 'I live alone.'

'You are the Vicar?'

'Of course I'm the Vicar. This is the Vicarage and I am the Vicar.'

'I see, sir. And your name is?'

'The Reverend St John Froude. F . . . R . . . O . . . U . . . D . . . E.'

'Quite sir, and you definitely don't have a woman in the house.'

'Of course I don't have a woman in the house. I find the suggestion distinctly improper. I am a . . .'

'I'm sorry, sir, but we just have to check these things out.

We've had a call from Mrs Wilt, at least a woman claiming to be Mrs Wilt, and it came from your phone ...'

'Who is this Mrs Wilt? I've never heard of a Mrs Wilt.'

'Well sir, Mrs Wilt ... it's a bit difficult really. She's supposed to have been murdered.'

'Murdered?' said the Rev St John Froude. 'Did you say "murdered"?'

'Let's just say she is missing from home in suspicious circumstances. We're holding her husband for questioning.'

The Rev St John Froude shook his head. 'How very unfortunate,' he murmured.

'Thank you for your help, sir,' said the Sergeant. 'Sorry to have disturbed you.'

The Rev St John Froude put the phone down thoughtfully. The notion that he was sharing the house with a disembodied and recently murdered woman was not one that he had wanted to put to his caller. His reputation for eccentricity was already sufficiently widespread without adding to it. On the other hand what he had seen on the boat in Eel Stretch bore, now that he came to think of it, all the hallmarks of murder. Perhaps in some extraordinary way he had been a witness to a tragedy that had already occurred, a sort of post-mortem déja vu if that was the right way of putting it. Certainly if the husband were being held for questioning the murder must have taken place before ... In which case ... The Rev St John Froude stumbled through a series of suppositions in which Time with a capital T, and appeals for help from beyond the grave figured largely. Perhaps it was his duty to inform the police of what he had seen. He was just hesitating and wondering what to do when he heard those sobs again and this time quite distinctly. They came from the next room. He got up, braced himself with another shot of whisky and went next door. Standing in the middle of the room was a large woman whose hair straggled down over her shoulders and whose face was ravaged. She was wearing what appeared to be a shroud. The Rev St John Froude stared at her with a growing sense of horror. Then he sank to his knees.

'Let us pray,' he muttered hoarsely.

The ghastly apparition slumped heavily forward clutching the shroud to its bosom. Together they kneeled in prayer.

'Check it out? What the hell do you mean "check it out"?' said Inspector Flint who objected strongly to being woken in the middle of the afternoon when he had had no sleep for thirty-six hours and was trying to get some. 'You wake me with some damned tomfoolery about a vicar called Sigmund Freud ...'

'St John Froude,' said Yates.

'I don't care what he's called. It's still improbable. If the bloody man says she isn't there, she isn't there. What am I supposed to do about it?'

'I just thought we ought to get a patrol car to check, that's all.'

'What makes you think ...'

'There was definitely a call from a woman claiming to be Mrs Wilt and it came from that number. She's called twice now. We've got a tape of the second call. She gave details of herself and they sound authentic. Date of birth, address, Wilt's occupation, even the right name of their dog and the fact that they have yellow curtains in the lounge.'

'Well, any fool can tell that. All they've got to do is walk past the house.'

'And the name of the dog. It's called Clem. I've checked that and she's right.'

'She didn't happen to say what she'd been doing for the past week did she?'

'She said she'd been on a boat,' said Yates. 'Then she rang off.'

Inspector Flint sat up in bed. 'A boat? What boat?'

'She rang off. Oh and another thing, she said she takes a size ten shoe. She does.'

'Oh shit,' said Flint. 'All right, I'll come down.' He got out of bed and began to dress.

In his cell Wilt stared at the ceiling. After so many hours of interrogation his mind still reverberated with questions. 'How did you kill her? Where did you put her? What did you do with the weapon?' Meaningless questions continually reiterated in the hope they would finally break him. But Wilt hadn't broken. He had triumphed. For once in his life he knew himself to be invincibly right and everyone else totally wrong. Always before he had had doubts. Plasterers Two might after all have been right about there being too many wogs in the country. Perhaps hanging was a deterrent. Wilt didn't think so but he couldn't be absolutely certain. Only time would tell. But in the case of Regina *versus* Wilt *re* the murder of Mrs Wilt there could be no question of his guilt. He could be tried, found guilty and sentenced, it would make no difference. He was innocent of the charge and if he was sentenced to life imprisonment the very enormity of the injustice done to him would compound his knowledge of his own innocence. For the very first time in his life Wilt knew himself to be free. It was as though the original sin of being Henry Wilt, of 34 Parkview Avenue, Ipford, lecturer in Liberal Studies at the Fenland College of Arts and Technology, husband of Eva Wilt and father of none, had been lifted from him. All the encumbrances of possessions, habits, salary and status, all the social conformities, the niceties of estimation of himself and other people which he and Eva had acquired, all these had gone. Locked in his cell Wilt was free to be. And whatever happened he would never again succumb to the siren calls of self-effacement. After the flagrant contempt and fury of Inspector Flint, the abuse and the opprobrium heaped on him for a week, who needed approbation? They could stuff their opinions of him. Wilt would pursue his independent course and put to good use his evident gifts of inconsequence. Give him a life sentence and a progressive prison governor and Wilt would drive the man mad within a month by the sweet reasonableness of his refusal to obey the prison rules. Solitary confinement and a regime of bread and water, if such punishments still existed, would not deter him. Give him his freedom and he would apply his newfound talents at the Tech. He would sit happily on committees and reduce them to dissensions by his untiring adoption of whatever argument was most contrary to the consensus opinion. The race was not to the swift after all, it was to the indefatigably inconsequential and life was random, anarchic and chaotic. Rules were made to be broken and the man with the grasshopper mind was one jump ahead of all the others. Having established this new rule, Wilt turned on his side and tried to sleep but sleep wouldn't come. He tried his other side with equal lack of success. Thoughts, questions, irrelevant answers and imaginary dialogues filled his mind. He tried counting sheep but found himself thinking of Eva. Dear Eva, damnable Eva, ebullient Eva and Eva irrepressibly enthusiastic. Like him she had sought the Absolute, the Eternal Truth which would save her the bother of ever having to think for herself again. She had sought it in Pottery, in Transcendental Meditation, in Judo, on trampolines and most incongruously of all in Oriental Dance. Finally she had tried to find it in sexual emancipation, Women's Lib and the Sacrament of the Orgasm in which she could forever lose herself. Which, come to think of it, was what she appeared to have done. And taken the bloody Pringsheims with her. Well she would certainly have some explaining to do when and if she ever returned. Wilt smiled to himself at the thought of what she would say when she discovered what her latest infatuation with the Infinite had led to. He'd see to it that she had cause to regret it to her dying day.

On the floor of the sitting-room at the Vicarage Eva Wilt struggled with the growing conviction that her dying day was already over and done with. Certainly everyone she came into contact with seemed to think she was dead. The policeman she had spoken to on the phone had seemed disinclined to believe her assertion that she was alive and at least relatively well and had demanded proofs of her identity in the most disconcerting fashion. Eva had retreated stricken from the encounter with her confidence in her own continuing existence seriously undermined and it had only needed the reaction of the Rev St John Froude to her appearance in his house to complete her misery. His frantic appeals to the Almighty to rescue the soul of our dear departed, one Eva Wilt, deceased, from its present shape and unendurable form had affected Eva profoundly. She knelt on the carpet and sobbed while the Vicar stared at her over his glasses, shut his eyes, lifted up a shaky voice in prayer, opened his eyes, shuddered and generally behaved in a manner calculated to cause gloom and despondency in the putative corpse and when, in a last desperate attempt to get Eva Wilt, deceased, to take her proper place in the heavenly choir he cut short a prayer about 'Man that is born of Woman hath but a short time to live and is full of misery' and struck up 'Abide with me' with many a semi-quaver, Eva abandoned all attempt at self-control and wailed 'Fast falls the eventide' most affectingly. By the time they had got to 'I need thy presence every passing hour' the Rev St John Froude was of an entirely contrary opinion. He staggered from the room and took sanctuary in his study. Behind him Eva Wilt, espousing her new role as deceased with all the enthusiasm she had formerly bestowed on trampolines, judo and pottery, demanded to know where death's sting was and where, grave, thy victory. 'As if I bloody knew,' muttered the Vicar and reached for the whisky bottle only to find that it too was empty. He sat down and put his hands over his ears to shut out the dreadful noise. On the whole 'Abide with me' was the last hymn he should have chosen. He'd have been better off with 'There is a green hill far away'. It was less open to misinterpretation.

When at last the hymn ended he sat relishing the silence and was about to investigate the possibility that there was another bottle in the larder when there was a knock on the door and Eva entered.

'Oh Father I have sinned,' she shrieked, doing her level best to wail and gnash her teeth at the same time. The Rev St John Froude gripped the arms of his chair and tried to swallow. It was not easy. Then overcoming the reasonable fear that delirium tremens had come all too suddenly he managed to speak. 'Rise, my child,' he gasped as Eva writhed on the rug before him, 'I will hear your confession.'

20

Inspector Flint switched the tape recorder off and looked at Wilt.

'Well?'

'Well what?' said Wilt.

'Is that her? Is that Mrs Wilt?'

Wilt nodded. 'I'm afraid so.'

'What do you mean you're afraid so? The damned woman is alive. You should be fucking grateful. Instead of that you sit there saying you're afraid so.'

Wilt sighed. 'I was just thinking what an abyss there is between the person as we remember and imagine them and the reality of what they are. I was beginning to have fond memories of her and now ...'

'You ever been to Waterswick?'

Wilt shook his head. 'Never.'

'Know the Vicar there?'

'Didn't even know there was a vicar there.'

'And you wouldn't know how she got there?'

'You heard her,' said Wilt. 'She said she'd been on a boat.'

'And you wouldn't know anyone with a boat, would you?'

'People in my circle don't have boats, Inspector. Maybe the Pringsheims have a boat.'

Inspector Flint considered the possibility and rejected it. They had checked the boatyards out and the Pringsheims didn't have a boat and hadn't hired one either.

On the other hand the possibility that he had been the victim of some gigantic hoax, a deliberate and involved scheme to make him look an idiot, was beginning to take shape in his mind. At the instigation of this infernal Wilt he had ordered the exhumation of an inflatable doll and had been photographed staring lividly at it at the very moment it changed sex. He had instituted a round-up of pork pies unprecedented in the history of the country. He wouldn't be at all surprised if Sweetbreads instituted legal proceedings for the damage done to their previously unspotted reputation. And finally he had held an apparently innocent man for questioning for a week and would doubtless be held responsible for the delay and additional cost in building the new Administration block at the Tech. There were, in all probability, other appalling consequences to be considered, but that was enough to be going on with. And he had nobody to blame but himself. Or Wilt. He looked at Wilt venomously.

Wilt smiled. 'I know what you're thinking,' he said.

'You don't,' said the Inspector. 'You've no idea.'

'That we are all the creatures of circumstance, that things are never what they seem, that there's more to this than meets ...'

'We'll see about that,' said the Inspector.

Wilt got up. 'I don't suppose you'll want me for anything else,' he said. 'I'll be getting along home.'

'You'll be doing no such thing. You're coming with us to pick up Mrs Wilt.'

They went out into the courtyard and got into a police car. As they drove through the suburbs, past the filling stations and factories and out across the fens Wilt shrank into the back seat of the car and felt the sense of freedom he had enjoyed in the Police Station evaporate. And with every mile it dwindled further and the harsh reality of choice, of having to earn a living, of boredom and the endless petty arguments with Eva, of bridge on Saturday nights with the Mottrams and drives on Sundays with Eva, reasserted itself. Beside him, sunk in sullen silence, Inspector Flint lost his symbolic appeal. No longer the mentor of Wilt's self-confidence, the foil to his inconsequentiality, he had become a fellow sufferer in the business of living, almost a mirror-image of Wilt's own nonentity. And ahead, across this flat bleak landscape with its black earth and cumulus skies, lay Eva and a lifetime of attempted explanations and counter-accusations. For a moment Wilt considered shouting 'Stop the car. I want to get out', but the moment passed. Whatever the future held he would learn to live with it. He had not discovered the paradoxical nature of freedom only to succumb once more to the servitude of Parkview Avenue, the

Tech and Eva's trivial enthusiasms. He was Wilt, the man with the grasshopper mind.

Eva was drunk. The Rev St John Froude's automatic reaction to her appalling confession had been to turn from whisky to 150% Polish spirit which he kept for emergencies and Eva, in between agonies of repentance and the outpourings of lurid sins, had wet her whistle with the stuff. Encouraged by it's effect, by the petrified benevolence of the Vicar's smile and by the growing conviction that if she was dead eternal life demanded an act of absolute contrition while if she wasn't it allowed her to avoid the embarrassment of explaining what precisely she was doing naked in someone else's house, Eva confessed her sins with an enthusiasm that matched her deepest needs. This was what she had sought in judo and pottery and Oriental dance, an orgiastic expiation of her guilt. She confessed sins she had committed and sins she hadn't, sins that had occurred to her and sins she had forgotten. She had betrayed Henry, she had wished him dead, she had lusted after other men, she was an adulterated woman, she was a lesbian, she was a nymphomaniac. And interspersed with these sins of the flesh there were sins of omission. Eva left nothing out. Henry's cold suppers, his lonely walks with the dog, her lack of appreciation for all he had done for her, her failure to be a good wife, her obsession with Harpic ... everything poured out. In his chair the Rev St John Froude sat nodding incessantly like a toy dog in the back window of a car, raising his head to stare at her when she confessed to being a nymphomaniac and dropping it abruptly at the mention of Harpic, and all the time desperately trying to understand what had brought a fat naked -- the shroud kept falling off her -- lady, no definitely not lady, woman to his house with all the symptoms of religious mania upon her.

'My child, is that all?' he muttered when Eva finally exhausted her repertoire.

'Yes, Father,' sobbed Eva.

'Thank God,' said the Rev St John Froude fervently and wondered what to do next. If half the things he had heard were true he was in the presence of a sinner so depraved as to make the ex-Archdeacon of Ongar a positive saint. On the other hand there were incongruities about her sins that made him hesitate before granting absolution. A confession full of false-hoods was no sign of true repentance.

'I take it that you are married,' he said doubtfully, 'and that Henry is your lawful wedded husband?'

'Yes,' said Eva. 'Dear Henry.'

Poor sod, thought the Vicar but he was too tactful to say so. 'And you have left him?'

'Yes.'

'For another man?'

Eva shook her head. 'To teach him a lesson,' she said with sudden belligerence.

'A lesson?' said the Vicar, trying frantically to imagine what sort of lesson the wretched Mr Wilt had learnt from her absence. 'You did say a lesson?'

'Yes,' said Eva, 'I wanted him to learn that he couldn't get along without me.'

The Rev St John Froude sipped his drink thoughtfully. If even a quarter of her confession was to be believed her husband must be finding getting along without her quite delightful. 'And now you want to go back to him?'

'Yes,' said Eva.

'But he won't have you?'

'He can't. The police have got him.'

'The police?' said the Vicar. 'And may one ask what the police have got him for?'

'They say he's murdered me,' said Eva.

The Rev St John Froude eyed her with new alarm. He knew now that Mrs Wilt was out of her mind. He glanced round for something to use as a weapon should the need arise and finding nothing better to choose from than a plaster bust of the poet Dante and the bottle of Polish spirit, picked up the latter by its neck. Eva held her glass out.

'Oh you are awful,' she said. 'You're getting me tiddly.'

'Quite,' said the Vicar and put the bottle down again hastily. It was bad enough being alone in the house with a large, drunk, semi-naked woman who imagined that her husband had murdered her and who confessed to sins he had previously only read about without her jumping to the conclusion that he was deliberately trying to make her drunk. The Rev St John Froude had no desire to figure prominently in next Sunday's *News of the World*.

'You were saying that your husband murdered ...' He stopped. That seemed an unprofitable subject to pursue.

'How could he have murdered me?' asked Eva. 'I'm here in the flesh, aren't I?'

'Definitely,' said the Vicar. 'Most definitely.'

'Well then,' said Eva. 'And anyway Henry couldn't murder anyone. He wouldn't know how. He can't even change a fuse in a plug. I have to do everything like that in the house.' She stared at the Vicar balefully. 'Are you married?'

'No,' said the Rev St John Froude, wishing to hell that he was.

'What do you know about life if you aren't married?' asked Eva truculently. The Polish spirit was getting to her now and with it there came a terrible sense of grievance. 'Men. What good are men? They can't even keep a house tidy. Look at this room. I ask you.' She waved her arms to emphasize the point and the dustcover dropped. 'Just look at it.' But the Rev St John Froude had no eyes for the room. What he could see of Eva was enough to convince him that his life was in danger. He bounded from the chair, trod heavily on an occasional table, overturned the wastepaper basket and threw himself through the door into the hall. As he stumbled away in search of sanctuary the front door bell rang. The Rev St John Froude opened it and stared into Inspector Flint's face.

'Thank God, you've come,' he gasped, 'she's in there.'

The Inspector and two uniformed constables went across the hall. Wilt followed uneasily. This was the moment he had been dreading. In the event it was better than he had expected. Not so for Inspector Flint. He entered the study and found himself confronted by a large naked woman.

'Mrs Wilt ...' he began but Eva was staring at the two uniformed constables.

'Where's my Henry?' Eva shouted. 'You've got my Henry.' She hurled herself forward. Unwisely the Inspector attempted to restrain her.

'Mrs Wilt, if you'll just ...' A blow on the side of his head ended the sentence.

'Keep your hands off me,' yelled Eva, and putting her knowledge of Judo to good use hurled him to the floor. She was about to repeat the performance with the constables when Wilt thrust himself forward.

'Here I am, dear,' he said. Eva stopped in her tracks. For a moment she quivered and, seen from Inspector Flint's viewpoint, appeared to be about to melt. 'Oh Henry,' she said, 'what have they been doing to you?'

'Nothing at all, dear,' said Wilt. 'Now get your clothes on. We're going home.' Eva looked down at herself, shuddered and allowed him to lead her out of the room.

Slowly and wearily Inspector Flint got to his feet. He knew now why Wilt had put that bloody doll down the hole and why he had sat so confidently through days and nights of interrogation. After twelve years of marriage to Eva Wilt the urge to commit homicide if only by proxy would be overwhelming. And as for Wilt's ability to stand up to cross-examination ... it was self-evident. But the Inspector knew too that he would never be able to explain it to anyone else. There were mysteries of human relationships that defied analysis. And Wilt had stood there calmly and told her to get her clothes on. With a grudging sense of admiration Flint went out into the hall. The little sod had guts, whatever else you could say about him.

They drove back to Parkview Avenue in silence. In the back seat Eva, wrapped in a blanket, slept with her head lolling on Wilt's shoulder. Beside her Henry Wilt sat proudly. A woman who could silence Inspector Flint with one swift blow to the head was worth her weight in gold and besides that scene in the study had given him the weapon he needed. Naked and drunk in a vicar's study ... There would be no questions now about why he had put that doll down the hole. No accusations, no recriminations. The entire episode would be relegated to the best forgotten. And with it would go all doubts about his virility or his ability to get on in the world. It was checkmate. For a moment Wilt almost lapsed into sentimentality and thought of love before recalling just how dangerous a topic that was. He would be better off sticking to indifference and undisclosed affection. 'Let sleeping dogs lie,' he muttered.

It was an opinion shared by the Pringsheims. As they were helped from the cruiser to a police launch, as they climbed ashore, as they explained to a sceptical Inspector Flint how they had come to be marooned for a week in Eel Stretch in a boat that belonged to someone else, they were strangely uncommunicative. No they didn't know how the door of the bathroom had been bust down. Well maybe there had been an accident. They had been too drunk to remember. A doll? What doll? Grass? You mean marijuana? They had no idea. In their house?

Inspector Flint let them go finally. 'I'll be seeing you again when the charges have been properly formulated,' he said grimly. The Pringsheims left for Rossiter Grove to pack. They flew out of Heathrow next morning.

21

The Principal sat behind his desk and regarded Wilt incredulously. 'Promotion?' he said. 'Did I hear you mention the word "promotion"?'

'You did,' said Wilt. 'And what is more you also heard "Head of Liberal Studies" too.'

'After all you've done? You mean to say you have the nerve to come in here and demand to be made Head of Liberal Studies?'

'Yes,' said Wilt.

The Principal struggled to find words to match his feelings. It wasn't easy. In front of him sat the man who was responsible for the series of disasters that had put an end to his fondest hopes. The Tech would never be a Poly now. The Joint Honours degree's rejection had seen to that. And then there was the adverse publicity, the cut in the budget, his battles with the Education Committee, the humiliation of being heralded as the Principal of Dollfuckers Hall ...

'You're fired!' he shouted.

Wilt smiled. 'I think not,' he said. 'Here are my terms ...'

'Your what?'

'Terms,' said Wilt. 'In return for my appointment as Head of Liberal Studies, I shall not institute proceedings against you for unfair dismissal with all the attendant publicity that would entail. I shall withdraw my case against the police for unlawful arrest. The contract I have here with the *Sunday Post* for a series of articles on the true nature of Liberal Studies – I intend to call them Exposure to Barbarism – will remain un-signed. I will cancel the lectures I had promised to give for the Sex Education Centre. I will not appear on *Panorama* next Monday. In short I will abjure the pleasures and rewards of public exposure ...'

The Principal raised a shaky hand. 'Enough,' he said, 'I'll see what I can do.'

Wilt got to his feet. 'Let me know your answer by lunch-time,' he said. 'I'll be in my office.'

'Your office?' said the Principal.

'It used to belong to Mr Morris,' said Wilt and closed the door. Behind him the Principal picked up the phone. There had been no mistaking the seriousness of Wilt's threats. He would have to hurry.

Wilt strolled down the corridor to the Liberal Studies De-partment and stood looking at the books on the shelves. There were changes he had in mind. *The Lord of the Flies* would go and with it *Shane*, *Women in Love*, Orwell's *Essays* and *Catcher in the Rye*, all those symptoms of intellectual con-descension, those dangled worms of sensibility. In future Gas-fitters One and Meat Two would learn the how of things not why. How to read and write. How to make beer. How to fiddle their income tax returns. How to cope with the police when arrested. How to make an incompatible marriage work. Wilt would give the last two lessons himself. There would be objections from the staff, even threats of resignation, but it would make no difference. He might well accept several resignations from those who persisted in opposing his ideas. After all you didn't require a degree in English literature to teach Gasfitters the how of anything. Come to think of it, they had taught him more than they had learnt from him. Much more. He went into Mr Morris's empty office and sat down at the desk and composed a memorandum to Liberal Studies Staff. It was headed Notes on a System of Self-Teaching for Day Release Classes. He had just written 'non-hierarchical' for the fifth time when the phone rang. It was the Principal.

'Thank you,' said the new Head of Liberal Studies.

Eva Wilt walked gaily up Parkview Avenue from the doctor's office. She had made breakfast for Henry and Hoovered the front room and polished the hall and cleaned the windows and Harpicked the loo and been round to the Harmony Community Centre and helped with Xeroxing an appeal for a new play group and done the shopping and paid the milkman and been to the doctor to ask if there was any point in taking a course of fertility drugs and there was. 'Of course we'll have to do tests,' the doctor had told her, 'but there's no reason to think they'd prove negative. The only danger is that you might have sextuplets.' It wasn't a danger to Eva. It was what she had always wanted, a house full of children. And all at once. Henry would be pleased. And so the sun shone brighter, the sky was bluer, the flowers in the gardens were rosier and even Parkview Avenue itself seemed to have taken on a new and brighter aspect. It was one of Eva Wilt's better days.

Tom Sharpe
Riotous Assembly £3.50

A crime of passion committed with a multi-barrelled elephant gun
... A drunken bishop attacked by a pack of Alsatians in a swimming
pool ... Transvestite variations in a distinguished lady's rubber-
furnished bedroom ... Famous battles re-enacted by five hundred
schizophrenic Zulus and an equal number of (equally mad) whites.

'Crackling, spitting, murderously funny' DAILY TELEGRAPH

Indecent Exposure £3.50

The brilliant follow-up to *Riotous Assembly* ... another of Tom
Sharpe's hilarious and savage satires on South Africa ...

'Explosively funny, fiendishly inventive' SUNDAY TIMES

'A lusty and delightfully lunatic fantasy' SUNDAY EXPRESS

Blott on the Landscape £2.99

'Skulduggery at stately homes, dirty work at the planning inquiry,
and the villains falling satisfactorily up to their ears in the minestrone
... the heroine breakfasts on broken bottles, wears barbed wire next
to her skin and stops at nothing to protect her ancestral seat from a
motorway construction' THE TIMES

'Deliciously English comedy' GUARDIAN

Porterhouse Blue £3.50

To Porterhouse College, Cambridge, famous for rowing, low
academic standards and a proud cuisine, comes a new Master, an
ex-grammar school boy, demanding Firsts, women students, a self-
service canteen, and a slot machine for contraceptives, to challenge
the established order – with catastrophic results ...

'That rarest and most enjoyable of products – a highly intelligent and
funny book' SUNDAY TIMES

James Herriot
If Only They Could Talk £3.50

The genial misadventures of James Herriot, a young vet in the lovely
Yorkshire Dales are enough to make a cat laugh – let alone the
animals, if only they could talk.

Vet in a Spin £3.50

Strapped into the cockpit of a Tiger Moth trainer, James Harriot has
swapped his wellingtons and breeches for sheep-skin boots and a
baggy flying suit. But the vet-turned-airman is the sort of trainee to
terrify instructors who've faced the Luftwaffe without flinching. Very
soon he's grounded, discharged and back to his old life in the dales
around Darrowby.

'Marks the emergence of Herriot as a mature writer'
YORKSHIRE POST

'Just as much fun as its predecessors. May it sell, as usual, in its
millions' THE TIMES

The Lord God Made Them All £3.99

The war is over, the RAF uniform has been handed in and James
Herriot goes back to where he ought to be – at work in the Dales
around Darrowby. Much has changed, but the blunt-spoken
Yorkshire folk and the host of four-legged patients are still the same.
So is their vet, not knowing that literary success is just around the
corner.

'A joyous book, a celebration of life itself' PUBLISHERS WEEKLY

All Pan books are available at your local bookshop or newsagent, or can be ordered direct from the publisher. Indicate the number of copies required and fill in the form below.

Send to: **CS Department, Pan Books Ltd., P.O. Box 40, Basingstoke, Hants. RG21 2YT.**

or phone: 0256 469551 (Ansaphone), quoting title, author and Credit Card number.

Please enclose a remittance* to the value of the cover price plus: 60p for the first book plus 30p per copy for each additional book ordered to a maximum charge of £2.40 to cover postage and packing.

*Payment may be made in sterling by UK personal cheque, postal order, sterling draft or international money order, made payable to Pan Books Ltd.

Alternatively by Barclaycard/Access:

Card No.

Signature:

Applicable only in the UK and Republic of Ireland.

While every effort is made to keep prices low, it is sometimes necessary to increase prices at short notice. Pan Books reserve the right to show on covers and charge new retail prices which may differ from those advertised in the text or elsewhere.

NAME AND ADDRESS IN BLOCK LETTERS PLEASE:

....

Name ————————————————————————————

Address ————————————————————————————

————————————————————————————————

————————————————————————————————

————————————————————————————————

3/87

PRIVA   O

To the   ts new clothes:
               ent for virtue.

Eric Linklater (1899–1974), was born in Wales and
educated in Aberdeen. His family came from the Orkney
Islands (his father was a master mariner), and the boy
spent much of his childhood there.

Linklater served as a private in the Black Watch at the
close of the First World War, surviving a nearly fatal
head wound to return to Aberdeen to take a degree in
English. A spell in Bombay with the *Times of India* was
followed by some university teaching at Aberdeen again,
and then a Commonwealth Fellowship which allowed
him to travel in America from 1928 to 1930.

Linklater's memories of Orkney and student life informed
his first novel, *White Maa's Saga* (1929), while the success
of *Poet's Pub* in the same year led him to take up writing
as a full-time career. A hilarious satirical novel, *Juan in
America* (1931), followed his American trip, while the
equally irreverent *Magnus Merriman* (1934) was based on
his experiences as Nationalist candidate for a by-election
in East Fife.

Linklater joined the army again in the Second World War,
to serve in fortress Orkney, and later as a War Office
correspondent reporting the Italian campaign, and later
writing the official history. The compassionate comedy
of *Private Angelo* (1946) was drawn from this Italian
experience.

With these and many other books, stories and plays to his
name, Linklater enjoyed a long and popular career as a
writer. His early creative years were described in *The Man
on my Back* (1941), while a fuller autobiography, *Fanfare
for a Tin Hat*, appeared in 1970.

Eric Linklater

Private Angelo

Introduced by Magnus Linklater

CANONGATE
CLASSICS
44

First published in Great Britain in 1946 by
Jonathan Cape Ltd. This edition first published
as a Canongate Classic in 1992 by Canongate
Press Plc, 14 Frederick Street, Edinburgh EH2
2HB. Copyright © Eric Linklater 1946. Introduction © 1992 Magnus Linklater.

The publishers gratefully acknowledge general
subsidy from the Scottish Arts Council towards
the Canongate Classics series and a specific grant
towards the publication of this title.

Set in 10pt Plantin by Falcon Typographic Art
Ltd, Fife, Scotland. Printed and bound in Great
Britain by BPCC Hazells Ltd.

Canongate Classics
Series Editor: Roderick Watson
Editorial Board: Tom Crawford, John Pick

British Library Cataloguing-in-Publication Data
A catalogue record for this book is available
from the British Library.

ISBN 0–86241–376–1

Introduction

Adventure was an important word in Eric Linklater's vocabulary. It meant surprise, discovery, excitement, sometimes disappointment, but more often enjoyment, and all of these he relished as an escape from what he described, 'in despair of a closer definition', as 'normal life'. He liked to recall his own past experiences as a series of adventures, full of light and colour, and to tell stories about them which became richer with age. The title he gave his rectorial address to Aberdeen University in 1945, the year he wrote *Private Angelo*, was 'The Art of Adventure' and in it he suggested to his young audience that sooner or later it would fall to most of them to be confronted with a choice between the routine and the unexpected. It was, he said, like walking out through a familiar door:

> There, on that doorstep, you are confronted with a momentous choice: you may regard life either as the general adventure or the general burden. That much of it is burdensome, no one can deny — the daily task of shaving is a nuisance, to listen politely to one's elders is tedious, to pay one's taxes an Egyptian load — but if from the beginning you think of life as a burden, you will immediately feel tired, and thereby suffer a disadvantage: you will lack energy that might have procured enjoyment. It is more profitable to see life as an adventure: not as something to be carried, but as something to be broken into.

One of the great adventures in Eric's own life was the six-month period he spent as the War Office's official historian in Italy in 1944, following the Allied attack north from Sicily, through Naples and Rome to Florence. He saw scenes of terrible devastation and great suffering; he witnessed bravery and cowardice; but he also saw the Pope in the Vatican wearing red embroidered carpet slippers, and was introduced to King Umberto, and discovered the Uffizi's greatest paintings only 2000 yards from the German forward positions, stored for safety in the Castello di Montegufoni where, memorably, he took advantage of his intimacy with one of the most famous pictures in the world and planted a kiss on the lips of the pregnant Venus, the loveliest of the Graces in Botticelli's 'Primavera'.

These adventures he spoke and wrote of long after the anguish of war had faded into a dark and gloomy backcloth. But above all he remembered and cherished Italy and the Italians. *Private Angelo* is a celebration of a country and a people with whom he felt immediate and instinctive sympathy. That its central character is a self-confessed coward and its supporting cast is studded with thieves, cheats and black-marketeers, has not prevented it becoming, amongst Italians themselves, one of the very few books by a foreigner which is recognised, with admiration and affection, as presenting an authentic picture of their native character.

Angelo himself, he who lacks *il dono di coraggio*, the gift of courage, is the universal soldier, like Jaroslav Hasek's *The Good Soldier Schweik*. He witnesses scenes of great violence and horror, but he retains throughout a touching innocence which allows him to turn his experiences of war into a philosophy for peace. From the vantage point of his essential simplicity, he resolves for himself the moral complexities of war, to say nothing of the moral complexities of his own amorous nature, and from it constructs a testimonial to the virtues of common humanity. Angelo's true ancestor is plainly Voltaire's *Candide*.

But if that sounds sententious, or even sentimental, then it is misleading. *Private Angelo* is wonderfully, gloriously, funny. It is shot through with wit and great good humour, full of wry observation and the warmth of what the Italians call *commedia*. In fact, its structure seems on occasion closer to the Italian *commedia*, or *opera teatrale*, than it does to the conventions of the novel. The plot, as such, is at best sketchy, at times positively unruly. But rather than search for the plumbline of a straight narrative, it is better to see each chapter as a dramatic set-piece, a theatrical scene, frequently opening with a duet which could easily translate onto the stage of a small Italian opera house — the Fenice in Venice would do very well. In one, for instance, Lucrezia, Angelo's long-suffering fiancée, is talking of life and love and the absence of her beloved, with her sister Lucia. '*Come triste la vita*' she sighs, as the two pluck hens in the green shade of a trailing vine, and one can almost hear the *continuo* as it leads up to a much-loved *aria*.

Angelo himself, like Figaro, is ill-equipped for war. He freely admits that he lacks the *dono di coraggio*:

> Courage is a great gift indeed, a great and splendid gift, and it is idle to pretend that any ordinary person can insist on receiving it; or go and buy it in the Black Market. We who have not been given the *dono di coraggio* suffer deeply, I assure you. We suffer so much, every day of our lives, that if there were any justice in the world we should receive sympathy not reproof.

War, he learns, teaches above all the art of survival. His patron, the Count of Pontefiore, survives by transferring his allegiances smoothly from Mussolini to the Germans, and then to the Americans for whom he conceives the warmest admiration, largely for their generous nature and their essential practicality; their greatest gift to Italy after the war is, in his view, the sewing machine. Angelo's friend, Sergeant Vespucci, survives by villainy — plundering petrol, food, even army lorries, and disposing of them on the black market at inflated prices. He too is a kind of hero, achieving freedom from the tiresome constraints of ordinary life by breaking the rules that hold most of his fellow citizens back – a quality which, as the Count points out, might be of value to others:

He plunders all nations without pride in one or prejudice against another. He despises frontiers — and what an unmitigated nuisance a frontier is! In bygone times any educated man was free to live or travel where he chose, but now it is only your rascals who claim such a privilege; and there is nothing international in the world but villainy. Sergeant Vespucci, who certainly deserves to be shot, might serve a better purpose if he were given the chair of philosophy in one of our universities.

But it was, perhaps, the women of Italy for whom Eric, romantic by nature, conceived the greatest admiration. He spoke of seeing them in the uneasy months of the Germans' slow retreat, emerging from the basements and the attics of the houses where they had sheltered, into the warm sunlight of the streets, and he recalls how vividly their pale oval faces and auburn hair reminded him of the madonnas he had seen so often on the canvases and frescoes of the Renaissance, faces from the hand of Ghirlandaio or Filippo Lippi. They seemed to him at the same time fragile yet immensely resilient, and in *Private Angelo* they are undoubtedly the stronger, and certainly the more sensible sex.

Lucrezia, who survives the bombing of her little village by both sides, and rape at the hands of a Moroccan 'goum', is briskly down to earth when it comes to explaining to Angelo how, in his absence, she has acquired a child which is plainly not his. He has, after all, been away for three years: 'Was it not more unnatural for you to become a soldier than for me to become a mother?', she asks. She is often ahead of Angelo in his attempts to make sense of the world, and when he tells her that he may have acquired a measure of courage in the course of his experiences, she is unimpressed: 'Courage is a common quality in men of little sense — I think you over-rate it. A good understanding is much rarer and more important.'

In the end, as the sound of warfare dies away, it seems that the greatest survivor is Italy herself. Roughly wooed by the Germans, pulverised by the Allies in the name of rescuing her, she sometimes wonders who her friends are. As Angelo mildly puts it at one stage: 'If our old friends and our new ones both remain in Italy, we shall soon have nothing left at all.'

Out of the destruction, however, comes the rebuilding of 'normal' life, a process which, after the brutal adventure of war is a sufficient adventure in itself. Eric sees the strength of Italy and her ability to survive in the durability of the Tuscan landscape, the beauty of her art, the timelessness of her towns and villages, and above all in the good sense and amiability of her people. He applauds the pleasure they take in ordinary life, 'doing nothing in particular to justify their existence, but nothing at all to perturb it . . . talking and gesticulating . . . contemplating eternity and abusing the present.'

He dedicated his book to the Eighth Army, for he loved soldiers and enjoyed their company. But it is doubtful if the Eighth Army would have had much truck with Private Angelo or with his unconventional wisdom. Indeed, Angelo's summary of the perils of war and the virtues of peace would have been regarded by the military hierarchy of any nation as positively subversive: 'What have you learned, Angelo, while you have been away all these years?' asked the Countess.

'That before the war I was better off than I realised: there is one thing. That soldiers can suffer much and still survive, but are not always improved by their suffering: there is another. That if men are as cruel at home as they are abroad, then their wives have much to complain of . . . and finally, that if living at peace were as simple as going to war, we might have more of it.'

M.L.
March 1992

'THE TROUBLE with you, Angelo,' said the Count severely, 'is that you lack the *dono di coraggio*.'

'That is perfectly true,' said Angelo, 'but am I to blame? Courage is a gift indeed, a great and splendid gift, and it is idle to pretend that any ordinary person can insist on receiving it; or go and buy it in the Black Market. We who have not been given the *dono di coraggio* suffer deeply, I assure you. We suffer so much, every day of our lives, that if there were any justice in the world we should receive sympathy, not reproof.'

With the back of his hand he rubbed a tear from his cheek, and turned away to look through the tall window at the splendid view of Rome on which it opened. In the westering sun the walls of the buildings were the colour of ripe peaches; the domes of several churches rose serenely, firmly round and steeply nippled like the unimpaired and several breasts of a Great Mother whose innumerable offspring, too weak to drain them, had even lacked sufficient appetite to use them much; while in half a dozen places, within easy reach of sight, Victory in a four-horsed chariot drove superbly through the golden air. Soft green foliage clothed the river-bank, and somewhere a military band was playing a gallant march. How beautiful was Rome, how beautiful all the land of Italy!

Sitting behind his handsome large table – inlaid with intricately patterned brass about its flanks and furnished with a brass inkstand as big as a couple of flower-pots, with a statuette in bronze of the Wolf and the Twins, and a signed photograph of the Duce – seated in state though he was, the Count felt a softening of his heart, and his hands which had lain flat and severe upon the table half-rose, half-turned their palms, in a little gesture of understanding and sympathy; a gesture like the prelude to a softly acquiescent shrug. Angelo was a good-looking boy. True, he was very dirty, his ill-made uniform was sweat-stained and caked with dust, his left knee showed through a long rent in his breeches, his right boot was tied with string to keep a loose sole in position, and he stank a little; but his black hair curled and the bones of his face were as comely as if Donatello in his prime had carved them; he had eyes like his mother's, and in his voice the echoes rose and fell of hers.

With the fingers of his left hand the Count played a small tune upon the table and thought of Angelo's mother when she was seventeen. His estate of Pontefiore, in the Tuscan hills between Siena and Florence, had always been renowned for the prettiness of its peasant-girls and the excellence of its wine, but in a year when the vintage was better than anyone could remember, and the girls – or so it had seemed to him, in the flush of his own youth – were more enticing than ever before, Angelo's mother had stolen all the light of the sky and left in shadow every other prospect of pleasure. Her lips and her long fingers and the suppleness of her waist! The round of her hips and the white of her knees when she stooped with a lifting skirt over the washing-trough with the women and the other girls; and then, when she turned to speak to him, the darkness and the laughter in her eyes! And how short, how tragically brief, had been their time together.

Desolation like a sudden storm enclosed him in its hail and darkness when he thought of those vanished years. He, like Angelo, was now in need of sympathy, and for a moment his impulse was to rise, embrace him, and let their tears flow in a common stream of sorrow.

But as he moved, restless in his chair, his glance encountered the Duce's portrait: the autograph, the massive jaw, and the unyielding mouth. Though the Duce had lately been dismissed from his high office, and his Grand Council dissolved, the Count still kept the portrait on his table, for it was signed *Your friend Mussolini*, and he prided himself on loyalty. How often had those piercing eyes inspired him! They inspired him still, and with an effort, with reluctance, he dismissed his tender thoughts. Stiffening his muscles and sitting bolt upright, he cast out sadness like a recognized traitor, and instead of tears forced into his eyes the atrabilious gleam of the eyes in the photograph. Not only was he Count of Pontefiore, Angelo's patron and once the lover of his dead mother; he was also Commanding Officer of the 914th Regiment of Tuscan Infantry, the Sucklings of the Wolf. He was Angelo's Colonel, and when he spoke it was in a colonel's voice.

'You are a soldier and it is your duty to be courageous,' he said loudly. 'The illustrious regiment in which you have had the honour to serve, and I the honour to command, is even now fighting with the most glorious courage in Calabria. By this time, perhaps, your comrades have slaughtered the last of the English invaders or driven them into the sea. And you, you alone deserting and disgracing them, have run away! You have run all the way from Reggio to Rome!'

'The last time I saw my comrades,' said Angelo, 'they were all running away. I looked over my shoulder once or twice, and they were running as hard as they could. But none of them was so swift and determined as I, and therefore I am the first to arrive. But if you will have a little patience, I am sure that you will presently see your whole regiment here.'

'Silence!' cried the Count. 'No one in my presence shall ever deny, or even dispute, the indomitable valour of my gallant men!'

He struck with an ivory ruler the gleaming surface of the table, and then, frowning a little, leaned forward and asked, 'Is it really as bad as that?'

'Quite as bad,' said Angelo. 'It has taken us a long time to lose the war, but thank heaven we have lost it at last, and there is no use in denying it.'

'It is treason to say that.'

'It is common sense.'

'You are still a soldier,' said the Count, 'and you have

no right to talk about common sense. You are subject to military law, and since by your own confession you are guilty of cowardice and desertion – well, my friend, you know the penalty for that?'

'Death,' said Angelo in a gloomy voice.

'If I do my duty, you will certainly be shot.'

'The English have been trying to shoot me for the last three years. In Cyrenaica I had the greatest difficulty in avoiding their bombs and bullets and shells. I had to run hundreds of miles to escape being killed. And now, after three years of that sort of thing, I come to see you, my patron and Commanding Officer, and almost the first thing you say is that you too want to murder me. Is there no difference at all between friend and foe?'

'There is a great deal of difference,' said the Count, 'but a soldier's duty is the same wherever you go.'

'It is, however, only a very good soldier who always does his duty.'

'That is worth bearing in mind,' said the Count thoughtfully. 'I am not eager, you must realize, to have you shot, for it would create an awkward precedent if, as you say, my whole regiment is now on its way to Rome. And yet, if I were openly to condone your cowardice, and wholly ignore the fact of your desertion, I should bring myself down to your level. I should stand shoulder to shoulder with you in dishonour.'

'It would be a new experience for you,' said Angelo. 'During three years of war you have never stood shoulder to shoulder with me or with any of your men.'

The Count replied a trifle haughtily: 'It is perfectly true that while you served with the regiment in Africa, I commanded it from Rome. But it is quite absurd for you to refer to the fact in so unpleasant a tone of voice. For you cannot deny that I set you a splendid example, since I have never abandoned my post, nor ever, in three years of war, run a single yard. And who else in the regiment can make such a boast?'

'I give you my word,' said Angelo, 'that I was speaking

with perfect respect. I made a short and simple statement of fact, and I can't see why that should be regarded as unfriendly criticism.'

'You are old enough to realize,' said the Count, 'that a statement of fact is nearly always damaging to someone. And furthermore,' he continued in an animated voice, 'you should ask yourself what would have happened if, as you appear to think proper, I had indeed commanded you in the field. I myself can perceive three possibilities. I might have been killed; I might have been seriously wounded or taken prisoner, and in either case debarred from further service; or I might have been dismissed from the Army for incompetence. And a pretty pickle you would be in to-day, if any of those things had occurred! You wouldn't be standing before an old friend who is devoted to your welfare, but confronting a total stranger who didn't care what happened to you!'

'I confess,' said Angelo, 'that I hadn't thought of that. I am only a private, and common soldiers often fail to appreciate the plans and the methods of senior officers. Your very habit of thought, indeed, sometimes appears strange and foreign to us.'

'Lack of understanding is the greatest evil in the world,' said the Count. 'My God! If understanding came to our minds as readily as condemnation to our lips, how happy we should be! – Or should we?'

While the Count was pondering this question Angelo discreetly turned his back, and tearing the wristband from a ragged sleeve of his shirt, blew his nose on it. The sweat was cold on his body, and he had begun to shiver. He was very tired.

He had folded the damp wristband, and was putting it into his trouser-pocket, when the inner door of the room was thrown noisily open, and a fat white-faced captain with very short legs and a nearly bald head came clumsily in and stammered, 'The radio! the radio! They are going to make a special announcement!'

'Who is going to make an announcement?' asked the Count. 'The Duce?'

'No, no! It is the Allies, it is the Americans, it is General Eisenhower himself who is going to speak!'

'Nonsense!' said the Count.

'But I have just heard them saying it, and the voice had an American accent. Stand by, it said. Stand by for one minute and you will hear General Eisenhower make an important announcement.'

'Who gave you permission to listen to foreign broadcasting?' asked the Count. 'It is a grave and serious offence, as you well know.'

The Captain wiped his forehead with a yellow silk handkerchief, and stammering again, muttered, 'But if I had not been listening I could not have told you about General Eisenhower's announcement.'

'That is so,' said the Count. 'It is a tolerable excuse, and I must admit that to show a strict regard for every trifling piece of legislation would lead us, eventually, into the deplorable ways of our good friends the Germans; which God forbid. – I shall come and listen to your illegal instrument.'

He rose, and with dignity led the way into the inner room, an office with maps upon the wall, where two smart young subalterns stood expectantly before a small wireless set. It was emitting the angry sounds of a far-off electric storm, but these suddenly gave way to what might have been the voice of a man with a hurricane in his lungs and a throat like the dome of St Peter's.

One of the subalterns hurriedly made an adjustment, the voice was reduced to human volume, and its accent became recognizably American. The tone was flat, the voice was soberly inflected. A plain man was speaking plainly, but every word he uttered was momentous, every sentence affected millions of lives, and he spoke with authority. Here was one of the decisive utterances of history. They were listening, thought the Count with enthusiasm, not merely to an American general, but to Clio herself. – And then the voice grew smaller, it receded to an infinite distance, and the electric storm was heard again, angrier than before, and now, as it seemed, filling all space.

'However,' said the Count, 'we have had the gist of it.
We have been offered peace on honourable terms, we have
accepted the offer, and an armistice has been signed. The
war is over!'

Angelo threw himself on to his knees, and grasping
the Count's left hand, covered it with kisses. 'Peace!' he
exclaimed. 'Peace has been restored to us, and now you
will not require to have me shot!'

'No, of course not,' said the Count. 'Of course not!'

'And I shall no longer be miserable because I have not the
dono di corragio. In time of peace one can live well enough
without courage, like everybody else.'

'It is the eighth of September in the year nineteen forty
three,' said the Count. 'It is five-and-twenty minutes to
seven. We must forever remember the hour and the day,
for they are part of our history. At this moment we and
all Italy are stepping, like joyous pilgrims, into a new and
happier age!'

The fat Captain was again wiping his forehead with his
yellow handkerchief. 'Do you suppose, sir,' he asked, 'that
we shall be compelled to resign our commissions?'

'Immediately,' said the Count. 'Now that the war is over,
what need have we of commissions?'

'I need mine to keep a roof over my head,' said the
Captain.

'Farewell, my mistress,' murmured one of the subalterns.

'*Our* mistress,' corrected the other. 'You see, sir,' he
explained, 'on a subaltern's pay it is impossible to maintain
a mistress who is both agreeable to the senses and presentable
to one's friends; but by using every economy Luigi and I
have, for some time past, been able to share such a one.
Now, of course, we shall have to relinquish her, and because
she has spoiled my taste for any coarser fare, I can see for
myself no prospect but emotional famine.'

'Come, come,' said the Count, 'you are unduly pessimistic.
We shall all have to make certain minor adjustments to
accommodate ourselves to new conditions, and some of
us, during the brief period of transition, may even suffer

small inconveniences. But we must not fret about them, we must ignore them, because at last, after three long years of fighting, we have won that for which we have always striven: Peace! Whatever trials you may have to endure, gentlemen, never forget that on the eighth of September, at five-and-twenty minutes to seven, you entered, after an eternity of suffering, the promised haven of peace.'

At that moment the windows rattled in their frames, and the fat Captain said, 'A thunderstorm is a bad augury for peace.'

'It is not thunder,' said Angelo in a trembling voice. 'It is gunfire.'

'Guns!' exclaimed the Count. 'Whose guns, and why should they be firing?'

'They may be firing a *feu de joie*,' said the younger subaltern with a cynical smile.

'That is undoubtedly the explanation,' said the Count. 'They are shouting their welcome to peace!'

'Perhaps they are firing against the English,' said Angelo.

'Impossible,' declared the Count. 'The English are hundreds of miles away.'

'They were coming very fast when I last saw them.'

'But it's unthinkable! And even if they have achieved the impossible, and arrived at the gates of Rome, why should they continue to fight against us when Clio herself, borrowing the lips of General Eisenhower, has declared an armistice?'

'They may not have heard about it,' said Angelo. 'The English are frequently unaware of what goes on in Europe.'

'Then we shall go and inform them,' declared the Count. 'You and I, my dear Angelo, shall be the first to give them the good news that henceforth we and they must live together in perfect amity and mutual assistance. Come, Angelo, let us waste no time.'

The windows rattled more violently as the gunfire grew louder, and Angelo tried to evade his errand with one excuse after another. But the Count would listen to none of them, and presently they were driving out of Rome towards the aerodrome that lies along the Appian Way. For that was the direction from which the firing came.

The evening was now darkening, and against the first veils of twilight the flashing of the guns was faintly hued with orange. Every shell that was fired made Angelo wince as though he were equipped, like the field-pieces, with a recoil-mechanism; but the Count was deeply interested in what he saw.

'Why, bless my soul,' he declared, 'they are Germans. It's a German battery! The poor Tedeschi, they have not heard the news. No one ever tells them anything!'

Briskly leaving his motor-car he approached the German officer in command, saluted him smilingly, clapped him on the shoulder with his other hand, and with a great deal of geniality started to explain that an armistice had been signed, and the war was over.

The German, already in a vile temper, listened for five seconds only, and then interrupted to abuse the Count in a loud voice and with vulgar detail.

'So you also are a traitor!' he shouted. 'You too are a rebel, are you, like the mutinous swine over there whom we are now liquidating?'

'Mutinous? Surely the English have not mutinied?' asked the Count.

'Not the English, you blockhead, but those garlic-eating Judases, your fellow-countrymen!'

'It is impossible!'

'They told us the war was over – and this is our answer.'

'You cannot be serious. You are not firing against Italian soldiers?'

'They may have been soldiers once,' said the German. 'Most of them are corpses now.'

'But we are your allies,' exclaimed the Count. 'You cannot fire against us! Good heavens, even a German should realize that this is no way to behave.' And turning toward the nearest gun-crew he shouted, 'Cease fire immediately!'

The German officer at once drew his revolver, and pressing the muzzle against the Count's stomach, declared in a voice so hoarse that it drew a little blood – which he swallowed noisily – 'You are under arrest. Move one inch or utter a single word, and I shall kill you!'

The Count was hard put to it to comply, for there were twenty things he wanted to say, but fortunately, before the strain became intolerable, there was a compelling sound in the air, a sibilance that swiftly grew louder and came nearer, and with a common impulse he and the German threw themselves flat on the ground.

Within half a minute the Count had recovered consciousness, and sitting up he perceived that the shell, which seemingly had landed within a yard of the nearby gun, had instantly killed all its crew, while the German officer had been mortally wounded by a heavy splinter. Towed by their tractors, the remaining guns of the battery were moving to a new position.

Though beyond human aid the German officer was still conscious, and the Count was able to deliver, without interruption, a brief lecture on the evils of intolerance.

'You Tedeschi,' he concluded, 'have persistently underrated us, and made light of our military qualities. The excellence of our artillery, for example, is quite generally admitted by impartial observers, and our gunners have frequently used it to great advantage. But have you ever praised them? Never! It may be, of course, that until now you have never seen for yourself what they can do –'

A barely human sound came from the German's lips, and his booted heels twitched on the ground. The Count, after stooping to examine him, shrugged his shoulders and murmured, 'They will never learn.'

He returned to his car and was about to drive away when, from somewhere on the ground, a voice in agitation cried, 'A moment, please! Wait a moment, do!'

'My dear Angelo,' said the Count, 'I had quite forgotten you. Where have you been? Underneath the car?'

'Of course I have,' said Angelo. 'It was the obvious place to choose.'

'And while you were lying there, safe and snug, I came

near to losing my life,' said the Count. 'Several Germans, less fortunate than I, were killed outright.'

'By the English?' asked Angelo.

'No, no!' cried the Count. 'Really, my dear boy, your appreciation of the situation is woefully at fault. They are Italian gunners, our own splendid soldiers, who are now engaged in battle with the Germans. Look there! Oh, bravo, bravo! They have found the range again. I have always maintained that our artillery is first-class – and who will deny that now?'

'Do you mean to tell me,' asked Angelo, 'that now, when we have stopped fighting against our enemies, we must go to war against our allies?'

'Surely there is some better way of expressing the situation,' said the Count, and driving slowly while he considered the problem, turned the car towards Rome. Behind them the night was loud and the sky lurid with gunfire. 'From what we have just seen,' he continued, 'we may reasonably infer that the Germans are no longer, in fact, or strictly speaking, our allies; and if that is indeed the case, we must, before we can discuss the situation clearly, find some new and more accurate title for them.'

'They will become our gaolers,' said Angelo bitterly. 'If they have turned against us they will hold the mountains to the north like a great door between us and the rest of the world, and all Italy will become a prison. We shall be the starving convicts and they will be the gaolers with whips in their hands.'

'But you must remember,' said the Count, 'that now we have powerful friends who will come to rescue us. The English and the Americans will not allow the Germans to ill-treat us. The English are already in Calabria, and we expect the Americans to land somewhere near Salerno either to-morrow or the day after. – That is in confidence, of course. – We may indeed be in the toils of Germany at this moment, but soon, very soon, the Americans and the English will come and liberate us. *Pazienza!* It will not be long.'

'*Speriamo*,' said Angelo.

CHAPTER TWO

SHORTLY AFTER NOON on the following day the Count was driving home to lunch. He was displeased to observe an unusual number of German soldiers on the streets, and the occasional sound of distant gunfire brought a little frown to his forehead. But when he entered the Piazza di Spagna his attention was taken by the exceptional colour of the flower-sellers' stalls, and ordering his driver to stop, he got out and bought, in wilful defiance of the hour, a bunch of every variety displayed. These he sent, by a convenient boy whom he found waiting beside the stall, to his dear friend the Marchesa Dolce, who lived in a small house high above the Piazza. The boy with his many-coloured, scented burden slowly climbed the steps, and the Count returned to his car.

Having lunched alone he sent for Angelo, and at once complimented him on his improved appearance. Cleanly shaved and diligently washed, smartly attired in a new uniform, Angelo now looked a credit to his regiment. Embracing him, the Count lightly stroked his hair and said with a sigh, 'Mine still grows as thick as yours, but it's turning grey. The first of the winter snow has fallen on it.'

'In the most attractive manner,' said Angelo.

'It is not uncomely, I have been assured of that,' the Count agreed, 'but white hairs are a warning of the coldness that comes with age, and I do not like them. – That, however, is a topic we can discuss at some more convenient time. There is an affair of the moment that we must talk about now. The fact of the matter is that we are living in difficult and dangerous days.'

'Have the English and the Americans changed their minds? Are they not coming to liberate us?'

'Of course they are, but the process may take some weeks, and in the meanwhile the Tedeschi are in power. The King and Marshal Badoglio have fled from Rome, and General von Kluggenschaft, whose troops control the city, has made it perfectly clear that he no longer regards us as his loyal friends and indispensable allies.'

'How many of our soldiers have the Tedeschi killed?' asked Angelo.

'Several score, I believe – but we must not let emotion obscure intelligence. We must remember, my dear Angelo, that the soldier's anticipation of a violent end is part of his contract. The shadow of the recruiting sergeant is very like the shadow of death, and a soldier's life, even in our army, is a flimsy structure. We must be practical – and to come to the point, I want you to take some of my pictures to Pontefiore, where, I think, they will be safer for the next few weeks than they might be in Rome.'

'That is prudent indeed. You are sending the Piero della Francesca?'

'That, and my little Raphael, the two small Bronzinos, and Simone Martini's portrait of Petrarch. I have several others packed up; the Filippino Lippi, and the Lorenzo di Credi with the light blue sky. Indeed, the best of my small collection is going, and though I do not for a moment suppose that the Germans would take them from me, I shall feel happier when they are in Pontefiore, where the Countess will be able to find secure hiding-places for them.'

'But how am I to take them there?'

An arrangement had been made, the Count assured him. Several weeks before, in preparation for an emergency, he had had the pictures packed in wooden cases, and that very morning he had called on General von Kluggenschaft to ask for the loan of two German army lorries.

'So you and the General are friends, are you?' asked Angelo.

'Far from it,' said the Count. 'He has a revolting personality, and whenever I see him I have to be extraordinarily polite in order to prevent an open quarrel. But as I needed his lorries I offered to sell him some wine if he would provide me with the necessary transport to bring it here. I mentioned an absurdly low price, his greed was instantly aroused, and when he had further diminished my figure we closed the bargain. Come, now, and let me show you the vehicles in which you will travel.'

In a small courtyard the lorries were already loaded, and their drivers, in German uniform, stood beside them. With wooden precision they came to attention and saluted.

'You need not be very frightened of them,' said the Count. 'Like so many people in the army of our late ally, they are not real Germans, but wretched prisoners forced into service. This one is a Czech, and that, I believe, some sort of a Russian who was taken captive in the Caucasus.'

'They don't look very happy,' said Angelo.

'They have very little reason to,' replied the Count, and unlacing the canvas cover of the nearer lorry he revealed how well it had been loaded. The pictures in their wooden cases were only a small part of the cargo. The bulk of it was softly filled sacks among which the cases stood, gently held and firmly guarded.

Angelo fingered one of the sacks and exclaimed, 'But this is flour.'

'That is so,' said the Count.

'And is the other lorry loaded in the same way?'

'In precisely the same way. I had been wondering how to protect these old and immensely valuable pictures against the jolting and tremors of a long journey, when I happened to remember that I had a certain stock of flour available.'

'How very fortunate,' said Angelo.

'A lucky chance,' agreed the Count, and having told the drivers to be ready to move within half an hour, he invited Angelo to have a glass of wine before he set off.

They drank a glass or two in the small library where Angelo had already been received. Neither spoke for a few minutes, and then the Count asked, 'Were you ever hungry when you were in Africa?'

'We came near to starvation once or twice,' said Angelo.

'Those English submarines sank hundreds of our ships,' said the Count. 'At certain times they were sinking so many that it really seemed useless to send you any stores at all. Ship after ship we loaded, and what happened to them? They went to the bottom of the sea. Our labour and our goods were wasted. Utterly wasted. And now and again I felt that I could no longer be a partner in such destruction. My whole being rebelled against the idea of sending, to no other destination than the engulfing waves, great shiploads of boots and shirts and guns and ammunition and oil –'

'And flour,' said Angelo.

'And flour,' the Count agreed.

'The lorries, then, are loaded with what should have been sent to your regiment in Africa?'

'And if the regiment had been commanded by a man less prudent than I, it might indeed have been dispatched,' declared the Count. 'And what would have happened to it?' he demanded. 'It would have gone, like so many other cargoes, to the bottom of the sea. What horrible and wicked waste, when all over Italy our peasants are in just as great a need of flour as ever our poor soldiers were!'

'So you are sending it to Pontefiore to be given away to anyone who is hungry?'

'Not *given*,' said the Count. 'Our Tuscan peasants are proud people who would not ask to live on charity. I am too much devoted to their welfare to wish to pauperize them. No, no! But my steward has orders to sell the flour at a fair and just price, and it will, I am sure, be very welcome to all my people. – And now, Angelo, it is time for you to leave. Here is your pass, and the permission signed by von Kluggenschaft for two motor lorries to go to Pontefiore for some urgently needed military equipment. I do not think you will have any difficulty on the road, but if you are stopped, by some officious Tedescho, you will find in each lorry a dozen bottles of wine, and that will certainly dissolve the obstruction. God bless you, my boy, and give this letter to the Countess. Tell her that I am well, in spite of my grey hairs.'

Angelo was appreciably moved by the kindness with which the Count had treated him, and he was forced to admit that there was something to be said for the prudence which had saved so much flour from the British Navy, and now, with an equal regard for the appetite and dignity of a Tuscan peasant, was sending it where it would certainly be useful. Stammering a sentence or two of gratitude, he took his leave, and, descending to the courtyard, elected to travel in the lorry driven by the Czech soldier. The Czech was a smaller man than the Russian.

Suddenly a vision filled his mind, an enchanted view of the home that he had not seen for three long years, the landscape lighted with the dark green candle-flames of the cypress trees, and his boyhood's sweetheart. Ah, the black eyes and the milk-white throat of dear Lucrezia! He was going home, and as he spoke the words aloud, to give them reality, his eyes filled with tears and he failed to notice the German staff-car that stopped before the Count's front door at the very moment when the flour-laden lorries drove past.

The Count was composing himself for his siesta when he was informed that two German officers desired to see him. He returned the answer that at three o'clock in the afternoon he could receive no one, but his reply was ignored and a moment or two later the library door was thrown rudely open, and two heavy-footed steel-helmeted Germans marched in.

What louts they are, thought the Count, and in his most courteous voice inquired, 'To what am I indebted for this honour, gentlemen?'

'You are Lieutenant-Colonel the Count Agesilas Piccolo-grando of Pontefiore?' asked the senior and more repellent of his visitors.

'I am.'

'Then you are under arrest.'

'Really,' said the Count. 'May I offer you a glass of wine?'

Unhappy Angelo, he thought, I suppose they were waiting for him when he went down. But I cannot believe that this is going to be a serious matter. The flour is not theirs, and never was, and I fail to see that they have any legal claim to it now. Nor did von Kluggenschaft specify for what purpose the lorries were to be used on the outward journey . . .

These musings were interrupted by the German who had already spoken, and now, having swallowed his wine, said harshly, 'Last night you treacherously endeavoured to interfere with certain gunners of a German battery then in action against a regiment of Italian rebels and traitors.'

'Last night?' said the Count, who was much surprised. 'Last night? Why, yes, I remember now. Of course I did. So that is what has brought you here. Well, well!'

'Your attempt to obstruct the gun-crew in the execution of its duty was observed by Major Fluchs, commanding the battery, who promptly put you under open arrest.'

'Poor Fluchs. And now he is dead.'

'Before he died, however, he regained consciousness long enough to inform Captain Bluther of his action.'

Captain Bluther, the other officer, looked proudly over the Count's head and spoke in a loud voice: 'With his last breath Major Fluchs did his duty as a German should, and expressed the wish that the Count Piccologrando should be punished for his swinish behaviour with appropriate severity.'

'I am amazed,' said the Count. 'I thought he was dead when I left him. Had you asked me, I should have said that he died in my arms. But there is, of course, no truth in those last rambling words of his. Poor fellow, his mind was wandering. You cannot be so foolish as to arrest me on no surer evidence than a fragment of delirious conversation which I shall totally deny, and which you cannot substantiate by witnesses; for none of them survives.'

'The word of a German officer does not require witnesses to prove it nor evidence to substantiate it, and is utterly indifferent to events which contradict it or enemies who deny it.'

'In that case,' said the Count, 'I think I had better telephone to General von Kluggenschaft, who is my very good friend. You will excuse me?'

'You will be wasting your time. The General is no longer in command.'

'He was in command this morning. I know that, because I saw him.'

'He is now on his way to the Führer's Headquarters. He was replaced an hour ago by General Hammerfurter.'

'But why? I cannot understand it. He was an excellent soldier. He did his work with admirable efficiency, and he was universally popular.'

The senior of the German officers smiled sourly, but Captain Bluther indignantly explained: 'General von Kluggenschaft had formed a most undesirable friendship in Rome. He was on intimate terms with a woman of vicious character whose other associates were known to engage in subversive conversation.'

'That is slanderous!' declared the Count fiercely. 'Your statement contains a monstrous and abominable slander!'

'What are your grounds for saying that?'

'General von Kluggenschaft was on intimate terms with one lady only in Rome, and of all her sex she is the most lovely, prudent, and desirable. He was entirely faithful to her – and had he ever been unfaithful, he would have had to deal with me!'

'You refer to the Marchesa Dolce?'

'As the name is known to you – I do.'

'So you know her also, do you?'

The Count's brief anger subsided. For a moment he stood, very straight and still, and then, his slim figure losing its rigidity like a tall reed when the morning wind blows up the river-bed, he slightly bowed and very quietly answered, 'For seven years she has been my dearest friend.'

Captain Bluther shuffled his feet, coughed behind his hand, and was clearly embarrassed; but his senior and more repellent companion lost his temper, raised his voice, and began to abuse his prisoner in violent language. The Marchesa Dolce was widely known to be a beautiful, witty, and cultivated woman, and this poor German, who had been on close terms only with some ungainly girls in Wuppertal and Bochum, and with overworked foreign prostitutes, was wildly jealous of the Count – whose nation he despised – and therefore became furiously angry with him, because of his good fortune and superior happiness in knowing such a charming person as the Marchesa.

The Count did not know how to reply. He was in no degree frightened of the German, but so deeply shocked by the display of violent rage that he could not protect himself against it. And in this state of helplessness, urged on by a pair of automatic pistols, he was presently marched out of his house, into the waiting car, and removed to a large villa on the outskirts of Rome which was maintained by the Schutzstaffel for their own peculiar purposes.

CHAPTER THREE

ANGELO'S JOURNEY was uneventful. He was halted several times by German soldiers, but the gift of a bottle or two of wine quickly persuaded them that he was fully entitled to travel where he liked; and the two drivers, of whom he had been somewhat afraid, showed clearly their desire to be friendly, and before very long were telling him their troubles.

To avoid driving in the dark they spent the night in a villa – one of the Count's smaller properties – on the eastern shore of Lake Bolsena, and there, after they had all drunk a good deal, the Czech and the Russian very earnestly sought his advice. They were both anxious to desert, and they wanted the help of someone who could guide them through the mountains to the southernmost parts of Italy, which, as they knew, had now been liberated by the English. Did Angelo know of such a person? Or would he himself show them the way?

For a long time they discussed the technique of desertion, as they had learnt it from the legendary exploits of those who had succeeded and the sad tales of their friends who had failed in the attempt; and Angelo promised, with much repetition, that when they returned to Rome he would introduce them to the most reliable accomplices that could be found. Then, having embraced each other warmly, they retired to sleep. They dreamt of happiness, and early in the morning resumed their journey.

It was an hour or so short of noon when they turned the last corner on the steeply climbing road to Pontefiore, and saw, like a crown of coloured stone on the hill-top, the old castle and the tightly gathered village. A narrow ravine divided the southern slope of the hill, and this, in one noble arch, was spanned by an ancient bridge whose abutments, at the proper season of the year, were overhung by blossoming trees. Even in Tuscany, where a handsome view is the merest commonplace, Pontefiore was notable for its dignified yet gentle beauty, and there was little wonder that Angelo, prone as he was to weeping, poured from his eyes a flood of delighted tears to see again its yellow roofs, the cobbled streets, and the castle tower rising among cypresses against a clear blue sky.

He called excited greetings to some eighteen or twenty people whom he recognized in the doorways of their houses, but dutifully did not stop until he had reached the castle, and there, with a sudden dignity, he requested an indoor servant to inform the Countess of his arrival.

She came out at once, for she did not believe in wasting time. She was small and trim, and though the prettiness of her girlhood had long since gone, much of its charm and some of its vivacity remained. Her hair was faded but her eyes were bright, and she still spoke Italian with an English accent. Had she spoken English, indeed, her accent would have been that of Yorkshire. She had formerly been a school-teacher in Bradford, and she had first met the Count in the railway station at Florence, during a holiday-fortnight that should have been devoted to the art of the Renaissance. She had won immediately while waiting for a train to Pisa – the Count's most passionate interest, and though their early friendship had been greatly troubled, and scarred by tragedy, she now, after twenty years of marriage, enjoyed his profound respect and the assurance, generally from a distance, of his enduring affection.

'So you've come back safe and sound after all?' she said to Angelo. 'Well, I'm glad to see you. How long have you been away?'

'Three years, madam.'

'And now, I hope, you're ready to do some honest work for a change?'

'No, madam, I can't do anything of that sort. I am still in the army, you see.'

'Haven't you had enough of it yet?'

'Oh, more than enough!'

'Has it done you any good?'

'None at all, so far as I am aware. It has taught me, indeed, that I shall never be a good soldier, but I was pretty sure of that before they called me up. Because, of course, I have not the *dono di coraggio*.'

'Don't you think you should keep that to yourself?'

'How can I, when all my actions reveal it? – But I am forgetting my duty. Here is a letter from Don Agesilas, who asked me to tell you that he is very well, though his hair is turning a little grey.'

The Countess read the letter quickly, for she had no interest in the art of correspondence, but was merely impatient to learn the news. Then she remarked, 'He's behaving quite sensibly, for a change. But where could he have got two lorry-loads of flour at a time like this?'

'How should I know, madam?'

'He says that you can explain everything.'

Angelo thought for a moment, and then said with a certain hesitation, 'Since all our soldiers in Africa have been taken prisoner, they are being fed by the English, and so our Government has no use for the food that was ready to be sent to them. And I remember, now, hearing that it was to be sold quickly, before it went bad, and that Don Agesilas had bought some flour for a small price. A very small price, I think.'

'Well, it will come in handy, there's no doubt of that. And you brought the pictures too?'

'Yes, madam.'

'Then we'll get them unpacked at once.'

But Angelo, blushing a little and speaking very rapidly, asked leave to go now on business of his own, and being pressed to explain it, admitted that he was burning with desire to see Lucrezia, his boyhood's sweetheart.

'You mean Lucrezia Donati, whose father sells charcoal?'

asked the Countess. 'But she was only a chit of a girl when you left here.'

'I was not very old myself.'

'Has she been writing to you?'

'Yes, three or four times.'

The Countess was about to ask another question, but checked herself and looked at Angelo in doubt, then tightened her lips to a line of thin severity and thought again, and finally said, 'Be kind to her, Angelo.'

'Be sure of that,' cried Angelo, laughing loudly and happily. 'I'll be as kind to her as she will let me, and all I hope is that she will be one half as kind to me.'

He turned to go, but saw at that moment a young man who had newly come in to the hall and stood now, as if uncertain where to go, at the far end of it. He had a fair complexion and light brown hair, a lively look, and small neat features. He was about the same height and figure as Angelo himself. He stood a moment longer, then swiftly turned and went out again.

'Who is that?' asked Angelo. 'I have not seen him here before.'

'Italy nowadays is full of people whom no one has ever seen before,' said the Countess, 'and sometimes your best course will be to look the other way when you meet them, and then forget about them.'

'That does not seem very courteous.'

'Not to see a man who doesn't want to be seen is the very height of courtesy,' said the Countess.

'But you are quite right! I had not thought of it in that way,' said Angelo. 'And you can be sure of this: that as soon as I clap eyes on Lucrezia I shall forget everything else in the world – except your kindness to me, which I shall always remember.'

Nearly everybody in the village wanted him to stop and talk. The women sitting in their doorways hailed him and asked for news of their sons and husbands who had gone with him to Africa, and men crossed the road to greet him and ask him to drink wine with them. But Angelo put them off, one and all, saying there would be plenty of time for gossip, but now he wanted to see Lucrezia. Where was Lucrezia Donati? he demanded. At the washing-place, they told him, at the end of the village.

He started to run, and though the way was downhill he was out of breath when he arrived and saw the girls and the women bending over the great stone trough in which they were soaping and wringing and beating their linen. It was a charming and familiar scene, and even while his eyes were searching for Lucrezia, and his lungs labouring for breath, he took the greatest pleasure in it nor wholly denied an errant wish to embrace, not his sweetheart only, but all these brisk and buxom creatures. How gaily they chattered, and how lovely was their laughter and the sound of the splashing of water! And there, in the middle of the row, was one with the prettiest pair of legs he had ever seen, so properly plump, as smooth as a chestnut and almost as brown, then paler behind the knee where the soft skin dimpled, and pale above – for now she was stooping forward and rubbing the linen so vigorously that her prim little bottom looked like a pair of apples when a boy is shaking the branch they grow on; and the back of her short skirt lifted higher still. White above her dimpling knees rose two entrancing columns into the modesty of occluding shadows, and really, thought Angelo, though legs and arms are the commonest things in the world, there are certain pairs of them with so remarkable a texture and shape that their effect upon the sensitive observer may be almost overwhelming.

His heart beat so hard that he lost his breath again, and while he stood there panting, the girl with the long brown legs, conscious of someone staring at her, suddenly straightened herself and turned to see who it might be.

Angelo's voice was no louder than a whisper when he spoke her name. That was the first time. Then a little strength came to it, and he said 'Lucrezia!' as a man in a dark room might say it. But the third time his voice was so loud he might have been hailing a ship at sea.

'Lucrezia!' he cried, 'I have come home again, and you

are more beautiful than ever! I thought it was impossible for you to be more beautiful, but you have wrought a miracle and made perfection lovelier than it was, and that is why, in the first moment that I saw you, I did not recognize you. O Lucrezia, let us be married immediately!'

As if by the pulling of a blind on a summer morning, joy had flushed Lucrezia's cheeks and lighted her eyes when she first saw Angelo, and she had made a swift movement as though she meant to run straight into his arms. But then she halted, still as a statue, and her eyes grew round with fear, and she lifted a hand to her mouth like a child restraining a cry of pain. Her fingers were wrinkled, her wrists pink from the washing-trough, and drops of water, running down her arm, fell hesitantly from her elbow.

Then Angelo, seeing her like that, laughed and embraced her, kissing her wet hands, and her startled eyes, and her warm neck. The women and the other girls, gathering in a close circle round them, laughed loudly and applauded. Some of them, impatient to hear of their own menfolk or eager for recognition, pulled Angelo by the sleeve and clapped him on the shoulder. But Angelo paid no attention, for by now Lucrezia's arms were tightly round his neck. She was whispering endearments and a practical suggestion to go and look for some more private place where they could talk in peace.

'*Pazienza!*' he cried to the women, all of whom were now clamouring for news. 'I shall be here for two or three days, and before I go I shall tell you everything I know about the regiment. But first of all I must talk with Lucrezia.'

They spent the rest of the day together, and Angelo had supper in the house of Lucrezia's parents, a sturdy and honest pair who in twenty years of married life had produced eleven children without loss of interest in each other or diminution of affection for them. The youngest, a fair-haired boy of about twelve months, was remarkably vivacious, and Angelo was about to congratulate Signor Donati on such a testimony to his vigour when it occurred to him that the child might be the son of Lucrezia's elder sister, who certainly had one or two of her own, and whose husband had recently been arrested on a false charge and sent to a labour battalion in Germany. Before he could make up his mind on this point, Signor Donati had refilled his glass, and the matter no longer seemed important. They drank a great deal of wine, and ate black figs and the well-cured ham of a black pig.

In the morning Angelo had another conversation with the Countess, and the day was spent in selecting safe hiding-places for the pictures. Two were stored in a winecellar among gigantic tuns whose perfume made the mere air intoxicating, and others were laid in the dry lofts of nearby farmhouses. But the Adoration of the Shepherds, which Piero della Francesca had painted, was hung in a little-used bedroom in the castle, and this was done because Angelo argued, with a great deal of feeling and considerable eloquence, that a work of such divine perfection should not, even for its own safety, be imprisoned in darkness or humiliated by confinement in a farmhouse attic.

'Let it remain where it can give happiness and consolation to at least a few,' he said. 'There is more life and truth and beauty in this picture than you will find in forty living villages – and you would not bury what is alive? It is very seldom that a man has shown so greatly and so triumphantly his power to create, which he inherits from the Creator himself, and we should not conceal what proves quite clearly that some of us are certainly the children of God, and therefore all of us may be; for evidence of that kind is extremely rare. You can buy security at too high a price, and I say that a world which buried and forgot its Piero della Francescas would not be a world in which we could take any pride. I do not ask you to put it in some very public place, for that would be indiscreet, but hang it where those who know of its existence can go from time to time and breathe the air which it ennobles. We have a lot of bad company now in Italy, and therefore the greater need to associate with what is good.'

The Countess was not uninterested in painting, but her

appreciation of it was more detached than Angelo's. She could not share his emotion, but she was moved, none the less, by his argument. For she had her own enthusiasm.

She was devoted to the novels of Ouida, and in every one of the several houses belonging to the Count there was a complete set of her works. Here, in Pontefiore, was the finest of them all. Bound in a soft white leather adorned with golden blossoms, it had been Ouida's own property – the title-pages bore her signature – and poor Ouida had sold it in the sad years before her death when she was selling nearly all her treasures to feed her dogs. Now all this commotion about pictures had set the Countess to wondering if it would not be wise to put her own favourite masterpieces in hiding, and she had been cogitating what would be a good place. But when Angelo spoke so bravely about Piero's Adoration, she decided to be equally courageous with her Ouidas; for what he said about the painter applied, in her opinion, with equal force to the novelist.

'Very well, then,' she said. 'We'll hang the picture in the small bedroom under the tower, and lock the door of the corridor that leads to it, and trust in Providence to do whatever else is necessary. Does that satisfy you?'

But Angelo made no answer. All his mind – and this had happened a hundred times before – was full of wonder at the skill with which Piero had painted the Blessed Virgin's coif, for the pallor of her unlined forehead showed clearly through the whiteness of the lawn, and its transparent folds were as firmly shaped as the forehead itself. And what mild dignity lay in the curve of the temples, what calm assurance in the wisdom of the eyes, and though the chin, perhaps, was a little heavy, the lips were drawn with grace ineffable. – They were the very shape of Lucrezia's, though hers were more brightly red.

Suddenly he returned to the mortal moving world about him, and with a little cry of distress exclaimed, 'But I am late, and she is waiting for me! Oh, madam, may I leave you, for I promised to meet Lucrezia, and it is long past the time we set? Oh, please, may I go at once?'

'Was she glad to see you?' asked the Countess.

'Of course! She has been waiting three years for my return, and she has been very lonely. But now I am here to comfort her, and presently we shall be married, and neither of us will ever be lonely again.'

'Hurry up,' said the Countess. 'If she is still waiting for you she may be feeling lonely now, and there are limits to what a girl can bear.'

So for the second day in succession Angelo left the castle at a run. In the short avenue of cypresses that led to the main gate he encountered the strange young man with light brown hair who had roused his curiosity on the day before; but now he paid no attention to him, except from the corner of his eye, and ran past as though the stranger were invisible. This is true courtesy, he thought. The stranger, indeed, paused and made a little gesture as if he were willing to talk. But it was too late. Angelo had gone.

A pair of tall white oxen with widely sweeping horns stood on the bridge, while their driver, with Lucrezia beside him, leaned upon the parapet in contemplation of the depths below. They had their backs to Angelo, their elbows were touching, they were talking in soft voices. Roberto Carpaccio, the driver of the oxen, was a clever young man who had evaded conscription by feigning epilepsy, and taken to the hills whenever German press-gangs appeared in the neighbourhood. He was about Angelo's age, and not ill-looking.

Angelo spoke to them sadly. 'Here I am,' he said. 'I am sorry that I am late.'

'But are you late? I hadn't noticed it,' said Lucrezia.

'I am very late,' said Angelo, and looked so extremely sad that Roberto laughed aloud, and laughing still bade Lucrezia a gay goodbye, called to his team, and went off in high good-humour.

'What is the matter with you?' asked Lucrezia.

'You did not realize I was late. You were so interested in what Roberto had to say that you forgot me altogether.'

'Am I not allowed to talk to anyone but you? Dear Angelo, how silly you are! I never have forgotten you, and never shall.'

'You are not in love with Roberto?'

'Not a bit.'

'Nor with anyone but me?'

'Nor with anyone but you!'

'Darling Lucrezia! And you never have been in love with anyone but me?'

Lucrezia put her arms round his neck, kissed him several times with the most agreeable warmth, and said, 'What a lot of foolish questions you ask! Tell me what you have been doing all day, and why you were so dreadfully late that I remembered, all over again, how unhappy I used to be while you were in Africa.'

'Were you very unhappy?'

'Oh, terribly so!'

'All the time, and every day?'

'You would like me to tell you so, wouldn't you?'

'Well yes, in a way I should.'

'Would it really please you to know that I had been miserable for more than three years? With never a moment of pleasure in all that time?'

'I should be very sorry for you. It would make me promise to do everything possible to give you happiness in the future, and help you to forget the past.'

'But why do you make conditions? Promise now that you will!'

'Lucrezia, I promise.'

'Truly and faithfully?'

'Truly and faithfully! Dear Lucrezia, let us be married very soon!'

But Lucrezia pushed him away, and leaning over the parapet again, looked down into the ravine. 'No, not yet,' she said.

'But why not? Don Agesilas will give me leave of absence –'

'I will not marry you while you are in the army, and while Italy is still at war.'

'But we are no longer at war with the English. They are coming to liberate us, not to fight against us.'

'You said last night that some of our soldiers are fighting against the Tedeschi, and the English certainly are fighting, and the Americans also, and they are all fighting here in Italy.'

'But I shall not fight again, if I can help it. And I am so bad a soldier that Don Agesilas, I think, will let me leave the army, and then I shall come home and stay here.'

'Then someone else will take you away. No, Angelo, I will not marry you until the war is truly finished, for I do not want to be a wife for two or three weeks, or only for two or three days, perhaps, and then be left alone. It is not good for a girl who is newly married to be left alone.'

'You mean,' said Angelo, 'that it would be like starting to read a new book –'

'Or sitting down to dinner –'

'Then someone borrows the book –'

'The plate is snatched away –'

'You want to know what happens in the next chapter –'

'You are hungrier than you were before you began –'

'But if you have strength of mind,' said Angelo –

'You can carry a great burden,' said Lucrezia. 'But there are limits.'

'On every road in Italy you see women carrying enormous burdens.'

'And their backs are bent, their faces tired, and they are old before their time. So also if you put too grievous a load upon their minds – no, Angelo. I will not do it.'

Nothing he said would change her opinion or undo her decision, and Angelo, in spite of his disappointment, became aware of a new respect for her. He even felt a little draught of fear that was somehow quite delicious. Sooner or later he would marry Lucrezia, and then he would be at the mercy of this strength she had developed in the years of absence, he would surrender himself to an unknown power. Though the prospect was alarming it was also alluring, and with some curiosity he perceived that fear is not always a deterrent to action. It may be, he thought, that I am a poltroon in war not merely because I am afraid of being hurt, but also because I do not enjoy fighting, neither the act of it nor the idea. For I now perceive that I am a little bit afraid of Lucrezia, yet I have no intention of running away from her. I should say not! So I am not altogether a coward, it seems.

Comforted by this reflection he accepted her refusal, and walked home with her in the darkness in a cheerful mood. It was Lucrezia, some little while later, who was reluctant to part, but now Angelo was quite firm, and with no regard for what lay upon her mind, bade her goodnight.

He spent the following day talking to everyone in the village, the evening was passed in tender conversation with Lucrezia, and early the next morning he set off for Rome. The lorries were now laden with wine in great vessels of green glass jacketed in straw; and they arrived without misadventure.

Pleased and self-important about the safe conclusion of his mission, Angelo demanded to see the Count.

'He is not here,' replied a middle-aged butler. 'Very soon after you left us, two German officers arrived, and a little while later he went away with them in a motor-car. I have not heard of him since.'

'*Dio mio*! He has not been arrested?'

'It happened several days ago. I do not think that anyone would stay so long with the Tedeschi of his own accord,' said the butler.

CHAPTER FOUR

LORENZO THE BUTLER, a timid man who went in great dread of the Germans, had done nothing to ascertain the Count's fate or his whereabouts, and for safety's sake had even concealed what he knew from the several people who had inquired for his master.

'If anyone has heard of him it will be the Marchesa Dolce,' said Angelo.

'She knows nothing,' answered Lorenzo. 'She has telephoned every day to ask for him.'

'And what did you tell her?'

'What could I tell her? The Tedeschi listen to all our conversations, and if you so much as mention them your name is noted as that of a person interested in politics; and that is the end of you.'

'I had better go and see the Marchesa,' said Angelo thoughtfully. 'She is a person of great accomplishment, she will know what to do about this.'

He went immediately to the house that overlooked the Piazza di Spagna, and after only a short delay was admitted to the Marchesa's presence. She was a very beautiful woman with a long nose and long slender hands. Her habitual expression was sedate and serious, a permanent reproof, as it were, to those who were first attracted by the voluptuous quality of her admirable figure.

'I remember you quite well,' she exclaimed. 'Where is Don Agesilas?'

'That is what I hope to find out,' said Angelo, and repeated the alarming tale he had heard from the butler.

'What a fool that man is! I telephone every day, and he replies that his master has gone out. Nothing more than that. If I had known a little earlier . . .'

She was silent for a while, and then, with sadness in her voice, said, 'It is going to be difficult. I do not think I can secure his release without help of some kind. I need advice, I must borrow a little wisdom. What have you learnt, Angelo, while you have been away all these years?'

'That before the war I was better off than I realized: there is one thing. That soldiers can suffer much and still survive, but are not always improved by their suffering: there is another. That if men are as cruel at home as they are abroad, then their wives have much to complain of –'

'Your time has not been wholly wasted,' said the Marchesa.

'And finally,' said Angelo, 'that if living at peace were as simple as going to war, we might have more of it.'

'That is probably true,' said the Marchesa, 'but the discovery, if it is one, is not helpful. Listen to me, Angelo. The Count, your master, has certainly been arrested by the Germans, and is therefore in grave danger. Until recently the senior German general in Rome was von Kluggenschaft, a person of unpleasant character but normal temperament, over whom I had some influence. He, unfortunately, has now been replaced by a man called Hammerfurter, who is different. That is to say, his nature is different. With him I can do nothing. He is greedy and could be bribed, of course, but I am not a wealthy woman.'

'I have just brought two lorry-loads of wine from Pontefiore,' said Angelo. 'Don Agesilas was going to sell it to General von Kluggenschaft, but it might serve for a bribe instead.'

'Not for a general,' said the Marchesa. 'Generals put a high price on their integrity. – But is it good wine?'

'No, not very good, but there is a large quantity of it.'

'There is an unpleasant little man called Colonel Schwigge who might be influenced,' said the Marchesa. 'One could offer such a bribe to a colonel without much fear of giving offence, I think. He could not, I am afraid, secure the release of Don Agesilas, but he might tell us where he is.'

'What, then, shall I do with the wine?'

'Have it unloaded and I shall let you know.'

The Marchesa had no difficulty at all with Colonel Schwigge, who, as it happened, was being blackmailed by a brother officer and stood in urgent need of money. He knew where he could sell the wine for a good price, and in return for it he quickly discovered that the Count was a prisoner of the Schutzstaffel. He gave the Marchesa his address, and informed her that the person in immediate charge of the prisoners there was a Corporal Hisser.

'I have two other favours to ask you,' said the Marchesa. 'Here is a gold watch belonging to Don Agesilas: perhaps it might be sent to him. And I should very much like to meet this Corporal Hisser.'

The watch was a valuable one, and Colonel Schwigge, quickly appraising it, was grateful for the tactful way in which it had been offered to him; for the Marchesa quite understood that he would keep it. He readily undertook to arrange the meeting she desired, and telephoned that evening to say that the Corporal would be waiting, at noon the next day, in the gardener's lodge of the Schutzstaffel villa.

The Marchesa arrived at five minutes before the hour, and found the Corporal expecting her. In his smart black uniform he made a handsome figure, and though the Marchesa had little cause, at that moment, to feel much liking for the Germans, she had to admit that Hisser was an excellent example of Teutonic youth. He had flaxen hair, the ruddy skin of perfect health, and candid blue eyes. Here indeed was an advertisement for the Nordic myth. His manner, moreover, was engagingly correct, and he accepted the present she offered without loss of dignity.

Yes, he would do what he could to make Count Piccolo-grando as comfortable as possible. Not that the Count had anything to complain of, except loss of liberty, for all the prisoners were well treated and accommodated in excellent rooms. He agreed, however, that prison-diet was apt to be monotonous, and that private addition to it would be welcome. – The Marchesa would like to have special meals for the Count sent in? But certainly! Nothing was easier than that to arrange, and he himself would see to it that the Count received them punctually and decently served.

The Marchesa was delighted, and said to herself: We must not be too hasty in our judgment. If we knew the Germans better we should discover, I am sure, that many of them are like Corporal Hisser. – She had a basket that contained a pot of anchovies, a cold roast chicken, a small cheese, and a bottle of wine. This she gave to the Corporal with a little note for the Count – he had no objection to that – and having thanked him again, returned to her car with a lighter heart than she had known for several days.

As soon as she had gone the Corporal took the basket to his own quarters, and setting out its contents on a clean white cloth, made an excellent lunch. Then he went to inspect the prisoners.

There were only ten of them at that time, including the Count, and they all lived in a cellar. When the Corporal opened the door the smell was unpleasant, but he had long since grown accustomed to the disabilities of humankind, and he uttered no complaint. He carried a large electric torch, and most of the prisoners, blinking in the white glare, rose hastily to their feet and stood at attention as he entered. Two of them, however – elderly men and therefore clumsy – were slow to move, and to induce a proper alertness the Corporal had to knock them down two or three times.

'Discipline,' he said, 'is the basis of all decent living. You must learn discipline. I had ordered a very good lunch for you to-day – anchovies and white bread and butter, roast chicken, some fine cheese and excellent wine – but now, because of the lax behaviour of those two ridiculous old men, I shall be compelled to countermand the order, and you will get nothing. Take this lesson to heart, and improve your discipline.'

Carefully locking the door, he returned to his own room, and having taken off his tunic and his boots stood for a moment yawning on the balcony. His blue eyes were as clear as the pellucid sky, and in their candour there was no deceit. It was quite a simple pleasure that he took in beating his prisoners, and he enjoyed the smarting pain of his own torn knuckles. When he lay down he slept like a dog on a rug, twitching and yelping in his dreams.

Every day for several days Angelo took a basket of food for the Count and delivered it to Corporal Hisser, who never failed to enjoy it. Angelo and the Marchesa were greatly comforted to think that Don Agesilas was not only well-treated but now, by their effort, well fed. They could not, however, discover why he had been arrested, nor could the Marchesa find anyone to offer hope of his release. It was worrying, but '*Pazienza!*' said Angelo.

Then one day, returning from his usual errand, he avoided by a handsbreadth a motor-cycle in the Via Quattro Novembre. It was one of a pair, ridden by German soldiers, that preceded a large open car. All three vehicles came fast round the corner. The motor-cyclists in a sudden blare sounded their sirens, Angelo nimbly jumped aside, and a cab-horse took fright and swerved into the middle of the street. Braking hard, the driver of the motor-car swerved the other way but could not avoid the cab. He struck it hard, knocked it over, and came to a halt with his bonnet between its spinning wheels. The elderly horse lay sprawling and kicking till Angelo, with great presence of mind, sat upon its head and held it still.

The motor-cyclists, quickly returning, dispelled with threatening gestures the small crowd that was gathering, and General Hammerfurter, rising in his car, condemned everyone within hearing of his harsh voice for their unexampled ineptitude, their bestial appearance, and malignant intentions. The cabman, dazed by his fall, lay bleeding on the ground. One of the German soldiers kicked him in the ribs, and the other, taking Angelo by the collar, was about to drag him from his seat on the horse's head when the General shouted 'Stop!' and at this command, which sounded like the splitting of a sail, they all became intently still, and the scene took on the likeness of a complicated group of statuary.

The General was immensely tall, and his long narrow body was elegantly uniformed. His hairless face was the colour of a turkey's egg, pale and mottled, and round the jaw were the scars of an old skin-disease. He stared at Angelo with a concentrated interest.

To avoid interference from the military, Angelo had put away his uniform and was wearing a pale grey suit belonging to the Count. It fitted well, and excellently became him. He was hatless, and his face a little flushed by exertion. A breeze played lightly in his curling hair.

The General spoke angrily to the soldiers and said, 'That young man is the only person here who has not behaved like a fool. – Come here, young man.'

The nearest soldier took his place on the horse's head, and Angelo approached the General's car.

'Who are you?'

Angelo, who spoke German fairly well, explained that he was private secretary to a gentleman in Tuscany, and had but recently arrived in Rome. He mentioned the Count's name. General Hammerfurter had apparently not heard it before.

'Where are his estates?'

'The principal one is between Siena and Florence.'

The General continued to study Angelo so intently that Angelo felt himself blushing. Then the General asked, 'Is it true that a very good sort of Italian is spoken in those parts?'

'In Siena, where I went to school,' said Angelo, 'they speak with a greater correctness and a purer accent than anywhere else in Italy.'

This information evidently pleased the General. 'Good, very good!' he exclaimed. 'Now come into my car. You will have lunch with me. There is something of much importance that you and I must talk about.'

Then he spoke sharply to his driver and the other soldiers. Leaving the cabman and his struggling horse to look after themselves, the soldiers remounted their bicycles, the driver steered clear of the overturned cab, and they resumed their journey to the accompaniment of shrieking sirens. Angelo, concealing as best he could his fear and confusion, sat straight and prim beside the General.

Their conversation at lunch was hardly more than a monologue in which the General described his affection for the Italian people, his admiration for their works of art, and his enthusiasm for natural scenery of every sort. Primarily, he said, he had come to Italy as a soldier, and his immediate purpose was to defeat and destroy the barbarous English and Americans who were desecrating its classic soil. But secondarily, he explained, he was a lover; a lover of Italy and all its life, and nothing would make him happier than to serve its charming people and promote their welfare. But how could he serve them, wisely and efficiently, without knowing their language? He must learn Italian, and quite certainly his teacher must be one who spoke the very best sort of Italian.

'And so I consider it a great stroke of fortune, my dear fellow,' he said, 'to have met you, who were educated in Siena. For now that I have explained myself to you, laid bare my heart and confessed my love, you will not, I am sure, refuse my proposal. You will not grudge me your time, but will become my teacher and help me to know my Italy as I desire. Yes? I think so. Have some more brandy.'

'But I am quite inexperienced,' said Angelo unhappily.

'Good, good!' exclaimed the General. 'It is better so, for so we shall both make our blunders, very laughable blunders no doubt, and have sympathy one for another. We Germans are famous for our sympathy because we have so good an understanding of people. – Let me show you how to make what is one of my favourite drinks: a glass of benedictine and a glass of cognac: mix them together. It is quite simple and very good. You try it. – Now tell me, my dear fellow, what is the Italian for "a true friend"?'

'What is the German for "a helpless captive"?' asked Angelo in Italian; and when he had translated his question the General laughed immoderately, complimented Angelo on his wit, and with honest affection pinched the lobe of his left ear so tightly that Angelo's eyes filled with tears.

Not until four o'clock was he permitted to leave, and then, after walking in the gardens of the Pincio for half an hour to collect his thoughts, he went to call on the Marchesa Dolce.

'Have you any news?' she asked.

'I have just been giving an Italian lesson to General Hammerfurter. I have become his tutor.'

'But what an achievement! How did you manage it?'

'The appointment was not really one I sought,' said Angelo, and described the street accident which had caused them to meet. 'Though he speaks in the friendliest way the General is very fierce and masterful,' he said. 'I am extremely frightened of him.'

'What does that matter?' asked the Marchesa warmly. 'It would be too paltry – selfish and paltry and mean – if in such a time as this you were to attach the smallest weight to your own feelings. It is not of ourselves we must think, but of Don Agesilas. By the greatest good fortune in the world you have made the acquaintance of General Hammerfurter, and now you must take every possible advantage of it. Play your cards properly, and we may look forward to the very early release of an unhappy prisoner. But if you are petty and small-minded, if you run away, why, then he may lie for ever, without hope or mercy, in his German prison.'

'That is what I have been thinking,' said Angelo sadly.

'Tell me what the General spoke about,' said the Marchesa.

'Chiefly about himself. About his love for Italy, the sympathy and good understanding which characterize all Germans, and so forth.'

'Good,' said the Marchesa. 'Now when you return to give him his next lesson, you must impress upon him the belief that those are the things of which Italy is most in need, and in return for his sympathy and understanding we should quite certainly, and almost immediately, offer him our passionate allegiance. – Do not hesitate to credit him with great ambition, it can do you no possible harm. – Then in the third lesson you must introduce the name of Don Agesilas. Mention, in a light and conversational way, his admiration for some aspect of German life –'

'He has none.'

'Then your invention will be untrammelled. Proceed more lightly still, with a careless laugh and a flutter of the hands, to the revelation that he is now in gaol. "Mistakes will occur," you must observe, "but how ironical that such a great lover of Germany should by error now lie in a German prison!" Add to that, as quickly as possible, the information that Don Agesilas is a very wealthy man . . .'

Angelo paid close attention to the Marchesa's advice, but found some difficulty in putting it into practice. With his native regard for order and authority, the General preferred the smoothness of monologue to the ragged give-and-take of ordinary conversation, and rarely would he consider any topic not of his own choosing. 'I wish to explain myself to you,' he would say. 'I have a remarkable character, and you will be deeply interested to hear about it. I am, for instance, equally capable of tragic perception and Homeric laughter. Intrinsically I am a nobleman, very simple and honest and kind-hearted, a true aristocrat of the old sort. But also I have a modern understanding so subtle that often I am amazed at myself. – But how German! you will say. For you, being intelligent yourself, know how typical of the German soul is its universality. How do you say, in Italian, "the universality of the German soul"?'

Talk of this kind, which Angelo found very tedious, prohibited any reference to the Count and his affairs for several days. And then one afternoon, when the General in a mood of languor toyed with a melancholy silence, Angelo found opportunity and a sufficient courage to broach the subject. How greatly his master the Count would enjoy their conversation, he said. Few Italians, he ventured to think, were more deeply interested in the complexity of the German mentality or more truly impressed by its grandeur, than Count Piccologrando.

'Where is he living?' asked the General.

'He is now in prison,' said Angelo.

'What a scoundrel he must be.'

'No, no! It is entirely by mistake that he is in prison. Two officers arrested him –'

'A German officer never makes a mistake.'

'Of course not! It must have been the Count, my master, who made a mistake. Like many rich men – I mean exceedingly rich men – he is sometimes very careless.'

'So? He is rich?'

Angelo named, in succession of value, the Count's several estates.

'But what is wealth compared with happiness?' exclaimed the General. 'It is my peculiarity that I despise mere riches. I have seen more true contentment in a humble cottage on the Baltic than in all your Roman palaces. Ach, when I think of the cabbages in the garden, and old men smoking their pipes, and everywhere our little swine running to-and-fro! How beautiful a scene, is it not? – Ring the bell, my dear fellow. Let us drink a bottle or two of champagne, and I shall tell you about my Prussian home.'

Angelo was sadly convinced, when he went home that evening, that the General had utterly forgotten the Count's existence. – I have been wasting my time, he thought. I detest my employment, and I have submitted to it only in the belief that somehow it might help me to secure the release of Don Agesilas. If that is not so, then *basta!* Enough! I shall never return to the house of that hateful and boring old man.

In the morning, however, he decided to make one more trial of his persuasive power, and was infinitely surprised to find the General not merely in a brisk and businesslike frame of mind, but waiting to discuss the very subject which Angelo had so often found impossible to introduce.

'I have had inquiries made,' he said, 'and found it to be true that this man whom you call the Count Piccologrando is in a German prison. Therefore, of course, he is a criminal. But I found also that he is not charged with any specific offence, for the two officers by whom he was arrested were too busy to make a detailed statement, and are now in some other part of Italy. And so it was quite easy to deal with him. I decided to fine him an appropriate sum, and release him.'

'How noble of you!' cried Angelo. 'How truly wise and clement you are! What an administrator you would make for all Italy!'

Unmoved by these compliments, the General continued in a cold and formal voice: 'I have ascertained that his bank is the Banco di Santo Spirito, and I have informed the manager that the Count Piccologrando is about to draw a large cheque in your favour.'

'Why in my favour?' asked Angelo; but the General ignored him and went on with his story.

'From his residence I obtained his cheque-book, which I had conveyed to him in his prison, with the information that he had been found guilty and fined the sum of so many lire. I also gave him my own word that he would be released as soon as his cheque had been honoured. After some discussion he perceived the justice of my sentence and the mercy of my intervention. Here, then, is the cheque. You will go to the bank, cash it, and return immediately. The signature is a trifle shaky, but it will serve. If you have any trouble, let me know.'

'But good God!' cried Angelo. 'This is a cheque for five million lire!'

'The Count is a very wealthy man.'

'Not so wealthy as he was.'

'Had he not valued his freedom he would not have purchased it. – No, I have no time at present for discussion. My car will take you to the bank, wait for you, and bring you back. The quicker you go, the sooner will the Count be free.'

The General had made excellent arrangements, and Angelo had no difficulty in cashing the cheque. One of the soldiers who accompanied him had brought a leather bag into which they packed the notes, and within ten minutes of their return the General had counted them with a methodical and yet not ostentatious care, and signed an order for the Count's release. He counted the money again before locking it into a safe, and then, after a moment of solemn thought, his mood quite suddenly altered. He unbuttoned his tunic, became boisterously genial, and from a silver bucket pulled a slender green bottle and poured brim-full two enormous glasses of primrose-coloured wine.

'Let us drink!' he exclaimed. 'Now that we have settled all that dull work let us enjoy ourselves for a change, and drink! And today, my Angelo, we shall drink German wine, which is the best in the world.'

The General smacked his lips and refilled his glass. With interest and some foreboding Angelo saw that the silver bucket held half a dozen bottles.

'Ach, how I hate the sordid claims of business! It is only the inferior breeds of people who take pleasure in money-making,' said the General. 'We are poets, we Germans, and our natural communion is with the eternal thoughts of nature. And mark how nature has blessed our understanding by giving us vineyards that grow a poet's wine. Already I feel my spirit soaring! I am so sensitive, I respond as quickly as a woman – but with a truer perception, of course, of the eternal values. Yes, we are poets! Let me tell you about our German soul . . .'

It was late before Angelo was allowed to leave and the sky was darkening when, with the utmost impatience, he hurried home to greet the Count. It was almost a lover's eagerness, or the tyrannical hunger of a child, that he felt, now, for the sight and the sound and the touch of that handsome trim figure, the musical and witty voice, those delicate and accomplished hands. Dear master! he thought. My wise, graceful, kindest master, how I long to welcome you!

He was sadly taken aback when the butler told him that the Count was in bed, and the doctor who had been called in had given orders that he was on no account to be disturbed. – But the butler was a dull creature, with no faculty but for misunderstanding. He was always making mistakes. Angelo decided to go and see for himself.

With feather-soft fingertips he tapped upon the bedroom door, tapped again, and waited. In a little while it was opened, and Angelo was surprised to see, against a shaded light, the Marchesa Dolce. She came out, closing the door behind her, and spoke in a whisper. Angelo listened with bewildered sorrow.

Then she said: 'You must not stay very long, and do not let him see that you are surprised by his appearance. The bandage, after all, makes a lot of difference.'

Angelo promised to behave with composure, and went gently in. Bending low to the pillow, so that the Count might recognize him, he uttered the hope that his master was already feeling better.

'To meet old friends again cannot fail to make me better,' said the Count with a courteous gesture of the hand which had not been hurt. 'But the truth is, my dear boy, that I am not so well as I used to be. Neither so well nor so well-off. My physical health is depreciated, and my account at the Banco di Santo Spirito is overdrawn. The poet Shelley, now happily buried in this city, once compared life to a many-coloured dome. And how right he was! For my poor body is black and blue, and to the Holy Ghost I am altogether in the red.'

ANGELO GAVE no more Italian lessons to General Hammerfurter. He had a generous nature and the springs of gratitude flowed freely in his heart – having been educated in an old-fashioned way he had never learnt that gratitude is a sign of inferiority and should therefore be suppressed – but after carefully weighing the evidence, for and against the General, he had come to the conclusion that he owed him nothing. True, the Count was at liberty, and that was through the General's influence; but the Count had paid five million lire for his freedom, and would need several weeks of careful nursing before he could enjoy it. 'I abhor a mean or grudging temperament,' said Angelo to the Marchesa, 'but facts are facts and should be recognized. We owe that man nothing!'

The Marchesa, though she disliked the General for more reasons than one, would have preferred a continuance of his friendship with Angelo, for the sake of peace and the possibility of further benefit; but when she perceived the strength of Angelo's feelings she made no more attempt to persuade him. She merely said, 'You must try to avoid an open quarrel. Tell him that you have to return to Pontefiore.'

'I shall tell him nothing,' said Angelo.

He trembled, even as he spoke, to think of the consequences of such heroic stubbornness, but escaped them, as it turned out, with the help of the butler's timely stupidity. The General sent his orderlies, and finally his aide-de-camp, to ask what had happened to Angelo; and always the butler answered with disarming frankness, 'He has gone out. No, I do not know where, and I do not know when he will come back. To tell you the truth, I know nothing about him.'

Angelo, in the meantime, had more than once met the two soldiers, the Czech and the Russian, with whom he had driven to Pontefiore. They had reminded him of his promise to help them escape, and because he now felt a certain prejudice against the German authorities, he had bestirred himself to find someone who could give them practical assistance. He met one evening an old comrade of his own regiment, who had deserted by feigning death in battle, and succeeded in returning to Italy from Cyrenaica. This man now earned a precarious living by reproducing, where they were needed, the purple die-stamps on official documents, which he did in a very simple but ingenious way; and after some discussion with Angelo he promised to introduce him to a person called Fest.

Within a limited circle, it appeared, Fest was well known, though no one could tell much about him except that, for reasons of his own, he was hostile to the Germans. He spoke Italian fluently, but with a clumsy guttural accent, and his appearance was remarkable. His thick growth of pale brown hair was streaked with grey, and he wore a monocle of clouded tortoiseshell to conceal the loss of his left eye and the burnt lids that betrayed the manner of its destruction. A deep scar, breaking the bridge of his nose, extended to his left cheek-bone, and half a dozen parallel scars, bone-white and thin as a knitting needle, ran from his forehead into the thickness of his hair. He dressed with distinction, his manner was cold, his carriage upright.

Angelo met him in a trattoria near the little Piazza dei Satiri that was commonly used by cabmen, flower-sellers, and petty agents of the Black Market; and there he spoke diffidently of his friends' desire to escape from German service. Fest appeared to be sympathetic and said he would make some necessary inquiries.

Two days later Angelo met him again, and Fest invited him to bring the Czech and the Russian to the trattoria on the following evening. The four of them spent nearly an hour together, and the two soldiers spoke at great length on the injustice they had suffered, the hardships they had endured, and their hatred of the Germans. Fest listened attentively, without saying much in reply, and made another appointment. He would then be able, he said, to let them know what arrangements had been made for their escape, and give them their instructions.

To Angelo's surprise the soldiers brought a stranger to this meeting. He was a short broad-shouldered man in the uniform of a German private. His expression was amiable, and according to the others he was a Lett from Dvinsk. He also, it appeared, was eager to desert, and having overheard the Czech and the Russian discussing their plans, he had asked as a great favour to be allowed to join their party. Angelo thought they had been indiscreet, but there was nothing he could do to redress the situation. They sat down together, ordered wine, and waited for Fest.

The trattoria was unusually empty, and Fest was late. The Lett paid for another flask and asked Angelo how many soldiers he had smuggled out of the country. Angelo answered with a knowing look and a shrug of the shoulders. They finished the flask, and still Fest did not come. The Czech and the Russian had begun to look worried, and the Lett was turning sullen. 'I think you have been deceiving us,' he said. 'I do not think your friend means to come.'

'Perhaps he has been prevented.'

'By whom?'

'How should I know?'

'Who else should know? It was you who introduced these men to him, and asked him to arrange their escape. You are responsible for the whole plan.'

'I offered to help them if I could –'

'That is enough,' said the Lett, and knocked the flask off the table. This was evidently a signal, for a few seconds later the door was thrown open and a sergeant of the Schutzstaffel came in, followed by four troopers, all carrying revolvers.

'Where's the other one?' demanded the sergeant.

'He hasn't come,' said the Lett.

'Why not?'

'This one tipped him off, I think,' and the Lett pointed to Angelo.

'We'll hammer your liver into paste for that,' said the sergeant.

Angelo and the would-be deserters were in a white trance of fear, and when the troopers dragged them from the table, to which they feebly clung, their loosened knees could scarcely bear their weight. They were hustled to the door while the other drinkers, the few who had come to the trattoria that night, shrank into dark corners or huddled against a wall, and watched them in a silence broken only by a flower-vendor's nervous hiccup.

They were driven to the prison called Regina Coeli, where for an hour or two they were questioned, not about their intentions – which had already been revealed by the Lett, who was an agent of the police – but about Fest. As none of them knew anything, however, they could tell very little; and because their interrogators had had a busy day, and were tired, they escaped with little worse than a formal beating for their incompetence.

Angelo, the Russian, and the Czech spent fourteen miserable days in the Regina Coeli gaol among some thirty or forty nondescript prisoners, none of whom dared speak freely to anyone else for fear he was talking to a German agent. Angelo and his two companions were so disconcerted by the Lett's betrayal of them that they regarded each other with mutual dread, avoided conversation almost entirely, and were reticent about the torture they suffered. They were all beaten every second or third day, but Angelo's interrogators were either bored by their duty or physically exhausted by it, and his injuries were superficial. The Czech and the Russian were less fortunate and they regarded Angelo with ever-increasing suspicion.

He was rescued from this unpleasant atmosphere by a sudden order, one night, to parade in the prison yard. A group of about two hundred men stood there under a fine rain, while guards moved about them, shouting. Presently they were marched to the railway station, where two smaller companies were waiting, and after a tedious delay during which the most alarming rumours were discussed, they were hustled with a sudden feverish haste into the open trucks of a waiting train. There they remained, cold and shivering, till dawn, when the train started.

All day the rain fell from low clouds. From time to time the train stopped, and the prisoners were ordered from their trucks to repair the line, which had been bombed in several places. Night was falling when they entered a mountain gorge, and quickly the sombre hills disappeared in a general gloom. It became very cold, and some of the prisoners were much distressed. Fortunately for Angelo the truck in which he was travelling was grossly overcrowded, and his companions engendered a natural heat which greatly comforted him. Towards morning, however, he was annoyed by an oldish man who, held against him by the crowd, fell sound asleep in his arms. Angelo supported him, partly because he was good-natured, partly because it was very difficult to get rid of the fellow; but it was unfair, he thought, that a stranger should use him so. Not until morning did he perceive that the oldish man was dead.

They were now in a very wild and rugged part of the country, but the weather was fair again, and as they descended from the mountains into the coastal plain the sun warmed them, and the steam of drying clothes rose above the jolting train. Several of Angelo's companions now felt sure that they were going to Ancona, though for what purpose none could guess.

But when the train reached the coast it went northward away from Ancona. Angelo squeezed and pushed his way to the right-hand side of the truck, and looked with pleasure at the pale blue sea that stretched so far, in silky calm, beneath a milk-white sky. It was the first time he had ever seen the Adriatic, and though he disliked the means by which he had come there, he was glad to increase his knowledge of the world.

They arrived at the little port of Pesaro, where they left

the train and were marched to the outskirts of the town, from which the native inhabitants had been removed. They slept in some empty houses, and in the morning began to knock them down.

Most of the houses were quite new, and well-built. The furniture remained in some of them, and when the Germans had taken all they needed for themselves, such as beds and cooking-pots and blankets, they sold what was left to the people who had been evicted. These unhappy creatures used to come every day to watch their houses being demolished, and some of the women cried aloud when they saw the walls tumble. The German officer who was in charge of the work was a pale young man, with the eager but careworn look of a student, who believed there was no virtue like efficiency. Angelo and his fellow-prisoners were compelled to break the houses down to single bricks, and spread the debris flat. Then the officer would smile and say, 'Good, very good! That is beautifully done!'

He appeared to be a kindly young man, and one day Angelo plucked up courage to ask him what was the purpose of this destruction.

'I suppose it is hard for you to understand,' said the officer. 'You feel guilty, you poor Italians, because you have betrayed us and broken our alliance. And because you feel guilty you fear that we shall desert you, and leave you to your fate. But no! A German promise is a sacred thing, and cannot be broken. You do not understand that, but nevertheless it is so. And therefore we are still fighting for you, and here in Pesaro we are making the most careful preparation to defend your country to the last. Have no fear! We shall never allow the English and the Americans to destroy your beautiful Italy.'

'Would they destroy it as carefully as we are doing?' asked Angelo.

'No, no! They are a lot of bungling amateurs,' said the officer. 'It is only we Germans who are truly efficient.'

'In that case,' said Angelo respectfully, 'I think Italy would be better off if you did desert us.'

'Shut up, swinehound!' shouted a sergeant who had been listening to their conversation, and with the back of his hand struck Angelo across the face so heavily that he fell upon a pile of bricks, and the Sergeant kicked him in the ribs.

'Do not be too severe,' said the officer. 'He comes of an inferior race, they lack understanding.' And he went busily to inspect the destruction of another house.

The demolitions were intended to open fields of fire for certain guns which the Germans were mounting, and when their work in Pesaro was done the prisoners were marched along the high road that runs inland from there, and whenever they came to a village they stayed in it until they had knocked it flat. Then they were ordered to fell all the trees on the flat river-fields south of the road, and Angelo grew sadder every day to see how thoroughly a country had to be ruined in order to be saved.

He was too unhappy to make friends with the other prisoners; many of whom, indeed, were in the same mood as he. Though never for a moment alone, he and those of his temper lived solitary lives and nursed their grief like a young widow suckling her orphan babe.

The Germans, about this time, were much alarmed by the success of the Allied landings, and contemplated a long retreat to the mountains north of Florence. Hurriedly they had chosen defensive sites, and were fortifying them to create from coast to coast what was later known as the Gothic Line. But then their Führer perceived the moral impossibility of abandoning Rome to the barbarians, and with the approach of winter – a potent ally – resolved to fight for it in the southern passes. So work on the Gothic Line came to a stop, no more houses were demolished, and for a week or two Angelo and his companions, with nothing to do, were lodged in a large school on the seashore south of Pesaro. The ejected pupils, enjoying their unexpected holiday, gave three cheers for every German they saw, and the prisoners were comforted by several days of fine warm weather.

They spent most of their time on the beach, and their

favourite occupation was to watch the fisherfolk hauling their nets.

The nets were towed out to sea in a great semi-circle, and then the fisherfolk would lay hold of the end-ropes and slowly, with a small formal step, drag them ashore. Most of the haulers were old men and women and girls. As the nets came in, running water from the mesh, the bare-legged, bare-armed women would kilt their skirts high above the knee. There was a girl there who reminded Angelo of Lucrezia; not by any physical resemblance, but because she stirred something of the same emotion in him. She was little and childishly plump, though she wore a wedding-ring, and when she had gathered her skirt to the waist, and was leaning far back on the rope, and the salt sea-drops fell with a tiny splash upon her smooth round thighs, then Angelo thought of Lucrezia at the washing-trough, and his lungs contracted as though a ghostly arm encircled him.

One day, observing a yard of rope unoccupied behind her, he stepped forward, took hold and helped to pull. She turned her head, and smiled.

Angelo soon discovered that it did no good to heave and strain, but when he lay upon the rope there presently came, as if the sea were lifting it, an easing of the weight, and then he must take – one-two, like dancing – a little step, and somewhere behind him a fathom of slack would be coiled upon the sand. The net came in, the circle narrowed and became a bag. Two score small fishes, wriggling silver, were gathered from it. Softly the girl asked him, 'Why do you look so unhappy?'

'I am a prisoner,' said Angelo.

'So is my husband.'

'To be separated from you must make him the unhappiest man alive.'

'Are you married too?'

'She said she would not have me until the war was over,' said Angelo.

'I think she is wise,' said the girl. 'But my husband is going to escape.'

'How?'

'Come back to-morrow, and I shall tell you.'

'What is your name?'

'Annunziata.'

The next day Angelo took his place on the rope behind Annunziata as though it were his right, and addressed her so warmly that she frowned at him, pointed her glance at an old grey-bearded man, and whispered through careful lips, 'Be sensible! He is my father-in-law.'

But Angelo, with hope like a bubble in his blood, answered, 'Dear Annunziata! Tell me how your husband is going to escape, and if he fails perhaps I can succeed and take his place.'

When they began to haul he fell easily into the rhythm of it, and once or twice put an arm round Annunziata's waist, when she leaned far back, and pressed her to him. She grew offended, or made a pretence of it, and would not talk to him until they were pulling-in for the third time. Then she said, 'You must volunteer for the front line.'

'Oh, no!' said Angelo. 'I should hate to do that.'

'That is how my husband is going to escape. He was taken away and set to work as you have been, but then the Tedeschi asked for volunteers who would join their army and serve them where they are fighting. Mario, my husband, said to himself, "If they send me to some place where there is a battle, I shall be quite near to the English or the Americans, and therefore it will be much easier to escape and join the other side." So he volunteered, and by now, perhaps, he has already deserted.'

Angelo said in a subdued voice, 'Perhaps your husband is a brave man?'

'He is quite fearless,' answered Annunziata. 'He has been in prison three times for fighting, he is beautiful and strong and absolutely courageous.'

'I am not in the least like that,' said Angelo.

Annunziata let down her skirt. 'But you are very kind,' she said. 'You have helped us greatly, and I hope you will be rewarded by good fortune. – No, I must not talk any longer, for my father-in-law is watching us, and he is very stern. Goodbye!' said Annunziata.

Angelo thought very earnestly indeed about her suggestion, and the more he considered it, the more he hated the prospect of going anywhere near the firing-line. He lay awake all night and frightened himself into a fever by picturing the horrors of war. He saw himself dying in dreadful agony, unable to rise from the little icy pool in the cup of a bomb-crater, while Lucrezia in her lonely bed lay weeping three hundred miles away. His fever broke, and a cold sweat bedewed him. When morning came he felt so weak that he could hardly get up.

But during the day he thought: How else can I escape? There isn't the smallest chance of running away from here, for I am quite ignorant of this part of the country, I shouldn't in the least know where to make for, and the English and the Americans – who are still fighting along the river Volturno, they say – might as well be in the moon for all the help they can give me. This business of liberation, about which there was so much talk, is going to be a slow process, and I may grow old waiting for it. The sensible thing, if it were not so dangerous, would certainly be to go and meet it half-way. Ah, if only I had the *dono di coraggio*!

During the day some of the prisoners heard a rumour, and quickly spread it, that they were to be taken to Germany and set to work at clearing the damage in some cities which had lately been bombed by the Royal Air Force. – That will be Essen and Cologne, said some. Berlin and Stettin are more likely, said others. Or Munich, suggested a third party.

Angelo's fellow-prisoners at this time were all Italians, and whenever they heard that a German city had been bombed they were delighted, for they hated the Tedeschi and also it was worth remembering that bombs which fell in Germany could never be used against Italy. But none of them had any wish to go and see for himself what damage had been done. The idea of being sent to Germany was their greatest fear, and no one was more profoundly affected by it than Angelo.

He slept that night, for he was too tired to stay awake, but his sleep was haunted by a dreadful nightmare in which he saw himself labouring in the horrid ruin of a German street, while a monstrous armada circled in the white-striped sky above, and the roar of its engines for ever threatened the louder roar of an exploding bomb. He woke, and felt more tired than ever. The nightmare had been even worse than his waking thoughts of war.

The greater fear diminished the less, and now that the alternative, as it seemed, was to labour like a slave in Germany, he longed to be engaged upon a battlefield in Italy. He decided to take Annunziata's advice as soon as the opportunity occurred.

He had not long to wait. About a week later an elderly German major arrived, the prisoners were paraded, and the major made a speech about the honourable profession of arms, and the still enduring friendship between Germany and Italy, the crimes that were daily being committed by the Allies, and so forth. Then he asked for volunteers to serve at the front in a pioneer regiment.

Angelo was the first to step forward.

CHAPTER SIX

'WE DO NOT get enough sleep,' said the Count.

'What is sleep?' demanded the Marchesa. 'Pure negation, and why you should want to enlarge a mere nothing, I cannot think. It is, moreover, so boorish. It puzzles me that you, who are otherwise courteous, should be so ready to turn your back upon a friend.'

'I have two friends,' said the Count with a gentle yawn, 'and the other is repose.'

'I think of sleep as a rehearsal for death,' replied the Marchesa, 'and as I feel sure that when the last night comes I shall wear my coffin with conviction, I see no purpose in wasting time on unnecessary practice.'

'I have a simpler mind than yours, and less vitality. I enjoy both the prospect and the process of going to sleep; and I need a great deal of it.'

'People in our position should not require very much. It is different for the poor, of course. Their life is so horrible that naturally they do not wish to endure consciousness for more than a few hours at a time. But we are different –'

'We have become like the poor in one respect: we are equally vulnerable nowadays.'

'Our life remains interesting. It is precarious, perhaps, but still furnished with beauty.'

'It is possible to over-furnish either a room or your life,' said the Count.

'That would be foolish, of course.'

'It is always surprising to see how many fools win the love, or at least the companionship, of beautiful women. – Or is it surprising? Perhaps not. Let us admit that a beautiful woman may be the desire of the noblest, and

56

should be the reward of the bravest among us. But a woman requires to be wooed, and who make the best wooers? Fools, because they have the time for it, and the necessary frivolity of mind.'

'I dislike you when you grow introspective, dear Agesilas.'

'I am sleepy,' said the Count.

Among her many excellent qualities the Marchesa owned a single disability. She had an unusually quick digestion. She ate heartily and often during the day, and she rarely passed a night without waking for a meal in the middle of it. Sometimes she would be satisfied with a glass of milk and a biscuit or two, but generally she wanted something with more bulk and substance in it. The Count had never quite reconciled himself to this idiosyncrasy, and since his release from prison he had found it more and more trying. He had recovered his health but not all his equanimity, and he blamed his own weakness as much as hers for the annoyance he suffered. But to be fair about it did not, he found, diminish the annoyance.

A maid, who had been roused for the purpose, brought into the little drawing-room a tray that bore a large omelette well stuffed with mushrooms and ham, a loaf of bread and a dish of butter, a bottle of wine, a small decanter of brandy, a bunch of grapes, and some pastry. For friendship's sake the Count accepted a small portion of the omelette and a glass of wine. It was an excellent white wine from Orvieto, and presently he began to feel more cheerful. He drank a little brandy, and started a discussion on political life.

'Mussolini was my friend,' he said, 'and I shall never conceal or deny it. Nowadays he is being adversely criticized by people who are as devoid of gratitude as they are incapable of memory. They have, for example – these ingrates – entirely forgotten the ubiquitous, the general, the inescapable corruption that made the life of Italy shameful, and so crippled our resources before the advent of Fascism.'

'There was plenty of corruption under Fascism.'

'But how tidy it became! In the same way as he drained the Pontine marshes he drained great lakes of bribery and peculation, and canalized their flow into official channels and official pockets. You must admire the magnitude of his work.'

'He was vulgar,' said the Marchesa.

'What else would you have had him? No person of true refinement can take a prominent part in public life, except perhaps, as an unwilling martyr; by no possible chance could such a person become a dictator. A dictator, being the product of social indigestion, is by nature as vulgar as a smell. You must not hold it against Mussolini that he made no effort to conceal his origin. No, no! The man was my friend, I tell you.'

'You are no better for his friendship now,' said the Marchesa, and helped herself to the last of the omelette.

'I am a little wiser, I think, and if others shared my perspicacity they also might be wiser. He did excellent work – this you cannot deny – in bringing the business of government into disrepute. This was desirable because popular education has been accompanied by, if it has not deliberately promoted, a growth of superstitious faith in government. The people have come to believe that government can procure for them, not merely prosperity, but happiness. Side by side with this nonsensical delusion there has marched the increasing professionalism of government. Many astute people have seen the business of government as a business indeed, and therefore, into the council chambers of the world, there has come a great deal of rascality. Now Mussolini, with real genius, perceived this tendency and pushed it to its logical extreme: he created a government that was frankly criminal, and then for universal enlightenment – or so I think, for I believe the man to have been misunderstood – he led it by a route congenial to criminals, a route congenial, that is, to certain elements in every government upon earth, to a destined and complete disaster. For that disaster, of course, we ourselves are fundamentally to blame, because our ridiculous credulity let us repose in his government all the faith a savage African has in his wooden idol, and with as much reason. Mussolini – and the world will remember him for this – exposed our folly to the depths, and like another Moses cast down the idol of total government. The corollary is obvious: We must grow up, we must cultivate ourselves. Our goal must be a world in which every man is his own republic –'

'Good God!' exclaimed the Marchesa. 'Who are you?'

A man stood in the doorway. He was tall and well built. His light brown hair was streaked with grey and in his left eye he wore a monocle of clouded tortoiseshell. He closed the door as quietly as he had opened it, and came into the room.

'I have some disturbing news for you,' he said.

The Marchesa had risen in alarm. Her breast rose and fell, her nostrils were slightly dilated, and she pulled her *saut-de-lit* more tightly round her with hands that slightly trembled. The Count remained in his chair, apparently calm, having adjusted his dressing-gown to conceal the agitation of his knees.

'Who are you?' repeated the Marchesa, while the Count declared, a little hoarsely, 'This is an extraordinary visit, sir! What do you want?'

'My name is Fest,' said the stranger. 'Some weeks ago I became acquainted with a protégé of yours, a young man called Angelo –'

'Where is he now?'

'I don't know. He was taken by the Germans, and, I believe, drafted into one of their labour battalions. But I have failed to discover what has happened to him. It was while I was seeking information about him that I heard of a new intention to arrest you.'

'Me?' exclaimed the Count. 'But that is impossible. I have already been arrested, and also set free.'

'You paid too handsomely for your release,' said Fest. 'You gave Hammerfurter five million lire to get out of prison, and now Brilling, the new chief of the Gestapo here, has heard of that and is going to have you arrested to see what he can squeeze for himself.'

'No, not again!' cried the Count. 'I have been squeezed enough. I cannot endure it again!'

'I thought as much. And so, if you will take my advice –'

'But who are you? What is your purpose in coming here? Why should you go to the trouble of warning me, and incur danger to help me?'

'I have a hobby,' said Fest, 'a simple hobby that gives me, nowadays, all the pleasure I know. It is to annoy the Tedeschi.'

The Count no longer made any attempt to conceal his perturbation. He walked up and down, wringing his hands, and glancing sideways at Fest in a grimacing alternation of anguish, appeal and suspicion. The Marchesa, who had been standing silent and still, now asked him, 'When are they coming?'

'Within a few minutes,' said Fest.

'What are we to do?'

'Find him a hiding-place.'

'My house is very small. There is nowhere a man can hide and be safe.'

'Nowhere,' exclaimed the Count. 'I know every inch of the house, and there is not room to hide a dog. My late father, in similar circumstances – a jealous husband was looking for him – once hid behind a woman's skirts, but nowadays that is quite impossible. The modern architect and the contemporary dressmaker have no sense of responsibility. Their creations are paltry, they offer neither protection nor concealment. No, no, I am already a prisoner!'

'The modern woman,' said Fest, 'is appreciably bigger than her mother. You have given me an idea. Lie down on that sofa.'

The Count was suspicious, a trifle querulous, and foolishly concerned about his dignity. Fest, however, disclosed a masterful temper, and the Count yielded. The sofa was long and broad. He lay down and was covered with cushions, of which there were many in the little drawing-room. The Marchesa took her place in the tableau with a look of restrained indignation. Fest instructed her to recline on the cushioned sofa in the attitude of Madame Récamier in the portrait by David; but he was dissatisfied by the picture she

represented. She lacked repose, and the displacement of a
cushion revealed one of the Count's feet and gave her the
appearance of possessing three.

'Have patience,' he said, and went into the adjoining
bedroom, from which he returned with a hairbrush and a
mirror.

'I concealed some clothes belonging to the Count,' he said,
'and now we must make adjustments here. It is absolutely
necessary to cover his feet, and if you will take off your
dressing-gown I shall drape it carelessly over this end of
the sofa.'

'My night-dress is very thin,' said the Marchesa coldly.

'You need have no fear. Even the Gestapo has admitted
my self-control.'

With manifest displeasure the Marchesa put off her
dressing-gown and resumed her seat. Fest gave her the
mirror.

'The Germans,' he explained, 'are incurably sentimental,
and take immoderate pleasure in the contemplation of
domestic bliss. I propose to show them a romantic scene
in a homely setting. You, with pardonable vanity, must
look at your mirror while I, with a delicate and adoring
hand, brush your hair.'

'In your overcoat?' asked the Marchesa.

'I was about to remove it,' said Fest, and threw it on a
chair. The Marchesa loosened her hair.

'You are not without practice,' she said, as she felt the
first strokes of the brush.

'But my pleasure, if I give you satisfaction, is without
precedent.'

The Marchesa settled herself more comfortably. 'Poor
Agesilas,' she said. 'I hope I am not stifling him.'

'Be calm now,' said Fest. 'Here they come.'

The front door of the Marchesa's house was stoutly
built, but the lock yielded to the blow of a sledge-hammer,
and this rude entry woke the maid, now dozing in the
kitchen, and set her screaming. It woke another in an
attic room, who piercingly replied. Male voices roughly

exclaimed, and heavily booted feet drummed upon the stair.

'Sit still!' said Fest.

'I have not moved. It is Agesilas,' whispered the Marchesa.

Three Germans in dark uniform, an officer and two others, entered the room with unnecessary violence. With a protective hand on the Marchesa's shoulder, the brush still engaged in her dark hair, Fest turned toward them his glaring eye and a face that was apparently convulsed with rage.

All three pointed their pistols at him, and the officer brusquely inquired, 'Are you the Count Piccologrando?'

Fest answered him in German. His voice was harsh and arrogant. 'You blundering misbegotten fool!' he said. 'You ill-advised untimely ape! What in the devil's name do you mean by bringing your insanitary press-gang into a lady's house at this time of the morning?'

'I am acting under instruction. My orders are –'

'What's your name?'

'Bloch.'

'Have you no manners, Bloch? Has no one ever told you how to address a senior officer?'

Lieutenant Bloch grew unhappy and perplexed. His face, gone pale about the mouth, was patched with red over the cheek-bones. He appeared to swallow a crumb or two, then straightened to attention and saluted.

'That's better, Bloch. Now take off your hat and tell me what you want.'

'I have come here to arrest the Count Piccologrando.'

'And why do you suppose that I am interested in your miserable ratcatcher's job?'

'You are not he?'

'God in his scorching heaven, do I look like an Italian? Do I sound like an Italian?'

'I was told that I would find him here,' said Lieutenant Bloch, and looked at the Marchesa, and looked away again, embarrassed. His two policemen stared at her without shame.

'And now that you have discovered your mistake,' said Fest, 'I suggest that you leave us, Bloch, and take your dung-rakers with you.'

A third policeman, a stolid sergeant, appeared in the doorway and reported that he had searched the lower part of the house and found no one.

'So your flatfeet have been rummaging, have they?' demanded Fest.

'My orders were to search the house, and I cannot leave until that has been done.'

Fest confronted him with a deeper frown, but Bloch muttered, 'I cannot!'

Then the Marchesa spoke. 'Let them go where they please. They will find nothing.'

Fest raised her hand to his lips and said loudly, 'I apologize for the manners of my fellow-countrymen. – Hurry, Bloch, and get your rummaging finished.'

Lieutenant Bloch spoke in a low voice to his policemen, who, after looking behind the curtains, went into other rooms. He himself remained, awkward and uncomfortable.

'Sit down!' said Fest sharply, and to the Marchesa: 'I am inexpressibly sorry for this outrage. Tomorrow, in other quarters, I shall have more to say about it, but tonight I am dumb with shame.'

'It is a lunatic world,' said the Marchesa, 'and I am no longer surprised by its oddities. You must not fret yourself. – Dear friend, you had promised to brush my hair. You have not forgotten?'

'In such gracious employment I may forget my anger,' said Fest.

Softly but strongly, with earnest but caressive strokes, he began to brush her darkly gleaming hair from brow to the curving crown of her head, from crown to the hidden nape of her neck. She held her head high, straining a little against the pull of the brush. She lifted the mirror and looked at her reflection and the youthful sharpening of her features as the muscles tautened. Then, stooping as the brush went down to her neck, she made little forward movements like a bird preening.

Lieutenant Bloch looked at her with sorrowful and hungry eyes. The blush had faded from his cheeks, he was pale as a plank of wood by now, and his short hair was the colour of a sponge. He sighed, and his lips began to whisper. He sighed again and in a soft voice recited:

> Nun muss ich gar
> Um dein aug und haar
> Alle tage
> In sehnen leben.

'How charming of you,' said the Marchesa.

'So you're a poet, are you?' asked Fest.

'That is not my own composition,' said Lieutenant Bloch, 'but nevertheless I am a poet. We Germans – are we not all poets?'

'Poets and policemen,' said Fest. 'My poor Bloch!'

The Lieutenant flushed again and said angrily, 'I have been doing my duty. I am not ashamed of it!'

One after another his policemen returned. 'Well?' he asked.

'There's no one else here, sir, except the servants.'

'So now you can go with a clear conscience,' said Fest.

The Lieutenant hesitated, but then said stubbornly, 'You must inform me who you are.'

'So that your ratcatchers can tell everyone where I pay my calls? I don't think so, Bloch.'

'I shall have to make my report. I cannot say there was no one here.'

Fest rubbed his chin and for a moment or two was thoughtful. Then in a friendlier voice he said, 'I am thinking of more than my own reputation. I wonder if I – if we – can rely on your discretion?'

'I am by birth a gentleman, sir!'

'A poet, a gentleman, and a policeman! – No, do not be angry, my dear Bloch, I am only making a little joke, as one does between friends. Well, come here.'

He bent and whispered closely in the Lieutenant's ear. Bloch retreated a step and gravely bowed. He ordered his policemen to go. Then, with a sudden fluency, he made an elaborate apology for his intrusion. The Marchesa gave him her hand to kiss and he bent profoundly. He found his cap, but held it under his arm and was clearly reluctant to leave. Fest took him by the arm and led him downstairs. He stood and watched him go. Then he moved a carved chest to hold the broken outer door in place, and returned to the drawing-room.

The Marchesa had lifted a couple of the cushions and was looking at the Count with some anxiety. His face was darkly coloured and he was breathing very slowly and laboriously. His eyes were half-closed. Fest raised him to a sitting position and gave him a glass of brandy.

The Count laid his hand upon the Marchesa's and said wearily, 'I was sure that you had been putting on weight, my dear.'

'I am thinner than I have been for several years,' said the Marchesa, and slid on her *saut-de-lit*. Then she rang a little silver bell. 'Let us have an early breakfast,' she said.

'That will suit me very well,' said Fest, 'for I should like to stay here for an hour or two in case they are watching the house. – The Count, I suggest, should leave Rome as soon as possible. You also, for a little while at least.'

'There is a small house belonging to Agesilas in Montenero. It is easy to reach, we might go there.'

A few minutes later she asked, 'Did you tell the policeman your true name?'

'That would not have been helpful.'

'Then whose did you give?'

'You must realize that these people are quite ignorant,' said Fest, 'and it is easy to deceive them. I invented a very simple name, but gave myself a good address. I told him that I was their Military Attaché at the Vatican.'

IT WAS NIGHT, it was raining, and Angelo was drunk. The wind blew coldly, and he was alone on the mountainside.

In his mind, like a bird in a wood before morning, a voice was crying, 'Free, free, I'm totally free!' But he was extremely frightened, and the voice increased his fear. If the gods should hear it, swaggering like a blackbird, they might take him by the heels and haul him into captivity again. He tried to silence the voice, but it would not be quiet. Sometimes it was more like a meadow-rill chuckling deeply through summer grass: 'Happy Angelo, lucky Angelo.'

Below him in the darkness a pebbly torrent fell with a hiss and a rumble into a granite linn. The mountainside was patched with pale shapes of snow, and sagging from the southern sky hung a black and monstrous cloud. He stumbled and slipped on the rutted path, his feet gathered great overshoes of mud, and he felt upon his legs the coldness of his sodden clothes. 'Free, free!' sang the wilful voice, and he looked dreadfully over his shoulder to see if he were followed. There was a German army behind him.

For ten weeks he had served it, and for much of that time his body had felt like a scoured egg-shell. There was no substance in it. Fear had emptied it with a spoon whenever a shell burst near him, and the last month had shed all its withered days under shell-fire. He had seen five of his fellow privates killed, and for ten days he had been lousy. He tripped again. The sole was coming off his right boot, and tears ran down his rain-wet face to contemplate such gross injustice. The blackbird voice no longer sang, and he remembered his friend Giuseppe who, an hour ago, had also been drunk and free. But Giuseppe had been unlucky in the minefield. They had not known about the mines until Giuseppe set his foot on one.

It was Giuseppe who had found the bottle of grappa that gave them both the courage to escape. They had been rebuilding a bomb-ruined bridge not far behind the front line, and Giuseppe had discovered the bottle in a cupboard that had survived the shattered walls of a nearby cottage. When dusk descended they had privily returned to the cottage, and their company had been assembled and marched away without them.

They resolved to take their chance of deserting, and Angelo with dutch courage went out to reconnoitre. Sixty yards away, beside another shell-torn house, he heard German voices and lay discreetly behind a tumbled wall to listen. A German officer was talking to a friend who had newly returned from leave with two bottles of Spanish brandy in his haversack. They had to visit their forward positions, and then they proposed to spend a pleasant evening. The Fundador, they decided, could be left safely under their blankets.

Angelo waited until they had gone. Then, without difficulty, he found the haversack and took it back to Giuseppe, who promptly knocked the neck off one of the bottles, took a good draught, and handed it to Angelo.

Never in their lives had they tasted such brandy. It mingled with the strong grappa in their blood, and made the business of escaping seem an easy jest. They felt no need to make a plan, no need for caution. They would simply walk out. Giuseppe corked the broken bottle with a rag, and Angelo put the other in his pocket.

The rain fell in black cascades. Before they had gone a dozen yards they lost each other in the darkness, thought it comical that this should happen, and shouted till they met again. Then they fell into a panic to think that someone might have heard them, and hand-in-hand began to run.

They were lucky. They knew the way by daylight, and unthinking memory guided them. They knew where there was a thicket of barbed wire, for they had helped to lay it. The rain fell harshly from a viewless sky, and no one challenged them.

Then Giuseppe complained of a stitch, and lagged behind. Angelo forgot him and went on. When the mine exploded he threw himself flat on the mud and lay there while machine-guns hammered nervously behind and strong lights, bursting in the sky, made visible like rods of brilliant wire the slanting rain. The firing did not last long, and presently he got up and began to run again. A sensation of relief, as though he had vomited and were rid of a load of sickness, was all he felt at first, but soon it became a bubbling happiness that he could not repress, and the blackbird voice began to sing and he could not quieten it.

But now, remembering Giuseppe, he cried most bitterly for the death of his friend and for the loneliness in which it left him. He sat on a rock and tried to repair his torn boot, but a sudden consciousness of guilt swept over him like a curving wave, and left him shuddering.

He was to blame for Giuseppe's death. It was he, Angelo, who had first whispered of desertion, and how shameful that now appeared! The Germans had fed him and clothed him and trusted him, and he had deserted them. He had already deserted his own army, the men with whom he had lived and the officers to whom he owed obedience: he had taken to his heels at Reggio and never seen them again. He was twice a deserter, he had broken faith with both sides.

He felt the cold eyes of the world upon him, and he could not escape their scorn. Now, thought Angelo, my poverty is immeasurably increased, since I, who never had much to live on, have now got nothing to live for. No one will ever trust me again, or want my company, and what is life worth without friends, a little respect, and a little liking?

He sat for a long time spellbound in grief. It was only to break the spell that at last he got up and with fumbling steps continued his journey. 'I have nothing to live on,' he said aloud, 'because I have rejected the bread of both sides. I have nothing to live for, because both sides despise me. I am a man only because I suffer.'

His loose sole caught in a root, and falling heavily he struck his knee against a sharp rock. Physical pain expelled his moral agony, and he remembered the Spanish lenitive he carried. He sat in the mud, rocking to and fro, and with a knife dug out the cork. He tilted the bottle to his lips, and after swallowing three or four times felt the pain diminish to a fiery patch. Tenderly, tentatively, he began to rub the injured bone.

'My poor little knee-cap!' he groaned. 'Oh, what a blow it was! Oh, how sore it is! Oh, my misery, miserable me!'

Little knee-cap! he thought, and with cold fingers explored its smooth round edge. It was like a pebble on a beach, a white pebble polished for a thousand years by that old craftsman the Sea. By the monstrous hands of the Sea. The Sea had carved for his own delight the Sporades and Cyclades, and drawn with a whimsical finger fantastic bays between the feet of soaring mountains, and polished in his idle hours a million multitudes of smooth white pebbles to scatter on his beaches. The gods were cruel, but God, what artists! And here, beneath his bruised and dirty skin, lay like an ocean-jewel his own dear knee-cap on a throne of ivory clothed with satin. He had seen a knee-joint stripped for inspection by a shell-splinter, and he remembered how beautiful were its smooth surfaces. Like an archaeologist in the Sila discovering a temple to Diana, a piece of metal had revealed the architecture of a soldier, and Angelo had stood amazed.

'But now, my little knee-cap,' he announced, 'I realize that I also am a masterpiece, for lovely though you are, *cara rotellina*, you are not the only marvel in my territory. I have, for instance, a pair of kidneys that perform the most remarkable tasks, and other glands that contain a family-tree which Adam planted. As a telephone system my nerves are astonishingly good, and they also carry power to my remotest parts, with the most gratifying efficiency. I have, moreover, a brain that in time of drought can always turn on the tap for tears, and in better seasons will instruct my tongue to utter the most intricate and delightful thoughts. My tongue is a highly skilled performer, and obeys upon the instant. Listen to him now: he's doing very well, isn't he? Oh, my dear *rotella*, I am a truly remarkable person, I do assure you. And also – note this! – I am free! And do you know what freedom means? It means that some day we shall go home to Pontefiore and be re-united with my adored Lucrezia.

'There will be many nights like this in the years to come, but you and I won't be out in them. Not a bit of it. We'll be snug indoors, and we'll listen for a minute or two to the wind howling and the rain beating on the window, and then we'll think how blessed we are to have a roof above us: and I shall turn and tuck the sheet round Lucrezia. What bliss awaits us, my *rotelleta*! To turn our back upon the darkness and the cold, and tuck a sheet round Lucrezia!'

He drank a little more brandy, put the bottle in his pocket, and got to his feet again. His colloquy with his knee-cap had greatly comforted him, and he went on his way, somewhat unsteadily, but with fresh resolution. He had a very vague and slender notion of where he was, but after some time it occurred to him that if he had been walking in a straight line he must now be very near, if not within, the Allies' outpost line. He perceived that he was walking on a road again. It would be a good thing, he thought, to warn the Allies of his approach. So he began to shout.

'Hallo, Englishmen! Hullo, Englishmen!' he shouted. 'Please do not shoot me, because I am a friend. Do not shoot me, I am a friend.'

He was answered almost immediately. From somewhere in the darkness a voice called, 'Then stop making that disgusting noise, and come and help me.'

Angelo, surprised, looked left and right but could see no one. The swollen black cloud had passed, and in the southern sky were the grey embers of dead stars. Above him was a pale hillside, a snowfield roughly combed by the rain, and below him the ground fell steeply and was dark.

'Hurry up!' said the voice.

'Where are you? I cannot see you,' said Angelo nervously.

'Don't argue. Come and get me out of this hole.'

Angelo went slowly forward. The road curved to the left, and was built like a terrace on the slope of a hill. Twenty yards on, to the right of the road and below him, Angelo discerned four wheels, and beneath them a motor-car of some small kind.

'How much longer are you going to keep me waiting?' demanded the voice. 'Don't stand up there admiring the view, come down and get busy.'

Angelo scrambled down, and lying beside the overturned jeep peered into the hole beneath. It had fallen like a lid over a small trench, that might sometime have been a machine-gun position, and in the cavity sat a figure whose pale face was now very close to Angelo's. 'See if you can lift it,' the prisoner suggested.

Angelo, with great willingness but no effect, did his best. First from the one side and then from the other he heaved and he strained, but his feet slipped in the mud, his strength was insufficient, and when he stood to get his breath he felt his arms trembling with exhaustion. 'I am not powerful enough,' he confessed.

There was a little pause, and then the voice said, 'Well, if you can't, that's all there is to it, I suppose. It's not your fault.'

Angelo sat down where he could converse more easily. 'I am truly sorry,' he said.

'Who are you?' asked the voice.

'I am a deserter,' said Angelo with some flavour of pride in his words.

'From us or from them?'

'From the Tedeschi, of course!'

'Where did you learn to speak English?'

'At school in Siena.'

'You were educated, were you? With education a man can go anywhere. Look where it's taken me.'

'Are you wounded?' asked Angelo respectfully.

'I have a cut on the head, a fractured collar-bone, and a twisted ankle. If it hadn't been for this hole in the ground, into which I fell like a well-played red loser, I would also have a broken back. So I don't complain about my injuries, which are trivial. It's the cold that's worrying me. I'm freezing from the feet up, I'm sitting on a stone that was deposited here in the Ice Age, and I shall probably be dead before morning.'

'I have a bottle of very good brandy,' said Angelo. 'If it would comfort you –'

'Brandy!' exclaimed the voice. 'Are you St Bernard himself?'

'My name is Angelo,' said Angelo, and passed the bottle to the man in the hole.

Half a minute later his voice had become warm and friendly. 'Spanish brandy!' it said. 'I've changed my mind. I'm going to live for a hundred years. Where did you get it?'

'It formerly belonged to a German officer. I acquired it by good fortune.'

'My honest co-belligerent! I drink to you with enthusiasm.'

Angelo was deeply touched. 'Thank you very much. That is most kind of you,' he said. 'May I ask to whom I have the honour of talking?'

'My name's Telfer.'

'An officer?'

'A substantive lieutenant, a temporary captain, and an acting major: three in one, divisible yet not divided. It's a trinity of officers that you have rescued, my dear St Bernard.'

'My name is Angelo,' Angelo repeated.

'Then you were well christened. Take a drink from your own bottle, and tell me how it all happened.'

Encouraged by the brandy, Angelo told his story at considerable length, and when at last he had finished he was disconcerted by Major Telfer's silence. He waited and repeated his concluding sentences; and still there was no comment, no reply. Nervously he thought that Telfer might have fainted, and reaching into the hole he grasped him by the shoulder and gently, then more forcibly, shook him.

Telfer was sleeping soundly, but Angelo succeeded in waking him. He apologized very handsomely for falling into a doze during what must have been a most interesting story.

A few minutes later he said, 'I'm feeling sleepy again, and I don't want to go to sleep. I don't believe it would be a good thing in the circumstances. What can you do to keep me awake?'

'Shall I talk to you about my early life?'

'No, don't do that.'

'Would you like me to sing?'

'That will depend on your voice. I don't want to be soothed.'

'I sing rather loudly,' said Angelo, 'and I have a good memory. Do you like Verdi?'

'Very much,' said Telfer.

'I also.' And after a little thought Angelo sang the duet of Manrico and Azucena from *Il Trovatore*; which inappropriately began, '*Riposa, O madre.*' Then, more suitably, he doubled the Conte di Luna and Manrico: '*Tace la notte,*' observed the Count; '*Deserto sulla terra,*' replied the other.

'And now,' said Telfer, 'let us each drink a little brandy. You have a splendid voice, it keeps me wide awake. – Drink up, and sing on.'

'*Libiamo, libiamo ne' lieti calici,*' sang Angelo, and then he sang fragments, large or small, of *Aïda*, *Otello*, and *Un Ballo in Maschera*. He sang a couple of songs from *Falstaff* and most of *Rigoletto*. His throat grew rough but his memory did not fail him. Telfer praised him judiciously and encouraged him as though he were a horse. They finished the brandy.

Dawn rose slowly with a grumbling wind, and when the sky about the eastern mountains was no darker than a grey goose-wing, and Angelo had no more voice than a goose, they heard in the distance a rattling noise on the road, and presently a Bren-carrier came in sight. Because Angelo was stiff with cold he had difficulty in getting to his feet and raising his arms in recognizable surrender; and for a moment or two he was in some danger of being shot. Then one of the carrier's crew came forward, covered by its gun, and as soon as he heard Telfer's voice appreciated the situation correctly and signalled to his comrades.

Within a few minutes the jeep had been set on its wheels, and a tow-rope attached to the carrier. One of the soldiers took the steering-wheel and the jeep was hauled on to the road. With clay-cold limbs and a face as grey as an old sandbag Angelo sat huddled in the back seat, and as well as he could supported Major Telfer, who was colder than he and white as marble. Slowly, for the steering-gear had been damaged, they drove southward. It began to rain again.

CHAPTER EIGHT

MAJOR SIMON TELFER of the 2nd Carabiniers (The Duke of Rothesay's Dragoon Guards) was a healthy young man, tall of stature, with a lean face that grew a large fair moustache, who had originally joined the Army in order to play polo for his regiment. He quickly achieved his ambition, and when war broke out he had a handicap of six goals and grave anxiety about the cumulative products of concussion, from which he had suffered a good deal. Two years of arduous campaigning in the Desert, however, had done him a world of good, and he was now – save for the effects of severe exposure, a broken collar-bone, a sprained ankle, and a lacerated temple – in excellent shape and spirit.

He had lately transferred from his own regiment to a less formal body known as Force 69. There were several such irregular formations in the British Army, and all who belonged to them were regarded with greenest envy by the disciplined majority that remained in regimental employment and were subject to a constant supervision, standing orders, and regular administration. The members of Force 69 were, from time to time, required to risk their lives in strange adventure. They made perilous voyages to hostile islands in fragile craft that amateur sailors navigated; they had reconnoitred, by routes that camel-ribs signposted, the farthest Libyan oases; they dropped by parachute on mountainsides in Albania; they drove their jeeps through the enemy's lines to join Partigiani in the Apennines – and so on and so forth, but they never drilled, they avoided contact with senior officers, they grew beards if they felt inclined to, they rarely returned a parade-state, they cocked a long snook at the bureaucracy, and in a world of dour obedience congratulated themselves every morning on the freedom they enjoyed, while their friends with equal regularity complained loudly of the chicanery and favouritism by which they had won it.

To join and remain in Force 69 it was necessary that an officer should be naturally brave, uncommonly resourceful and know a great number of people by their Christian names. In common with all other civilized armies the British Army used many thousand tons of paper to promulgate its orders, instructions, plans and policies; but that was merely to conform with modern practice and provide a livelihood for elderly majors and disabled captains in areas remote from battle. Operations in the field were governed otherwise, and decisive action was taken only in consequence of something that General Oliver or Colonel Peter had said to Dicky This or Nigel That. The executive order usually wore the look of a friendly suggestion, and the officer who loosed the fury of a barrage or led his squadron to death and glory was almost certainly responding to the syllables that had dripped upon his infant face with the water of baptism, or with which he had been labelled in the Lower Fourth. Battles were fought and won by Christian names – and many privileges were granted to those who knew them.

Simon Telfer knew at least three hundred, and as in addition to that good fortune he was brave without effort, and unusually resourceful, he had been allowed to join Force 69.

The jeep that he had capsized he had taken by piracy, only a few hours before, from a German officer who had captured it in ambush from a British patrol on reckless reconnaissance. Simon had been returning from a mission to partisans in the Abruzzi, and though he had used great caution during most of his journey, the taking of a jeep had filled him with exuberance and exuberant driving had lifted him off the road. Good fortune, however, had not wholly deserted him, for he soon discovered that the carrier patrol which came to his rescue belonged to a battalion commanded by an old friend called Michael. The battalion was at present holding a slight salient not far from Alfedena, and shortly after their discovery Simon and Angelo were brought safely to its advanced headquarters.

Their appearance created no particular surprise, for Michael, a lieutenant-colonel at twenty-seven, had long since grown accustomed to the unheralded entrances and sudden exits of his fellow-actors in the war. Simon's broken collar-bone was quickly set, and he was given what comfort could be provided in a ruined village in the mountains. Angelo received equal hospitality because Simon loudly proclaimed that he, with his singing and his brandy, had saved his life. The Intelligence Officer of Michael's battalion, moreover, regarded him as a welcome guest, for Angelo was willing to talk at great length about the Germans' battle-positions and life in their army.

A little after noon on the following day, in a wintry sunshine, they were sitting outside the house in which Michael had established his headquarters. It was a house of two storeys, painted salmon-pink. The front of it was splinter-scarred, an upper window had been raggedly enlarged by a shell, a chimney knocked off by another, and the roof holed. It wore the dumb and sorrowful expression of a man who had been beaten by hooligans.

While Michael and Simon were casually gossiping, and the Intelligence Officer corrected a typewritten copy of the information that Angelo had given him, Angelo sat and regarded them in grave perplexity. A pause in the conversation gave him the opportunity for which he had been waiting.

'Excuse me, please,' he said, 'but do you no longer wear uniform in the British Army?'

They turned and gazed at him with mild astonishment. 'Of course we wear uniform,' said Simon. 'What sort of stories have the Germans been telling you?'

'I have heard no stories,' said Angelo. 'I have been looking at your trousers.'

Michael and Simon wore sheepskin jackets, the Intelligence

Officer a fisherman's blue jersey. Tied round their throats were brightly coloured scarves. Michael was bareheaded, Simon wore a bandage, the Intelligence Officer a stocking-cap of rakish pattern. All three wore corduroy trousers: Simon's were grey, the Intelligence Officer's green, and Michael's a dark brown tucked into gum-boots. With a transient curiosity they considered their own and each other's small-clothes.

'Oh, yes,' said Michael. 'I see what you mean.'

'We do dress informally at times,' said Simon, 'but comfort is the main thing, isn't it?'

'It began in the Desert,' said the Intelligence Officer.

'In Africa,' said Simon, 'one felt a resurgence of individualism.'

'I would give a great deal to be there now,' said Michael.

Simon agreed with him. 'There's a lot to be said for Libya.'

'It's ideal country for a war,' said the Intelligence Officer. 'You can't do any damage there, except to yourself and the enemy.'

'One had a lot of freedom in Libya,' said Simon, 'but the landscape needed colour to give it variety: that's where we began to wear chokers.'

'It's a pity we had to come into Europe,' said Michael. 'I enjoyed myself in the Desert.'

'One had so many friends there,' said Simon.

'Everybody knew everybody else,' said the Intelligence Officer. 'Of course it was uncomfortable from time to time, but on the whole –'

'At its best,' said Simon –

'Taking it all round,' said Michael, 'it was good.'

For a full minute they sat in silence, revolving behind reminiscent eyes nostalgic thoughts of quivering heat, engulfing dust-storms, and immensities of barren soil; till Angelo, in a voice hoarse with amazement, interrupted.

'Excuse me, please,' he said again, 'but are you truthfully saying that you enjoyed the war in Libya?'

'In a way I think we did,' said Michael. 'Didn't you?'

'It was fearful, it was horrible!' cried Angelo with passion. 'I hated every single hour of it!'

'What bad luck,' said Michael.

They looked at him curiously. They tried to be sympathetic, but they were puzzled by his attitude and disappointed in him. Simon had said he was one of the best fellows alive. 'He carries Spanish brandy and his voice doth murder sleep. He sat in the mud and sang to me all night, and saved my life.' That was what Simon had said, and now Angelo was talking about their war in Africa with embarrassingly bad taste. Foreigners were full of complexities and self-contradiction, they felt.

Then Simon's attention was taken by a pair of newcomers. 'Who,' he asked, pointing to the end of the village street, 'are your enterprising friends?'

The farthest houses had collapsed into grey mounds of rubble, and in a space between them, as if in a small ravine, stood two soldiers of savage and repellent aspect. Their faces were blackened, they wore stocking-caps like the Intelligence Officer's, their battle-dress was dark and filthy, over their shoulders were slung tommy-guns, and one had a long knife in his belt, the other a bludgeon. Each carried, dangling to the ground, a dead goose and a turkey.

'They're two of my battle-patrol,' said Michael. 'Corporal McCunn and Private O'Flaherty, I think. – Come here!' he shouted.

The two soldiers, as though overcome by a sudden shyness when they saw their Commanding Officer, had halted between the ruined houses; and now, with an assumption of careless ease, were retreating in the direction from which they had come. They stopped reluctantly when they heard the Colonel's voice, looked round, and with a philosophic acceptance of the situation marched towards him.

'Sir,' said Corporal McCunn.

'Where did you get those birds?'

With a far-away look the Corporal thought for a moment and answered, 'From an old farmer.'

'In a small farm on the hill beyond,' said Private O'Flaherty. 'He was very grateful to us, sir.'

'For liberating him and his family from the Germans,' said Corporal McCunn.

'He was that grateful,' said Private O'Flaherty, 'that he told us we could liberate as many as we needed of his geese and his turkeys, sir.'

'But we weren't wanting to be greedy,' said the Corporal, 'and we couldn't easily carry more than the two apiece.'

'So we just liberated the four of them, and that's the whole truth of it,' said Private O'Flaherty.

'I see,' said Michael. 'Well, I'm glad you weren't greedy.'

'If we'd happened to have any money with us,' said Corporal McCunn, 'we'd have been glad to pay for the birds.'

'Now don't overdo it,' said Michael. 'Your story, I mean, not your goose. A goose like that needs to be cooked for about an hour and a half.'

'Thank you, sir.'

'I am very fond of those two,' said Michael when they had gone. 'I have a good battalion, and my battle-patrol is quite excellent. In private life Corporal McCunn used to sell children's toys in a shop in Glasgow, and O'Flaherty was a steward in a passenger-ship. After earning their living by cosseting people, and persuading people to buy things, they find spiritual refreshment in their present occupation – which gives them a chance to assassinate people.'

'Excuse me,' said Angelo, 'but when I went to school in Siena, I was taught that to liberate means to set free. Is that so, please?'

'It is,' said Michael.

'And in September we were told that you and the Americans were coming to liberate Italy.'

'And now we have come,' said Michael coldly.

'But those soldiers, who said they had liberated the turkeys and the geese, had taken a most drastic way of giving them their freedom. I do not deny that turkeys and geese, especially in winter, lead a very dull and disagreeable and apprehensive life. So do many human beings, however, and if the Allies have decided that all who are unfortunate can be liberated only by wringing their necks –'

'I'm afraid I can't spend the whole day gossiping,' said Michael, and stood up. 'I have work to do.'

'So have I,' said the Intelligence Officer.

'I usually take a short drink about this time,' said Simon.

Angelo was left alone with his troubled thoughts. He got up and walked slowly down the village street, then stopped to look at a house which had been hit by a bomb. It had been a good house, with a portico and pillars and well-proportioned large windows, but now, cut diagonally in two, a half of it lay in a heap of untidy masonry as though it had been caught and melted by a draught of infernal flame, and run to waste. On the remaining fragment of an upper floor stood a carved armchair upholstered in wet red velvet.

A passing soldier of Michael's battalion, a burly man with a great red face, also stopped to look at the wasted house. He gave Angelo a cigarette, and said, 'It makes you think, doesn't it?'

'It does,' said Angelo.

'In the olden times, before people like you and me were educated and enlightened,' said the soldier, 'they used to go to war to capture towns, and when they had captured them, they enjoyed them. There was drink, there was loot, and there were women. The victorious army went into winter quarters and had a good time. But nowadays we're fighting for something fancier than towns. We're fighting for ideas about freedom and justice, so we despise mere stone and mortar, and consequently knock it to bits. So the wine runs down the gutters, and the women pick up their skirts and scuttle, and the conquering soldiers don't find any winter quarters. We're living in uncomfortable times, and you've got to admit it.'

'Would you say that this village had been liberated?' asked Angelo.

'Oh, properly liberated,' said the soldier. 'There isn't a roof left in it.'

'It makes me sad to look at such destruction,' said Angelo. 'I am Italian, you see.'

'You ought to have a look at Coventry,' said the soldier. 'It was a big town, as towns go in England, and they laid most of it as flat as a plate. That's where I come from: Coventry.'

'And surely it made you very sad to see your native town in ruins?'

'Sad?' said the soldier. 'Don't you believe it. I'm a brick-layer by trade, and as soon as this war's over, and I get back to Coventry, I'm going to be worth my weight in gold.'

'You Englishmen are very practical,' said Angelo in a melancholy voice.

'Yes and no,' said the soldier. 'We're more practical than many, I grant you, but we fall short of perfection, there's no denying that. Now I'm a bricklayer, as I've just told you, and consequently I'm not only valuable but important. But is my importance recognized? No. Would I myself live in one of the houses that I built before the war, or that I'm going to build after the war? No. And why not? Because they were shoddy, and they'll be shoddy again. I used to live in a house that was built in seventeen-sixty, when people built well because they thought it important to build as well as they could. – Now take my wife's eldest brother, he's a different case. He was a farmer, and he went to live in New Zealand. Why? Because he was a good farmer, and in 1930 England didn't believe that farmers were important, so England lost him. – Then there's a nephew of mine, he was never fit for honest work because of his kidneys, but he learnt to play the fiddle, and he played it well. And what's he doing now? Playing the sort of stuff that makes you sick to listen to, and earning thirty pound a week in a dance band. – Now you see what I mean, don't you? As a people we can still hold our own, because in my opinion nobody's much good nowadays, and everybody's going down hill; but we're going slower than the rest. But I often feel we're not as good as we used to be, or as good as we ought to be, and the reason is that our feeling for what's really important is part-worn, and most of us don't know why it is important anyway. And nobody's really practical who doesn't recognize at sight that some things are valuable, and other things are trash. Here, have a cigarette.'

Angelo spent the rest of the day in solitary thought, and an hour or two before dusk was rescued from so depressing an occupation by a sudden storm of shells and mortarbombs that fell upon the village. Ten minutes later the Germans made a small but resolute attack, which was energetically repulsed, and for some hours there was intermittent gun-fire and sufficient excitement to put a stop to intellectual exercising. Shortly after midnight the noise diminished, and Angelo slept.

In the morning Simon Telfer decided that he was able to travel. His captured jeep had been repaired, and it was tacitly assumed that Angelo would go with him. Simon had not only taken a liking to him – despite his heretical views about the Libyan campaign – but acquired a possessive pride in Angelo's singing voice and his knowledge of English. With his broken collar-bone, moreover, he needed a driver. So Michael lent them a spade, and they set off soon after breakfast.

Only twice had Angelo to dig deeply, to extricate them from snowdrifts, and without untoward incident they reached a village near Piedimonte d'Alife where a detached company of Force 69 was then quartered. Simon immediately discovered that he was no longer a major. During his mission to the Abruzzi partisans a senior officer had arrived from England, and Simon in consequence had to revert to the rank of captain. But he had long since recognized that promotion in war-time was like a greasy pole, or a game of snakes-and-ladders, and was philosophical about the change; though Angelo was indignant.

Simon's reduction in rank, however, did not impair his friendship with useful Christian names, and he had no difficulty in arranging that Angelo should be attached to the Force as an interpreter. Angelo was given a suit of battle-dress, a small stipend, and a place in the sergeants' mess. His official adoption by the army of liberation pleased him immensely. A few qualms that he felt to begin with – the queasy offspring of his experience in the mountain village – he quickly put aside as unmanly and trivial, and he set himself zealously to acquire the sangfroid and practical outlook of the Englishman. Within a week or two he was putting on weight, and the sergeants' mess thought highly of him as a vocalist.

Because the detached company was enjoying one of its idle seasons, Simon was able to remain with it while his collar-bone mended, and under his patronage Angelo quickly extended his knowledge of England and the English.

Much of what he learnt surprised him. He had always heard that the English were an arrogant, wealthy, and aggressive people; and he was astonished to find that they thought of themselves as very mild and easy-going creatures, chronically hard-up, and habitually deceived or over-ridden by their continental neighbours. They did, however, take a pride in their sense of justice, and to Angelo this was quite incomprehensible; for he had often read of the many millions of Indians, Canadians, Australians, New Zealanders, Basutos, Zulus, Kikuyus, Scots, and Irish whom they held in slavery.

They were curiously heartless, he decided, for although they were far from home he never saw them weeping and sighing for their distant wives, their deserted lovers, and their half-forgotten children. They wrote, indeed, innumerable letters, but said remarkably little in them. They ate enormously, and were continually making jokes that no adult European could understand: Angelo did his best, but was forced to conclude that their sense of humour, though deceptively robust, was quite elementary. The private soldiers grumbled prodigiously and professed a fearful cynicism about the intentions, practice, and good faith of their Government; yet strangely continued to serve it with zeal and do their duty with alacrity. They appeared to become dirty very easily, for they were always washing themselves. They talked a good deal about fornication, but looked askance at the Americans for their excessive indulgence in it. They all regarded football as a more exacting and therefore more praiseworthy art than making love, and many of them preferred it.

Angelo one day persuaded Simon to speak of English politics. Did Simon, he asked, truly believe in democracy?

'Yes, I think I do,' he answered. 'It doesn't work very well, of course, but what does?'

'Would not the ideal government,' asked Angelo, 'be that of an autocratic ruler who was also a philosopher?'

'Not in England,' said Simon. 'No one would admit that it was ideal, in the first place, and in the second we regard philosophy as a rarefied sort of entertainment, like chess or the more difficult crosswords.'

'You are a Conservative, I suppose?'

'Yes,' said Simon, 'yes, I suppose I am. I have never actually voted, but then I am also a member of the Church of England, and except for an occasional wedding I haven't in fact been to church since I left school. The Conservative Party and the Church of England are rather similar in that respect: you can belong to both of them without doing much about it. – I belong to two or three very good clubs, now that I think of it, that I never use though I still pay my subscriptions. – But what I do believe in most devoutly is the party system, because when you get tired of the party in power you can always kick it out. You can kick it fairly hard, indeed, throughout its tenure of office. I should say that democracy is really represented by a party with a mind that knows how to act, a tender bottom that tells it when, and a well-shod electorate.'

'I find that very interesting,' said Angelo, 'but how are you going to ensure that your electorate can afford good shoes?'

'That's a problem, isn't it? Some people say that we shall have to work very hard and export everything we make; others maintain that we must work even harder, but buy it all ourselves; and others again declare that our real difficulty is to know what to do with our spare time. To tell you the truth, we're in something of a muddle, and that is just what you would expect if you knew us better. We have been in a muddle for so long that most of us now regard it as our normal environment. And probably it is.'

Angelo regarded him gravely. He did not like to say that he had studied at school the long course of England's history, and often heard his teachers expound and deplore the cold calculation, the Oriental persistence, the diabolic art of English statesmen through the ages. Muddle indeed! – But more recently he had discovered that the English hated to be asked about their history, for none of them remembered it. So tactfully he changed the subject and asked, 'Are English women very passionate?'

'Between their tennis-playing in girlhood and their later addiction to the card-table, there is a season during which they are not indifferent to love,' said Simon.

'But the war has affected their traditional way of life, has it not?'

'It has indeed. They have gone into the Services, they have gone into factories and offices. They have given up tennis altogether, and postponed their bridge.'

'And their season of love?'

'Love has adopted a war-time policy like that of the farmers,' said Simon. 'With equal enthusiasm it has cultivated both field and furrow; and assisted by the foreign troops now quartered in Britain it has ploughed thousands of hitherto neglected acres.'

Time passed agreeably. Thin blue skies and a hint of warmth in the morning breeze foretold the return of spring. On the southern slopes of the mountains the snow-line grudgingly retreated and exposed a wet black earth. Hail-storm and sleet-squall blew with a slattern's fury, but never lasted long. Winter was fighting a losing battle and retiring slowly to the north. Every day the sun rose a little earlier, and sometimes shone with a brief but splendid promise.

Simon one day proposed to visit some friends near Venafro, and invited Angelo to go with him. On the way there he spoke of a great air-assault that was going to be directed against the enemy's hitherto impregnable position at Cassino. All winter, in a frozen landscape like the mountains of the moon – but besmeared with blood and lashed by fire – the Allies had been fighting with a sorrowful heroism for possession of Monte Cassino, and now at last Cassino and all the Germans in it were to be blasted out of existence by the concentrated attack of a huge fleet of bombers. By noon of the next day, said Simon, Cassino would be merely a scar on the landscape. It was the fifteenth of March.

Simon's friends, whom he was visiting, were on the staff of a general whose camp was pitched on a wooded hillside. Angelo was by now on very easy terms with his English co-belligerents, for his command of their language persuaded them that he was of superior character to the majority of Italians; he had learnt to speak respectfully of the campaign in Libya; and Simon told everyone he met that Angelo had saved his life. Simon's friends invited him to have a drink, and he listened with great interest to what they were saying about the coming air-attack.

It began soon after breakfast on the following morning. They stood outside the mess-tent and watched the attacking fleet pass overhead, and listened to the rolling thunder and blunt reverberating echoes of myriad bursting bombs. Hidden from sight by the mountains, Cassino was about twelve miles away as the bomber flew.

Presently they went in to drink another cup of coffee, and a flight-lieutenant described, with professional enthusiasm, the extraordinary accuracy of the bomb-sight by which missiles could be successfully aimed from prodigious heights at targets far below them. But a nervous member of the company made some comment on a drumming noise of aeroplanes directly overhead, and his uneasiness affected the others. They went out from the tent and again stared upwards at the sky. They were just in time to see the sunlight glinting on a shower of swiftly falling objects, and to throw themselves flat on the ground.

Only a few of the bombs exploded near them, and as soon as they had decided that the attack was not likely to be repeated most of them rose again, wiping stains of grass and mud from their battle-dress, with no graver injury than a shocked surprise. A young captain, however, an officer with a pale and intellectual cast of features, whom a large fragment of hot metal had missed by a few inches only, was so annoyed as to be openly critical of the flight-lieutenant who had spoken about the accuracy of aerial bombardment. But the flight-lieutenant explained that a good bomb-sight was still good though a navigator might bring it to bear on the wrong target.

'It is as a target that I am speaking,' said the Captain bitterly.

'You were very nearly hit,' said the flight-lieutenant. 'You cannot deny that the bombing, as bombing, was excellent bombing.'

'Art for art's sake,' said the Captain.

'I admit,' said the flight-lieutenant, 'that a bomb is no respecter of persons.'

'If persons are not entitled to respect,' asked the Captain, 'why are we fighting this war?'

'It is easy to criticize,' said the flight-lieutenant.

'On the contrary,' said the Captain. 'For those who could criticize you with the authority of personal experience are too often left speechless.'

They stared at each other with some dislike, until another officer asked, 'Where are Simon and his Italian friend? Has anyone seen them?'

They were discovered, close together, on a narrow shelf of the hillside. Angelo lay unconscious, having been clouted on the head by a flying clod as big as a tea-tray; and Simon with a disconsolate expression sat holding his left thigh which had been laid open by a bomb-splinter. Angelo was bleeding from the nose, and to a hurried examination Simon's wound appeared to be co-extensive with the damage to his trousers, which were torn from the knee to the haunch. An ambulance was quickly summoned and the two casualties, roughly bandaged, were removed to a field-hospital without delay. There it was soon discovered that neither of them was seriously injured, for Simon's wound, though fifteen inches long, was little deeper than a scratch, and Angelo was merely bruised, bewildered, and very angry.

'Do I, in any way, resemble Cassino?' he asked Simon, as soon as he was allowed to visit him.

'There is no apparent similarity,' Simon answered.

'Then why was I bombed?'

'We all make mistakes from time to time.'

'We do not all carry bombs. To make a private mistake in your own house is one thing, but to make a public mistake with a bomb of two hundred and fifty kilogrammes is different altogether.'

'Year by year,' said Simon philosophically, 'science puts more power into our hands.'

'So that we may throw bombs at the wrong people?'

'Science like love,' said Simon, 'is blind.'

'I prefer love,' said Angelo. 'It makes less noise.'

He was still angry, and not to be pacified until Simon told him that in a day or two they might be going to Sorrento. Simon was on terms of friendship with the senior surgeon of the hospital – they called each other by their Christian names – and his contention that such wounds as theirs would heal most quickly in convalescence by the sea had not been seriously disputed.

Angelo was momentarily pleased. 'It is very beautiful in Sorrento,' he said. 'Many people used to go there for their honeymoon.' – And then he fetched so deep a sigh that Simon asked him what the matter was.

'For the last two days,' said Angelo, 'I have been thinking about nothing but bombs, and whenever I fell asleep I had a nightmare. And now I have begun to think about my sweetheart Lucrezia and the honeymoon we cannot have until the war is over; and that is worse than bombs, for I shall not be able to sleep at all. It is very difficult to be happy.'

'LET US MAINTAIN our good temper,' said the Count. 'Let us keep a sense of proportion. There are seven deadly sins and only two redeeming virtues, which are faith and love –'

'I should include good manners,' said the Marchesa.

'So should I, if I had my way,' the Count agreed. 'I should include tolerance, a judicious taste in music, a preference for the baroque in architecture, a certain refinement in the apprehension of physical beauty and one's responses to it, a talent for imparting gaiety to conversation, and so forth. These would all be redeeming virtues if I were the ultimate authority and final court of appeal; but there's no use pretending that I am any such thing. It has been decided otherwise, and we have to recognize facts. The essential virtues are two, the deadly sins are seven, and therefore the virtues are in a permanent minority and we should not be surprised that sometimes they suffer a heavy defeat. We should not, that is, be so destructively surprised as to fall into a state of wrathful despair before the scene of a human battlefield from which the virtues have fled shrieking in dismay, and on which the triumphant sins for a little season strut and revel, maltreat their captives, and quarrel among themselves. It is tiresome, I admit –'

'My maid refuses to leave Rome,' said the Marchesa. 'The perfume that I have used for ten years is unobtainable in this paltry village, and today the hairdresser, clumsy to begin with, was finally insolent. The few clothes that I was able to bring here now seem like a vulgar admirer whom one has allowed to perform some opportune but regretted service: their excessive familiarity has become revolting. There is, moreover, no company in Montenero, and what is hardest of all to bear, you have turned philosopher.'

'No, no,' said the Count. 'That is too kind of you. I explore the fringes of thought, I contemplate human affairs with a certain interest, but that is all. I am not yet conscious of a complete and orderly system of cognition.'

'You should be glad of that,' said the Marchesa, 'for it is sheer misfortune to be much aware of any system, whether physical, political, or merely plumbing. The plumbing in this house has now finally collapsed, and no one can be unconscious of the fact. And except for a few hours in the middle of the day we live in such gloom as only good eyesight can distinguish from total darkness.'

'It was the Germans who cut off the electric light,' said the Count.

'And an English or an American bomb that cut off the water. If our old friends and our new ones both remain in Italy, we shall soon have nothing left at all.'

'And then upon the stony soil of our destitution the seven deadly sins may dwindle and faint with hunger, and by strenuous cultivation the redeeming virtues will show their heads again.'

'Do you look forward to the prospect?'

'No,' said the Count, 'I cannot bear to contemplate it. – I am going for a walk.'

'I shall not come with you,' said the Marchesa, 'for I cannot afford such an expense of shoe-leather.'

The little town of Montenero di Roma, where they had been living in seclusion for several weeks, had formerly been a popular resort of tourists. There were several good churches in it, the largest being that of Santa Maria Maggiore, which had an elaborate façade and contained four large paintings of the Holy Family by Luini. There were also a palace that had once belonged to the Orsini, in which there were frescoes by Ghirlandaio, and two restaurants well-known for their cooking. The municipality had built a new sulphur bath below the ruins of that which had been more splendidly created for Diocletian, and but for a surplus of statuary the public gardens would have been charming. The main street, a narrow thoroughfare smoothly paved, curved like a half-hoop round the hill, and in summer time the houses were decked with red geraniums that grew in little balconies of wrought iron beneath their windows. From many places there were broad views of the Campagna, far below and reaching spaciously to the north, and of St. Peter's dome, small in the distance, in the flat haze of Rome. The town was built upon a wooded hill-top in a broad bay of the mountains, and above it, on either flank and behind it, rose their wrinkled sides. But the wrinkles were hardly visible in winter, when the snow filled them.

How cold it was! thought the Count. How different from the warm seasons when tourists had filled the streets with their clamorous tongues from Birmingham and Bremen and Minneapolis! Heigh-ho for progress: what a lost beatitude that genial vulgarity now appeared!

The sun shone with a pallid glitter, and the snowy breath of the wind came shrilling down a *salita* on the right-hand side of the street. The Count turned up the collar of his coat: it was lined with Persian lambskin, tightly curled. Two plump and red-legged girls with scanty dresses ran past him, laughing loudly. An old man stood in the gutter, begging, but seemingly indifferent to the frozen air. A burly fellow with a bare head and his shirt open to the waist stood in the mouth of a lane and shouted to a friend on the other side of the street . . . There were gradations of sensibility, thought the Count, and no one should generalize on social affairs until everyone had been furnished with an equally efficient circulation of the blood.

The smoothly paved and curving street led to the Piazza Santa Maria where, in the tourist season, a fountain had risen from the triple source of three dolphins' mouths and splashed the generous forms of two nereids clinging to the knees of a benignly bearded Neptune. There was no fountain now, and the basin was half-full of dirty snow. Printed posters, signed by the German commandant, defaced the columns of Santa Maria Maggiore on the north side of the square. There was a scattering of German soldiers among the idly moving people. – 'And how superfluous and out of place they are,' murmured the Count with a sudden distaste for their strong but awkward figures. The Italians, the several score of them who loosely filled the piazza, were doing nothing in particular to justify their existence, but nothing at all to perturb it. They were talking and gesticulating, they were contemplating eternity and abusing the present, they were behaving like the digits and fronds of a great anemone that reasonably filled its own sea-cove; but the Germans were manifestly a foreign growth and stood out like proud flesh.

Their alien condition became still more obvious when a senior officer approached in company with a person in civilian clothes who walked with the self-conscious strut of someone whose importance was considerable, but not long established. His hands were clasped behind his back – though with difficulty, for his arms were so short that his fingers barely met each other – and his head had been characteristically moulded by a Teutonic pelvis. They crossed the square, and with a harsh contraction of their muscles the soldiers stiffened to attention and saluted as they passed. In the north-east corner of the square, near the church, there was a little shop whose proprietor sold silversmith's work, intaglios, and reputed relics of the Etruscans' art. The officer and his civilian friend paused for a few seconds to look through the window, then went inside.

The Count knew by sight most of Montenero's German rulers, but these were strangers, and beneath a small cloud of anxiety he was wondering who and what they might be when he caught a glimpse, in the shadowed portico of the church, of a tall and unforgettable figure. The figure had swiftly vanished, presumably into the church, but the Count had no doubt as to who it was.

It was Fest, his mysterious visitor whom he had not seen since the night when he had been nearly suffocated in the Marchesa's house above the Piazza di Spagna. – Circling a stolid group of dark-clad peasants, narrowly avoiding a running child, dodging between idle talkers, the Count hurried across the square and ran up the steps of the church. There was no one in the wide porch who looked like Fest. He pushed open a creaking door and went in.

Before one of the side altars a priest in a shabby white chasuble was marrying a thin young man to a plump young woman in the presence of fourteen of their friends and relations. On the steps of another altar a kneeling girl had been so overcome by fear or grief that she crouched like a beaten child, leaning against the wall, her shoulder and her yellow head on the black stone. The Count passed her, then paused and looked discreetly back. She was a pretty girl. Poor creature, he thought, it is the pretty ones who suffer most. But then he caught sight of another woman who was by no means pretty, nor ever had been in all her fifty years of unfulfilment, and on her hatchet face, as she lifted her squinting eyes to the darkness under the roof, there was a misery so forlorn and unrelieved that the Count looked hurriedly away and muttered to himself, 'No, no, I was wrong, I was very wrong. *Dio mio*, how unhappy it always makes me to come into a church.'

He walked round again, to make sure that Fest was not there, and while re-passing the wedding-group he observed that the bride, though young, had a hard and greedy look, and the bridegroom, but little older, was nervous and ill-tempered. The walls of the chapel in which the ceremony was taking place had been painted with graceful exuberance to represent the marriage at Cana in Galilee. The principals in the picture, and all their guests, were strikingly handsome. Shrugging his shoulders, the Count bent and whispered to an astonished woman, a cousin of the bridegroom's father, 'We must be patient, we must be very patient.'

The creaking door closed behind him, and he breathed more happily the colder air outside. But he wondered, with annoyance at his failure to find him, where Fest had gone. And then he saw him.

He saw a figure come gently but swiftly into sight at

the north end of the portico, and flatten itself behind the farthest column. He was about to go forward and claim acquaintance, when the figure withdrew its right hand from its overcoat pocket and swung it slowly back like a man who is about to throw, very carefully, a rubber ball to his little boy. With a sudden pulse beating in his throat the Count looked outward, in the direction of the projected throw, and saw that the German officer and his square-headed civilian friend had newly come out of the shop where intaglios and objects of reputed Etruscan art were sold, and for a moment stood in conversation.

The percussion bomb burst at their feet, and within a second another had followed it. The Germans fell with a curious violence, as if trying to leap away from or over the explosion, and the shattered windows of the shop flung upon them a wild confetti of broken glass. The Count felt a sea-sick rising of his tripes, and in a slow horror looked round again at the figure behind the left-hand column. Fest recognized him and turned so that the Count saw his monocle of clouded tortoiseshell and his smiling lips. With a courteous gesture Fest raised his hat, and then, swift as a sprinter starting his race, vanished round a corner of the church into an alley that steeply descended to the lower parts of the town.

The explosion of the bombs had first thrown the crowd into a wild confusion during which people screamed loudly, ran hither and thither, and waved their arms about in a dark fluttering of limbs and garments that looked like the frightened rising of a cloud of rooks. But soon their panic-movement was seized and held, their legs were haltered and their thoughts captured by overmastering curiosity. With a force like gravity curiosity drew them all, their scattered circumference gathering tightly in, to the blood-stained doorway of the shop that had sold Etruscan statuettes to tourists.

The Count moved slowly at first, yielding reluctantly to a horrible attraction, but when other spectators began to push him aside and unfairly thrust themselves in front of him, he became insistent on his equal rights and struggled for a good place with the best of them. He was entirely taken by surprise when a cry of alarm went up and the crowd again began to run. The Germans had acted promptly, and, now, in a very methodical manner, were dealing roughly with the sight-seeing inhabitants of Montenero. The Count offered no resistance to arrest, but while one German soldier seized him by the arm, another hit him on the head with a rifle-barrel.

He appeared to recover consciousness fairly soon, but for some time took no interest in his surroundings. When he did he found himself, with twenty or thirty other men, in a classroom in an infants' school. A score of little desks stood on the floor, and the walls were gaily decorated with a fresco of the farmer's year. On a blackboard, in large white figures, there was a simple sum in addition. Concussion had left him with a headache, but the Count's mind was now clear, and quickly it filled with apprehension and dismay when he perceived that all his companions – or all but one – were in a state of extreme dejection. Some were quietly weeping, others noisily expostulating to friends who paid no attention, and a few sat on the floor in a silent surrender to grief that reminded him of the girl in church. The one person who retained his composure was an elderly small man with a red nose, a scanty combing of dyed hair across his half-bald head, and a well-worn but decent suit of professional black. The Count knew him slightly. His name was Toselli, and he was a retired school-teacher. The Count beckoned, and Toselli joined him in a corner of the room beside the blackboard.

'What is the explanation of all this?' asked the Count. 'What has happened, and what is going to happen?'

'Several things and one thing,' answered Toselli. 'What has already happened is a tangle of events, what is going to happen is a single event. At six o'clock tomorrow morning we are going to be shot.'

'But why?'

'To expiate the murder of two German visitors who

seem to have been people of some importance. I have heard many suggestions as to who they were, but none of us really knows. From the behaviour of some German officers, however, which I observed with interest, I think the inference is justified that they were highly regarded by their own people, and I gathered that they had only recently arrived from Berlin.'

'But the man who murdered them isn't here,' said the Count.

'Oh no,' said Toselli. 'They are searching for him, of course, but if they catch him they will certainly not execute him in a hurry, like us. They will examine him, and interrogate him, for days and days. But we are people of no importance. We are no more than those chalk figures on the blackboard. We are merely integers in a German sum, and can be rubbed out as easily. One German life, they say, must be paid for by twelve Italians – so here we are.'

'There are more than twenty-four people here,' said the Count.

'They may have thrown in a few extra for good measure,' said Toselli carelessly. 'We were chosen without much consideration. There is little Ercole the boot-black, and there old Bartolomeo who is a great-grandfather. You recognize blind Roberto who begs in the streets, or used to? You, my dear Count, represent the nobility, and I the learned professions – but fortuitously, I assure you. We are a casual collection, and who cares though the sum is not exactly correct?'

'How can you speak so lightly of this appalling crime?' demanded the Count. 'You yourself are going to die; how can you sit and talk with such inhuman composure?'

'I have for long been indifferent to life,' answered Toselli. 'Why should I not be indifferent to death?'

'Surely they are not identical?'

'We may be subject to new illusions, or merely cease to be plagued by those with which we have grown familiar. I cannot suppose there is anything else to suffer or worse to fear.'

'I do not want to die,' said the Count.

'Neither do our companions here, yet who among them has had even the illusion of a happy life? They fear to die because they have been taught that life is good, and therefore they are alarmed by the thought of losing it; but if they had never heard such nonsense –'

'Their senses would have told them so, and reason convinced them.'

'The human senses are very poor guides to reality, for it is well known that one man's meat is another's poison. A Hottentot beauty would excite only derision in Rome, the table delicacies of Tibet would nauseate a French epicure, and where you shivered with the cold an Eskimo would throw off his shirt and complain of the heat. – No, my dear Count, you can repose no great trust in the senses, and as for reason, that is simply a product of time and locality. Reason can prove anything, but it does best of all at turning somersaults.'

The Count was silent for a few minutes, and then he said again, 'I do not want to die.'

'It is a word,' said Toselli, 'but is it anything more? Death may be only a name-plate on an empty house. Neither of us knows, and I do not care. My master is the philosopher Pyrrho, who was probably the wisest man who ever lived, and he knew nothing and knew that he knew nothing. A friend of his, a Greek of Byzantium, after dining with him one day went home and wrote, proleptically, his epitaph. It may be roughly translated like this:

'"And oh, dear Pyrrho! Pyrrho, are you dead?"

"Alas, I cannot tell," dear Pyrrho said."'

But the Count was no longer listening. He was overcome by a plain and quite intolerable sorrow to think that he must die so soon. The bare and simple fact of living became unutterably dear to him, and the prospect of being shot implied so huge a deprivation that his natural fear was swallowed in a vast engulfing grief.

All the days of his life joined themselves together to make a Chinese scroll of the most rich and delectable entertainment; to tear it would be unforgivable. Yet the scroll did not lie, and many of the pictures, very clearly drawn, showed him haggard with pain. He saw himself swollen with the toothache and badgered by the ear-ache; and he thought of those suffering days, so long ago, with wild regret. In spite of its aches and pains, life was good.

He saw in sharply drawn pictures the countless humiliations to which he had been subjected. Public snubbing and secret rebuff, a friend's forgetfulness, a girl's indifference: he had suffered them all and kindred shames beyond counting. Sleep-walking at seven, a clap at college, the piles at forty – he had fallen from his horse in the Pincio, he had choked on a fish-bone when dining with the Colonnas, he had gone to the races with his buttons undone – oh, the stabs of minor misfortune that drove so deep and left so hot a wound! And yet, though they were ten times as many, life would still be good.

He thought of graver torment. He remembered Angelo's mother, and the liquefaction of his heart when she died. He saw upon the scroll the death of later love and the dull hue of women's bodies when it was no longer possible to see them in the light of love. What arrant flesh they then became, a something that might be weighed but had no other meaning; and how lonely he used to feel, at such a time, to think he had lain with those cold strangers. But even love in its most melting warmth had never quite dissolved his knowledge of his loneliness, nor hidden totally the outlines of his immanent incommunicable singularity. Every man was alone, born in a caul of solitude that none could tear. He must live in the narrow confinement of himself, and into his cell disaster came to beat him cruelly. Yet life was good.

He wept, and as the tears ran down he remembered that other men had died. He recalled, with a sudden horror, how many and how many had lately died, and all had lost a life as dear to them as his. Chinese and Ethiopians had perished by the thousand, a multitude of Russians and Germans had gone back to clay with Englishmen and Poles, with his own fellow-countrymen, with Norwegians and Frenchmen and

Jews – and never had he given a thought to the sad infinity
of farewells they spoke, before the bullets parted them from
their distracted lives. They had felt as he felt now, and their
fate had never troubled him, never touched the hardness of
his heart. That was the great vulgar sin of these dishevelled
times, hardness of heart. – But he would die as he had lived,
he promised himself.

'Do you believe in honour?' he asked Toselli.

'No,' said Toselli.

The Count dried his eyes. 'I have just perceived,' he said,
'that I am under a certain obligation of decency. During the
last few years a vast number of men have died, and I have
not pitied them. Therefore it would be indecent and wrong
to pity myself. I shall go to my death unweeping.'

'I see no occasion for tears,' said Toselli.

'I do,' said the Count.

'Nor, if it comes to that, for refraining from them.'

'Again I do.'

'The great world will certainly not weep for us, because
it has grown too much accustomed to what was once called
tragedy. Though men are still upset by their own misfortunes, they have acquired wisdom enough to be indifferent
to others.'

'That is not wisdom,' said the Count.

Toselli yawned and lay down, and appeared to sleep.
He tied a handkerchief round his eyes, for the room was
brightly lit. Throughout the night a dynamo throbbed, and
the unshaded lights filled the room with a radiance that
threw quivering shadows. The door of the classroom had
been taken off its hinges, and two soldiers stood in the
opening. Other soldiers in heavy boots passed and re-passed
in the corridor. The Germans had commandeered the school
to serve as an emergency prison and accommodate some
of the additional troops they had brought into Montenero.
For most of the night there was a mingled noise of harsh
voices, doors slamming, ponderous feet on wooden floors,
and occasionally a nightmare scream; but in the harsher
coldness before dawn there was comparative silence. Then,

with a sudden clamour, the prison woke to a simmering fury and the day's business began.

New snow had covered the school playground, but so thinly that feet printed it with black. Large flakes of snow were falling from a still darkness. A dozen soldiers with rifles stood at the gate, and there were two motor-lorries on the road outside.

The Italians were marched out in single file. Soldiers were on either side and dragged forward those who hesitated, passing them on as if they were tubs of water to put out a fire. The lorries were filled, and set off slowly through the darkness. In a whisper the Count repeated again and again, 'I had no pity for others, I owe none to myself.' He was so intent on believing this that he heard nothing of what the others were saying.

About two miles from Montenero, in the hillside some eighty yards above the road, there was an opening like a long and very shallow arch. It was between five and six feet high in its middle part, and the cave behind it was extensive. There was a little space of flat ground in front of it.

The lorries halted on the road below, and the Italians were dragged or driven up the hill to the narrow level in front of the cave. There were some German soldiers already there, and an officer with a powerful torch whose beam he swung slowly from end to end of the huddled line. Within the cave, shining erratically in its darker gloom, were other lights, and men moving behind them.

'How many of them are there?' demanded the officer with the torch.

'Twenty-eight,' answered the lieutenant in command of the escort.

'That's too many.'

The lieutenant did not reply, and the officer with the torch shouted, 'That's more than I want, I tell you!'

The lieutenant approached him, and they argued in low voices. Then he with the torch exclaimed loudly, 'I must have authority, that's all. I don't care how many I take, but I won't do it without authority. If you say it's all right –'

'It is,' said the lieutenant.

'Then for God's sake let's get a move on.'

He began to make a short speech to the Italians, but was interrupted by a fit of coughing. He coughed as if his throat were being torn, and spat in the snow. Then hoarsely went on with his speech. The Germans, he said, had improved the Hebrews' law of an eye for an eye and a tooth for a tooth. They had put up the price of German eyes, and required a dozen in payment.

At this point the philosopher Toselli, who was standing beside the Count, began to scream; and when a soldier clapped a hand over his mouth he bit it, and hacked the soldier's shins. In the darkness Toselli had caught a glimpse of reality, and lost on the instant his indifference to life and contempt for death. His example upset the other prisoners, most of whom also began to struggle and scream, and for a minute or two there was wild confusion. When order was restored they all turned their heads to listen to the noise, very loud in the gloom, of a motor-cycle climbing the hill.

The motor-cycle came to a stop beside the lorries, and the officer with the torch sent a soldier to see who had come and ask what he wanted. The soldier quickly returned with a dispatch-rider. The two officers, their shoulders touching, read his message by torchlight, and then the senior fell into another paroxysm of coughing.

When he recovered he announced, as though it were a matter of no importance, 'Your execution has been postponed. The actual murderer has been captured, and you will be taken back to Montenero to await a final decision as to what is to be done with you.'

He lighted a cigarette, but his throat was sore and he could not smoke it. He threw it away, and little Ercole the boot-black picked it up.

On the way back to Montenero the Count felt that his legs were made of green cheese, but his chest was like a barrel bursting full of new wine, and he could not restrain himself from talking very volubly to all his fellow-travellers, who listened to never a word, for all were talking with an excitement no less than his.

They were taken to the school again, and into the class-room decorated with pictures of the farmer's year. Shortly after their return the Count saw Fest. With a soldier on either side, and one behind him, he walked past the open door. His head was high, and he seemed quite calm. He still wore his monocle of clouded tortoiseshell.

Later in the day a squadron of Allied bombers attacked some German transport on the road near Montenero. A few of their bombs fell in Montenero itself.

CHAPTER TEN

MOVING BRISKLY on his crutches, Simon Telfer was walking along a high cliff-road in Sorrento with Angelo beside him. At the entrance to a large white villa, temporarily occupied by the military, stood a tall sentry, gravely still. As Simon approached he sprang to attention, with smart and sudden action clapped his rifle on to his left shoulder, and with a hard hand resounding on the small of the butt, saluted. At every movement a small thick cloud of dust rose from his clothing as though he were an ancient carpet that someone was beating with a cane.

From the cone of Vesuvius across the bay rose thick columns, densely spiralling, of purple smoke shot with a fierce flush or melting glow of pink. High into the tall and clouded sky they rose in oily whorls, until the upper wind caught and bent them suddenly, and sent them flying over the sea in a flat brown canopy from which descended the close volcanic dust. Oozing from the crater's lip and trickling down the upper slope of the mountain came scarlet rivulets, thick and slow, of molten lava. Below them, under clouds of evil smoke, the glaciers of iron-dark cinders crawled down hill, filling the hollows, shirking heights and promontories, and crushing houses, tumbling pines and chestnut-trees in their sluggish flow.

Angelo coughed and blew his nose, and turning to shake his fist at Vesuvius exclaimed, 'This is too much! It is really too much!'

'I agree with you,' said Simon. 'Whatever else one may ask from a landscape, one does expect stability.'

Angelo smacked a puff of dust from either shoulder. 'My poor Italy,' he said. 'Now your stuffing is coming out.'

They were on their way to visit two of Simon's friends, brother-officers who were spending a few days' leave with an Italian family which, before the war, had occasionally acquired an American stepmother, sometimes an English daughter-in-law. Their villa commanded a view of the clouded bay, and there were about twelve or fourteen people in a handsomely furnished but somewhat chilly drawing-room. A well preserved woman of fifty, with dark eyes and gleaming teeth, was loudly declaring as they went in that the eruption had been caused by a treacherous airman who had privily dropped into the crater of Vesuvius a bomb weighing two thousand kilogrammes, which had acted like a violent emetic.

A brisk debate on the weather followed, and everyone agreed that the exceptional severity of the winter, so unlike the temperate climate to which they were accustomed, was due to the air being shaken and battered by gunfire. A gentleman with a jaundiced eye said that the future of the world was dark indeed, for its atmosphere would be increasingly tormented by aeroplanes, ships in the stratosphere, and wireless; with appalling consequences.

'Everywhere the climate will deteriorate,' he said. 'On five days out of seven there will be rain or sleet, and neither corn nor fruit will ripen.'

An English daughter-in-law – pretty, plump and petulant – was describing to a lieutenant of the Royal Navy the hardships of life in Sorrento during time of war. A saturnine young man, passing with a bottle of Italian vermouth in one hand, a bottle of Plymouth gin in the other, halted and turned his head to listen. 'For many years to come,' he said, 'the world is going to be full of people competing for attention with stories of what they have suffered. And those who have suffered the least will have the most to say. It will be extremely boring.'

In a corner of the room Simon was looking at a replica, in bronze, of a whimsical piece of some ancient statuary's work that one of his friends had recently bought in Herculaneum or Pompeii. It represented a satyr making satyric love to a briskly co-operating nymph.

'Our follies,' he said, 'have such antiquity that it is almost impossible not to respect them.'

'But our virtues,' said his friend, 'are like a litter of puppies untrained and delicate. Some are gun-shy, some will chase rabbits, and all require worming. Their noses cannot distinguish between a skylark and a grouse, their mouths are untaught, and most of them will be carried off by distemper.' – With his forefinger he drew an arabesque on a dusty table-top, and added, 'There's brimstone in the air today. Oh, damn Vesuvius!'

Angelo took the bronze and looked at it with eyes that swam in unshed tears. 'Does it not make you sad,' he said, 'to think of all the beautiful girls there have been, whom we never knew and could not enjoy? To have missed so much: I can hardly bear it! I imagine them turning their heads so neatly on their little white necks to look at me as I come in, and their voices when they are soft and husky, and their slim round arms – and then I remember they are dead, they are the dust that the wind blows round the corner, and I am overcome by the cruelty of life.'

'You must look forward, not back,' said Simon. 'Think about meeting and marrying Lucrezia –'

'But there again I see the unfairness that rules the world!' cried Angelo. 'Because I am in love with Lucrezia I am faithful to her; or very nearly faithful. And therefore I am deprived of a hundred enjoyable experiences that a person less sincere, or not quite so sensitive as I, could quite easily obtain! It is wrong to suppose there are principles of natural justice in life, or that life is ever peaceful. Life is war, and we who are virtuous may well lose every battle but the last one.'

'That,' said Simon's friend with noticeable stiffness, 'is the prerogative of the English.'

'Because you are good?' asked Angelo.

'It is an attractive hypothesis,' said Simon.

'There was a time when we aspired to goodness,' said his friend, 'and the world regarded us as hypocrites. Then we decided to pose as realists; and the world said we were effete.'

'But why do you win your last battles?' asked Angelo.

'We are amateurs,' said Simon's friend with a noisy yawn, 'and the amateur lasts longer than the professional.'

At night the molten lava, creeping slowly in blunt-headed streams, shone like wet silver, and the dark air smelt more strongly of sulphur. So long as the eruption continued Angelo was melancholy and given to superstitious fear or dubious philosophy, but as soon as the volcano recovered its equilibrium he regained his good spirits, and discovered the truth of the matter. Vesuvius had felt the need to purge itself, and having purged was better. There was the symbol. Now Italy must take heed of it, and would. And oh, the content, the relaxed and satisfied euphoria that follows a deferred and large purgation! Yes, he declared, the future was bright.

Some days later Simon received an official letter which informed him that he had now, as a result of his wound, been absent from duty for three weeks, and had in consequence been reduced in rank from captain to lieutenant. This was in accordance with an old-established regulation of the War Office which saved the taxpayer money and dissuaded junior officers from staying in hospital longer than was strictly necessary. It also discouraged unruly ambition; for the British War Office has always set its face against militarism.

Simon took a balanced view of his diminished status, made a hurried calculation, and thought it might save him a few pounds of income tax; but Angelo was deeply mortified and for several days refused to speak English, which, he said, was the language of injustice and ingratitude.

Simon was in no hurry to return to duty until he heard that some part of Force 69 was about to begin training for a new operation, when he at once presented himself for medical examination, was declared fit, and promptly set out for Benevento, whither his company had lately removed. An elaborate secrecy enclosed their training programme, and Angelo, to begin with, had no part in it. But the general preparation for large events could not wholly be concealed, and as April vanished from the calendar and May came in, expectancy grew large and taut like a balloon plumping for the ascent.

The battle began a little before midnight on May the eleventh. From the mountains beyond Cassino to the lighted water of Gaeta's gulf a thunderstorm of gunfire bellowed among the hills and over the sea, and filled dark valleys with reverberant echoes. An army mustered from the five continents of the world advanced to the attack, to destroy the opposing army of Germany and its subject peoples, and to open the gates of Rome. On the Allied side there were Poles and Englishmen, Frenchmen and Scots, Irish and Welsh: that was the European contribution. There were New Zealanders who looked like Cromwell's Ironsides and fought with pride and professional severity: that was the Antipodean levy. There were small and merry highlanders from the mountains of Nepal, tall ones from the passes of the Afghan frontier, bearded plainsmen from the Punjab, the heirs of Rajput chivalry and Shivaji's Mahrattas: they were the voluntaries of Hindustan and High Asia. There was on the coast an American army enlisted from New England and California, from Oregon and Kansas and the Carolinas, and at the mountainous end of the line a Canadian corps: that was the New World's share in the venture. From the fifth continent there came an armoured division, some of English stock and some of Boer descent, with black auxiliaries, and panting for the signal to start a wild and huge array of tribesmen from the Atlas mountains; and the latter, who were compendiously known as Goums, were the *semper aliquid novi* out of Africa.

The Eighth Army had already won fame enough to make its story live, but none of its battles had been so fierce and hard as this, and the blood of many valiant men ran with the waters of the Rapido and the Garigliano to the Great Sea. In the mountains beyond Cassino the Poles were checked, and British troops and Canadians found the entrance to the Liri Valley held strongly against them. On the coast the

Americans of the Fifth Army made progress, but slowly at first. Soon they would go like a river in spate, but to begin with their advance was hardly won. It was on the high hills near the middle of the line that the German defences were most decisively broken in the early days of the battle, and the troops who went through them, farther and faster than anyone else, were the wild men from Morocco: the Goums.

Quickly they created, not merely a salient pointing like a spearhead to the north, but a legend of fear and a fabulous renown. They worked in silence and by night, and terror was their ally. They killed with long steel blades, and in lonely farmhouses the women dreaded them for another reason. Many a German sentry lay headless behind their patrols, and many a woman, it was said, looking up to see the swart and narrow face of a Goum at the window, had miscarried on the spot. In the broad pathway of their advance German outposts betrayed themselves by the chattering of their teeth, and the *contadine* fled from evening shadows screaming '*Gli Marocchini, gli Marocchini!*'

When the battle had been raging for nearly a fortnight, Simon sent for Angelo and said to him in a casual way, 'We are going to have a little party of our own. There is a rumour that the Germans are about to do something that we take a poor view of, and I'm going to see if I can put a stop to it. It will be quite a small party, but I've got permission to take you with us. You will be very useful, knowing your way about Rome as you do, and I thought you might like to come. We start tomorrow.'

'And where is your party going to be?' asked Angelo.

'In Rome,' said Simon. 'Didn't I make that clear?'

'But Rome is still occupied by the Germans!'

'That will add to the interest of it, don't you think? – Why, what's the matter?'

Before Simon could catch him, Angelo fell to the ground in a dead faint. Simon made haste to turn him over, to loosen his belt, to pour water on his face and chafe his hands. As soon as he showed signs of recovery, Simon gave him rum in an enamel mug, and Angelo sat up, pale and shivering.

'What is the matter?' Simon repeated with anxiety in his voice. 'Are you ill?'

Angelo stared at him with wide-open, terrified eyes. Never in his life had he heard a more fearful proposal than this calm suggestion that he should join a party of desperadoes to break through the German lines, and enter by stealth the enemy's citadel! The shock of hearing it had frightened the blood from his brain – and who, he thought with a passion of returning fear, who could blame it for retreating before so monstrous a prospect? Never, never would he consent to put himself in such agonizing jeopardy, and throw his life away to crown it! And yet, when he tried to speak, he could not find the words of refusal. He looked at Simon and thought: He and his friends are going, and they have asked me to join them because they regard me as a friend. They are very brave, they do not think deeply but they laugh a great deal, and in a careless way they are very kind: it is a good thing to have such friends, but O my God, what a price to pay! If I refuse to go, if I admit that I am too frightened, I shall lose their friendship for a certainty; and if I agree, and make myself one of them, I may very well lose my life, and how much good will friendship be then? What a choice for a May morning!

'Give me some more rum,' he said, and emptied the mug.

He gasped and shuddered slightly, but soon felt a warmth inside him like a great lusty visitor coming with a laugh and a heart-stirring greeting into a cold quiet house. That was excellent. The visitor was most welcome, and when he laughed again it sounded throughout the house, and lamps were lighted in every room. But then, surprisingly, the visitor took charge of the situation, and borrowing Angelo's vocal chords, his palate and teeth and tongue, addressed Simon in quite unforgivable terms and offered an explanation of the fainting-fit that was wildly mendacious. – It was the idea of seeing Rome again, long before he had considered the possibility of such happiness, that had keeled him over, he said. An emotional type was Angelo, quite unlike the English, and his lack of self-control must be forgiven him. – So said the rum-bold swaggering visitor, and a moment later, to make things infinitely and irretrievably worse, declared: 'And I shall, of course, be delighted to come with you. We are a band of brothers and nothing shall divide us!'

An hour later Angelo lay in his tent and felt his heart beating against his ribs like a funeral bell, with a slow and melancholy stroke. He had signed away his life, he was convinced of that, and in return for the indifferent friendship of a score or so of young men as callous as they were reckless – a friendship that would be long-lived if it lived for a week – he had done no more than ensure that his last week upon earth would be spent in a torment of gathering dread. Never a thought came into his mind that he could survive the adventure. Danger had always filled him with such awe that any danger had seemed allpowerful to destroy, and this was no common danger but stark peril for a hero to gamble with. He was self-doomed, there was no doubt of it, and he listened as he lay to his heart that beat a funeral-knell.

In the morning the face in his shaving-mirror looked at him so whitely, from such dark enormous eyes, that he was at first startled and then impressed by it. His cup of warm water grew cold while he studied it. It was the reflection, he thought, of a tragic but romantic figure. It was the face, he told himself, of a man of destiny. It had caught its pallor from the coldness of fate, and he could not avoid his allotted task however deeply his eyes might mourn the necessity. – This perception did not exactly give him courage, but lent him a kind of resignation, or hypnotized his wilder fears, and let him pass the next few days without drawing much attention to his utter unsuitability for service with Force 69.

Simon, quickly promoted to captain again, was to command the foray. His party consisted of two subalterns and a score of men. They were all heavily armed, and though

Angelo knew most of them fairly well, and had seen photo-graphs of their wives and sweethearts that made him feel very much at home with them, he was deeply impressed by their appearance in battle-array. How little, he thought, their wives and sweethearts really knew of them.

They went first to Naples, and there before nightfall embarked in a very small ship for the port of Anzio. Fortunately the sea was calm, and nothing interrupted their passage. The starlit darkness was warm as new milk, and Simon, sitting under the lee of the deckhouse in a mood of pleasant anticipation, told Angelo what they were proposing to do.

Allied sympathizers in Rome had reported that the Germans were preparing to blow-up the bridges over the Tiber. The Allies, who were looking forward to pursuing a defeated Ger-man army across the bridges, would be seriously hindered by their destruction, and Simon's task was to prevent it. The circumstances, he said, would probably favour him, because the Germans would not explode the charges until they had withdrawn all but the last rearguard of their troops, and by then there might be some confusion in the city. There would be a period favourable for attack, and if he could strike in the very bull's-eye of opportunity, they might well be successful. They would enter Rome from the north . . .

The canopy of the sky was wearing thin. The moths had been there, and through it in prickle-points shone the brilliant vacancy beyond. Nothing was real, thought Angelo. They were ghosts on a sterile sea, and there were holes in the sky. This mad adventure was certainly unreal, for only in the fantasy of a dream could he have embarked upon it. He listened to Simon with the accompaniment of a running prayer that he might wake up.

But in the morning, at Anzio, he had to admit the reality of the scene, though it was different from his expectation of it. The sun shone brightly on a calm sea and about fifty soldiers, stark naked and as brown as chestnuts, were noisily bathing in the clear boulder-strewn water on the outer side of the breakwater. The little harbour was full of strange craft, and men were shouting, working, hurrying to and fro, with unceasing busyness. Inland the view was screened by a wall of artificial smoke, and a rumble of gunfire came from the invisible hills beyond it. The tall painted buildings along the water front, scarred and torn by shellfire, looked calm and decorative among their companion-trees. Though vibrant with activity, the scene was unexpectedly peaceful.

Simon marched his little company up the cobbled wharf through part of the town, and into a scrubby wood. The wood was thickly populated and strewn like the floor of a gigantic customs-shed with military stores in great variety and vast abundance. Wherever they went they saw little dumps of oil and food and ammunition. Shells here, cheese and pickles over there. Elsewhere blankets and barbed wire, pick-helves and canned peaches and more ammunition, and grenades in wooden boxes. The air also was crowded, and full of odours. It smelt of a sickly vegetation, of sweat and leather, of acrid smoke and dung. There were soldiers everywhere, working or sleeping, smoking and brewing tea and eating ration beef out of the tin. Many wore nothing but khaki shorts, and the sun had burnt their shoulders to flaming red or polished brown. Their common expression was a tough indifference, and their language was shocking.

Simon was shown a small unoccupied area in which his party might bivouac, and after he had given some necessary orders he walked idly towards Angelo, who was standing deep in thought at the edge of a large hole. A German shell, falling by chance on a store of ammunition, had exploded it and opened an untidy crater; and now in the loose earth of its circumference a border of scarlet poppies bloomed.

'After the last war,' said Simon, 'they took those flaming weeds for a symbol of remembrance. But the poppy is the flower of oblivion, and the poppy did its own work in its own way.'

'There are always poppies at this time of year,' said Angelo. 'I wasn't thinking about them, but about the Emperors Nero and Caligula, who were born here. In Anzio, I mean.'

'Had they any voice in the matter? They could no more choose their landfall than the soldiers who are here today.'

'Of course not. But in such a time as this it is refreshing to think about the lives of wicked Emperors. They sinned for their pleasure, and in good style.'

Ambulance-jeeps, laden with wounded men, came slowly down the road from the front of battle. The troops so long confined in the narrow acres of the bridgehead had now broken their perimeter and were fighting their way through a gap in the Alban hills to the Via Casilina. American soldiers from the main front, advancing through the flooded Pontine Marshes, had joined the beleaguered garrison in Latium, and both were striking tumultuously at the Germans' seaward flank. For the next few days Simon spent most of his time observing the battle at close quarters, but Angelo put off several invitations to join him, and passed the time in wistful melancholy on the sea-shore.

North of Anzio there are low cliffs of a soft stone that breaks easily into caves. Some of the caves had been enlarged, and soldiers were living in them. They spread their washing on the rocks, and the shore had something of a domestic look. Lying on the warm sand or swimming in the mild sea there were always soldiers, free from duty for a little while, making a brief holiday of opportunity. Gunfire seemed no more than thunder in the hills, and Angelo would swim out to sea and wish that he might meet a friendly dolphin. In classical times, as he had learnt at school, it was no uncommon thing for a young man to win a dolphin's regard and be carried on its back to some delectable island. But he wished in vain, and searched to no purpose the silver-sprinkled sea. The character of dolphins, like that of Emperors, had presumably suffered a change.

The day came when they must go forward with their adventure, for now the fall of Rome was imminent. For their transport Simon had procured two half-tracked German vehicles, captured from the enemy, and a sufficiency of soft, long-snouted caps, such as were worn by the Africa Korps, to give his party a rough disguise. At sunset they embarked with their vehicles aboard a sheer-sided ungainly craft with a blunt bow, and put to sea and headed to the north under the rising moon.

Their landfall was a point on the coast some twenty miles beyond the mouth of the Tiber, and they made it in the darkness between moonset and dawn. A pair of partisans, with two dim lanterns in line, guided them in. Their vessel grounded on a shelving beach, the door in the bow was lowered, and Simon's party in their vehicles drove ashore. The partisans led them through a minefield and a wood. A couple of miles to the south there was much excitement on the beach, for the Germans had discovered what appeared to be an attempted landing. Two motor-gunboats had caused the alarm to divert attention from Simon's invasion, and after manoeuvring off-shore at high speed and firing several thousand rounds of coloured ammunition, they drew away and set their course for Anzio again. Simon's party, by this time, was motoring comfortably towards the farmhouse where he proposed to go into hiding.

The vehicles were concealed, the soldiers brewed-up and ate a hearty meal, then most of them lay down in a barn and went to sleep. A guard was inconspicuously posted, and Simon with one of the subalterns set off to an appointed rendezvous. They had not long to wait. Within half an hour two excited Italians appeared, who at once declared that the Germans were in full flight from Rome, and that Allied aircraft were now bombing their transport on the main roads north of the city.

They knew nothing about the bridges over the Tiber except that they were strongly guarded. The rumour was still current that they had been prepared for demolition, but now a counter-opinion declared that the Germans had no intention of destroying them. A story was also to be heard that some of the bridges had already been blown-up, and both the Italians said they had been alarmed during the night by loud noises that must have been demolitions of some kind. – So much they told, with great pleasure and volubility, constantly interrupting each other and repeatedly breaking their narrative to describe with animated and expressive gestures the weary, hang-dog, and shamefaced air of the retreating enemy. What a contrast, they exclaimed, to the arrogance with which the Tedeschi had entered Rome, their bands a brazen triumph, their great boots thumping the road, and their stupid faces starched with pride!

Simon put many questions without getting much more information, and after some thought he said to his subaltern, 'I think we had better start.'

'I believe you're right,' said the subaltern.

They returned to the farm and roused the soldiers. Simon said to them: 'We're going to start in half an hour. So far as I can learn, the Hun is pulling out of Rome as fast as he can, so we haven't any time to lose. I think our two half-tracks, going as fast as they can in the opposite direction, will have a good chance of getting through. You look quite ugly enough, in those caps, to be mistaken for Germans, and till we get on the main road we'll take turns in leading so that we can all get a good coating of dust. We shan't fight unless we have to. If we're held up, we'll try to bluff and run. If we get separated, we'll continue independently to our rendezvous on the outskirts of Rome. Then we'll go to ground again until we've done a further reconnaissance. Is that quite clear?'

The soldiers briskly began to wash in the green water of a long stone trough. They propped-up fragments of mirror and shaved. They were quite calm, but their language, as they discussed their prospects and their commanding officer, was shocking. They themselves, it appeared, were shocked. Not by their language, but by Simon, who asked too shocking much from them, they said. But they took pride, as it seemed, in being so deeply shocked, and no one had a word to say against Simon himself. Not a shocking word. It was just the shocking demands he made.

'Shock me,' said a tall brown fellow with long hairy arms and a long lean jaw, screwing his mouth to tauten the skin for scraping, 'shock me if that shocker gives a shock for any shocking Jerry that ever shocked. I'll be shocked if he does.'

'What about the shocking tea?' shouted another. So they brewed-up again, and quickly ate another hearty meal, then climbing into their open vehicles sat there as primly upright as if they had indeed been Germans.

To begin with they drove along a country road where there was little chance of meeting traffic. Two of the partisans had volunteered to go with them. On the landward side the country was lightly wooded, but towards the sea it fell gradually in broad uncovered slopes. They could see where they were going, and drove with confidence. But the country road led to the main road, the Via Aurelia, and they must use that for some three or four miles. Then, if they were fortunate so far, they could turn inland on a vagrant lesser route that served a rural traffic only, where they might hope to avoid interference and circumvent such minor obstacles as they would encounter.

A little distance from the Via Aurelia they halted under cover, and Simon with a sergeant went forward to regard the scene. – A German convoy was moving northwards at high speed, with long intervals between the lorries, and a battalion of infantry, immensely elongated, was on the march. Two staff-cars came in sight, travelling fast, and in succession overtook a heavy-laden lorry. The footsoldiers made way for them. Then quite suddenly, as if they had that instant crystallized in the bright air, three white-starred aeroplanes appeared at no great height above the road, and sped along it in a swift assassin's flight, and left behind them the roaring wash of their propellers, and dead men tumbling on the verges, and burning wreckage. Both staff-cars were hit, and leaping from the road turned somersaults into a field. The marching infantry scattered like minnows in a pool, save the sluggards who lay still. And a canvas-hooded lorry slewed sideways and stopped abruptly, then toppled over and palely flowered into shimmering grey-tipped flame.

Simon and the sergeant ran back to their vehicles, beckoned the drivers to start, and mounted quickly. The heat of the burning lorry scorched them as they passed it, and two soldiers bending over a wounded comrade looked up and shouted angrily. An officer who had belatedly brought a light anti-aircraft gun into action held up his hand against them, but Simon made a sweeping and dramatic gesture that persuaded him to stand clear. Half a mile farther on they passed three lorries, halted close together, and a corporal who stood on the road and abused the drivers. He also signalled them to stop, but Simon repeated his gesture with good effect.

They crossed a bridge that engineers were preparing for demolition. Red cakes of explosive lay on the parapet. Here they excited suspicion and three men pursued them for a few yards, one of them firing his revolver. Road and railway now ran side by side, and more engineers were tying small cutting charges to the rails. An officer stood at the roadside, in argument with another, pointing furiously at his watch. These also turned and stared with suspicious curiosity at Simon's troop, but did nothing more than stare. Ahead of them, marching wearily, was another battalion of infantry, but before they reached the leading files the partisan who sat by Simon pointed to the left, and with barely moderated speed they turned into a side road. Three soldiers at the corner were laying mines in the verges.

For some distance ahead the lesser road was empty, and all of them felt in their muscles a small but pleasant relaxation. All but Angelo, that is. Angelo, sitting with his eyes tightly shut, was praying that he might die without pain. His refusal to observe the situation was due to his realization that in no other way could he endure it. He had not opened his eyes since leaving the farm, nor did he open them when, some few miles from the Via Aurelia, the two vehicles came abruptly to a halt.

They were on a curving road with a wood to the right of it and a high bank to the left. Round the corner towards them, moving faster than their custom, came a herd of thirty or forty cattle. They were the great white cattle of the Tiber valley, standing as high as a Guardsman at their tallest, and immensely horned. They filled the road, and within a few seconds the vehicles were two islands, close together, in a turbulent milky sea. The partisan beside Simon stood up and exclaimed, 'They are being driven!'

Simon also stood up. 'Germans,' he said. 'I can see eight of them, and there may be more behind.'

He gave his orders: 'Two men and the driver stay in each truck. The rest of you get into the wood, quickly, and we'll take them from the flank and rear.'

Nimbly the men leaped out, and Angelo, buffeted by their movement, but with his eyes still grimly closed, asked faintly what the matter was.

'Just a little parcel of Jerries,' said someone.

The word was too much for his resolution. He could not sit and wait for death, but while strength to run was in him, he would run. He laid his hand upon the rail, and scarcely looking where he might land, jumped out.

His descent was negligible, for he fell astride the tallest ox in the herd. He pitched forward, and to save himself grasped the loose hide over its withers. The ox in great alarm struck sideways with its mighty horns, goaded a cow into movement, and found a space ahead of it. It made a ponderous and futile attempt to buck, then broke into a lumbering trot. Angelo held tightly on.

Still driven by the Germans behind, and excited by the soldiers in its midst, all the herd was moving more quickly now. The great ox thrust its way to the front, and by example and contagion increased the general pace. The herd stampeded.

In comparison with the half-wild cattle of the South American pampas, or fighting bulls on a Spanish ranch, its speed might have been considered slow; but to Angelo it seemed a wild and furious progress. He was tossed and shaken as if he had been abroad on some wild ocean. On either side of him, like the billows of a stormy sea broken to white, were galloping shoulders and tumultuous pale haunches. Long gleaming horns were the naked spars of tall ships running before a gale. The broad beast under him rolled and plunged as though it were meeting confused and contrarious waves. He began to feel slightly sick, but as he was heaved further forward on the ox's back, he took a new grip on a loose roll of skin, and grimly kept his seat.

The great ox began to outstrip the rest of the herd, and turning suddenly from the road it entered the wood by a narrow path. Low branches struck cruelly as they charged beneath, and brambles tore at Angelo's legs. He lowered his head and shut his eyes again. All his muscles were aching with the effort to maintain his seat.

How long his ride had lasted, and how far he had travelled, he had no notion when at last the pace grew slower, the gallop became a trot, and the trot a walk. Angelo sat up and opened his eyes. They were approaching a farmyard, and in a cartshed two men and a woman were watching them. Spouting its steamy breath out of distended nostrils, foam dripping from its mouth and vast flanks heaving, the ox stood still. Angelo dismounted, and on failing knees tottered to the cartshed.

One of the men there was broadly built, with a fat unshaven face and a swollen paunch. He wore a soft black hat, black trousers, a white shirt fastened at the throat with a brass stud, and red braces. He carried his coat over his left arm. His voice was an over-ripe, husky bass.

'So you have joined the cavalry?' he said. 'When you left us at Reggio I realized that we of the infantry were too slow for you. Have you had a good ride?'

Angelo wiped the sweat from his eyes and recognized him. 'Sergeant Vespucci!' he exclaimed.

CHAPTER ELEVEN

A COUPLE OF HOURS later Angelo and Sergeant Vespucci
sat facing each other across a table on which were scattered
the fragments of a substantial meal. Flies buzzed and fed
upon the gravy smears, on cherry-stones and breadcrumbs.
An empty fiasco stood among the plates. From another, half
empty, the Sergeant was pouring red wine with steady care
into Angelo's glass. His own was brimfull. In the wrinkles
below his eyes the sweat glistened like seed-pearls, and
his leathery cheeks shone with a general moisture. Great
dew-drops stood upon his forehead, and his shirt clung
damply to his chest.

He set down the flask and said, 'So that's how I became
a Distributer.'

Angelo looked at him with admiration. Sergeant Vespucci
was a veteran of his own regiment who had served in Africa,
and it was good to meet an old comrade again and learn that
he was doing well in life, not only for himself but for his
country. They had told each other all their adventures, and
Angelo had listened with deep respect to the Sergeant's tale.
How prudent he had been, and how successful!

When the retreat began at Reggio he had rescued from
the administrative chaos some two dozen pack-mules which
would otherwise have fallen into the enemy's hands. He
had promptly set up as a carrier, serving refugees who
were anxious to save their household goods, and loading
other beasts with produce of the countryside. He had led
his caravan through the Sila, through the mountains of
Lucania and Campania, all the way to Naples, keeping
ahead of the Eighth Army and avoiding the Germans.
Some of his refugees travelled only a short distance to

village relatives, but there were always others who needed accommodation, and the traffic was lucrative enough. So was the sale of country produce, for the usual means of transport had vanished, and when goods were scarce people would pay fancy prices for them.

In Naples he had thought of settling down, but the typhus epidemic frightened him, so he had sold his mules and gone to Rome. There, with the useful capital he had acquired, he purchased a motor lorry, permission to move freely, and a forged certificate that entitled him to acquire petrol from the military authorities. In favourable circumstances he developed the business he had begun by chance, and buying produce where it was abundant, carried it to some neighbourhood in which it was scarce and sold it at an agreeable profit.

'I've always been a student of affairs,' he told Angelo, 'and it's a long time since I first discovered what's really wrong with the world. The life of the world, you see, depends on three things: Production, Consumption, and Distribution. Now in our time, if you care to put it so, Science has gone to bed with Production and produced Abundance. So that's all right. As for Consumption, the world is full of Consumers, a new one is born every minute, and their nature is such that they will consume anything that is put before them. So there is no difficulty there. But Distribution is a different bottle of wine altogether. Distribution has become Politics, and Politics is something that enables people who can find no other sort of pleasure to purse their lips and say, "No, you cannot do that until I give you permission!" Oh, politics is a powder to make a man spew! And I do not like that, Angelo, I do not think it is good. So then, when I am able to do so, I decide to dissociate myself from political distribution and be a Free Distributer. And what is the result? I make a lot of money and everybody is glad to see me. I feed my fellow-men, and I feed myself. I am a benefactor and I grow rich – and all because I have been thoughtful, I made plans! I saw what was desirable. I found the means to perform it, and with an abundance of good will I set to work.'

Angelo drank a little wine, and reaching across the untidy table shook Sergeant Vespucci by the hand. 'It is admirable,' he said. 'You are a good man, Sergeant. And in Rome, I suppose, you sell most of your produce in the Black Market?'

'Naturally,' said the Sergeant, 'I have my agents in the Black Market. For a Free Distributer it is the only way.'

'Have you not found the German authorities very troublesome?'

'On the contrary,' said the Sergeant. 'No, I have had no difficulty with them. They are commercial, you see, and if a man is commercial you can deal with him. They are greedy, of course, and very suspicious, but if you flatter them and pay them lavishly you can get on very well with them. During the last few months I have been able to distribute German rations and German petrol, to the value of many thousands of lire, among Roman citizens who were greatly in need of them. – But what is going to happen now? That is what I ask myself. Will the Allies co-operate in so reasonable a manner? *Speriamo*, we say, and we can say no more.'

'And when will you return to Rome?'

'As soon as possible. I came here the day before yesterday, to avoid trouble of any sort, and when I can return without trouble I shall. And now let us have one more glass of wine, and then I should like to sleep for an hour or two.'

The farmer in whose house they were was one of Sergeant Vespucci's business acquaintances. He, while they slept, went to the wood where Simon's little column had met the white cattle – he had recognized Angelo's description of the scene – and on his return reported that a vast number of dead Germans lay upon the road and among the trees, but there was no sign of the Englishmen or their vehicles. Close questioning reduced the bodies he had seen to ten, but he still insisted that all of them were German, and Angelo was infinitely cheered by the inference that Simon and his men had survived the encounter. The farmer also brought news of the German retreat. The Tedeschi, he said, were leaving Rome that night, there was no doubt about it. The countryside was full of rumours and tense with excitement. People were going to and fro, with increasing boldness, and every one of them had some new story of the enemy's plight.

None of them went to bed, and several times during the night men came in, singly or two or three together, to ask what news they had and bring in exchange their own most recent information. At six o'clock in the morning a boy pushed open the kitchen-door and shouted, 'They're in! The Americans are in Rome!' Then he disappeared, and though they at once pursued him, clamouring for details, they saw nothing more of him than his backside and the rear wheel of his bicycle. Stooped over the handle-bars, he was racing for the city.

Sergeant Vespucci told the farmer's wife to make some coffee, and went to harness his horse and trap. 'Are you coming?' he said to Angelo.

'Do you think it is safe?'

'I shouldn't be going if I didn't.'

The coffee was excellent. 'American,' said the Sergeant, 'from Naples. The Americans have very good rations, better than anyone else. Drink up, Angelo, I am becoming impatient!'

There was a freshness in the air that made the mere acts of moving in it and breathing delightful. In the east a narrow border of clouds looked like sheeps' wool caught on a wire fence, but elsewhere the sky was a pale undifferenced blue. A pair of young jays fled noisily into a bush, the mother-bird chattering behind them. Webs of gossamer gleamed in the hedge-high sun.

Sergeant Vespucci touched his mare with the whip. 'She is a good one,' he said. 'Ten years old, but she had never done any work till I bought her. No real work; nothing but hunting. I bought her cheap, because her owner couldn't feed her. But I am able to give her some corn, thank God.'

They went at a great pace and met no soldiers on the road until they came within a mile or two of Rome. Then they encountered an American armoured car, and passed another, stationary, whose commander was watching the progress of the first. Some distance farther on they were stopped and questioned by an officer who, in the open top of his car, had been volubly conversing with someone unseen by radio-telephone. Their papers were in order, the officer accepted Angelo's story that he had fallen sick while on a mission with a detachment of Force 69, and they were allowed to proceed. Then they approached a squadron of tanks. In the shade of tall trees they looked like monsters of a new pleiocene twilight, and as dinosaurs after breakfast might smell of blood, so these stank of petrol. The long gun that projected from the leader's turret travelled slowly from side to side like the long stiff neck of a brontosaurus sniffing the breeze. On the road beside it a major was eating a dough-nut. He beckoned to Angelo and the Sergeant, spoke to them with his mouth full, and after questioning let them go.

Their road returned them to the Via Aurelia, where they saw a long line of soldiers moving out from Rome. Their drab uniforms were stained and dirty, they were laden with the tools and weapons of the infantry. They were bent by the weight they carried, and as if their potshaped helmets were intolerably heavy, their heads were bowed. The pallor of long fatigue lay on their faces, and it was many days since they had shaved. They took little interest in where they were going, but with downcast eyes followed the heels of the man in front.

'And they have won their battle!' said the Sergeant. 'What in God's name do the losers look like?'

'What a dreadful burden victory must be!' said Angelo.

But when they entered Rome it became evident that the populace thought differently, and regarded the Allied victory as an occasion at least as splendid as the production of a new opera. Everywhere on the streets there were Romans who applauded the passing troops, held their hands high and clapped them loudly, tossed flowers into jeeps and tank-turrets, and boisterously demanded in exchange caramels, and biscuits, and cigarettes.

Angelo and the Sergeant crossed the Tiber – 'So they did not blow-up the bridges!' said Angelo thankfully – and on the other side found more numerous crowds and listened to ever more jubilant applause. In every quarter the Americans were hailed as actors in a gala performance, and for some considerable time they responded very graciously. Like artists bestowing their autographs, they threw cigarettes, caramels, and biscuits to their admirers wherever they went.

Sergeant Vespucci complained loudly against this prodigality. 'It is bad for trade,' he said. 'They are worth a lot of money, all those cigarettes and biscuits, and they should be distributed in a fair and orderly manner to those who can pay for them. The Germans gave nothing away, they were very correct.'

He stabled his mare in a little street not far from the Piazza dei Satiri and the trattoria where Angelo had once conferred with Fest and the German deserters, and then they went out to mingle with the crowd and share the common pleasure. The morning was fine, the air grew warm, and the sun shone with a genial glow on walls the colour of honey or the colour of the ripe flesh of a melon. Even Sergeant Vespucci yielded to the general infection, and taking some flowers from a pair of little girls who did not know what to do, threw them to the crew of a passing field-gun.

Presently, drifting with the crowd, they found themselves near the Campidoglio, and hearing that some ceremony was toward, climbed the steps to see what it might be. At the far end of the Piazza the double flight of Michelangelo's staircase rose over a fountain to the great stone balcony of the Palazzo del Senatore. On the balcony stood a little cluster of Generals – in dress distinguishable from the common soldiers only by the white stars painted on their helmets – who, with maps spread before them on the broad stone balustrade, were busily conferring, active with their index fingers, and seemingly unaware of the spectators who stood below and gazed intently at the scene.

'What are they looking for on their maps?' asked Angelo. 'Do they not know where they are?'

'It is always the same with Generals,' said the Sergeant. 'They and their maps, they are like a woman with her knitting. When there is nothing else to do, out it comes.'

There was at sudden commotion in the small crowd as two cars drove up, and from them, before they had stopped, sprang a dozen men so fierce of aspect, so ponderous yet quick in movement – they ran with a jungle-stoop – that Angelo caught his breath in a momentary gasp of fear. He thought, in that startled second, they were assassins and this a plot to murder the victorious Generals in their hour of triumph. But then he perceived that the newcomers wore American uniform, and the implements they carried were merely cameras.

Some of the photographers, disdaining the marble stair-case, ran up the balustrade that curved like an elevated bow high above the fountain, and presented their cameras at the Generals on the balcony as if they had been highwaymen and were holding them to ransom. The Generals affected disregard of their presence but assumed a more intense interest in their maps, or a more authoritative demeanour. Then, to placate the photographers who had arrived by the normal route, they turned attractive profiles in their direction and put on expressions of sapient authority. Every new pose excited the photographers to fresh demands, and some of them now clambered to window-sills above the group, so that they could secure a picture of helmets bent in studious contemplation; while others, clinging with one great hand to the balustrade, like apes in an equatorial forest, lowered themselves to some perilous roost on a scanty foothold of baroque ornament, and tilted their cameras upward to obtain a view of military jawbones in steely outline and soldier-nostrils adequately distended.

What terrifying faces they have, and with what passion they go about their business, thought Angelo as he contemplated a photographer poised like a chamois on a little peak of carved stone – another hanging like a sailor from the yard-arm – a third press closely in like a throat-specialist with his laryngoscope – and a fourth like Death himself command his victim to be still. And how meekly, yet in what comely postures, the Generals obeyed!

Posterity, said Angelo to himself, will look at these pictures and admire them. But posterity will know nothing of what I have seen, and that is the bloodshot eyes of the photographers who took them, their maniacal expression, and long simian arms. How I wish that I could live for ever and tell my great-great-grandchildren about life!

His thoughts were interrupted by a dearly loved and well-known voice. 'Angelo!' it said. 'My dear boy, how are you, and what have you been doing all this time?'

He turned, and with a blink of astonishment recognized the Count. Astonishment, because the Count had changed so much. He was bare-headed, and his hair was white as growing cotton. He still carried himself jauntily enough, but his clothes, though they were not exactly shabby, had the look of a suit that is worn without much relief. His shirt was in its second day, and his shoes had not been cleaned that morning.

'Oh, my dear – my dear Don Agesilas!' cried Angelo. 'What has happened to you?'

'Come, come,' said the Count, 'do I look like the victim of circumstance?'

'No, not at all,' said Angelo in a hurry, 'but it is so long since we have met that something or other must have occurred. No one, in times like these, can live for more than a week or two without things happening to him.'

'That is perfectly true, and when I tell you the whole tale of my adventures you will, I have no doubt, be properly astonished. But I should not like to think that I show any sign of misfortune, or carry the visible scars of unhappiness.'

'No, indeed you do not,' said Angelo. 'You are looking very well, and white hair suits you wonderfully.'

'Not white!' exclaimed the Count. 'I admit to a touch of grey above the ears, such as you might expect in a man of my years, but surely you cannot call it white?'

'It is the way the sunlight falls upon it,' said Angelo apologetically. 'But now when I look at it more closely – oh yes, I was quite mistaken.'

'You gave me a little shock,' said the Count with a smile, 'but think no more of it. Tell me, instead, about your own affairs. What fortune have you had, and why do you wear that uniform?'

'I am now serving with the English,' said Angelo, and turned to speak to Sergeant Vespucci and bring him into the conversation. But the Sergeant had gone, and as he was about to comment on his disappearance it occurred to him that Vespucci, perhaps, was unwilling to meet his late commanding officer for reasons best known to himself. So Angelo said nothing about him, but asked the Count what news he had had from Pontefiore.

'None at all,' said the Count. 'Very little news comes to me now, for I am, in truth, little better than a ghost. Officially I died in early March. But come, let us find a quiet place in which to talk and exchange our stories in peace.'

A short distance from the excited streets they found the old Forum empty and calm and still, like the garden of a deserted house, so they sat themselves comfortably on the turf under a large tree, and the Count told Angelo about his flight to Montenero, his arrest by the Germans after Fest had killed the two strangers, and his nightmare journey to the cave. Angelo fell into an extreme agitation as he listened, and the Count, seeing what an appreciative audience he had, spared no pains to make his recital as dramatic as possible.

After their last-minute reprieve, he explained, they had been taken back to the school, and there he had seen Fest, himself a prisoner, walking between his guards. They had had an hour or so in which to contemplate with tears and wonder their good fortune, and then the bombers had come. Only a few bombs had fallen in Montenero itself, but they had caused great confusion and laid open the school as if it had been a doll's house. How many of the prisoners succeeded in escaping from that smoky chaos the Count did not know, but he thought a good many, and perhaps nearly all of them. He himself had spent most of the day in a barber's shop, wrapped in a sheet with lather on his face, and whenever the Germans came in, searching for the fugitives, the friendly barber was shaving him. But in the evening the barber had grown frightened, and refused to help him further. The Count had passed a miserable night, playing in the streets a desperate game of hide-and-seek, for the Germans were still hunting the runaways, because Fest was among them. He had heard this news in the barber's.

'And then in the early morning,' said the Count, 'when I was very nearly at the end of my tether, I found safety. To be precise I smelt it. There was a baker's shop at the end of a lane down which I was slinking like a thief. He, poor fellow, was already at work, and the scent of his labour was delicious. I was drawn to it like a starving kitten to a saucer of milk. And then, as I approached the open door of the bakehouse, I heard a woman's voice raised in anger. Cautiously I peered in, and there was the baker's wife berating and denouncing her little husband for some newly discovered fault, I know not what. He was a scrubby fellow, black-avised, with the flour showing white on his hairy arms and smearing his unshaven cheeks. But she was splendid! She had crossed the lane, from their house on the other side, on her bare feet, clad only in her night-gown, and against the light of an oil-lamp I could see the shape of her body. It was a body of the sort that one turns to for comfort. Nothing of grossness about it, I assure you of that, but rather for the winter than a warm May. So I waited until the connubial dispute was done, and when she came out I spoke to her.

'She was quick-witted and no great argument was necessary. She told me to follow her, and closed the door of the house behind us. I saw then that her face also was handsome, in the hardy way of our countrywomen, and her age about twenty-eight or thirty. She smelt of new bread and the warmth of a pillow, and I almost forgot the distress I was in. Bless her heart, she was good to me and kept me hidden all that day, and later she smuggled me out of Montenero into the country where she had a sister who had married a farmer. An older sister, a dozen years older perhaps, but in her day she had been just such another as the baker's wife, and though she had lost her looks she liked to have a man in the house to make much of. And I needed care by then, for I was suffering like one of the damned from all the fears that I had previously kept at arm's length, but now came crowding in upon me like chickens to be fed. What I needed was simple kindness, and I found it in a very simple house.'

'It was no more than common courtesy to look after you,' said Angelo.

'Is such courtesy so common? I am glad to hear it. But these people, mark you, were also tactful. For it fell to the farmer's lot to inform me that I was dead, and he did it with the utmost delicacy yet with genuine feeling, and assured me that his regard for me was undiminished. The Germans, you see, had announced the execution of all whom they had arrested for the murder of the two men killed by Fest. Many of us, perhaps most of us, had certainly escaped, but the Germans had their dignity to consider, and the inevitability of their justice had to be asserted. So they put up a notice that said we had been shot.'

'That could not hurt you very deeply,' said Angelo.

'It hurt me bitterly,' said the Count. 'True, I did not feel the hurt until a few days ago, when I came into Rome, a refugee. I entered with some forty or fifty companions, expelled from their houses because the Germans were going to blow them up or fortify them. – I do not know which, and it would make very little difference in the long run. – I came back to Rome, I tell you, and discovered that after the announcement of my death my property had been seized and my furniture sold. I am a homeless pauper, Angelo! And because I am dead, I cannot even complain!'

They discussed this lamentable predicament for some time, and then the Count, with a flyaway motion of his fingers and the politest affectation of a yawn, dismissed his own affairs as being of small interest, and commanded Angelo to tell his adventures. These he listened to with close attention, and having sympathized with Angelo for the hardships he had endured, congratulated him most warmly on the success with which he had survived them.

'And now,' he said, 'let us go to lunch.'

LORENZO, THE Count's butler, disliked having to serve a dead man. He held the dish of spaghetti at arm's length, and shook his head with timorous disapproval when the Count asked for wine.

The Germans had told him that his master had been shot, and never had he dared question anything which they said. He had discussed the tragedy long and lugubriously with his friends, and then put the Count away in a cupboard of his memory that he kept for those who had met a violent end. He had watched the removal of the furniture and the formal closure of the house, and no doubt remained in his mind – such as it was – that he had finished with the Count forever. He himself suffered no inconvenience, for he had been left in possession of his own quarters, at the back of the house, as a caretaker.

When the Count appeared and demanded to know what had happened, Lorenzo had been frightened out of the few wits he possessed, and had it not been for Giulia his wife the Count would have fared poorly. But Giulia had welcomed him with tears of joy and a bustle of preparation for his comfort. She had put clean sheets on her bed and contrived a shakedown in a sort of cupboard for herself and her husband; on which Lorenzo used to lie and shiver to think of the ghostly visitor in the room beyond. The Count enjoyed whatever amenities could be provided in so humble an abode, and, as he told Angelo, he had no scruple about enjoying them; for Lorenzo, despite his stupidity, had robbed him right and left for years.

It was late in the afternoon, after the Count had slept for an hour or two, when Giulia came in to tell them that if they wanted to hear *Papa* they had better hurry. It was half-past five, she said, and at six o'clock the Holy Father was going to speak to his people, who were now gathering like a swarm of bees, like twenty swarms and many of them carrying banners as well, in St Peter's Square.

Immediately the Count was in a great hurry to go, for not only was he in a fine mood for thanksgiving, he said, but the Pope would assuredly give them his blessing, and in his present state he was in urgent need of benediction. So he and Angelo became part of the multitude that was going from every direction to St Peter's. So vast a number of people filled the roads that it seemed as if, not Rome, but all the world was on its way, and in the din of voices there was high expectancy, and the host of faces of every sort and shape and variety all wore a look of exhilaration.

'These Romans,' said the Count complacently, 'are a very wicked people, as most people are, and extremely proud. But every now and then they reveal their faith with a simplicity that is pure as a child's. You may have noticed that although they have been applauding the Americans with great good will, there has been a certain reserve in their manner? They threw flowers in plenty, but they did not throw their hearts as well. They are Romans, and Rome has seen many conquering armies and the concluding act of many well-performed historical dramas. They recognize the Americans as accomplished actors, and they give them the plaudits due to actors. But not for a moment do they believe that either the Americans or the English wrote the play. No, indeed! And that is why they have been saving their enthusiasm, and why they are going to show it now. For now they are going to shout for the author.'

They arrived at the far end of the Square as the bells began to ring, and though they were a great distance from St Peter's still, even far from the enfolding colonnades, they could make little more progress, for in front of them was such a host of people, tightly crammed together, as they had never seen before. They were indeed carried slowly forward before the impetus of some thirty, forty, or fifty thousand late arrivals, but their further movement was involuntary. They became a little part of the crowd, and moved with it or not at all.

Two diminished beings came out of a window high on the broad face of the Church, and hung from a balcony a large crimson carpet with a dove embroidered at the centre. With six reverberant strokes the hour was struck and the white figure of the Pope appeared on the balcony with a pair of attendant officers. Wave after wave of prodigious cheering rolled across the Square and broke upon the Church, and such was the turbulence of waving arms and shaken banners that it seemed as though a great gale had instantly burst from the sky and set all those hands to frantic motion like the leaves of a vast forest. Then, as suddenly as it had broken, the gale was stilled, the whole level of the Square subsided, and the huge crowd knelt.

Amplifiers gave the Pope's voice a more than human power, and every phrase came clear and resonant from the mouth of a trumpet. He offered thanks for the safety of the City, and commanded the Romans to show themselves worthy of the grace they had received. 'Shape your lives to the gravity of this hour,' he said. 'Cease from discord. Lift up your hearts!'

The gale of applause broke again, and roared for several minutes. The Pope returned to the balcony and waved a white-winged arm. The applause was renewed.

'What did I tell you?' demanded the Count. 'Rome has been saved, and who did it? You can't deceive the Romans!' And cupping his hands to his lips he shouted, 'Author! Author!'

The Pope returned, and lifted both his wings.

Nobody was in a hurry to leave the Square. The crowd made little effort to disperse, and no one tried to disperse it, but very gradually it melted. Parts of it, in the process, piled-up on other portions like ice-floes in a river when the thaw has begun. Among the many tens of thousands of people there were hundreds of vehicles, of all sorts from horse-drawn market-gardeners' wagons to scout-cars of the

Fifth Army, and when the outward movement began these were quickly boarded by pedestrians, most of them young women. Jeeps that began the afternoon with a load of four doughboys now carried in addition half a dozen well-grown girls and a couple of little brothers belonging to one or other of them. Drivers endeavoured to steer through the crowd with a girl on either knee and a prancing young man on the bonnet waving an ensign big enough for a battleship. Old men, bewildered but happy, found snug seats on the wings of a staff-car, and stout women, squawking like delighted geese, were hauled into troop-carriers. Flagstaffs were thrust into unprotesting faces, children were rescued from a thousand deaths, everybody was shouting or singing, and not an inch of soldiers' khaki but had about it a soft foliage of printed cotton, white linen, or flowering silk.

With an arm of prodigious strength an American sergeant saved the Count from the wheels of a command-car. Angelo, tightly confined by the crowd, saw Simon's troop some twenty yards away, their two vehicles so packed with nubile girls that they looked like haywains loaded with apple-blossom. Another American handed the Count a large cigar. Angelo kissed a girl who had just been given a drink by a corporal from Minnesota, and a moment later was embraced by another whose mouth was full of chewing-gum, the gift of an ammunition-number from Rhode Island. The Count was riding on a guntractor with a long lad from Arizona who was inviting him to come and visit the Double L Ranch near Tucson. Nobody cared if the traffic jam should last all night. *Papa* had said, 'Lift up your hearts!' and their hearts were glad.

An hour later, walking idly in a street that was but thinly peopled, the Count said, 'This is the temper in which all the world should live for ever.'

'That would be most agreeable,' said Angelo.

'Our besetting sin, as I discovered in my darkest hour, is hardness of heart. Take off, my dear Angelo, the tough and leathery jacket, like a bull's hide, that encloses your natural heart.'

'I do not think it has any such covering,' said Angelo. 'I have often wished for some protection of that nature, but all in vain.'

'You are fortunate,' said the Count. 'If your heart is tender, and naked to every pinprick and every joy, then you are truly fortunate.'

'It is a new way of looking at things,' said Angelo with doubt in his voice.

A little while later the Count said, 'I should like to invite some three or four hundred of these charming Americans to my house, and give them a party.'

'All your doors are locked,' said Angelo.

'We could break them open.'

'But your rooms are unfurnished.'

'That is true, unhappily. But would it matter?'

'You have no food or wine to offer them.'

'No,' said the Count with sudden melancholy, 'I have nothing. How miserable it is to have nothing for one's friends.'

Angelo was silent, and the Count said, 'You are not very sympathetic tonight.'

'I am thinking of Lucrezia,' said Angelo. 'If she were here to share our happiness, I should be happy indeed, and I might be tolerably happy if only I could forget her. There was a girl in the crowd who pleased me very much, and I was getting on well with her till I remembered Lucrezia. And then I let her go.'

'To be in love,' said the Count, 'is to suffer a perpetual torment for the sake of relieving it, from time to time, with a dab of delicious ointment. It is a ridiculous state of affairs, and the only cure for it is to grow old. But you have to grow very old.'

On the next day Rome had returned to its normal mood, and to some approximation of its normal conditions. The shops were open, a few tramcars were running, and the Army of Liberation had become merely the latest of the many armies which, in the long course of its history, had entered the city for some purpose of their own. Those who had anything for sale, be it a fountain-pen or their person, were still attentive to the foreign soldiers, but clearly regarded them as heaven-sent customers rather than divinely inspired liberators. The solid citizens went about their business, intent upon their own affairs, and charming girls in summer frocks rode their bicycles uphill and down with never a glance for the perspiring soldiers who had come to their rescue. Only the Count was still faithful to them.

All morning he and Angelo walked in the principal streets for no other purpose than to enjoy the spectacle of the relieving soldiery in holiday temper. Nine out of ten were Americans, but here and there was a little group of English or Scots from the bridgehead in Anzio. The Count was disappointed in the British, who went to and fro without displaying any emotion at all. They looked at the Colosseum and agreed that a lot of work must have gone into the building of it. They stared dubiously at the well-supplied shop-windows, and said that Rome couldn't have known there was a war on. They said that St Peter's reminded them of St Paul's.

The Count wasted little time on the British, but courted American society with ever-growing pleasure. Britannic phlegm and Roman indifference had no diminishing effect on the exuberance of the Americans, who paraded the streets with boisterous enthusiasm or sat upon the pavements with endearing familiarity and offered conversation to everyone who passed, but especially to young females.

'They are all so friendly,' declared the Count, as two lieutenants stopped their jeep beside a couple of girls and invited them to come for a ride. 'And what boundless hospitality they offer!'

'See how confidently they make themselves at home,' he said, a little while later, and pointed to three privates who, with their backs to a shop-window, were sitting comfortably on a pavement in the Piazza Barberini. 'Truly they are citizens of the world who can make themselves at home wherever they go. And how full of fun they are,' he added as the nearest soldier seized the ankle of a young matron who was rash enough to pass within arm's reach. 'What did he say to her, Angelo?'

'He said, "Hiya, toots".'

'Hiya, toots,' repeated the Count. 'I like that. It is the felicitous expression of a young people who are making their own language, and making poetry of it. It is brisk as a challenge, yet genial and democratic. Yes, I like it.'

An acquaintance of his own walked by: a tall lady in black with a long grey face and heavy eyelids. 'Hiya, toots,' said the Count.

'But look at him!' he went on, pointing to a thickset doughboy with a truculent expression who stood upon the edge of the pavement. On his left breast he wore several ribbons and some brooches, and from each of his hip-pockets protruded a bottle of wine. 'Now he,' said the Count, 'is quite obviously a man of sterling character and wide experience. To carry one bottle shows forethought, to carry two indicates hospitality. One for himself and one for his friend: yes, you can say with certainty that he is both provident and generous.'

An impudent little boy approached the doughboy with outstretched hand. '*Niente sigaretti!*' shouted the doughboy. '*Niente caramelli, niente biscotti! Via!*'

'Oh, the poor fellow!' said the Count, 'he has given away everything he possessed.' And with a smile of understanding he offered a packet of cigarettes that he himself had recently acquired.

'Aw, nuts,' said the doughboy, and pushed him on to the road, where he narrowly escaped being run over by an amphibious jeep that came at great speed round the corner from the Via Vittorio Veneto. It was driven by an enormous negro who wore a pair of white-rimmed sunspectacles and was smoking a cigar. He drove his curious vehicle twice round the square, and then, still at high speed, disappeared down the Via Tritone.

'Their vitality is amazing,' said the Count. 'Quite, quite amazing.'

They walked slowly on, up the tree-lined curving street,

but turned to the left before they reached the Pincio gate. Outside an hotel were some twenty military cars, of various kinds, and in the doorway stood a group of officers, talking. They were British, and Angelo, suddenly exclaiming, ran across the street and with a delighted smile saluted one of them with the characteristic high-handed gesture he had learnt in Force 69.

'And where have you been?' asked Simon. 'Did the cow give you a good ride?'

'It was an ox,' said Angelo, 'and quite uncontrollable. I had to ride it for many miles in the most horrible discomfort. I am still a mass of bruises.'

'Well,' said Simon, 'you've turned up at the proper time. We are going south again tomorrow, and you can come with me if you like. I found a jeep that had no visible owner, and I am using it.'

'I should like to introduce,' said Angelo, 'the Count Piccologrando of Pontefiore.'

For a few minutes the Count and Simon exchanged small talk and compliments, but their conversation developed no warmth, and the Count's attention visibly wandered when a large car went by filled to overflowing with American soldiers and self-assured young women of the town. In his festival mood the British were no good to him. He still desired American company, and declining Simon's invitation to lunch he walked briskly down the Via Francesco Crispi towards more populous streets where he would be certain of meeting, in large numbers, the New World's uninhibited defenders.

Angelo came running after him. 'You understand,' he said, 'that I am bound to go with Captain Telfer? I am in British service now.'

'Have no qualms,' said the Count. 'You can leave me here in the assurance that I shall fare well and find a sufficiency of friends.'

'I dare say the Marchesa Dolce will soon be returning.'

'She is in Rome now. She came back a month ago, but she is indisposed. In her rustic exile she put on a little weight, and until her masseuse has restored her to her customary proportions she does not care to be seen.'

Standing in front of a jeweller's shop two khaki-clad girls were seriously inspecting the display in the window. 'Look!' said the Count in sudden excitement. 'They are Americans! American women!'

'I think they are nurses,' said Angelo.

One of them walked slowly on, the other lingered. With a quick handclasp the Count said good-bye to Angelo, and approached her. He bowed with the grace of an older world. 'Hiya, toots,' he said.

Angelo sighed and went to look for a sergeant of Simon's troop whom he had been told to find. He tried to console his loneliness by thinking of Lucrezia, but with indifferent success.

In the morning he and Simon drove out of Rome by the Via Appia and they soon began to overtake the slow traffic of returning refugees. Nearly all carried heavy loads and were bent beneath their burdens; but some were remarkably cheerful. They were going home, and few of them yet knew what had happened to their homes.

The pleasant little towns along the Appian Way had suffered, quite suddenly, such a change in their appearance as could only have been effected – without the help of science – by long eras of disaster. Our age of steel and explosives had shown itself very like the Ice Age in its ability to alter the face of a landscape, create lacunae, and remove excrescences. Wedding-chamber and warm kitchen, the smithy and the grocer's shop and the notary's office had been reduced to rags and dusty rubble by a stick of bombs that caught the sunlight as they fell. With a huff and a puff the metallurgist and the chemist had blown away the long toil of many simple masons, and whole families who had spent their arduous and patient years in the growing of corn and wine had vanished in a little acrid smoke. A bridge that had served a thousand needs, and many thousand brisk and busy people, and filled its valley with arcs of beauty and proud columns, had been demolished with boisterous success by a cartload of guncotton . . . Of all the triumphs that had marched the Appian Way none had so spaciously shown the enormity of human power as this great spectacle of destruction; and the pity was that the refugees could not appreciate it as it deserved. The refugees were unimpressed by the march and the majesty of science. They were thinking only about their homes. Tired as they were, and stumbling under their burdens, they hurried on towards their abandoned villages with hope in their straining muscles, hope in their bright eyes. And when they came to their villages they sat down and wept.

Some of them, bracing their arms against the backboard of an overloaded cart or heaving at the spokes of a wheel, laboured to keep their cargo moving while the rack-ribbed horse between the shafts trembled with exhaustion and pecked uncertainly on the uphill road. On top of the corded pile of feather-beds and chairs and cooking pots might be a shrivelled grandmother in dusty black and a couple of astonished children.

'If there is any creature in the world more miserable than a refugee,' said Simon, 'it is a refugee's horse.'

'There is no liberation for horses,' said Angelo.

'None,' said Simon.

Angelo sighed. 'They have at least been spared that.'

They passed a very old man who was pulling a handcart loaded with a chest of drawers, a mattress, the frame of an iron bed, two saucepans and a variety of articles tied in a red blanket, and a goose in a basket.

'All these people,' said Angelo, 'have been liberated and now they have nowhere to live. And before the war is over you will have to liberate northern Italy and France, and Greece and Yugoslavia, and Holland and Belgium, and Denmark and Poland and Czechoslovakia.'

'It may take us rather a long time,' said Simon.

'And when you have finished no one in Europe will have anywhere to live.'

'You mustn't exaggerate. It won't be as bad as that.'

'*Speriamo*,' said Angelo.

The lately reclaimed fields of the Pontine Marshes lay drowned under great lakes of gleaming water, and the roofs of many little houses showed above the surface like tiny red islands. Of trees that had been planted for summer shade there remained in sight only tufts of branches like currant-bushes. A man in a boat tied his craft to a chimney and began to fish.

'I was very glad,' said Angelo, 'to see that the bridges over the Tiber had not been blown up.'

'Apparently the Germans made no attempt to blow them,' said Simon. 'Our journey wasn't necessary, as things turned out, but we had a very interesting time. After you mounted your cow –'

'It was an ox,' said Angelo.

'We fought a very successful little battle, and we had another skirmish, almost as good, at a cross-roads five or six miles further on. But when we came into Rome we had nothing to do except buy a few souvenirs. I got a dozen pairs of silk stockings and some very good perfume, and that was a great piece of luck, because by now, with all those Americans there, every shop will be stripped to the boards.'

'But surely looting is forbidden – at least in Rome?'

'Oh, they don't loot, you mustn't say that about them. The Americans aren't like that at all. They just go shopping. They have so much money there is no need for them to loot.'

'From where do they get so much money?'

'It is the same as we use,' said Simon. 'It is printed in the United States and it comes over by the ship-load.'

'And when the war is finished, and you and the Americans have all gone home, and there is nothing left in Italy but the money you have spent – will it be any good to us?'

'That is an interesting question.'

'Would it not be simpler to let your soldiers loot?'

'Angelo,' said Simon, 'there are occasions when you become tiresome.'

'I am not being unfriendly,' said Angelo in his most earnest voice. 'You must not think that, please. We are very grateful to you for coming to liberate us, but I hope you will not find it necessary to liberate us out of existence. When I think about the future –'

'Your future,' said Simon, 'is bound to be complicated by the fact that Italy came into the war quite wilfully, and then was quite decisively beaten.'

They were approaching the coast and Angelo pointed to the promontory ahead of them. 'There is Gaeta,' he said, 'which was so named by Aeneas after his nurse. I think people were more affectionate in those days. And there' – he pointed across the glinting sea – 'there to the westward is Monte Circeo, where Circe the Great Enchantress turned twenty-two of the companions of Ulysses into swine. But when Ulysses came to their rescue, and persuaded Circe to give them back their proper shape, he did not punish them very much for the disgusting things they did when they ran about on four feet. He was magnanimous.'

'Ulysses,' said Simon, 'had advantages that we have lost. In his time no one had heard of economics, and a popular leader was not responsible to a hungry electorate, but only to the gods. It was relatively easy to be magnanimous.'

WHEN NEWS OF THE Count's death came by devious routes to Pontefiore, his English Countess had been sustained in sorrow by her sturdy conviction that a person in her position, in time of general loss, could not afford much indulgence in private grief. She also admitted her native belief – Yorkshire was her birthplace – that foreigners met a violent end far more often, and more naturally, than the English; and a little while later she remembered, with appreciable comfort, the mourning she had been obliged to buy, a couple of years before, for an old uncle of Don Agesilas, a gentleman known as the Noble Signor of Rocca Pipirozzi. She had grudged the expense of it, for wealth had never obscured in her memory the narrow circumstances of her girlhood and youth in Bradford, and to spend more than five pounds or so, on anything that could not be regarded as an investment, always gave her a feeling of guilt. She found, therefore, in her great bereavement, a little quiet satisfaction in thinking that the extravagance with which she had mourned the Noble Signor would now be redeemed when those dreary and expensive garments became her widow's weeds.

She continued to go about her business of looking after Pontefiore with an apparent composure and real strength of mind that the villagers and the peasants thought most unnatural; but upon which they more and more came to rely as the front of battle was pushed northward into Tuscany. From the earliest days of her marriage she had busied herself among the people and with the affairs of her husband's estate, and now, when she had become the sole guardian of their interests, and life and property were equally menaced, she set about the problem of securing them, as far as possible, with great vigour and a constant anxiety.

For nearly three years her greatest solace had been the presence in her house, or in its vicinity, of the young man whom Angelo had seen and recognized as a stranger in Pontefiore, when in the previous autumn he had come home with the Count's pictures and two truck-loads of flour. This young man was an English soldier, a corporal in the Royal Engineers, Tom Trivet by name, who had been taken prisoner in Libya in the summer of 1941, and made his escape very soon after from a transit camp for prisoners of war near Bari. He had the advantage of knowing where he wanted to go, for his father had married a Miss Goodge, whose elder sister, a teacher in Bradford, had married Don Agesilas. So Tom Trivet, with the help of innumerable people on the way, had walked from Bari to Pontefiore and remained there ever since. But now, to his aunt's distress, he was about to leave.

Very soon after the surrender of Italy partisans had begun to appear who, in some parts of the country, declared for the Allies in a bold and forthright manner, but in other parts in a rather shy and tentative way. In the neighbourhood of Pontefiore they were neither numerous nor reckless, but a little company had gradually come into being under the leadership of Tom Trivet and a former member of the Guardia Civile called Pasquale; and some slight contact had been established with the Allied armies. Quite recently a signal had been received that included certain instructions for Corporal Trivet.

A few hours before he was due to leave he was sitting with the Countess in the small drawing-room that she always used in summer, for it was cool and overlooked a formal garden in which she took continual pleasure. The room itself was full of flowers, two canaries made small noises in a cage, and pale behind the mullioned glass of a bookcase showed the white and gold bindings of her favourite edition of Ouida.

A stranger, overhearing their conversation, might well

have denied the Countess's affection for her nephew; for with her northern sense of duty she was taking advantage of her last opportunity to lecture him for his ill behaviour, and her disapproval was enriched and fortified by a Yorkshire accent that seemed to accuse, not Corporal Trivet only, but all the Italian landscape of sins and follies unknown to Bradford.

'That my own sister's boy should act like that,' she was saying, 'and in a foreign country too, where it's our duty to set an example to people less fortunate than ourselves – no, Tom, no. I shall never forgive you. Though they may be the last words you'll ever hear from me, I can never forgive you.'

'You've forgiven me half a dozen times already, Aunt Edith.'

'And what's been the result? You just get worse and worse, and now you're completely shameless. And it's a falsehood to say that I forgave you. I may have agreed to overlook what happened, for the sake of peace, but that was the farthest I ever went. And it isn't as though it was one occasion only, as you know well. And you a married man!'

'I was married for five days, and I've had four years to think about it. If I'd taken four years to think about it first, I wouldn't have been married even for five minutes.'

'You never thought about the meaning of marriage, that was the mistake you made. There's nothing in life more serious than marriage, but you weren't serious at all. You were only thinking about a few days' pleasure, and how to guard against interruptions to it.'

A soldier in the Territorial Army, Tom Trivet had gone to France in the winter of 1939 and returned to England, in a motor-boat from Dunkirk, in the following May. In the peculiar circumstances of the time he had thought it reasonable to marry a girl of his own age – which was then twenty – whom he had known for some years, but who had never excited his emotions until war, and escape from battle, and the prospect of returning to battle had so heated them that any girl's breath could have blown them to flame. So they married and had their honeymoon in five days of leave, and six weeks later Tom had embarked for Egypt. Several months went by before her letters began to reach him, and when the first ones came, a whole parcel of them, he was dismayed. He had waited for them in a torment of emotional hunger, and when he sat down to read them, in a stony landscape dyed with the setting sun, he had found them as empty of nourishment as the sand that lay in crevices of the rock. There was a great deal in them, but nothing sweet or sound or satisfying.

In the weeks and months to come he read more and more of her letters, and as he thought of the well-turned limbs, the sleek yellow hair, and the innocent round face he had married, he grew increasingly puzzled and more and more depressed by the cloud of dust she created whenever she bent her head and shook out her brain over the writing-table. When Tom Trivet was captured, and his captors searched him, they found her last two letters in his pocket, unopened.

Now, to his aunt the Countess, he said sadly, 'We've had all this talk before, and it doesn't do any good, does it?'

'If it doesn't,' she answered, 'that's your fault and not mine. All you young people believe that because you want a thing, you're entitled to get it. But when I was young we were made to recognize our obligations. My generation was taught responsibility.'

'Not very well.'

'No, not very well. Human beings are full of imperfections, and you can't cure them overnight. But we tried.'

'And we're trying to do something quite different. You tried to make out that your way of life was worth preserving for ever, and we're trying to understand what it's all about.'

'By making love to half a dozen girls in Pontefiore!'

'They've taught me quite a lot,' said Tom.

'Nothing but self-indulgence.'

'And that's something too. I never had much chance to indulge myself in Bradford, and it wasn't till I came here that I realized how enjoyable life could be. I've been happier in Pontefiore than I ever was in my life before. It's an odd thing to say in the circumstances, but it's true enough and I feel all the better in consequence.'

'And the poor girls – do they feel better?'

'From time to time I've been led to believe so. – No, don't look at me like that, Aunt Edith. I didn't invent human nature.'

'You would have done, if you'd had the chance. You're brazen enough.'

Their arguments always followed the same pattern. The Countess would open the attack, and Tom defend himself with energy enough to make her deploy some early principles, a little moral indignation, and the zest that comes with berating a member of one's own family. Then when her eyes were sparkling and her lips compressed, he would begin his retreat – throwing out a few excuses to impede the pursuit – and when he saw the time was ripe for it, would offer his surrender. An acknowledgment that she was right, and he wrong, was all she ever asked for. She would assume that the past was dead and the future a clean page on which, with better fortune, no blot would ever fall. He, with a proper embarrassment, would accept her conclusion, and then for half an hour they would exchange kindly reminiscences of their native place. That was his only penance.

But now, when he had made his peace, discomfort remained in the atmosphere and with a renewed emotion, that neither would dream of mentioning, they remembered their impending separation. The Countess covered her feelings by inquiry about his socks and shirts, and Tom disguised his reluctance to leave by assuring her that he would soon return.

'I've got to go and meet this Captain Telfer,' he said, 'and there's only two things he can expect me to do for him. One is to show him the way about this part of the country, and the other is to help him with the partisans. I dare say I'll bring him straight back to Pontefiore.'

'But you won't stay here. The war has caught you up

again and your holiday's over. But we mustn't grumble,
I suppose. You've had nearly three years of it, and that's
a longer holiday than anyone gets in Bradford. And I've
enjoyed having you here, in spite of your behaviour.'

'Now don't start that again, Aunt Edith.'

She shook her head, and pursed her lips, and said, 'You'd
better go now and say goodbye to her. And I wouldn't be
in your shoes for a hundred pounds.'

A girl called Bianca was waiting for him on the bridge.
She was tall and pretty, with an oval face and enormous
eyes, one of which squinted a little. Her nature was warmly
affectionate and her figure suggested that prudence had been
no match for the ardours of her temperament. Tom Trivet
had been in love with her for several months, and if his
feelings were no longer so completely engaged as they had
been, the diminishment was more than made good by the
increase of her devotion. She held out her hands to him.
Her lips were tremulous, her eyes brim-full of tears. Tom
led her into the little wood beyond the bridge, and in the
humid heat of her embrace remembered the dry impersonal
kiss with which his aunt had bade him goodbye. Her kiss
had embarrassed him almost as much as Bianca's. More,
perhaps, for he had not cared to return it with any warmth
– though he wanted to – and while to begin with he was
reluctant to give Bianca measure for measure, he soon
perceived what decency required, and then found it easy
enough. There was a great deal of protestation, argument,
tears, and renewal of promises before he was allowed to
leave, but eventually Bianca appeared to find some comfort
in his assurances, and he set off for his rendezvous with
Captain Telfer.

At night, however, Bianca became hysterical and wept
noisily for more than an hour, after which she fell asleep and
dreamed that she was walking, blind and naked, in a strange
land where dreadful voices made unending lamentation; but
because she was blind she could not see who the mourners
were, and her hands could not find them, for their bodies
had no substance. A dozen miles from Pontefiore Tom Trivet

lay in the darkness and tried to guess how far away were the two German soldiers whom, from time to time, he could hear talking. He felt quite as lonely and friendless as Bianca.

The Countess spent most of that evening with her house-keeper and an elderly steward. So that they might avoid conscription by the Germans, she had given orders that all the younger people of the village should take to the woods, which as they reached the higher parts of the hills concealed the entrances to many caves; and to preserve the proprieties the young women had been directed to the woods east of Pontefiore, the young men to those west of it. She listened to reports of the exodus, and came at last to the conclusion that she had done everything possible for the safety of her tenants. 'Except, perhaps, for the Donati girls,' she said. 'For Lucia and Lucrezia, whom I sent some time ago to the Noble Lady of Rocca Pipirozzi. Do you think they will be safe?'

'*Speriamo*,' said the housekeeper.

'The house of the Noble Lady is some distance from the nearest road,' said the steward. 'It is a house that may well be disregarded by the Tedeschi.'

'It is, in any case, too late to make other arrangements for them,' said the Countess, 'and so they must trust in Providence. I should be happier if they were in a cave, but as that is impossible Providence will have to take the responsibility.'

The steward and the housekeeper agreed, and presently the Countess went to bed and slept as well as could be expected. The next day passed quietly, but on the morning after, as the Countess in her summer drawing-room was busy with her household accounts, she heard an unfamiliar voice, and going to the window saw a German soldier climbing over the garden wall. He was followed by two others, and then the three of them, who all carried ungainly automatic pistols and had bombs hung at their belts, stood in a group and were manifestly uncertain what to do next. The Countess was also in a state of strong incertitude, and until she could make up her mind remained in tactful concealment behind a curtain. The soldiers in the garden continued to argue, and the Countess felt her heart beating with, as it were, a disagreeable importunity. Then she heard other voices, the crash of breaking glass, and the housekeeper came in, agitated in voice and manner, to tell her that three German officers were in the hall, who demanded to see the owner of the house at once.

The senior of the three, a Captain Schlemmer, was in appearance by far the most interesting. Of medium size, of good and powerful build, the cast of his features was so handsome as to suggest the emulous work of a new Praxiteles; but some equally strong agent had ruined the tone of his facial muscles and the texture of his skin so that his beauty, though he was still young, showed itself only in the decay of what had been. An extreme, a fervent debauchery might conceivably have been the cause, but the Countess, who in her old-fashioned way had been brought up to believe not only in Good but in Evil, was convinced as soon as she saw him that he had sold his soul to the Devil. She regarded him in consequence with horror, but also with a respect that his companions failed to inspire. Lieutenant Peiss was a short strong man, dark of eye and chin, in no way remarkable; and Lieutenant Hofmeister was a tall youth with a foolish expression, a loose mouth, and flaxen hair that had not recently been cut. All three wore the blue overalls of a Parachute Regiment.

'You are the proprietor?' asked Schlemmer in easy Italian. 'Good! We have taken over your house, and you will do what I tell you. I want for myself a large room with a comfortable bed and a good view. Where is one that would please me?'

'My housekeeper will show you the way,' said the Countess.

'You will show me the way,' said Schlemmer.

'I can do it no better than she,' said the Countess, but led him upstairs.

All three officers followed her and in silence looked into several rooms as she, silent also, opened their doors. Then Schlemmer said, 'These do not satisfy me. Where is your own room?'

The Countess, who realized that her only policy was acquiescence, turned back across the upper hall that was flanked by the broad stone balustrade of the main staircase.

'A minute, please,' said Schlemmer, and stopped to examine one of a pair of large black and red Etruscan vases that stood upon the balustrade. 'A poor barbaric design,' he said. 'I do not like it at all.' And with a dismissive gesture he pushed it away. It fell with a loud crash into the hall below.

'You are quite right,' said the Countess calmly. 'They are just a bad imitation of the real thing, made for tourists only, and so I told my husband when he bought them.'

'That is a lie!' cried Schlemmer angrily. 'Do you think that I could be deceived by any modern fraud? I who have always been a lover of the arts? They are genuine Etruscan pottery, I tell you. Push the other one over, Hofmeister.'

Hofmeister with a snigger obeyed, and there was a second crash. 'I told my husband he was wasting money on them,' observed the Countess.

'You speak a very curious Italian,' said Schlemmer. 'Where do you come from?'

'I was born in Yorkshire.'

'In England? Oh no, it is too good to be true! We have an Englishwoman for our hostess, gentlemen. A lady, I beg her pardon. And so we shall be well looked after, for now I shall certainly insist upon that. Show me your room!'

He walked round it, lifted a few toilet articles, glanced out of the window, and said, 'It is not bad. I may use it, or if not Lieutenant Peiss can sleep here. What sort of rooms are over there?'

'Quite small,' said the Countess. 'That is the old part of the castle.'

Schlemmer was turning away when Hofmeister, at the entrance to a narrow corridor, exclaimed, 'This door is locked.'

'Open it,' said Schlemmer.

'It leads to some rooms that are never used,' said the Countess.

'Open the door,' said Schlemmer.

The Countess returned to her bedroom for the key, and when the door was opened a room hardly bigger than a closet was discovered. But beyond it was a larger chamber, and on one of its walls hung the Adoration of the Shepherds by Piero della Francesca. Schlemmer went close to examine it.

'That is genuine,' said the Countess.

'That is unlikely,' said Schlemmer. 'It is well done, but I am not inclined to think it is an original.'

'It was painted by Piero della Francesca.'

'Or by a skilful copyist. – Has the bed been aired?'

'Not for a long time.'

'Then have the sheets changed before night. I shall sleep here. Hofmeister and Peiss, you can go and choose rooms for yourselves. I recommend the Countess's for one of you. No, Countess, do not go. I want to order breakfast first.'

'It's long past breakfast-time,' said the Countess.

'It is breakfast-time when I want breakfast,' said Schlemmer, and throwing himself on the bed he dug his dusty heels into its blue silk covering, and doubled the pillows under his left arm for greater comfort. 'Since you are English', he said, 'it will give you pleasure, of course, to serve me with an English breakfast. You have bacon? And eggs? That is good. I shall have three or four slices, well fried, and three or four boiled eggs. Some toasted bread and cherry jam. All that is very English, is it not? But I do not want your English tea. Bring me instead a bottle of your best white wine, and a bottle of brandy. But not Italian brandy, which I do not like. In a house such as this you must have plenty of cognac. And send a girl to take off my boots.'

He lay alone, staring at the picture of the Adoration. It was, he admitted, a masterly piece of work. The quality of the paint was right. There was none of that fulsomeness with which a copyist, striving to do his subject justice, so often betrays himself; but all the tones had the gentleness of old colour that has lost its ostentation to the centuries. The gentleness of an aged champagne found in a forgotten bin that has outlived its effervescence. The gentleness of dawn and sunset in the older countries of the world where civilization has long since given docility and form to the reflecting earth. Yes, it was good. But the Englishwoman had said it was genuine, and she of course was lying. She was lying to deceive him for some purpose of her own; and therefore the picture was no better than a copy could be.

His breakfast came. He ate quickly, drank half the bottle of wine, and filled a claret glass with brandy.

It could be an old copy, even a contemporary copy. But the drawing of the mother's head had the firmness that suggests the originality of genius. Something is made, by genius, and nothing before it was ever quite the same, and nothing after will be. The novelty of genius is so strong that straightway it seems inevitable, it could have been done no other way; but it cannot be done again. If the Englishwoman had not said it was by Piero della Francesca it would have given him great pleasure to recognize the master's work. But she, there was no reason to doubt it, had been lying. Why should she tell the truth to him, her enemy? He finished his glass of brandy, and went out.

Under the supervision of Peiss and Hofmeister his company – it was much depleted – was hard at work. Preparations were being made for the demolition of the bridge, and packages of a red explosive lay on an abutment wall. 'We've got none too much,' said Peiss. 'This old masonry was built to last.'

'Make a proper job of it,' said Schlemmer.

Some of the houses at the far end of the village offered a wide field of fire, and German soldiers were reinforcing the ceilings of their outer rooms with timber. Schlemmer walked away from the village, down a slope that would be hidden from the approaching enemy, and chose positions for his mortars. He returned to the castle, sent for the Countess, and said to her, 'There is no one in the village but old men and women, and small children. Where are the young people hiding?'

'There are no young people here,' she said. 'They have all been taken for work of some kind or another.'

'By us?'

'By you or the Republicans.'

'Is that true?'

'If I swore it was true a hundred times you wouldn't believe me.'

Schlemmer stared at her for a few seconds without speaking, then turned abruptly and went back to his men. He gave orders that no one was to leave the village, but all its inhabitants must stay indoors, and continued his direction of the preparations for defence till it began to grow dark.

At dinner he was taciturn, and Hofmeister and Peiss, following his example, also ate silently. But despite the lack of conversation the meal was slow and deliberate, for Schlemmer from time to time would push away his plate, and leaning on his forearms stare unspeaking into a web of thought. They drank between them five bottles of red wine and half a bottle of brandy. 'The same cognac as you gave me for breakfast,' Schlemmer had ordered.

Then, rousing himself, he repeated with clarity and exactitude his instructions for battle, if the battle should come before morning, and saying good night, went to his room in the old part of the castle.

The electric light was still working, and because the shutters had been closed for several hours the air was stuffy. He undressed, poured himself another glass of brandy, and sat gazing at Piero's Adoration. 'If it is genuine it is good in the highest degree,' he muttered. 'But if it is a copy, it cannot be so good. I should know which it is, but I do not know. Why do I not know? Why cannot I say with certainty *This is good*, or *This is not so good*?'

The difficulty of answering this question induced a little self-pity, and he thought querulously of the Countess. 'It is her fault,' he said to himself. 'If she had not told me a lie, I should know what to think. They tell lies too cleverly, the English. They have no scruples, they are unfair.'

Quietly, and without pain, he began to cry, and remembered how in his childhood he had often wakened crying at night. But in spite of that he had been happy as a boy, and now his early years seemed all to have been lived in sunlight or among green trees. There were gleams of yellow and gold in his memory, of oranges and honey and the dining-room curtains on a morning of summer wind. He thought of his mother's large white arms, and his father's stubble hair. His father had been a professor at Freiburg, and he one of five children. He remembered the ridiculous family procession to church, every week, all in stiff clothes, and his father's cigar on the homeward walk. One Sunday there had been a strange preacher, a distinguished visitor to the university, who had slowly climbed the pulpit stair and before beginning his sermon had stood, for a long time as it seemed, looking from one to another of his congregation. Then quietly, as if disclosing a secret, he had said, '*Seid stille, und erkennt, dass ich Gott bin.*' 'Be still,' the strange pastor had repeated, 'and know that I am God.' Believing the words to be a statement of fact, he, still a child, had been badly frightened.

When he grew up he had quarrelled with his father, and later his father had been imprisoned because he held dangerous political views, and called himself a Liberal. His father had been a talkative man, given to expounding with great energy his views on every subject conceivable to man, but readily silenced by his wife's voice. 'Now Heinrich,' she would say, 'you are becoming tiresome. It may be so, and it may not be so. You should not go too far. Let us talk now of something else.'

'How do I know,' cried Schlemmer, starting from his chair, 'if it is good or not? How do I know, how do I know?'

He heard his own voice, and became cautious. 'Quiet now,' he murmured, 'be quiet. Take a sleeping draught, that's the thing. You've been out in the sun too long, your eyebrows are white as bleaching clothes. Take a sleeping draught.'

He filled the claret glass with brandy and drank it too quickly. He filled it again, took a little more, and hiccuped. Then, turning out the light, lay down and with hoarse breathing fell asleep.

In the last darkness before dawn he woke in fear. A nightmare that he could not remember had evicted him from sleep, and for a little while he lay in a panic, not knowing where he was. Then he found the switch, and light fell on Piero's Madonna, on the confident Child and the adoring Shepherds.

Schlemmer sat up frowning, biting his nails, and began to study the picture as though he had been wakened for the single purpose of learning its meaning. Though the child is confident, he thought, it is the mother who really knows its purpose. The shepherds, who are the base of the triangle, are eager to believe; but the mother, whose head is the apex, knows. That is quite clear. Nor is there any suggestion that she has been at pains to acquire her knowledge. It has come to her naturally, or she has heard a voice saying *Seid stille, und erkennt, dass ich Gott bin*. She is very grave, but she is happy.

'She is happy,' he said aloud, and a moment later, with a violent shudder, he screamed, 'It is a myth, the whole story is only a myth, and in any case the Englishwoman lied! It is not even the original, it is merely a copy!'

His breast heaved, he sat gazing at the picture. 'It is not true,' he whispered. 'It cannot be true. For if it is true – no, no! It must not be true!'

In the shuttered room the air was hot and still. The walls enclosed a little space in which all the light fell on Piero's Madonna, and she with a mild sublimity looked under white eyelids at the innocent assurance of her Son.

'It is not true, it is not true!' screamed Schlemmer, and stretching a shaking hand to the bedside table took from it a clumsy Schmeisser pistol and opened fire on the adoring shepherds.

The stuttering bullets raced up and down the picture, and before the last echo was dead there were voices at the door. Lieutenant Hofmeister was shouting, asking what had happened, and the Countess in a breathless voice as hoarse as a grasshopper was making the same inquiry of the Lieutenant.

Schlemmer opened the door and coldly inquired, 'What do you want here?'

'You are safe?' exclaimed Hofmeister. 'Who is in there? What has been happening?'

'I wished to see if you were alert. Is Peiss also at his post?'

'Yes, sir.'

'That is good. You can go now.'

'If you are going to behave in that way again,' said the Countess, 'will you give me warning?'

'Do not refer to my behaviour!' shouted Schlemmer. 'It is you: your lies – but no! You are of no importance now. Your day is over. You also can go.'

He locked his door again, turned out the light, and opened the window. He smelt the acrid pistol fumes as they drifted out, and breathed deeply of the morning air. Ten minutes later he lay down and slept soundly till his servant wakened him.

A little before noon a dispatch-rider appeared and gave Schlemmer a written order to withdraw his company from Pontefiore before midnight, and prepare for defence another position some three or four miles to the north of it. He read his instructions moodily, and sent for Peiss. 'Get ready to move,' he said.

'Already? What for?'

Schlemmer showed him the order.

'It's always the same,' said Peiss. 'They don't know their own minds, that's the trouble. You sweat your soul out, digging and working, and then all your effort's wasted.'

'We should get bombed in the morning, if we stayed,' said Schlemmer.

'I don't think they saw us.'

'They always see us.'

An aeroplane on reconnaissance, high in the blue sky, had flown to and fro above Pontefiore early that morning. The Germans had made no movement while they were under observation, and all their defensive works had been well concealed; but the appearance of a second aeroplane, an hour later, had made Schlemmer complain that the camouflage was still insufficient.

Now he said, 'There are some good draught-oxen in this village. We shall take them with us.'

'There's plenty of pigs too.'

'Have some of the oxen harnessed and put what pigs you want in the carts. We shall move as soon as it is dark. Now I shall go and look at this other village, and see what work we must do there. And Peiss –'

'Yes, sir?'

'You can tell the soldiers that I am not fond of Pontefiore, and if in the process of withdrawing there should be some damage to property, I shall have no time to listen to complaints.'

When he returned in the early evening, he walked for some little while in the castle grounds and found much to admire in the gentle formality with which they had been planned and planted. He admired the ingenuity of the topiarist, and thought the art a pleasing one. In front of him two living peacocks strutted nervously down a path between a pair of enormous peacock-images cut from the dense foliage of yew trees. The path was lined with other trees that had been clipped to the likeness of double candle-shades, and led to a stone balcony that overlooked a pool where among water-lilies goldfish swam, and a Triton in hoary stone blew his shell upon the bank. The lower terrace, patterned with a doubled design of dwarf hedges, was enclosed by a semi-circle of tall cypresses, all of equal stature, and beyond them the great slopes of Tuscany were clothed with the mellow evening light.

It has taken a long time, he thought, to make this beauty. From the beginning the hills were there, and the valleys divided them, but they were bare and meaningless before man came, with his art and purpose, to give them significance and define their form. The Etruscans did so much, the Romans more, and at the Renaissance they began again. They were good husbandmen who lived here. They desired beauty and they created it. It is a country

I also could live in, if we possessed it. I am sorry to leave it.

His hands were swollen with the heat. He knelt and cooled them in the goldfish pond, then rising, shook the water from his fingers and squaring his shoulders walked briskly back to the castle.

In the small garden below the Countess's drawing-room he stopped, hearing above him voices raised in anger or distress. From the open window, fluttering in its descent, a book flew out, and with it an angry scream. Another book came tumbling through the air, and Schlemmer perceived that both were bound handsomely in white leather. He listened for a moment or two, and then with a pleased smile went in.

Lieutenant Hofmeister rose from his chair, and the Countess, who had entirely lost her usual composure and was struggling in the grasp of two German soldiers, greeted Schlemmer with the strangest demand. 'My Ouidas, my Ouidas!' she exclaimed. 'For God's sake, save my Ouidas!'

'I should explain,' said Hofmeister, 'that I came in to choose a few books to take with me, and as I read a little English and wanted something light –'

'Light!' said the Countess. 'She is a great writer!'

'– I chose these novels by the woman who called herself Ouida. They are very prettily bound.'

'They are my dearest possession,' said the Countess.

'That interests me very much,' said Schlemmer. 'But why,' he asked Hofmeister, 'why did you throw some of them out of the window?'

'That was after she had refused to make me a present of them,' said Hofmeister. 'She had the impertinence to snatch one from my hands –'

'I slapped your face!' said the Countess.

'– so I had her put under restraint, and informed her that as a German officer I had the right to dispose of her property in any way I chose.'

'But naturally,' said Schlemmer. 'If, for example, you decided they were subversive, and should be destroyed –'

'Like this,' said Hormeister, and grasping one of the volumes by its elegant boards, he tore out the pages.

The Countess whimpered like a child, and tears ran down her cheeks to her quivering mouth. Schlemmer laughed softly and said, 'I disapprove of female writers. They are an evil influence in the world, they set a bad example, for women should bear children, not books. You had better destroy them all.'

'Let me keep one,' said Hofmeister, and put *Moths* in his pocket.

The small drawing-room was in a state of extreme dishevelment when they left it, but the village piazza, to which they walked together, presented an even stranger appearance; for it was littered with bedclothes, mattresses, and furniture that the soldiers had gathered from the houses of Pontefiore, and were now throwing into a large untidy heap. At nightfall they set fire to the heap, and many of the villagers, beside themselves with rage and despair, came rushing out of their houses in a vain attempt to save their precious goods from the flames. They were quickly driven back, however, when the Germans opened fire on them.

After the main body had marched away, Lieutenant Peiss remained with a rearguard to blow up the bridge. This he did an hour before sunrise, and was very well pleased with the demolition.

On the outskirts of the village he noticed, in a small orchard, half a dozen straw beehives. 'Why should they have honey to eat, when we are going into battle?' he asked.

A sergeant grinned, and took from his pocket a box of matches and some old letters. The straw was dry, and the beehives burnt fiercely.

CHAPTER FOURTEEN

'COME TRISTE LA VITA!' sighed Lucia, and lifted and stretched her plump brown arms, and opened her wide red mouth in a desolate yawn. The day was hot, and little yellow feathers clung to her fingers and stuck to her wrists. 'Nothing ever happens,' she said. 'Life goes by and leaves us here, alone and idle, without our men and therefore without pleasure or purpose in our existence. Oh, I am so dissatisfied, Lucrezia!'

She and Lucrezia, her younger sister, had been plucking a pair of hens in the green shade of a great vine that half-covered the wall and overhung the back door of a farmhouse. Beyond the farmyard the ground fell steeply to a narrow glen, and rose again to a round hill like a pudding-basin, but patched with trees and circled by a climbing path that here and there showed white among them. On the other side of the farmhouse was the large, squarely-built mansion of the Noble Lady of Rocca Pipirozzi.

The Noble Lady had been obliged to give hospitality, some weeks before, to a prolific niece and her seven children who had fled from their own house near Chiusi when the Germans entrenched in its grounds. As the Noble Lady lived in straitened circumstances, the Countess of Pontefiore had come to her help, and to augment her small domestic staff had sent her Lucia and Lucrezia Donati. They had come willingly enough, pleased by the offer of a change of scene, but soon had grown weary of a house duller than they had been accustomed to, and dominated now by a woman with a grievance and her numerous unattractive family. In memory, even so short a memory, Pontefiore and their own overcrowded home acquired a charm and a gaiety they had never, or never fully, appreciated till now. They longed to return, and with a desire sharpened by ennui they yearned for the company of their lovers.

'It is no life at all,' Lucrezia agreed, and holding up a naked hen she plucked from its loose skin a few remaining pin-feathers. Lucia clasped the other bird in her hands, and leaning forward, stared with mournful eyes at a daydream of her lost husband.

'It is more than a year since Enrico was taken,' she said, 'and who knows now whether he is alive or dead?'

'It is ten months since Angelo came home and went away again,' said Lucrezia, 'and I do not know whether he – he, my Angelo – is alive or dead.'

'You were not married,' said Lucia. 'It is not so bad for you.'

'It is worse for me,' said Lucrezia, 'because my nature is more affectionate than yours.'

'You have not so much self-control: that is what you mean, and we know that already.'

'I have so much self-control that often I am astonished at myself.'

'I remember one occasion when you astonished every body.'

'That is the sort of occasion you would remember. But there are other occasions, which may be very numerous indeed, to which no one pays any attention; and they are the very important occasions on which a person conducts herself with virtue and restraint. All that goes quite unnoticed, but if for a moment or two a person is ill-advised in her behaviour, then everybody stares.'

'Enrico's absence has made no difference at all in my behaviour. I have been strictly faithful to him.'

'Your nature is comparatively cold, Lucia.'

'Well, that is a new discovery! Nobody ever said that before. Enrico never said so, and if anyone should know, it was Enrico.'

'Enrico, it may be, was easily contented.'

'Enrico was a husband that any woman might be proud of. Enrico was a true man –'

'Oh, do not tell me about Enrico! Be quiet, Lucia. I want to think about my Angelo, and how can I do that while you are shouting *Enrico, Enrico, Enrico?*'

'If I thought he could hear me, I would shout till my throat split in two!'

They were silent for a little while, and then Lucia cried, 'I must talk about him to someone! You are so selfish, Lucrezia, that a conversation with you is no pleasure at all. I shall go and talk to Emilia Bigi. She will listen to me, and be glad to listen.'

'Emilia Bigi has never had the chance to learn about men for herself, but only from women who have been deserted or betrayed, and go to her to confide their troubles.'

'She is truly sympathetic!' Lucia shouted, and without waiting for an answer threw down the hen she had plucked and set off with indignant speed, her short skirt in a flurry above her bare legs and her arms swinging to and fro like a soldier's. Quickly she disappeared from sight in the narrow glen, then reappeared a few minutes later on the path that girdled the round hill beyond it. Lucrezia watched her – intermittently in view among the farther trees – without much interest, and listened with no interest at all to the distant sounds of battle. Somewhere to the east and somewhere to the west the foreign armies were fighting each other. Field-guns were firing, but the explosion of their shells was muffled by intervening hills. Sometimes a machine-gun fired and was answered, as it seemed, by a boy rattling his stick along iron railings. Lucrezia sat in the very midst of war, but the war was not near enough to be frightening, and presently, with her hands folded in her lap and her head drooping, she fell into a light and pleasant sleep.

She began to dream about a harvest field, and herself cutting with a steady sickle the dry varnished stems of the wheat. Then, quite suddenly, panic took her, for another reaper had seized her hair in mistake for a handful of corn, and was pulling it towards him, ready to cut. She woke with a gasp of fear, and felt indeed the tug of a strong hand. Her head was jerked back, her eyes that were still half-full of the dream saw a familiar face come swiftly down, and her lips that were opening to scream were closed by an imperative warm kiss. The back of the wooden chair on which she was sitting broke with a crack, she tumbled to the pavement, and Angelo came down with her. Brown feathers that had been gathered tidily on a sheet of newspaper were scattered here and there as they lay for a minute in a commotion of mutual embraces. But then they sat up, and Lucrezia stared at Angelo, and cried, 'No, be still! I want to look at you, I want to be sure it is you. Dear Angelo, in my dream you were going to cut my head off!'

'I like it very well where it is,' said Angelo. 'Even in your dreams you should be aware of that. You must be getting morbid, darling Lucrezia, and the only cure for that is to be married. When shall we be married?'

'Oh, soon, quite soon, I think. But first of all tell me how you are, and what you have been doing, and how you came here. Listen! The guns are firing again. Oh, my dear, it must have been dangerous for you to come. Where did you sleep last night?'

'In a cave in the woods not far from Pontefiore. Some men I knew were also sleeping there, and it was from them that I learnt you were here. But if you want to know everything I have done since I last saw you, you will have to listen for a long time, because I have had many adventures.'

'Do not tell me about the adventures, tell me about yourself. Do you still love me, Angelo?'

Several minutes passed before he was allowed to explain his presence. He had come through the German lines, he said, on a perilous and important mission. No, he had not been alone. An English officer, a Captain Telfer, had come with him, and the manner in which he had first met Captain Telfer, many months before, was extremely interesting. To make his story comprehensible, he suggested, he should really begin at the very beginning –

'There will be time in plenty for that,' said Lucrezia. 'We have all our lives before us.'

'Indeed, I hope so,' said Angelo, 'though in times like these a long life is by no means certain.'

'Oh, do not be so gloomy when I am full of happiness to see you again. Was it not wonderful, Angelo, that I should be dreaming of you at the very moment when you arrived? Tell me about yourself, tell me everything!'

'That is what I am trying to do, dear Lucrezia.'

'Did you ever dream about me when you were away?'

'Yes, often.'

Lucrezia moved nearer to him, sighed, and leaned her head against his shoulder. 'Tell me more,' she whispered.

'Certainly,' said Angelo. 'As I was saying, Captain Telfer and I broke through the German lines in what was undoubtedly a very hazardous enterprise; though I do not wish to boast about it, for we' – Angelo cleared his throat – 'we of the Eighth Army do not find it either necessary or seemly to boast about ourselves.'

Lucrezia disappointingly made no comment, and Angelo continued: 'I was chosen for this duty because, of course, I know all the country here quite intimately. But I did not know the German dispositions, so we were met by a young Englishman called Corporal Trivet, who escaped from the Germans a long time ago and has been living in Pontefiore. I saw him when I went there last year.'

'Yes,' said Lucrezia.

'Did you know him?'

'Everybody knew him.'

'Was he well liked?'

'By some, yes. There are always certain people who will make much of a stranger.'

'I found him very friendly and agreeable,' said Angelo.

'By those who came to know him quite well, however, it was agreed that he was shallow and deceitful and incapable of true feeling; as all the English are.'

'Did you, then, meet a lot of Englishmen while I was away?' asked Angelo.

But Lucrezia was no longer listening. She was sitting upright and staring with dilated eyes at two figures that had appeared, in a gap among the trees, on the basin-shaped hill in front of them. They were a considerable distance away, but the light fell sharply on them and their costume was distinctive. They wore long hooded cloaks of grey wool.

'*Marocchini!*' she exclaimed.

'They are Goums,' said Angelo. 'They advance very quickly, and often they arrive in parts of the country where nobody expects them. But you need not be alarmed, they are on our side.'

'Not if you are a woman,' said Lucrezia; and in fierce words related the legend that these wild irregulars from the Atlas had created for themselves in their swift advance from Ausonia to the bare downs of Siena. They were devils incarnate, she said. Even the Tedeschi dreaded them, and to women they were the personification of all the terrors that walk by night. Her own cheeks grew pale as she spoke, and Angelo was infected by her fear. But he tried to reassure her, and himself as well, by calling attention to the deep shade in which they sat, that would make it difficult if not impossible for the Goums to see them. 'And look!' he said, 'they are moving now, they are going in the opposite direction.'

'Towards the house of Emilia Bigi,' exclaimed Lucrezia, 'where Lucia went an hour ago to talk about Enrico her husband.'

'That will do her no harm.'

'It will do her harm enough if she encounters two *Marocchini* on the way back. Angelo, you must go and warn her!'

'I see no necessity for that.'

'It is my own sister of whom we are talking! Lucia, my sister, is about to be raped, and you do not see the necessity to warn her!'

'You are becoming excited, Lucrezia.'

'In the circumstances that is not unnatural. Would you remain calm and unperturbed if your sister were in immediate danger of being assaulted, outraged, and assassinated?'

'I should first of all ask myself if the danger were real or imaginary.'

'And while you were arguing on this side and that, and never reaching any conclusion, your sister would have been waylaid and maltreated, undone and destroyed!'

'The situation is unlikely to occur,' said Angelo stiffly, 'because, as you are well aware, I have no sister.'

'But I have, and already she may be in the clutches of the *Marocchini*. You must go and rescue her, Angelo!'

She rose and dragged him to his feet, and as he felt in the strength of her grasp the intensity of her emotion, Angelo's heart began to beat with uncomfortable speed. Nervously he exclaimed, 'But you do not understand! The Goums are, it is true, our allies, and they have many good qualities. But they are sensitive people, they are easily offended. If I were to interfere with two men who are merely taking a quiet walk in the country, they would of course feel insulted.'

'You are afraid of them,' said Lucrezia.

'That is not the point.'

'You who belong to the *Ottava Armata*, who boast about your Eighth Army, are afraid of two poor ignorant *Marocchini*.'

'They are very redoubtable, everybody knows that.'

'You carry a revolver at your belt, and yet you are afraid. You are no use to me, Angelo.'

'If it were possible to gather a party, a fairly large party –'

'There is no one here but old women and children. The men have all gone.'

With a pitiable expression and a stammer beyond control, Angelo said, 'You know that I have a certain weakness. I have never tried to conceal or deny it, and all my friends are well aware of it. Many people possess the *dono di coraggio* in great measure, and never pause to think how fortunate they are. But I, who was born without it, know that life can be very miserable to those who lack it.'

'I am not thinking about your misery, but about Lucia's,' cried Lucrezia. 'If you want to stay here and pity yourself while Lucia is being ravished and strangled, you can do so. But do not ask me to stay beside you, and never ask me again to listen to your adventures, which I should not have believed in any case. – I give you a last chance: will you go and rescue her?'

Angelo hung his head and whispered, 'What you said is quite true. I am afraid.'

'Then give me your revolver,' said Lucrezia, and beating down his protesting hands she seized him by the belt, unfastened the holster, and took out the pistol. 'If you will not go, I must,' she exclaimed, and ran across the farmyard and down into the narrow glen.

Angelo followed her, crying breathlessly, 'No, no, you must not! You must not, Lucrezia. Those men are dangerous, you do not realize how dangerous they are!'

Lucrezia made no reply, but roughly pushed him away when he tried to hold her, and with swift steps climbed out of the glen and strode resolutely over the rising ground beyond it. They passed through a belt of woodland, Angelo at her heels still begging her to return, and came out on the path that ran upward round the side of the basin-shaped hill.

Now Lucrezia's pace grew a little slower, and when Angelo pleaded with her yet again to think of the danger she was inviting, she answered not unkindly, 'It may be dangerous for you also. I thought you were too much afraid to come.'

'What do I matter? I am thinking about you, Lucrezia. Oh, come back! Come back before it is too late.'

'I am thinking about Lucia,' she said, but walked closer to him and took him tightly by the hand.

Slower and slower became their pace, but both were breathing as deeply as if they had been climbing a mountain at utmost speed. Nervously they peered ahead, and furtively from side to side. Where the path ran bare beneath the sun they felt as though a thousand eyes were watching them, and when they walked beneath overarching trees they dreaded instant capture. But still, with faltering steps, they went on.

The guns were no longer firing, and the silence of a

summer afternoon lay heavy on the little hill. Then suddenly, as if the silence were a curtain caught in a madman's hand, it was torn again and again by frightened screams.

'Oh, Lucia!' cried Lucrezia.

'But that was a man's voice,' said Angelo.

White and trembling, they stood and stared at each other. 'Take this,' said Lucrezia, and gave him the pistol.

'It is not loaded,' said Angelo.

'Then load it, for God's sake load it!'

With nerveless fingers he fumbled at the stiff button of his cartridge-pouch, but before he could unfasten it Lucrezia uttered a shuddering cry and fell in a dead faint at his feet. Two yards away a man rose from behind a bush, a man who wore a grey woollen cloak striped thinly with bearish brown. His black eyes glittered like a hawk's, his nose had a hawkish curve. His cheeks were rather grey than brown, and the downward crescent of his narrow moustache was like a dreadful grin.

'Good afternoon,' stammered Angelo, and let his empty pistol fall. He bent to retrieve it, and with the speed of a stooping hawk the Goum leapt forward and struck him on the back of his head with a heavy cudgel.

The pain of the blow was so momentary that Angelo hardly felt it until he began to recover consciousness, and when that returned he grew aware of a further unhappiness that divided his mind evenly between it and his aching skull. The sun was now at tree-top height, and the guns were firing again. The explosions struck his sore head like little blows, and every movement he made brought a gyre of giddiness. He longed to lie still, to remain quiet and undiscovered in the cool shadow, but his fearful anxiety for Lucrezia gave him the resolution and the strength to get up.

He found her a few yards away, and the sight of her distress came near to banishing his own. Kneeling beside her, he undid the strips of her dress with which her hands had been tied and her mouth gagged, and taking her into his arms he held her for a long time until her sobbing stopped, and she lay so quietly that he thought she must be sleeping.

But presently, without raising her head, she spoke to him. 'And now,' she said, 'you will never marry me.'

He held her more tightly, but did not answer, and a little while later she said again, 'You will not want to marry me now. You could not, Angelo, could you?'

'Darling Lucrezia,' he said, 'in the hope that you may find comfort in another's misfortune, I think I should tell you that I am in somewhat the same plight as yourself. For I also have been humiliated. But there is nothing to be gained by going into mourning for misfortunes that come to us through no fault of our own. True, I forgot to load my revolver, and that was negligence, but even had it been loaded in all chambers my hand was so tremulous that I could not have fired to any purpose; so I do not think my negligence mattered very much. No, Lucrezia, we are not to blame, so the best we can do is to let bygones be bygones, and thank God we are still alive.'

EMILIA BIGI'S HOUSE was not very far away, and Emilia and Lucia, who was still there, did everything that was possible to solace and comfort them. Emilia, an angular woman of nearly fifty, was indeed somewhat tiresomely complacent about her own escape from calamity, and perplexed them by her frequent exclamations in praise of boiling water. It was boiling water that had saved her and Lucia from the attentions of the other Goum, for there happened to be a pan of it on the stove when he came in, and Emilia had promptly thrown it in his face, scalding him so severely that he ran away making a noise, she boasted, of great lamentation.

When Angelo and Lucrezia congratulated her on her enterprise, she told them, with a mingling in her voice of pride and bashfulness, that it was not the first time she had preserved her virtue in such a way, for when she was sixteen a friend of her eldest brother had made her both frightened and angry, and without a moment's reflection – for luckily she was in her mother's kitchen at the time – she had rebuked him with a saucepan from the fire. 'And ever since then,' she continued, 'I've kept a pot boiling, and more than once, while I was still young and tender, I just grabbed it in time! Oh, I wouldn't be without boiling water for anything! I don't often leave home nowadays, just for that reason, because it's difficult to carry with you. But so long as I stay within a few yards of the stove, I'm as happy as a woman can be.'

Both Lucrezia and Lucia were unwilling to return to the house of the Noble Lady of Rocca Pipirozzi while the countryside was so unsettled, but in the evening of the following day Lucrezia decided that she must return immediately to Pontefiore. She would give no explanation of this strange resolve, and though the others all tried to dissuade her from so rash a project, they did not care to oppose her too roughly, for she was still in a condition of some nervousness, and prone to tears. Pontefiore, indeed, was little more than ten miles away, but who might be moving in the space between?

'I think,' said Angelo, 'that we are on the right flank of the French troops, with whom the Goums are serving, and on the left flank of the British, and perhaps there is a little space between them. But we cannot be sure of that. The nearest British troops, it may be, are Indians.'

'O God!' cried Lucrezia, 'they will be as bad as the *Marocchini!*'

'Not at all,' said Angelo. 'In battle the Indians fight with the greatest bravery you can imagine, but out of battle they are extremely gentle. Many of them are vegetarians, and their religion forbids them to kill any living creature except their fellow-men; and that they only do when commanded to by the English. There are no soldiers in the world who have better manners.'

'It is good treatment that begets good manners,' said Emilia Bigi. 'India must be a happy country.'

'I have heard different opinions about that,' Angelo replied, 'and I cannot tell you the truth of it. But I promise you that if we meet any Indian soldiers, they will behave with perfect courtesy.'

'Then let us go at once!' cried Lucrezia. 'I cannot bear to stay here any longer. I want to be in Pontefiore.'

'It would be wiser,' said Angelo, 'to wait and see whether Pontefiore is going to be liberated, or lucky enough to be ignored.'

'Are you not eager for it to be liberated?' asked Lucia.

'It is sometimes necessary to go to the dentist,' said Angelo, 'but I have never seen anyone eager to go; and this is a more serious operation than the pulling of a tooth. In the first place, before a town or village can be liberated it must be occupied by the Germans, and the Germans will rob it of everything they can find; but that is of no importance, that is merely the Overture. Liberation really begins when the Allied Air Forces bomb the town: that is the First Movement, *Allegro*, so to speak. The Second Movement is often quite leisurely but full of caprice: it occurs when the Allied artillery opens fire to knock down what the bombers have missed, and may be called *Andante Capriccioso*. After that has gone on for some time the liberating infantry will rush in, that is the Third Movement, the *Scherzo*, and though the Allied soldiers do not loot, of course, they will find a number of things, such as geese and hens and wine, that apparently belong to no one – for the local inhabitants have taken to the hills or are hiding in their cellars – and to prevent the wine and the geese from being wasted, the soldiers will naturally take care of them. Then comes the Last Movement, when the officials of the Allied Military Government arrive and say to the inhabitants, "No, you cannot do that, you must not go there, you are not allowed to sell this, and you are forbidden to buy that. If you want to live here you must apply for our permission, and it is against the law for you to be domiciled anywhere else." Yes, that is the *Finale*, and then you may say that the process of liberation is complete.'

None of them believed a word he was saying, but Lucia and Emilia Bigi listened indulgently, as they would have listened to any young man of good appearance who chose to exercise his wit on great affairs. Lucrezia, however, grew more and more impatient, and he had scarcely finished before she said again, with great vehemence, 'I must go to Pontefiore! Will you take me, Angelo, or shall I go alone?'

Angelo sighed deeply and tried to explain the peril of moving in what might already be, or quickly become, a battle-field. He did not know how far the Allied soldiers had advanced in the last few days, nor in what parts of the country the Germans were retreating. The line of battle curved and recurved across the country, here reaching forward like a long nose, there leaning back like a receding chin. They were, perhaps, in some no-man's-land between

the armies into which both sides would presently charge
with the most savage intention. Or, he admitted, because
the roads in their immediate neighbourhood were neither
good in themselves nor led anywhere in particular, it was
just possible that neither army would come that way at all.

'Why, then, do we not go at once?' asked Lucrezia.

'There will, of course, be patrols moving here and there,
and if we encounter the Goums again –'

'Bullets never strike the same place twice,' said Lucrezia.

'That may be the rule,' said Angelo, 'but can we be sure
that the Goums will obey it?'

'Do you wish to drive me mad?' she inquired; whereupon
Angelo, forsaking all other argument, pointed to the time
and said, 'It will be quite dark in an hour, and though I
know the way to Pontefiore, by an unfrequented path, it
will be difficult to follow it at night. But if we wait till about
three o'clock in the morning the last of the moon will be in
the sky, giving a little light, and if we start then we should
arrive, with good fortune, about sunrise or not long after.
Go to bed now, Lucrezia, and rest yourself; and I shall wake
you at three.'

The others agreed that this was the best plan, and Lucrezia
allowed herself to be persuaded. She and Lucia slept in one
bed, Angelo in an adjoining room; but Emilia Bigi stayed
in the kitchen, and from time to time replenished the pan
of water that bubbled all night upon the fire.

The air of early morning was cold, and the moon no
brighter than a candle when they went out. But innumerable
stars shone from a clear dark sky, and soon, when they
could more easily distinguish substance from the shade, they
walked with a firmer step. But in the sombre stillness they
felt lonely, and clung together, and made slower progress
than they had expected. A dozen times they threw themselves down, quivering with excitement, and hid behind a
rock or a bush until the soldiers they had seen turned out
to be merely another rock, or the stump of a tree. It began
to grow light when they were still three or four miles from
Pontefiore, and then they walked more quickly. They met

no one on the way and heard nothing but occasionally the distant rattle of a machine-gun firing, and before sunrise, during the morning chorus of the birds, a loud explosion that rumbled and re-echoed through the quailing air.

They halted on a wooded slope from which they could look across a valley at the road leading to Pontefiore, and at Pontefiore on its cleft hill. Lucrezia was impatient to go on, but Angelo said they must wait for a little while to see if there was any movement of troops on the road, and if so, whether they were friendly or hostile troops. They lay for five minutes and saw no one stirring. Lucrezia said again, 'There is no purpose in waiting here,' but Angelo caught her by the wrist as she was going to rise, and said, 'I think it is safe enough, but let us stay a little longer and make sure.' They could not see the bridge from where they lay.

Then they heard – faintly at first, but quickly it grew louder – a noise that was more like a sensation of feeling than of hearing; for it rubbed upon their ears. Gleaming like beads of ice, with the morning sun upon them, the bombers looked very pretty under the tall arch of the sky.

It was unfortunate that the pilots' information was not up to date. They knew that the Germans had occupied Pontefiore, but no one had told them that the Germans had left it. Their bombs, that fell with great accuracy on the chosen targets, were in fact wasted; and so indeed was Pontefiore. A thunderstorm seemed to break upon the little town, and from it rose fountains of rubble that smeared the pale blue sky with grey dust. In the lower darkness of the storm red flames began to leap, and here and there a wooden beam or a large piece of masonry was thrown far above the general upheaval. The roar of the bombers, fretting eardrums, persisted through the thunder.

Shocked and dismayed by the spectacle, Angelo and Lucrezia rose and stood speechless for a little while, hand clasped in hand. Then Lucrezia began to moan, very quietly, and went slowly down the hill towards her home. Angelo seemed scarcely to notice that she had left him. But of a sudden he uttered a little cry of pain, and followed her.

Both were unsteady in their gait, stumbling from time to time as if they were drunk or very tired, and neither seemed aware of the other's presence. The storm was nearly over when they reached the floor of the valley, and between the last few claps of thunder there were long intervals. A solitary dark spout of smoke and ruin burst from the castle, and spread against the sky, and slowly subsided as the noise of the bombers diminished. They were returning to their base, their mission completed.

When they had climbed the opposite slope and were on the road to Pontefiore, Angelo and Lucrezia began to run, but quickly were stopped by the destruction of the bridge. Between broken parapets the road crumbled into the gulf below, and at the bottom of the ravine lay a mass of shattered masonry. The bridge, their beautiful and famous bridge, had fallen down! The discovery appalled them, for the bridge had been so old that it had seemed as much a part of nature as the hill itself, and in their lives it had been something so important that neither, for a moment, could think of anything more important. Here on the bridge they had met with quickening hearts in the dusk of evening, and the bridge was their way to the world, and the way home again. And now it was gone, it lay broken before them, and the ravine – though in fact it was not very deep – seemed an impassable gulf between them and everything with which they were familiar.

But smoke was rising from a dozen places in the ruins beyond, and when they had recovered sufficiently to notice it, they remembered their separate purposes and saw that it was easy enough to climb down into the ravine and up again on the other side. Lucrezia never gave a thought to Angelo as she reached the farther edge, but with the smell of burning rafters in her nostrils ran desperately, crying 'Tommaso! Tommaso! Where are you?'

Angelo, for a moment only, wondered if he should follow her, but then, with tightened lips and fear in his eyes, began to climb the nearest pile of rubble, that blocked the main street of Pontefiore, and ran faster still towards the castle.

He was sickened by the sour stink of the crumbled houses, and once he stopped to help a woman who was crawling out of a cellar, and again he had to scramble across a rampart of crumbled stone; but with a single thought in his mind he hurried on.

The main door of the castle hung aslant from broken hinges, so that was no obstacle. A small fire was burning in a corner of the hall, but he hardly noticed it. A passage on the storey above was blocked by a room that seemed to have burst over it, but he clambered across the wreckage and made his way on yielding boards to a door that opened into a narrow corridor.

In the inner room he found the Adoration of Piero della Francesca lying face down upon the floor, and when he lifted it the near end broke off with a crack along a line of bullet-holes. More carefully he raised the larger fragment, and turned it over. Bullet-holes ran across it too, and the shepherds had suffered irreparable damage from some blunter assault; perhaps of a boot. But the head of the Madonna was unhurt and unsullied. The bullets had drawn a triangle on the panel, and the punctured lines enclosed her head.

Angelo sat on the floor, and his mind fell captive again to the pale brow and the gravity of the eyes. The coif about her head was white with starch, and through its transparency – what a miracle of painting was there! – the different whiteness of the forehead was stretched upon the bone that shaped it. The stillness of the face was something caught in the midst of movement, but the movement had never been swift or ungainly. Her peace was native to her, and the composure of her beauty was the reward of perfection. How strong were the cheekbones, how delicate the nostrils!

To Angelo's nose came faintly the smell of burning, but rapt in his admiration he thought nothing of it. He had found what he had run so far to look for, he was satisfied, and being satisfied had no attention to spare for anything else. The ruin of the picture as a whole, the excoriation of the shepherds, meant little to him, for his relief at finding the Madonna's head unspoilt had been so great that he had instantly accepted their loss as the reasonable price of her preservation. It was she whom he adored: she who was the product of Piero's paint and Piero's genius at work on some forgotten but immortal model. Angelo had fallen in love with her when he was sixteen, within a few days of his falling in love with Lucrezia, who was then a plump and vivacious child of twelve. Which had been the first to rouse his emotion he could not remember, but they had shared his thoughts and his fidelity – the ideal and the real – in the happiest division. He had never analysed his feelings for them, but had given to each the sort of devotion to which she was entitled, and for this simplicity had been repaid by complementary emotions. His twin attachment had contented him, and sooner or later the one side of it always reminded him of the other, because Piero had given to his Madonna lips that were remarkably the same shape as Lucrezia's; though Lucrezia's were the redder.

What depths of affection there were in Lucrezia's heart! Not many girls, he thought, would have shown so desperate an anxiety as hers for the safety of her old father and mother and her many brothers and sisters. He remembered the intensity of her fear, that had quite separated her from him as they ran together into Pontefiore, and he marvelled at the richness of her nature that could give so generously to those she loved. But how had she fared among the smoke and falling ruins of the town? It occurred to him that he had been neglectful of her, in his solicitude for the Madonna, and that now he had better go quickly and see what help Lucrezia needed.

He had no hesitation about taking the Madonna with him. Violence had very nearly released her from her context, and it was easy enough to complete the separation with a jack-knife. Like so many others, she was a victim of war, and though Angelo was well aware of his good fortune in discovering her, like a lost mistress on the road with refugees, he told himself that he was giving her protection and a home when he cut the panel along the line of bullet-holes, and wrapped the severed triangle in a pillowslip from the bed.

The Countess, he admitted, might not have understood the propriety of his action, but she, by happy chance, was not there to see and dispute it. The Countess . . .

Among the rubble in the corridor Angelo halted with a new question in his mind. Where was the Countess? He had assumed, so far as he had given her a thought, that she had long since fled from the castle; but what reason had he for thinking that, except the natural but possibly misleading hope that it was so? She could still be there, lying wounded in a corner, unconscious probably, or imprisoned by a wall's collapse. Sorely though Lucrezia might need him, he could not leave the castle until he had made sure of the Countess's escape. With the Madonna's head under his arm he returned down the quaking corridor to the summer drawing-room that overlooked the garden.

The floor was covered with torn paper, and the Countess lay upon a couch. She was breathing hoarsely, snoring a little indeed, but though her face was unnaturally pale she did not appear to have been hurt.

Angelo knelt beside her and gently shook her arm. She groaned, but her eyes did not open, and he was puzzled by an unusual odour in the room. He took her by the shoulder and shook her more roughly.

'Oh dear,' she said at last. 'Oh dear, oh dear! Do go away and leave me.'

'Madam,' said Angelo, 'the castle is on fire.'

'I'm not surprised,' she said. 'I feel as if all the world was coming to an end, and a good thing too.'

'You must get up,' said Angelo. 'We really shouldn't waste time.'

'There's too much time,' said the Countess. 'That's the trouble with life. Oh dear,' she repeated as she sat up and looked at the enormous litter of torn paper. 'Oh dear, I do feel ill.'

'Are you wounded?'

'No, not now. I was, but that was a long time ago. They tore up my books, all my lovely Ouidas, and I didn't know how I could live without them. But then I remembered something. In time of sorrow, I remembered, people often take to drink. So I thought I'd try it too. And it works. Oh dear, it works! You drink a bottle of brandy, and when you wake up you don't feel anything at all except your stomach rising and your head going round. Do go away, Angelo, I want to go to sleep.'

'But the castle is on fire, madam!'

'Why should you worry about that? It isn't your castle.'

'But you, madam –'

The Countess groaned and lay down again. Then she whispered, 'There's a bottle of champagne in the little cupboard in the corner. Open it, Angelo, and look for a glass.'

The cork hit the ceiling and Angelo held to her lips a gently foaming goblet. She emptied it as though it had held a doctor's draught, and he poured another dose.

'It's certainly surprising,' said the Countess, 'how quickly you learn vicious ways, once you start them. They seem quite practical too, and that's a thing I never realized before. Have a glass yourself, Angelo.'

'Madam,' said Angelo, 'we must hurry. We really must!'

'And so we shall, as soon as we've drunk some champagne and my head's a little clearer. It's getting clear already. Very clear indeed. Oh, I'm not deluding myself, Angelo. I know that self-indulgence ought to be followed by repentance, but the fact of the matter is that champagne suits me better. Give me a little more, and help yourself when you're at it.'

'Do try to realize what a serious situation we are in,' said Angelo in a voice of distress. 'The castle is burning, you can smell the smoke.'

'It reminds me of home,' said the Countess. 'The drawing-room chimney always used to smoke. We only used it on a Sunday, and whenever the wind was in the north or the east, or if it was raining, the chimney smoked. We were well brought up, in Bradford, and a happy family too.'

Angelo made a gesture of despair. 'I also have happy memories,' he said, 'and because of them I do not want to stay here and be burnt to a cinder. I want to go and look for Lucrezia. Half the houses in Pontefiore are in flames –'

'Good God!' exclaimed the Countess, rising from the sofa and swaying slightly. 'Have the Germans set it on fire?'

'Not the Germans,' said Angelo, 'but the Allies. They came over this morning and bombed it.'

'Don't talk nonsense,' said the Countess.

'But it is true! They made a mistake, I dare say, but a bomb has no political opinions and will explode in the wrong place quite as loudly as in the right place. Pontefiore, I give you my word, is now in ruins.'

'Then why do you let me sit here drinking and gossiping when there's work to be done? You're no sense of responsibility, Angelo, that's the trouble with you. Now give me your arm, and stop talking.'

The Countess quickly recovered herself, and when they found that the fire in the hall had burnt itself out, she accused Angelo of wilfully exaggerating the damage in order to frighten her.

'I assure you,' said Angelo, 'that a little while ago the smoke was most alarming.'

'It took more than a little smoke to alarm us in Bradford,' said the Countess, and with only an occasional stumble set off at a good pace for the village. There, having quickly perceived the extent of the damage, she wasted neither time nor breath on exclamations of astonishment or grief, but organized as many people as she could find – they had now emerged from their hiding-places to gaze with impotent sorrow on the wreckage of their homes – and set them to work to search the ruins for other survivors, to save whatever could be saved, and knock down such walls as would otherwise tumble of themselves and might claim more victims in their fall. With the deepest gratification she remembered her decision to send the young people of the village into the woods. There would have been many more casualties had they remained.

Angelo took the earliest opportunity of escaping from her benign conscription, and still carrying the Madonna's head in its pillowslip, went feverishly in search of Lucrezia. But nowhere in the village could he find her, and no one he met had lately seen her. The Donatis' house was unhurt, but the door stood open and none of the family was in. He grew almost frantic with fearful imaginings of her fate, and returned again and again to streets he had already traversed and to houses he had searched twice or three times in vain. Then, wandering haphazardly on the outskirts of the village, he came to a little garden where small pear trees grew among beds of homely vegetables, onions and the like, and frogs were croaking in a brick-sided pond till someone, splashing the water with a stick, frightened them to silence. He looked over the wall and saw Lucrezia sitting on stone steps that descended from the house, and near her, by the waterside, a sturdy child some two years old whom she watched with a doting joy. Angelo's delight in finding her knew no bounds, but she, apparently, took little pleasure in being discovered. She answered all his questions in the shortest way, and made no response whatever to his many protestations of love and gratification. He sat down beside her, but she refused his embrace and presently there was silence between them. The child continued to beat the water with a stick.

'Who is that little boy?' asked Angelo.

'His name is Tommaso.'

'Whose child is he?'

'How should I know? There are many children in the village.'

'But everyone in Pontefiore knows everyone else.'

'Not now. Things are different now. People come and go, and one does not inquire too closely who they are, or what they leave behind them.'

'I see,' said Angelo, and sighed. 'It is a pity when things like that happen. He is a fine-looking child, however, much fairer than most of the children here. Has his mother also gone away?'

'That would have been the wisest thing for her to do.'

'Tommaso,' said Angelo, frowning now. 'His name is Tommaso? Lucrezia, when you left me this morning, and ran off on your own, that was the name you were shouting. You were calling *Tommaso, Tommaso!*'

'Somebody has to look after these poor children who have no fathers.'

'But you were very agitated.'

'Naturally.'

'I don't understand.'

'Is it not natural to worry about an orphan child who is being bombed and murdered and possibly burnt to death before your very eyes?'

'Oh. Well, yes, I suppose it is.'

'Well, then.'

Lucrezia, expressionless, stared straight in front of her, and Angelo could not think what to say next. In his mind a monstrous suspicion had come suddenly to life, and though he was very properly ashamed of it, he could not quell it, and Lucrezia's words had done nothing to dispel it. She had merely made it difficult for him to ask more questions, unless he made a very blunt unmannerly inquiry; which he dared not do.

The orphan Tommaso continued to beat the water with his stick, but otherwise an embarrassed silence lay upon the garden. Then came a louder splash, a childish cry, abruptly muffled, and for a moment Tommaso's legs appeared like sunburnt branches among a foliage of silver leaves. Briefly he vanished below the greenish surface of the water, and Lucrezia with a hoarse scream leapt to her feet and a moment later was groping in the wavy pool. Quickly she found and hauled ashore the choking boy, and clasped him dripping-wet to her bosom, and passionately kissed his distorted features. He yelled for half a minute, then recovered from his fright, and asked what had become of his stick. In a loving voice Lucrezia scolded him, took off his soaking clothes, and roughly dried him with her skirt. He escaped her grasp and ran naked to the other side of the pool. There he caught sight of a small green lizard panting on a warm stone, and stood stock-still to gaze at it. Lucrezia, sitting on her heels, watched him with adoring eyes.

Angelo's voice, when he spoke to her, was so tremulous that he could hardly shape his words. His lips were dry,

and the blood receding from his brain had left his cheeks
a little pale, and made him feel weak and ill. 'Lucrezia,' he
stammered, 'that child –'

'He is mine,' she said.

He knelt beside her, speechless now. 'You were away for
three years,' said Lucrezia.

'You cannot blame me for that. It was not by my own
choice but by force of circumstance that I became a soldier.'

'Was it not more unnatural for you to become a soldier
than for me to become a mother?'

'So you are going to defend yourself?' cried Angelo. 'You
are shameless, are you?'

'I must speak for myself, because no one else will. Women
are less fortunate than soldiers. The poets and historians
of the world are always at hand to argue that soldiers are
justified in their horrid trade of destroying life, but if a
woman is guilty of creating life she can find no advocate
but herself.'

'This is not a proper occasion to become philosophical!'
said Angelo indignantly. 'Philosophy is all very well in its
way, but when a woman betrays the man who loves her,
philosophy is merely an impertinence.'

'I have done worse than that,' said Lucrezia sadly. 'I have
betrayed the man whom I love.'

'You have the hardihood to say that? You have the audacity
to say that you still love me?'

'I do,' said Lucrezia.

'You have chosen a strange way to prove it.'

'I had other ways in mind. I had hoped that one of my
sisters would look after Tommaso –'

'To conceal your fault? You meant to go on deceiving me?'

'You might have been happier if I had.'

Angelo hid his face in his hands, and in a muffled voice
asked, 'Who is the father?'

'Why should I tell you that?'

'I insist on your telling me!'

'You have no right to know, unless you mean to forgive
me.'

'How can I forgive you unless I know all the circumstances?'

Lucrezia said slowly, 'He is nothing to me now. Indeed, he is less than nothing, for we quarrelled long ago when he showed himself to be quite an untrustworthy person with whom, when I discovered his true character, I had no wish to associate.' Her manner grew warmer, her voice more rapid. 'Imagine my feelings,' she said, 'when I found that he was making love to other girls! Even before Tommaso was born he was having an affair with Vittoria Carpaccio, and then another with Francesca Cori, and quite lately he has got Bianca Miretti into trouble, who suffered already from a squint in one eye, about which she was extremely sensitive, and very soon she will have a great deal more to be ashamed of. That is the sort of man he turned out to be, after he had taken advantage of the little friendship that in decency I could not refuse him, and the sympathy that his plight demanded. No, Angelo, you need have no fear. He means nothing to me now, except as a type of selfish inconstancy that I heartily despise.'

'But who is he?' asked Angelo.

'Do you remember the Englishman whom you saw in the castle when you came here last year?'

'You mean Corporal Trivet?'

'Does my conduct seem worse to you because he is a foreigner? But Angelo, that in fact was the reason for my weakness. He was so far from home, he was so lonely and terribly unhappy that I, being ignorant then of his true character, was sorry for him. It was pity that moved me, nothing else.'

'You became his lover,' said Angelo, 'purely out of charity?'

'I am sure that is the correct way to think of it,' said Lucrezia.

'He has a very pleasant way with him,' said Angelo.

'Until you know him really well,' Lucrezia admitted, 'he is an agreeable companion.'

'And he is quite good-looking.'

'Most certainly!' said Lucrezia. 'Do you think I would

have misbehaved with anyone whose appearance was repulsive? I am not so wicked as that, I hope. Trivet has good features, white teeth, and truly handsome eyes. Tommaso has inherited his father's eyes.'

'You liked him, did you?'

'But of course!'

'So you let him make love to you,' said Angelo, 'not merely because you were sorry for him, but because that was what you wanted.'

'How can you make such a dreadful suggestion!' exclaimed Lucrezia. 'No, Angelo, it is one thing to like a person, but quite another thing to want him to become the father of your orphan child. That I never desired. But I was sorry for Trivet in his loneliness, I felt for him in his unhappiness, and to comfort him I gave him my sympathy. There is the truth of the matter, whether you believe it or not.'

'All over Italy,' said Angelo, 'there are girls who have become the mothers of orphan children whose fathers, for whom they felt no love but were infinitely sorry, were homeless Germans, disconsolate Englishmen, yearning Americans, melancholy Poles, miserable negroes, afflicted Greeks, desolate Scotchmen, woebegone Japs – yes, there are Japanese fighting on our side in the American army – and weeping Brazilians and suffering Goums.'

'No, no!' cried Lucrezia. 'It is impossible to be sorry for a Goum.'

'Perhaps you are right,' said Angelo. 'But all the others can inspire sympathy, I suppose, and because of that and the nature of women, there are orphans of every kind and colour in all the towns and villages of Italy, and their mothers have but the one excuse: it was charity that did it. They were kind to strangers, they were sympathetic beyond all care for themselves, and that is why their cradles are full and babies are crawling on every doorstep in the country. And this is happening, not only in Italy, but throughout the world. In England there are English girls who have been sorry for nice young men from New York and San Francisco, from Amsterdam and Bergen and Paris and Lyons, from Brussels and Warsaw and Montreal. In France they were sorry for the soldiers who first of all came from Birmingham and Leeds and Edinburgh, and then from Hamburg and Munich and Dresden, and now are arriving from Chicago and Pittsburgh and Philadelphia. All over the world it is the same, and everywhere young women, with their orphan children in their arms or clinging to their skirts, cry to their startled sweethearts and bewildered husbands, "But we did it out of charity!" – And what are the men to say? Are they to remove their hats and lower their eyes, look humbly to the ground and say, "You are nobler creatures than we ever realized. Thank God and you for this lesson you have taught us!" Or are they to say, "You were wantons from the beginning, and now you are liars in addition, so out of my house with you and never return!"'

'It will be better for everyone,' said Lucrezia, 'if they believe.'

'That charity was the motive?'

'Yes,' said Lucrezia. 'For charity is the Christian virtue. On charity our faith must stand or fall.'

'But if their plea is false?' demanded Angelo. 'Suppose there was no charity in the act, and nothing but simple lust? What shall a man do then?'

'If a woman pleads that charity was the motive,' said Lucrezia, 'it shows that she is aware of the high place that charity should have in life. It is an aspiration to virtue on her part that she should lay claim to charity. She has the seeds of virtue in her, if not virtue itself, because she knows the poor world's need of charity. Give her credit for that, and believe her if you can.'

'I must think it over,' said Angelo.

'I have been thinking it over for a long time,' said Lucrezia.

Silence again fell upon the garden, and silence again was broken by a loud splash. Tommaso for the second time had fallen into the pond. Now it was Angelo who pulled him out, and dried him on the pillowslip in which he had been carrying the head of Piero della Francesca's Madonna.

CHAPTER SIXTEEN

SOME DAYS LATER Angelo was sitting by the side of an empty road that climbed on the one hand to the pinewoods of Vallombrosa, and on the other descended to the Arno. He was waiting, with considerable trepidation, to play his part in a small but daring assault upon the enemy. About sixty yards away, on the other side of the road where trees grew closely, Captain Telfer and Corporal Trivet lay hidden; and a little farther to the east the partisan Pasquale, who had once been a Guardia Civile, played shepherd to a flock of brown-skinned docile sheep. Also in the vicinity were half a dozen local partisans whom Telfer did not wholly trust. His hopeful intention, and the purpose of the ambush, was to capture two senior German officers, one of them a General.

On the day of the bombing of Pontefiore, Simon and the Corporal had reconnoitred the road, and twenty-four hours later had returned to the village to wait for an Allied agent who for some time had been living in Florence, which the Germans still occupied. They waited a day longer than they had intended, but the agent did not come. He sent a message, however, to confirm the information they already had. The General, he said, drove every evening from Florence to his headquarters in Vallombrosa, and he was usually accompanied by a Colonel of the Schutzstaffel who was organizing Republican resistance in Florence. If they set the ambush for such-and-such a time, he, the agent, would meet them at the appointed place on the road. Simon, though ill-pleased with this new arrangement, and well aware of its danger, had decided to accept the added risk and proceed with his plan.

Angelo, most unusually, had welcomed the prospect and the menace of action. Now that he was on the verge of it he was, indeed, acutely frightened, and wished with all his heart that he was elsewhere, and thought with regret how easily he could have twisted an ankle, or even broken it, in their swift and secret march across the Tuscan mountains. In Pontefiore, however, the idea of a skirmish in enemy country had been a timely comfort. It had rescued him, like a sailor pulled from a stormy sea, from a raging conflict of emotions.

A dozen times a day, for several days, he had fallen violently out of love with Lucrezia, and as often and as violently fallen in again. He had told himself, with a persistent hope of believing it, that her conduct had been as natural as the warmth of summer, even laudable if one could believe her defence of it, and reprehensible only to the most intemperate of moralists; but a little while later he would be sure to see it in another light, in which the betrayal of their love became intolerable, and her unchastity a barrier between them that he could never cross. Her character, he could then perceive, had been vitiated beyond redemption; and a great pity it was that he must also admit she had grown more beautiful than ever.

But what of that, he would cry in quick despair, for what is beauty but a little paint on a rotten house, and paint does not last a lifetime, but withers in the sun and cracks upon the wall and time strips it. Beauty is no argument.

To which another voice would answer, Beauty is everything, and everything is forgiven it.

But how unfair! he would protest. Justice should be a constant thing, and beauty has no right to look for leniency and special terms.

You will find it very pleasant to be lenient, said the voice. It is a fine thing to be magnanimous, and to be magnanimous to a lovely creature like Lucrezia is really quite a luxury. Try it and see.

Then he would remember the child, and see clearly that little Tommaso, yearly growing taller, would forever cast a shadow on his marriage and perpetually remind him that once upon a time – oh, not once, but often, he supposed – Lucrezia had surrendered herself to Corporal Trivet, as now to him. And how could happiness ever live with so noisy a reminder of her infidelity and the rival who had preceded him?

To which the voice would reply: That is nonsense indeed. You have no concern with what is past and over, you are concerned with the present. A man who broods upon past injustice, early hardship, and the youthful vagaries of his wife, is like a nation that cannot forget its history: he has not the slightest chance of happiness. As for the boy, he is Lucrezia's child, well-built and friendly, and you may become very fond of him. When you have three or four children of your own he will be no more than one of the family, and you will never trouble yourself to think how he came there. Confess now, that when you dried him with the pillowslip in which you had been carrying the head of Piero's Madonna, you felt your heart already warming to him?

It is true, Angelo would then admit, that I have no animosity against the child, but that is a different thing from forgiving his mother. And if, as you say, beauty is everything, the pillowslip contained a paradigm of perfect beauty, that is now in my possession. One, moreover, that cannot change and grow old, put on grey hairs and fat, and wear wrinkles for its winter fashion. I have Piero's masterpiece, and with her upon the wall of my room I can live happily enough.

Try it and see, said the voice. You will need something more than perfection hanging on a wall to keep you happy . . .

On and on went the passionate argument, till Angelo was exhausted by its double vehemence; and the order to march, the invitation to a brush with the enemy, had come like the blissful ease of holiday. They had crossed the tall ridges of Tuscany, waist-high in bracken, upon which the wind blew gale-strong, though in the dark valleys the air was warm and still, and every mile had strengthened the illusion of release and fortified his frail desire to bid Lucrezia goodbye and forget her forever. She had failed him, she had no claim upon him, he was a free man and henceforth he would enjoy his freedom. So he thought in the fine soldierly spirit of a soldier who is not yet in touch with the enemy.

Though to begin with he had been gloomy in the presence of Corporal Trivet, his embarrassment had been lessened by the discovery that Trivet himself was much perturbed by the claims of Bianca Miretti. She was a stupid girl, as Angelo well knew, but stupidity has never prevented a good-looking young woman from engaging a man's interest, and thereafter lying on his conscience; and having perceived that Trivet, like himself, was the victim of unruly love, Angelo began to regard him as a fellow-sufferer. He did, at first, feel an occasional wild impulse to assault the Corporal, but because his good sense told him that the sequel might be uncommonly painful, he always managed to suppress this foolish inclination; and when Trivet showed himself to be friendly – he was very generous with his cigarettes – Angelo soon became sympathetic, and from time to time he was convinced that they had both been deeply wronged.

For a whole day, indeed, he had been almost persuaded that he was done with Lucrezia, and would never see her again; but his resolution had weakened in the half-hour he had been waiting at the roadside, and now she returned to his mind very vividly as an image of comfort. Now again he desired her, and admitted his desire. The minutes passed and the time approached when he must boldly break cover, and expose himself to flying bullets, and keep his hand steady to shoot in reply; and in this horrible situation he longed for the shelter of Lucrezia's arms, the concealment of her hair, and the warmth of her body that would enclose him like the walls of a house. He was just about to take off his hat, to make a solemn declaration that he had forgiven her infidelity, and would go back to her as soon as this dreadful adventure was done with, when he saw that Pasquale the partisan was already driving his flock of sheep down the road towards him.

Angelo, sitting by a bend in the road, had a long view of it in both directions, but Pasquale could see it only as far as the corner, and travellers coming from the opposite direction would not see Pasquale and his sheep until they turned the corner. Angelo's task was to hold Pasquale in conversation, or give the appearance of doing so, and by clumsy shepherding of the flock help him to block the road about twenty yards west of the corner. The General for whom they were waiting was a person of regular habit, and they knew, within a few minutes, when to expect him. As soon as he saw the car coming from the west, Angelo was to walk down the road to meet Pasquale.

Now, with a sudden feeling of guilt – for he had been sitting with his eyes tight-closed to think more clearly about Lucrezia – he looked westward and saw, not the car, but a peasant riding a donkey and leading another that carried a great load of firewood. Angelo for a moment was puzzled by this unexpected appearance, for he could see two hundred yards down the road, and the last time he had looked that way it had been empty; but now the peasant was barely a stone's throw from him. He must, he realized, have been daydreaming of Lucrezia for a couple of minutes, and by his neglect might well have ruined Telfer's plan. Conscience pinched him hard, and in deep remorse he determined to make amends by playing his part in it with high courage.

Before time and the working of imagination could weaken his resolution he saw the car coming, and with a quickly-beating heart and a dry mouth went to meet Pasquale. He turned for a moment to look at the peasant on his donkey, and saw that he was a tall, sturdily-built man, roughly dressed, with an old black hat pulled far down over his eyes.

'They're coming!' shouted Angelo to Pasquale, but his voice cracked and the words were no louder than the breaking of a dry twig in a wood. Pasquale with a long staff was keeping his flock in the middle of the road, and because there had been a thunderstorm in the early afternoon, and their fleeces were still wet, the strong smell of the sheep was like an invisible cloud carried by the downhill wind. They stood stock-still when Angelo was five yards from them. He said again, hoarsely, 'They're coming!' He could hear the increasing noise of the car, and now Pasquale was watching, not only his flock, but the bend in the road twenty yards away. Quite suddenly he made a little jump, all his muscles twitched, his eyes dilated and his hands flew out, like a man who has had an electric shock; and Angelo turned swiftly to see what was happening.

The peasant on the donkey had reached the corner a moment before the car overtook him. As it approached he bent towards the other donkey, and from a funnel in the load of wood on its back swiftly drew a tommy-gun, with which, very calmly and accurately, he opened fire on the car as it passed him.

The shriek of skidding tyres covered the staccato of gunfire, and the heavy car, after rocking this way and that, fell with a deafening bang into the ditch beside Angelo, on the north side of the road, crushing beneath it a couple of small brown sheep. The engine stopped, and the silence that followed was startling in its intensity. The tall peasant, who had dismounted, came running up and, before anyone could stop him, carefully fired three more shots into the wrecked car. 'That will save trouble,' he said, and with a smile asked Angelo, 'How is my friend Don Agesilas?'

Angelo, gaping and tremulous, perceived that the peasant was blind of one eye; but before he could speak, Simon Telfer and Corporal Trivet were beside them, and Simon was asking questions in a loud angry voice.

'Who the devil are you?' he demanded. 'What are you doing here? Who gave you permission to shoot on my ground? You damned poacher!'

The peasant took from an inner pocket a monocle of clouded tortoise shell, which he adjusted over his blind eye, and said urbanely, 'You are Captain Telfer, I presume? My name is Fest.'

'You're Fest, are you? Well, you're an unmitigated nuisance! You've spoiled the whole plan. First of all you leave me in the lurch, you don't turn up when I expect you, and now when you do come, you get in my way!'

Angelo had never seen Telfer so angry, but Fest was unperturbed. He made a small deprecatory gesture and said in a soothing voice, 'There is no need to be upset. Our mission has been accomplished and both the officers are dead. So, indeed, is their driver.'

Simon walked to the overturned car and looked into it. 'I wanted them alive,' he said. 'My orders were to take them prisoner.'

'That would have been too cruel,' said Fest. 'I could not, without straining my conscience, have assisted you in that.'

'Crueller to take them prisoner than to kill them?'

'Much crueller,' said Fest. 'I have been a prisoner myself, and I know.'

Simon, still angry, demanded, 'Why did you interfere in this affair? I can't understand you. It seems to me that you have shown a complete lack of responsibility.'

'I am self-indulgent,' said Fest. 'I have nothing in the world but my hobbies.'

'I admit,' said Simon, 'that you did your job very efficiently, though it wasn't done in the way I intended.'

'Thank you.'

'But we can't stay here gossiping. – Get in and search them, Trivet. See what papers they're carrying.'

'I shall help,' said Fest. 'I intend to take this officer's uniform, though it will require cleaning before I can wear it. I have long wanted to dress myself up as a colonel of the Schutzstaffel.'

Angelo, in the meantime, had been staring with a horrified fascination at the other dead officer. He had recognized his old pupil, General Hammerfurter, to whom he had once taught Italian, and though he had detested him when he was alive, he could not help feeling sorry for him now that he was dead. He thought Fest was talking utter nonsense when he said that it was crueller to take a man prisoner than to kill him; for Angelo had such a healthy appetite for life that he could imagine nothing worse than to be deprived of it. In the simplicity of his heart, moreover, he thought it strange and marvellous, an occasion for wonderment and awe, that so great a person as a general could be removed from the grandeur to which he was accustomed by a little piece of lead no bigger than an acorn. A bullet, he had supposed, was a private's ration. It was monstrous that a general should die of it.

While Angelo was musing in this unprofitable manner, and Fest was busily undressing the dead colonel, and Tom Trivet was searching for documents, they were interrupted by a little squall of bullets from the north, and then by another from the east. Some of the bullets struck and penetrated the car, others flew off it with a wicked whine, and a few scarred the surface of the road within a foot or two of where Simon was standing with Pasquale the partisan. Simon and Pasquale immediately leapt into the cover of some trees on the south side of the road, and were quickly followed by Fest and Tom Trivet; the former carrying the German colonel's uniform, and the latter a small packet of letters. But Angelo took shelter under the car.

A German patrol, on a periodic tour of the hills, had been attracted by the noise of the smash, and when the non-commissioned officer in charge of it saw three or four men gathered about the car, and a scattered flock of sheep and two donkeys in the vicinity, he immediately assumed that some local peasants had perceived an opportunity for looting. Dividing his patrol into two, and ordering both parties on to nearby hillocks that overlooked the road, he had given the signal to fire as soon as they were in position. When he saw Simon and the others make a dash for cover, he and half his patrol got up and ran towards the car.

'Angelo, Angelo!' shouted Simon. 'Oh, damn him, why didn't he come with us? Angelo! Get a move on, you fool!'

But Angelo, huddled in the ditch with his head between his hands, stayed where he was.

'I can't wait for him,' said Simon. 'He knows the orders,

he knows we can't stay and fight it out. We're not equipped for fighting.'

'I'll go and get him,' said Corporal Trivet, and before Simon could answer he was running across the road, firing as he went. Simon and Pasquale at once gave him covering fire, and the Germans, one of whom was hit, quickly went to ground. Fest had disappeared, and there was no sign of the partisans who should have been supporting them.

Trivet knelt and looked under the car. 'Come on,' he said, 'you can't stay here.'

'What else can I do?' asked Angelo.

'Get up and run. I'll take care of you.'

'Oh my God!' said Angelo. 'The road is very broad.'

'Hurry,' said Trivet.

Angelo, crouching, ran nervously towards the trees, and Trivet, after firing a burst in the direction of the Germans, followed him. He was hit and fell as he reached the other side. Simon pulled him into cover, and found a flesh wound in his left thigh. 'It's only a scratch,' he said, and began to unfasten a field-dressing. A German appeared thirty yards away, and Pasquale shot him through the head.

'You can walk all right, can't you?' asked Simon.

'I'm all right,' said Trivet.

'But your arm's bleeding, too –'

'They hit me twice. I'll tie that up later. It's nothing to worry about.'

'Angelo and Pasquale will go with you. I'll follow in a few minutes.'

The Germans were now moving with more caution, and Simon waited for more than a minute before one showed himself. He was the non-commissioned officer in charge of the patrol, and Simon shot him in the chest. He fell, and another man came to his assistance. Simon hit him also, and running behind some bushes about thirty yards to the right, fired several shots at random, and repeated the manoeuvre from another position still farther away. Keeping under cover, he then followed the others.

The site of the ambush had been largely determined by

the useful line of retreat which it offered. Here a little wood concealed him as he ran, and there the slope of a terraced hill and a grove of olive trees whose green and silver leaves were now straining in the evening wind. He soon overtook Pasquale, who told him that he would find Angelo and the Corporal a little farther on.

Pasquale, broadly grinning, was enjoying himself. 'That was good, that was fine,' he said. 'You saw him that I shot in the noggin? *Bic-boc!* like that, and he's bottom-up. A big Tedescho, six feet high. Oh, I'm good, but I was better still when I was a young man. We are all right now?'

'Yes, I think so. Will you do rearguard while I go on and see how Corporal Trivet is?'

'Have no fear,' said Pasquale. 'I will protect you.'

Tom Trivet, with one arm round Angelo's neck and the other hand tucked into his shirt, was keeping a good pace, but his cheeks were as white as a bone, his nose waxen, and his right sleeve drenched with blood. He was unwilling to stop, but when they came to a small stream Simon washed and examined the wound, and discovered that the tip of his shoulder-blade had been broken. He dressed and bandaged the wound as well as he could, and they continued their march to the south. Before it was dark they had reached a friendly farmhouse on the east bank of the Arno, where they waited for Pasquale and the cover of night.

Pasquale arrived about two hours later, still in high spirits, and said that the German patrol, now reinforced, had apparently picked up a false trail; the Tedeschi, he said, were watching the road and the river-bank in the neighbourhood of Rignano, well to the north of where they were. He himself had had no trouble.

Simon was a little worried and considerably annoyed by the disappearance of Fest. It was ridiculous, he told himself, to suppose that Fest would betray them; he had a long record of hostile acts against the Germans, and his assassination of a General, a Colonel, and their driver seemed to indicate, if not sympathy with the Allies, at least a genuine antipathy to their enemies. But from the military point of view his behaviour was most unorthodox, and his loyalty – well, loyalty was a difficult word to define, but even were it given its broadest definition, Fest would still appear to be deficient in it. He was fundamentally selfish, Simon decided. It was a vice that foreigners, and foreign countries, were much addicted to. They were selfish and irresponsible, and there were far too many of them in the world. – So thought Simon, brooding over Fest's unloyalty, and his mind discoloured by it.

His mood softened, however, when he turned to Pasquale, for Pasquale, his leathern face creased with delight and his broad hands filling the air with gestures, was describing for the tenth time how he had hit a giant Tedescho in the noggin, and laid him like a dead ox on the grass; and their hosts, a sturdy black-browed farmer and his broad-built wife, who were known for the help they had given to many British and American airmen who had been shot down and gone into hiding, were encouraging him with great exclamations of pleasure; and the farmer was filling, brim-full and spilling over, everyone's glass from a new flask of wine; and four children in the doorway, wide of eye and sucking their thumbs, were listening as though it were the first fairy-tale they were hearing; and the farmer's wife, without a thought for the morrow, was cutting for her guests' entertainment her last loaf of bread and the knuckle-end of her last smoked ham.

Suddenly regretting the ungenerosity of his thoughts, Simon raised his glass to Pasquale and said, 'You're a good fellow, Pasquale, and you've done well.'

'Right in the noggin,' said Pasquale happily. 'A Tedescho six and a half feet high, the biggest I ever saw, but *bic-boc!* and down he goes, arse over tip.'

'When the war is finished,' said Simon to the farmer, 'I shall come back to Italy.'

'Why not?' said the farmer. 'Before the war, all you English used to come to Italy. Italy is very beautiful. Naturally you will return, and perhaps quite soon.'

'*Speriamo,*' said Pasquale.

'But the war's not over yet,' said the farmer's wife.

'*Pazienza*,' said the farmer. 'Even wars come to an end.'

A few minutes later Simon left them to reconnoitre the river-crossing, and when he came back, with the news that all was quiet, Angelo went to wake Tom Trivet, who had been sleeping in the farmer's bed. Trivet woke in a fright and began to talk with rambling excitement; but a glass of brandy seemed to calm him, and presently they set out with Simon in the lead, Angelo and Trivet a hundred yards behind him, and Pasquale in the rear. The night was dark but clear, with clouds like black continents dividing a grapeskin sky, and the Arno running noisily, flushed with the day's rain. They had no great difficulty in fording it, however, and two hours later they were in the upland country to the west. Then Trivet collapsed, and they found that the wound in his leg was bleeding again.

They carried him into the shelter of a nearby copse, and Pasquale went in search of a neighbouring friend of his, another farmer who had, from time to time, succoured Allied soldiers who had escaped from their captors. He returned before dawn with a short ladder, half a dozen eggs, and a disconcerting account of the increased number of German troops in the neighbourhood. The farm where they had hoped to leave Trivet, in comfort and reasonable security, was occupied by the enemy.

All day they lay hidden, listening to the not-far-distant noises of an intermittent battle, and fed thinly on biscuits, chocolate, and raw eggs. For most of the time Tom Trivet slept, and when evening came he seemed better, though he was still too weak to walk. Both Angelo and Pasquale knew the country they were in, and after long discussion over a map Simon had come to the conclusion that by keeping to the higher slopes of the Chianti mountains they might break through the German lines and reach the nearest troops of the Eighth Army before another dawn.

'I don't think they're much more than ten miles away,' he said, 'and if we can average a mile and a half an hour, carrying Trivet, we can do it in seven hours, and that gives us a little margin of darkness for safety. What do you think, Pasquale?'

'By myself I could go through quite easily,' said Pasquale. 'Carrying the Corporal, it will be more difficult, and hard work. But not impossible.'

'Angelo?'

'We must do everything we can for him,' said Angelo very earnestly. 'He should be in hospital now, and delay may be dangerous.'

Angelo had spent the day keeping flies off the Corporal while he slept. His heart was full of gratitude, and devotion, and self-reproach. Not only had Tom Trivet saved his life, or saved him from captivity, and suffered grievous wounds in consequence; but he had set Angelo an example in generosity which he now saw as a great and humiliating lesson. He, Angelo, had committed a fault unpardonable in a soldier: he had sought safety in a ditch when his plain duty was to stand up – for the short time it would take to cross a narrow road – and thereafter fight or run as he might be ordered. He had failed in his duty, he had sinned against discipline. But Tom had forgiven him and proved his forgiveness by risking his own life to rescue him. How much more, then, should Angelo forgive his dear Lucrezia, whose fault he could pardon at no cost to his skin, but only a little wound to his pride? Yes, Tom had taught him a lesson. A man should be generous always – and the mere thought of his coming magnanimity filled his mind with the anticipation of its pleasure.

'Yes,' he went on, 'Corporal Trivet needs medical attention, and though it may be difficult to carry him through the German lines, I do not think we should be deterred by that.'

'Good for you,' said Simon.

'And afterwards, I very much hope that you will allow me to return to Pontefiore.'

'For any particular purpose?' asked Simon.

'I have set my heart on being married at the earliest possible moment,' said Angelo.

CHAPTER SEVENTEEN

WHEN THEY HAD TIED Tom Trivet firmly to the ladder which Pasquale had found, Angelo and Pasquale lifted it to their shoulders, inserting their heads between convenient rungs at either extremity, and began their night-march, led by Simon some forty yards in front of them. Good fortune and their choice of the most arduous route enabled them to avoid the Germans, but nothing could mitigate the burden of Tom Trivet. They had to carry him up steep hill-paths to lofty starlit ridges, where a boisterous wind assaulted them, and down again by tortuous rocky trails. They followed sheep-tracks across ground so perilously aslant that Angelo often feared they would lose their footing and go tumbling and rolling into unseen depths; and they forced their way through thickets of tall bracken. The poles of the ladder pressed deeper and deeper into their aching shoulders, or leaned horribly against their necks when they walked upon a slope. Whenever they were climbing, Tom Trivet's weight hung backward so that they were in danger of being garrotted, and when they went downhill their heads were bowed in agonizing obeisance. Long before midnight Angelo began to suspect that a wounded giant lay on the ladder. By two o'clock in the morning the giant had acquired some uncommonly heavy luggage: his tombstone, perhaps, the field-gun that he used for a fowling-piece, two thousand demijohns of the local wine, and so forth. A couple of hours later, pain had created a fantasy more malignant still, and the giant was an ogre whose monstrous thumbs were pressing Angelo and Pasquale, like drawing-pins into a board, deep into the resistant earth. Angelo wept and prayed, Pasquale groaned and swore. Tom Trivet was silent, for he was unconscious again. And Simon, with no mercy for himself or them, still sought improbable paths and compelled them to follow.

When daylight came they were some three hundred feet below the crest of a great green hill, at the upper corner of a straggling wood that climbed its southern slope, and there was nothing to be seen of the enemy, nothing of the English army. Simon at last gave the order to halt and rest, and Angelo, so weary that he could no longer bear even the sight of other men, staggered a little farther downhill, a hundred yards or more, and falling into a clump of ferns at the edge of the wood was sound asleep within the instant.

He was awakened, when the sun stood overhead, by the iron growl and screech of approaching tanks, and immediately was seized with a fear of their crushing him where he lay hidden among the ferns; but as he did not know whether they were British or German he dared not get up and run away, lest he expose himself to the enemy. The leading tank halted not far from him, and a little while later Angelo heard men's voices. He held his breath to listen, and then had to bite his fingers to keep his teeth from chattering. It was not English they were speaking.

'*En wat is daar nou te doen noudat ons hier aangeland het?*' said one of the invisible soldiers.

'*Ons Kan die natuurskoon bewonder,*' replied another. '*Daar is, goddank, niks anders om te doen nie.*'

There was a pleasant tune in their voices that was certainly not German, but the words were more like German than anything else, and Angelo was well aware that the enemy had recruited foreign legions who spoke in many tongues. He lay still for three minutes more, tormented by doubt as well as fear, and then, with relief that merged quickly into gratitude and pure happiness, heard other voices and words – familiar English words – that now seemed inexpressibly kind and comforting.

'Shock me,' exclaimed a hoarse and breathless Cockney, 'if ever I want to see a shocking mountain again! It's like that shocking old nursery rhyme, this shocking war is:

> The good old Duke of York,
> He had a thousand men,
> He marched 'em up to the shocking top of a shocking
> > hill,
> And shocking well marched 'em down again.

I'm browned off, I am, and my shocking feet are on fire.'

How sweetly they fell upon his ears, the homely English syllables! He was free, he must be free, in the company of these good fellows who spoke the tongue that Shakespeare spake; and crawling softly through the fern he saw presently some half-a-dozen tall soldiers, wiping their sweaty brows, of the Grenadier Guards, and with them the crews of two tanks of the South African Division. They appeared to be on terms of the warmest friendship, and the voices that had lately been speaking Afrikaans now joined with Cockney in genial debate. Angelo, not yet revealing himself, watched them and listened with the greatest pleasure until a Guardsman, coming into the fern on business of his own, tripped and fell on him. This caused some confusion, and Angelo for a moment or two was in near danger of his life, but saved it by his own command of English.

'I am not a shocking spy!' he exclaimed indignantly. 'I am a shocking co-belligerent!'

They listened to him then, both Englishmen and South Africans, with a proper respect, and readily went with him to look for Simon and Pasquale and Corporal Trivet.

Simon, they discovered, had already met the Grenadiers and was talking to one of their officers who happened to be an old friend of his. Tom Trivet had been carried away and put in the doctor's care, and Pasquale, who had never before seen tanks on a mountain-top, was patting their steel flanks with admiring hands, as though they had been fat cattle.

For a little while, in this small segment of it, the war had the innocent look of some old pastoral foray. The day was fine, and the great shoulders of the green Chianti hills showed firm and muscular beneath a tall blue sky. A gentle wind rustled the bracken and whispered in the branches of some lonely trees. Two officers with field-glasses, patient and quiet as deerstalkers in a Highland forest, searched the opposing mountainside for a possible head; and the Guardsmen and the South Africans – the sons of Queen Victoria's infantry and of Kruger's long-sighted riflemen – lay gossiping together and drinking tea.

A tank moved slowly forward, and its gun was depressed till its barrel lay on a downward slant like the slope of the hill. Three shots were fired, and from the wall of a farmhouse in the valley below floated small clouds of dust. A man, crouching, ran from the farm into a copse behind it, and in the flat fields to the east little khaki figures could be seen advancing. Three aeroplanes, circling their target, stooped like hawks upon it, and as they climbed again tall plumes of smoke rose behind them. The sound of distant machine-gun fire mingled with the stridulation of grasshoppers.

Angelo and Pasquale ate some bread and bully, and went to sleep again. Then Simon sent for them, and they found him, half a mile downhill, sitting with a Guardsman in a borrowed jeep. They had no difficulty in returning to Pontefiore, for the curving front of battle was now several miles to the north of it, and peace, with a look of stunned surprise, lay upon the ruined village. In the castle they found Fest drinking white wine with the Countess.

Simon's manner, when they met, was cold and constrained, but Fest was bland and smiling, and the Countess took such obvious pleasure in his company that Simon had to master his feelings and assume a friendlier air than he had any mind to. What would otherwise have been an acrimonious discussion became in fact, at the Countess's table, a protracted dinner-party with Fest, on her right, playing the part of the distinguished guest, accomplished in conversation, until they retired to her drawing-room, where the Countess herself kept the talk going with anecdotes of her early life.

Angelo, in the meantime, had found Lucrezia, proposed immediate marriage to her, and been accepted. Lucrezia's objections to a wedding in war-time had seemingly vanished, and though Angelo warned her that he would certainly have to leave her again, she made no reference to the sad plight and many difficulties of a young wife, married one week and left alone the next, which had been the mainstay of her argument the year before. She had responded, indeed, with such a melting warmth as Angelo had never seen in her. She had hung upon his neck as though in utter abandonment to his will or care, and lying in his arms had looked up at him with eyes so lovely in their trust and gratitude that Angelo, at one moment ravished with delight, was at the next intoxicated with the pride of his triumphant manhood.

He was, however, somewhat taken aback by the coolness with which she listened to the tale of Tom Trivet's heroism and the wounds he had received. She made no concealment of her agitation when Angelo spoke of the danger that he himself had been in, when he found himself on the wrong side of the road; but the news of Tom Trivet's wounding did not affect her in the least.

'He is all right now?' she asked, with plain indifference in her voice.

'By no means!' said Angelo indignantly. 'He was hit in two places and it will be a long time before he is all right again. He will recover, certainly, but at this moment, I suppose, he is lying in great pain; while I, who owe everything to him, am alive and well and supremely happy.'

'Oh darling, how glad I am that you are alive, and very, very glad that you are happy!'

'But we must also think about Corporal Trivet –'

'Let us think about him some other time. Just now it is enough to think only about ourselves.'

On subsequent reflection he admitted that her loss of interest in Tom Trivet would be a decided advantage to their married state; but he was surprised, and dubiously hurt, and even alarmed a little by the completeness of her unconcern. That Tom had jilted her could not be denied, and to get a girl with child and then desert her was something, of course, quite unforgivable. But even so, the spectacle of unforgiveness was a trifle shocking; or so it appeared to Angelo.

He was, however, far too happy in his possession of Lucrezia to waste time in fault-finding, and early the next morning he sought the village priest and told him that he wanted to be married as soon as possible.

The village church and the village priest had both suffered badly in the bombing of Pontefiore. The church, with its west wall blown down and most of the roof gone, stood wide open to the sun and the rain, and the priest, having lost the placid view of life that had protected him for half a century, now seemed equally exposed to the elements. He shivered in the noonday heat, he was frightened of the dark, and when Angelo said firmly that the day after tomorrow would be most suitable for a wedding, he at once agreed. The sacraments, he said, were always available for those who needed them, and marriage was a sacrament like baptism and penance. 'Though indeed,' he said, 'I should not be happy if you had to be carried to it, as you were to your baptism, or returned for it again and again, as undoubtedly you will in penitence. Oh no! One marriage is enough for anyone, and you'll come to it on your own legs or not at all. – Bless you, my child. Our poor church is draughty now, but I dare say it will serve.'

All the villagers were delighted by the prospect of a wedding, for they saw in it a brave assertion that life must continue in its ordinary way, despite the outrages of war; and Lucrezia's mother laughed and wept alternately for the better part of a whole day, while the Countess with a stern and furrowed brow went to and fro to see what could be provided for a marriage feast. She found little enough, for the Germans had taken with them everything they could carry, and the general feeling of elation was quickly followed by a widespread gloom when it became apparent that the celebrations would be dulled by hunger.

Angelo was further depressed by a conversation he had with Simon. 'I have been thinking about your future,' said Simon.

'I am going to be very happy,' said Angelo.

'Yes, I hope you will be. But I think you should know that I've recommended you and Pasquale for transfer to one of the new Italian Brigades that are being formed. I'm going to one of them myself, as a liaison officer.'

'And what shall I have to do there?' asked Angelo.

'Training, to begin with. We're starting to train and equip a large number of Italian troops, so that by next year they'll be able to take their place in the line along with us and the Americans.'

'By next year? Is the war going to last as long as that?'

'Nobody knows how long it's going to last, but obviously we must be prepared for the worst.'

'I don't think I could live,' said Angelo, 'if I were truly prepared for the worst. Why should I, indeed? Why should anyone?'

'Now you're being obstructive. You are talking for the sake of talking, and that won't do you any good at all. What I mean is that we must face facts.'

'In an infantry regiment?' asked Angelo sadly.

'Yes, you're pretty certain to be posted to the infantry.'

'But why, why! Why must I go and spend month after month being drilled, and running to and fro carrying very heavy weights, and firing rifles and mortars and machine-guns, and throwing bombs of which I am extremely frightened, and lying out all night in the cold, and marching hundreds of miles without going anywhere in particular – and all to be killed in the most unpleasant manner by a total stranger in some part of the country that I have no wish to visit?'

'I think it is the proper thing for you to do,' said Simon stiffly.

'Oh my God,' said Angelo, 'now I am doomed indeed!' – For he knew that when the English say *It is the proper thing to do*, the inexorable laws of nature are supplemented by another that they discovered, and only they can understand. Oh, their wild notions of propriety! They are like sunspots, he thought, for they cannot be explained or foretold, and their effects are incalculable. Whether they have indeed certain absolute standards of behaviour, or merely a tribal instinct, or perhaps an hereditary taint – a sort of itch – it is impossible to say. But you can no more argue with them than you can dispute the law of gravity. – Yes, he admitted, I am doomed, and there is no escape.

'Lucrezia,' he said, 'will not be pleased when she hears that I am to become a soldier in the infantry again. It will be very difficult to say goodbye to her.'

'Well,' said Simon, 'that sort of thing is always difficult. But it has to be done, of course.'

Always difficult! thought Angelo in a sudden wordless rage. *Always* difficult indeed! He wanted to ask Simon – but dared not, for he knew it would be improper – he wanted to ask him how often he had bidden goodbye to a woman who loved him, and broken her heart, and comforted himself with the cold reflection that *it had to be done, of course*. Oh, they were insufferable, these Englishmen! They made life impossible – and the expectation of it highly improbable.

But he knew that he must hide his feelings, for though he had come near to losing his temper, he retained his manners; and the English, as he had learnt, disliked above all things a display of feeling. So with a stiffness like Simon's own he said, 'I shall do whatever you think it befits me to do. You can be sure of that.'

'That's good,' said Simon warmly. 'You're a good fellow, Angelo, though you talk a lot of nonsense, and I knew I could rely on you.'

Walking by himself, with desolated spirit, Angelo pondered this last remark and could not decide whether he had been flattered or insulted by it. Simon relied on him to do something which was quite unnatural for a man to do; something to which he was wholly disinclined; something that could only be justified by Simon's ridiculous notions of propriety. And Simon was clearly wrong in some of his ideas, for it was absurd to pretend that people should always be prepared for the worst. Shadowed by such a future, the present would be intolerable. To make the most of the present one should be prepared for the best, and risk a little disappointment. Yes, Simon was wrong in that, and so he might also be wrong in his expectation of a long war. The war might be over tomorrow, or next week, or at any rate before he had to return to the penal servitude of infantry training.

Hope crept into his mind, rosy-fingered as the dawn, and like the quick-rising sun swelled in imagination's sky to golden confidence. He was going to be married: that was the main thing, and nothing could prevent it now. As for the future, it was unpredictable. There might be fair weather or foul, but no one knew which till it began to blow. 'And if it is the former,' said Angelo, 'I shall enjoy it; if the latter, I must endure it. But what folly to start shivering now!'

On his wedding-morning he dressed himself carefully in a borrowed blue suit, that was somewhat tight over the chest and a little short in the leg, but looked smart enough with a clean shirt and a white tie and a flower in the buttonhole. Pasquale accompanied him to the church, where they arrived an hour and a half before anyone else appeared, and spent the time in trying to re-assemble the pieces of a ruined fresco, of the Flight into Egypt, that lay scattered on the floor of the north aisle.

In the midst of destruction the painted walls of the church were incongruously gay. The frescoes that covered them were cracked and torn, but their faded colours were brightened by the sun, and Saints and Martyrs, Shepherds and Madonnas and Patriarchs, all seemed to be in festival attire for their first sight of the outer world.

Angelo found the ears of the Ass, and said, 'It was Gozzoli who painted this.'

'They were good little animals that that fellow had on the road over by Vallombrosa the other day,' said Pasquale. 'It was a pity we had to leave them behind.'

'Gozzoli was an extraordinarily industrious painter,' said Angelo.

'It's a disease,' said Pasquale, 'Now what do you make

of this? Will it be the Ass's tail or the half of St. Joseph's beard?'

'It fits this piece here. – Do you really think that to be industrious is a disease?'

'I never caught it myself, but my poor wife died of it. – Put all these blue bits together.'

'I hope Lucrezia will be a good worker,' said Angelo.

'It's useful,' said Pasquale, 'but they're apt to be shrewish, those who are. And those who won't work are sluts, and that's worse.'

'Here's part of the halo,' said Angelo. 'I suppose you never get perfection in a woman?'

'I never heard of it. But you're sure to get surprises, so you might be lucky.'

'This, I think, is the Ass's tail.'

'Some of them change their character over night,' said Pasquale. 'You take what you think is the mildest and softest little creature you ever saw, and you give her a house of her own and a husband of her own, and as like as not she turns into a regular tyrant.'

'I think I'll go and sit in the shade,' said Angelo. 'The sun is hot this morning.'

Pasquale followed him and they sat on the pavement under a badly scarred representation of Sheba's visit to King Solomon.

'There are things that go on in the mind of a woman,' said Pasquale, 'that no man can ever guess at. And because of that there are things that happen in married life that you've got to experience before you can believe in them.'

'What sort of things?' asked Angelo nervously.

'Injustice,' said Pasquale in a graveyard voice, 'is one of the worst. They've got a longer memory than we have, and your own words will be used against you.'

'But surely, with a little patience and common sense, you can easily put right small misunderstandings of that kind?'

'No,' said Pasquale. 'There's something in women that can't ever be put right. You can't do anything about it. You've just got to suffer.'

'What, what is the time?' stammered Angelo.

'They ought to be here in about ten minutes now.'

'I think I'll go for a little walk first.'

'Don't go too far,' said Pasquale. 'It won't help you if you make a bad start by being late. That's the sort of thing they never forget.'

'O God!' said Angelo, walking very rapidly. 'Please give me courage! I mustn't run away now. I really mustn't. But oh, how I wish I hadn't been so impulsive! There was no need for me to get married – not yet – and though I do love Lucrezia, it may not suit either of us to be tied together for ever and ever. And she has such a strong character. I'm sure she can never be cured of that. Oh, I do wish I could have another chance.'

He was walking quite aimlessly, and only recognized the lane he was in when he was startled by a furious female voice, and, looking up, saw a figure in white running towards him, her dress furled high to the knees, and fifty yards in front of her a small child making what haste it could in the tumbling gait of a two-year-old. The child ran into a garden, and Angelo perceived that it was the garden where, so short a time before, he had heard Lucrezia's confession of infidelity. He also perceived that the figure in white was Lucrezia herself, and the child was Tommaso.

The need for action drove out fear. He too began to run and entered the garden side by side with Lucrezia, who in a voice breathless with anger and exertion told him how Tommaso, freshly clad in new clothes for the church, had at the last moment escaped her vigilance, and disappeared on some purpose of his own. A moment or two later his purpose became apparent: it was to look for the frog that croaked so loudly in the garden pool. They heard him smacking the water with a stick, and then they heard a louder splash. Tommaso had fallen in again.

Angelo pulled him out, and Lucrezia boxed his ears. Gasping and whimpering, he promptly attacked her, and Lucrezia pushed him away, fearful lest her white dress be soiled. Tommaso then began to cry in earnest, and went on crying with the implacable resolution of which only a simple child is capable. Two or three of Lucrezia's sisters arrived. They too were dressed in wedding finery, and Tommaso in a berserk rage assaulted them in turn. They screamed, and pulled their frocks away from his wet hands. Angelo picked him up and held him, dripping, at arm's length. Tommaso's anger subsided a little and his cries diminished to a small braying noise.

'What are we going to do with him?' asked one of the sisters.

'Do with him?' demanded Lucrezia. 'We must take him with us, naturally. There is no one else to look after him, and if we leave him alone he will drown himself. But he is going to be a good boy now. Put him down, Angelo, and he will walk with me.'

As soon as Tommaso's feet touched the ground he began to cry again with alarming vigour. He would have nothing to do with Lucrezia or her sisters, but clung passionately to Angelo's leg.

'Angelo knows how to manage him,' said one of the sisters.

'He would be quite good if Angelo carried him,' said another.

'He is going to spoil everything,' cried Lucrezia, on the verge of tears. 'It is my wedding day, and everything is going wrong. Look at my shoes. They are quite dirty already, and it is getting late. Oh, Angelo, what shall we do?'

'If you want me to,' said Angelo unhappily, 'I suppose I can carry him.'

Lucrezia with a radiant smile whispered in his ear and called him a darling. The sisters clapped their hands, and Angelo lifted the soaking Tommaso to his shoulder. Tommaso sat there with a look of grave satisfaction, and they set off for the church.

The whole village was assembled, either within the gaping building or among the adjacent ruins, and a murmur of sympathetic pleasure rose from the spectators when they saw that the wedding had already become a family occasion.

Angelo tried again to set Tommaso down, but a piercing howl was the immediate response, and Lucrezia once more showed signs of the most painful agitation.

Angelo by now was nearly as wet as the child. He shivered a little, straightened his tie, and hoisted Tommaso to the other shoulder. They walked up the open nave to a little chapel that had not suffered greatly, where the priest was waiting with the Countess and Simon Telfer and Lucrezia's parents.

The poor bomb-shocked priest was quite bewildered by the appearance of the dripping child, and to everyone's surprise he began to recite the service for public baptism. When the Countess informed him of his mistake, however, he showed no ill-will but proceeded to marry Angelo and Lucrezia with the utmost kindliness, and manifestly in a great hurry lest he go wrong again.

Tommaso sat solemnly on the bridegroom's left shoulder, little runlets of water trickled down the bridegroom's neck, and Lucrezia, gravely beautiful, put her hand in his. The cloudless sun lighted the ancient frescoes, and the Madonnas and the Saints, the Patriarchs and Angels that the industrious Gozzoli, and Pinturicchio, and Lippo Memmi had painted long centuries before, looked down in mild benignity. On the one side of them Saint Sebastian endured his martyrdom with astonishing equanimity, and on the other Noah discovered the secret of making wine with pious gratitude. Rubble from the broken walls was crumbled by restless feet, and as soon as the ceremony was over the villagers surrounded Angelo and Lucrezia in warm congratulation. Tommaso allowed himself to be transferred to the shoulders of Pasquale.

After that nobody quite knew what to do, and all stood talking in little groups among the shattered masonry, under the heat of the bright sky, hoping to hear some good suggestion for enjoyment of the day, but what they chiefly heard was the hunger rumbling in their bellies. The Countess's intention to offer a wedding-feast to the whole village had come to nothing, for the simple reason that there was nothing to eat. Or very little. Far too little to feed the assembled men, women, and children of Pontefiore. They were all aware of this, but still they waited with a lingering hope in their minds, their ears alert for better news, and their eyes turning wistfully in the direction of the Countess and her foreign guest.

She, for the third or fourth time, was telling Angelo of her failure and her disappointment, and her reluctance to sit down with a small party to the small meal that was all she had been able to provide, when the great majority must remain unfed.

'But what else can I do?' she asked. 'I can't work miracles and I don't know anyone who can, more's the pity. I could give them something to drink, for there's wine in plenty, but when you pour wine into empty stomachs you don't know what may happen, though you can make a good guess. And we've had trouble enough in Pontefiore without that. No, I'll just have to tell them all to go home, if they've got homes to go to, and wait for better times. It's cold comfort and I don't like the sound of it; but I can think of nothing else.'

Twice while she was talking Angelo heard the noise of a motor-horn some distance away, and now it sounded insistently. Some of the villagers were already moving in idle curiosity towards the ruined bridge, with children running ahead of them. The harsh irregular voice of the horn seemed increasingly to demand attention. The drifting movement of the crowd became a purposive current as more and more people joined it. The horn grew louder: a rasping noise with occasionally a fierce warbling note to break its monotony. Angelo and Lucrezia, Pasquale and the Countess and Simon Telfer and Lucrezia's parents, all followed the crowd. Everyone hurried towards the bridge.

The children who had led the way came running back, chattering excitedly. Their words were repeated, incredulously at first, and then in triumph, and became a noisy chorus. '*Il Signore!*' shouted the crowd. '*Il nostro caro Signore!*'

On the road, on the far side of the broken bridge, stood a

six-wheeled canvas-roofed military lorry with an American star painted on the bonnet. An American soldier sat in the cab and another, a huge fat man, stood beside it. As the crowd gathered about the near abutment a slim and handsome figure, slightly flushed by exertion, came climbing out of the ravine. It was Don Agesilas.

'*Ben arrivato!*' shouted the villagers. '*Ben arrivato!*'

The Countess pushed her way through the excited people and Don Agesilas, kissing first her hand and then her cheek, exclaimed, 'My dear! How long since we have met! Far, far too long. But how well you look, and younger than ever. I am devoted to you.'

'What's in that lorry?' she asked.

'It is what is called, I believe, a mixed cargo.'

'Is there any food?'

'It is full of food.'

'You've come just in time,' said the Countess. 'We're going to have a feast.'

'ONE OF THE advantages of living in a castle,' said the Count, looking up at the fallen ceiling, 'is that one recognizes a periodic destruction as part of its natural existence. In a town flat or a suburban villa a bomb or two, a little flight of shells, are catastrophic. But this small castle of mine, of no importance to anyone but myself, has survived all manner of disasters, and I cannot feel seriously perturbed by the present damage. The walls remain and the holes can be patched.'

He and Simon Telfer were sitting at the end of a long dinner table, empty now but for a bowl or two of fruit, the decanters, and their glasses. The villagers, abundantly fed, had long since returned to their ruined homes, and Angelo and Lucrezia had retired to the housekeeper's room, happily undamaged, which had been chosen as the nuptial chamber. The Countess had left the table early and nothing had been seen of Fest since the afternoon. He had attended neither the wedding nor the wedding feast.

'You were going to tell me something about the two American soldiers who came with you,' said Simon.

'Indeed I was,' said the Count. 'My attention was distracted for a moment by the fall of plaster – the cornice over there is also loose – but the case of the American soldiers is deeply interesting. They are, in fact, not Americans, but deserters from my old regiment who, by nefarious means of which I remain happily ignorant, acquired American uniform for a criminal purpose which, by pure chance, I was able to defeat. The senior of the two, the fat man, is Sergeant Vespucci, of whom you may have heard. Our dear Angelo knows him well. He and Angelo entered Rome together on the morning of its liberation.'

'Vespucci?' said Simon. 'Yes, I think I've heard Angelo speak of him.'

'What a scoundrel the man is,' said the Count complacently, 'and yet how much we could learn from him! For your true rascal is today your only true citizen of the world. He plunders all nations without pride in one or prejudice against another. He despises frontiers – and what an unmitigated nuisance a frontier is! We should all learn to hold them in contempt. In bygone times any educated man was free to live or travel where he chose, but now it is only your rascals who claim such a privilege; and there is nothing international in the world but villainy. Sergeant Vespucci, who certainly deserves to be shot, might serve a better purpose if he were given the chair of philosophy in one of our universities.'

'He stole the lorry as well as the uniform, I suppose?'

'Let me tell the story in my own way,' said the Count. 'I have in Rome a very dear friend, to whom I have been devoted for a number of years, called the Marchesa Dolce; whose circle of acquaintances is always large and sometimes influential. One of the latest to enter it is an American Colonel, now stationed in Rome. He is a man of great charm and his knowledge of the world has made him both wise and humane. He realizes that the war, almost certainly, will come to an end some day, and we shall then have to deal with the as yet unsolved problem of how to live together in peace. He is already doing what he can to ease the situation – into which we may be plunged without warning – by meeting some of our more liberal industrialists and discussing, quite informally, of course, the possibility of their resuming trade with his own firm. A prudent and far-sighted man is the Colonel. He, as an American, has access to many commodities, such as petrol and food and blankets, of which we are sadly in need; and we in our poverty have still an abundance of little pictures, *objets d'art*, and so forth, that he, being a man of culture, can appreciate. We have already made, through his agency, a number of transactions that, I like to think, have been beneficial to both sides.'

The Count paused to replenish his glass and Simon's, and continued: 'You can imagine how upset I was when the Colonel told me, only the other day, that the generosity and good-nature of his fellow-countrymen were being abused, and that some of our people, with a quite shocking impatience, were not waiting to be given such stores of food and clothing as the Americans could afford to exchange for little pictures and so on, but were actually stealing and exposing them for sale in the Black Market. The American Army, said the Colonel, was in fact being plundered by those whom it had come to liberate; and in consequence of its very grave losses the authorities had decided that in future they would have to take care of their stores. They had, in fact, adopted such a serious attitude that the Colonel himself was unable to bring the Marchesa Dolce a side of bacon, a sack of flour, and some cases of fruit that he had promised for her birthday.

'Only a day or two later,' the Count went on, 'I made a discovery that seriously perturbed me. I had recently given Sergeant Vespucci permission to keep a lorry or two, that he used in business, in the courtyard of my house in Rome; of which I had been dispossessed but where, by the kindness of my butler, I still slept. I had met Vespucci some time before, and he had apologized so handsomely for deserting my regiment that I was persuaded to forgive him; more readily, I must confess, because I myself, at that particular time, had had very little control over it. Vespucci told me that he had set up, in a modest way, as what he called a *Free Distributer*, and naturally I was pleased to help him, as I would be to help any old soldier whom I found striving, with the small means at his command, to make a humble place for himself in a world that is too prone to neglect old soldiers. I was more than a little worried, however, after my conversation with the Colonel, to see one night Sergeant Vespucci driving into my courtyard, not one of the shabby vehicles that he had formerly used, but a brand-new American lorry.'

Don Agesilas was interrupted in his story by the return of the Countess, who came in and took the empty chair beside him. 'I thought I'd come back and drink a glass of port wine with you,' she said.

'Nothing could give me more pleasure,' said the Count, rising to receive her with surprise in his voice and wonder in his eye. He reached for the decanter.

'I'm getting quite a taste for port wine,' said the Countess. 'I think it's better for you than brandy.'

'If drunk in the same quantity,' said the Count, 'brandy may produce unfortunate effects.'

'That's what I mean. And you can drink port wine without wincing: that's another advantage. – But go on with what you were talking about; I didn't intend to stop you.'

Don Agesilas found it difficult to conceal his astonishment at this unexpected development in his wife's character, who in all their life together had been abstemious to a degree that he thought dangerous to her health. He watched her, fascinated, while she sipped her port, and with a growing admiration refilled her glass.

'Go on,' she repeated. 'What were you talking about?'

'I really cannot remember,' said the Count.

'Sergeant Vespucci,' said Simon.

'Ah, yes. Yes, Sergeant Vespucci. Well, to put it as briefly as possible, he and a friend of his – another deserter from my regiment, I am sorry to say – had procured American uniform, stolen a six-wheeled lorry and with the aid of accomplices of whom I know nothing, filled it with American goods from the nearest American dump. Then he had the gross impertinence to conceal his booty in the courtyard of my house, and I found myself in a very painful dilemma. It went against the grain to return such a treasury of viands to the military authorities who, from my own observation, were by no means undernourished; but if I let Vespucci sell his loot on the Black Market – and, to give him his due, he offered me a very generous share of the profit – I should be unable to meet my friend the Colonel without embarrassment and a little sensation of guilt. What was I to do? A few minutes' reflection decided me, and I said to Vespucci: "Sergeant, you are a man of good feeling, and at the moment you are completely in my power. You call yourself a Free Distributer, and that is precisely what you are going to be. I am deeply concerned for the welfare of my people in Pontefiore. They have, as I hear, been plundered by the Germans and liberated by our Allies. They are in a sad plight and need comforting. We have here the wherewithal to comfort them. Your cargo, Vespucci, will go to Pontefiore!" – He protested, but ineffectually. I reminded him that I was still his Commanding Officer, and that though he had deserted with the rank of sergeant, I had the authority to reduce him to private. He has his pride, has Vespucci, and eventually he accepted my ruling. So northward we drove, that very night, and I am deeply happy to think that our arrival was so timely.'

'I never thought, when I lived in Bradford, that one day I'd eat stolen meat and be glad of it,' said the Countess.

'Our troops,' said Simon, 'occasionally help themselves to the produce of your country. A few weeks ago, west of Lake Trasimene, they were living very well on roast goose. Then there was a slight epidemic of jaundice, and the rumour got about that it was due to eating Christmas dinners in the height of summer. It was only jaundice that saved the geese from total extinction.'

'You can't expect people to have much respect for property when they're taught to have no respect for each other's life,' said the Countess. 'Whenever there's a war the first casualties are the Ten Commandments.'

'Another glass of port?' Don Agesilas suggested tactfully.

'I don't mind if I do,' said the Countess. 'And now tell me about Rome. What's happened to all the Fascists?'

'Many of them have become Communists,' said the Count. 'And really, can you blame them? After wearing a black shirt for twenty years, what a pleasure it must be to go out in a red muffler!'

'That hardly seems a sufficient explanation,' said Simon.

'It would be sufficient for me,' said the Count, 'but then I am a frivolous person. Many of my Roman neighbours, I admit, are extremely serious – serious and simple – and some are not so simple. There are those who say to themselves, "There is always someone who cooks the joint, and others who dip their bread in the gravy. Yesterday the chef wore a black shirt, and so did we. But now, if red is to be the fashion, let us go out quickly and buy a new handkerchief".'

Presently they retired to the small drawing-room above the garden. The windows had been blown out and the shutters broken, but the night was calm and the heavy curtains hung without motion to the floor.

The Countess halted on the threshold with an exclamation of surprise, and the others, looking over her shoulder, were momentarily startled to see, at ease in a tall chair, a man dressed in the sable uniform of the Schutzstaffel. They recognized him almost immediately, though he had contrived some alteration in his appearance, and slowly approaching regarded him with a puzzled and rather unfriendly curiosity. He had dyed his hair a dull yellow, and in place of his tortoise shell monocle wore one of frosted glass.

'The sleeves are a little short,' said Fest, 'but otherwise the tunic fits very well. There were one or two small holes in it which needed repair, but I am quite skilful with a needle; you hardly notice them, do you?'

'Why are you wearing those clothes?' asked Simon.

'You may call it a dress rehearsal,' said Fest. 'Tomorrow I am going to Florence, and from there, at the first opportunity, to Bologna.'

'But Florence and Bologna are full of Germans,' said the Countess.

'That is why I am going.'

'It's madness,' said Simon. 'You'll be caught immediately and shot out of hand. If you work with us, in a proper and orderly manner, you can do a great deal of good –'

'But I have no desire to do good. I want to amuse myself, that is all. My hobby, my only pleasure in life nowadays, is to annoy the Germans, and since working with your organization I have often been handicapped by its narrowly utilitarian aims. My hobby demands freedom of choice and freedom of movement.'

'The Germans,' said the Count, 'failed to find a small cellar in which I keep a few wines of some interest to myself, and so I can offer you this tolerable cognac, or this armagnac that I have often found uncommonly agreeable to one of my occasionally robust and youthful moods.'

'The armagnac, without a doubt,' said Fest.

'I am inclined to praise your decision,' said the Count. 'No, I do not mean your choice of the armagnac – though I shall follow your example there – but your resolve to play a lone hand against the enemy. I am bored by the spectacle of people moving hither and thither in great masses. One cannot even be sorry for a horde of people. It is only the individual who rouses either interest or compassion. But the lone fighter, the solitary genius, the inconversable artist; the outlaw, the eccentric, and the anchorite; the craftsman with his single-handed skill, the wandering gipsy with his fiddle, the neighbourless shepherd proudly sufficient in his wilderness – all these are being crushed, as if beneath a landslide, by the regimented multitudes of today. It is a day of Great Powers, great causes, great events – and how dull they are! I want to go and watch a lapidary at work in his lonely room, cutting a solitary gem. I want to read, not some great overstuffed history of the world's calamities, but the brief and well-told tale of one embittered man, moved by a single hatred, who cut his sweetheart's throat in a deserted house. I want to turn my back upon mankind in order to see, against the great horizon on the other side, a man alone. Yes, my dear Fest, your proposal pleases me; though it is most unwise.'

'I have had my fill of wisdom,' said Fest, 'and I want no more of it. For twenty years I was a serious person. I was a good man. I knew what was true and what was false, and I revered the truth. I saw where virtue pointed, where wisdom led, and I went that way. And at the end of the road the Gestapo was waiting for me. So now I am entitled to a holiday. A little holiday of unwisdom.'

'I understand you perfectly,' said the Count.

'No!' said Fest. 'You do not understand. You cannot. Nobody can understand what we are like, we who have been tortured. We are different from you.'

'I also,' said the Count stiffly, 'have been in a German prison.'

'So?'

'I was arrested in Rome. I was arrested again in Montenero, where I was very nearly shot in reprisal for one of your exploits.'

'I remember, of course. And what did you think about when you were in prison?'

'Generally about hot baths and food.'

'You cannot have been very long in your prison. When a man has been hungry for a long time – but really hungry, very near starvation – he is no longer worried by the thought of food. He becomes proud and indifferent. You cannot bribe him. That is an important difference, is it not? But it occurs. And torture, if he can survive it long enough, makes him indifferent to fear and pain. He does not even scream when they hit him. When he is back in his cell he may scream, but not at the time. No, no. Then he can be impudent. He can say mischievous things to his torturers, and defy them. He gives them cheek. And when he goes back to his cell he does not think about hot baths and a big dinner, he thinks of one thing only: am I still sane?'

Fest removed his monocle and with a handkerchief wiped his eyes. 'The blind one still weeps,' he said. 'May I have a little more of that good armagnac?'

No one spoke for a minute or two, and then Simon said, 'You can take your revenge far more effectively by working with us.'

'But then it would become your revenge,' said Fest, 'and I want my own, you see. I am quite selfish. No, you can do no good by argument, because we do not think alike. We are quite different people. – And now, if you will excuse me, I think I shall go to bed; for I must leave early to-morrow morning.'

'Look here,' said Simon –

'No,' said Fest. 'I am looking in another direction.' He bent and gravely kissed the Countess's hand. 'Good night,' he said.

Again there was silence, till the Count murmured, 'Poor fellow! I hadn't realized till this evening that he himself is a German.'

'Oh yes,' said Simon, 'he's a German. We know all about him.'

'He's going too far with that hobby of his,' said the Countess. 'But that's just like them. They always overdo things.'

'He was in a concentration camp for two years before the war,' said Simon. 'When he was released he went to Switzerland, where his wife was waiting for him. They lived together for a few months, and then she left him. That upset him badly, and when the war began he went back to Germany with the simple purpose, apparently, of making trouble. He was arrested again, but escaped from a camp in East Prussia. The Polish Underground took care of him, and then he disappeared in the Balkans. He was a steward in a Danube river-steamer for a little while, and for some time he lived in Bucharest. But we first met him in Syria.'

'He told me about his wife before you came here,' said the Countess. 'I'm sorry for him, but she had a lot to put up with too. He used to get up at night and play with the bedroom door. Just opening it and shutting it again. For a man who'd been locked up for years, he said, that was a very pleasant thing to do. But it got on his wife's nerves, and I don't wonder.'

'I ought to stop him,' said Simon. He rose and stood, irresolute, midway between his chair and the door. 'It's his own life, of course, and I suppose he has earned the right to do as he pleases with it. But he's throwing it away.'

'Socrates in his last hour,' said the Count, 'told his judges: "This is the time to say good-bye, and now we must part: you to live, and I to die. Which is the better, God only knows".'

'If Socrates said that, he was talking nonsense,' declared the Countess. 'Go and stop him.'

Simon followed Fest to his room, but when he got there he found it empty.

CHAPTER NINETEEN

'HOW EXTRAORDINARY!' said Angelo, speaking to himself, as he pulled a wallet from the pocket of a dead German and began to count the notes it contained. 'Three thousand, four thousand, five thousand – he must have robbed somebody – six thousand, seven thousand – oh, but here is a fortune! And how truly astonishing to think that I have killed one of them at last, and I myself am still alive!'

He sat down beside his late enemy, in the comfortable knowledge that the flood-dyke behind him was an adequate protection against most of the missiles of war, and with a feeling of grateful wonder contemplated the scene of battle. It was horrible, of course, and he disliked the cold flat fields of the river-plain; but because he had endured so much in the company of this earth, and helped in the winning of it, he now regarded the drab untidy landscape almost with complacency. To some degree, and after a fashion, it was his.

Another winter had gone, and though every afternoon the *bora* blew from pale skies like a fluency of melting ice, the ground was dry and the sun rose clear in the morning. The winter had been harsh and wearisome, and the soldiers of the Allied Armies had spent it, in sad persistence and complaining valour, under mountain-snow and mountain-rain. The Germans had entrenched themselves from sea to sea across the Etruscan Apennines, and against their ramparts of concrete and steel and cloud-swept hill there had striven, week by week for the advantage of another mile, the polyglot forces of democracy, born of many lands and bred to divers habits, but all alike in that all could shiver and bleed. On the left of the line, by the western sea, there had been

Brazilians and American negroes, and on the right, on the Adriatic shore, Greeks and Poles. In the mountains north of Florence men had given their orders to advance, and others had cursed them, in the accents of New England and the Middle West, in voices from the cornfields of Kansas and the cold plains of Nebraska, from the black soil of the deep South and the arrogant immensity of Texas. Voices from the Transvaal and the Cape had answered them, and to the eastward came a clamour of tongues from Hindustan. Soldiers had died with a sentence, half-spoken, of Urdu on their lips. They had called gently to each other in the night in Gurkhali and Mahratti, and heard the debate of comrades in the broad accent of Yorkshire, the lazy flow of Cotswold villages, the quick traffic of a London borough, and here and there the softness of Gaelic. Christchurch and Dunedin had spoken to Glasgow and Liverpool, Manitoba and Quebec to Warsaw and Athens. Pietermaritzburg had conversed with Little Rock, the Grampians with the Punjab, and tied each other's wounds. Hardly since the confounding of the people at Babel had such a diversity of tongues been heard, and month by month their hopeful or their weary speech had sounded a little farther to the north, till now, in the cold bright air of spring, the languages and lingos, the argots and parley and paronyms of half the world, to the orchestration of their innumerable artillery, were shouting for the kill.

Since the autumn Angelo had been serving in the Cremona Brigade of the new Italian army. He had been toughened and bored and drilled in the use of strange weapons during long weeks of training in the Marches, and in January his Brigade had gone into the line near Ravenna. Slowly the darkness of winter had grown lighter, April had come at last, and now, in what was to be the Eighth Army's triumphant last battle, Angelo, a troubled particle of its fame, was fighting among the stiff-sided streams of the valley of the Po. Somewhere not far away, invisible between its tall banks, flowed the Santerno. To his right was the highway that runs from Ravenna through Alfonsine to Ferrara. And beyond the dyke that sheltered him, about two hundred yards away, was a German machine-gunner watchful in his muddy embrasure.

But Angelo, for the present, hardly gave him a thought. He had not become indifferent to danger, nor acquired any surprising degree of courage, but the irritable mysticism of discipline, in this new army, had so deeply infected him that often he did not feel afraid for several hours at a stretch; and now his mind, after travelling a little in space and briefly in time, was occupied with one person only, and she was far away.

Pasquale, stooping cautiously, came to join him and offer a crust of bread and a piece of sausage. Pasquale had done well in the Cremona Brigade and was now a sergeant.

'I was thinking about Lucrezia,' said Angelo with his mouth full.

'She must be getting near her time,' said Pasquale.

'Very near. It may be today, it may be tomorrow, or perhaps it was yesterday. I should be with her.'

'There's nothing a man can do at such a time but look miserable and get in other people's way. If it's the first one he goes about snivelling with fear, and if it's the fourth he grumbles because there's no one to cook his dinner. That's all a man can do.'

'I could comfort her,' said Angelo.

'Don't you believe it. When his wife's lying-in, his home's no good to any man, and he's no good to his home.'

'She is all alone,' said Angelo.

'Except for her mother, and three or four of her sisters, and every woman in the village who can think of an excuse to go along and see what's happening,' said Pasquale.

A few hours later they attacked again. The air was full of the wild whistling of passing shells, the earth shook and rose in black fountains. Angelo waited, and because he was no longer alone, but one of many inspired by firm intention and welded by discipline, his fear no longer entered and destroyed him, but only hovered above him like a carrion bird that dares not strike a living man. Then Pasquale spoke. '*Andiamo!*' he said.

'*Andiamo!*' Angelo repeated, a trifle shrilly, and got up.

He climbed the flood-bank and bullets spat in his ear as they passed him. He splashed across the stream and clambered up the farther bank. *Piou, piou!* cried the bullets, and shells burst like lions roaring under a cliff.

Angelo ran with his elbows out and his head down. He was dimly aware of the men on either side of him – men who had become his friends – and their presence comforted him. But what he chiefly desired was to reach, as quickly as possible, some place of shelter. The smallest hillock, any meagre protuberance of mud behind which he could lie concealed, would serve his purpose. There, over there, was a little weal of earth and greenery. What bliss to reach it!

Then like a drowning man he gasped in the squall of a near explosion and something hit his left hand so hard that he spun round, facing the other way, and after a wild stumble fell flat upon his face. Fear and indignation, mingled together, poured into his mind. He had been wounded. Oh, what injustice, and ah, what misery! He looked at his hand, and was seized by an overwhelming sorrow for his poor body that had been so mutilated.

It was not long before someone came to help him, and as he returned unsteadily to the flood-banks from which the attack had started, he was surprised to find how near they were. He had been running, he thought, for a long time, but now he perceived that he had gone no more than forty yards before being hit.

He fainted when his wound was dressed, and his first anxiety when he recovered consciousness was for the safety of his wallet. He felt for it, with his good hand, and found it still in his pocket. He took great care of it on his way to hospital, and put it under his pillow as soon as he got to bed.

When he was told that his left hand would have to be amputated, he fell into a profound melancholy that was curiously charged with a feeling of guilt, and for some time he was convinced that the loss of his hand was a deliberate punishment. He could never decide, however, for what he was being punished, because the more deeply he searched his conscience the more sins he discovered, many of them grave indeed, and the innumerable little ones were so wanton that it was difficult to imagine how they had escaped correction for so long. But though justice had been tardy its penalty was severe, and night after night he wept for his cunning fingers and the fingernails that were the shape of almonds, the brown skin and the blanched knuckles, the strong palm calloused by work and scored with inscrutable lines, the sturdy thumb on its plump throne of muscle, and the adept strength by which he could hang from the branch of a tree or gently enclose a girl's soft arm. A marvellous thing was a hand, and a fearful calamity to lose it. His sin must have been grievous indeed, but still, out of so many that lay upon his conscience, he could not see which was the blackest nor decide for which he had been condemned.

And then, after days of anguished inquiry, it occurred to him one morning that he had been lucky beyond all hope or expectation. There he was, with all the sins in the calendar growing out of him, a vast crop of them every year, like figs fattening in August on an ancient tree, and by some great stroke of mercy he had been punished for only one of them, while hundreds had been ignored, perhaps even forgiven. What a marvellous clemency! He was still alive, and upon the stump of his wrist he could wear a smooth steel hook. A hook flashing in the sun, with which he could hold an ox by the bridle and with a gesture frighten small boys. A hook would be a fine appendage to his arm.

He sat up in bed and declared, 'Now I am going to get well!'

Almost immediately his health began to improve, and after a few weeks he was sent to a convalescent hospital in a village on the Adriatic coast south of Rimini. He was, he discovered, not very far from Pesaro, where in the service of the Germans, more than a year and a half before, he had helped to demolish a lot of houses. He remembered the officer who had commanded his company, the pale and earnest young man like a student, who had despised the Allies for their inefficiency; and wondered what had become of him. For by now the German army in Italy had surrendered, after its total defeat on the Po and beyond it; and the war was over and the Allies were the victors.

He was returning to hospital one evening, after walking on the pale bright beach, when he observed in the village street a girl with a baby in her arms who was trying to attract the interest of a group of soldiers. Though the soldiers wanted nothing to do with her, she was insistent. She took one of them by the sleeve, but he made an impatient movement and would not look at her. '*Niente mangiare!*' she was saying.

Angelo, who had stepped off the pavement to avoid them, paused to glance in her direction. '*Niente mangiare,*' she said again in a piteous voice, and suddenly he realized that he had heard her voice before.

In great confusion he spoke to her. 'Do you remember me?' he asked.

She was thinner than she had been, and the childish roundness of her cheeks had become a small sad oval. But her eyes were the larger by contrast, and the new fragility of her wrists was even prettier than the smooth sturdiness of her forearms when, a year and a half before, he had watched her hauling on the sea-wet rope.

She shook her head when he asked again if she remembered, and holding out her hand repeated dully, '*Niente mangiare.*'

'Oh dear,' said Angelo, 'this is a dreadful state of affairs. Well, you had better come with me, for it happens that I know of a place where we can get something to eat, and I have plenty of money at present. But I wish you remembered me.'

For a little way she walked beside him in silence, and then she said, 'You used to come and help us haul the nets. Your name is Angelo.'

'Of course it is! And you are Annunziata, I recognized you immediately.'

'You have been wounded?' she asked.

'At the battle of the Santerno. We of the Cremona Brigade suffered very heavily,' said Angelo proudly.

'Was that where the Poles were fighting?'

'No, they took Bologna, I think. – But is it true, really quite true, that you and your baby have nothing to eat?'

'Somebody gave us a meal yesterday, but it was only a little one.'

'And where is your husband?'

'He was killed. He was serving with the Tedeschi, and when he tried to escape from them, they shot him.'

'He was with the Tedeschi when I first met you. Did you never see him again?'

'No, not after that.'

'I am very sorry,' said Angelo, and looked at her and her baby, and deeply sighed. They said no more until they came to a small inn that Angelo sometimes visited when the meals at the hospital were not to his liking. The innkeeper served only those whom he knew, for he never had very much to offer, and what he had had usually been obtained in some clandestine manner. But Angelo, who was very well off with the money he had taken from the dead German, had become a favourite customer, and when he told the innkeeper and his wife that Annunziata was his sister, and the victim of evil circumstance, whom he had encountered in the nick of time, for she was starving – but before he could finish his explanation the innkeeper's wife had taken charge of the poor girl and her baby, and was bustling to and fro to prepare a meal, while the innkeeper stood watching her, shaking his head, and commenting profoundly on the sad state to which the world had fallen.

They would give her a bed, said the innkeeper, and Angelo could be sure that she would be well looked after. Annunziata said little, for she was too tired even to be surprised by what had happened. Her baby lay in her lap and sucked a thumb. It was a large child, fatter than she, and appeared to be about three or four months old.

When the meal was ready the innkeeper's wife took the baby and Annunziata pulled her chair to the table. She had been wearing a cotton shawl round her head, and when she took it off Angelo saw that her hair had been cut short. It was no longer than that of a young man who had neglected to go to the barber, and very ragged and untidy. Angelo did not stay much longer, but said he would return in the morning.

In his dreams that night he remembered his first meeting with Annunziata when she and the old fishermen, and their wives and their granddaughters, had been hauling their nets, and Annunziata with her skirts kilted high had leaned on the greenish rope, and little salt-water drops had fallen from it on her plump brown thighs. How pretty she had been! – And how pretty she is! he thought when he saw her in the morning.

Her eyes were bright again, and she had washed her hair and brushed it tidily. The innkeeper's wife had lent her a clean blouse and a skirt that was too big for her, and her legs were also well washed. She had recovered something of her spirit, and she began to thank Angelo so warmly for his kindness that he had to caution her, when the innkeeper and his wife were out of hearing, against showing too much gratitude. 'For you are supposed to be my sister,' he said, 'and a sister takes a great deal for granted.'

He gave her some money to buy new clothes, and two or three days later they went for a walk together. She tied a kerchief round her head, and said, 'You will not be ashamed to be seen with me now.'

'I shall be very proud,' said Angelo, 'for though I searched from Rimini to Ancona I do not think I could find a lovelier companion.'

'If I look well,' she said, 'it is due to your kindness. I have never had such nice clothes before.'

She took his wounded arm and said, 'Oh, your poor hand! It makes me sad to think how you have suffered.'

'Very soon,' said Angelo, 'I shall be wearing a fine steel hook. That will be very distinguished.'

They sat on the beach and looked in silence at the placid sea. Presently Annunziata said, 'When I asked you if there were any Polish soldiers fighting beside you, in the battle where you were wounded, I was hoping that you might be able to tell me about someone of whom I am very fond. I thought you might have met him. His first name is Stanislas, but I cannot tell you his other name. It was too difficult to say. He is very good-looking, with grey eyes and a dimple in his chin.'

'No,' said Angelo, a little sadly. 'I have never met him.'

'It is a long time since I have heard from him,' said Annunziata, 'and perhaps he has been shot. Then my poor baby will be an orphan.'

'It is Stanislas who is the father of your baby?'

'Oh yes, he is already very like Stanislas. If you knew him you would have no doubt about it. And I am not a bad girl, you must not think that. I have never gone with any other man. But when I heard that my husband had been killed my heart was quite broken for a long time, and I became very lonely. And then I met Stanislas, and he also was lonely.'

'And you were sorry for him,' said Angelo.

'Very, very sorry. But how did you know?'

'It is nearly always so. Women are constantly being sorry for foreign soldiers.'

'But no one could help being sorry for Stanislas, because he had no home to go to. He came from a city called Lwow – it is very hard to pronounce it – but Lwow is no longer in Poland, for the Russians have taken it, and Stanislas did not want to become a Russian. And I cannot understand why Russia should behave in such a way, for I thought that Poland and Russia were both fighting against Germany.'

'They were indeed.'

'And therefore they were on the same side, and surely it is very wicked to rob one's neighbours.'

'Hush, hush! You must not say such a thing, Annunziata, not even as a joke. Russia is a very dignified and important nation. She is, moreover, extremely sensitive about her reputation in the world, and any Russian who heard you suggesting that she was capable of robbery would be extremely hurt. You do not understand these things.'

'Do you?'

'It is quite certain that the Russians had some good reason for taking Lwow, though it is possible that no one in our position could fully comprehend it. Perhaps they thought they could look after it better than the Poles, and took it away from them, not because they wanted it, but because they felt it to be their duty.'

'And Stanislas, in consequence, has no home to go to.'

'We ordinary people always suffer when a great nation develops a sense of duty,' said Angelo.

'Even though he may be dead by now,' said Annunziata, 'I continue to be sorry for Stanislas. We were so happy together for a little time. He had a very deep voice and a way of saying things, even the most ordinary things, that made you quite sure he had some strong emotion about them. Everything he said sounded impressive, and it was most moving to listen to him. But often, of course, he was extremely unhappy, and then I also had to weep. I suffered in other ways because of my friendship with him. That was why they cut off my hair.'

'Because of Stanislas?'

'There were some young men at home who had been Fascists, as everybody knew, but when the situation changed they became Patriots. So naturally they wanted to do something to show that they were now Patriots, and prove their enthusiasm. They told me that it was wrong for an Italian girl to go out with a foreigner, and I must stop it. But by then I knew that I was going to have a baby, so it was too late to stop. And because I was in love with Stanislas I told them to mind their own business. So then they cut off my hair.'

Angelo took her hands and pressed them fiercely. 'What cruelty! I do not want to think about it.'

'They were rough with me,' said Annunziata. 'We are not all so good-humoured, we Italians, as we pretend to be.'

'I am certainly not good-humoured when I think of such hooligans! But how anyone could ever fail to treat you well, I do not understand. Everybody, it seems to me, should want to be kind and tender to you.'

'Life has by no means been like that,' said Annunziata.

'But it should be!' cried Angelo. 'I know it should. And why is it not so?'

'It would be very pleasant if it were,' said Annunziata, 'but I do not think we should expect too much from life. – And now we must go back. My baby is very good and sleeps well, but I have left him alone for a long time.'

As they walked towards the inn she asked him, 'Are you married now? Your sweetheart, I remember, said that she would not marry you until the war was over. But perhaps she changed her mind?'

'Yes,' said Angelo, 'I have now been married for nearly a year, and when I go home again I shall find more people in the house than when I left it. Our son is already two months old.'

'You must be very happy. It is a good thing to have a home.'

Every evening they walked together, or sat among the little fruit trees that grew behind the inn, and with good food to nourish her body and Angelo's flattering attention to please her mind, Annunziata became prettier and more cheerful day by day. The innkeeper's wife said that never in her life before had she seen a brother and a sister so devoted, but the innkeeper himself was increasingly suspicious and took to asking Annunziata certain questions that she found difficult to answer; and of which she made no mention to Angelo.

His suspicions grew darker as their evening walks became longer, and one night when their return was late indeed he told his wife that he was going to get the truth out of Angelo if he had to squeeze it out of his gullet.

That evening, as it happened, Angelo had accepted a great responsibility and asserted himself in a very proud and singular manner. He and Annunziata were sitting in a secluded hollow on the shoreward side of the dunes which, along that part of the coast, rise in tufted hillocks above a narrow beach. The night was starless and the sky so dark that the sea was invisible, and the earth no more than a palpable obscurity. There was no wind nor any sound to be heard except the lapse of little waves and the crumbling of the sand beneath their touch; until the silence was broken by Angelo's inquiring voice.

'Are you, by any chance,' he asked, 'behaving like this because you are sorry for me?'

'Dear Angelo,' she said, 'of course I am sorry for you. How could I be hard-hearted when you have suffered so, and lost your poor hand –'

'That is enough,' he said. 'I refuse to be an object of pity! If, like so many others, you regard your love as the bread of charity, I do not want it.'

'But Angelo –'

'You can do no good by argument. My mind is made up. There is, I am well aware, a widespread belief that because of the war a woman is entitled to be sorry for anyone who takes her fancy. But I do not share that belief. If it became the accepted rule, we should never have peace at all. – No, I am not going to listen. And I am not going to join the breadline for love, either yours or any-one else's.'

Annunziata began to cry. 'I don't know what you are talking about.'

'The gift of understanding is very rare,' said Angelo coldly.

'I love you because you have been so kind to me. You found me starving, and you helped me. You have been more generous to me than anyone I have ever known. I do not think that anyone has been generous to me before.'

'You are now admitting,' said Angelo, 'that our friendship began, not because you were sorry for me, but because I was sorry for you.'

'I know that! Do you not think I am grateful? But because you have been sorry for me, I do not see why you should not love me.'

'But this is a very different state of affairs,' said Angelo. 'This alters the situation entirely. – No, wait a minute. I must see to it that the difference is quite clear in your mind.

– Do you realize that if we become lovers, it will not be the result of your being sorry for me?'

'That is what you have been saying.'

'But it may well be the result of my being sorry for you?'

'How glad I am that you were!'

'Dear Annunziata! I knew that you could understand if you tried.'

It was not until they had returned to the inn that Annunziata asked, 'Will it make you angry if I admit that I still do not see why you had to decide which of us was sorry for the other? What difference did it make?'

'It was a matter of principle,' said Angelo.

Before the innkeeper could make up his mind to speak openly of his suspicions, and demand from Angelo the true account of his relations with Annunziata, the military authorities announced that his wound was now healed and he must go and be fitted with a hook, as he desired, and receive his discharge from the army.

'And what will happen to me?' asked Annunziata with misery in her eyes.

'It is going to be difficult,' said Angelo, 'but I dare say I can make her see reason.'

'Whom do you mean?'

'Lucrezia, of course. I shall tell her that as many young women have given hospitality, during the last few years, to lonely soldiers, I feel entitled to give similar hospitality to you, who are certainly as lonely as any soldier I have ever known.'

'I am entirely alone, except for my baby,' said Annunziata.

'Another baby or two will make very little difference in the house; if, indeed, I have a house to go to, about which I am still in doubt.'

'You are going to take me with you?'

'Had I allowed you to be sorry for me,' said Angelo, 'I might have deserted you without compunction. But when I insisted on being sorry for you, I accepted the responsibility for what has passed between us. I can do nothing else. Nor indeed – dear Annunziata! – do I wish to.'

STOOPING TO LOOK into the cradle, Angelo gave a gasp of horror, and turned to Lucrezia a face of consternation and dismay. 'But he is black!' he exclaimed. 'You never told me he was black!'

'Black indeed! Oh, how unfair! He is nothing of the sort. A little dark, I admit –'

'He is a Moor, there is no doubt of it.'

'He is my baby! I suffered a misfortune, you know that as well as I do, and such a thing often leaves an effect. But to say that he is a Moor is too much.'

'Why did you not tell me?'

'Until he was born, how should I know what his complexion was going to be? And after he was born, what could I do to change it?'

'I thought it was my child that you were carrying,' said Angelo.

'You do not think he resembles you, even a little?'

'No.'

'I am sorry,' said Lucrezia. 'I should be very happy if he looked like you. But during the war there were very few of us who had the chance to order our lives as we would have liked them to be. We were little better than sheep, and it was only by good fortune that we escaped the butcher. If my baby is too dark for your liking –'

'He is.'

'That is a vexation, of course, but only one of many that we have suffered. He is one of an infinity of vexations, and it is very sad for him as well as for us.'

'This is not the home-coming that I had looked forward to,' said Angelo.

'It is not precisely the home-coming that I had expected,' said Lucrezia, staring with no friendliness in her eyes at Annunziata and her baby.

'His name is Stanislas,' said Annunziata. 'His father came from Poland. He had no longer any home to go to, and he was very lonely.'

'So she took pity on him,' said Angelo.

Little Tommaso fell off the kitchen table and began to cry; but no one paid much attention except little Stanislas, who made it a duet.

'Oh, I cannot bear it!' shouted Angelo. 'What am I but a poor Italian soldier, who has done nothing wrong, unless under orders, and now I am expected to settle down as a married man with three children to care for, one of whom is an Englishman, another a Pole, and the third a Moor! It is too much, I say, and I cannot bear it!'

He ran out of the house and through the nearby fields in a kind of panic, and did not stop until he had climbed nearly to the crest of the hill opposite Pontefiore, where for about half an hour he lay exhausted, flat on the ground and staring at the sky. High clouds in the tideless blue were sailing slowly to the east. He watched them until he grew slightly giddy with a sensation that the earth was spinning westward, and then sat up, and with his right hand violently rubbed his face and head, and spoke aloud: 'But one does not run away. There was a time when I thought that I could always improve my position by leaving it; but that is not so. Even when we are outnumbered it is necessary to stay and return the enemy's fire. As a man grows older, moreover, the world appears to become smaller, so that every year there are fewer places available for refuge. No, I cannot run away.'

He let his mind accustom itself to this decision, and then he began to think: I have served in three armies, the Italian, the British, and the German, without wishing to serve in any, and now I have three children, none of which I desired. That is only a coincidence, of course, but coincidences are very interesting and should be useful. They should help to remind us that there are patterns in life, and design in the world, and a purpose in the universe; though God only knows if it is the sort of purpose we should be glad to know about. Even accidents, it may be, are not wholly accidental. – But how I wish that the youngest of my family had not been black! I shall have to call him Otello.

He looked about him and was enraptured, as so often before, by the rich and mannerly beauty of his country. – Oh, those Englishmen! he thought, remembering a conversation with Simon and two young officers in a wintry village near Alfedena. They loved the desert because it was empty! How incomprehensible they are. For I who adore this land of mine, this Tuscany of the green candles and the terraced hills that are crowned with men's houses, adore because it is complete. As the little grapes in the valley are sweet already and coloured with their ripeness, so Tuscany wears its bloom and is plump as a young grape with sweetness.

He said aloud: 'The land is very ancient, yet summer comes to it with the colour of a new invention. When Rome was but an angry thought, we were civilized and had our arts, and when the world was in its dark despair we woke it with our painting and our poetry and quarrelling. And still our olive trees are silver and green, and the olives grow fat. All the countries have come to us, either to conquer or to learn, in love or envy, and we are still Tuscany, and the grapes are ripening again, and in a little while from now my family – the Englishman, the *Marocchino*, and the Pole – will drink the vintage and be the better of it.'

He stood up, and walked to and fro, and declared: 'It is possible, it even seems probable, that I have a mission. I must demonstrate that all the peoples of the world – or four of them, at least – can make their home together in civilization. I shall bring up these children in such a way that they will have no obsession about their nationality, and that will be a very good thing indeed. For even the best of nations may have a bad influence on its subjects, and human nature being what it is, the majority of its subjects are likely to prefer that to anything else it can offer. But my family will merely retain a sentimental regard for the places where their fathers were born, and sentimentality, which can relieve itself in a song or two and an occasional tear, is an excellent thing.'

He stopped, and looking towards Pontefiore with a frown, thought: But I must not say anything of this to Lucrezia. If she were to suspect that I have discovered a mission in life, or a theory, let us call it, she would never let me forget it. She would refer to it at the most inconvenient times, and taunt me with it whenever the children happened to spill a bowl of soup on the dinner-table. For women do not approve of theories, but are jealous of them because they take up a man's attention. Nor do I blame them for that, because when a man's theory goes wrong it is a woman, of course, who must dry the table and wipe up the soup. – But that does not alter the facts of the case, and so I must remember to be discreet. I must also be firm.

He sat down again, a little worried by the thought, and exclaimed: 'This is a time – though the war is over – when I should be very glad of the *dono di coraggio*. I know exactly what I am going to say to Lucrezia, in the matter of Annunziata, but I do not relish the prospect of saying it. I have a good logical argument, but she has great strength of character and a formidable tongue: can logic prevail against such a combination? Not without courage, I fear. Or shall I use the little blackamoor to support my case? It will be unfair to Lucrezia, poor girl, but the whole situation is unfair to me and we must come to terms in some way. I had better consider our little Otello as part of the bargain.'

He contemplated his task with some reluctance still, and when a fly stung him on the ankle slapped thoughtlessly at it with his hook and deeply pricked himself. 'Well, that is a lesson,' he said. 'What strength I possess, when a mere gesture can draw blood! I had forgotten how much I have changed since going to the war again. Why should I be frightened of words – even a woman's words – when I have learnt to endure the screaming of shells and the extraordinary repetition of machine-guns? A moment in which to muster my arguments – and then, *andiamo!*'

He rose once more, and shaking his hook at another buzzing fly, set off at a steady pace for the ruined farm where Lucrezia had set up house. The previous tenants, an elderly man and his wife, had both been killed in the bombing of Pontefiore, their sons were either dead or prisoners of war, and their daughters had been carried off by various misfortune. The Countess had given Lucrezia permission to use what remained of the house – the kitchen and one other room were habitable – and promised the farm to Angelo if, on his return, he should want it. It was small and the ground was thin, but it was pleasantly situated.

When he arrived he found the kitchen full of women. Two of Lucrezia's sisters were living with her – Lucia, who still had no news of her husband, and a plump noisy girl of sixteen called Simonetta – and several neighbours had already come to make the acquaintance of Annunziata. She and the infant Stanislas were, indeed, the centre of the group.

Angelo from the doorway spoke coldly. 'Lucrezia! I have something to say to you.'

'In a little while,' Lucrezia answered. 'I am busy at present.'

'No,' said Angelo, 'I want to speak to you now.'

She looked at him again, surprised by the tone of his voice, and for a moment appeared to be on the point of making a brusque refusal. But then she thought better of it, and with tightened lips and an added colour in her cheeks came to the door. The other women, all silent now, watched her with a lively interest.

'Let us go for a little walk,' said Angelo. 'Gentle exercise calms the mind, and what I have to say must be considered without prejudice or heat. The fact is, my dear Lucrezia –'

'The fact is,' interrupted Lucrezia, 'that you have come home in very strange circumstances, and now are making matters worse by treating me without respect in the presence of my sisters and several of my friends. The fact is that I want to know, immediately and without beating about the bush, what your relations are with Annunziata.'

'Annunziata,' said Angelo, annoyed that he had been forced into explanation so early, 'is the daughter of a fisherman, and her husband was killed by the Germans –'

'All that I know. She has already told me her entire history, including her compassion for a Polish soldier named Stanislas, so far as her meeting with you when you were in hospital.'

'That was quite a remarkable coincidence,' said Angelo.

'Are you her lover?' demanded Lucrezia.

'I will not be questioned in this way –'

'My God!' said Lucrezia, 'if I have not the right to question you on such a matter, I who am your wife, then who has? Here is this woman whom you bring home with you, who has already had a baby by a Polish soldier on whom she took pity, and what I ask is whether you have succeeded the Pole. Has she been sorry for you also?'

'No!' shouted Angelo. 'There you are wrong indeed. There you show how little you understand me. It was I who was sorry for her!'

'What!' said Lucrezia.

'Sauce for the goose,' said Angelo, 'is sauce for the gander. You, some time ago, were sorry for Corporal Trivet, with a result that is likely to be with us for a long time –'

'So you would reproach me, now when we are married, with something that happened when I was a mere girl! I do not call that generous, or even kind of you.'

'I am not reproaching you,' said Angelo. 'I am simply stating a fact. And if you were sorry for Corporal Trivet, surely I have an equal right to be sorry for Annunziata?'

'No, no!' cried Lucrezia. 'A man cannot be trusted to be reasonable in these matters. A man has no sense of proportion, he is too self-indulgent. But a woman, because of her nature, has a proper responsibility, and I who have once been sorry for a man shall take good care never to be sorry for another.'

'And yet,' said Angelo, 'I come home and find that you are the mother, not merely of little Tommaso, but also of a little blackamoor –'

'Was it my fault? Am I to be blamed for that? Oh, but that is truly unfair!'

'It is very unfair indeed,' said Angelo, 'but the whole world is grossly unfair and we have to put up with it. Many husbands, perhaps a majority of husbands, would deeply resent the appearance of two little foreigners in their home, whatever might have been the manner of their arrival, and if I take a lenient view of the situation it is not because I like it, but because, whether I like it or not, I love you.'

'That I can well believe!' said Lucrezia bitterly. 'To browbeat a woman, to bully and humiliate her, is a well-known sign of love.'

'It may well be,' said Angelo sadly. 'For I have loved you so long that my love has become very stubborn, and neither of us, I think, will ever escape from it.'

'But now your love also includes Annunziata.'

'I have already explained my position with regard to her.'

'And if you expect me to be satisfied with that, you are going to be very much disappointed!'

'No, do not go!' cried Angelo as Lucrezia turned to leave him, and reaching with his left arm, took her by the shoulder. She uttered a gasp of pain and he, with a responsive cry, enfolded her in his arms – but now with extreme care – and babbled a little stream of endearments mixed with apology for his clumsiness. 'I am not,' he said, 'quite used to my new finger. I forget that it is harder than my old ones.'

'Give me your handkerchief.'

First with his right hand, then with his hook, Angelo felt in pockets and sleeves, clumsily but without appearing to care that he was clumsy, and then admitted, 'It does not seem that I have one today.'

Lucrezia watched him, his patience and his fumbling, then covered her eyes and turned away.

'Is it so painful?' asked Angelo. 'I am very sorry.'

'No, it is not that.'

'Then I think, perhaps, we should be going home. We have talked enough for tonight, and it is nearly dark.'

She turned again and flung her arms round his neck. 'Oh,

your poor hand!' she cried. 'Oh, Angelo! I have not been kind to you. I meant to be kind, I was going to ask you to forgive me, I was determined not to say a word that would anger you. But when you said the baby was black, and when I looked at that woman –'

'She is only a girl,' said Angelo.

'That makes it no better! But do not let us talk about her. – Angelo, do you swear to me that you love me still?'

'There is no doubt about it.'

She hung more heavily about his neck, and cried a little, and kissed him with a sort of desperation. 'His skin is going to be rather brown,' she said, 'but you cannot call him black.'

When at last they went home, walking slowly in the darkness, Angelo wondered if he had behaved as firmly as he intended. It cannot be denied, he thought, that to some extent it was Lucrezia who took the initiative, and whereas I was going to make it quite plain that I, on certain conditions, was ready to forgive her, she now believes that she has forgiven me. I have, I think, achieved what I set out to achieve, and that clearly proves that Lucrezia has a certain respect for me. But if we do succeed in living together on friendly terms, she will undoubtedly take the credit for it, and I really think the credit should be mine. – But what does it matter? Let her have the credit; it is a small price to pay for peace.

He was tempted to speak once more about Annunziata and make sure that her position had been properly recognized; but discretion intervened, and it occurred to him that Lucrezia might tolerate Annunziata's presence the more easily if she were not required to make a formal acceptance of it. I shall say no more, he decided, but await developments.

Despite his wisdom he was surprised, within the next week or two, by the quick growth of friendship between Lucrezia and her guest. They had discovered, it appeared, some common cause with which Lucrezia's sisters were associated in a less degree, but to which Angelo was certainly not a party. If, for example, Lucrezia made some small reference to his behaviour, his appearance, or an opinion recently uttered, Annunziata and Lucia and Simonetta would all laugh together, and it was evident that to them her words had a peculiar illumination and a special significance, though to Angelo they often sounded quite irrelevant.

All four women paid much attention to the infant members of the household, and not only were such practical matters as feeding and cleaning them taken seriously, but what, to any man, would have seemed the imperceptible vagaries of their inexistent characters were very gravely discussed. Into these activities Angelo had no wish to intrude, but he observed with interest that the four young women appeared to regard the three small children as their common responsibility – if not their common property – and that Tommaso, the young Stanislas, and the little blackamoor could equally depend on the service and interest of Lucrezia, Simonetta, Annunziata, and Lucia; whoever happened to be nearest responded to the cry.

When he proposed that the little blackamoor should be called Otello, they combined against him in open resistance and for several days the division in the house was manifest, and courtesy was strained. But Angelo saw clearly that if his wishes were flouted now, his authority would be denied before long, and with a firmness that gravely offended the others and deeply astonished himself he insisted on having his own way. Lucrezia's second child was called Otello.

The major factor, however, in maintaining peace in the family, or in restoring it after this and some other disputes, was not so much Angelo's authority as the abundance of work that had to be done. Though the farm had been neglected, the grapes and the olives had ripened, the fields had to be tilled with what primitive tools they could find, and the greatest need of all was to patch and fortify their ruined house against the winter rains and Christmas cold. Because the Germans had driven off so many draught oxen, the whole village had suffered during the past year from a grievous lack of beasts for the plough, and had it not been for the pictures that Angelo had once brought from Rome in a cargo of flour its plight would have been far worse.

When the Count – more than a year ago now – had returned in time for Angelo's wedding feast, he had found all but two of his pictures safe and in good condition. The Adoration of the Shepherds had been destroyed, and one of the small Bronzinos had been discovered by the Germans and removed, by a major who appreciated art, as a souvenir of the war; but the others remained, whole and intact, and on his return to Rome the Count took them with him in the six-wheeled lorry that Sergeant Vespucci had so opportunely stolen. Little had been heard of him since, but it was understood that he was very busily engaged in several schemes for the welfare of his tenants and the promotion of good relations between Italy and the United States of America. That he had sold one, two, or three of his pictures was easily inferred when two pairs of matched plough-oxen arrived in Pontefiore; for the Countess let it be known that Don Agesilas had had to pay the monstrous price of 900,000 lire for each pair.

The oxen worked hard but the villagers worked harder, and day after day laboured with their mattocks to open the fields for seed. Two of them were killed when their mattocks struck mines that the Germans had left in exchange for the beasts they stole.

Now winter came again, and everyone was cold, and often wet, and not seldom hungry. But all except some of the youngest and a few of the oldest survived, and went on toiling, and Angelo was widely envied because he had four women to work for him. He himself, however, sometimes thought with regret of the easy times he had had when the world was still at war, and he had nothing to worry about except his recurrent fear of being killed, or wounded, or taken prisoner, or punished for some breach of discipline. – The rain came through the roof, the fire smoked, the children cried in concert, and life was hard indeed. But there was consolation, he admitted, in the warmth of Lucrezia's love, though there was warmth in her anger too; but Annunziata had the sweetest of tempers. And hanging on the kitchen wall, mounted on a square of pale wood, was the head of Piero's Madonna that he had salvaged from the wrath of the German officer.

Angelo was by now quite sure that this was the perfect expression of all beauty, and to possess it, and be able to look at it every day, often seemed to him the very height and culmination of good fortune. For nothing in life either was or could be more agreeable to the senses than beauty to the eye, and to the understanding – or so he thought – there was no such justification of life, or much need of any other. 'What a blessing have I won from the wreckage!' he would say, and looking from Piero's Madonna to Lucrezia or Annunziata he would perceive in their comeliness the living tutor of Piero's art, and very often, in his delight at this relationship, embrace them one after the other in the heartiest manner. Sometimes, if he had been staring too long at the Madonna, so that his eyes were a little dazzled by her, he would turn and see her reflection against Lucia's wistful face or Simonetta's hoydenish red cheeks; and embrace them also. On such an occasion Lucrezia would be sure to utter one of her veiled remarks, that he could not see through, but which always made the others laugh.

Spring at last returned, and then the fact that they lived in a ruin became of no importance, for they hardly used it except as a place of darkness in which to sleep. All day they worked in a golden light or a green shade, and their thoughts, like the thoughts of everyone in Pontefiore, were flushed with an approaching triumph. Their famous bridge had been built again, and in a little while, when the road had been levelled across it, it would be opened to traffic.

All the young people thought the new bridge a vast improvement on the old, and their parents and their grandparents were hard pressed to find a single fault in it. The masons had worked with the cunning and craft of their forefathers. The stone had been nobly hewn and trimly dressed, the abutments ran sweetly into either bank, over the ravine the arch soared serene as a rainbow.

The day came when the road was finished, and while a few workmen sprinkled gravel on it – as though powdering its face for a party – the villagers stood at the near end and debated with loud good humour as to who should have the honour of being the first to cross. They were still arguing, and pushing and resisting, when some of them caught sight of an approaching motor-car. It was a very small car, black as a beetle and remarkably like a beetle in shape; and quickly recognizing the driver, they greeted him vociferously.

'My dear friends!' exclaimed the Count, emerging with difficulty from the tiny vehicle. 'What a beautiful bridge! What a magnificent achievement! Our national and domestic difficulties are still enormous, but now I am convinced that we shall overcome them. Indeed, I never doubted it. I have lost my fortune, but not my faith. Nations totter, empires crumble, crowns go tumbling down the abyss of time, tyrant states are blown out like candles, but man is invincible, man is the true phoenix, and our dear Italy is the native home of the *risorgimento*, the renaissance, the indefeasible and recurrent spring of beauty. Primavera shall walk across this noble bridge with a pledge of richer years, and I myself, preceding her like a herald, have brought you something that will give you pleasure, profitable employment, and the promise of security in your old age. Will someone fetch me, as speedily as possible, a table and a chair?'

While the furniture was being sought, the Count gossiped with his acquaintances – shook hands, clapped shoulders, patted cheeks, inquired for brothers, sisters, fathers, cousins – all in the liveliest manner; and when a chair and a table had been fetched, and set conveniently in the middle of the road, he raised his arms in the sort of gesture that the conductor of an orchestra makes to gather attention for the opening chords of a Beethoven symphony, and returning to his diminutive motor-car, dived into it like a rabbit entering a rudimentary burrow. For a moment or two his hinder parts were curiously agitated, and then he reappeared with a burden in his arms that was shrouded with a coverlet of green baize. He carried it to the table, set it down, and removing the cloth displayed the bright enamel and shining steel of a sewing-machine.

'My dear friends!' repeated the Count. 'After Noah had been afloat for forty-seven days – in great discomfort, one may assume – he sent out a dove from the Ark, and in the evening the dove returned with an olive-leaf in its beak. Now what was the significance of that? – It meant that normal conditions were returning, and the time was ripe for reconstruction!

'My friends, history repeats itself, and I am Noah's dove! We, like that sturdy patriarch, have seen the devastation of our world, and now I, like the dove, come to you with a promise of better times. Not an olive leaf – of which you have plenty – but a brand new model of America's finest sewing-machine, for the sale and distribution of which I have lately been appointed Principal Supervising Agent in Umbria, Tuscany, the Abruzzi, and the Marches. This sewing-machine is the favourite instrument of many of the most intelligent, cultured, and virtuous women in the Western Hemisphere. It is at once the ornament and the assurance of well-being in a million high-class, happy, and essentially modern homes in Canada and the United States. When it has been introduced into Italy in large numbers – as I hope and intend to introduce it – it will be a potent factor in the reconstruction of our country, which, no matter what political system we may enjoy or endure, must begin in the home and cannot be well founded unless it is founded on the prosperity and happiness of the home. With a sewing-machine in the house you can never be bored, you can never be listless; and with a sewing-machine like this in your house, your house will quickly become the envy and example of all your neighbours!'

Sitting down, the Count put a square of white linen in position and speedily stitched a broad hem in it with scarlet thread. This he handed to the nearest villagers for their admiration, and to others distributed leaflets that explained how a sewing-machine could be bought outright for so much, or by a series of fractional payments for a somewhat larger sum.

'I want you to realize,' he said very seriously, 'your good

fortune in being offered this machine, on such reasonable terms, in times that are still gravely perplexed by the evil legacies of war. Had it not been for my close friendship with an American officer, and our realization in the midst of war that we must prepare for the sterner tasks of peace, you could not possibly have been given such a marvellous opportunity. With all the force of which I am capable, I advise you not to neglect it.'

Having instructed an elderly man named Dino to look after the machine, and told him to let customers make a fair trial of it, the Count re-entered his motor-car and was about to drive to the castle when he caught sight of Angelo, who, somewhat embarrassed by his patron's latest activity, had till now remained on the outskirts of the crowd. The Count greeted him in the most amiable fashion and proposed that he should ride a little way with him.

'What times we live in!' he observed as they drove slowly through the ruined village. 'With what triumphant invention has science filled our lives – those of them, that is, which it has not destroyed. Inventions of all kinds, racing to perfection. Sewing-machines, aeroplanes, radio, rockets and bombs, and drugs that cure unmentionable diseases almost before one has time to mention them. Progress has become a race – and only man has not entered for it. Our sewing-machines are better than they used to be, our aeroplanes fly faster and have a greater expectation of arriving, our medicines are more deadly year by year; but man, dear whimsical man, shows no improvement whatsoever. And on the whole,' said the Count, 'I dare say that is a good thing. Try to imagine a human being, emulous of the machines, who had become perfect in all his parts and scientifically efficient. How horrible he would be!'

'Wait for me if you have nothing better to do,' he said when they had reached the castle. 'I must speak to my wife, but I shall not be long. I must let her know that I shall be dining with her.'

He returned in a few minutes wearing a look of worry

and perplexity. 'She is asleep,' he said. 'She never used to sleep at this time of day, but she is actually snoring.'

'The Countess is no longer quite young,' Angelo suggested.

'Nonsense,' said the Count. 'She's younger than I. – Well, it does not matter greatly. Let us walk in the garden, and you will tell me how marriage suits you, and how you are prospering as a farmer. Let me walk on your other side, dear boy. Your hook alarms me.'

He listened with the closest attention to Angelo's description of his household, and often exclaiming in admiration, made him repeat it twice so that he could memorize it in detail.

'It is magnificent, your menage!' he declared. 'I must come and visit you tomorrow.'

'Lucrezia is not looking her best at the moment,' said Angelo.

'You mean –?'

'Yes,' said Angelo, 'in about six weeks from now. We hope for a daughter this time.'

'What excellent news! I congratulate you most warmly. – But you will permit me to meet the other lady: Annunziata, is it?'

'It so happens that she is in a similar condition,' said Angelo.

'My dear fellow,' exclaimed the Count, 'let me embrace you! You are a credit to our old regiment. What a pity the war is over, for otherwise I should certainly have recommended you for a decoration. But have you any money?'

'A little,' said Angelo, who still had four or five thousand lire from the dead German's pocket.

'With a family so rapidly increasing as yours,' said the Count, 'you certainly need a sewing-machine. I had better put you down for one. I shall let you have it at a special price. – No!' he exclaimed, 'I shall do more than that. I shall make you a present of it. Though you did not win a medal, you have decidedly earned a sewing-machine!'

ANOTHER YEAR went by, and it could no longer be denied that the Countess had taken to drink. Her appearance suggested it – little veins whose presence had never been suspected showed themselves in a rosy reticulation upon her nose and cheeks – and her manner completely betrayed it. She was happier than she had been since the first few years of her marriage, and the villagers who had often quailed under her reprobation now found that their silly ways and venial sins were condoned with a chuckle of sympathy; while the elder servants of the castle were often invited to share a flask or two and exchange their native legends and the local gossip for tales of her idyllic youth in Bradford. Such comfort and such kindliness, such moral goodness and worldly prosperity, such jollity, such benignity of climate and handsome scenery were now ascribed by the Countess to her Yorkshire home that presently there became popular in Pontefiore – almost proverbial indeed – a mode of approval which ran: 'That's good, that's very good. That's good enough for Bradford.' No one thought worse of the Countess because occasionally she lost her way, and sometimes her balance, for everyone knew that she had had a great deal to put up with.

The Count came more frequently to Pontefiore, and though his affairs did not prosper as he had hoped, he kept his head above water. More and more he made Angelo his confidant.

'My old friend the Marchesa Dolce, whom you know very well,' he said once, 'is beginning to show her age, and for that I blame the Americans. Since they left Rome she has become careless about her figure. She had always a tendency to put on weight, and now she does little to control it. Her mind

254

is still brisk and youthful, but the mind is not everything; especially in women. A nimbleness, indeed, of thought and speech sometimes draws attention to the relaxation of the body. I wish they had remained in Rome: the Americans, I mean.'

With the Countess's weakness he was most sympathetic, when he had recovered from the surprise it caused him, and he told Angelo: 'I must confess that I have not been the ideal husband. There are men, a few of them, designed by nature for the married state, and they make women happy and destroy their souls. But I am not one of them. We had two or three years of mutual delight, and then a progressive disappointment in each other that was mollified by charity and good manners. Love and wine have much in common – though the former is apt to be exclusive, and the latter inclined to invite others to share its happiness – and if she can find pleasure in the bottle, I call it just compensation for the failure of bed and board. I have given her good advice. I have told her that she should drink nothing before lunch, and not much at lunch; for to drink in the morning obscures the outline and destroys the individuality of a day. And a day is something that dawn and sunset enclose, and should not be demeaned.'

At another time he asked: 'Do you remember a young man called Trivet? I knew nothing of him till recently, but my wife tells me that he spent several years here during the war, and that you shared an adventure with him. – It appears that he is not happy. After being wounded and discharged from the army he made some attempt to resume a domestic life, but without success, and volunteered for service in the Far East. Then the war against Japan came abruptly to an end, the unfortunate Trivet was again discharged, and now he is desperately anxious to escape from a wife whom he finds intolerable, but with whom circumstances compel him to live; for both families are thoroughly respectable in the peculiar fashion of the north of England. So he wants to come back to Pontefiore. Do you think that would be a good thing?'

'Yes,' said Angelo, 'I should like to see him again. – But no, it would not be a good thing. He was very popular with the girls here, especially with Bianca Miretti, Vittoria Carpaccio, and some others. Bianca is now married to Vittoria's brother Roberto, and Roberto has recently discovered that Bianca is still somewhat in love with Corporal Trivet. No, it would not be a good thing if he came back.'

'I shall tell my wife what you say,' said the Count.

About this time Angelo's labour on the farm was much lightened by a sturdy young man from the mountains north of Udine who, in the last days of the war, had had a series of unfortunate experiences in that part of the country which had persuaded him to leave it forever. He had joined a group of Italian partisans and fought in some small actions against the Germans. Then, for no reason that he could understand, his group had been attacked and he had been taken prisoner by Slovene partisans, who had used him with some brutality, and from whom he had escaped by the timely but inexplicable action of a band of Independent Croats who treated the Slovenes, so the Slovenes said, with great cruelty. Losing his head completely, the young man had fled to the north and fallen into the hands of a regiment of renegade Cossacks who were running away from the Bulgarians who were endeavouring to rescue them from the pluto-democratic forces of the Americans and bring them back into the arms of Soviet Russia. The Cossacks, when they had robbed him of everything he possessed, showed no further interest in him, and he succeeded in joining a company of Free Austrians who, because neither the British nor the Americans would recognize them, grew very morose and handed him over to a ridiculous little party of people who called themselves Werewolves. They, by mere chance, fell foul of a lost company of Ukrainian Separatists, who were also on the run but could not decide whither, and the young man presently found himself alone on a road between Judenburg and Graz. He was desperately anxious to escape – not from anyone in particular but from danger in general – but he found it difficult to decide which way to go; for on one side of the road there were many refugees trudging to the east, and on the other an equal number limping to the west. He finally decided to go west because a female Brazilian war-correspondent, having halted to ask him his political views, offered him a ride in her jeep as far as Klagenfurt.

After re-entering Italy he had managed to make a living for a year or two in the provinces of Lombardy and Emilia, but a persistent impulse to escape kept him moving south until he came into Tuscany and eventually to Pontefiore. There he had met Lucrezia's young sister Simonetta, by now a very handsome and lively girl, and having fallen wildly in love with her he had agreed to work for Angelo for a merely nominal wage.

One hot day when they were all busy in a field of barley, cutting with steady sickles, Angelo said he would go home to fetch a flask of wine, and Annunziata decided to walk with him to see if the children were safe and happy. There were by now five of them in the house. Annunziata's baby, a charming little girl just a year old, was a few weeks older than Lucrezia's, which was also a girl. Tommaso had been left to look after them. Tommaso, a well-grown boy of five, had developed a sense of responsibility and a serious manner, but the young Otello, though an extremely handsome child, was difficult to control, and the little Stanislas had moods of wild exuberance. Otello, now rather more than two years old, had sometimes shown a fondness for killing chickens, and Annunziata was always a little anxious about her infant daughter when he was in the vicinity. On this occasion, however, her fears were groundless, and under Tommaso's supervision the children were all peacefully occupied.

'Let us have a glass of wine before we return to the field,' said Angelo. 'Simonetta's young man is doing twice his share to show her how strong he is, so we shall not be missed.'

'He is nice,' said Annunziata, rubbing her wrists that the rough beard of the barley had scored with red. 'Oh, what a happy life we lead here!'

'Well,' said Angelo, 'it is far from perfect, but in comparison with many others we are fortunate. Pontefiore is a small place, of no great importance to the world, so we miss a lot of excitement, but miss a lot of trouble too.'

'That day when you saw me begging from the soldiers with my baby – look at him now! – was the luckiest day of my life.'

'Dear Annunziata! You have repaid that little kindness a thousand times.'

'I am very happy,' she repeated.

'Do you never regret your home by the sea? Are you truly contented in this landward place?'

'I should like some fish for dinner. Fresh fish. I cannot think of anything else I want.'

'Some day,' said Angelo, 'I shall go to Livorno and bring you some fish from there.'

'Then Pontefiore will be quite perfect.'

He kissed her and said, 'The wine here is better than anything you grew on the other side. Let us have another glass.'

When she returned to the field, Angelo made an excuse to remain and decided, a little later, that he was disinclined for more work. After thoughtfully drinking a third glass of wine he strolled into the farmyard, and where a broken wall threw a triangle of dark blue shadow lay down, and yawned a little, and presently fell fast asleep.

Voices, some time later, invaded his sleep, but not so strongly as to drive him out of it. He lay between waking and slumber, and listened to the words that were spoken without, at first, hearing anything strange in them or anything very relevant. There were two speakers.

One of them said, 'Well, there's no one here except those children. I suppose they're all at work.'

'They work hard,' said the other.

'What they've done,' said the first voice, 'is really remarkable. When you think of the state their country was in, and look at it now with the fields decently tended, and the crops growing, and bridges built again, you've got to give them credit. Credit for courage as well as hard work. It looked such a hopeless task. Here in Pontefiore, for example, and all down the Liri valley. Quite hopeless. But they tackled it and they did it. They've got courage.'

Angelo by now was sufficiently wide awake to realize what was strange about the voices. They were talking English! And one of the voices was well known to him, though he found it very hard to believe that the owner of it had returned to Pontefiore and now stood no more than a few feet away. While he considered this charming improbability, the other voice continued.

'I think I agree with you,' it said. 'You remember all those wretched little towns and villages that we bombed and shelled till you wouldn't think a human being could live in them? But when we went in there were always some people waiting to cheer us, and throw flowers and give us wine, though we'd smashed their houses and scattered them on the road. I couldn't do that, and I wouldn't if I could. Yes, we may have been wrong about them. We laughed at them in Africa, because they ran like rabbits from time to time, but we may have been wrong. They've got something. It's their own sort of courage, but they've got it.'

Angelo leapt to his feet, and clutching the flask of wine – which he had thoughtfully taken out with him – stepped round the ruined corner of the house and exclaimed, 'Oh, Captain Telfer, Major Telfer, or is it Colonel Telfer now? I am transported into bliss to see you again! And do you really and truly believe that I have the *dono di coraggio*?'

'Angelo, my dear fellow,' said Simon, 'how are you? We went to the castle and saw the Countess – she's beginning to feel her age, isn't she? – and she told us where you lived. This is a friend of mine: Major Crowther.'

'How do you do?' said Angelo. 'But is it true that I have the *dono di coraggio*?'

'You were listening, were you?'

'I was sleeping, but not quite asleep after you began to talk. – Let us have some wine: hold the flask and I shall get some glasses. But no! I have a house of my own now, you must come inside and we shall drink in comfort.'

He ushered them into the kitchen and then inquired, with

a little anxiety, 'You do not dislike children, I hope? We have rather a lot here.'

'Are they all yours?' asked Major Crowther.

'In one way, yes. In another, no,' said Angelo, and briefly explained the ancestry of his family. 'The babies, however, are truly mine.'

'Angelo,' said Simon, raising his glass, 'have no doubt about it. You possess the *dono di coraggio*.'

His face beaming with pleasure, Angelo replied, 'That is something I never expected to hear you say. It makes me very happy to hear it. – But tell me, what are you doing here?'

'We are on leave,' said Simon. 'We are on holiday, we are revisiting familiar scenes and reviving old acquaintance.'

'Then clearly,' said Angelo, 'we must have another drink. This is a day of celebration. And when you have refreshed yourselves we shall go and talk to Lucrezia and Annunziata, who are working in the fields.'

It was nearly an hour later when they set out for the barley-field, and as they left the house Angelo said, 'I must warn you that Annunziata, who in ordinary circumstances is quite uncommonly pretty, is at the moment not looking her best.'

'I am sorry to hear that,' said Simon.

'No,' said Angelo, 'there is nothing to worry about. It is quite natural.'

'Oh, I see.'

'I hear that your wife is extremely handsome,' said Major Crowther.

'Yes, I am very fortunate,' said Angelo. 'But Lucrezia too, just at present, is at some disadvantage so far as looks are concerned.'

Simon Telfer and Major Crowther stopped, and stood, and stared at him in astonishment.

'It is a remarkable coincidence,' said Angelo modestly.

'It is a good thing,' said Simon, 'that your fields are also bearing well.'

'Our country is very fertile,' said Angelo, and leading his guests through the barley, introduced them to Lucrezia,

Annunziata, Lucia, Simonetta, and the young man from the mountains north of Udine. 'Lucrezia,' he said, 'there can be no more work today. We have honoured guests. You must go home at once and prepare a meal for them.'

'There is not very much to eat in the house,' she whispered.

'There is *prosciutto*,' said Angelo, 'there are hens in the yard. Carve the one and kill the others. We must eat well tonight.'

'We are sleeping at the castle,' said Simon.

'But you will dine with me!'

It was late in the evening before they had had their fill of food and wine and talk, and not until his guests were about to leave did Angelo remember to ask if Simon had any news of a former companion, the strange adventurer who had worn a tortoiseshell monocle.

'You mean Fest,' said Simon. 'Poor Fest went to look for trouble, and found it. He was killed in Bologna. When the Poles went in they met a person in the uniform of a German colonel. He was eager to be friendly with them, so they shot him immediately. It was Fest.'

'I remember him clearly in that affair on the road to Vallombrosa,' said Angelo. 'He was very brave but rather selfish.'

He and Lucrezia walked a little way towards the castle with Simon and his friend, and when they had arranged to meet again in the morning, said good night.

'What a day it has been!' exclaimed Angelo as he turned homeward with Lucrezia. 'I was sleeping when they arrived, and when I woke I lay for some time and listened to them talking before I got up to greet them. There was one thing they said that pleased me greatly, whether it was true or not. They said I had the *dono di coraggio*.'

'Is that really important?' asked Lucrezia.

'It is highly important when one has had to do without it for most of one's life. It gave me so much pleasure to hear what they said that all day, whenever I have thought of it, I have wanted to sing. Shall I sing now?'

'No,' said Lucrezia.

'Just a little song? It would be appropriate, I think.'

'Courage is a common quality in men of little sense,' said Lucrezia. 'I think you over-rate it. A good understanding is much rarer and more important.'

'I have always had a good understanding of things,' said Angelo, 'and I assure you that it does not always make for happiness.'

'You did not show much understanding when you insisted on inviting your friends to dinner. I told you there was hardly any food in the house, and now there is none at all. We ate the last of the ham and there is no more *pasta*.'

'But when one meets an old friend,' said Angelo, 'one does not count the cost of entertainment. That would be base indeed.'

'It is not your way. I know that.'

'Darling Lucrezia! My way is to be so deeply in love with you that I am in great danger of drowning.'

'You are a little drunk, aren't you?'

'Perhaps – but only a little – and what does it matter? We are going to live for a long, long time, and to be always sober would be most ungrateful.'

'I hope life will become a little easier if we are to live so long.'

'It will. I am sure it will.'

'And some day, perhaps, we shall have enough to eat as well as enough to drink.'

'We shall have everything we need!'

'*Speriamo*,' said Lucrezia with a sigh.

'*Pazienza!*' cried Angelo. 'We have stood up to a great deal, we can stand what is still to come, whether it's poverty or plenty. For we have learnt the most useful of all accomplishments, which is to survive!'

Rome, August 1944 – *Orkney, August* 1945